tapas original

# THE WITCH'S THRONE

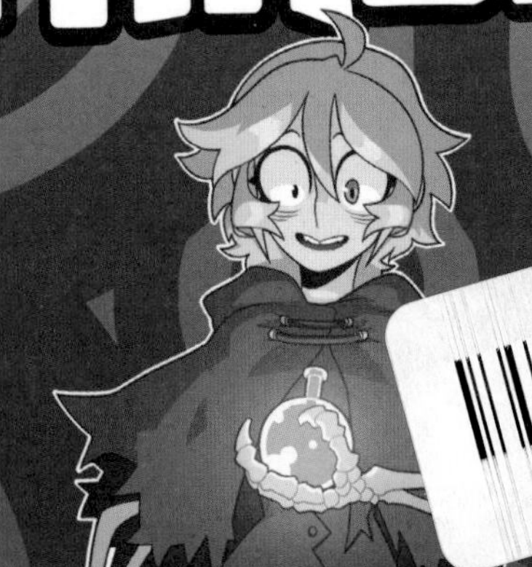



Cedric Caballes

Andrews McMeel
PUBLISHING®

Dear Reader,

*The Witch's Throne* is a love letter to all the things I enjoyed most in my childhood. Whether it was intentional or by accident, I created a story full of all the elements and aesthetics that I adored growing up. Video games and comics were the most prominent influences on my teenage brain. I stayed up late into the night playing the latest action RPG or reading the newest issue of a shonen manga where the protagonist yells the villain's name fifteen times in a row. When I was very young, I'd design a bunch of characters and give them names, backstories, and power descriptions akin to what I saw in my favorite games and comics. Most of those little characters and settings I created faded into memory, while others stuck in the back of my mind and became the story you're reading now.

Out of everything I want for this book, my greatest wish is for you to have fun while reading *The Witch's Throne*. This story grew out of the games and comics I cherished as a kid and young adult. Every trope, every trope subversion, every fight scene, every power-up, every screaming match between Agni and her friends—all of these stem from what I find to be endearing and enjoyable. I hope to convey these feelings of appreciation for childish whimsy and cartoonish romanticism through these pages.

Agni's journey to becoming a hero will be long and arduous, but I hope you find it to be just as fun and exciting as it was to create it.

# CONTENTS

# Prologue

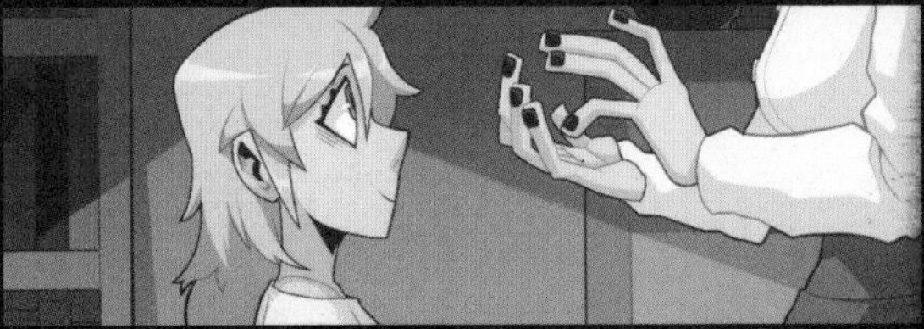

I REMEMBER WHEN I WAS YOUNG, I WOULD ALWAYS ASK MY MOTHER TO TELL ME MY FAVORITE STORY BEFORE I SLEPT.

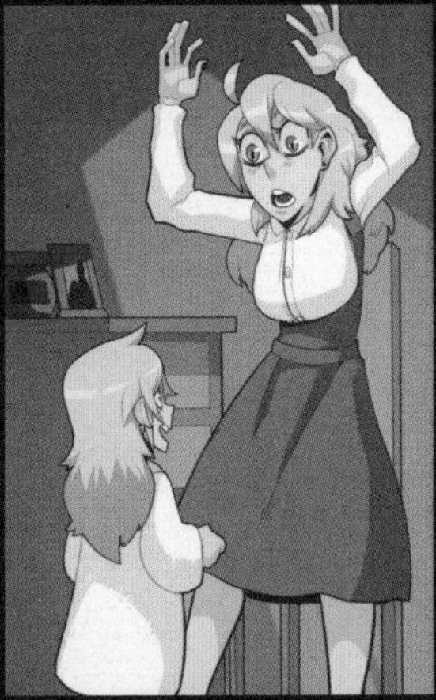

"THE THRONED PROPHECY."

THE TALE OF FOUR BRAVE HEROES...

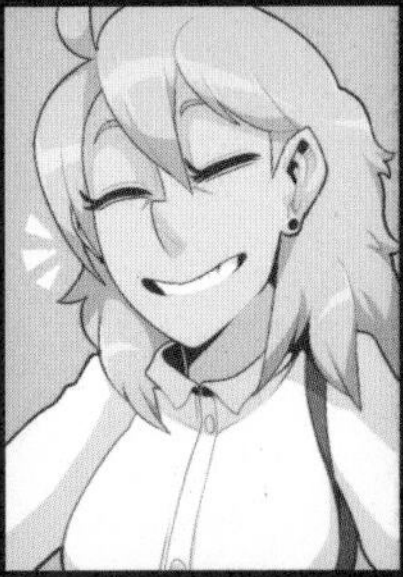

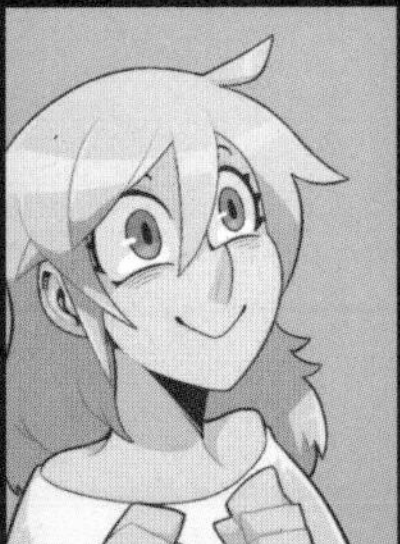

...AND A WITCH.

THE PROPHECY STATED THAT EVERY TEN YEARS, DURING A RANDOM MONTH, ON A RANDOM DAY, A SINGLE GIRL WOULD AWAKEN AS A WITCH.

HER RIGHT HAND WOULD CRACKLE AND CONVULSE WITH UNPARALLELED ARCANE POWER.

THE WHITES OF HER EYES WOULD BE DYED BLACK AS THE DARKEST ABYSS.

AND THE MAGIC IN THE AIR AROUND HER WOULD DANCE,

ENVELOPING HER IN A CLOAK OF SHADOWS—

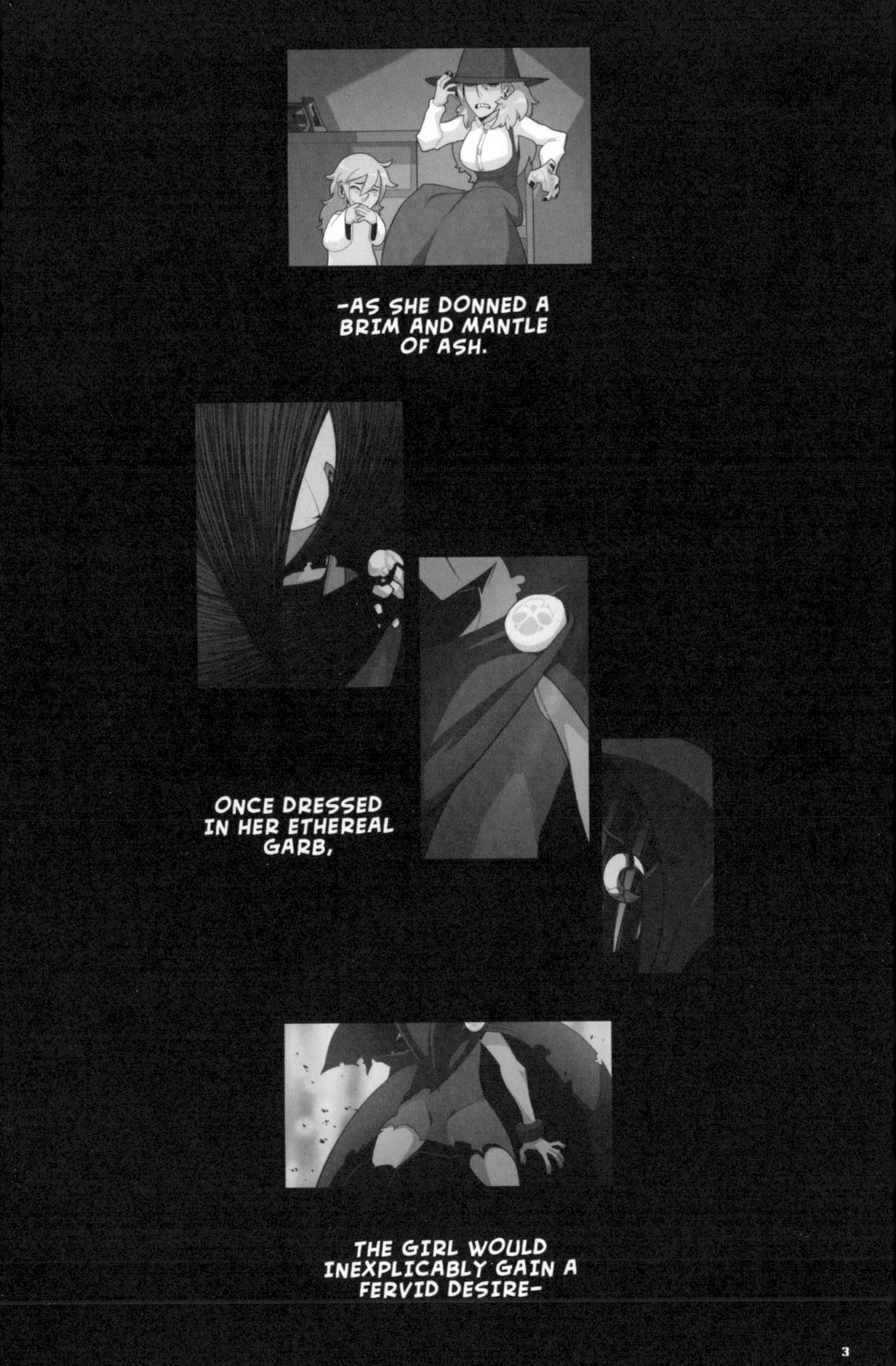
-AS SHE DONNED A BRIM AND MANTLE OF ASH.
ONCE DRESSED IN HER ETHEREAL GARB,
THE GIRL WOULD INEXPLICABLY GAIN A FERVID DESIRE-

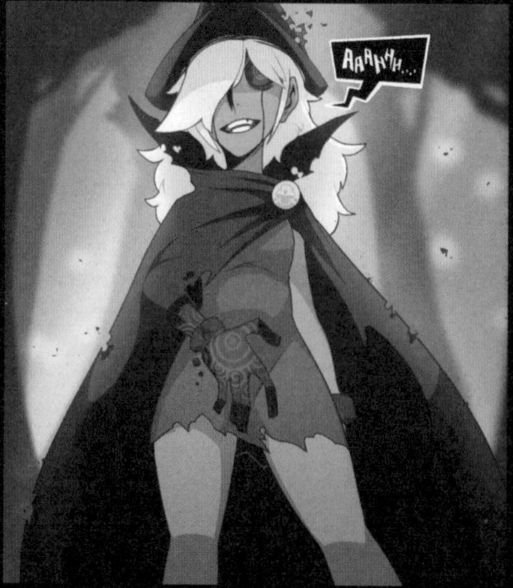

AAAHHH...


-TO ERADICATE
ALL LIFE.

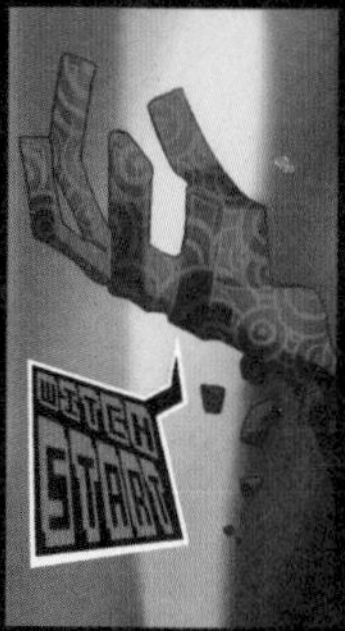

WITCH
START


THE WITCH WOULD
MARK HER COMING
WITH A SYMBOL OF
HER MIGHT-

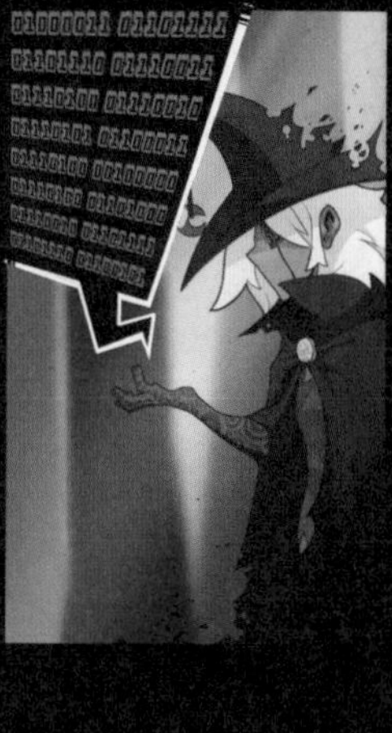

01000011 01101111
01101110 01110011
01110100 01110010
01110101 01100011
01110100 00100000


A TOWERING
THRONE OF
BONE AND
BRIMSTONE
THAT
ASCENDED
TO THE
HEAVENS,

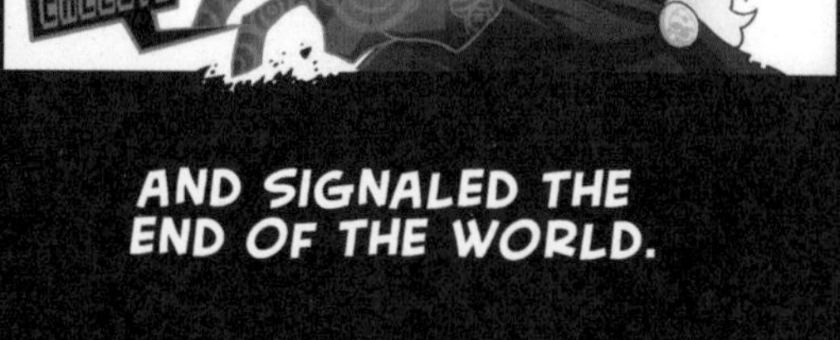

EXECUTE

AND SIGNALED THE
END OF THE WORLD.

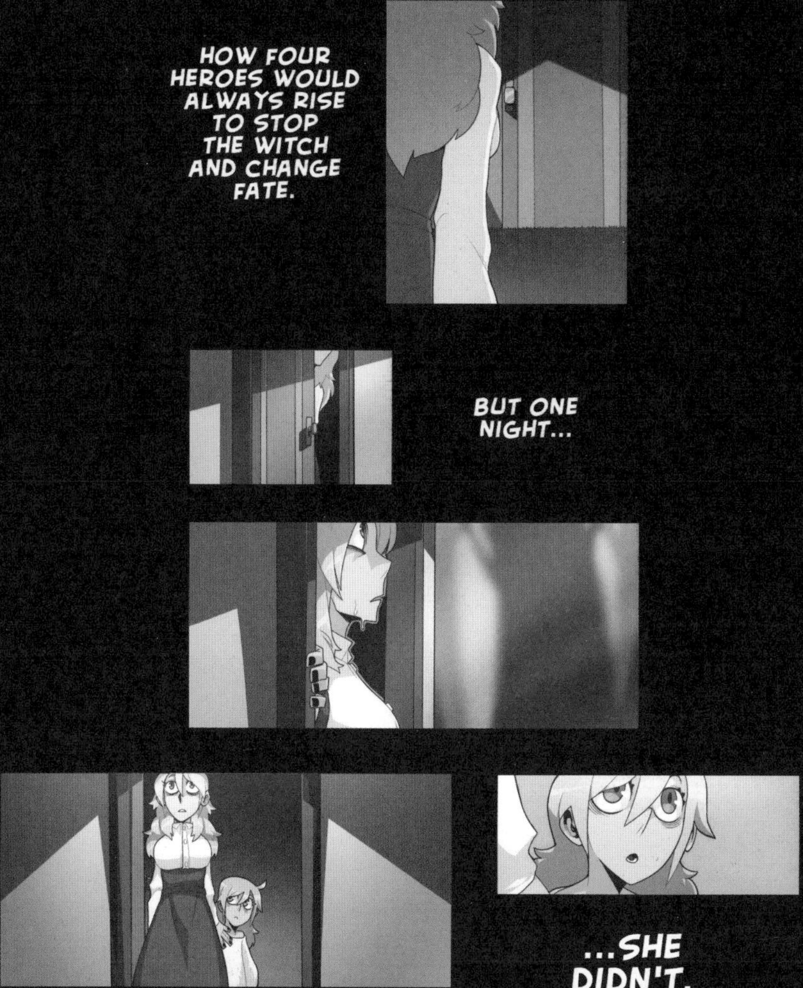
HOW FOUR HEROES WOULD ALWAYS RISE TO STOP THE WITCH AND CHANGE FATE.
BUT ONE NIGHT...
...SHE DIDN'T.

TO BE HONEST, I HAD ALWAYS THOUGHT THE WITCH WAS JUST A LEGEND,

AN INSPIRING FABLE ABOUT FOUR HEROES THAT WOULD HELP ME SLEEP AT NIGHT.

IT WAS ONLY UNTIL I SAW THE THRONE FOR MYSELF THAT I REALIZED THE PROPHECY WAS ALL TOO REAL.

BUT AT THAT MOMENT, FOR WHATEVER REASON...

I WASN'T SCARED.

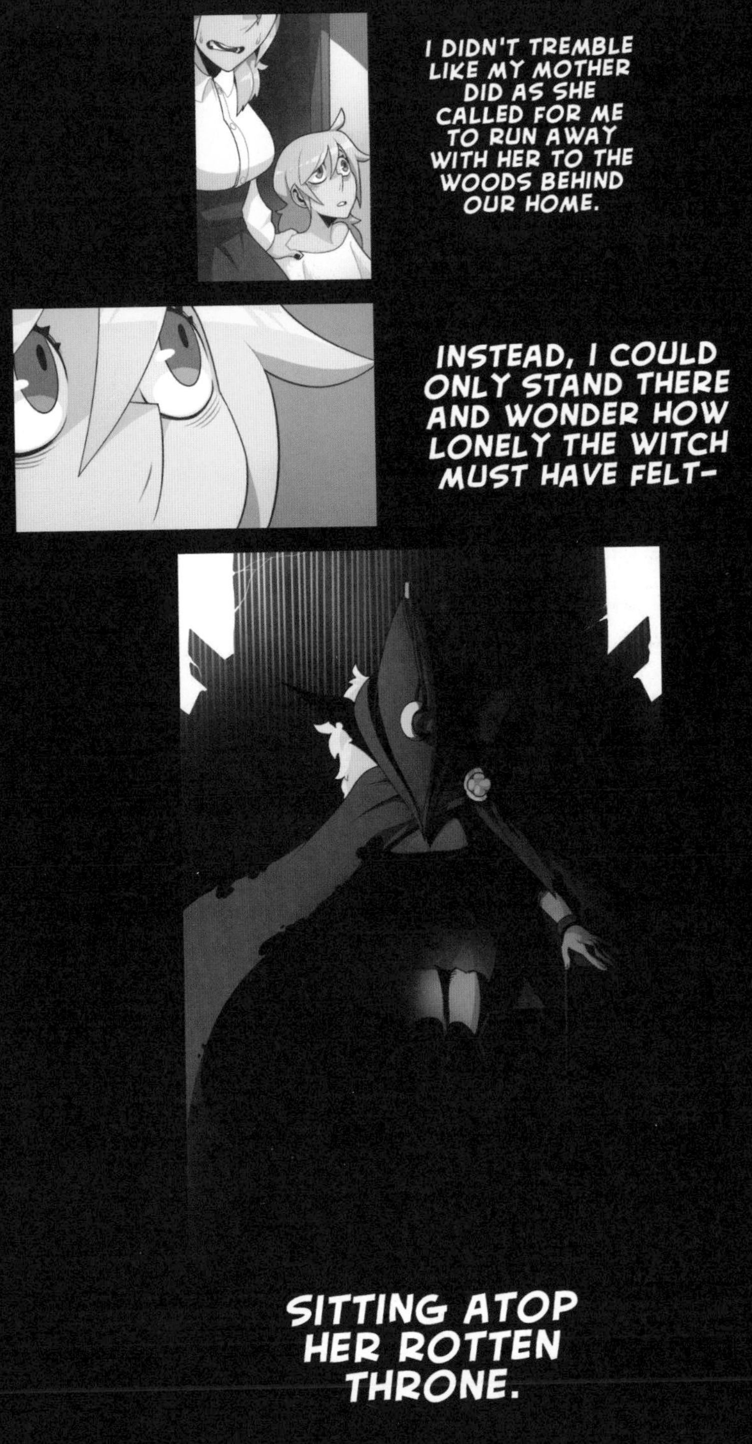
I DIDN'T TREMBLE LIKE MY MOTHER DID AS SHE CALLED FOR ME TO RUN AWAY WITH HER TO THE WOODS BEHIND OUR HOME.
INSTEAD, I COULD ONLY STAND THERE AND WONDER HOW LONELY THE WITCH MUST HAVE FELT-
SITTING ATOP HER ROTTEN THRONE.

# Chapter 1
# THE ALCHEMIST

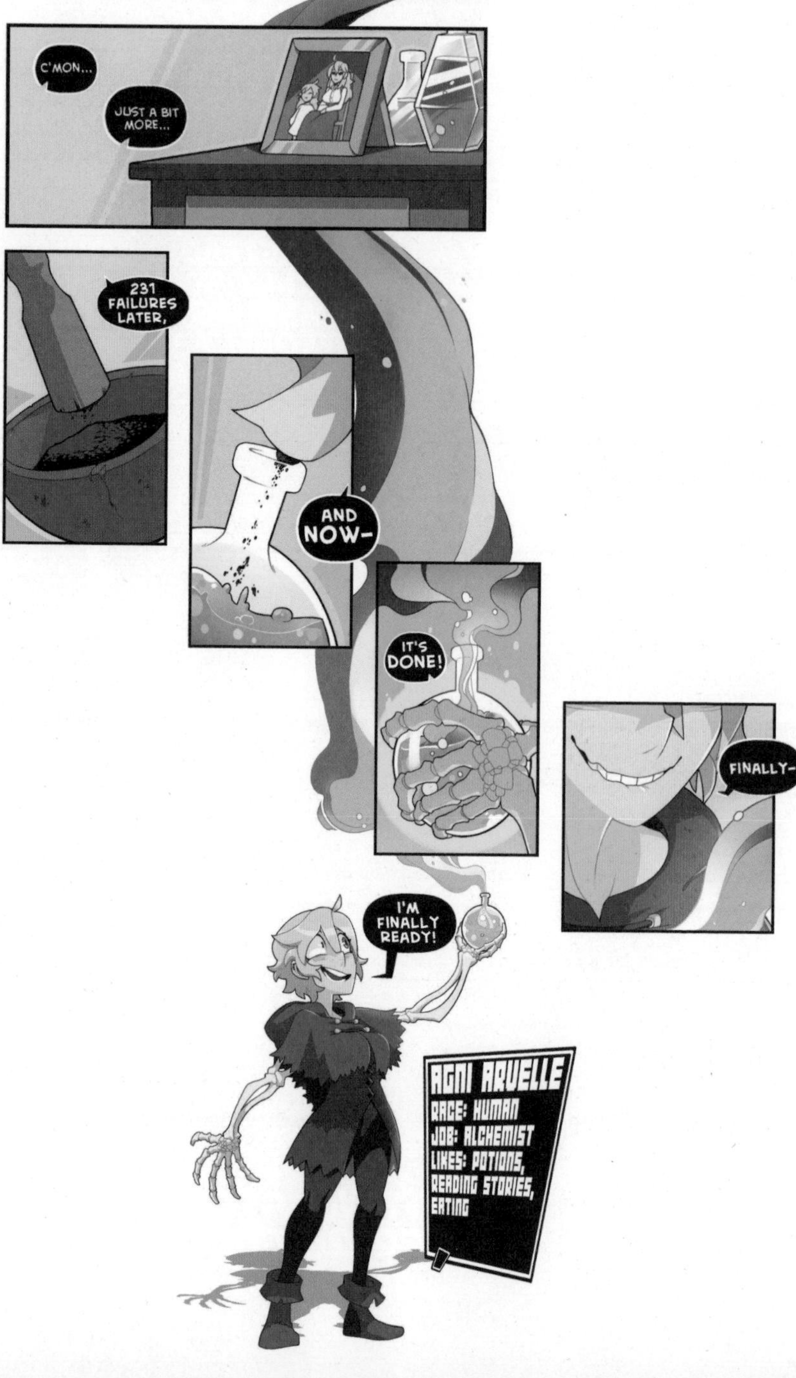

C'MON...
JUST A BIT MORE...
231 FAILURES LATER,
AND NOW-
IT'S DONE!
FINALLY-
I'M FINALLY READY!
AGNI ARVELLE
RACE: HUMAN
JOB: ALCHEMIST
LIKES: POTIONS, READING STORIES, EATING

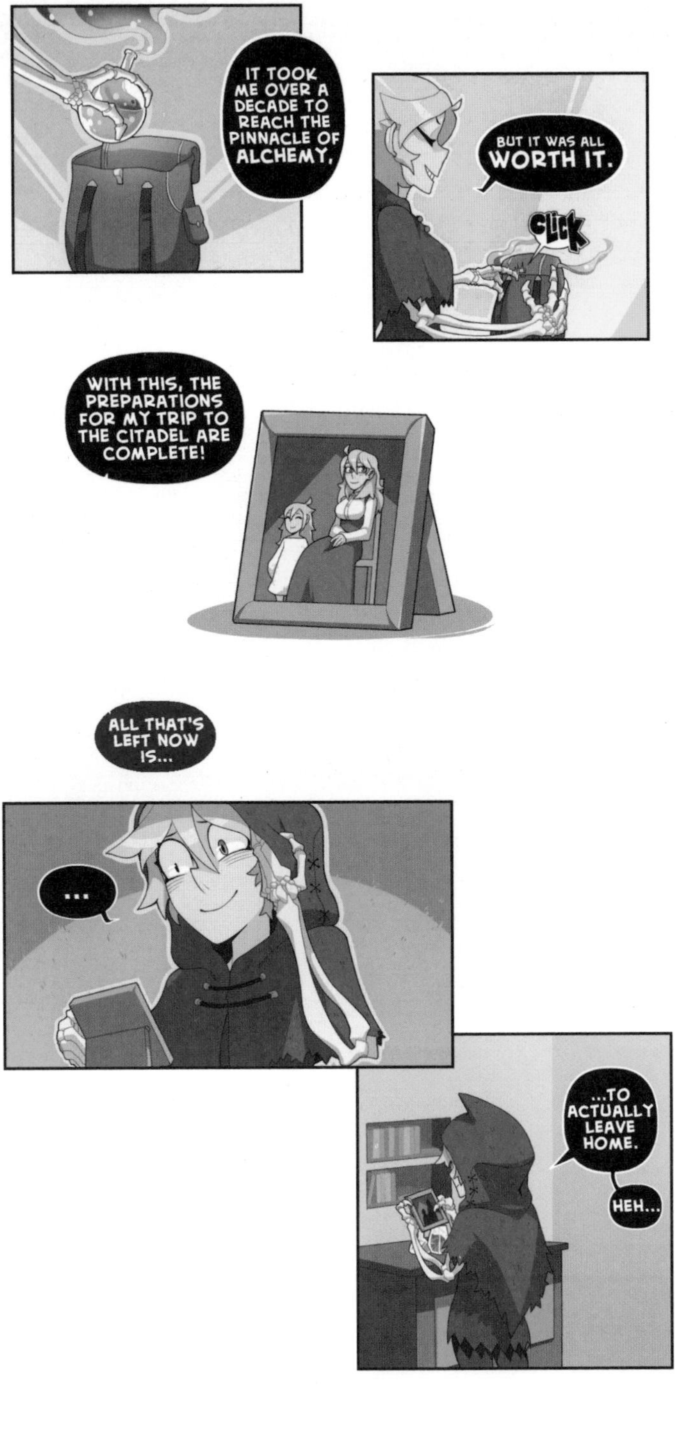
IT TOOK ME OVER A DECADE TO REACH THE PINNACLE OF ALCHEMY,
BUT IT WAS ALL WORTH IT.
CLICK
WITH THIS, THE PREPARATIONS FOR MY TRIP TO THE CITADEL ARE COMPLETE!
ALL THAT'S LEFT NOW IS...
...
...TO ACTUALLY LEAVE HOME.
HEH...

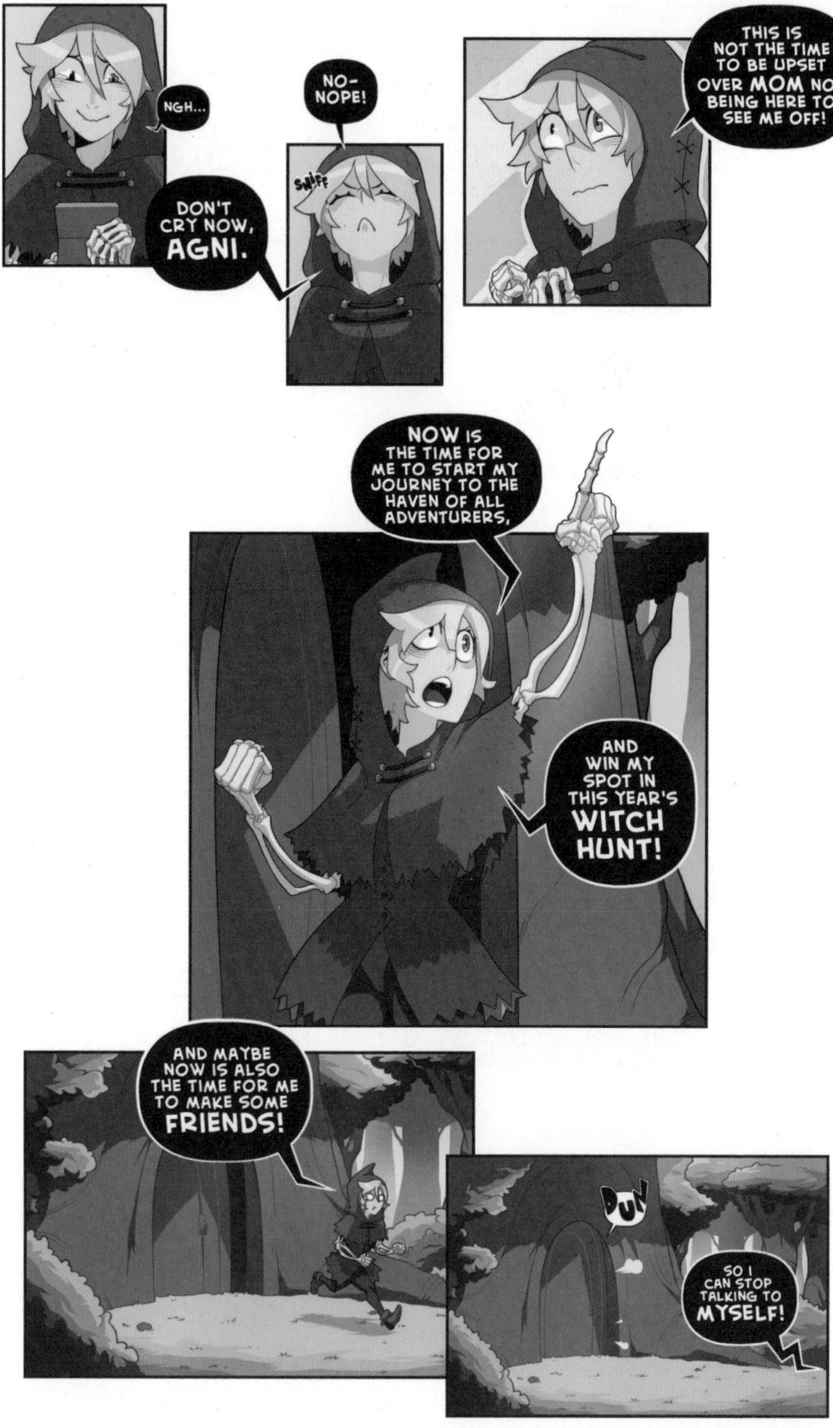
NGH...
DON'T CRY NOW, AGNI.
SNIFF
NO- NOPE!
THIS IS NOT THE TIME TO BE UPSET OVER MOM NOT BEING HERE TO SEE ME OFF!
NOW IS THE TIME FOR ME TO START MY JOURNEY TO THE HAVEN OF ALL ADVENTURERS,
AND WIN MY SPOT IN THIS YEAR'S WITCH HUNT!
AND MAYBE NOW IS ALSO THE TIME FOR ME TO MAKE SOME FRIENDS!
DUN
SO I CAN STOP TALKING TO MYSELF!

3 hours of walking later...

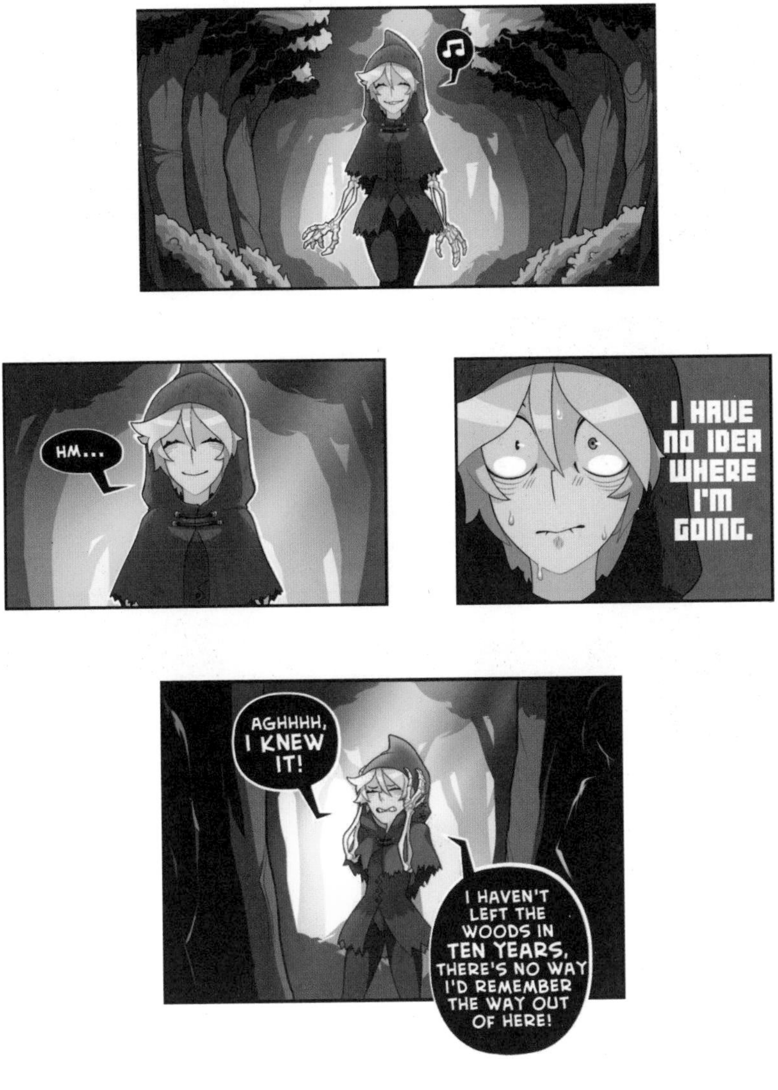

♫
HM...
I HAVE NO IDEA WHERE I'M GOING.
AGHHHH, I KNEW IT!
I HAVEN'T LEFT THE WOODS IN TEN YEARS, THERE'S NO WAY I'D REMEMBER THE WAY OUT OF HERE!

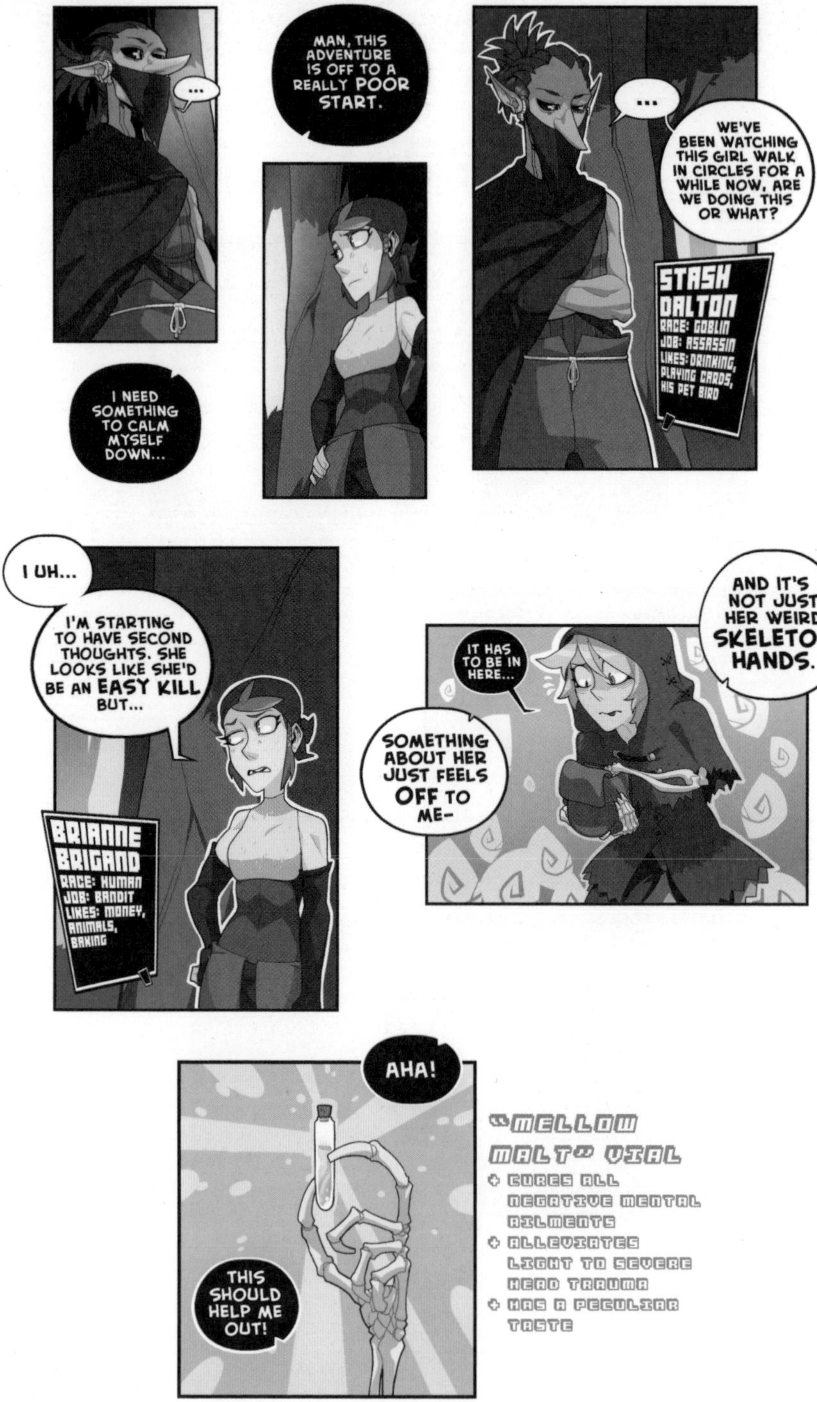

...
MAN, THIS ADVENTURE IS OFF TO A REALLY POOR START.
I NEED SOMETHING TO CALM MYSELF DOWN...
...
WE'VE BEEN WATCHING THIS GIRL WALK IN CIRCLES FOR A WHILE NOW, ARE WE DOING THIS OR WHAT?
STASH DALTON
RACE: GOBLIN
JOB: ASSASSIN
LIKES: DRINKING, PLAYING CARDS, HIS PET BIRD
I UH...
I'M STARTING TO HAVE SECOND THOUGHTS. SHE LOOKS LIKE SHE'D BE AN EASY KILL BUT...
BRIANNE BRIGAND
RACE: HUMAN
JOB: BANDIT
LIKES: MONEY, ANIMALS, BAKING
IT HAS TO BE IN HERE...
SOMETHING ABOUT HER JUST FEELS OFF TO ME-
AND IT'S NOT JUST HER WEIRD SKELETON HANDS.
AHA!
THIS SHOULD HELP ME OUT!
"MELLOW MALT" VIAL
+ CURES ALL NEGATIVE MENTAL AILMENTS
+ ALLEVIATES LIGHT TO SEVERE HEAD TRAUMA
+ HAS A PECULIAR TASTE

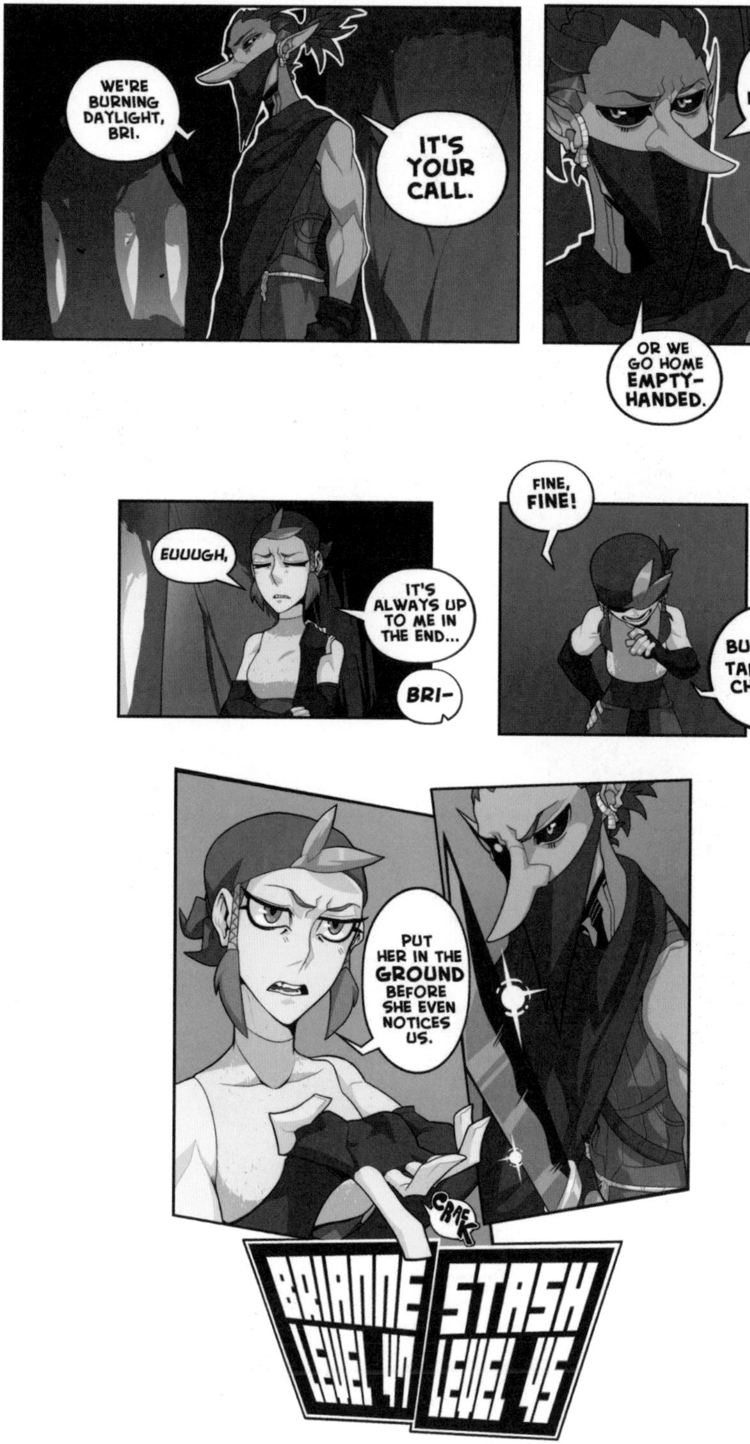
WE'RE BURNING DAYLIGHT, BRI.
IT'S YOUR CALL.
WE EITHER KILL HER FOR SOME QUICK EXPERIENCE AND LOOT,
OR WE GO HOME EMPTY-HANDED.
EUUUGH,
IT'S ALWAYS UP TO ME IN THE END...
BRI-
FINE, FINE!
BUT DON'T TAKE ANY CHANCES!
PUT HER IN THE GROUND BEFORE SHE EVEN NOTICES US.
CRAK
BRIANNE LEVEL 47
STASH LEVEL 45

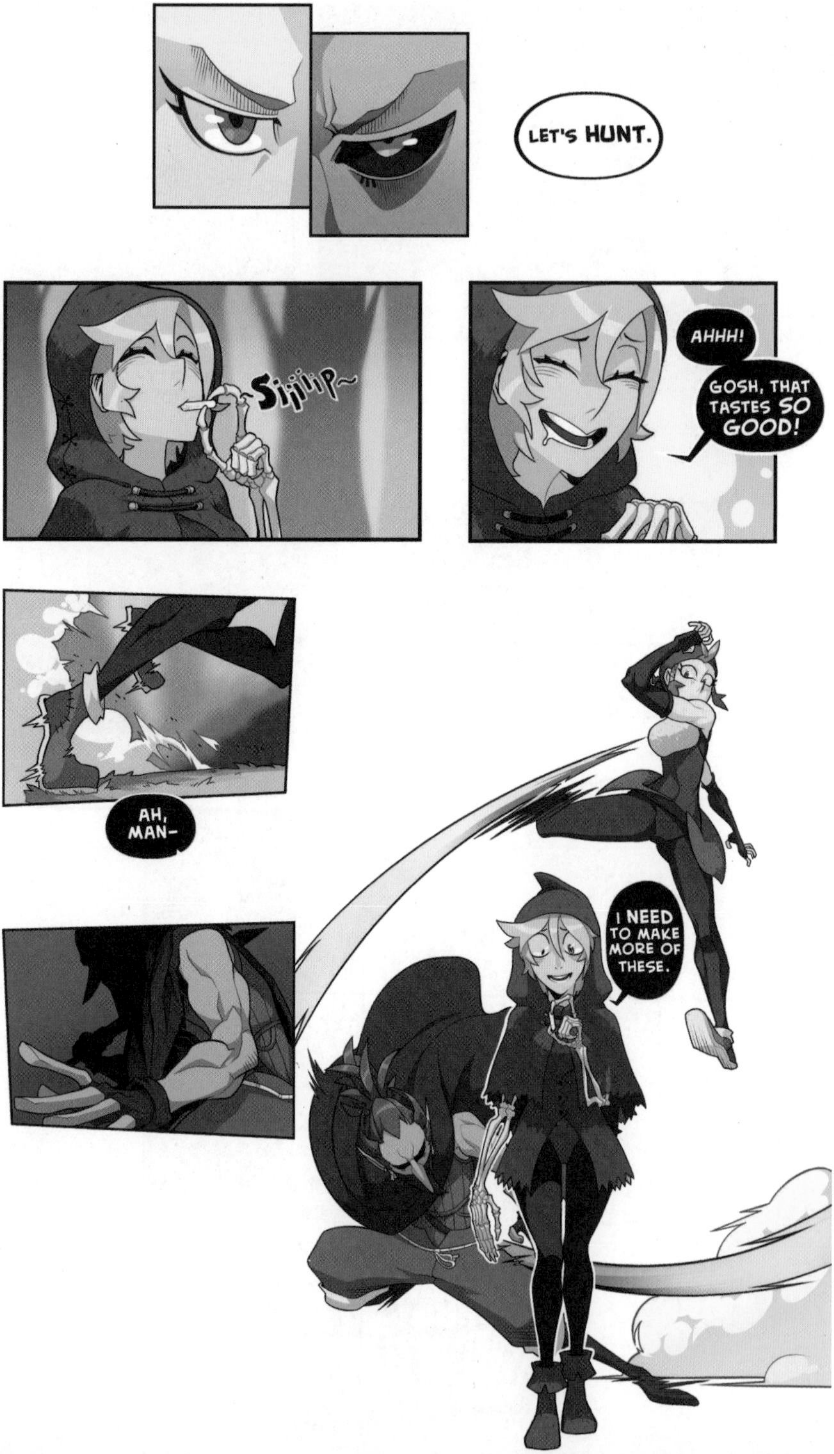
LET'S HUNT.
Siiiiip~
AHHH!
GOSH, THAT TASTES SO GOOD!
AH, MAN-
I NEED TO MAKE MORE OF THESE.

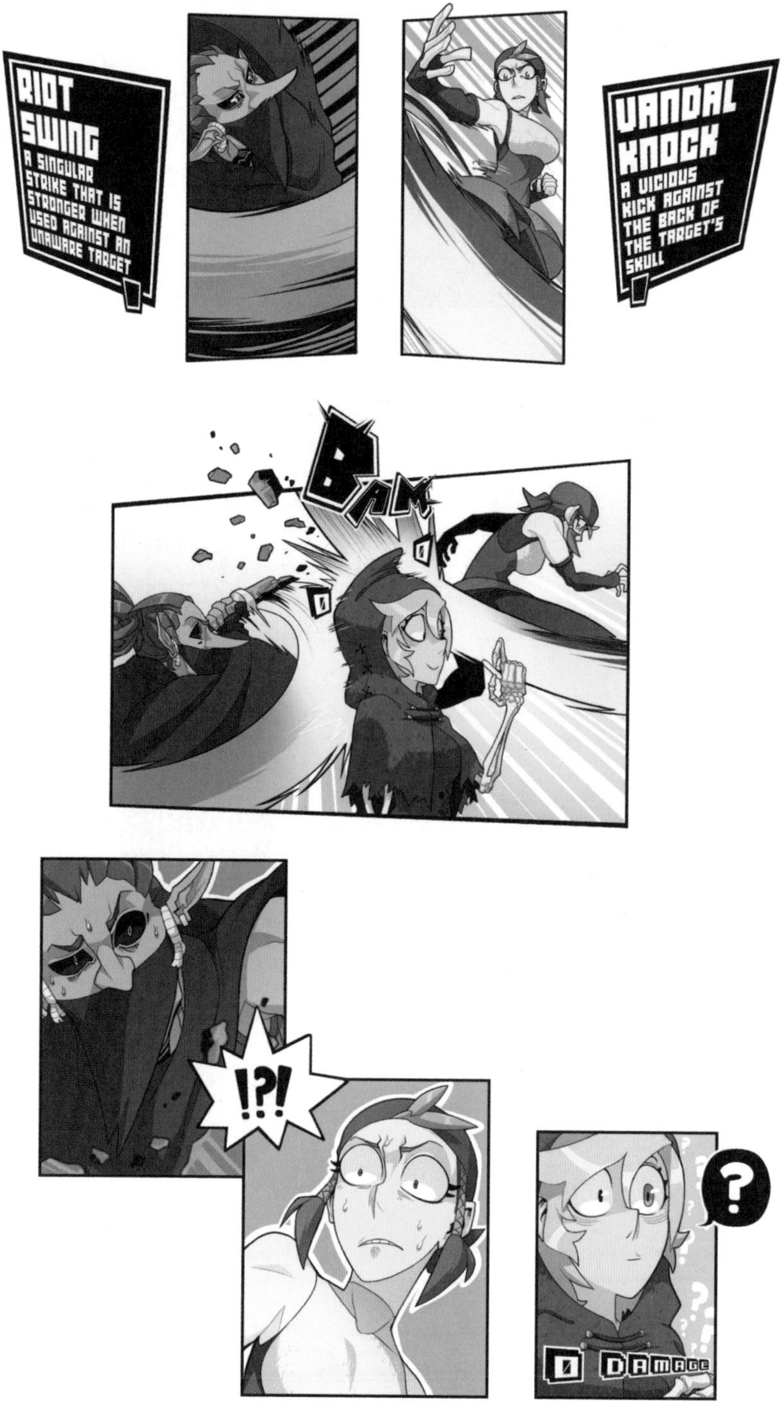
RIOT SWING
A SINGULAR STRIKE THAT IS STRONGER WHEN USED AGAINST AN UNAWARE TARGET
!
VANDAL KNOCK
A VICIOUS KICK AGAINST THE BACK OF THE TARGET'S SKULL
!
BAM
0
0
!?!
?
0 DAMAGE

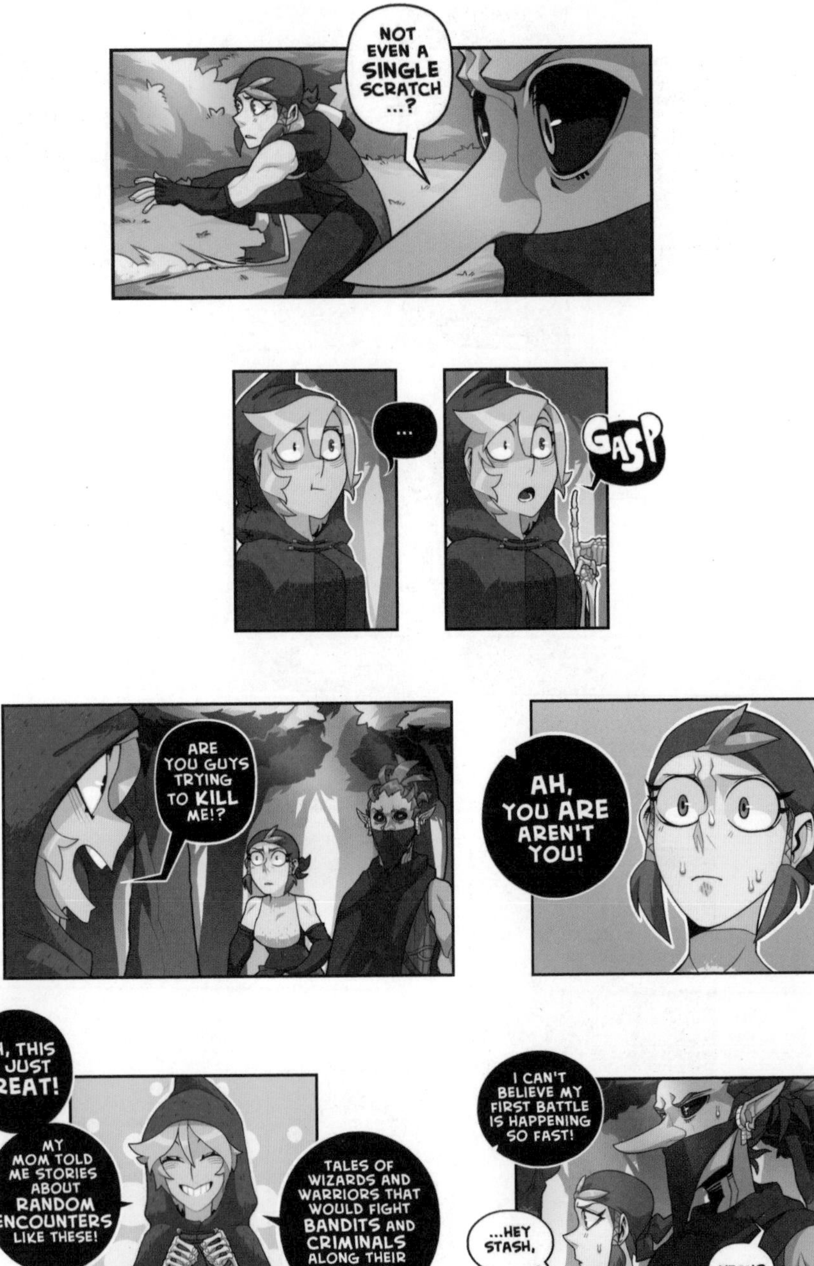
NOT EVEN A SINGLE SCRATCH ...?
...
GASP
ARE YOU GUYS TRYING TO KILL ME!?
AH, YOU ARE AREN'T YOU!
OH, THIS IS JUST GREAT!
MY MOM TOLD ME STORIES ABOUT RANDOM ENCOUNTERS LIKE THESE!
TALES OF WIZARDS AND WARRIORS THAT WOULD FIGHT BANDITS AND CRIMINALS ALONG THEIR TRAVELS!
I CAN'T BELIEVE MY FIRST BATTLE IS HAPPENING SO FAST!
...HEY STASH,
YEAH?

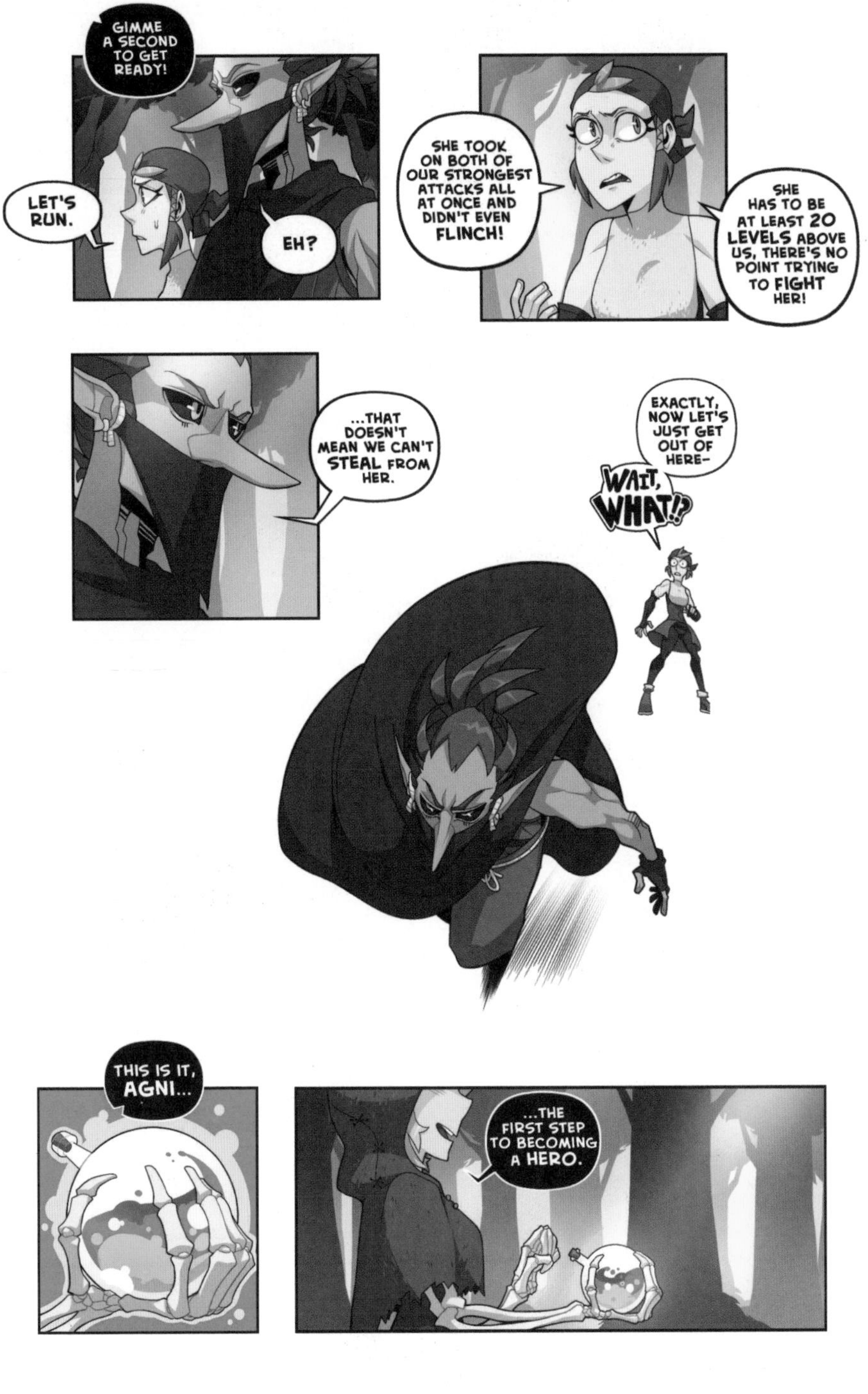
GIMME A SECOND TO GET READY!
LET'S RUN.
EH?
SHE TOOK ON BOTH OF OUR STRONGEST ATTACKS ALL AT ONCE AND DIDN'T EVEN FLINCH!
SHE HAS TO BE AT LEAST 20 LEVELS ABOVE US, THERE'S NO POINT TRYING TO FIGHT HER!
...THAT DOESN'T MEAN WE CAN'T STEAL FROM HER.
EXACTLY, NOW LET'S JUST GET OUT OF HERE-
WAIT, WHAT!?
THIS IS IT, AGNI...
...THE FIRST STEP TO BECOMING A HERO.

I'M NOT LEAVING THESE DAMNED WOODS WITH NOTHING,

JUST BECAUSE THIS NUTCASE HAS BETTER NUMBERS THAN ME.

**VULTURE'S GRASP**

SHATTER.

**FWOOM**

**ORIGINAL FLASK IRE OF AMADEUS**

18

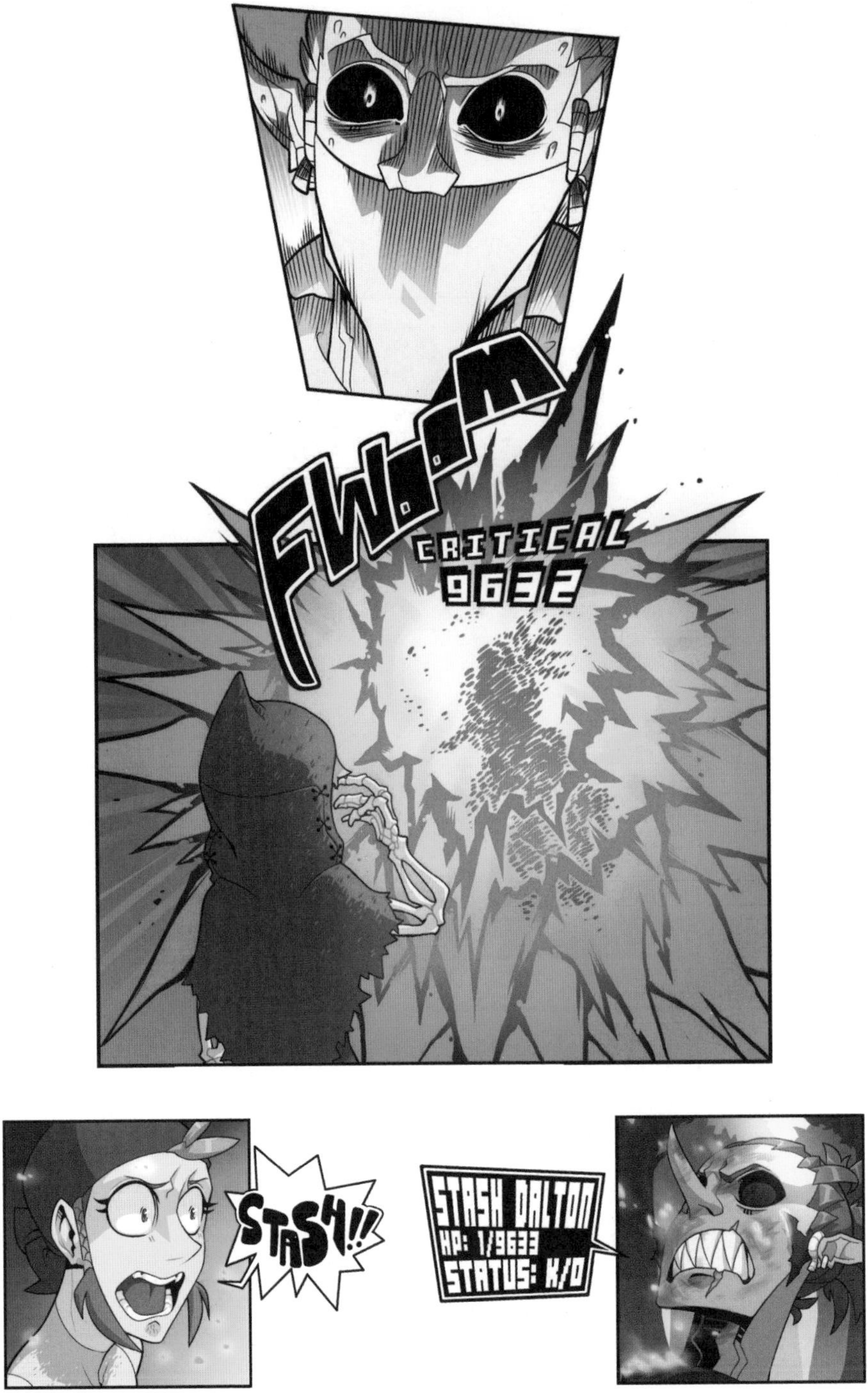
FWOOM
CRITICAL
9632
STASH!!
STASH DALTON
HP: 1/9633
STATUS: K/O

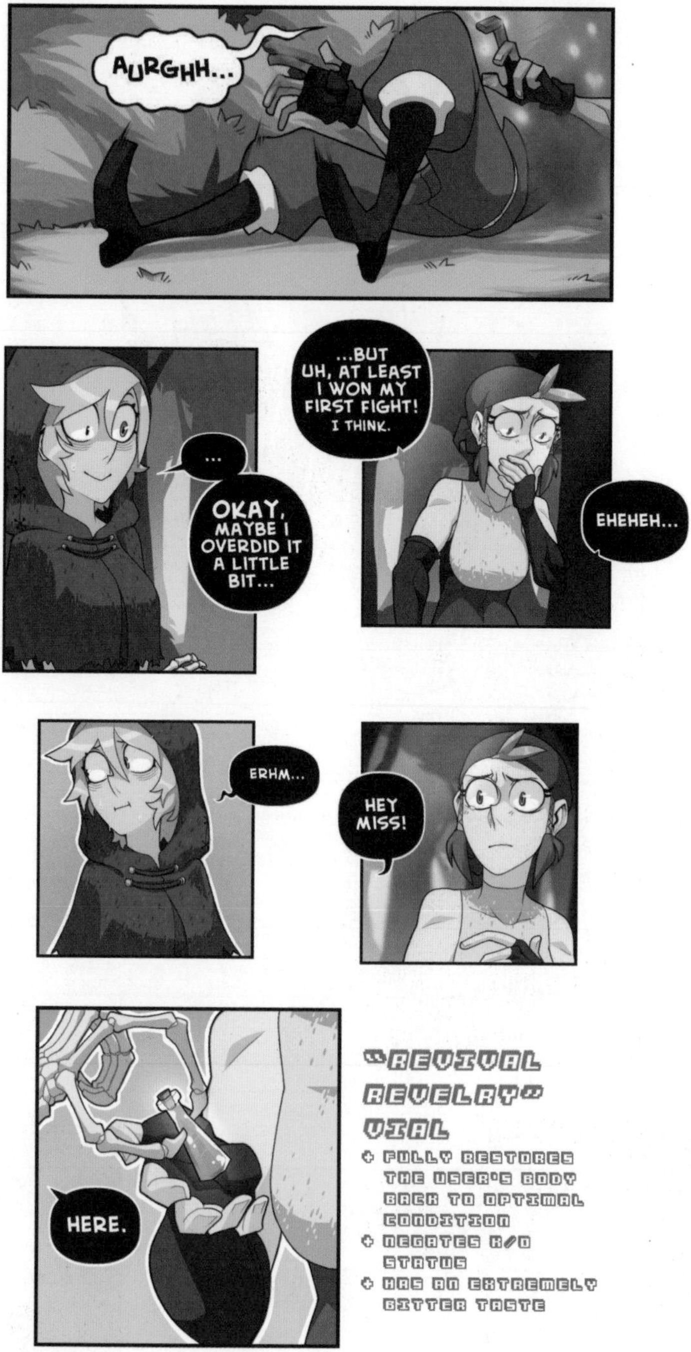
AURGHH...
...
OKAY, MAYBE I OVERDID IT A LITTLE BIT...
...BUT UH, AT LEAST I WON MY FIRST FIGHT! I THINK.
EHEHEH...
ERHM...
HEY MISS!
HERE.
"REVIVAL REVELRY" VIAL
+ FULLY RESTORES THE USER'S BODY BACK TO OPTIMAL CONDITION
+ NEGATES K/O STATUS
+ HAS AN EXTREMELY BITTER TASTE

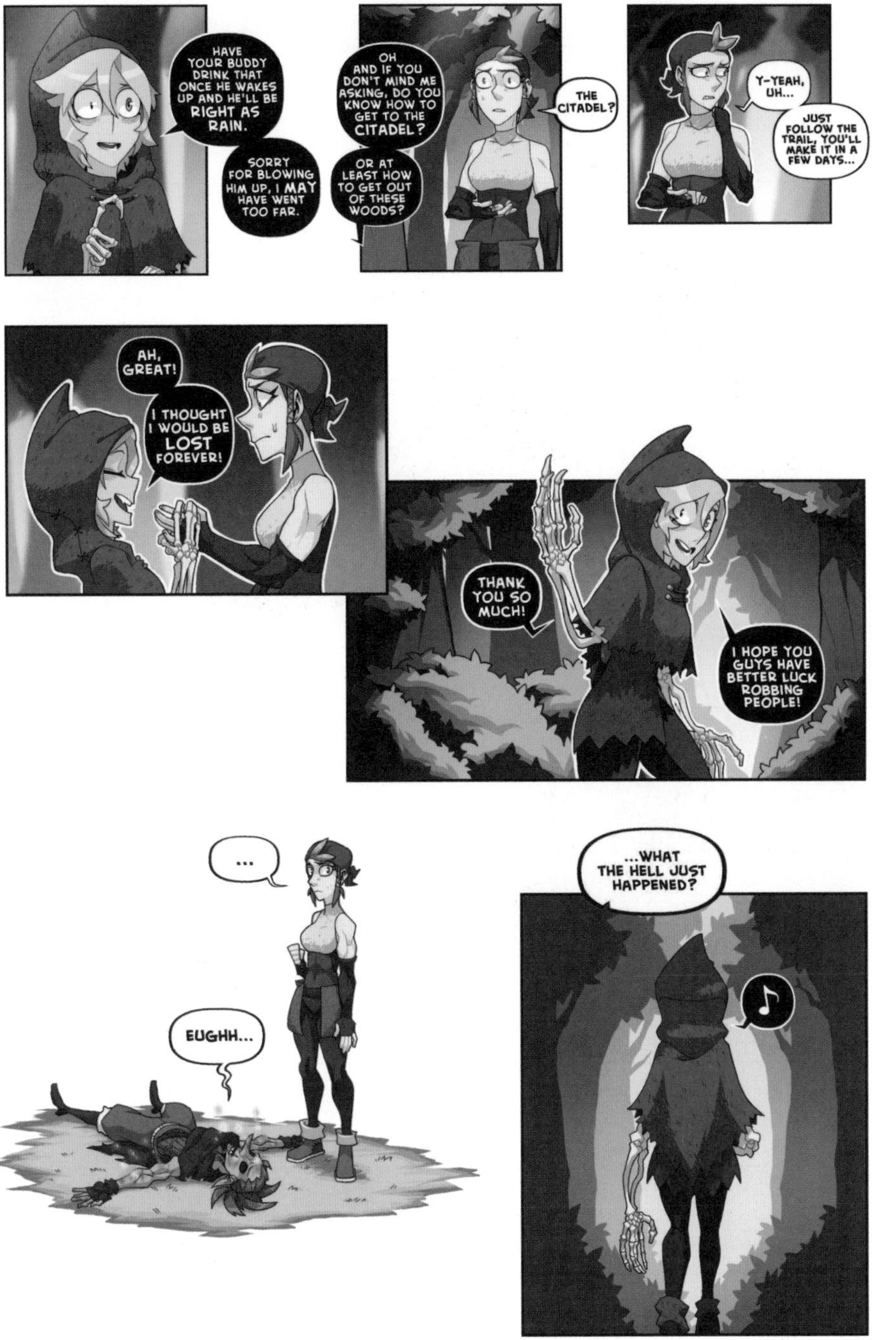
HAVE YOUR BUDDY DRINK THAT ONCE HE WAKES UP AND HE'LL BE RIGHT AS RAIN.
SORRY FOR BLOWING HIM UP, I MAY HAVE WENT TOO FAR.
OH AND IF YOU DON'T MIND ME ASKING, DO YOU KNOW HOW TO GET TO THE CITADEL?
OR AT LEAST HOW TO GET OUT OF THESE WOODS?
THE CITADEL?
Y-YEAH, UH...
JUST FOLLOW THE TRAIL, YOU'LL MAKE IT IN A FEW DAYS...
AH, GREAT!
I THOUGHT I WOULD BE LOST FOREVER!
THANK YOU SO MUCH!
I HOPE YOU GUYS HAVE BETTER LUCK ROBBING PEOPLE!
...
EUGHH...
...WHAT THE HELL JUST HAPPENED?
♪

## Chapter 2
# THE BLACKSMITH

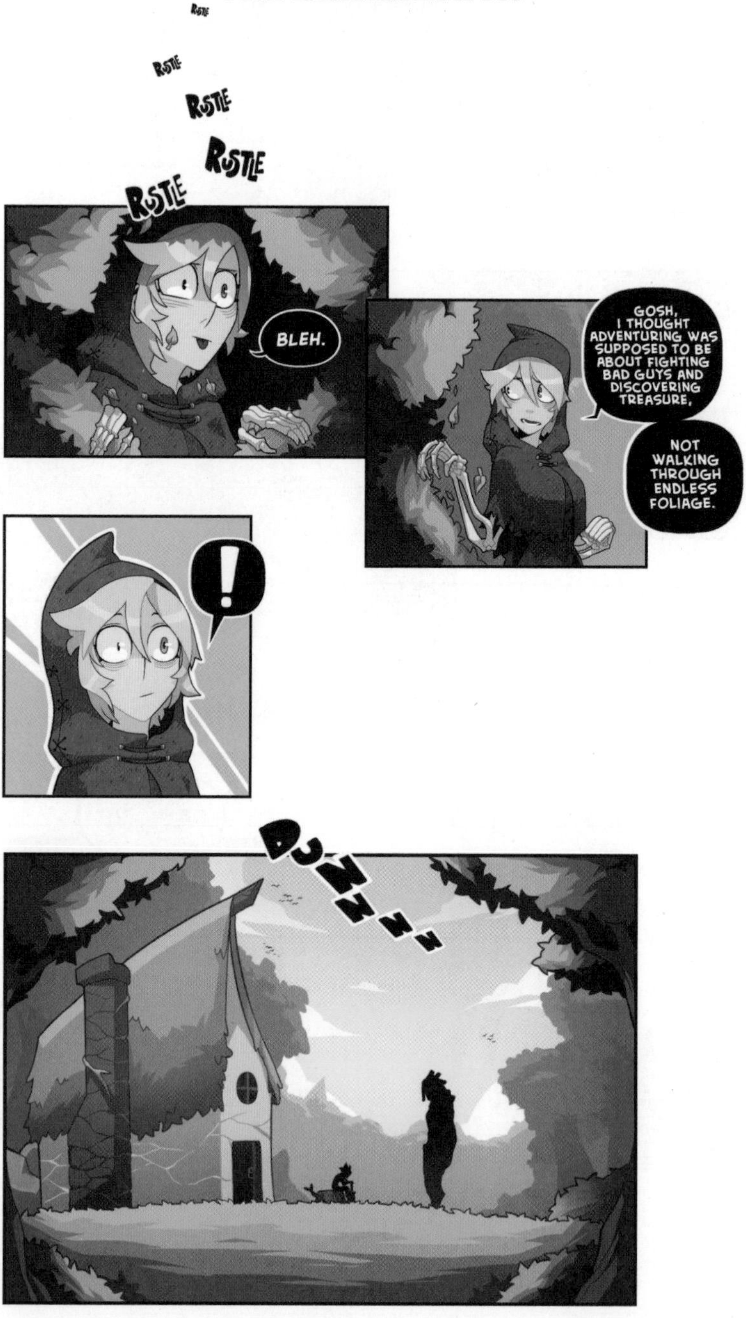
RUSTLE
RUSTLE
RUSTLE
RUSTLE
RUSTLE
BLEH.
GOSH, I THOUGHT ADVENTURING WAS SUPPOSED TO BE ABOUT FIGHTING BAD GUYS AND DISCOVERING TREASURE,
NOT WALKING THROUGH ENDLESS FOLIAGE.
!
DUNNNN

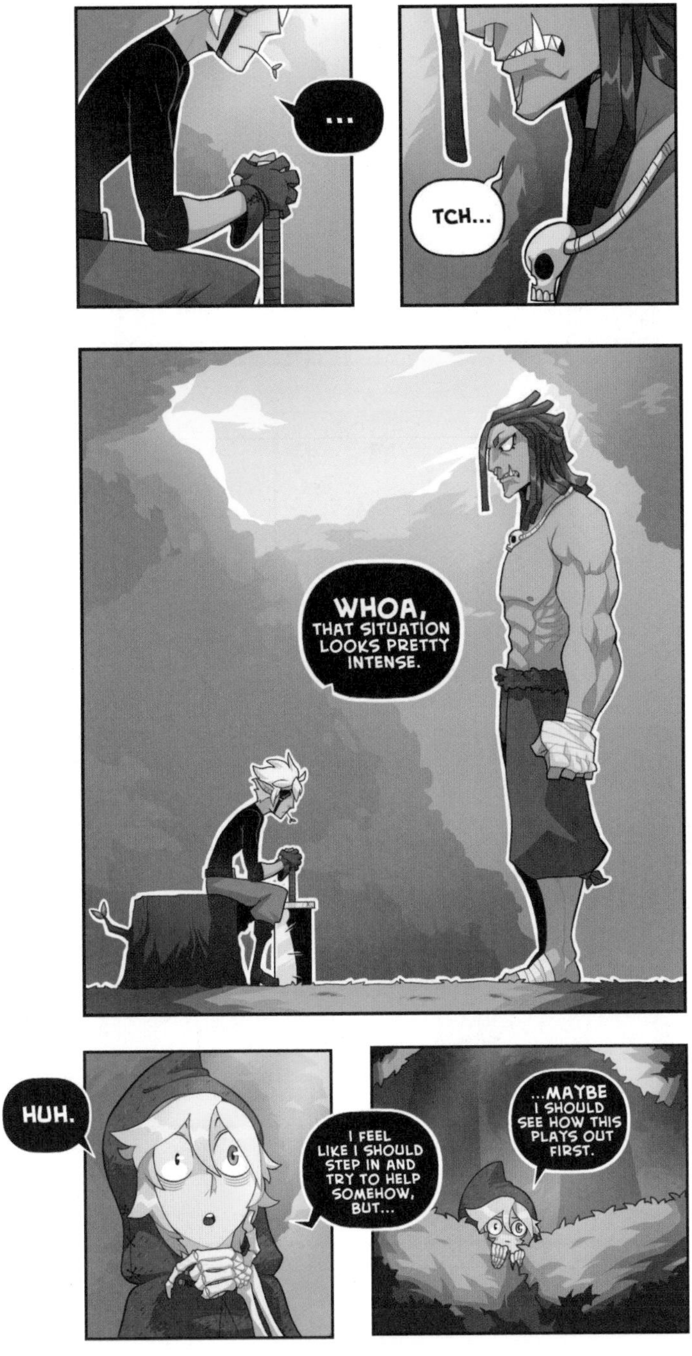
...
TCH...
WHOA, THAT SITUATION LOOKS PRETTY INTENSE.
HUH.
I FEEL LIKE I SHOULD STEP IN AND TRY TO HELP SOMEHOW, BUT...
...MAYBE I SHOULD SEE HOW THIS PLAYS OUT FIRST.

I REFUSE.
YOU REFUSE?
W-WHAT DO YOU MEAN?
I'M NOT INTERESTED IN FIGHTING YOU,
PLAIN AND SIMPLE.
Y-YOU CAN'T BE SERIOUS.
THE WITCH HUNT TOURNAMENTS START ONE MONTH FROM NOW, I NEED THIS FIGHT.

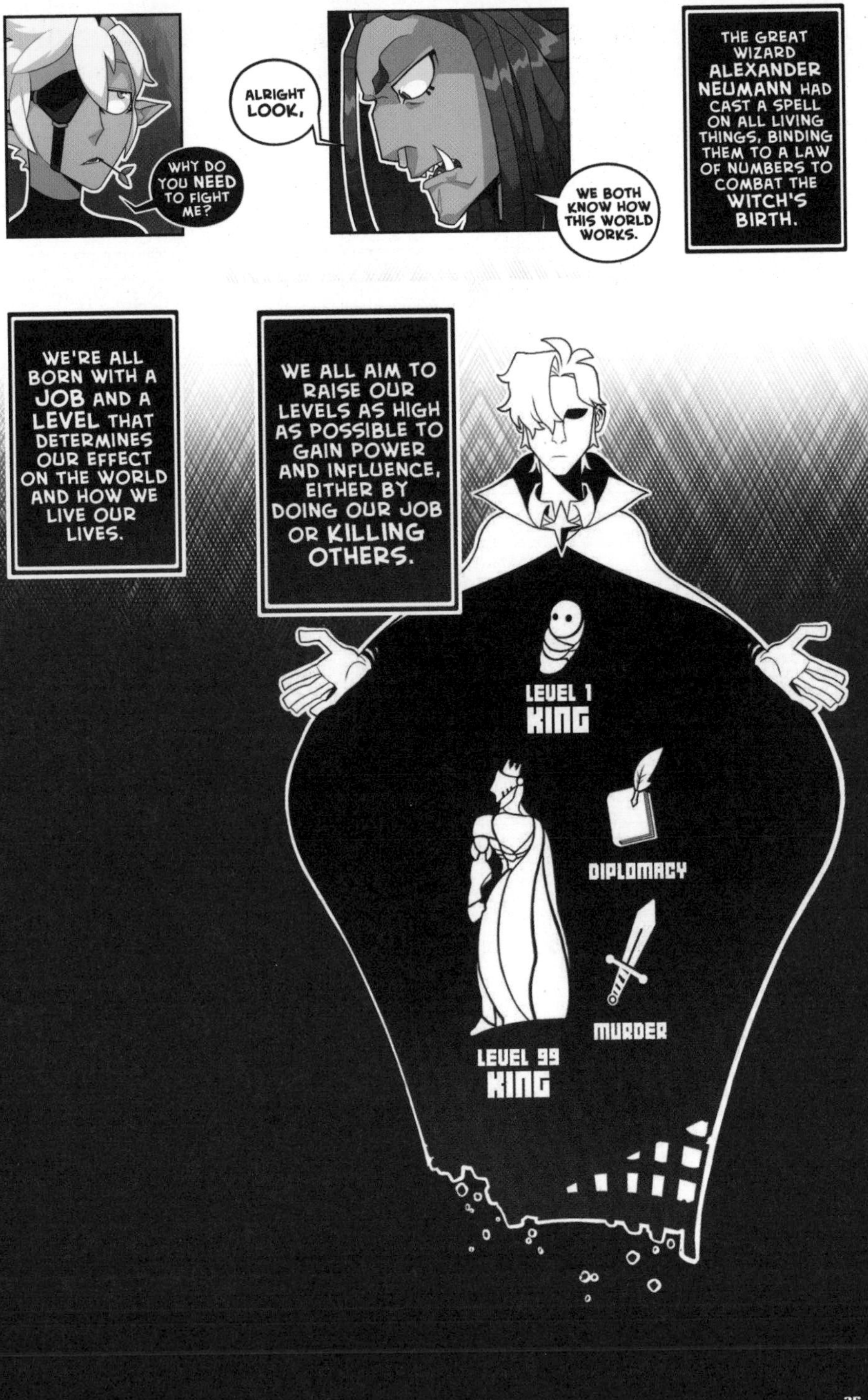
WHY DO YOU NEED TO FIGHT ME?
ALRIGHT LOOK,
WE BOTH KNOW HOW THIS WORLD WORKS.
THE GREAT WIZARD ALEXANDER NEUMANN HAD CAST A SPELL ON ALL LIVING THINGS, BINDING THEM TO A LAW OF NUMBERS TO COMBAT THE WITCH'S BIRTH.
WE'RE ALL BORN WITH A JOB AND A LEVEL THAT DETERMINES OUR EFFECT ON THE WORLD AND HOW WE LIVE OUR LIVES.
WE ALL AIM TO RAISE OUR LEVELS AS HIGH AS POSSIBLE TO GAIN POWER AND INFLUENCE, EITHER BY DOING OUR JOB OR KILLING OTHERS.
LEVEL 1 KING
DIPLOMACY
MURDER
LEVEL 99 KING

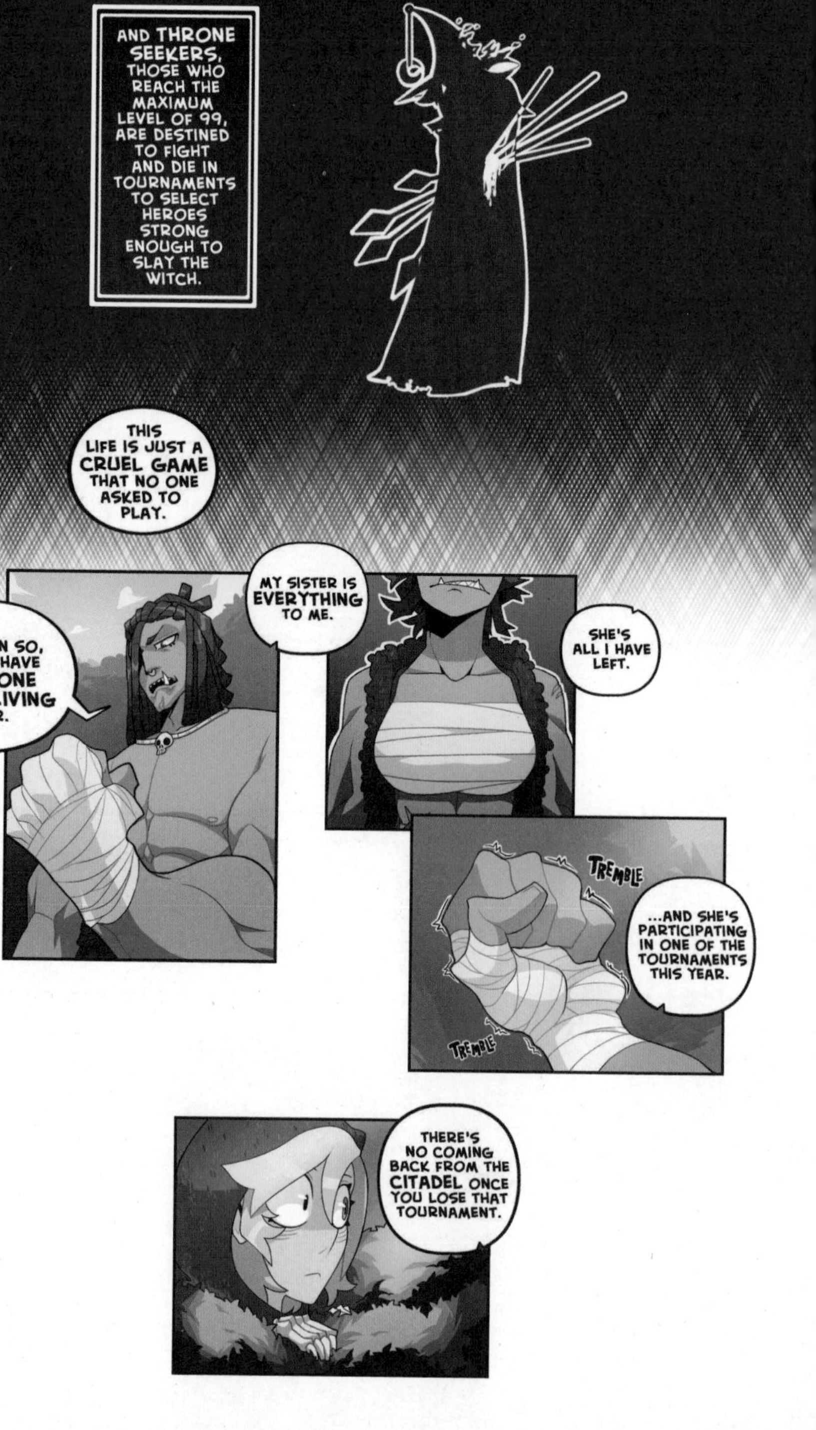
AND THRONE SEEKERS, THOSE WHO REACH THE MAXIMUM LEVEL OF 99, ARE DESTINED TO FIGHT AND DIE IN TOURNAMENTS TO SELECT HEROES STRONG ENOUGH TO SLAY THE WITCH.
THIS LIFE IS JUST A CRUEL GAME THAT NO ONE ASKED TO PLAY.
BUT EVEN SO, I STILL HAVE SOMEONE WORTH LIVING FOR.
MY SISTER IS EVERYTHING TO ME.
SHE'S ALL I HAVE LEFT.
TREMBLE
...AND SHE'S PARTICIPATING IN ONE OF THE TOURNAMENTS THIS YEAR.
TREMBLE
THERE'S NO COMING BACK FROM THE CITADEL ONCE YOU LOSE THAT TOURNAMENT.

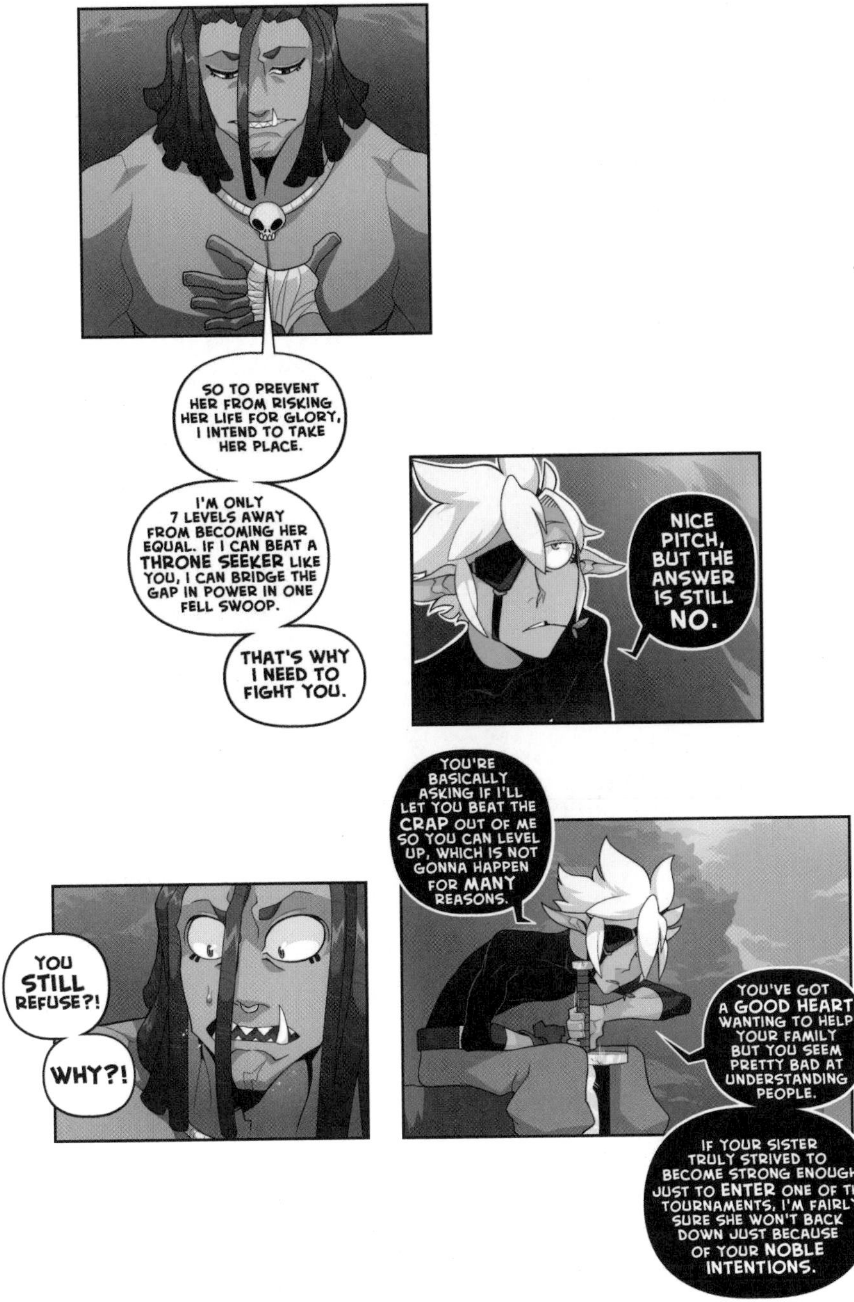
SO TO PREVENT HER FROM RISKING HER LIFE FOR GLORY, I INTEND TO TAKE HER PLACE.
I'M ONLY 7 LEVELS AWAY FROM BECOMING HER EQUAL. IF I CAN BEAT A THRONE SEEKER LIKE YOU, I CAN BRIDGE THE GAP IN POWER IN ONE FELL SWOOP.
THAT'S WHY I NEED TO FIGHT YOU.
NICE PITCH, BUT THE ANSWER IS STILL NO.
YOU STILL REFUSE?!
WHY?!
YOU'RE BASICALLY ASKING IF I'LL LET YOU BEAT THE CRAP OUT OF ME SO YOU CAN LEVEL UP, WHICH IS NOT GONNA HAPPEN FOR MANY REASONS.
YOU'VE GOT A GOOD HEART WANTING TO HELP YOUR FAMILY BUT YOU SEEM PRETTY BAD AT UNDERSTANDING PEOPLE.
IF YOUR SISTER TRULY STRIVED TO BECOME STRONG ENOUGH JUST TO ENTER ONE OF THE TOURNAMENTS, I'M FAIRLY SURE SHE WON'T BACK DOWN JUST BECAUSE OF YOUR NOBLE INTENTIONS.

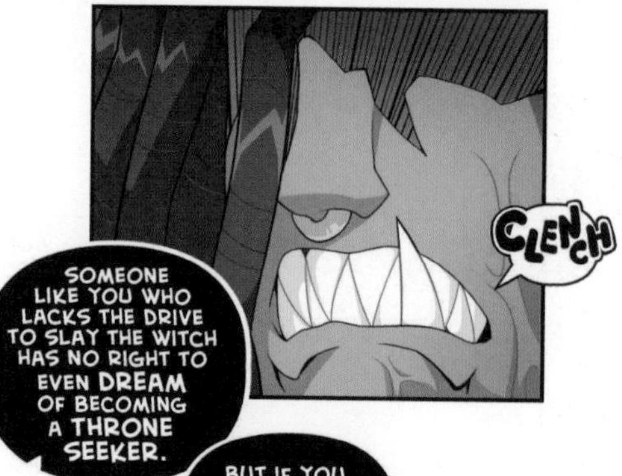
CLENCH
SOMEONE LIKE YOU WHO LACKS THE DRIVE TO SLAY THE WITCH HAS NO RIGHT TO EVEN DREAM OF BECOMING A THRONE SEEKER.

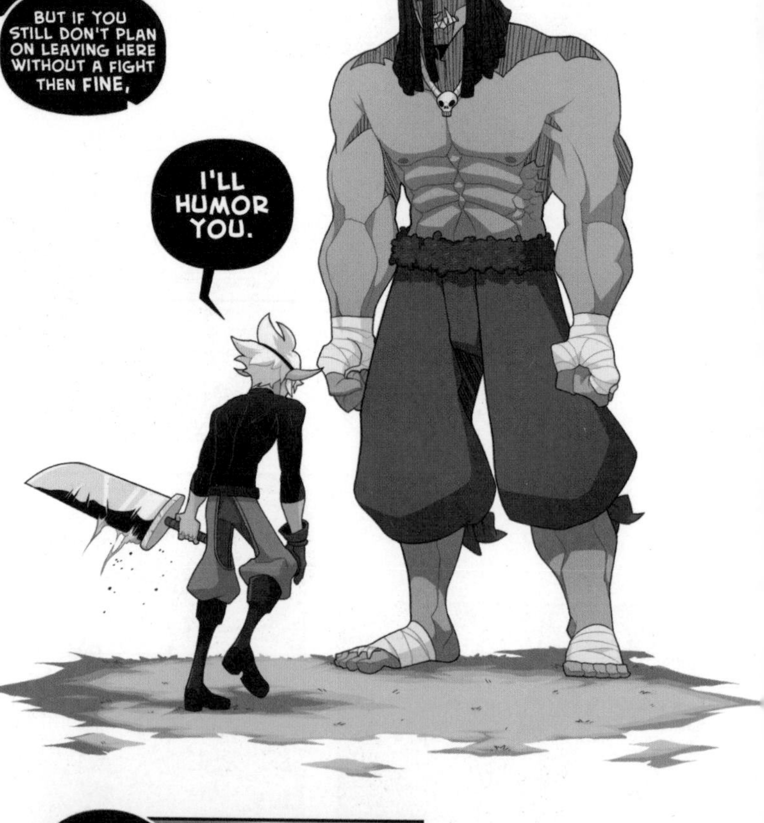
BUT IF YOU STILL DON'T PLAN ON LEAVING HERE WITHOUT A FIGHT THEN FINE,
I'LL HUMOR YOU.

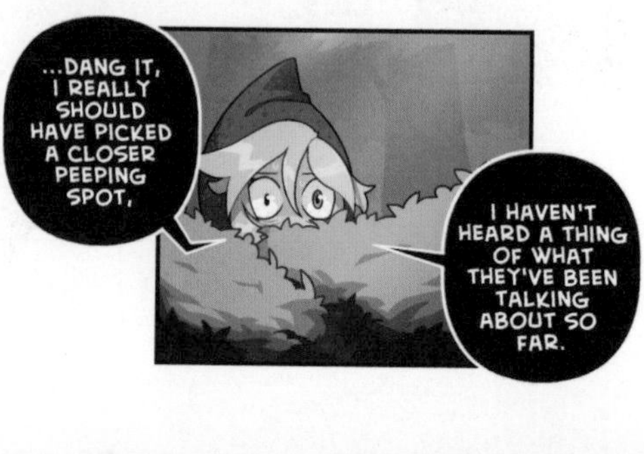
...DANG IT, I REALLY SHOULD HAVE PICKED A CLOSER PEEPING SPOT,
I HAVEN'T HEARD A THING OF WHAT THEY'VE BEEN TALKING ABOUT SO FAR.

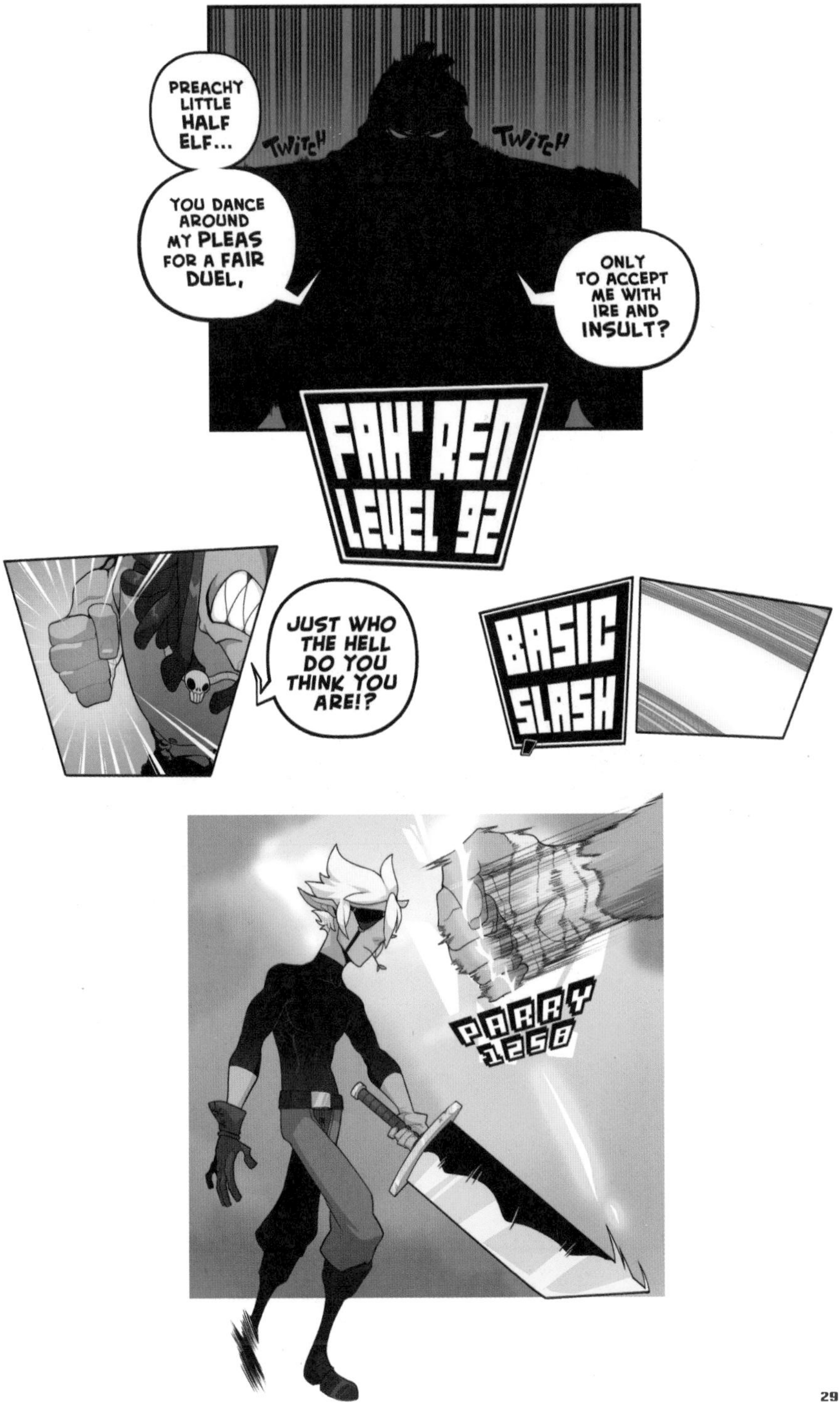
PREACHY LITTLE HALF ELF...
TWITCH
TWITCH
YOU DANCE AROUND MY PLEAS FOR A FAIR DUEL,
ONLY TO ACCEPT ME WITH IRE AND INSULT?
FAH'REN LEVEL 92
JUST WHO THE HELL DO YOU THINK YOU ARE!?
BASIC SLASH
PARRY 1258

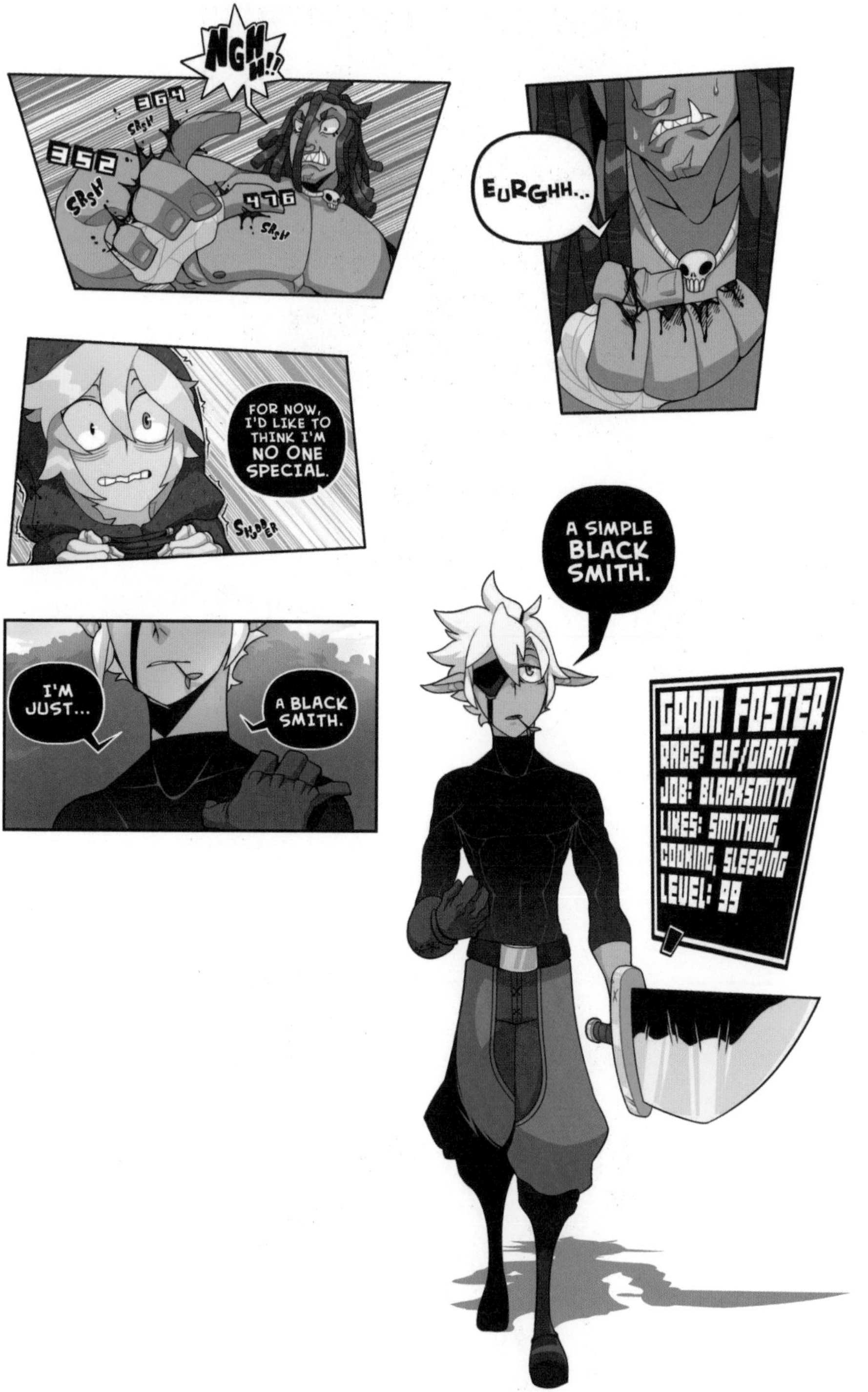
NGHH!!
364
SRSH
352
SRSH
476
SRSH
EURGHH...
FOR NOW, I'D LIKE TO THINK I'M NO ONE SPECIAL.
SHUDDER
I'M JUST...
A BLACK SMITH.
A SIMPLE BLACK SMITH.
GROM FOSTER
RACE: ELF/GIANT
JOB: BLACKSMITH
LIKES: SMITHING, COOKING, SLEEPING
LEVEL: 99

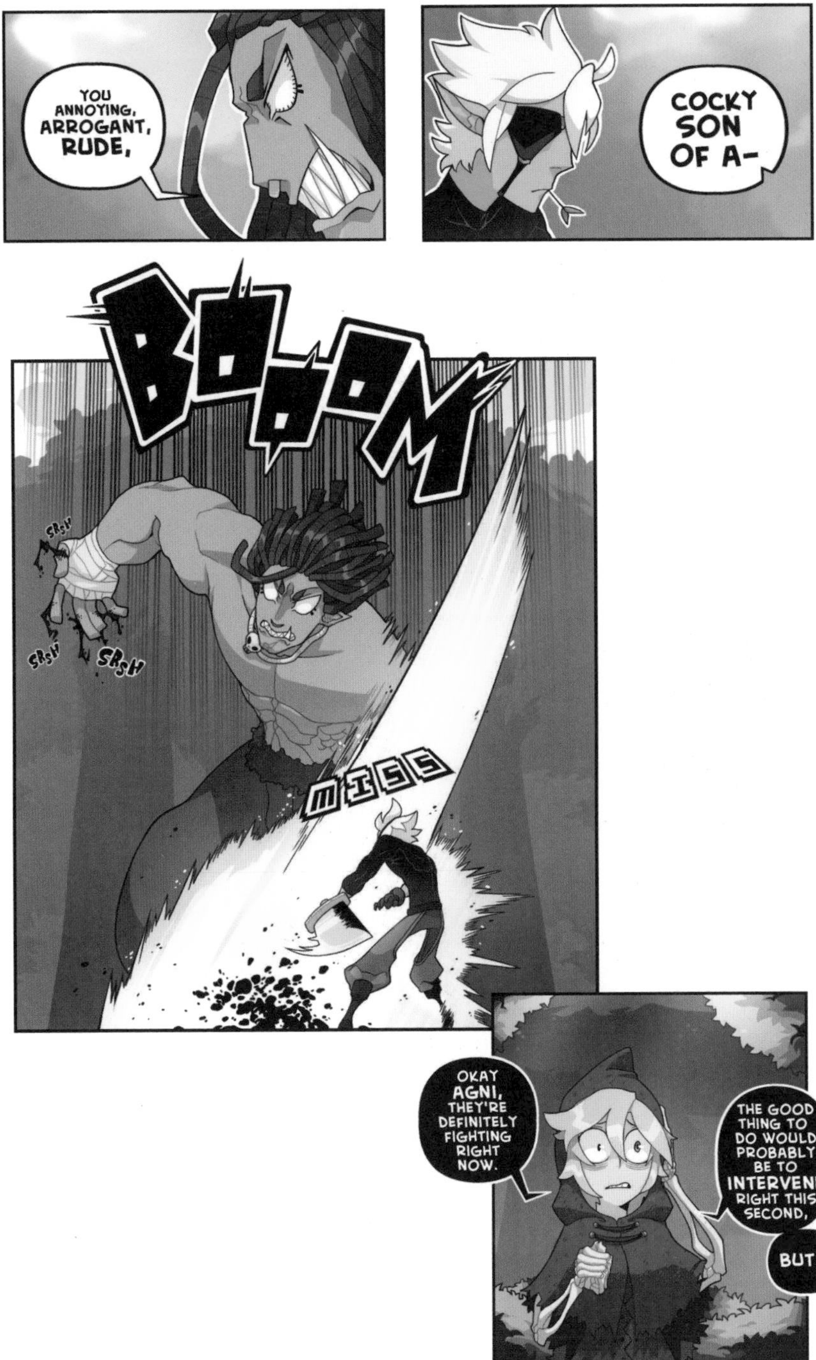
YOU ANNOYING, ARROGANT, RUDE,
COCKY SON OF A-
BOOOOM
SRSH
SRSH
SRSH
MISS
OKAY AGNI, THEY'RE DEFINITELY FIGHTING RIGHT NOW.
THE GOOD THING TO DO WOULD PROBABLY BE TO INTERVENE RIGHT THIS SECOND,
BUT...

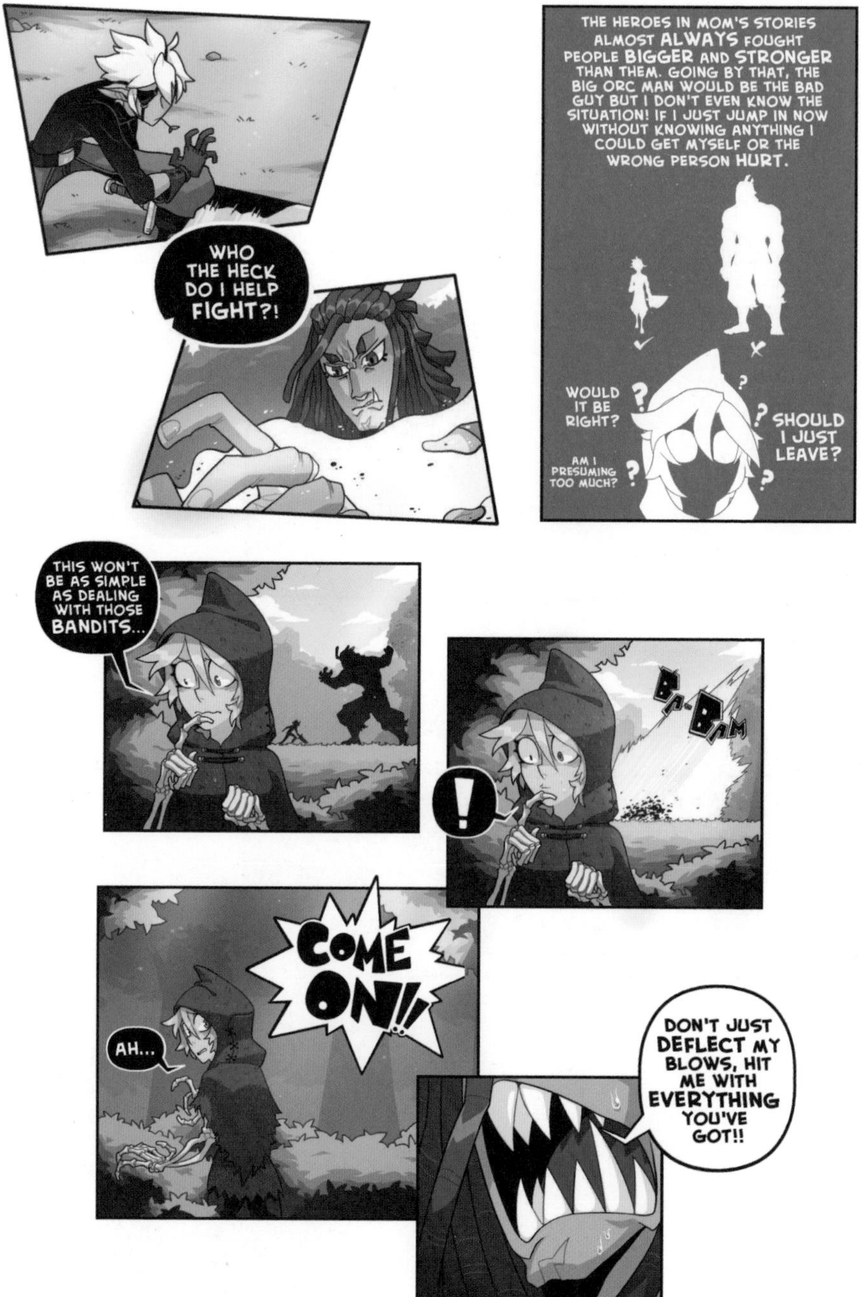
WHO THE HECK DO I HELP FIGHT?!
THE HEROES IN MOM'S STORIES ALMOST ALWAYS FOUGHT PEOPLE BIGGER AND STRONGER THAN THEM. GOING BY THAT, THE BIG ORC MAN WOULD BE THE BAD GUY BUT I DON'T EVEN KNOW THE SITUATION! IF I JUST JUMP IN NOW WITHOUT KNOWING ANYTHING I COULD GET MYSELF OR THE WRONG PERSON HURT.
WOULD IT BE RIGHT?
SHOULD I JUST LEAVE?
AM I PRESUMING TOO MUCH?
THIS WON'T BE AS SIMPLE AS DEALING WITH THOSE BANDITS...
BA-BAM
!
COME ON!!
AH...
DON'T JUST DEFLECT MY BLOWS, HIT ME WITH EVERYTHING YOU'VE GOT!!

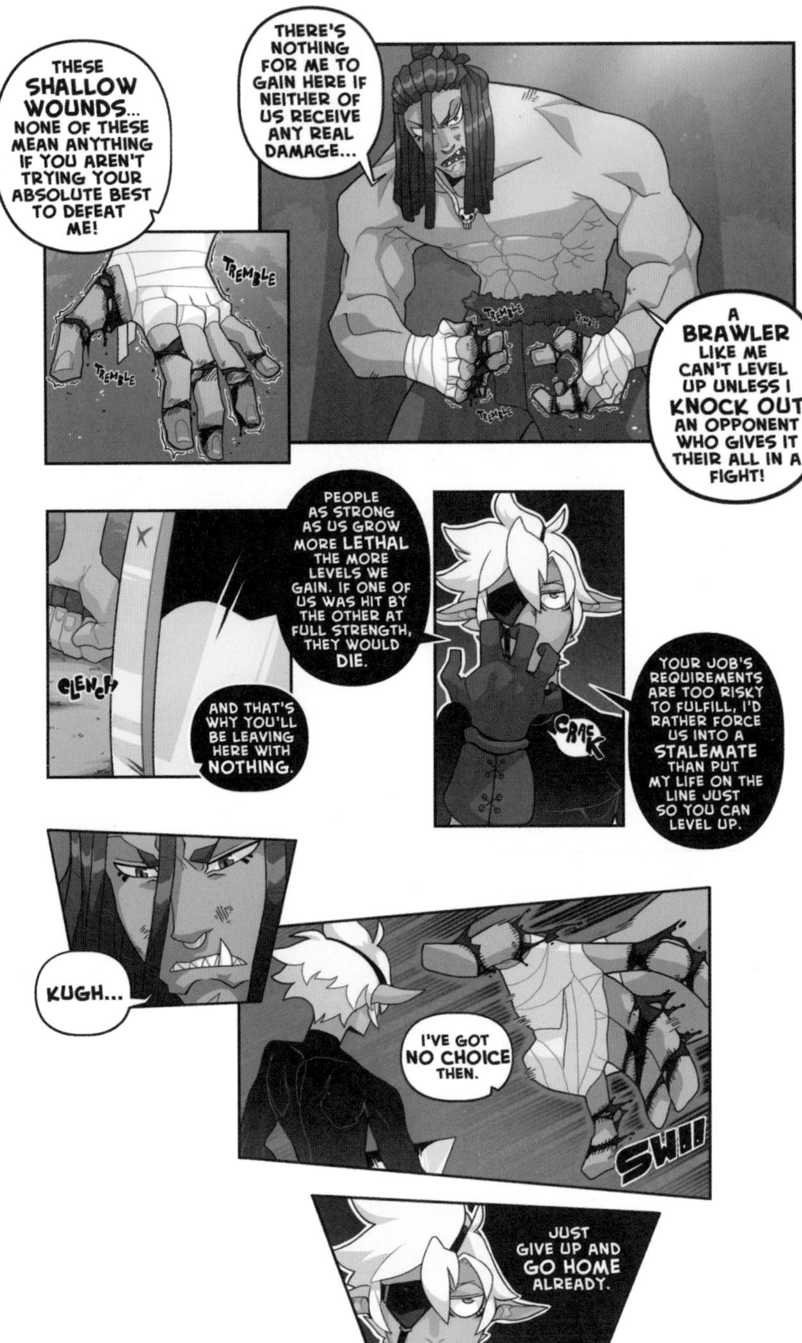
THESE SHALLOW WOUNDS... NONE OF THESE MEAN ANYTHING IF YOU AREN'T TRYING YOUR ABSOLUTE BEST TO DEFEAT ME!
TREMBLE
TREMBLE
THERE'S NOTHING FOR ME TO GAIN HERE IF NEITHER OF US RECEIVE ANY REAL DAMAGE...
TREMBLE
TREMBLE
TREMBLE
A BRAWLER LIKE ME CAN'T LEVEL UP UNLESS I KNOCK OUT AN OPPONENT WHO GIVES IT THEIR ALL IN A FIGHT!
CLENCH
PEOPLE AS STRONG AS US GROW MORE LETHAL THE MORE LEVELS WE GAIN. IF ONE OF US WAS HIT BY THE OTHER AT FULL STRENGTH, THEY WOULD DIE.
AND THAT'S WHY YOU'LL BE LEAVING HERE WITH NOTHING.
CRACK
YOUR JOB'S REQUIREMENTS ARE TOO RISKY TO FULFILL. I'D RATHER FORCE US INTO A STALEMATE THAN PUT MY LIFE ON THE LINE JUST SO YOU CAN LEVEL UP.
KUGH...
I'VE GOT NO CHOICE THEN.
SWII
JUST GIVE UP AND GO HOME ALREADY.

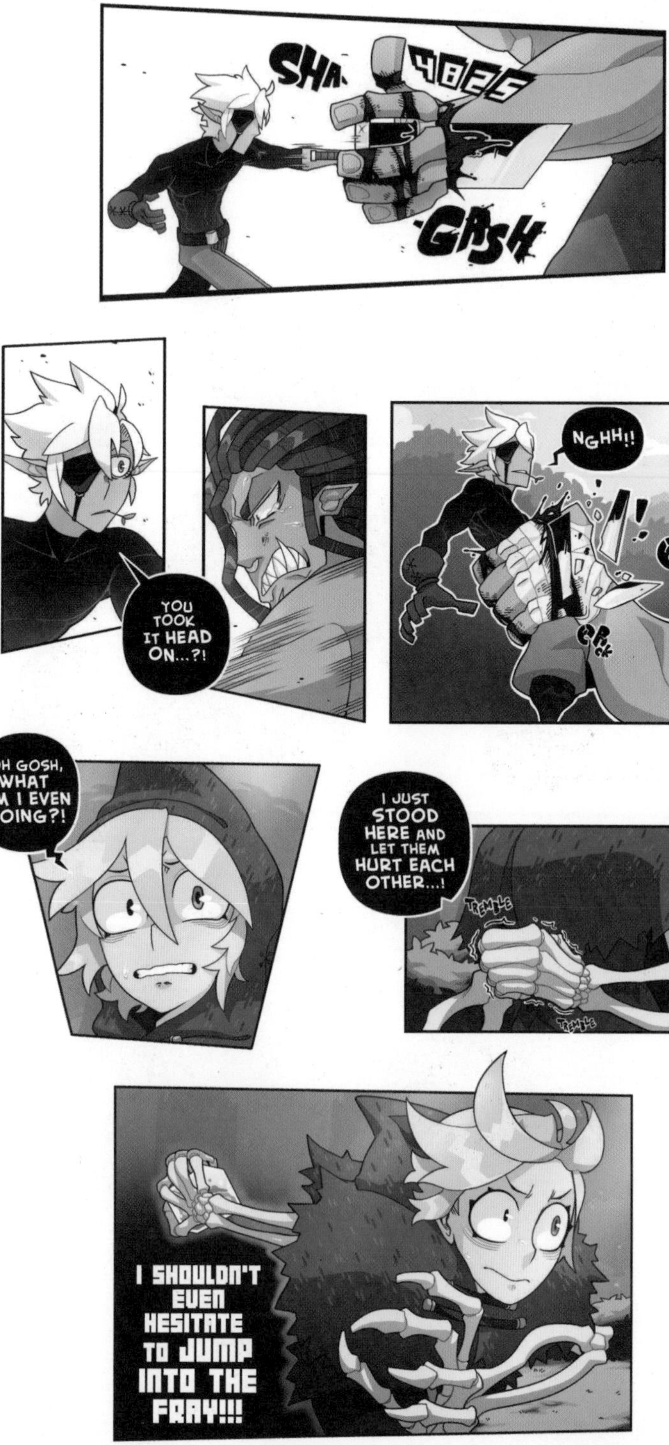
SHA-
4825
GASH
YOU TOOK IT HEAD ON...?!
NGHH!!
CRACK
CRACK
OH GOSH, WHAT AM I EVEN DOING?!
I JUST STOOD HERE AND LET THEM HURT EACH OTHER...!
TREMBLE
TREMBLE
IF I WANT TO ACTUALLY HELP THEM...
I SHOULDN'T EVEN HESITATE TO JUMP INTO THE FRAY!!!

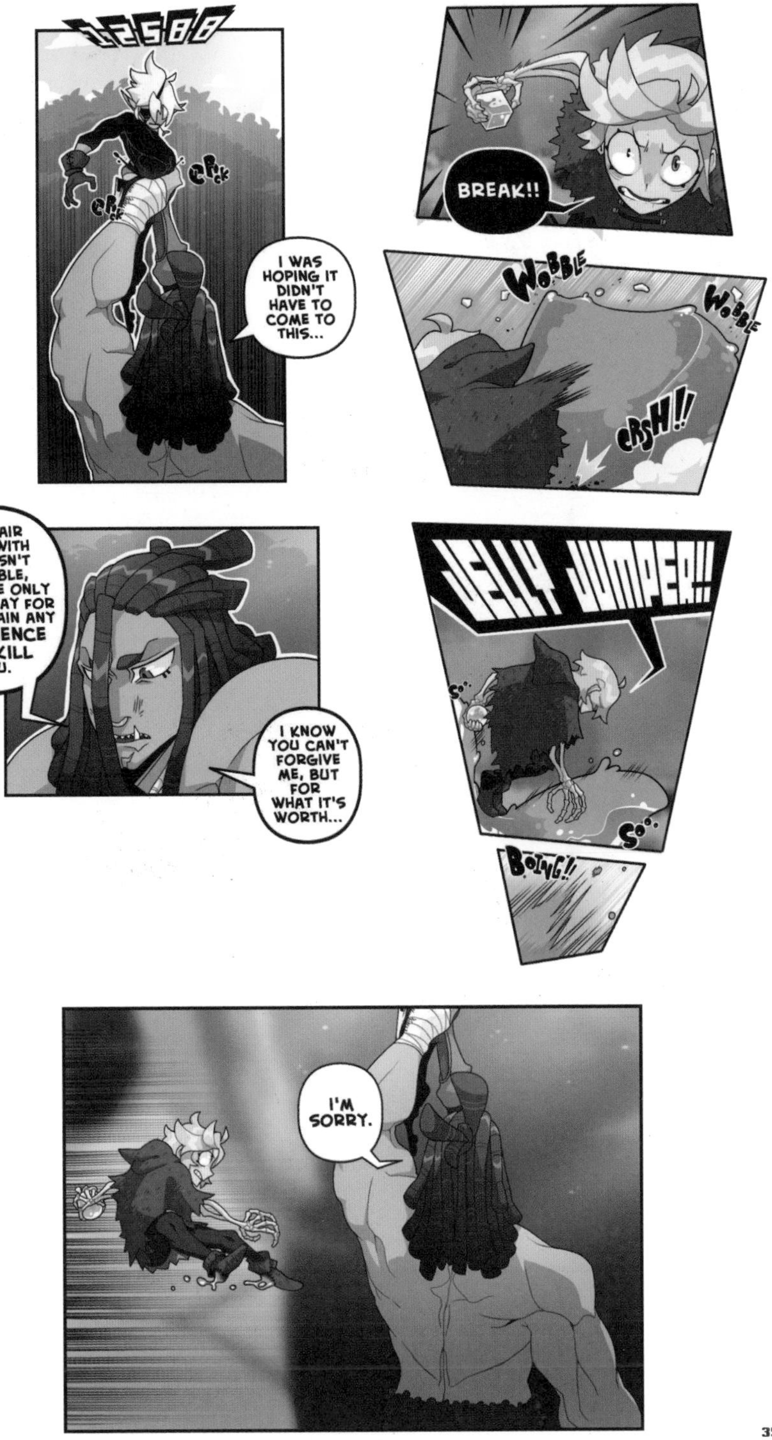
CRACK
CRACK
I WAS HOPING IT DIDN'T HAVE TO COME TO THIS...
BREAK!!
WOBBLE
WOBBLE
CRSH!!
IF A FAIR DUEL WITH YOU ISN'T POSSIBLE, THEN THE ONLY OTHER WAY FOR ME TO GAIN ANY EXPERIENCE IS TO KILL YOU.
I KNOW YOU CAN'T FORGIVE ME, BUT FOR WHAT IT'S WORTH...
JELLY JUMPER!!
BOING!!
I'M SORRY.

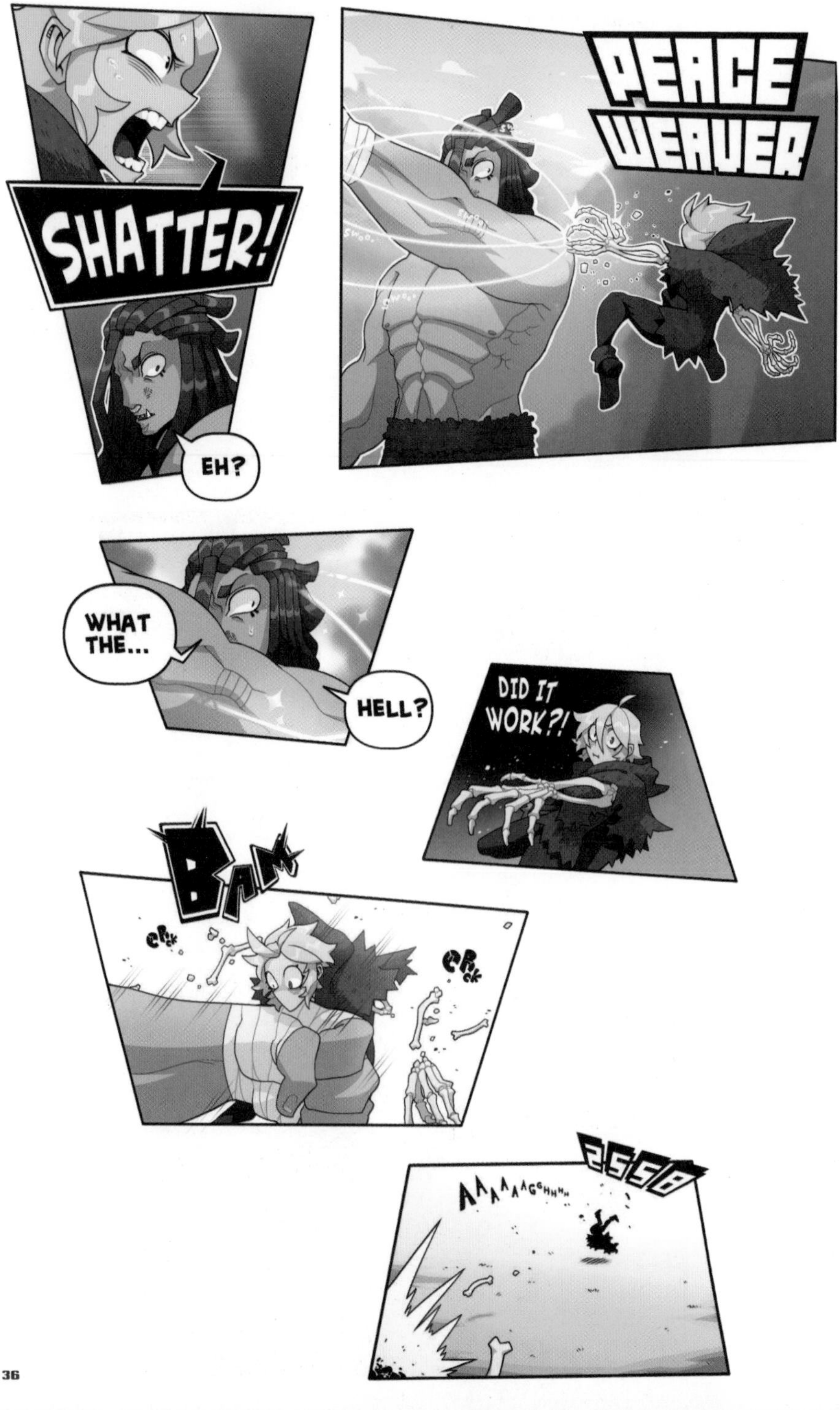
SHATTER!
EH?
PEACE WEAVER
WHAT THE...
HELL?
DID IT WORK?!
BAM
CRACK
CRACK
AAAAAAGGHHHH

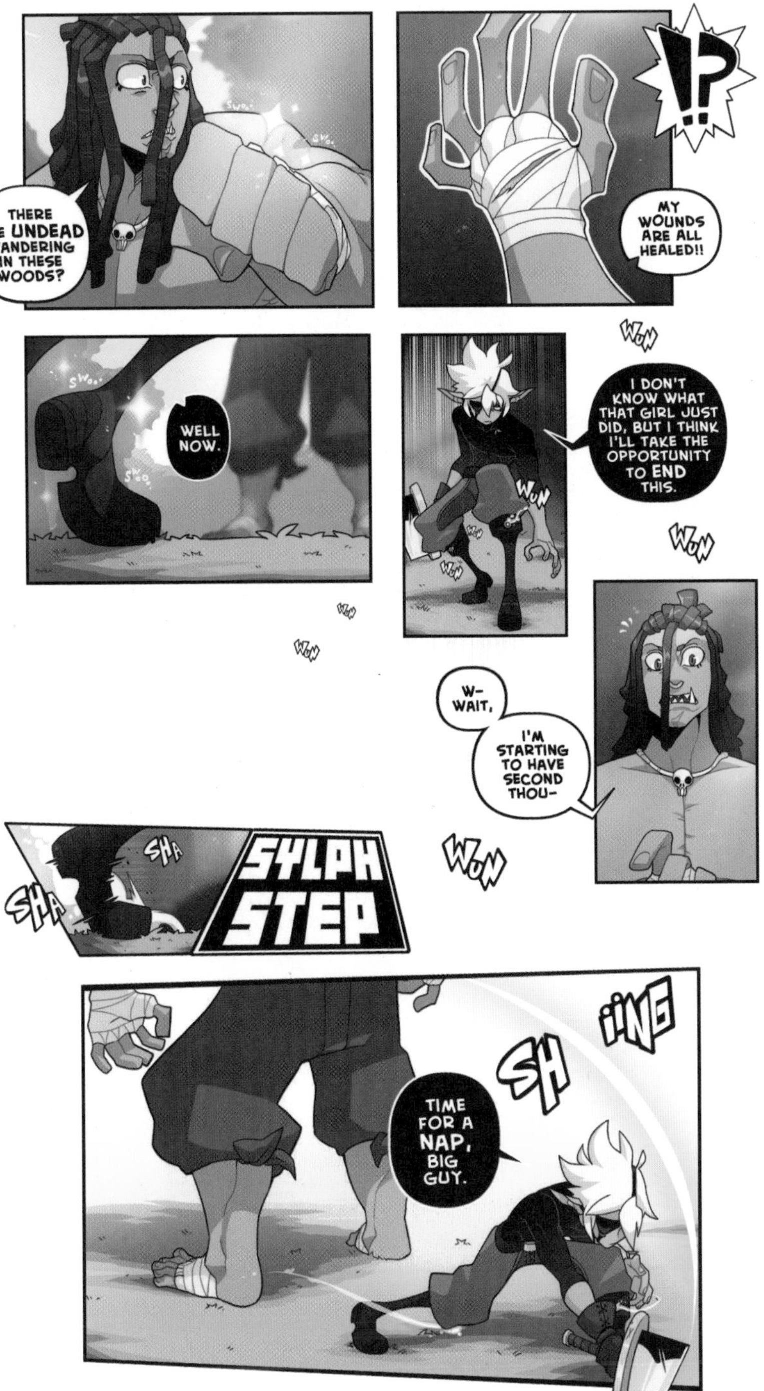
THERE ARE UNDEAD WANDERING IN THESE WOODS?
!?
MY WOUNDS ARE ALL HEALED!!
WELL NOW.
WUN
I DON'T KNOW WHAT THAT GIRL JUST DID, BUT I THINK I'LL TAKE THE OPPORTUNITY TO END THIS.
WUN
WUN
WUN
WUN
W-WAIT,
I'M STARTING TO HAVE SECOND THOU-
WUN
SHA
SHA
SYLPH STEP
SH
iiNG
TIME FOR A NAP, BIG GUY.

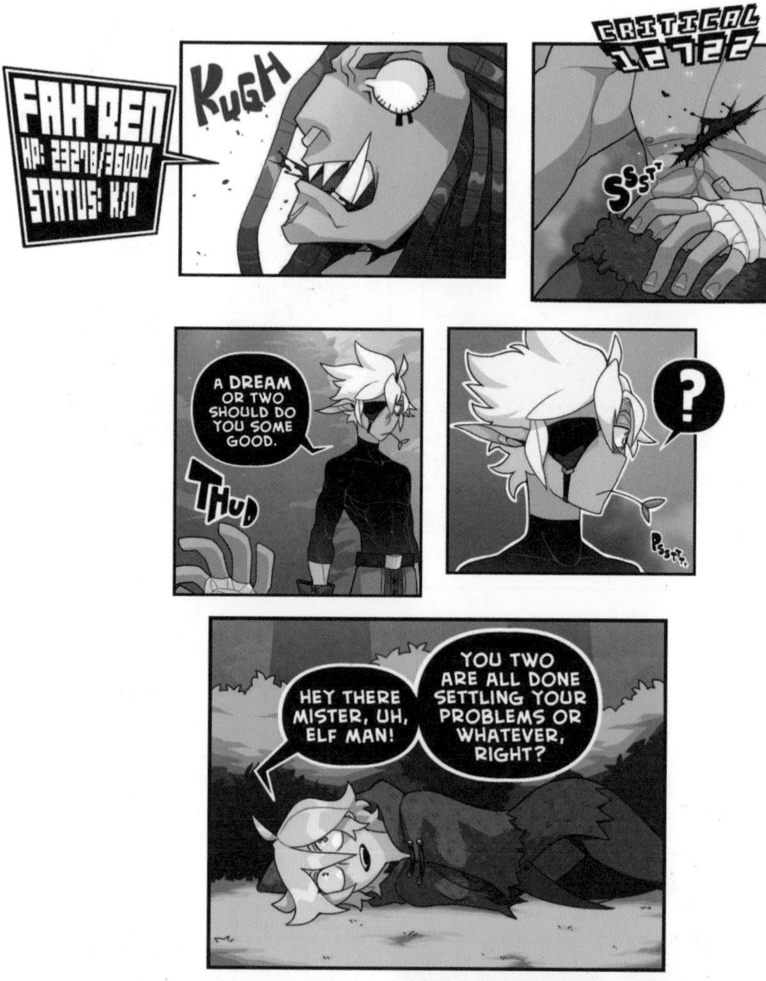
FAH'REN
HP: 23278/36000
STATUS: K/O
KUGH
CRITICAL
12722
A DREAM OR TWO SHOULD DO YOU SOME GOOD.
THUD
?
HEY THERE MISTER, UH, ELF MAN!
YOU TWO ARE ALL DONE SETTLING YOUR PROBLEMS OR WHATEVER, RIGHT?
OH, UHM... YES.
THANK YOU FOR HELPING WITH THAT, BY THE WAY.
I-ITS NO PROBLEM, HEHEH.
SPEAKING OF HELPING PEOPLE,
DO YOU MIND GIVING ME A HAND?

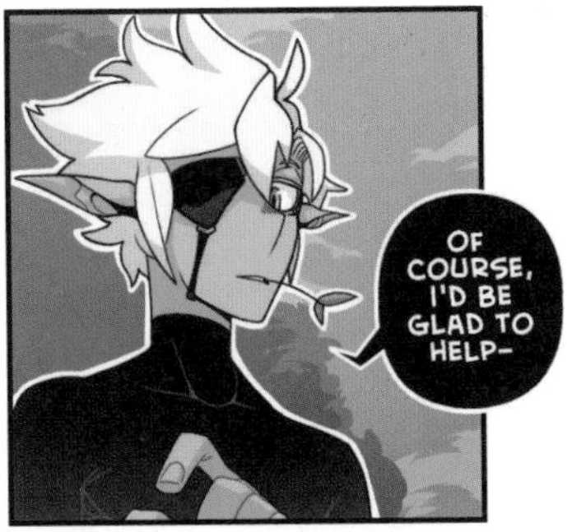
OF COURSE, I'D BE GLAD TO HELP-

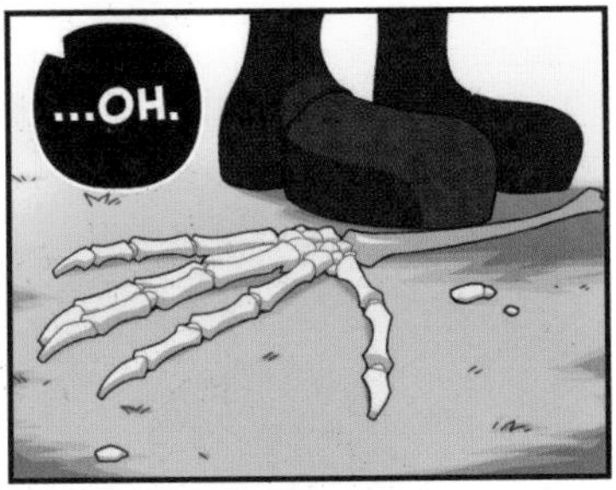
...OH.

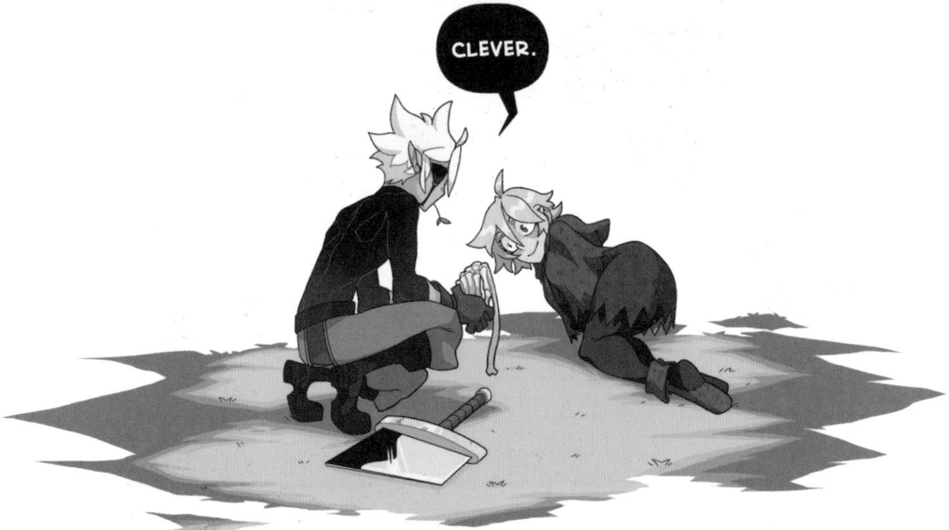
CLEVER.

## Chapter 3
# THE BREAKER

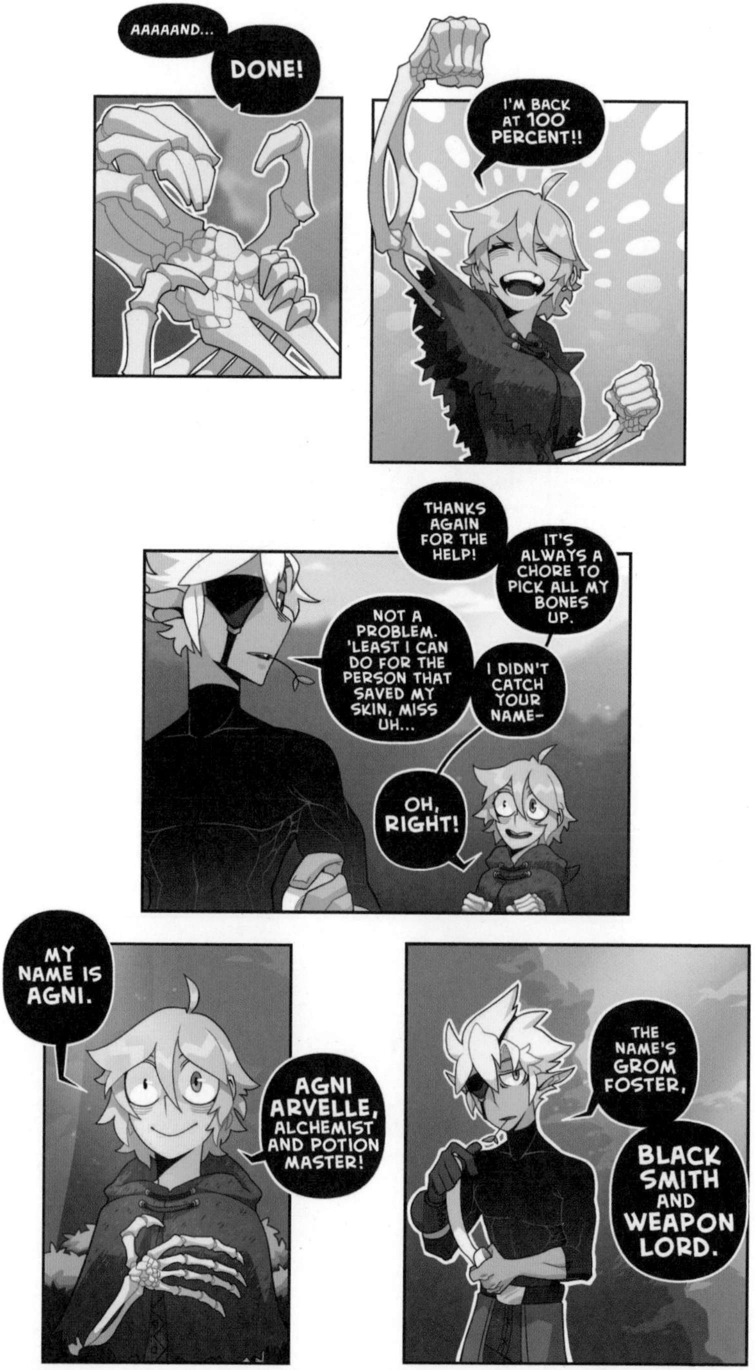

AAAAAND...
DONE!
I'M BACK AT 100 PERCENT!!
THANKS AGAIN FOR THE HELP!
IT'S ALWAYS A CHORE TO PICK ALL MY BONES UP.
NOT A PROBLEM. 'LEAST I CAN DO FOR THE PERSON THAT SAVED MY SKIN, MISS UH...
I DIDN'T CATCH YOUR NAME-
OH, RIGHT!
MY NAME IS AGNI.
AGNI ARVELLE, ALCHEMIST AND POTION MASTER!
THE NAME'S GROM FOSTER,
BLACK SMITH AND WEAPON LORD.

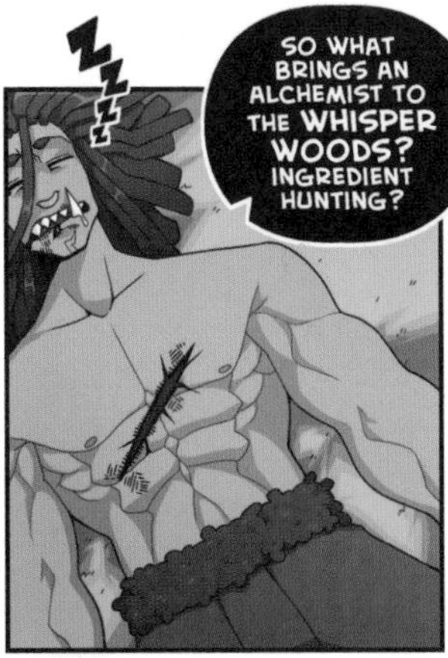
ZZZZ
SO WHAT BRINGS AN ALCHEMIST TO THE WHISPER WOODS? INGREDIENT HUNTING?

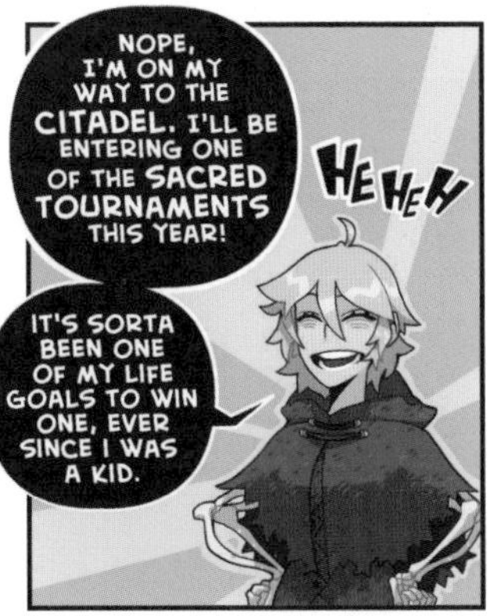
NOPE, I'M ON MY WAY TO THE CITADEL. I'LL BE ENTERING ONE OF THE SACRED TOURNAMENTS THIS YEAR!
HE HE H
IT'S SORTA BEEN ONE OF MY LIFE GOALS TO WIN ONE, EVER SINCE I WAS A KID.

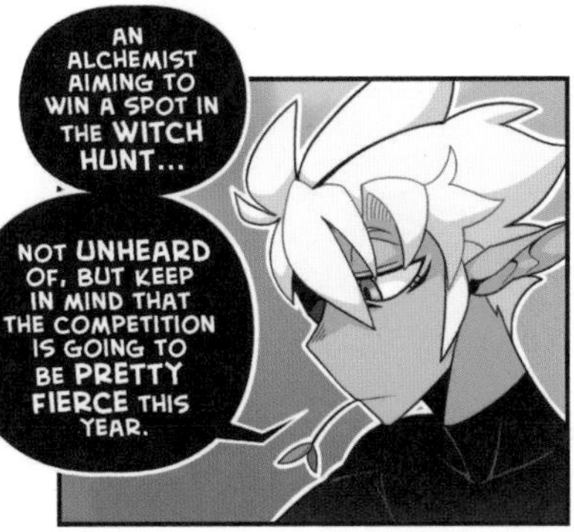
AN ALCHEMIST AIMING TO WIN A SPOT IN THE WITCH HUNT...
NOT UNHEARD OF, BUT KEEP IN MIND THAT THE COMPETITION IS GOING TO BE PRETTY FIERCE THIS YEAR.

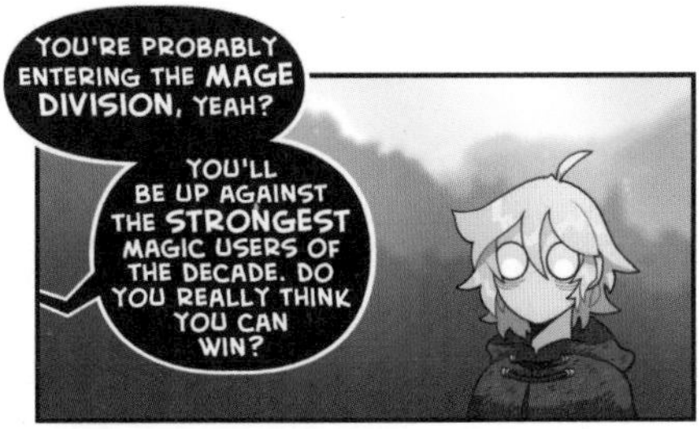
YOU'RE PROBABLY ENTERING THE MAGE DIVISION, YEAH?
YOU'LL BE UP AGAINST THE STRONGEST MAGIC USERS OF THE DECADE. DO YOU REALLY THINK YOU CAN WIN?

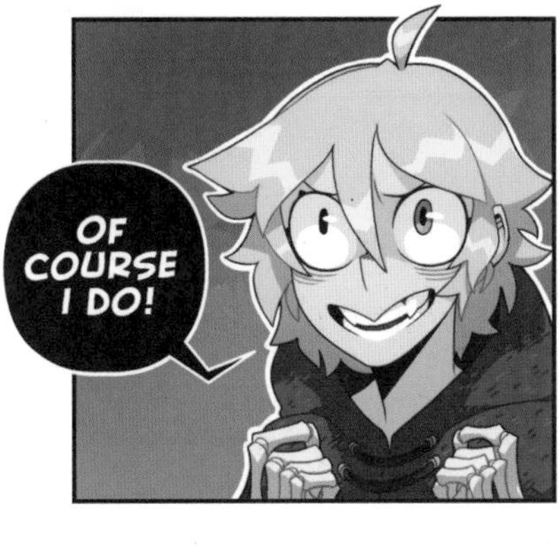
OF COURSE I DO!

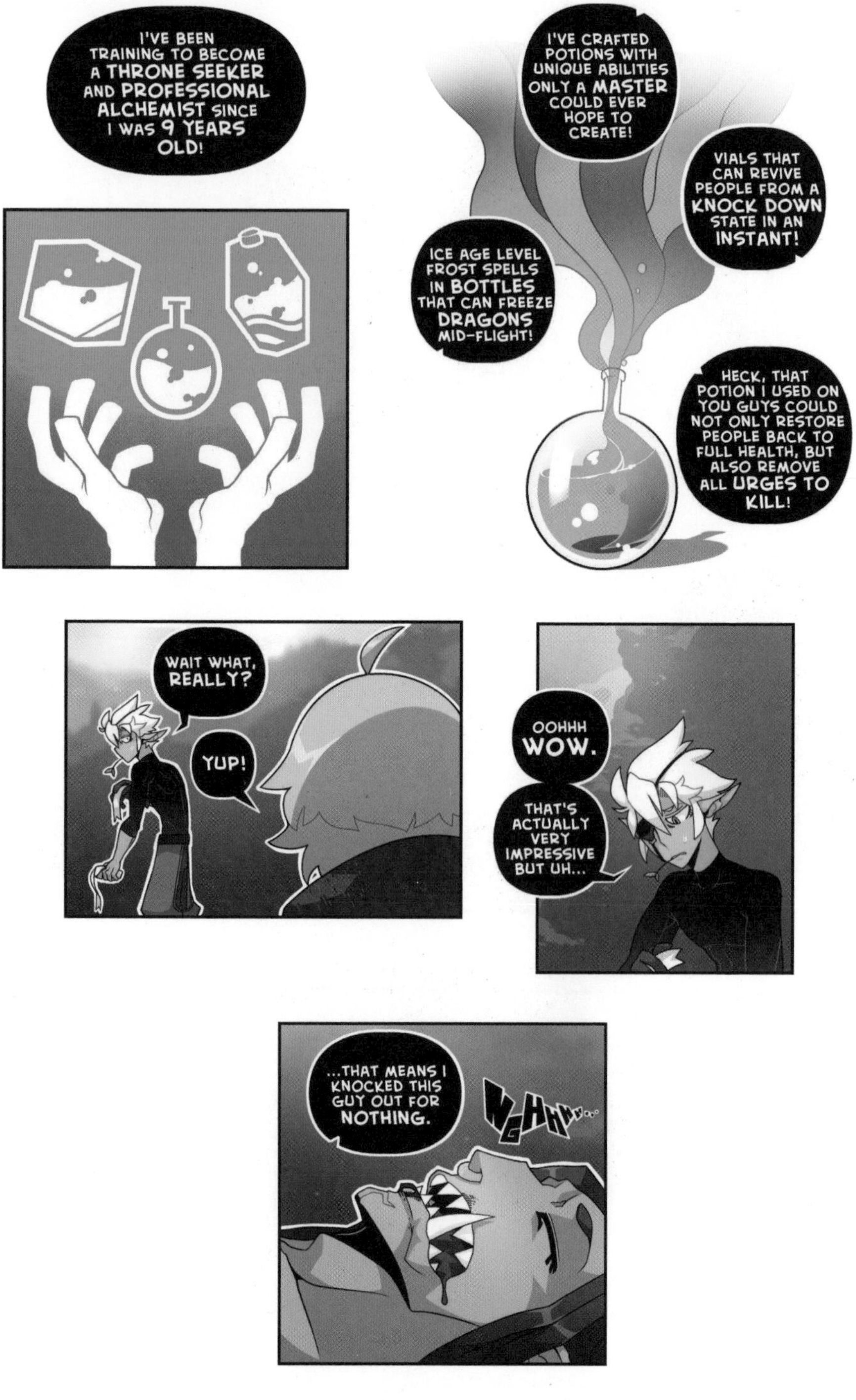
I'VE BEEN TRAINING TO BECOME A THRONE SEEKER AND PROFESSIONAL ALCHEMIST SINCE I WAS 9 YEARS OLD!
I'VE CRAFTED POTIONS WITH UNIQUE ABILITIES ONLY A MASTER COULD EVER HOPE TO CREATE!
VIALS THAT CAN REVIVE PEOPLE FROM A KNOCK DOWN STATE IN AN INSTANT!
ICE AGE LEVEL FROST SPELLS IN BOTTLES THAT CAN FREEZE DRAGONS MID-FLIGHT!
HECK, THAT POTION I USED ON YOU GUYS COULD NOT ONLY RESTORE PEOPLE BACK TO FULL HEALTH, BUT ALSO REMOVE ALL URGES TO KILL!
WAIT WHAT, REALLY?
YUP!
OOHHH WOW.
THAT'S ACTUALLY VERY IMPRESSIVE BUT UH...
...THAT MEANS I KNOCKED THIS GUY OUT FOR NOTHING.
NGHHH...

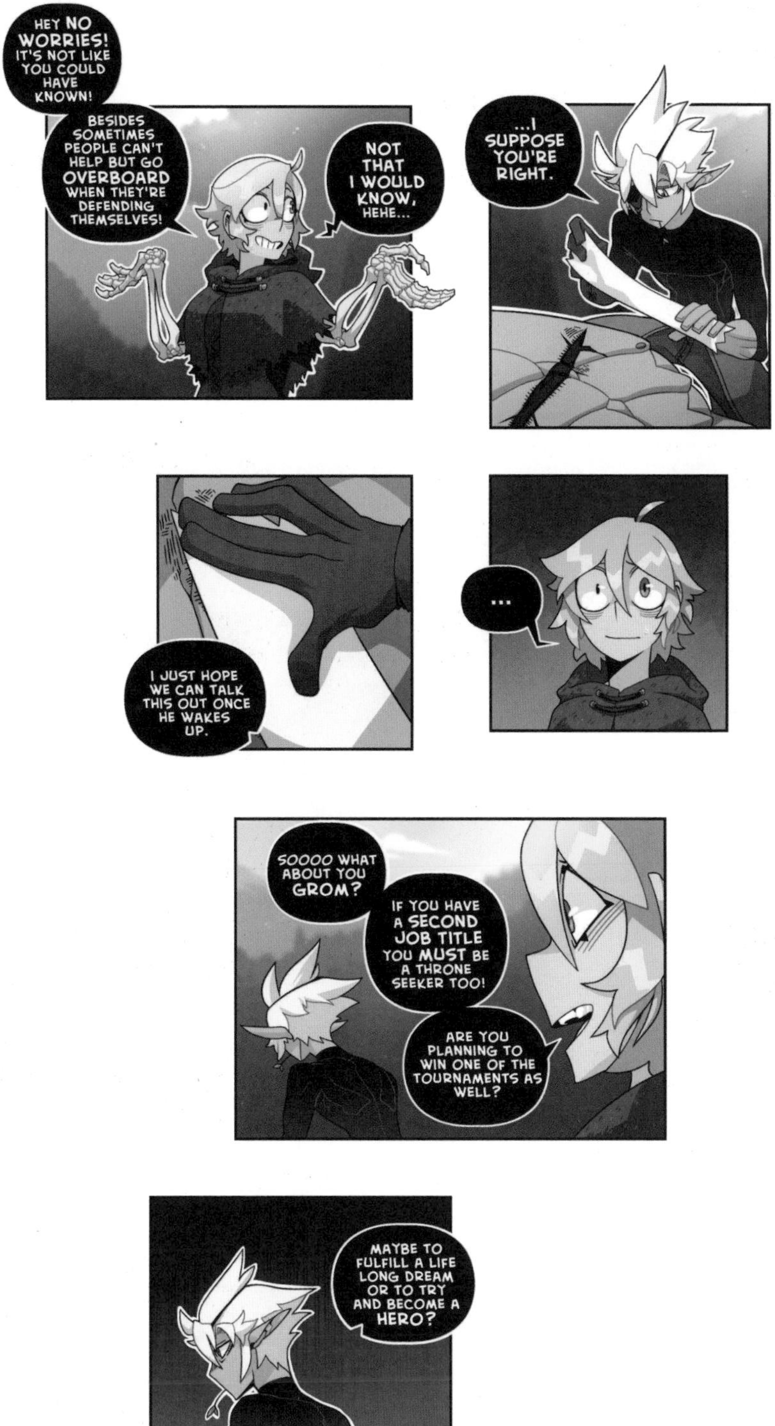
HEY NO WORRIES! IT'S NOT LIKE YOU COULD HAVE KNOWN!
BESIDES SOMETIMES PEOPLE CAN'T HELP BUT GO OVERBOARD WHEN THEY'RE DEFENDING THEMSELVES!
NOT THAT I WOULD KNOW, HEHE...
...I SUPPOSE YOU'RE RIGHT.
I JUST HOPE WE CAN TALK THIS OUT ONCE HE WAKES UP.
...
SOOOO WHAT ABOUT YOU GROM?
IF YOU HAVE A SECOND JOB TITLE YOU MUST BE A THRONE SEEKER TOO!
ARE YOU PLANNING TO WIN ONE OF THE TOURNAMENTS AS WELL?
MAYBE TO FULFILL A LIFE LONG DREAM OR TO TRY AND BECOME A HERO?

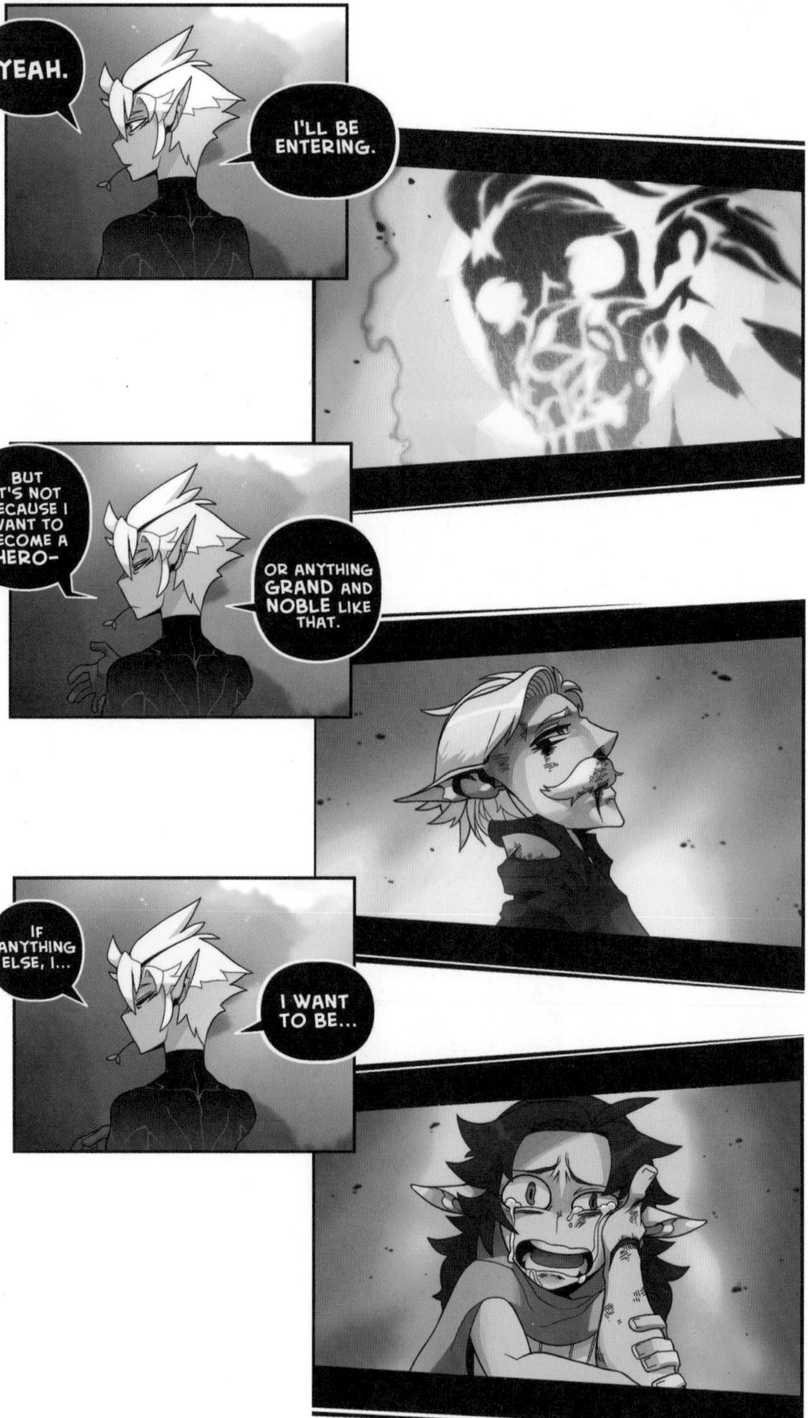
YEAH.
I'LL BE ENTERING.
BUT IT'S NOT BECAUSE I WANT TO BECOME A HERO-
OR ANYTHING GRAND AND NOBLE LIKE THAT.
IF ANYTHING ELSE, I...
I WANT TO BE...

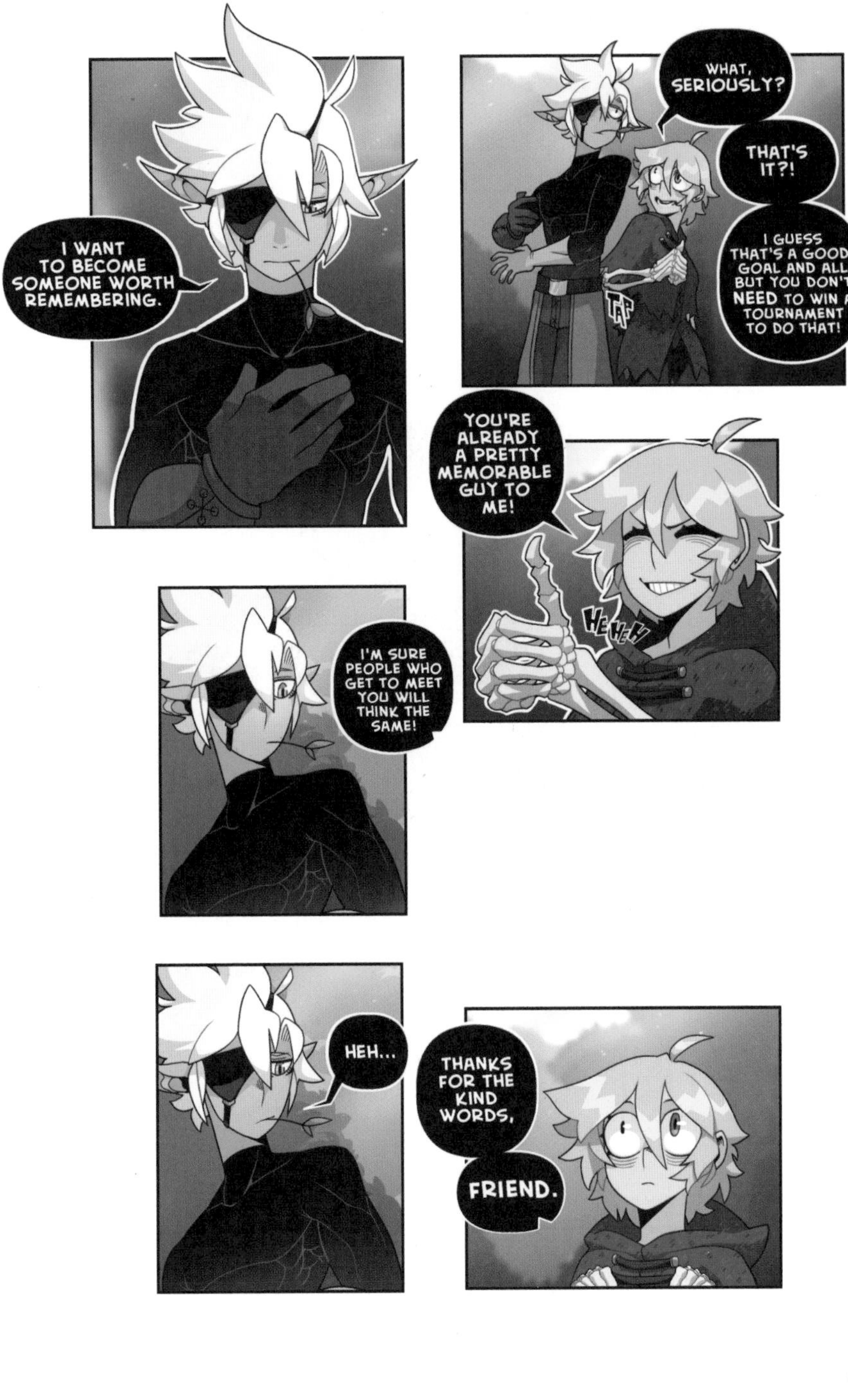
I WANT TO BECOME SOMEONE WORTH REMEMBERING.
WHAT, SERIOUSLY?
THAT'S IT?!
I GUESS THAT'S A GOOD GOAL AND ALL BUT YOU DON'T NEED TO WIN A TOURNAMENT TO DO THAT!
TAP
YOU'RE ALREADY A PRETTY MEMORABLE GUY TO ME!
HEHEH
I'M SURE PEOPLE WHO GET TO MEET YOU WILL THINK THE SAME!
HEH...
THANKS FOR THE KIND WORDS,
FRIEND.

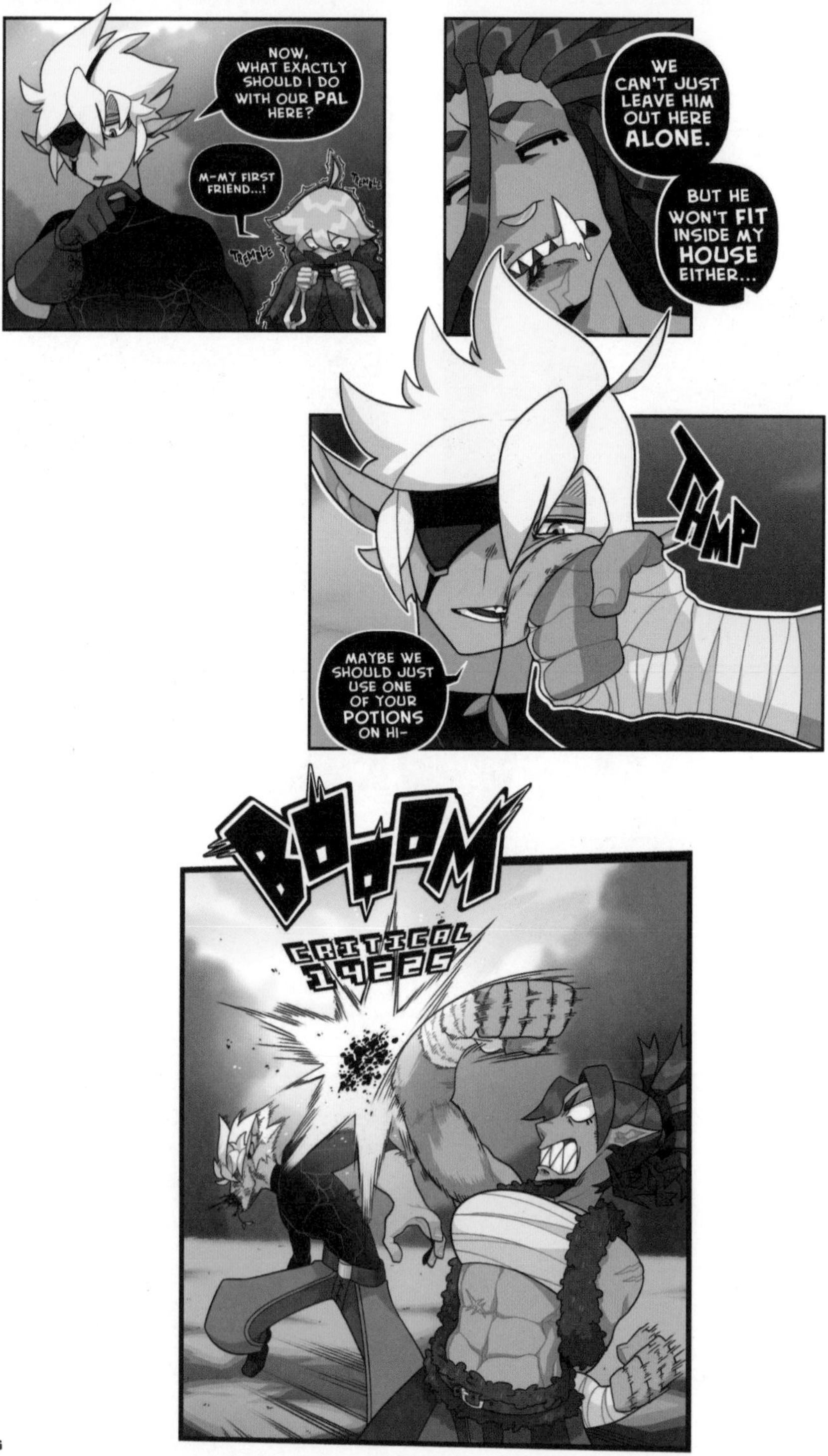
NOW, WHAT EXACTLY SHOULD I DO WITH OUR PAL HERE?
M-MY FIRST FRIEND...!
TREMBLE
TREMBLE
WE CAN'T JUST LEAVE HIM OUT HERE ALONE.
BUT HE WON'T FIT INSIDE MY HOUSE EITHER...
THMP
MAYBE WE SHOULD JUST USE ONE OF YOUR POTIONS ON HI-
BOOOM
CRITICAL 14225

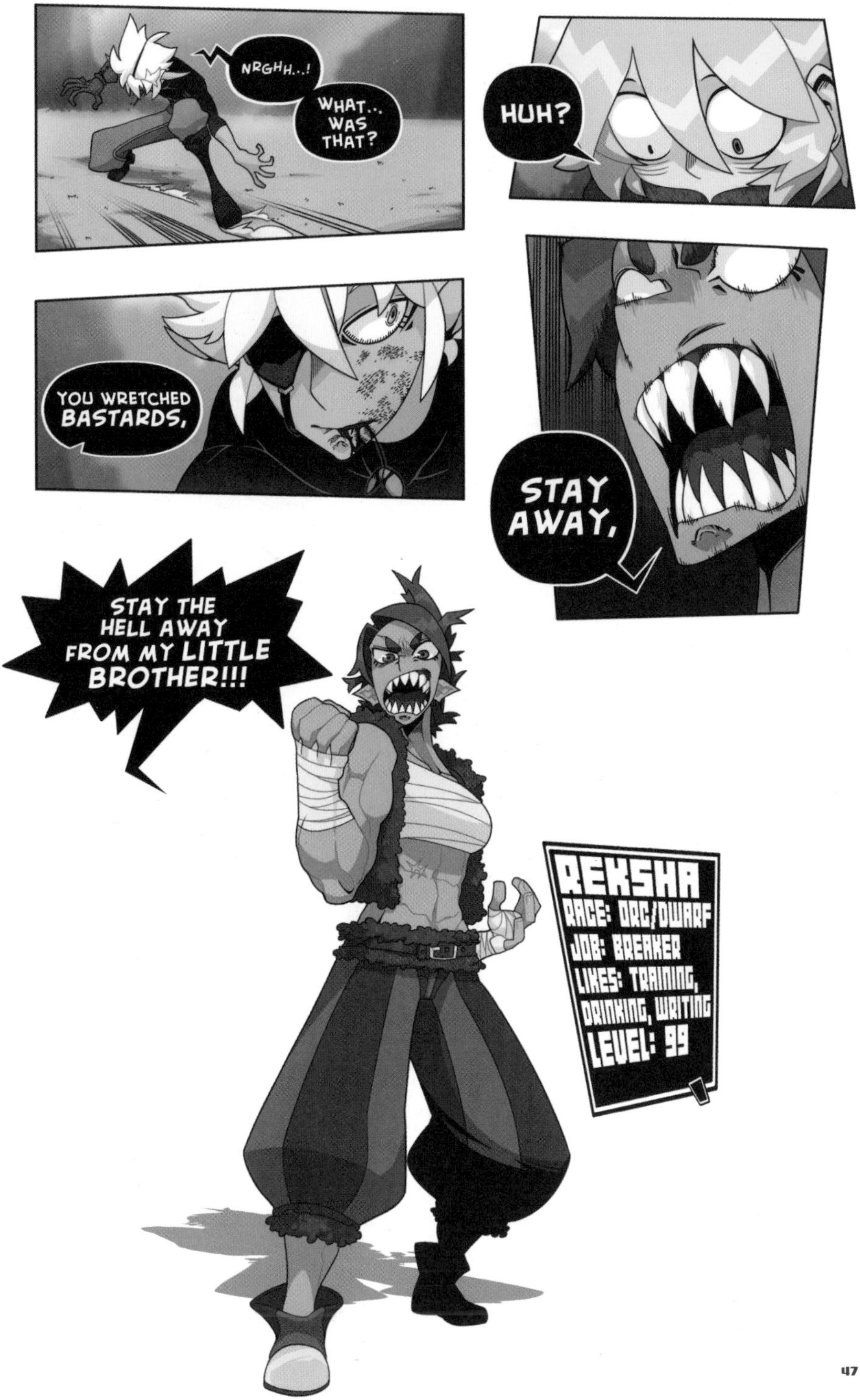
NRGHH...!
WHAT... WAS THAT?
HUH?
YOU WRETCHED BASTARDS,
STAY AWAY,
STAY THE HELL AWAY FROM MY LITTLE BROTHER!!!
REKSHA
RACE: ORC/DWARF
JOB: BREAKER
LIKES: TRAINING, DRINKING, WRITING
LEVEL: 99

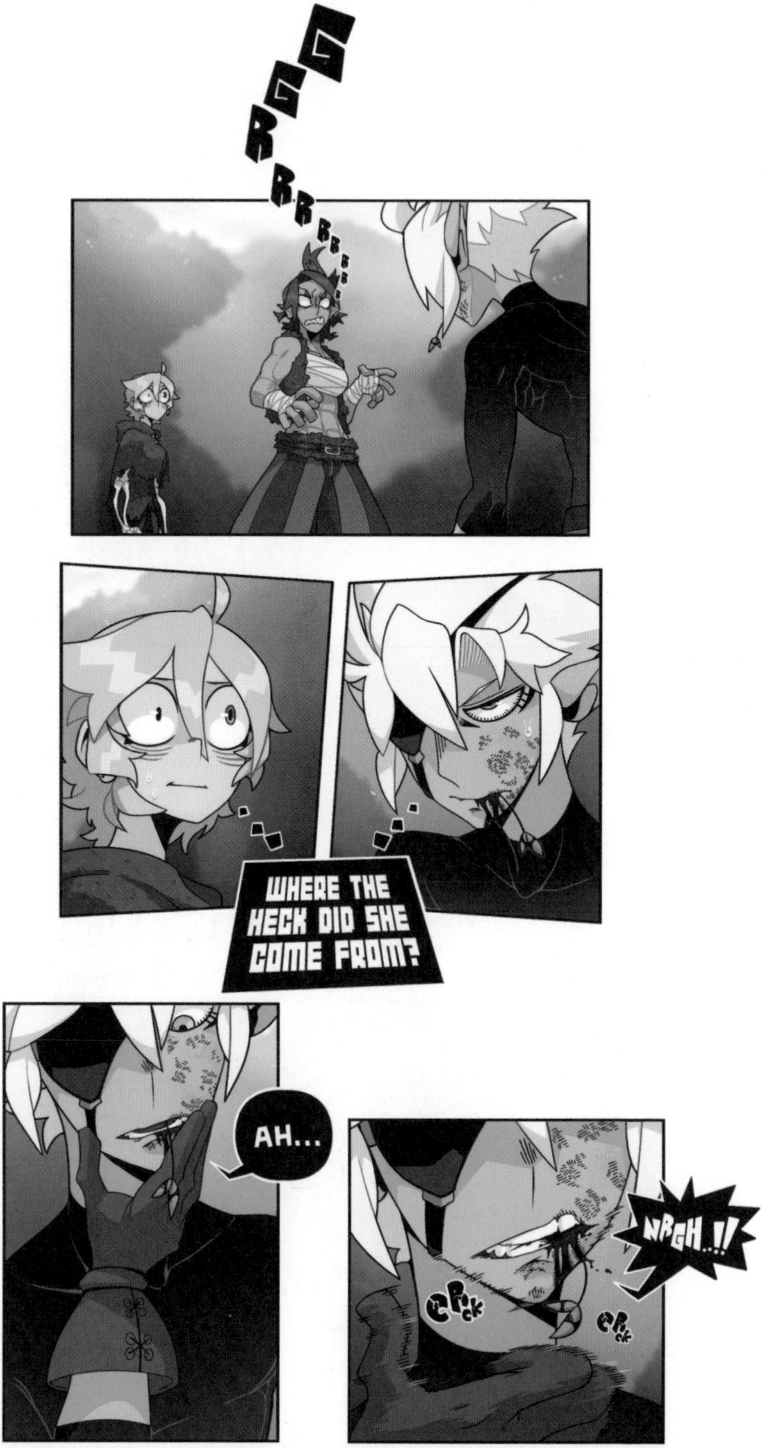
GGRRRRRRRR
WHERE THE HECK DID SHE COME FROM?
AH...
NRGH..!!
CRACK
CRACK

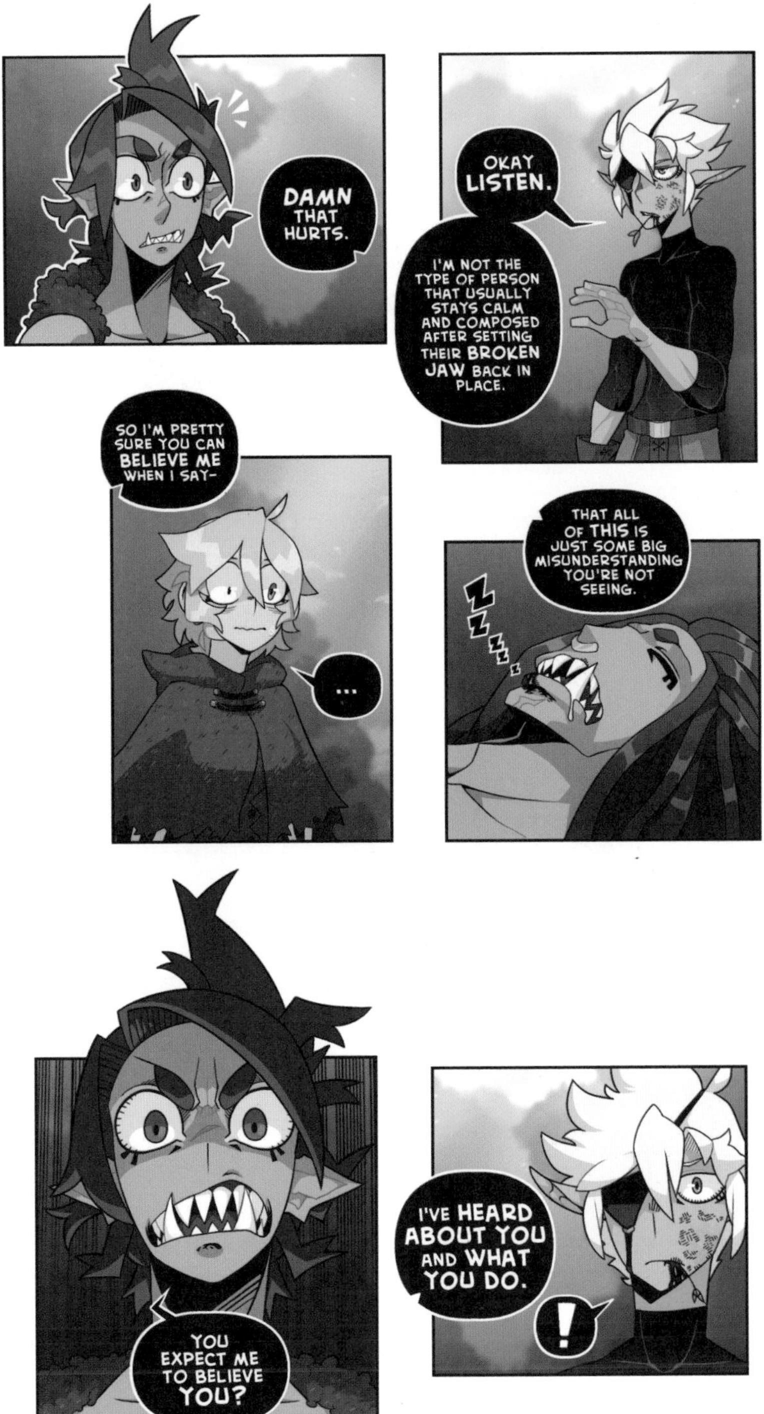
DAMN THAT HURTS.
OKAY LISTEN.
I'M NOT THE TYPE OF PERSON THAT USUALLY STAYS CALM AND COMPOSED AFTER SETTING THEIR BROKEN JAW BACK IN PLACE.
SO I'M PRETTY SURE YOU CAN BELIEVE ME WHEN I SAY-
...
THAT ALL OF THIS IS JUST SOME BIG MISUNDERSTANDING YOU'RE NOT SEEING.
ZZZZ
YOU EXPECT ME TO BELIEVE YOU?
I'VE HEARD ABOUT YOU AND WHAT YOU DO.
!

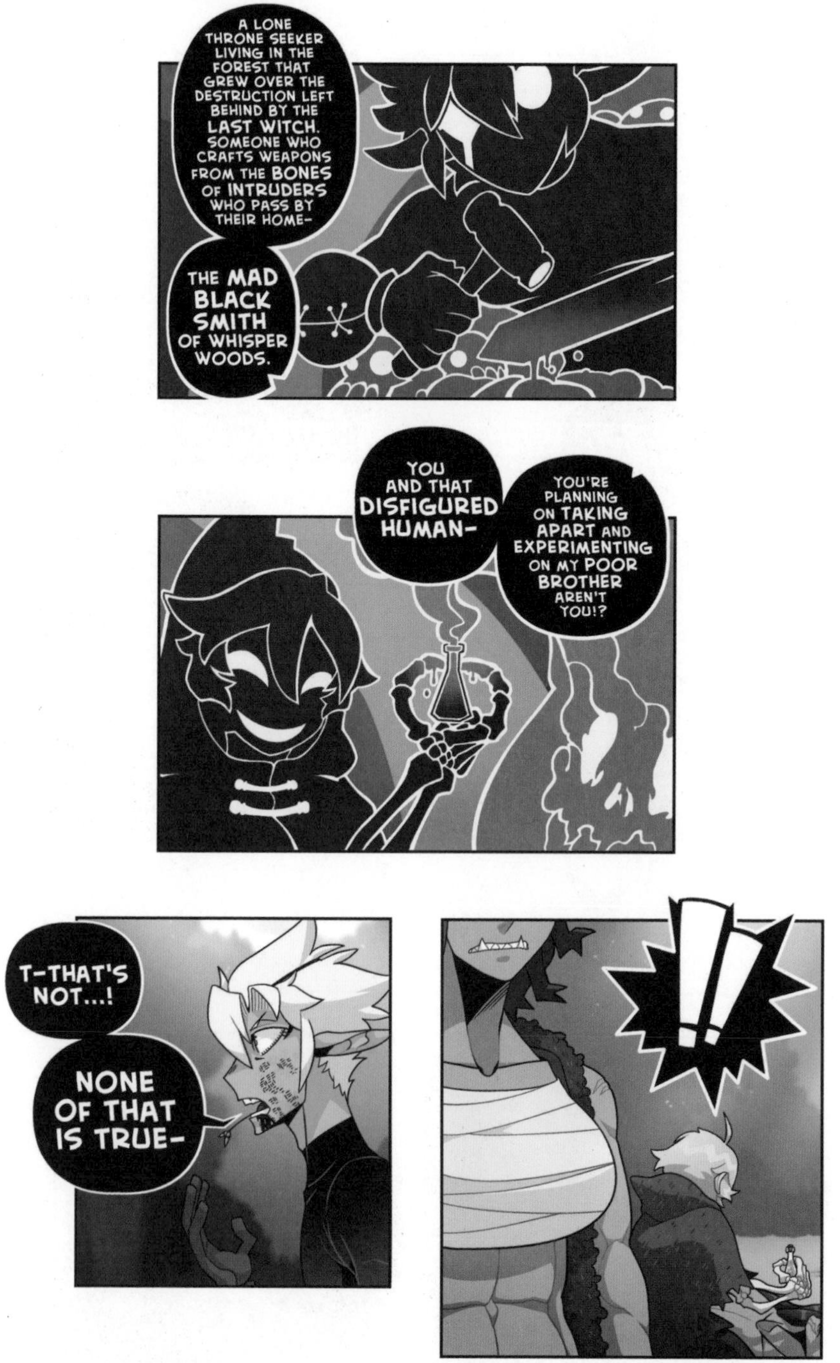
A LONE THRONE SEEKER LIVING IN THE FOREST THAT GREW OVER THE DESTRUCTION LEFT BEHIND BY THE LAST WITCH. SOMEONE WHO CRAFTS WEAPONS FROM THE BONES OF INTRUDERS WHO PASS BY THEIR HOME-
THE MAD BLACK SMITH OF WHISPER WOODS.
YOU AND THAT DISFIGURED HUMAN-
YOU'RE PLANNING ON TAKING APART AND EXPERIMENTING ON MY POOR BROTHER AREN'T YOU!?
T-THAT'S NOT...!
NONE OF THAT IS TRUE-
!!

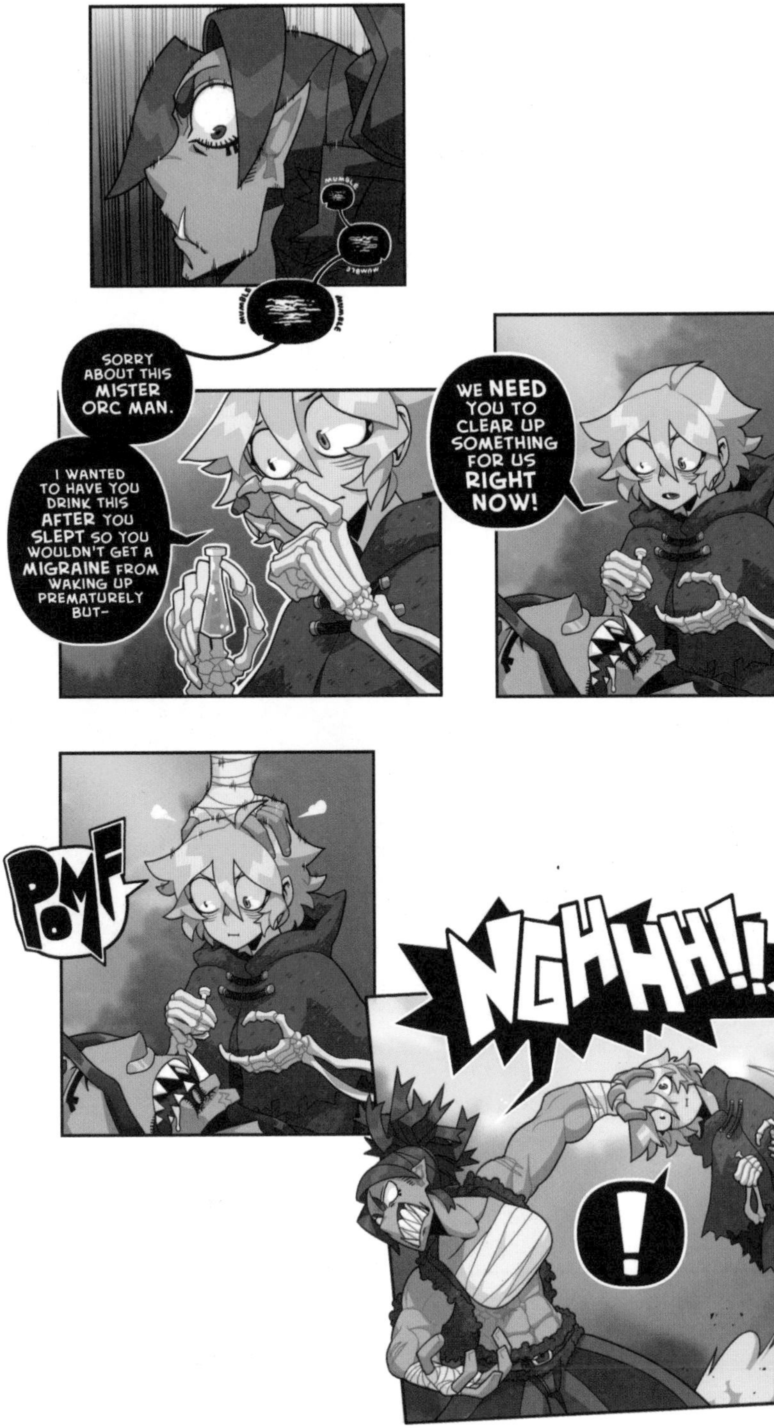
MUMBLE
MUMBLE
MUMBLE
MUMBLE
SORRY ABOUT THIS MISTER ORC MAN.
I WANTED TO HAVE YOU DRINK THIS AFTER YOU SLEPT SO YOU WOULDN'T GET A MIGRAINE FROM WAKING UP PREMATURELY BUT-
WE NEED YOU TO CLEAR UP SOMETHING FOR US RIGHT NOW!
POMF
NGHHH!!
!

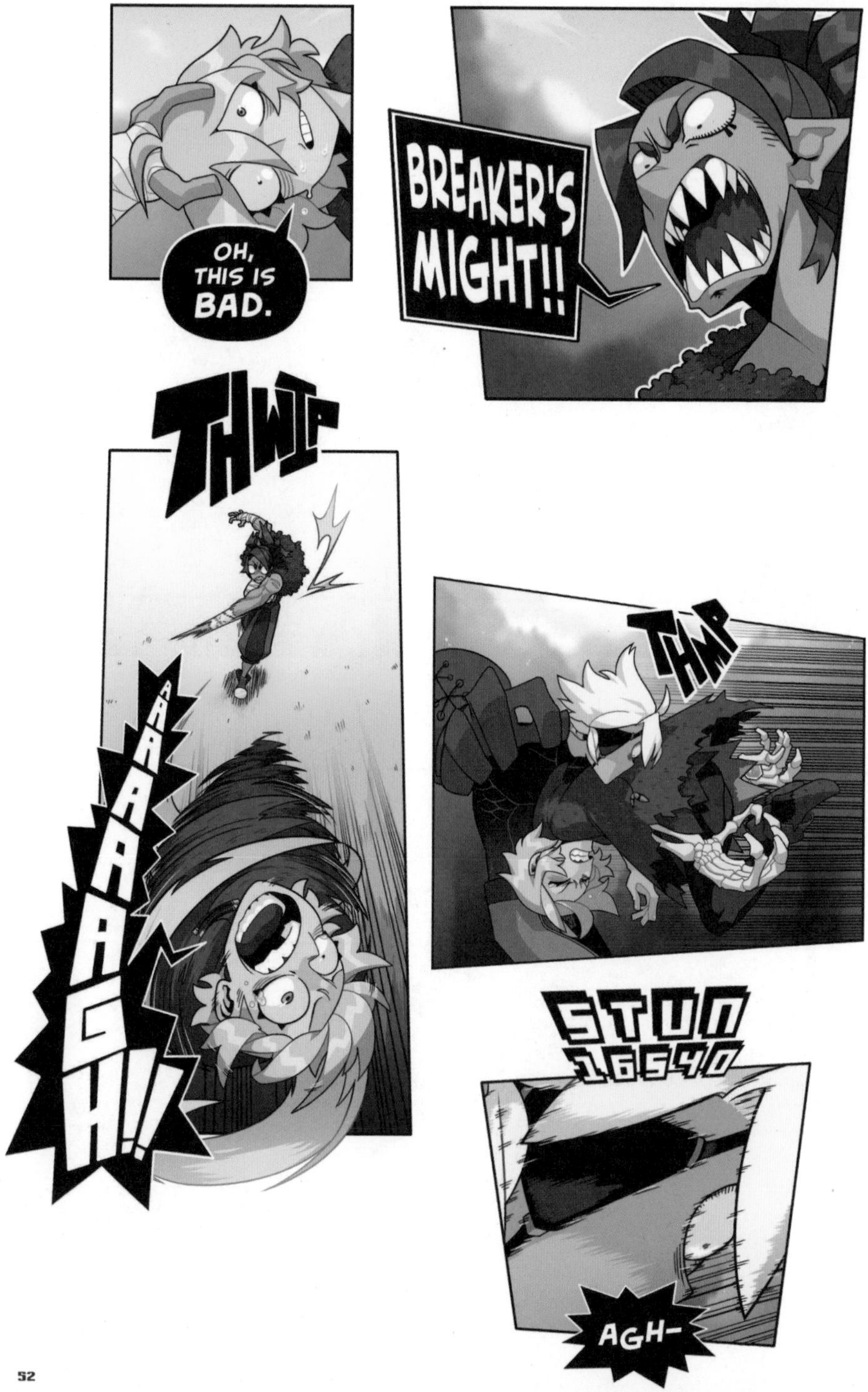
OH, THIS IS BAD.
BREAKER'S MIGHT!!
THWIP
AAAAAAAGH!!
THMP
STUN
16540
AGH-

THOOM
WAS THAT ENOUGH TO BREAK THEM?
...NO.

[redacted]

[redacted]

[redacted]

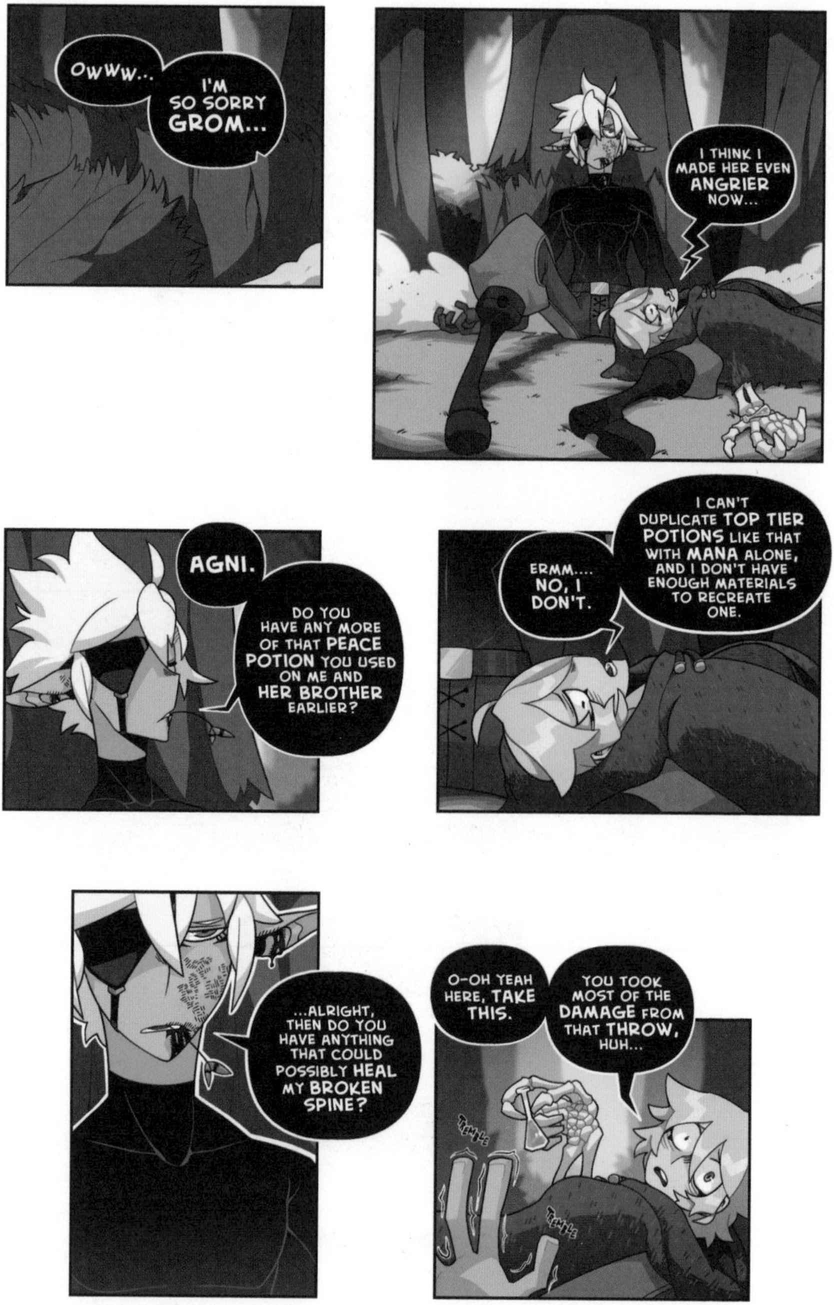
OWWW...
I'M SO SORRY GROM...
I THINK I MADE HER EVEN ANGRIER NOW...
AGNI.
DO YOU HAVE ANY MORE OF THAT PEACE POTION YOU USED ON ME AND HER BROTHER EARLIER?
ERMM.... NO, I DON'T.
I CAN'T DUPLICATE TOP TIER POTIONS LIKE THAT WITH MANA ALONE, AND I DON'T HAVE ENOUGH MATERIALS TO RECREATE ONE.
...ALRIGHT, THEN DO YOU HAVE ANYTHING THAT COULD POSSIBLY HEAL MY BROKEN SPINE?
O-OH YEAH HERE, TAKE THIS.
YOU TOOK MOST OF THE DAMAGE FROM THAT THROW, HUH...
TREMBLE
TREMBLE

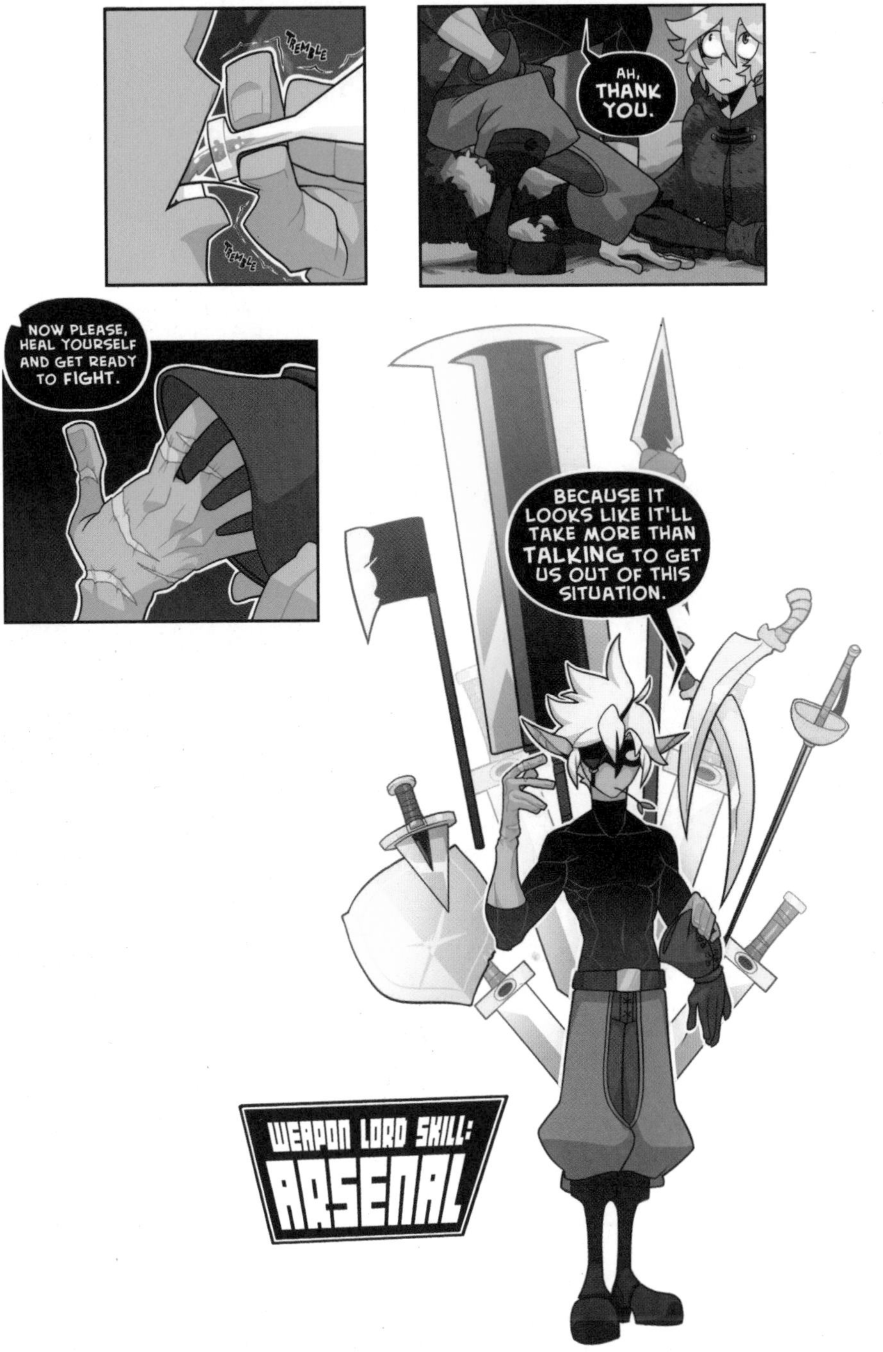
TREMBLE
TREMBLE
AH, THANK YOU.
NOW PLEASE, HEAL YOURSELF AND GET READY TO FIGHT.
BECAUSE IT LOOKS LIKE IT'LL TAKE MORE THAN TALKING TO GET US OUT OF THIS SITUATION.
WEAPON LORD SKILL: ARSENAL

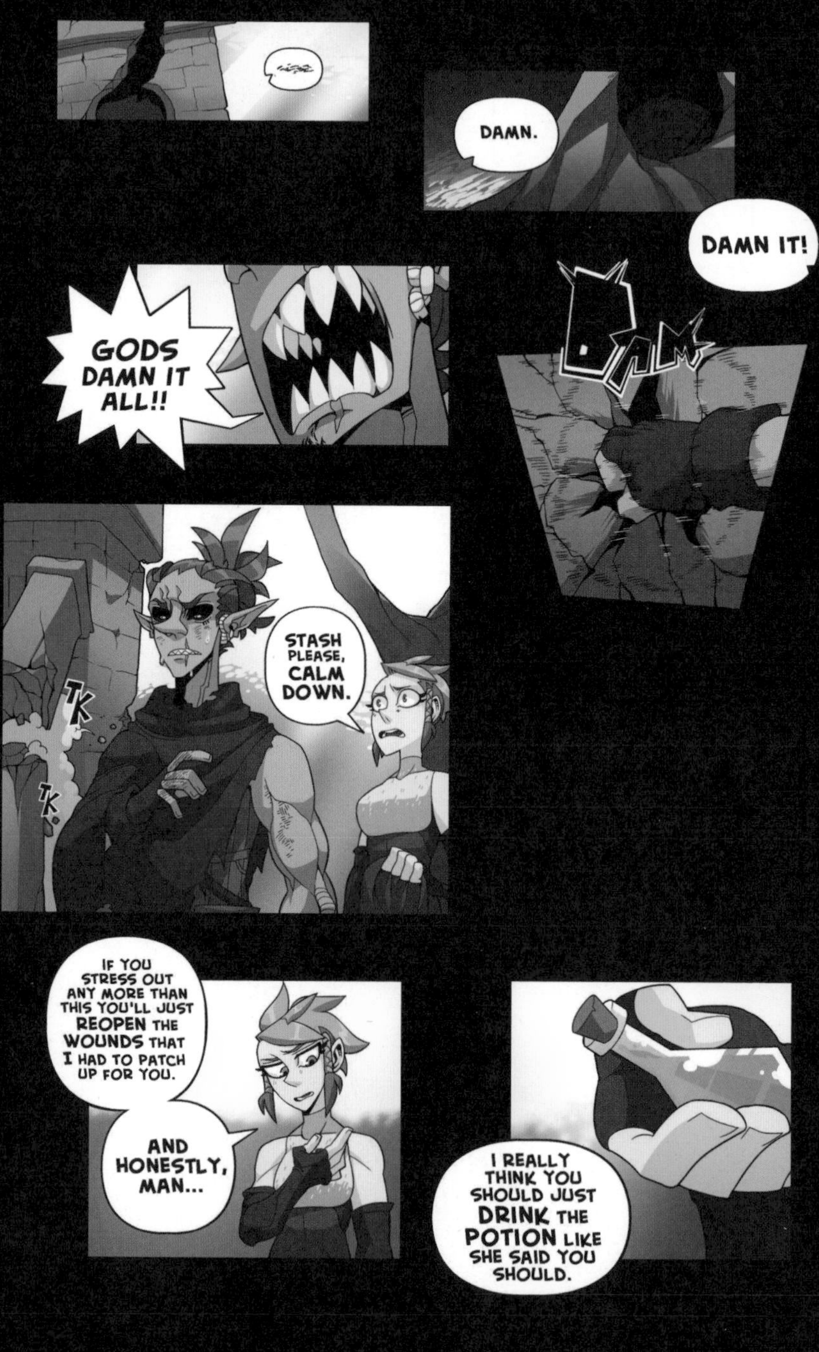
DAMN.
DAMN IT!
GODS DAMN IT ALL!!
BAM
TK
TK.
STASH PLEASE, CALM DOWN.
IF YOU STRESS OUT ANY MORE THAN THIS YOU'LL JUST REOPEN THE WOUNDS THAT I HAD TO PATCH UP FOR YOU.
AND HONESTLY, MAN...
I REALLY THINK YOU SHOULD JUST DRINK THE POTION LIKE SHE SAID YOU SHOULD.

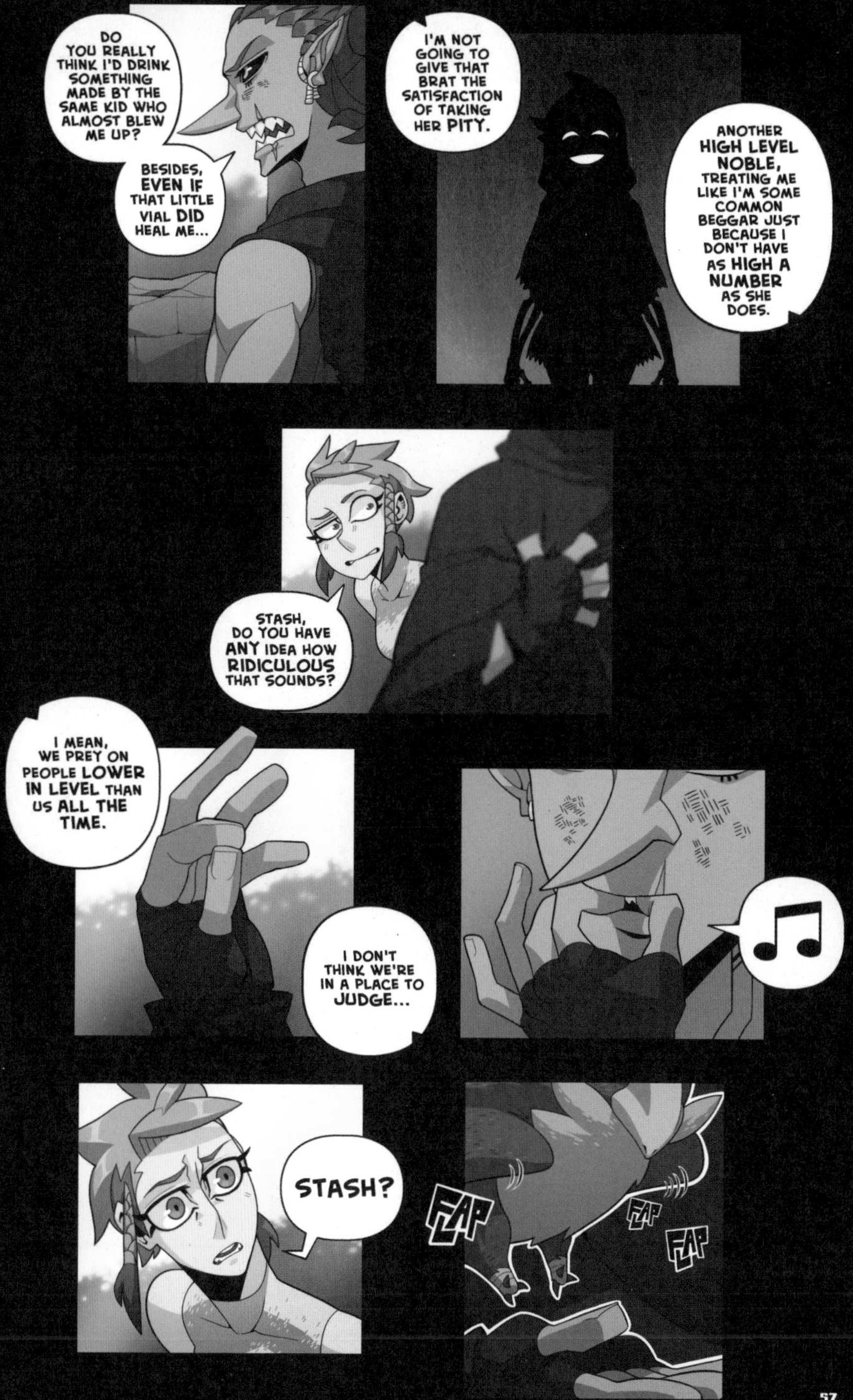

DO YOU REALLY THINK I'D DRINK SOMETHING MADE BY THE SAME KID WHO ALMOST BLEW ME UP?
BESIDES, EVEN IF THAT LITTLE VIAL DID HEAL ME...
I'M NOT GOING TO GIVE THAT BRAT THE SATISFACTION OF TAKING HER PITY.
ANOTHER HIGH LEVEL NOBLE, TREATING ME LIKE I'M SOME COMMON BEGGAR JUST BECAUSE I DON'T HAVE AS HIGH A NUMBER AS SHE DOES.
STASH, DO YOU HAVE ANY IDEA HOW RIDICULOUS THAT SOUNDS?
I MEAN, WE PREY ON PEOPLE LOWER IN LEVEL THAN US ALL THE TIME.
I DON'T THINK WE'RE IN A PLACE TO JUDGE...
♫
STASH?
FLAP
FLAP
FLAP

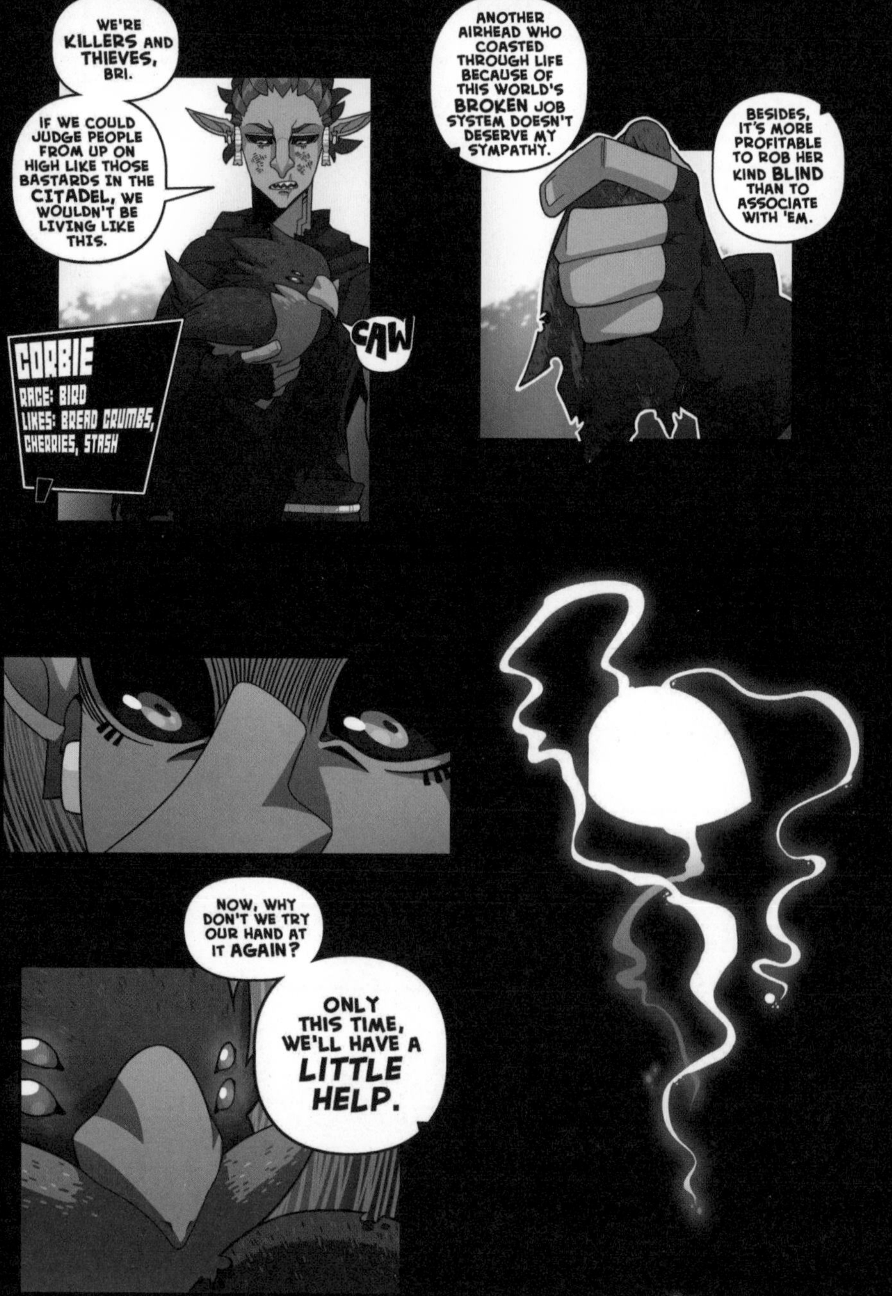
WE'RE KILLERS AND THIEVES, BRI.
IF WE COULD JUDGE PEOPLE FROM UP ON HIGH LIKE THOSE BASTARDS IN THE CITADEL, WE WOULDN'T BE LIVING LIKE THIS.
CORBIE
RACE: BIRD
LIKES: BREAD CRUMBS, CHERRIES, STASH
CAW
ANOTHER AIRHEAD WHO COASTED THROUGH LIFE BECAUSE OF THIS WORLD'S BROKEN JOB SYSTEM DOESN'T DESERVE MY SYMPATHY.
BESIDES, IT'S MORE PROFITABLE TO ROB HER KIND BLIND THAN TO ASSOCIATE WITH 'EM.
NOW, WHY DON'T WE TRY OUR HAND AT IT AGAIN?
ONLY THIS TIME, WE'LL HAVE A LITTLE HELP.

HAA
HAA
HAA...
TREMBLE
T-TOO FAST...
TREMBLE
THAT ALL HAPPENED... WAY TOO FAST.
THESE TWO... I COULDN'T FOLLOW THEIR MOVEMENTS AT ALL.
I'LL GIVE YOU... ONE MORE CHANCE... TO BACK OFF...

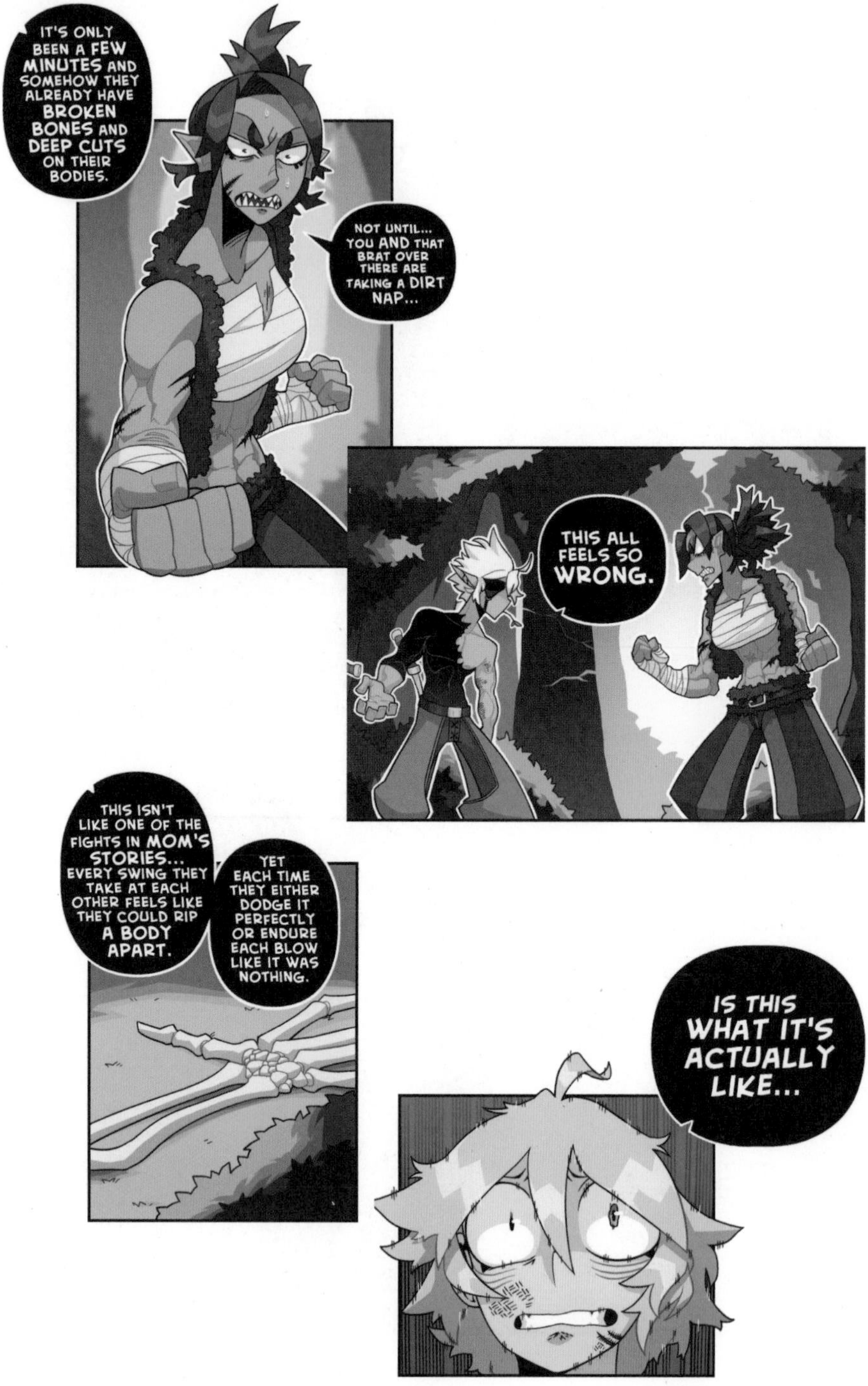
IT'S ONLY BEEN A FEW MINUTES AND SOMEHOW THEY ALREADY HAVE BROKEN BONES AND DEEP CUTS ON THEIR BODIES.
NOT UNTIL... YOU AND THAT BRAT OVER THERE ARE TAKING A DIRT NAP...
THIS ALL FEELS SO WRONG.
THIS ISN'T LIKE ONE OF THE FIGHTS IN MOM'S STORIES... EVERY SWING THEY TAKE AT EACH OTHER FEELS LIKE THEY COULD RIP A BODY APART.
YET EACH TIME THEY EITHER DODGE IT PERFECTLY OR ENDURE EACH BLOW LIKE IT WAS NOTHING.
IS THIS WHAT IT'S ACTUALLY LIKE...

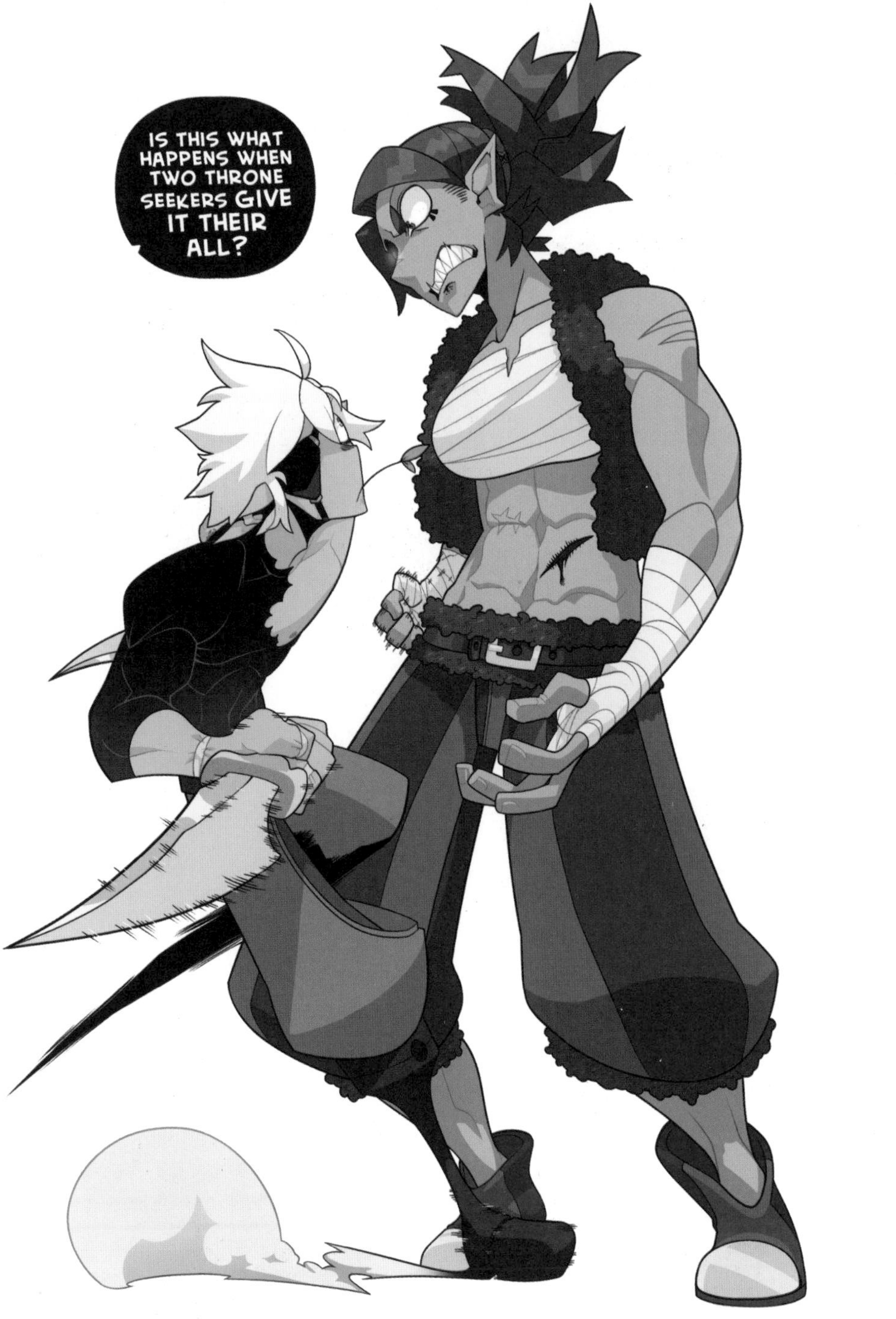
IS THIS WHAT HAPPENS WHEN TWO THRONE SEEKERS GIVE IT THEIR ALL?

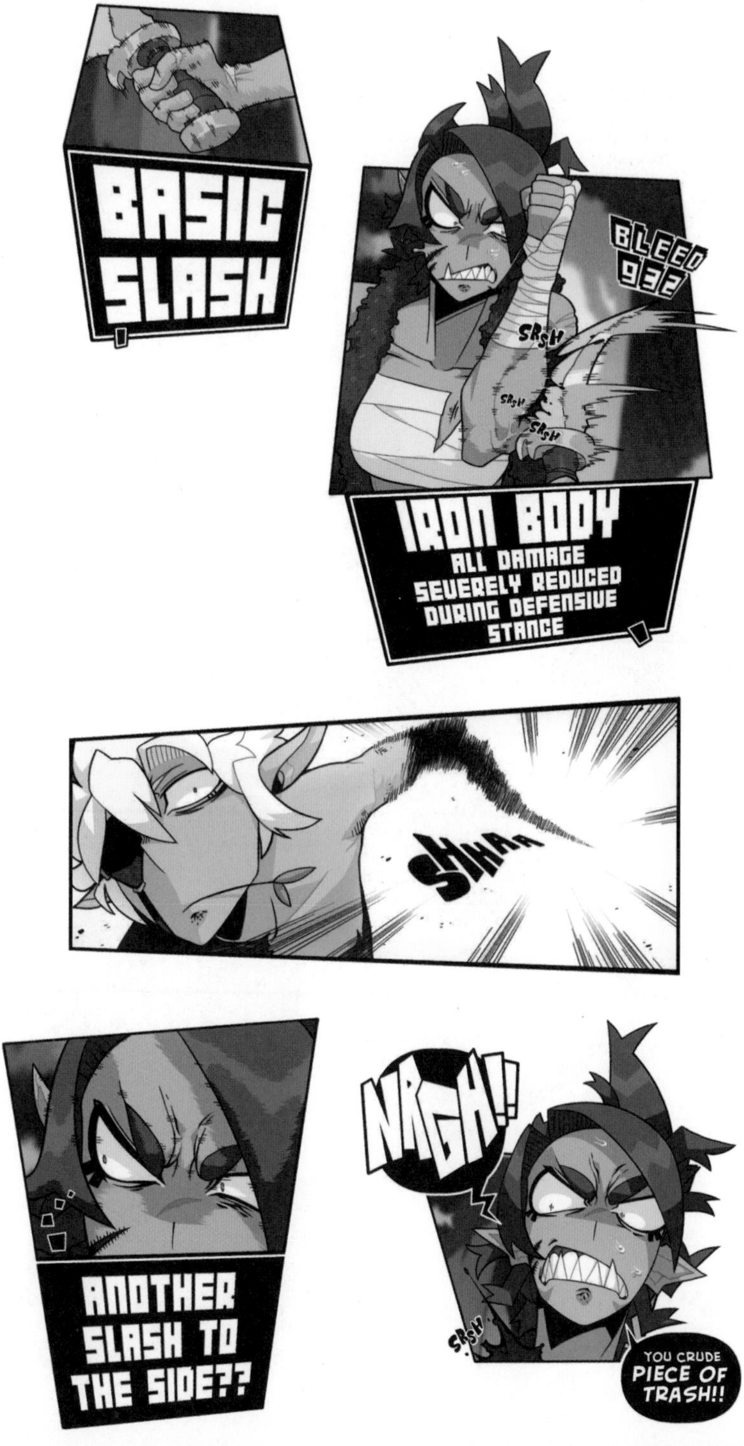
BASIC SLASH
BLEED 932
SRSH
SRSH
SRSH
IRON BODY
ALL DAMAGE SEVERELY REDUCED DURING DEFENSIVE STANCE
SHAA
ANOTHER SLASH TO THE SIDE??
NRGH!!
SRSH
YOU CRUDE PIECE OF TRASH!!

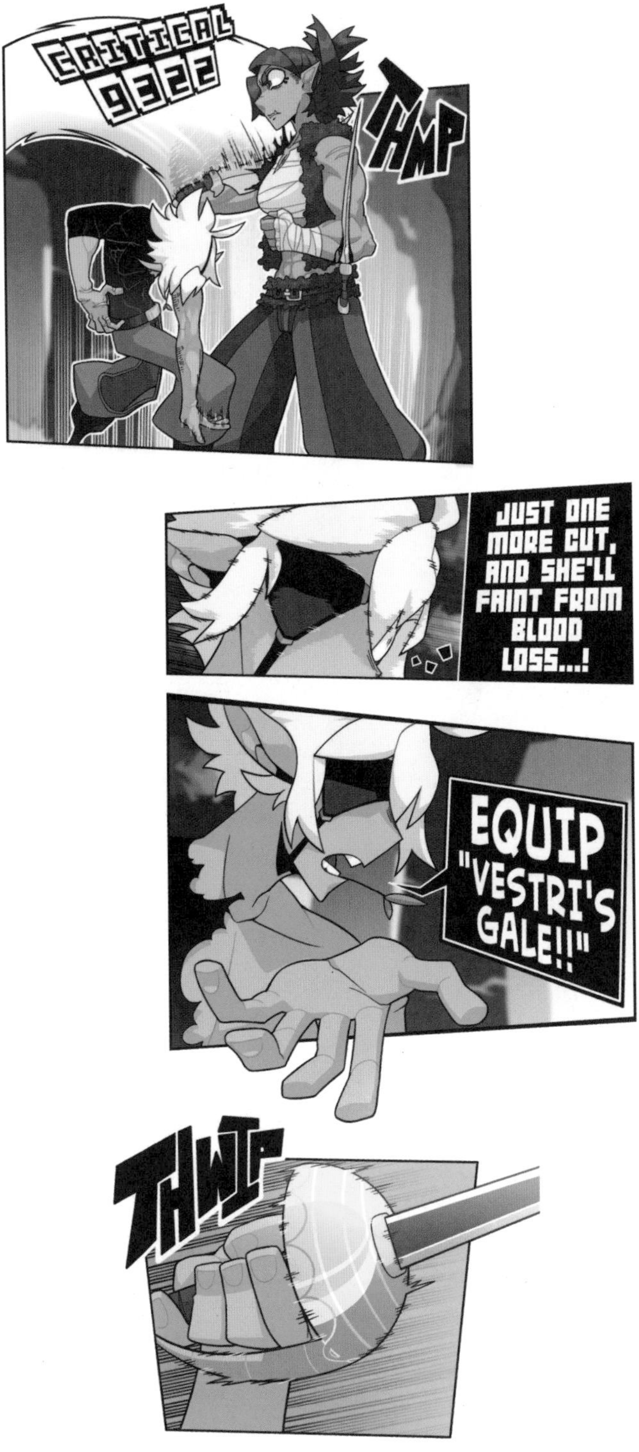
CRITICAL
9322
THMP
JUST ONE MORE CUT, AND SHE'LL FAINT FROM BLOOD LOSS...!
EQUIP "VESTRI'S GALE!!"
THWIP

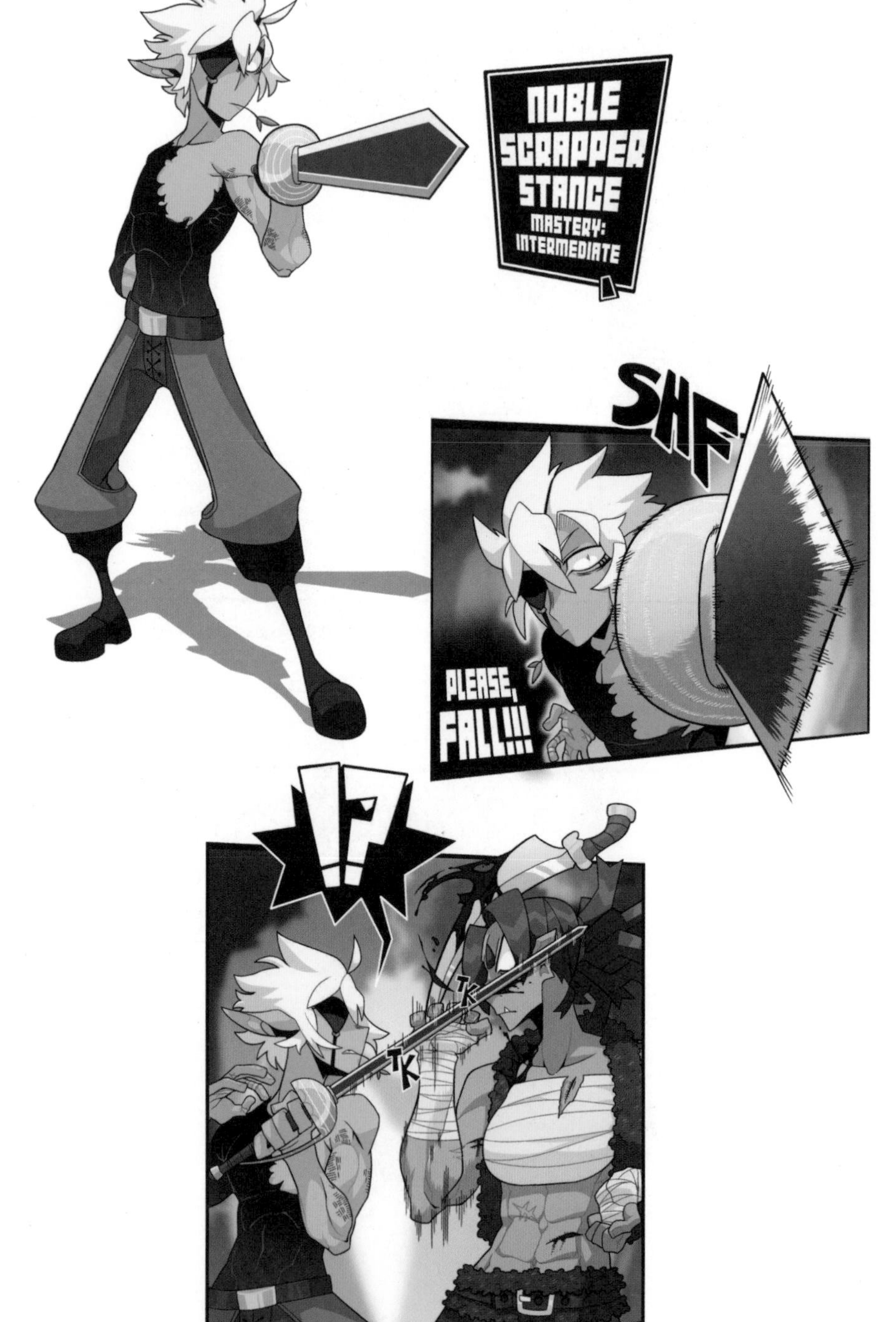
NOBLE SCRAPPER STANCE
MASTERY: INTERMEDIATE
SHF
PLEASE, FALL!!!
!?
TK
TK

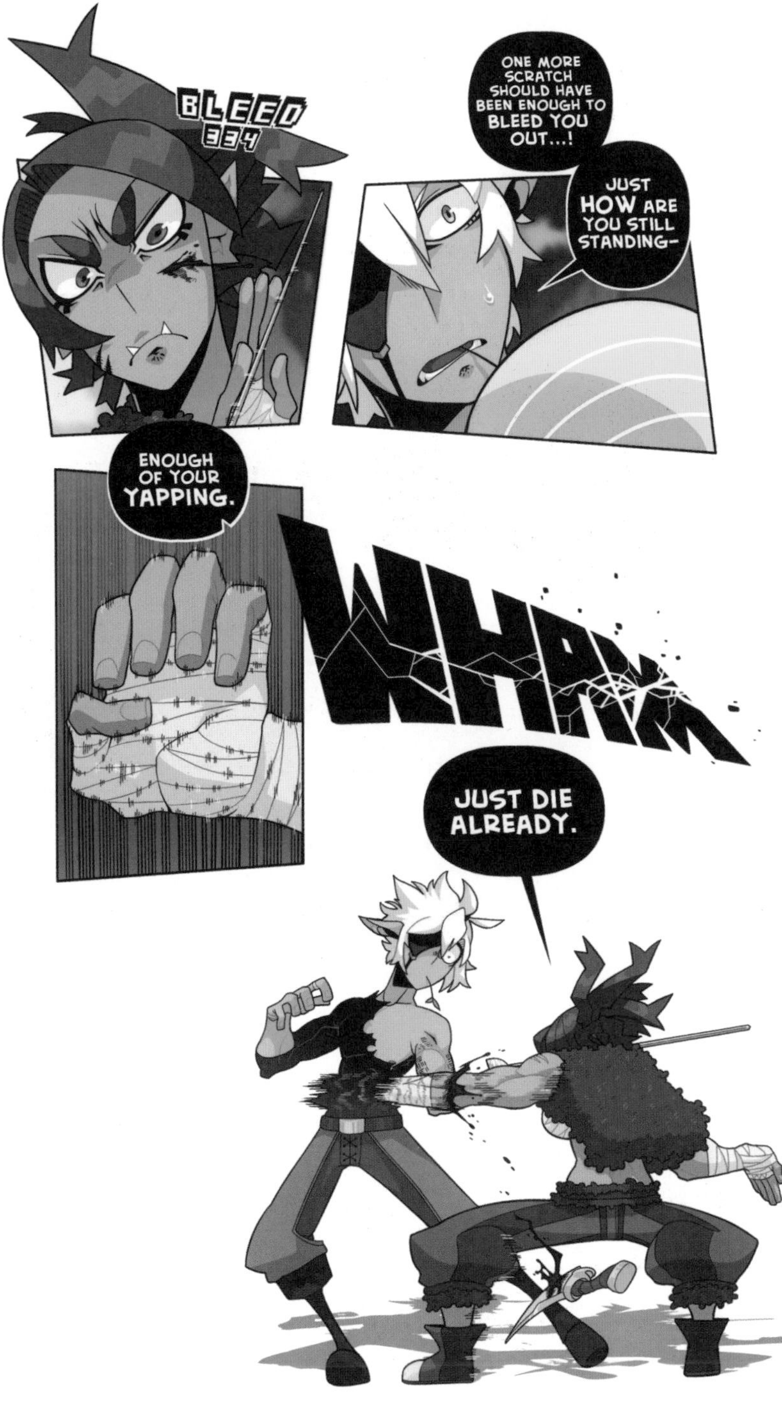
BLEED
334
ONE MORE SCRATCH SHOULD HAVE BEEN ENOUGH TO BLEED YOU OUT...!
JUST HOW ARE YOU STILL STANDING-
ENOUGH OF YOUR YAPPING.
WHAM
JUST DIE ALREADY.

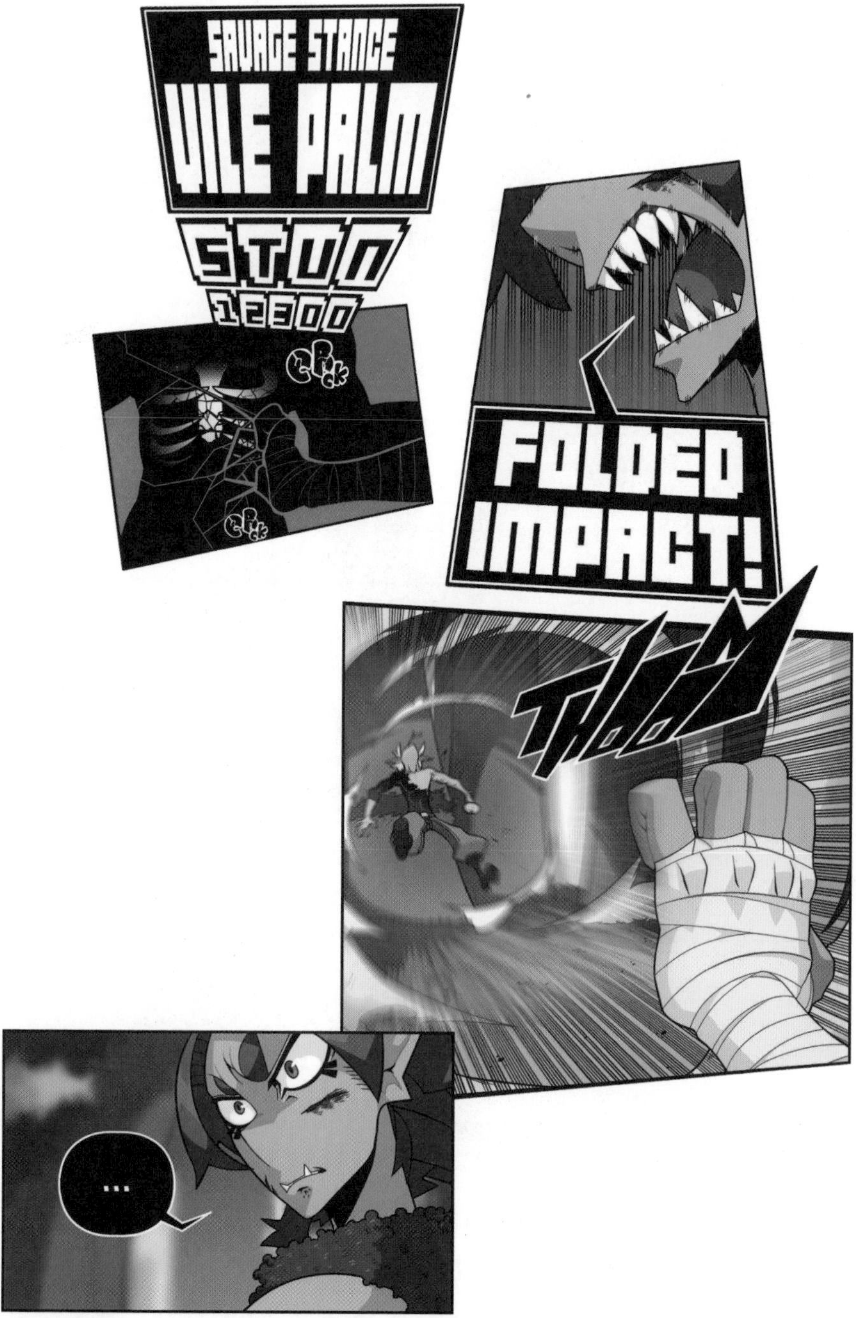
SAVAGE STANCE
VILE PALM
STUN
12300
CRACK
CRACK
FOLDED IMPACT!
THOOM
...

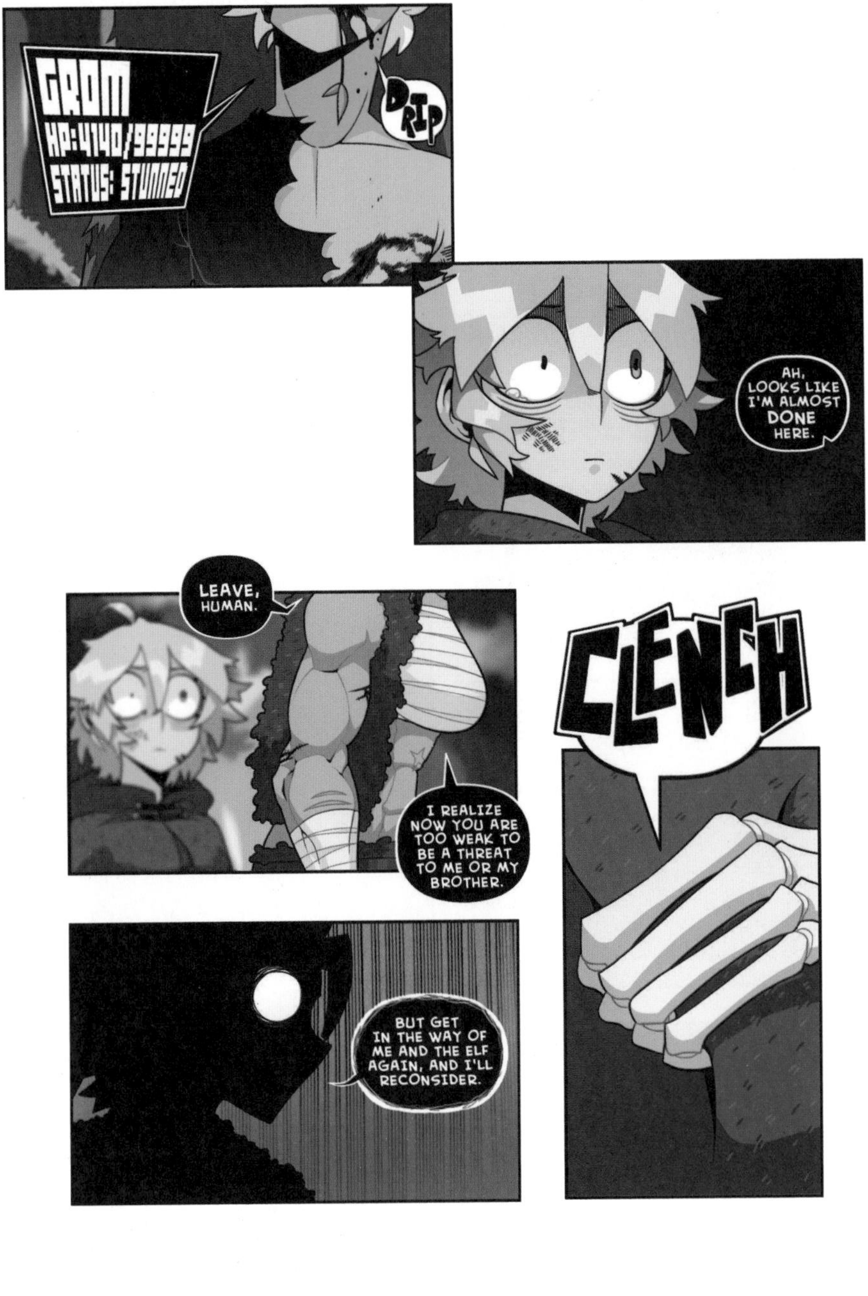
GROM
HP:4140/99999
STATUS: STUNNED
DRIP
AH, LOOKS LIKE I'M ALMOST DONE HERE.
LEAVE, HUMAN.
I REALIZE NOW YOU ARE TOO WEAK TO BE A THREAT TO ME OR MY BROTHER.
BUT GET IN THE WAY OF ME AND THE ELF AGAIN, AND I'LL RECONSIDER.
CLENCH

I AM WEAK.

I'M NOT STRONG ENOUGH TO HELP SETTLE A FIGHT BETWEEN REAL THRONE SEEKERS.

IN FACT, I'M PROBABLY BETTER OFF JUST LEAVING GROM BEHIND AND SAVING MYSELF THE TROUBLE.

BUT EVEN SO...!

I COULD NEVER LIVE WITH MYSELF IF I JUST ABANDONED MY ONLY FRIEND!!!

## Chapter 4
# THE UNDERSTANDING

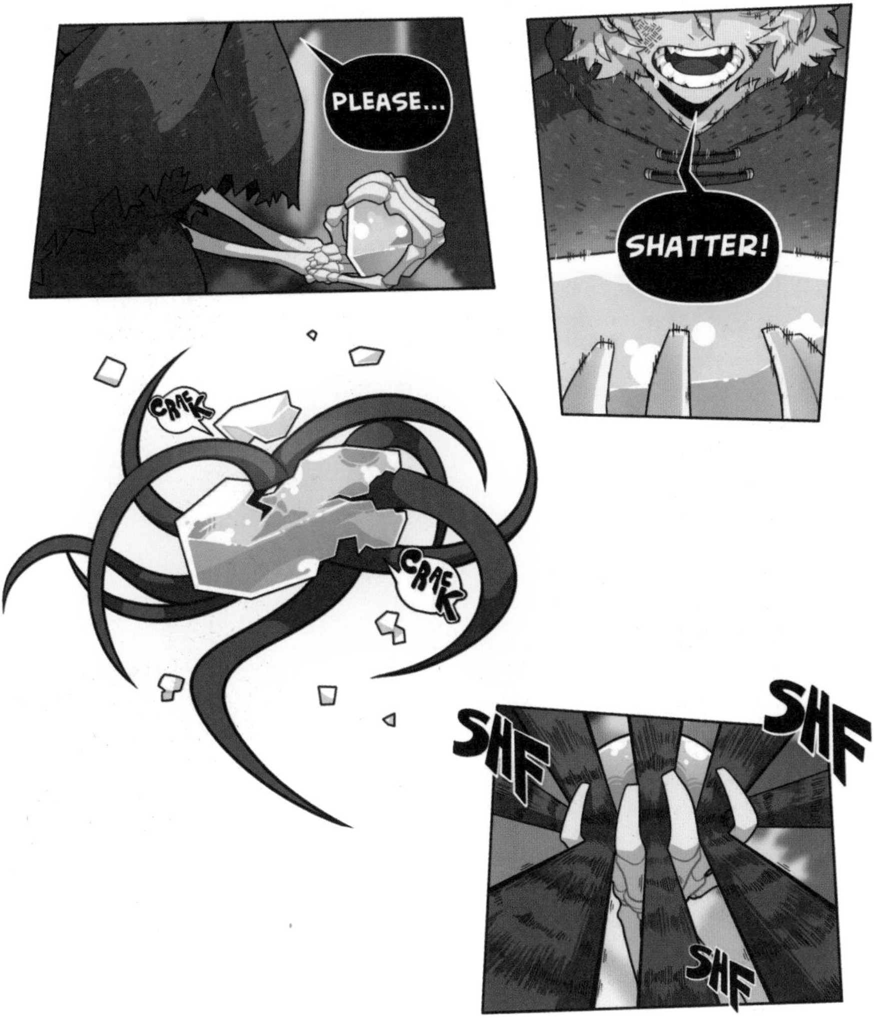
PLEASE...
SHATTER!
CRACK
CRACK
SHF
SHF
SHF

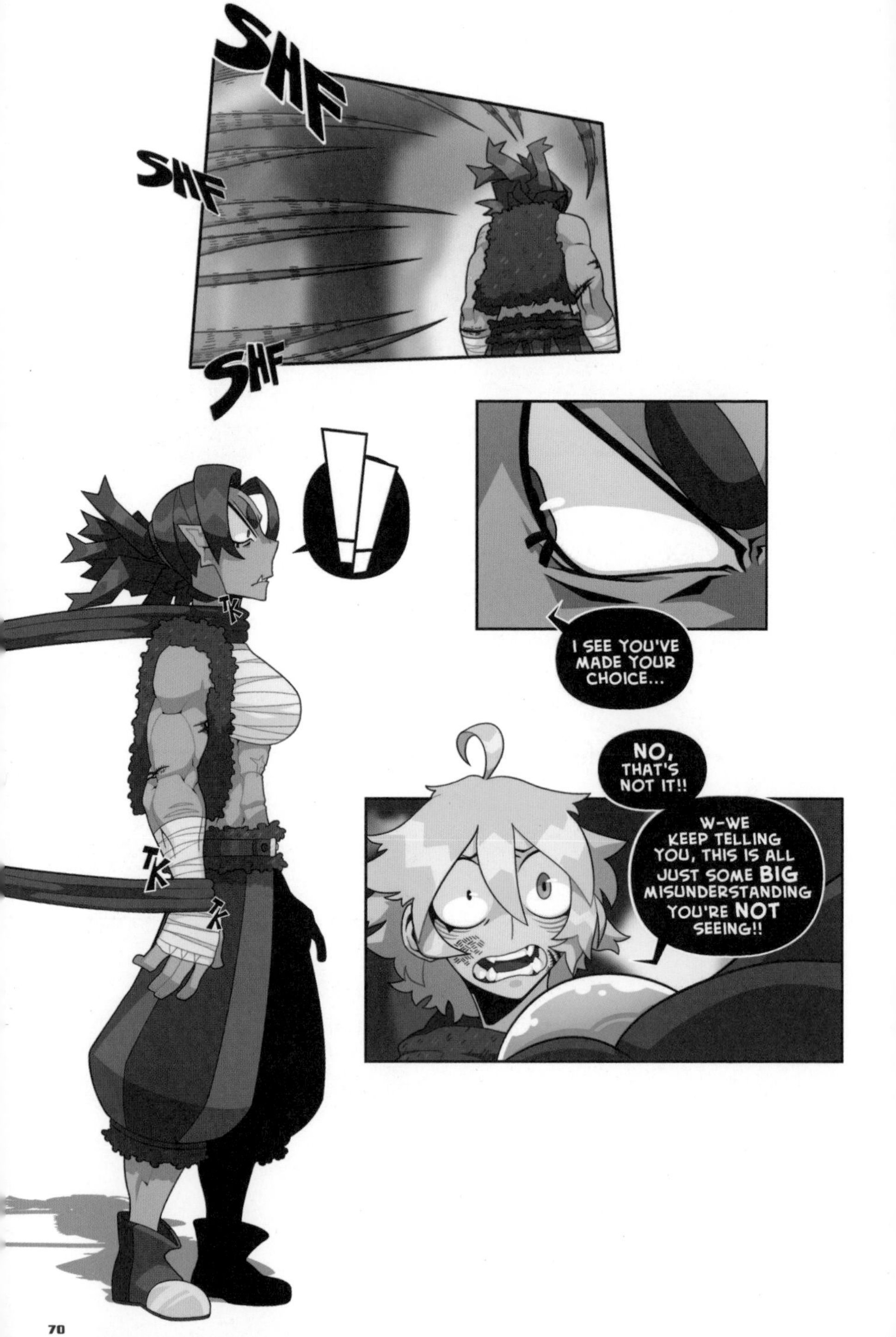
SHF
SHF
SHF
!
TK
TK
TK
I SEE YOU'VE MADE YOUR CHOICE...
NO, THAT'S NOT IT!!
W-WE KEEP TELLING YOU, THIS IS ALL JUST SOME BIG MISUNDERSTANDING YOU'RE NOT SEEING!!

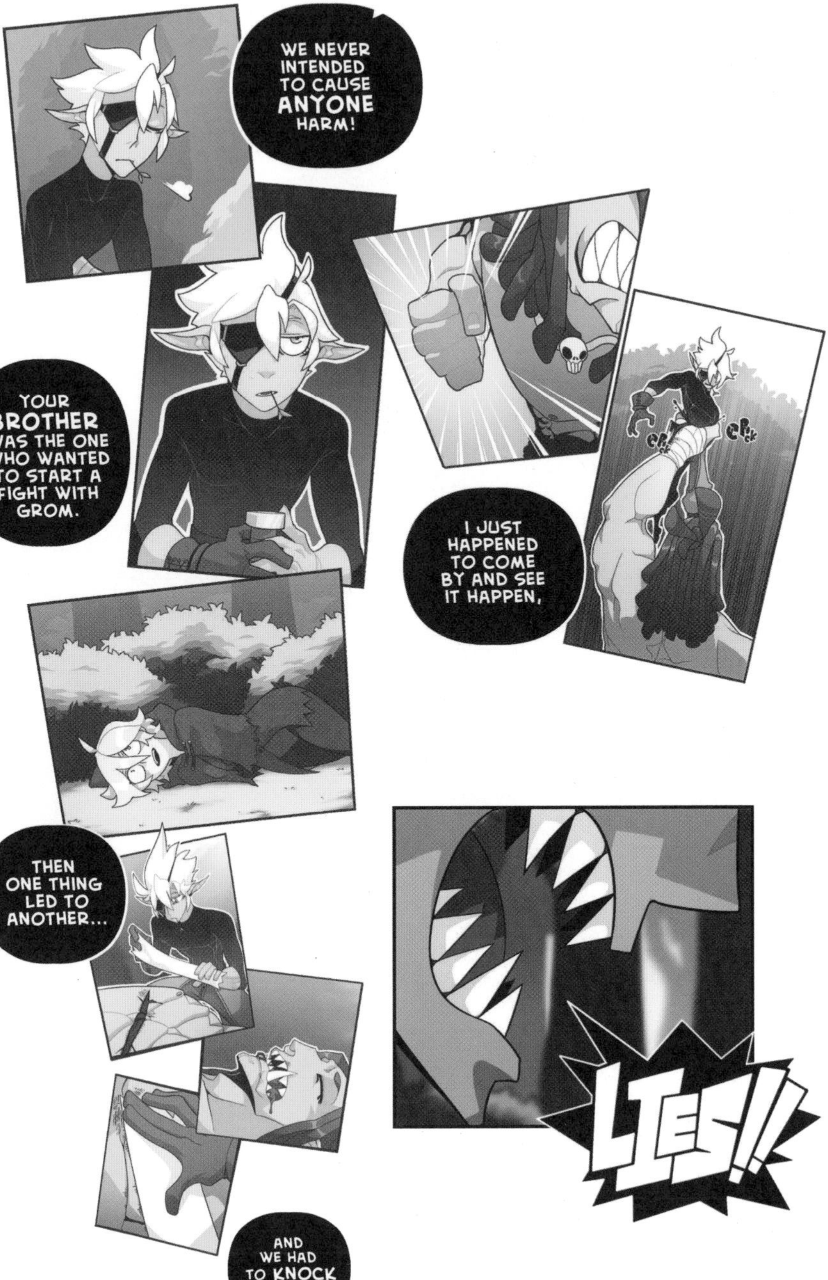
WE NEVER INTENDED TO CAUSE ANYONE HARM!
YOUR BROTHER WAS THE ONE WHO WANTED TO START A FIGHT WITH GROM.
CRACK
CRACK
I JUST HAPPENED TO COME BY AND SEE IT HAPPEN,
THEN ONE THING LED TO ANOTHER...
AND WE HAD TO KNOCK HIM OUT-
LIES!!

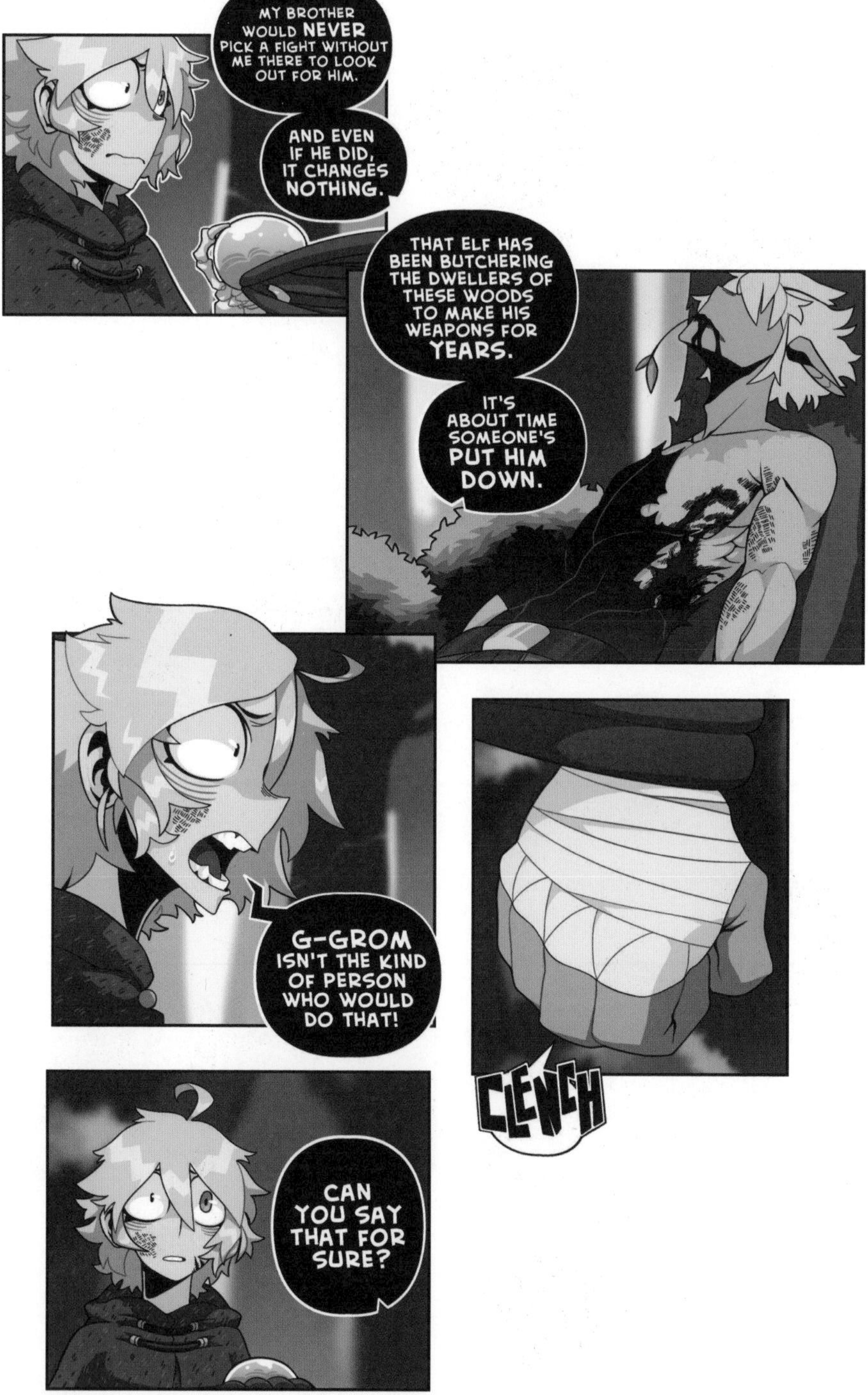
MY BROTHER WOULD NEVER PICK A FIGHT WITHOUT ME THERE TO LOOK OUT FOR HIM.
AND EVEN IF HE DID, IT CHANGES NOTHING.
THAT ELF HAS BEEN BUTCHERING THE DWELLERS OF THESE WOODS TO MAKE HIS WEAPONS FOR YEARS.
IT'S ABOUT TIME SOMEONE'S PUT HIM DOWN.
G-GROM ISN'T THE KIND OF PERSON WHO WOULD DO THAT!
CLENCH
CAN YOU SAY THAT FOR SURE?

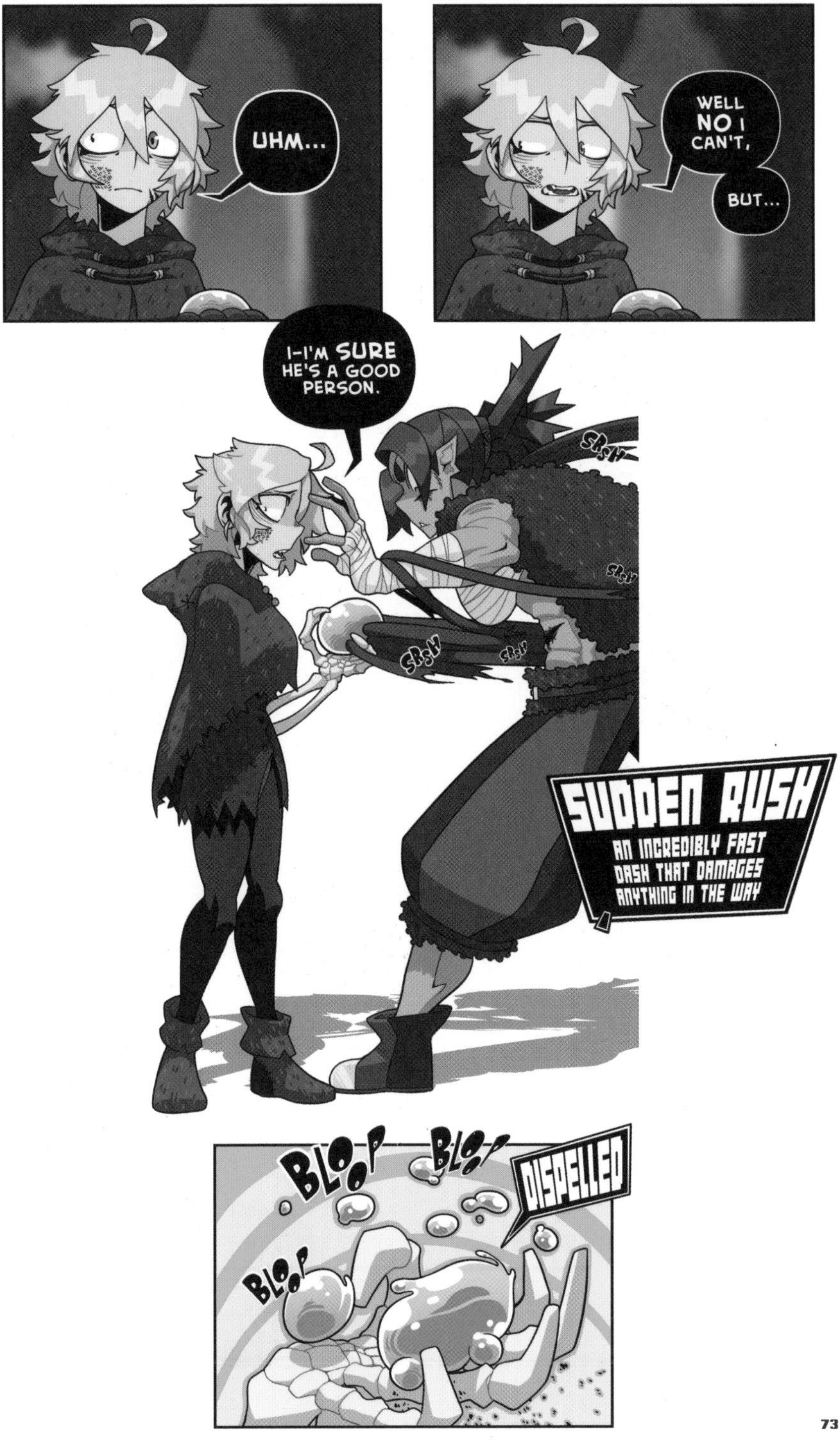
UHM...
WELL NO I CAN'T,
BUT...
I-I'M SURE HE'S A GOOD PERSON.
SRSH
SRSH
SRSH
SRSH
SUDDEN RUSH
AN INCREDIBLY FAST DASH THAT DAMAGES ANYTHING IN THE WAY
BLOOP
BLOOP
DISPELLED
BLOOP

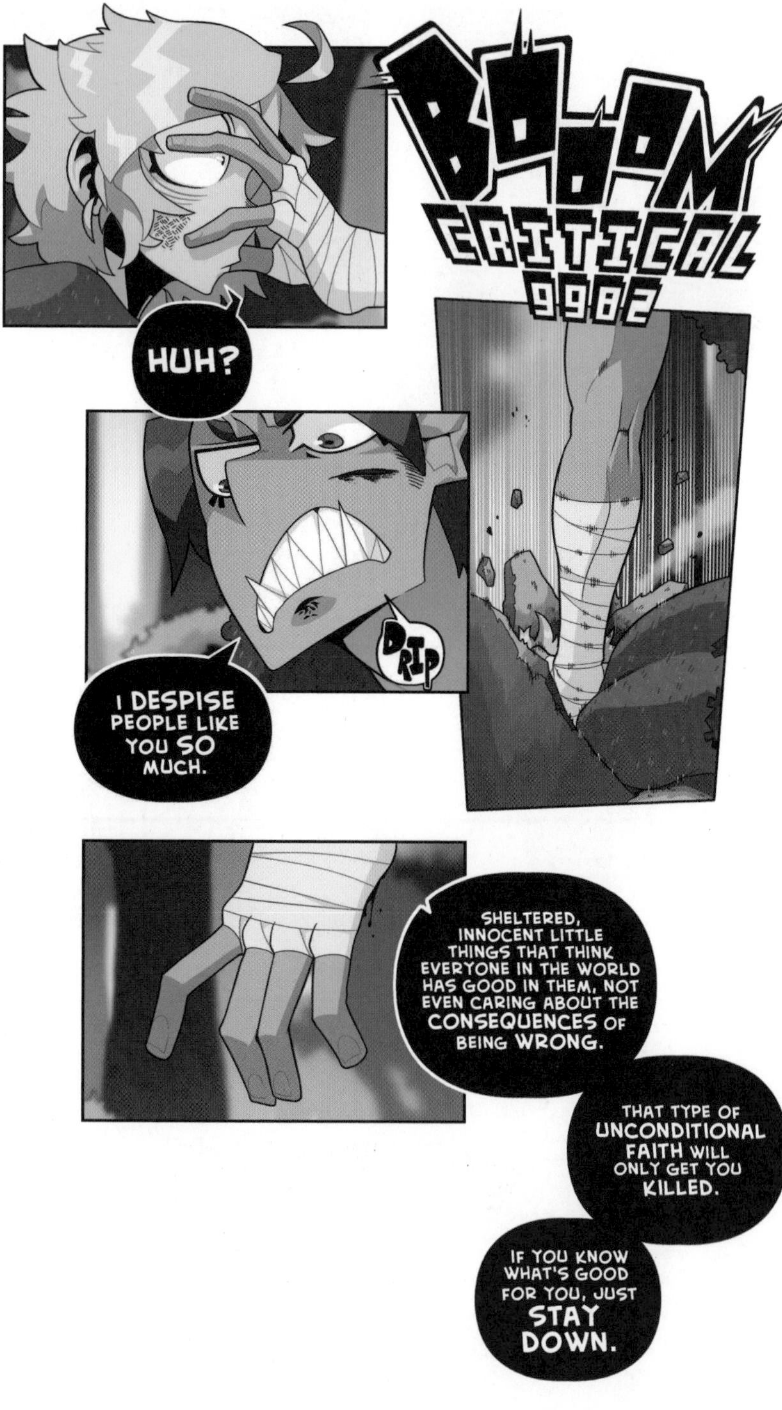
BOOOOM
CRITICAL
9982
HUH?
DRIP
I DESPISE PEOPLE LIKE YOU SO MUCH.
SHELTERED, INNOCENT LITTLE THINGS THAT THINK EVERYONE IN THE WORLD HAS GOOD IN THEM, NOT EVEN CARING ABOUT THE CONSEQUENCES OF BEING WRONG.
THAT TYPE OF UNCONDITIONAL FAITH WILL ONLY GET YOU KILLED.
IF YOU KNOW WHAT'S GOOD FOR YOU, JUST STAY DOWN.

PIERCE
1207
CRSH
SRSH
...WHAT?
THERE'S NOTHING... WRONG...
THERE'S NOTHING WRONG WITH BELIEVING IN PEOPLE...!!

## Chapter 5
# THE CALM

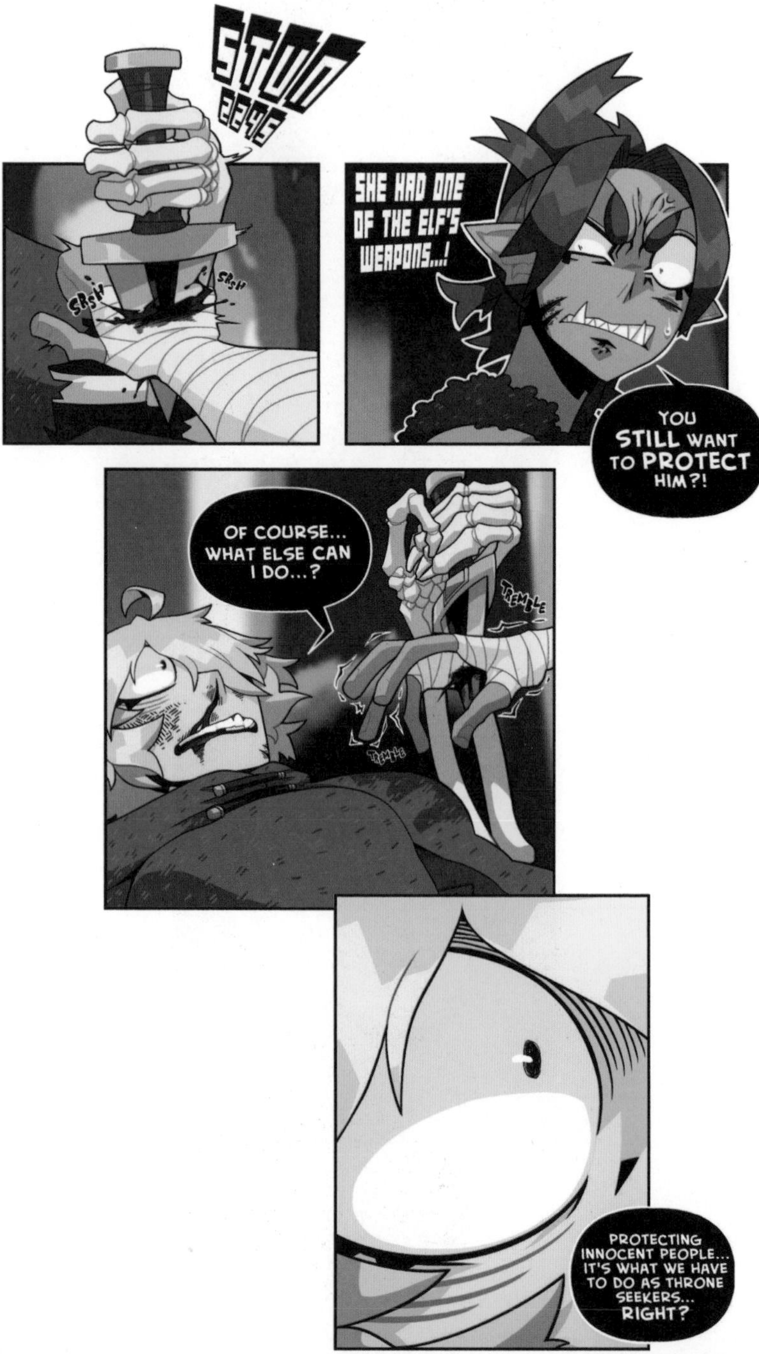
SRSH
SRSH
SHE HAD ONE OF THE ELF'S WEAPONS...!
YOU STILL WANT TO PROTECT HIM?!
OF COURSE... WHAT ELSE CAN I DO...?
TREMBLE
TREMBLE
PROTECTING INNOCENT PEOPLE... IT'S WHAT WE HAVE TO DO AS THRONE SEEKERS... RIGHT?

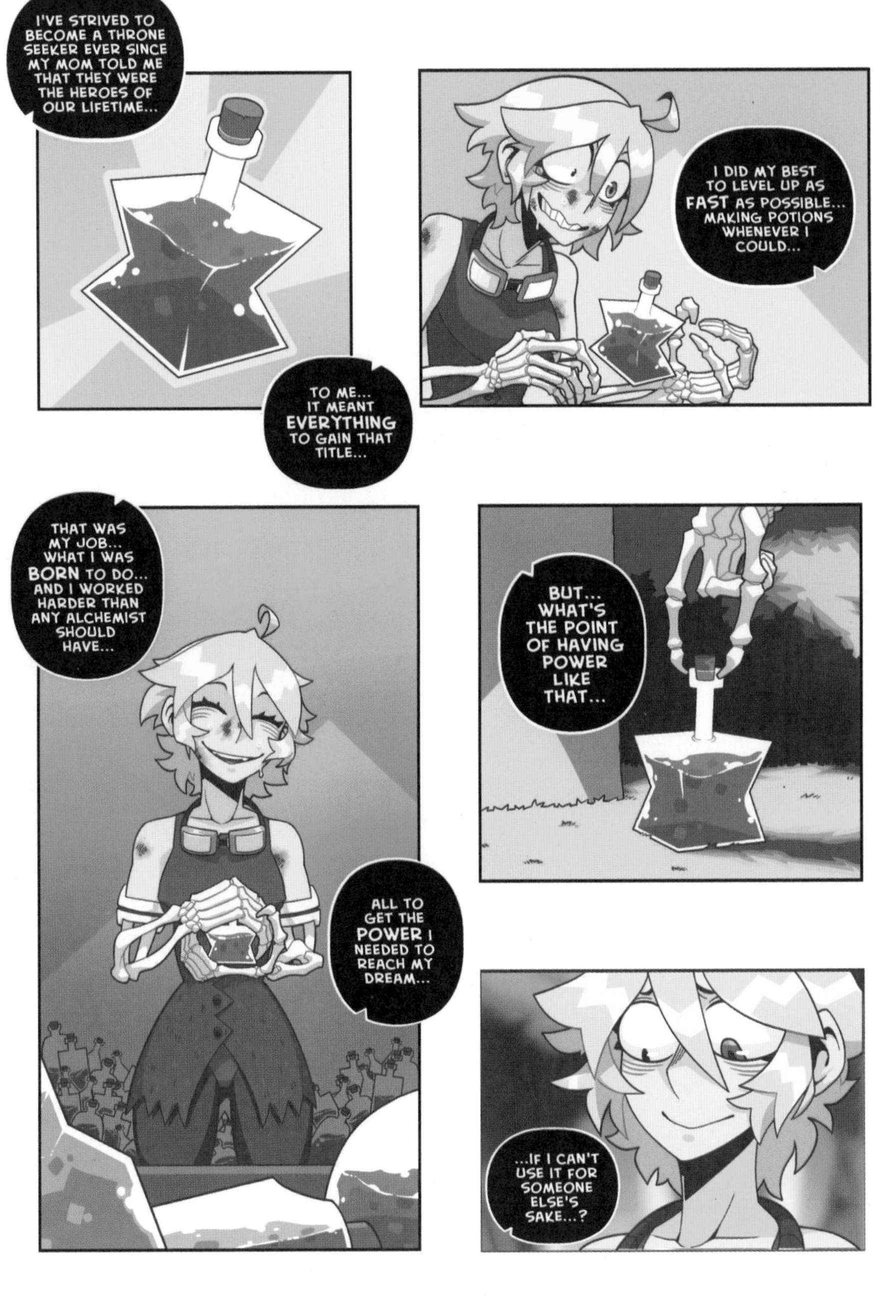

I'VE STRIVED TO BECOME A THRONE SEEKER EVER SINCE MY MOM TOLD ME THAT THEY WERE THE HEROES OF OUR LIFETIME...
TO ME... IT MEANT EVERYTHING TO GAIN THAT TITLE...
I DID MY BEST TO LEVEL UP AS FAST AS POSSIBLE... MAKING POTIONS WHENEVER I COULD...
THAT WAS MY JOB... WHAT I WAS BORN TO DO... AND I WORKED HARDER THAN ANY ALCHEMIST SHOULD HAVE...
ALL TO GET THE POWER I NEEDED TO REACH MY DREAM...
BUT... WHAT'S THE POINT OF HAVING POWER LIKE THAT...
...IF I CAN'T USE IT FOR SOMEONE ELSE'S SAKE...?

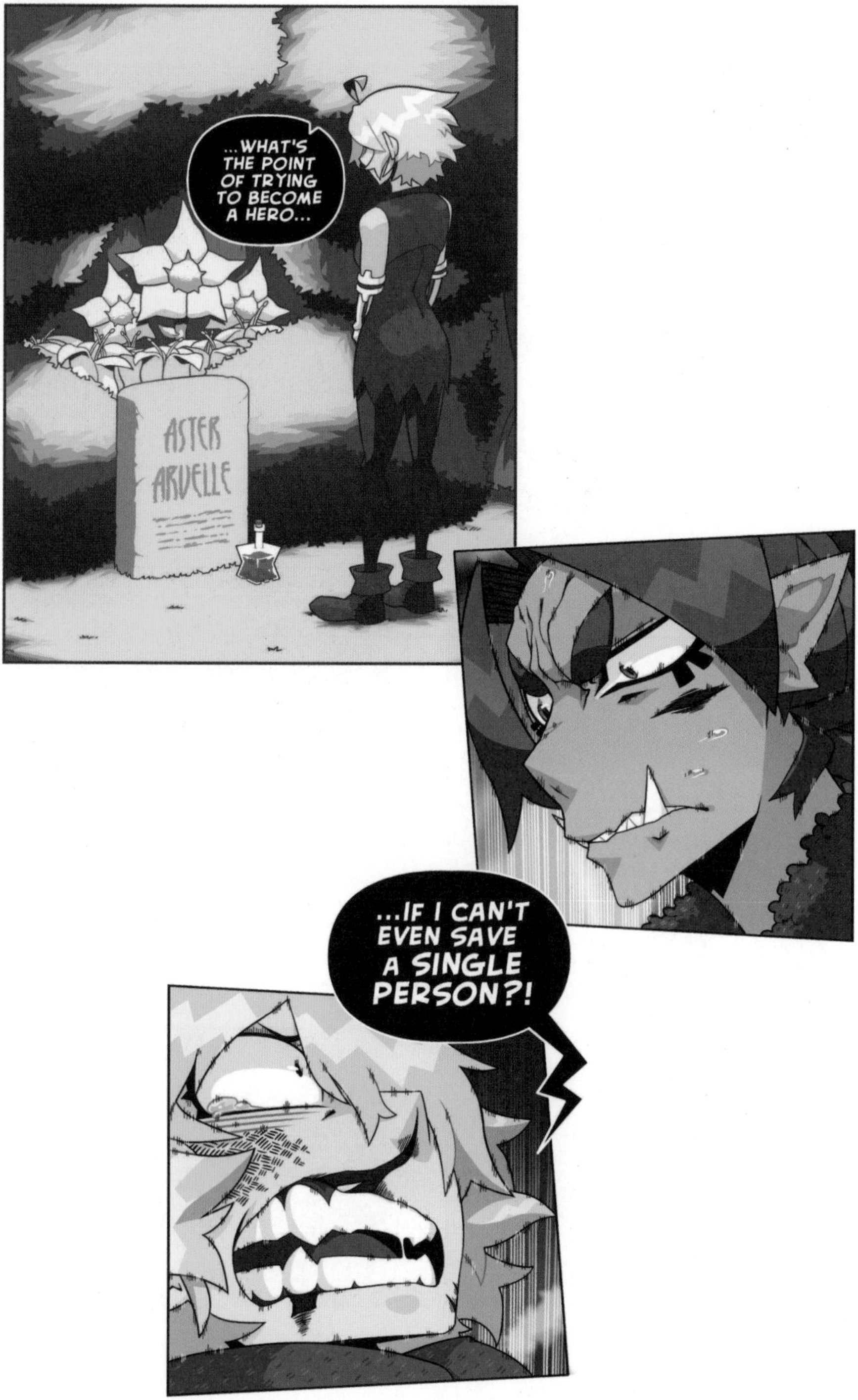
...WHAT'S THE POINT OF TRYING TO BECOME A HERO...
ASTER ARVELLE
...IF I CAN'T EVEN SAVE A SINGLE PERSON?!

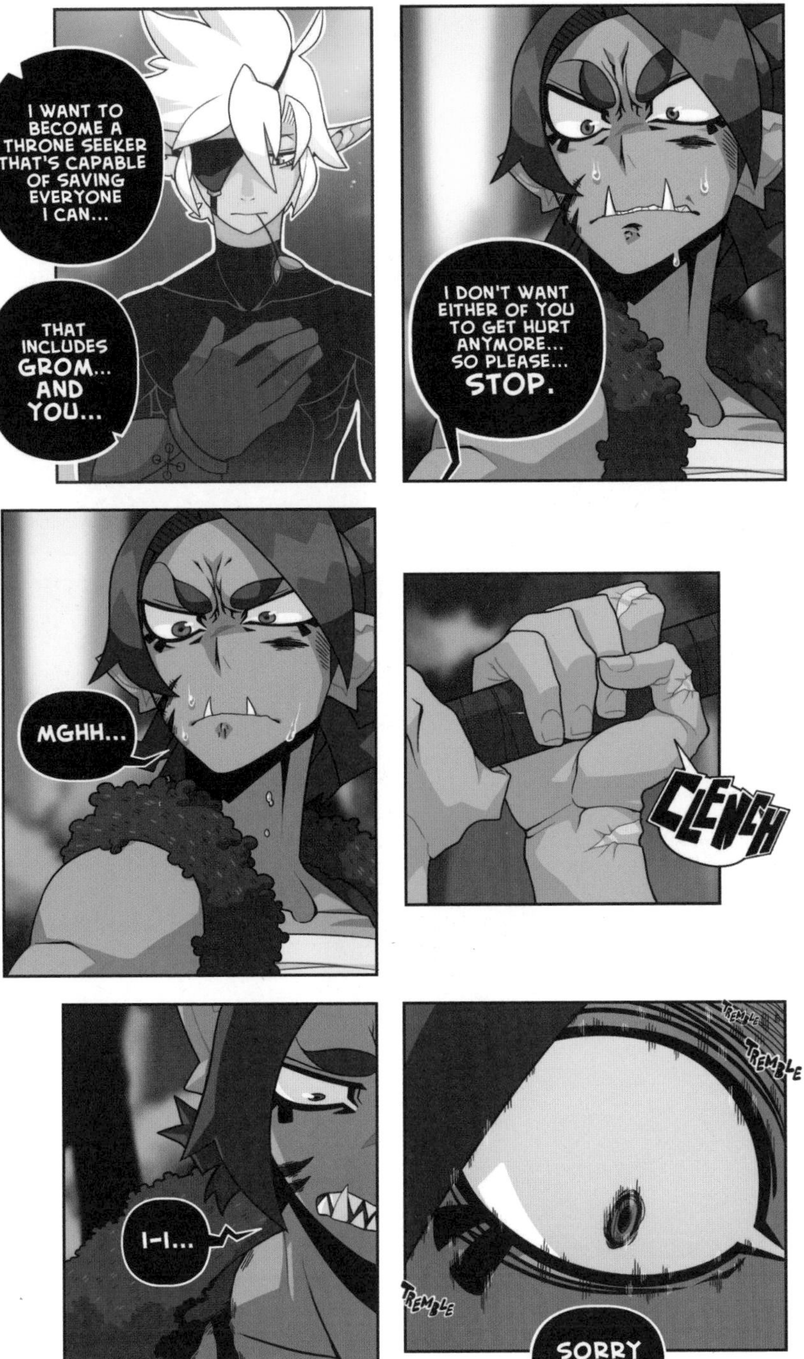
I WANT TO BECOME A THRONE SEEKER THAT'S CAPABLE OF SAVING EVERYONE I CAN...
THAT INCLUDES GROM... AND YOU...
I DON'T WANT EITHER OF YOU TO GET HURT ANYMORE... SO PLEASE... STOP.
MGHH...
CLENCH
I-I...
TREMBLE
TREMBLE
TREMBLE
SORRY AGNI,

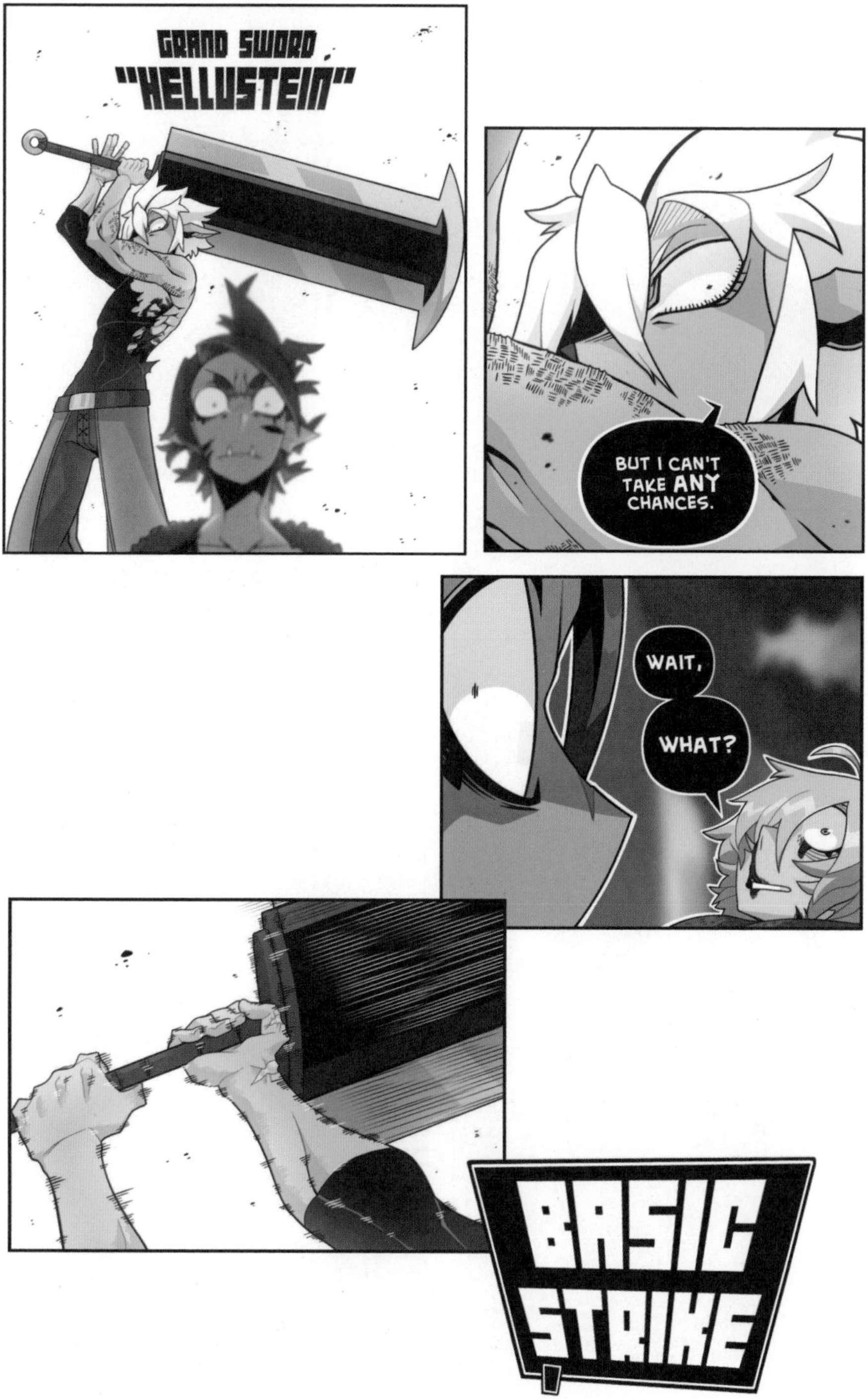
GRAND SWORD
"HELLUSTEIN"
BUT I CAN'T TAKE ANY CHANCES.
WAIT,
WHAT?
BASIC STRIKE!

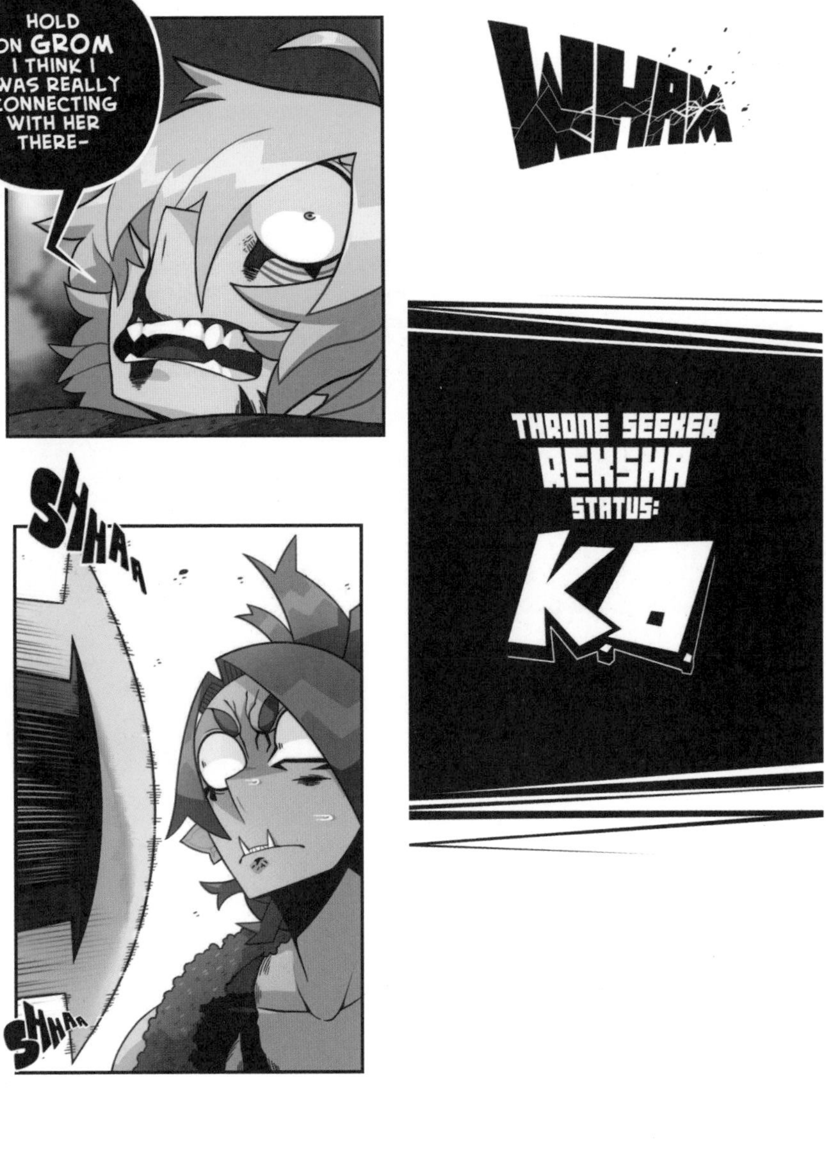
HOLD ON GROM I THINK I WAS REALLY CONNECTING WITH HER THERE-
WHAM
SHHAA
SHHAA
THRONE SEEKER
REKSHA
STATUS:
K.O.

# Chapter 6
## THE TALK

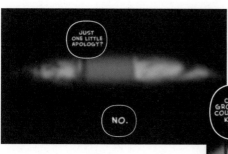

JUST ONE LITTLE APOLOGY?

NO.

C'MON GROM, YOU COULD HAVE KILLED HER!

BUT I DIDN'T, DID I?

YOU COULD AT LEAST FEEL A LITTLE BAD ABOUT IT...

SAME THING COULD BE SAID ABOUT HER.

WELL, YEAH BUT-

!

SHE'S AWAKE!

NGHH...

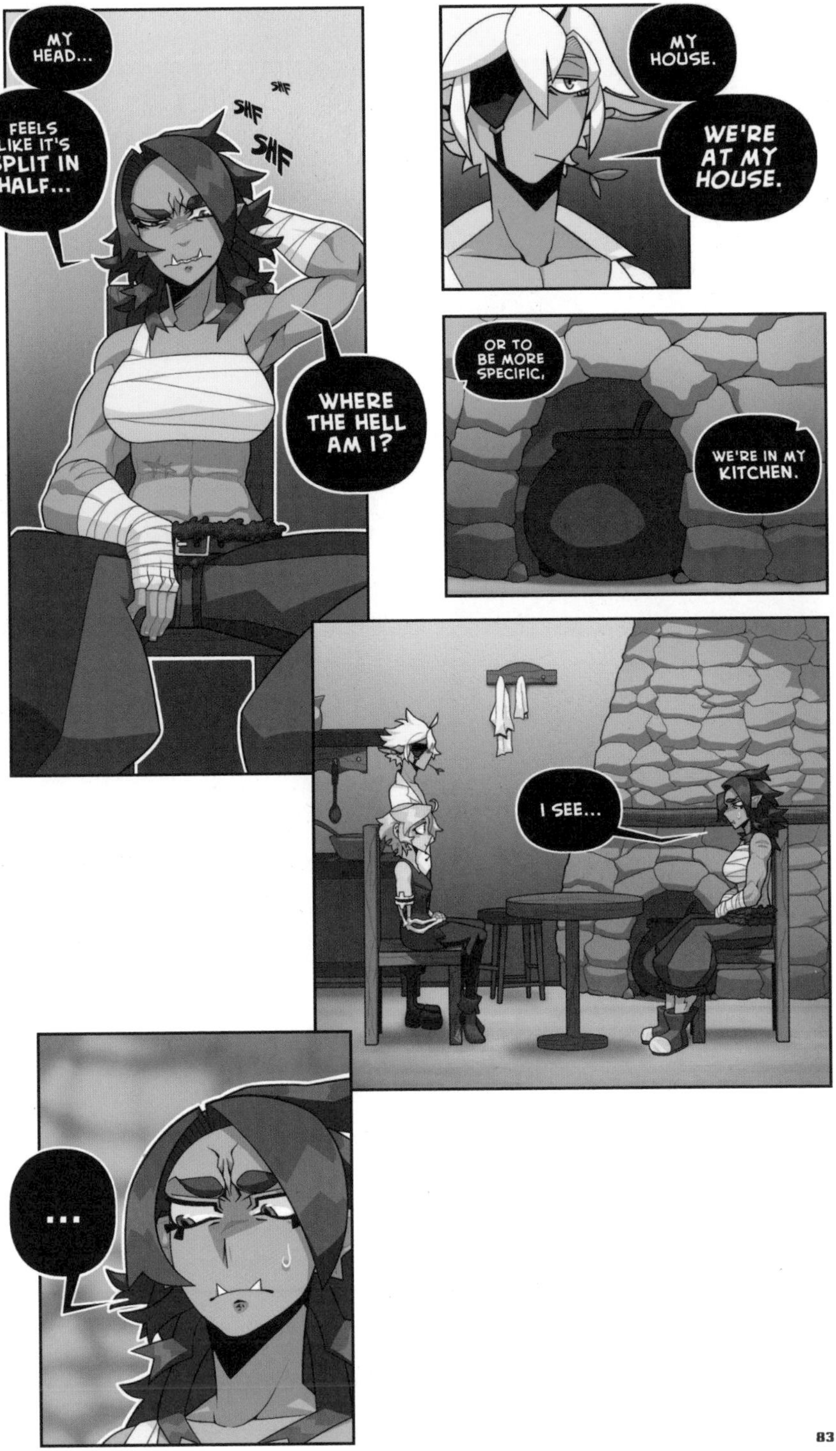
MY HEAD...
SHF
SHF
SHF
FEELS LIKE IT'S SPLIT IN HALF...
WHERE THE HELL AM I?
MY HOUSE.
WE'RE AT MY HOUSE.
OR TO BE MORE SPECIFIC,
WE'RE IN MY KITCHEN.
I SEE...
...

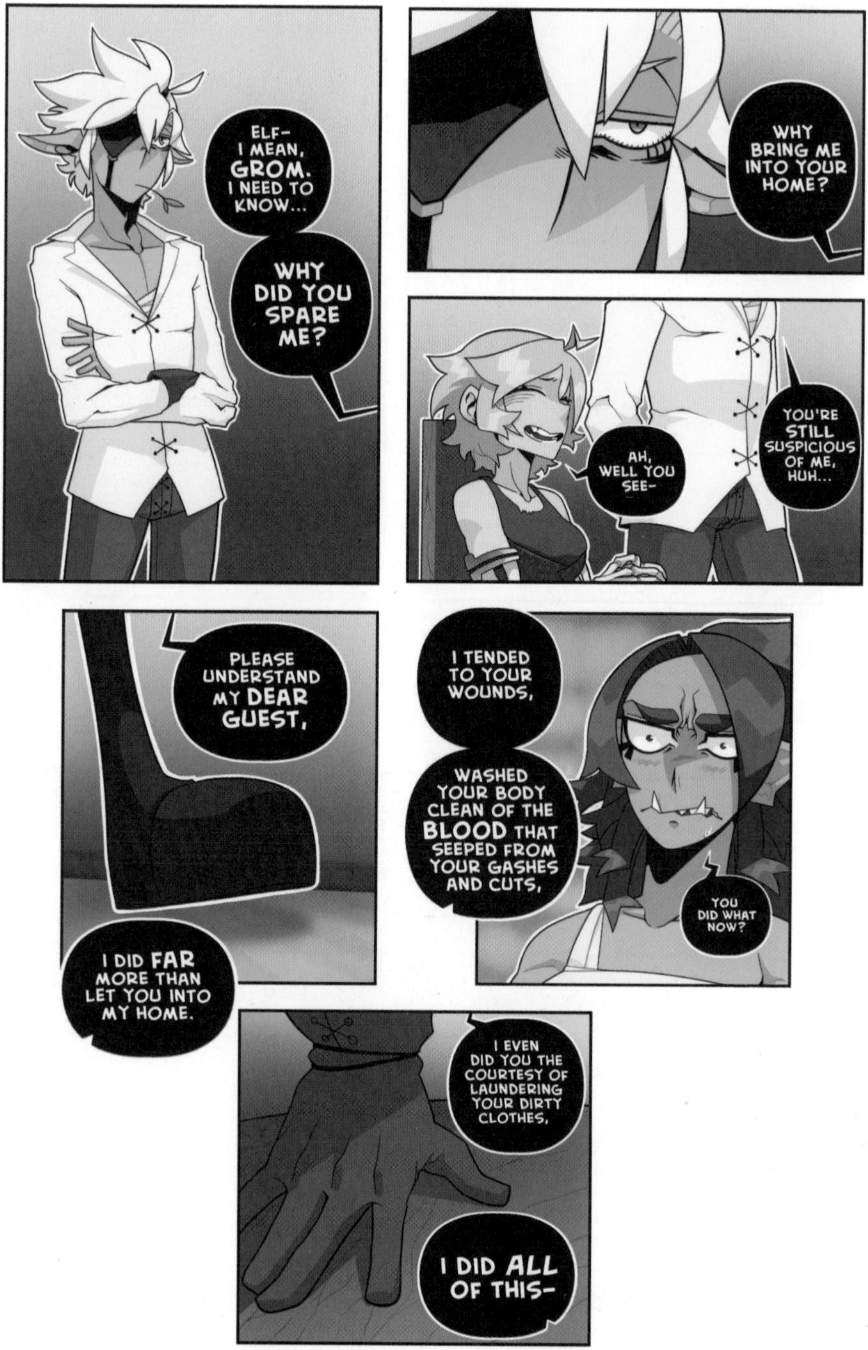
ELF- I MEAN, GROM. I NEED TO KNOW...
WHY DID YOU SPARE ME?
WHY BRING ME INTO YOUR HOME?
YOU'RE STILL SUSPICIOUS OF ME, HUH...
AH, WELL YOU SEE-
PLEASE UNDERSTAND MY DEAR GUEST,
I DID FAR MORE THAN LET YOU INTO MY HOME.
I TENDED TO YOUR WOUNDS,
WASHED YOUR BODY CLEAN OF THE BLOOD THAT SEEPED FROM YOUR GASHES AND CUTS,
YOU DID WHAT NOW?
I EVEN DID YOU THE COURTESY OF LAUNDERING YOUR DIRTY CLOTHES,
I DID ALL OF THIS-

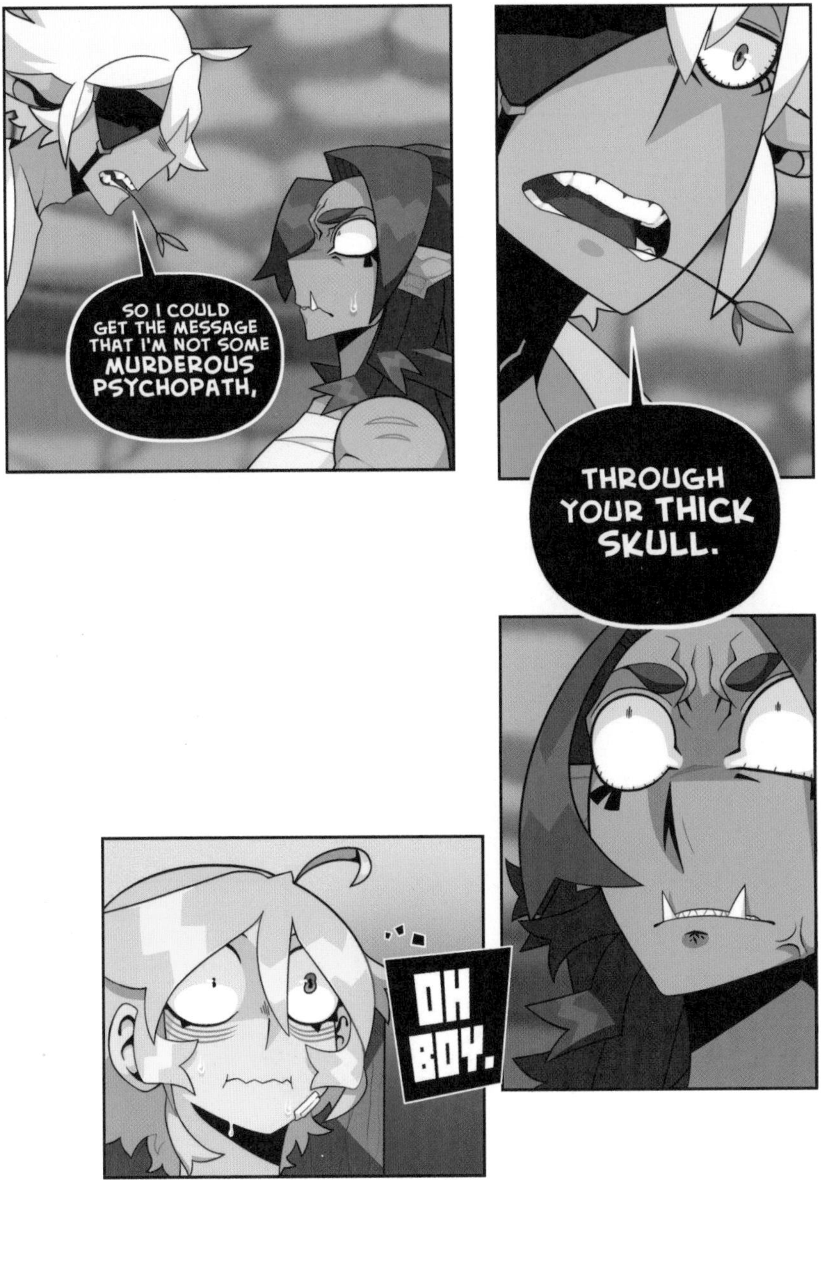
SO I COULD GET THE MESSAGE THAT I'M NOT SOME MURDEROUS PSYCHOPATH,
THROUGH YOUR THICK SKULL.
OH BOY.

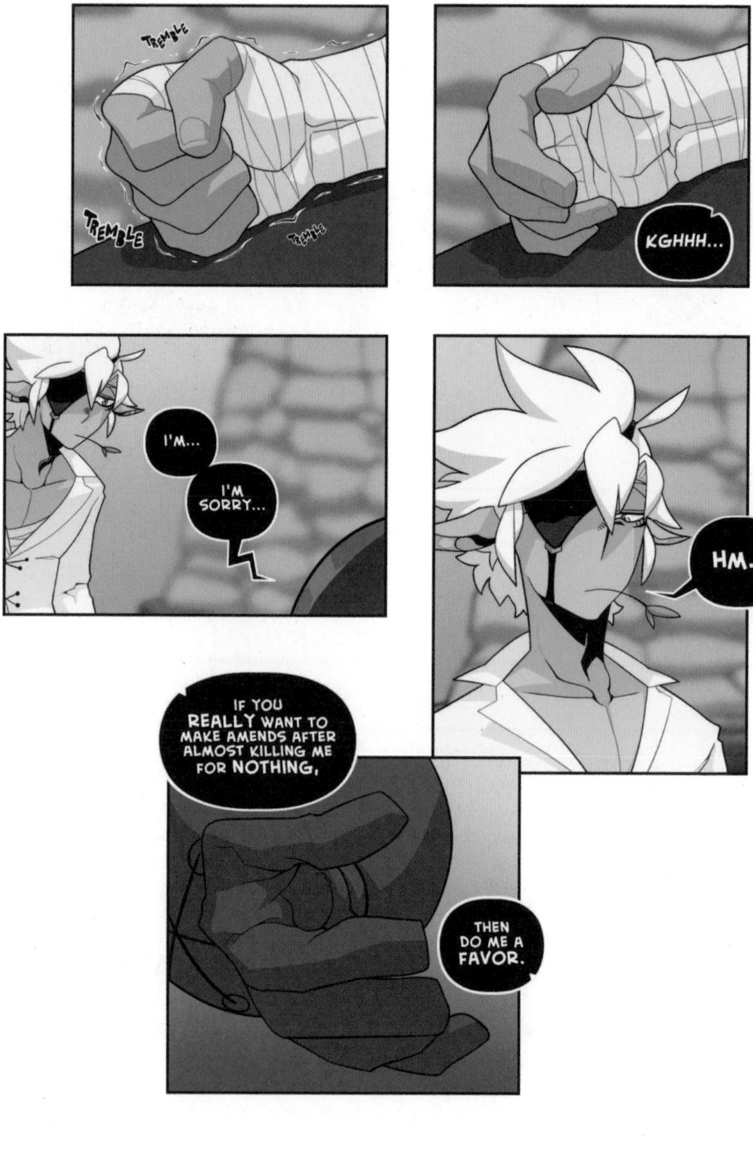
TREMBLE
TREMBLE
TREMBLE
KGHHH...
I'M...
I'M SORRY...
HM...
IF YOU REALLY WANT TO MAKE AMENDS AFTER ALMOST KILLING ME FOR NOTHING,
THEN DO ME A FAVOR.

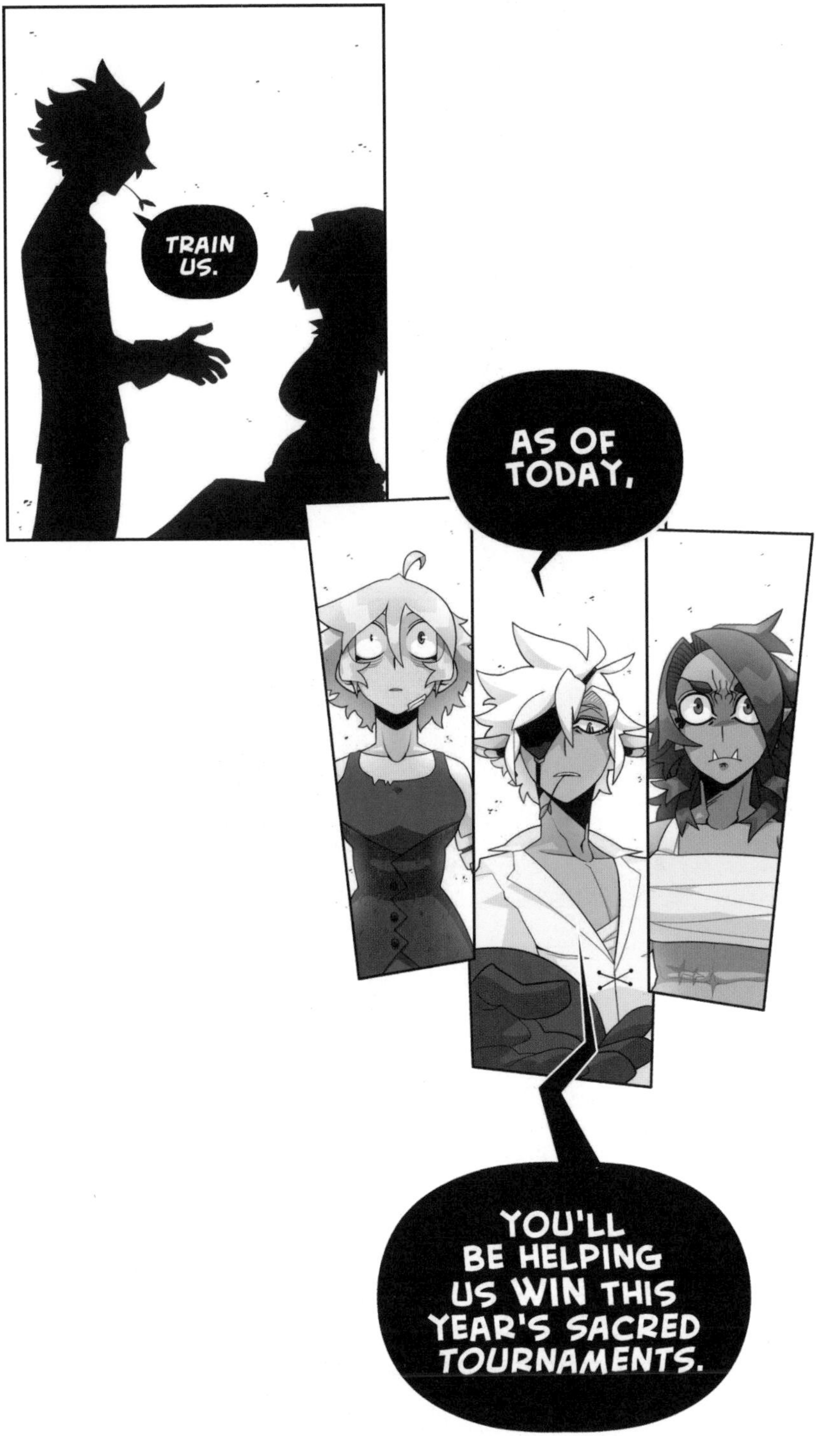
TRAIN US.
AS OF TODAY,
YOU'LL BE HELPING US WIN THIS YEAR'S SACRED TOURNAMENTS.

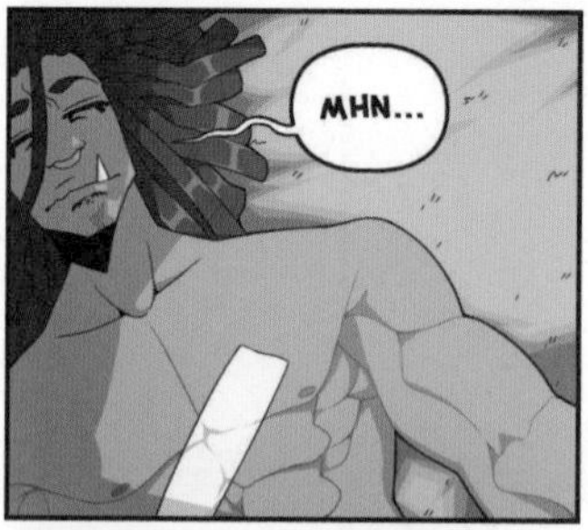
MHN...

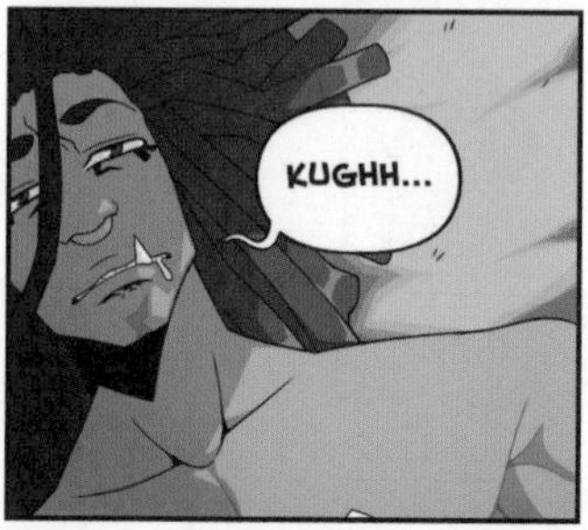
KUGHH...

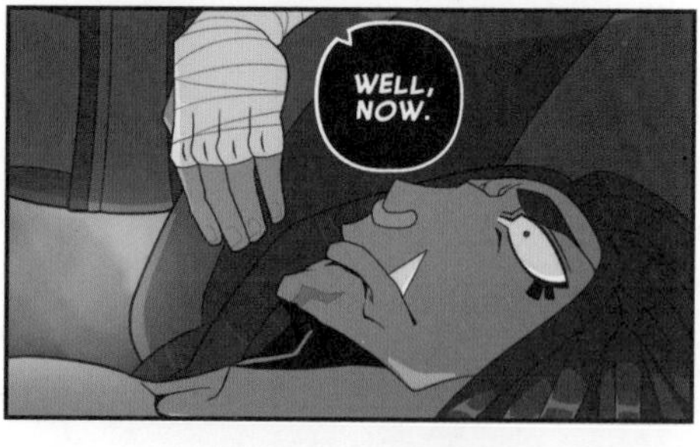
WELL, NOW.

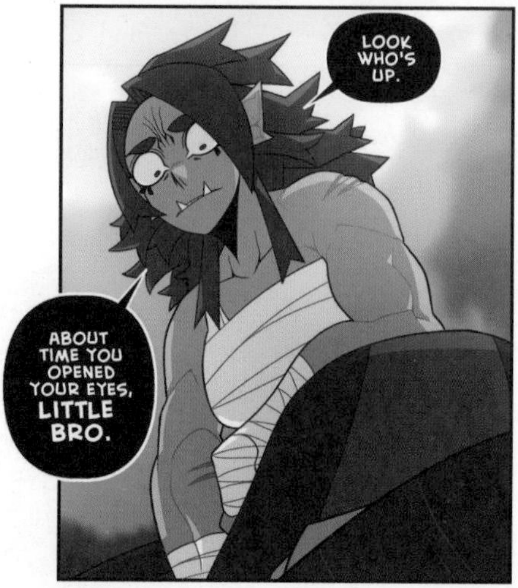
LOOK WHO'S UP.
ABOUT TIME YOU OPENED YOUR EYES, LITTLE BRO.

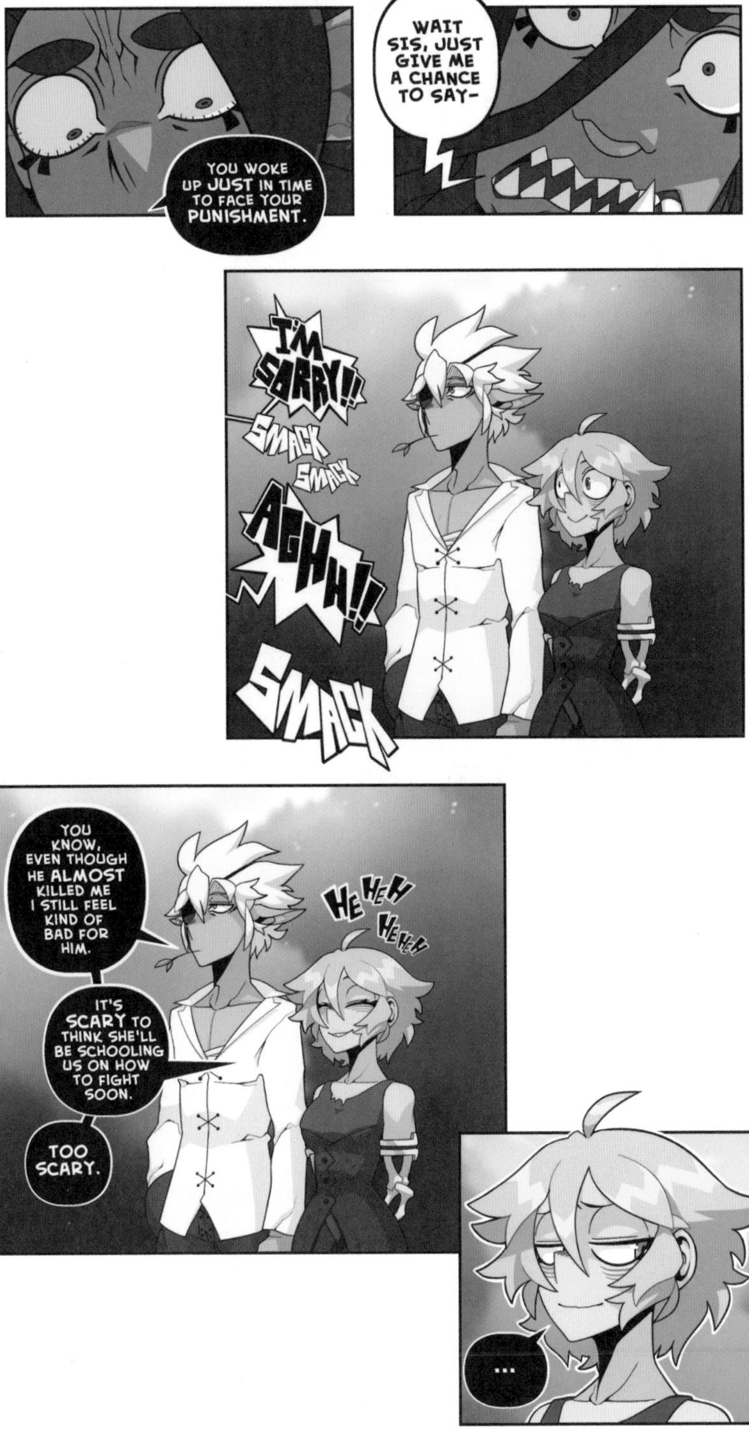
YOU WOKE UP JUST IN TIME TO FACE YOUR PUNISHMENT.
WAIT SIS, JUST GIVE ME A CHANCE TO SAY-
I'M SORRY!!
SMACK
SMACK
AGHH!!
SMACK
YOU KNOW, EVEN THOUGH HE ALMOST KILLED ME I STILL FEEL KIND OF BAD FOR HIM.
HE HEH
HE HEH
IT'S SCARY TO THINK SHE'LL BE SCHOOLING US ON HOW TO FIGHT SOON.
TOO SCARY.
...

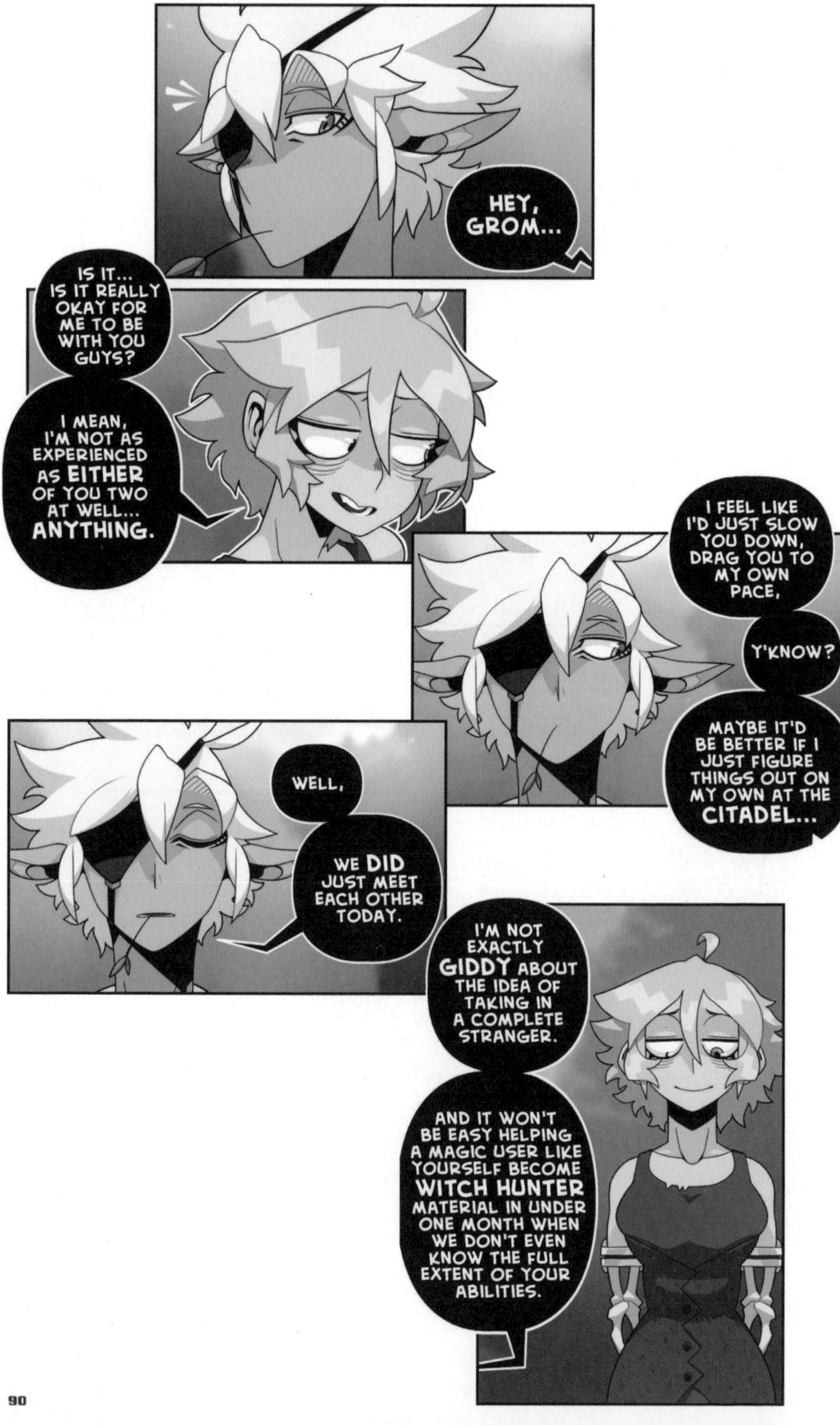

HEY, GROM...
IS IT... IS IT REALLY OKAY FOR ME TO BE WITH YOU GUYS?
I MEAN, I'M NOT AS EXPERIENCED AS EITHER OF YOU TWO AT WELL... ANYTHING.
I FEEL LIKE I'D JUST SLOW YOU DOWN, DRAG YOU TO MY OWN PACE,
Y'KNOW?
MAYBE IT'D BE BETTER IF I JUST FIGURE THINGS OUT ON MY OWN AT THE CITADEL...
WELL,
WE DID JUST MEET EACH OTHER TODAY.
I'M NOT EXACTLY GIDDY ABOUT THE IDEA OF TAKING IN A COMPLETE STRANGER.
AND IT WON'T BE EASY HELPING A MAGIC USER LIKE YOURSELF BECOME WITCH HUNTER MATERIAL IN UNDER ONE MONTH WHEN WE DON'T EVEN KNOW THE FULL EXTENT OF YOUR ABILITIES.

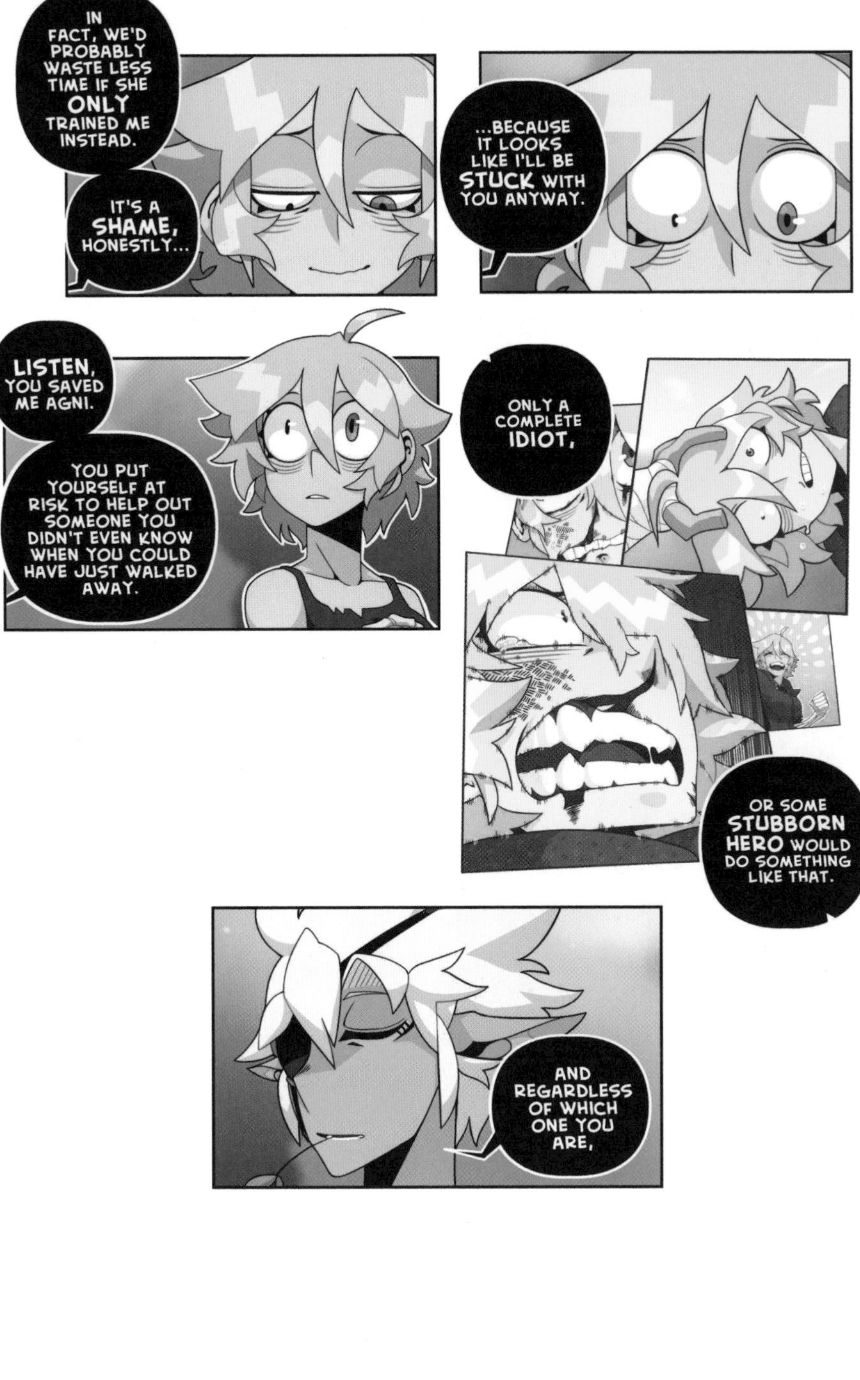
IN FACT, WE'D PROBABLY WASTE LESS TIME IF SHE ONLY TRAINED ME INSTEAD.
IT'S A SHAME, HONESTLY...
...BECAUSE IT LOOKS LIKE I'LL BE STUCK WITH YOU ANYWAY.
LISTEN, YOU SAVED ME AGNI.
YOU PUT YOURSELF AT RISK TO HELP OUT SOMEONE YOU DIDN'T EVEN KNOW WHEN YOU COULD HAVE JUST WALKED AWAY.
ONLY A COMPLETE IDIOT,
OR SOME STUBBORN HERO WOULD DO SOMETHING LIKE THAT.
AND REGARDLESS OF WHICH ONE YOU ARE,

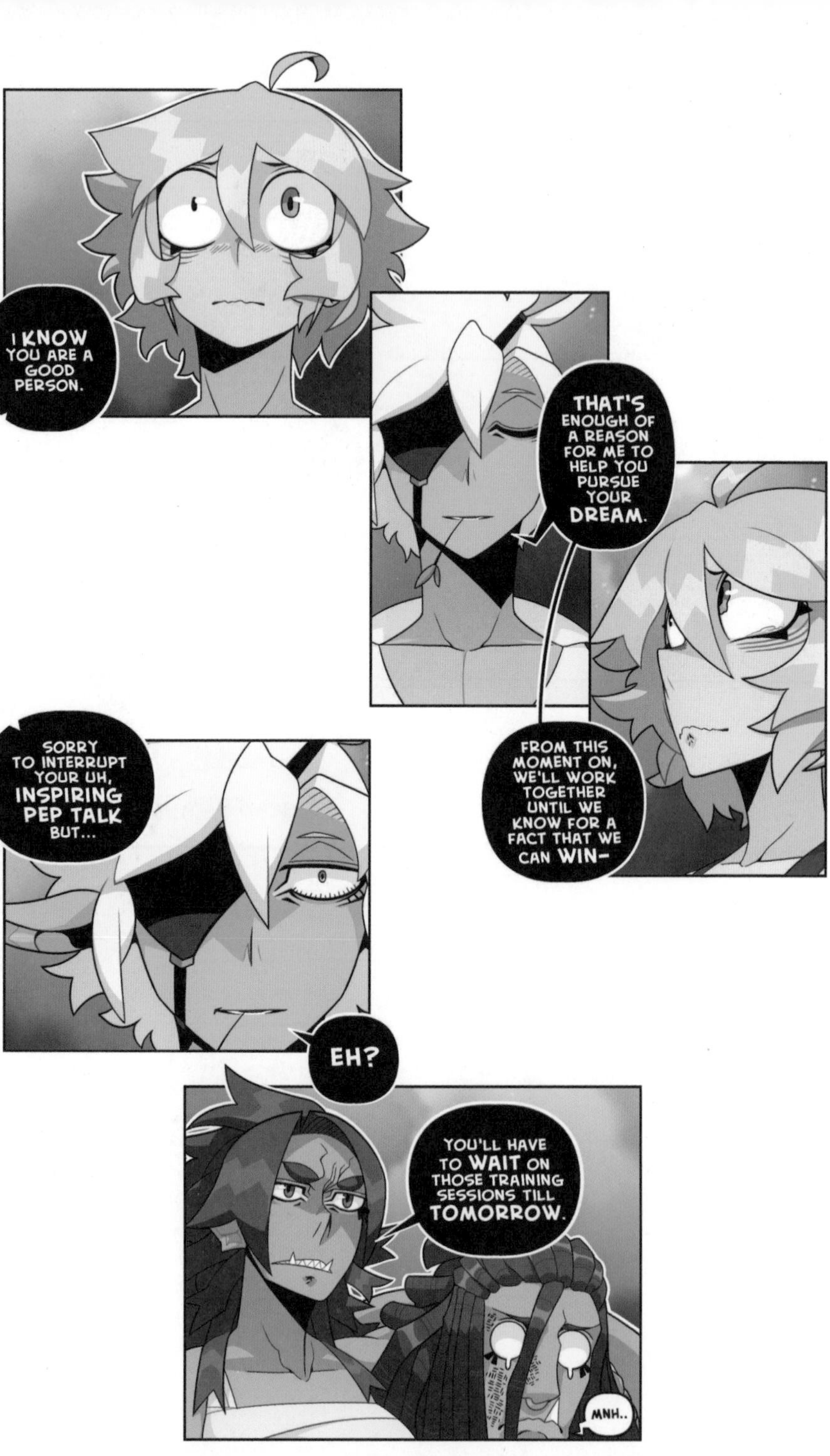
I KNOW YOU ARE A GOOD PERSON.
THAT'S ENOUGH OF A REASON FOR ME TO HELP YOU PURSUE YOUR DREAM.
FROM THIS MOMENT ON, WE'LL WORK TOGETHER UNTIL WE KNOW FOR A FACT THAT WE CAN WIN-
SORRY TO INTERRUPT YOUR UH, INSPIRING PEP TALK BUT...
EH?
YOU'LL HAVE TO WAIT ON THOSE TRAINING SESSIONS TILL TOMORROW.
MNH..

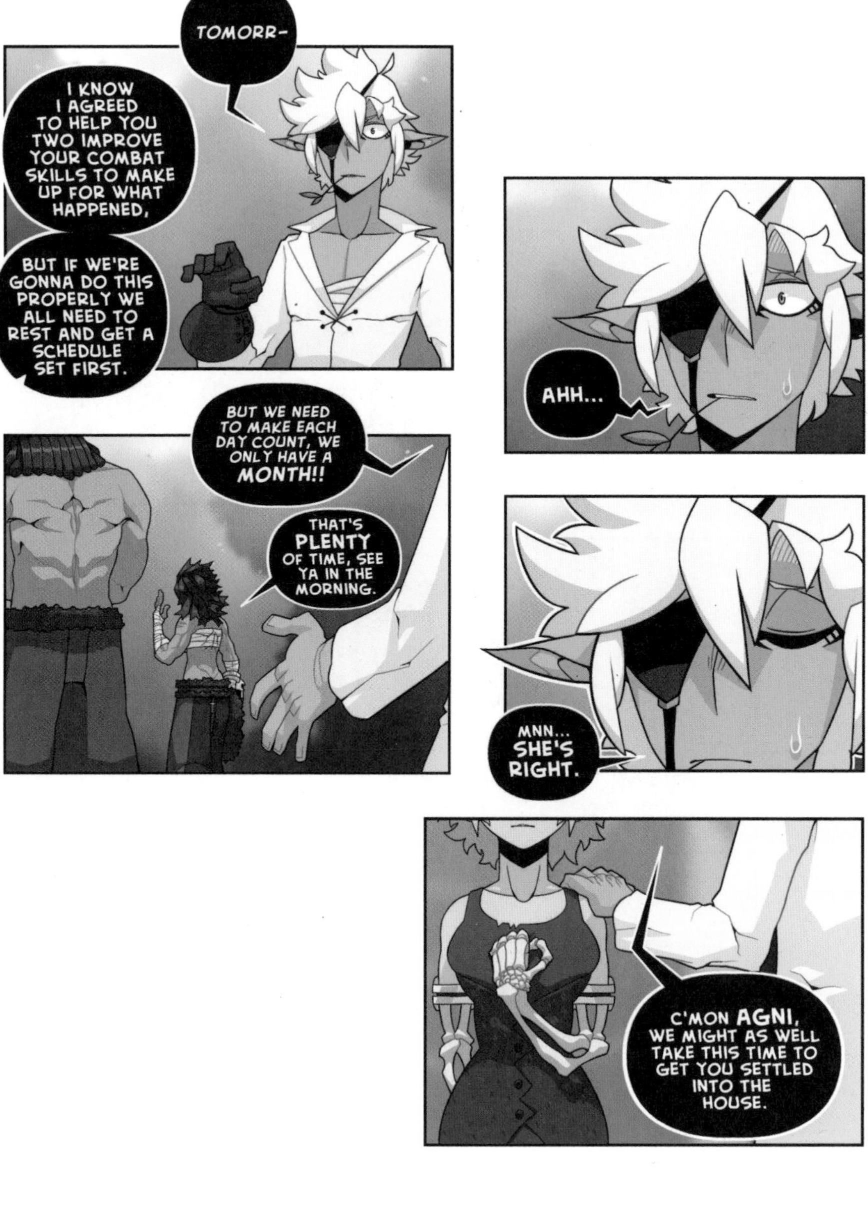
TOMORR-
I KNOW I AGREED TO HELP YOU TWO IMPROVE YOUR COMBAT SKILLS TO MAKE UP FOR WHAT HAPPENED,
BUT IF WE'RE GONNA DO THIS PROPERLY WE ALL NEED TO REST AND GET A SCHEDULE SET FIRST.
AHH...
BUT WE NEED TO MAKE EACH DAY COUNT, WE ONLY HAVE A MONTH!!
THAT'S PLENTY OF TIME, SEE YA IN THE MORNING.
MNN... SHE'S RIGHT.
C'MON AGNI, WE MIGHT AS WELL TAKE THIS TIME TO GET YOU SETTLED INTO THE HOUSE.

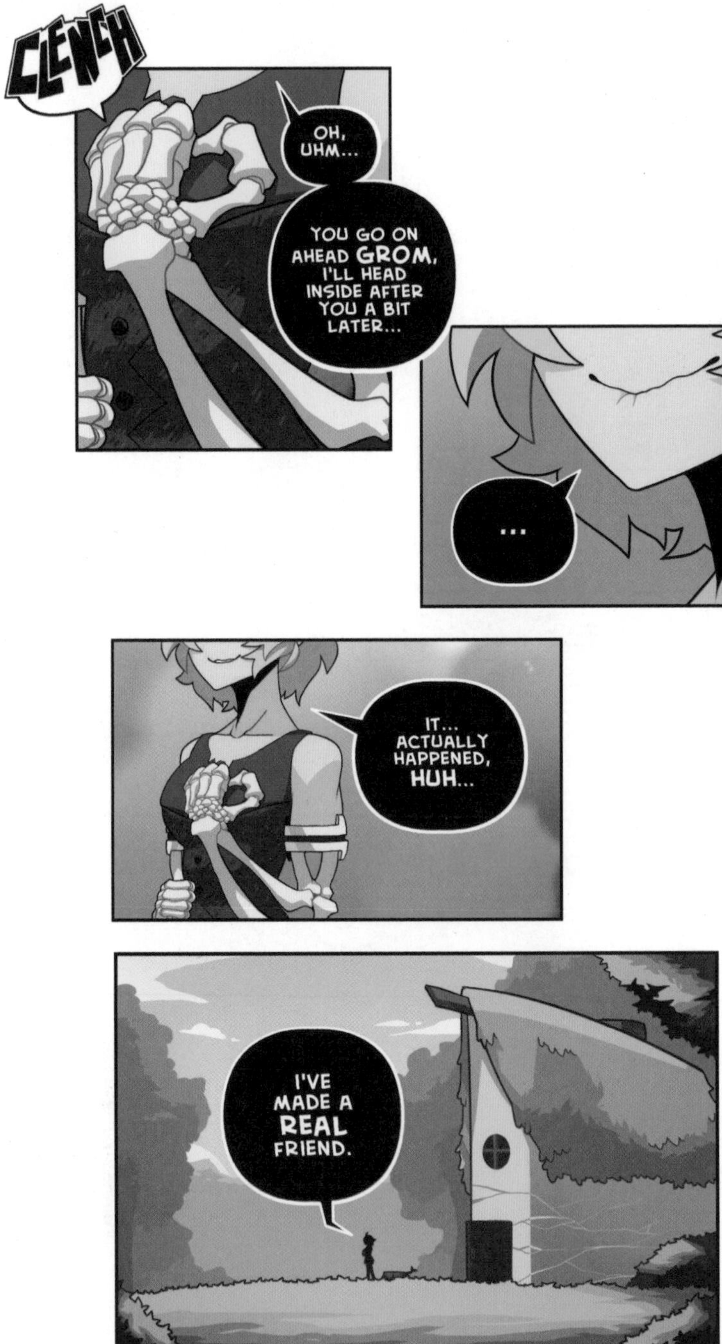
CLENCH
OH, UHM...
YOU GO ON AHEAD GROM, I'LL HEAD INSIDE AFTER YOU A BIT LATER...
...
IT... ACTUALLY HAPPENED, HUH...
I'VE MADE A REAL FRIEND.

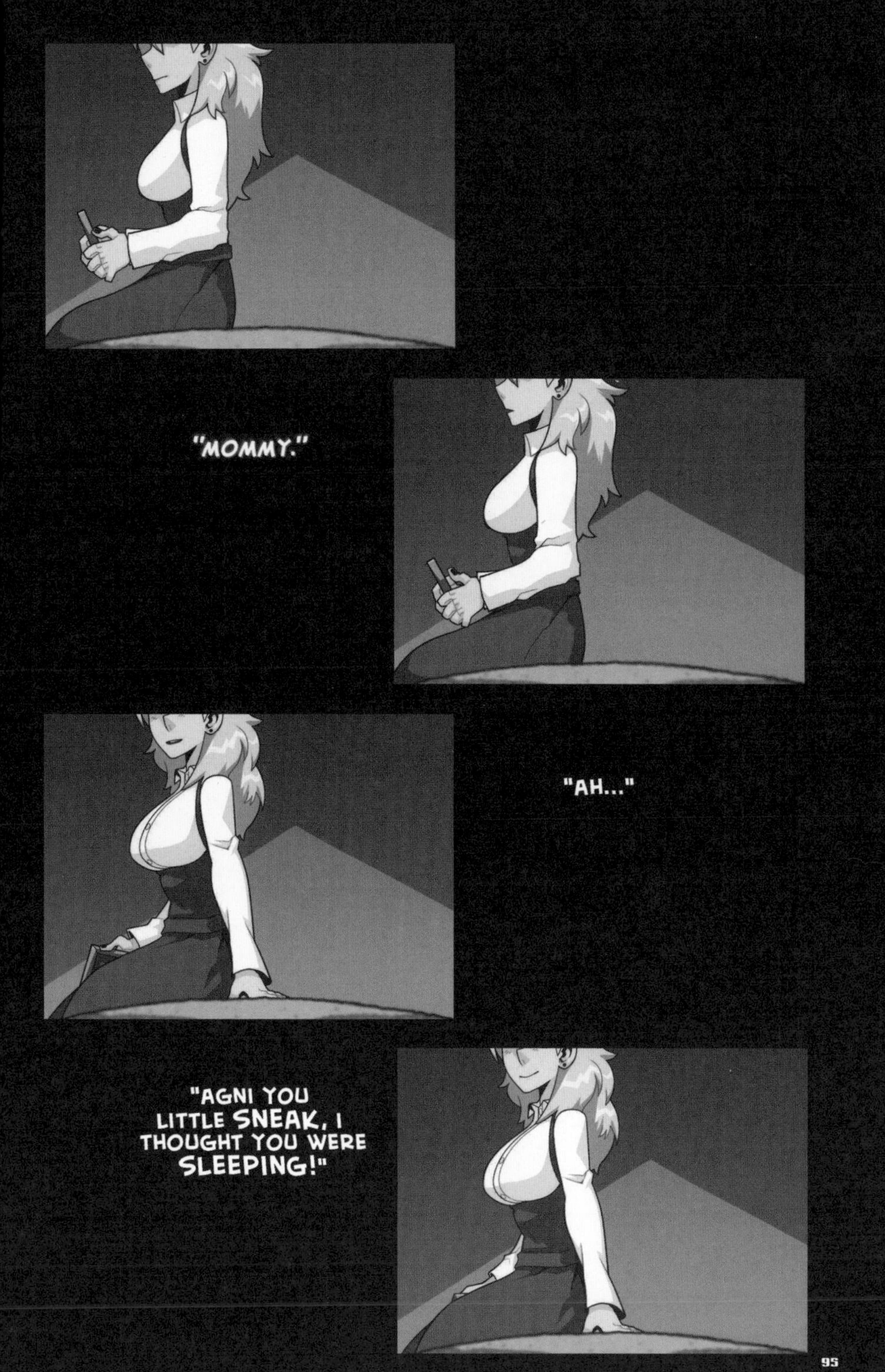
"MOMMY."
"AH..."
"AGNI YOU LITTLE SNEAK, I THOUGHT YOU WERE SLEEPING!"

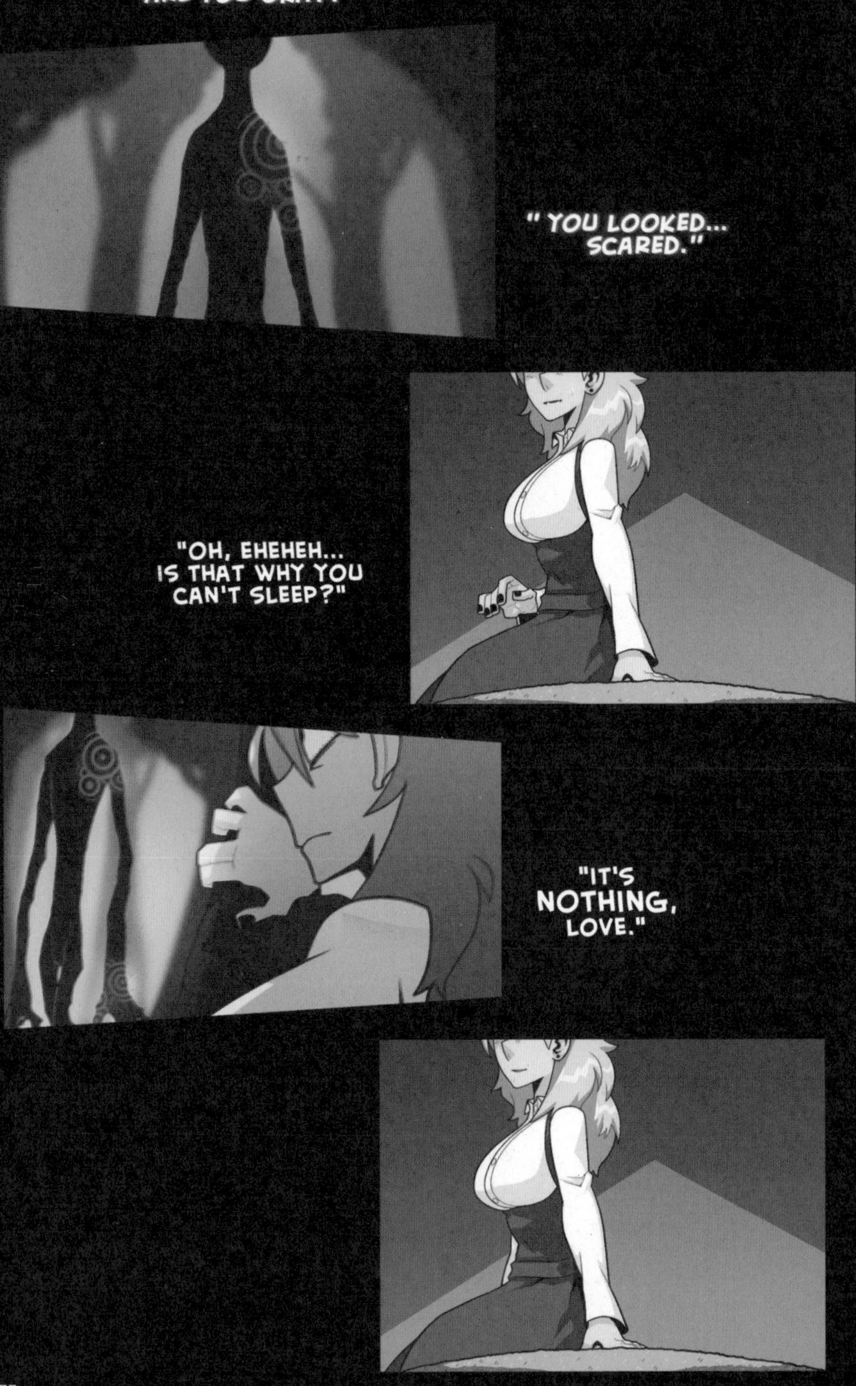
"YOU LOOKED... SCARED."
"OH, EHEHEH... IS THAT WHY YOU CAN'T SLEEP?"
"IT'S NOTHING, LOVE."

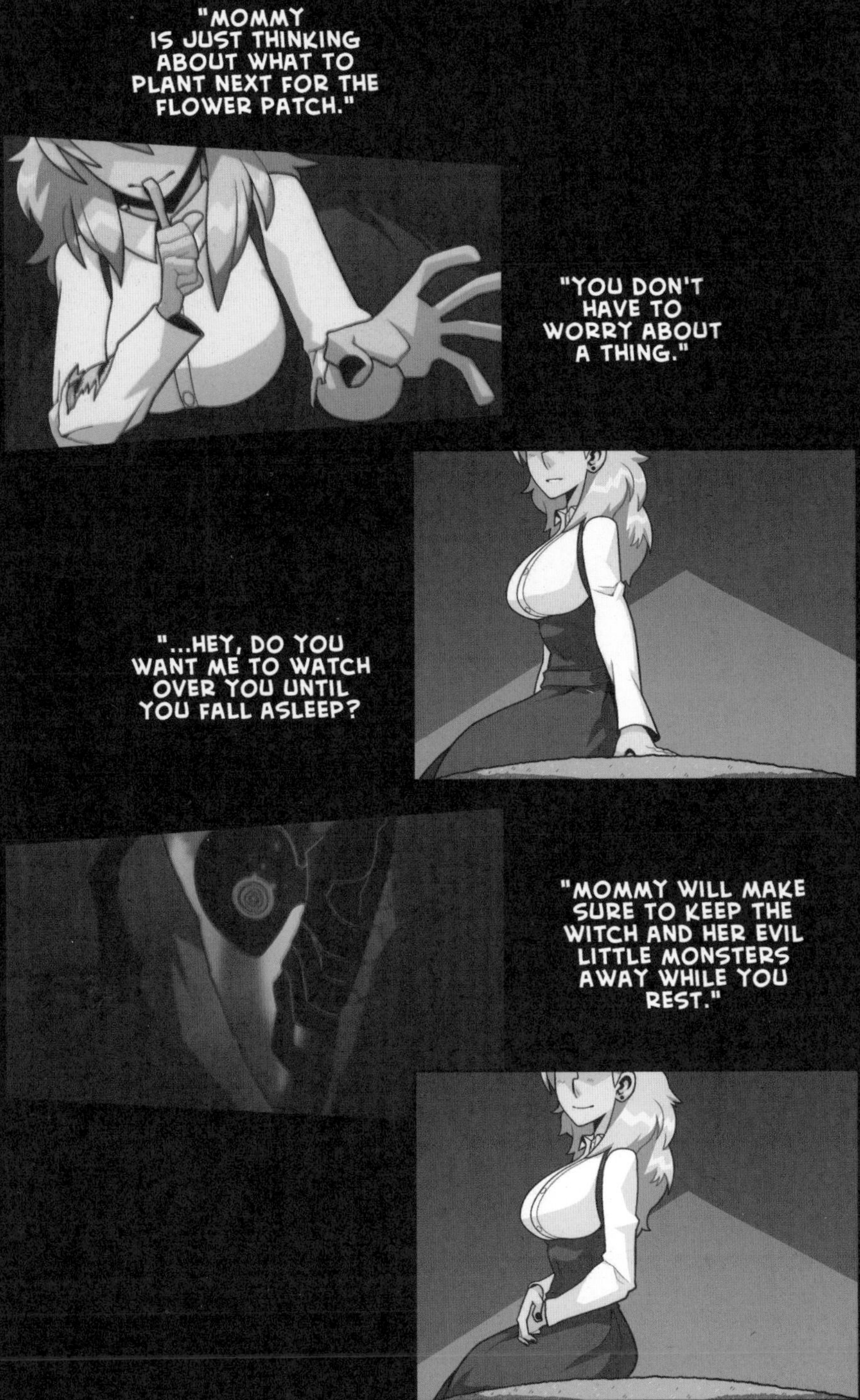
"MOMMY IS JUST THINKING ABOUT WHAT TO PLANT NEXT FOR THE FLOWER PATCH."
"YOU DON'T HAVE TO WORRY ABOUT A THING."
"...HEY, DO YOU WANT ME TO WATCH OVER YOU UNTIL YOU FALL ASLEEP?
"MOMMY WILL MAKE SURE TO KEEP THE WITCH AND HER EVIL LITTLE MONSTERS AWAY WHILE YOU REST."

"...DO YOU PROMISE?"

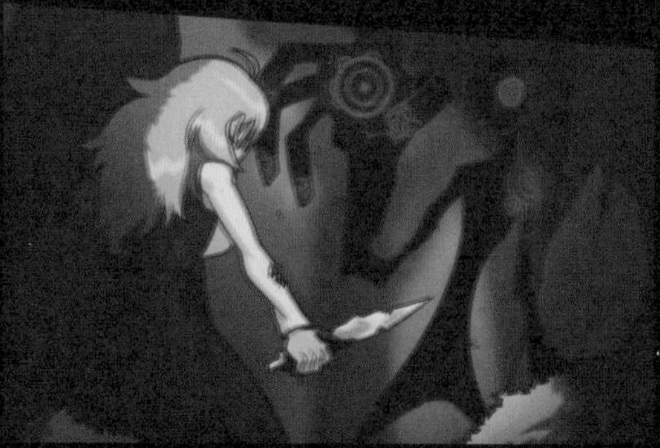

"OF COURSE LOVE,"

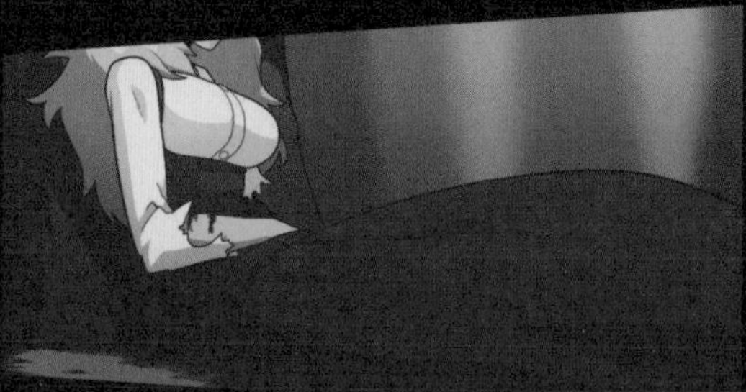

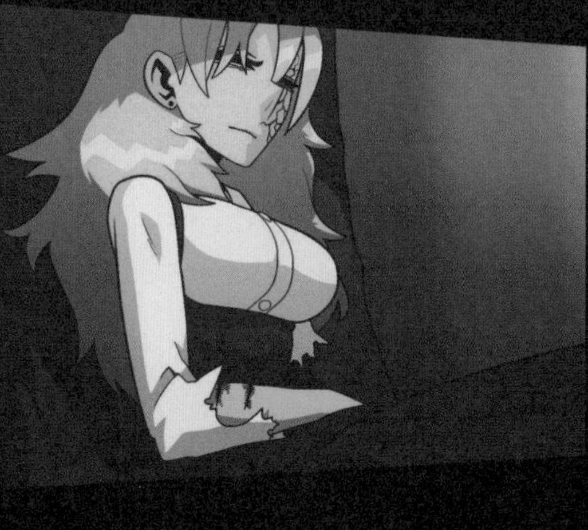

"I PROMISE."

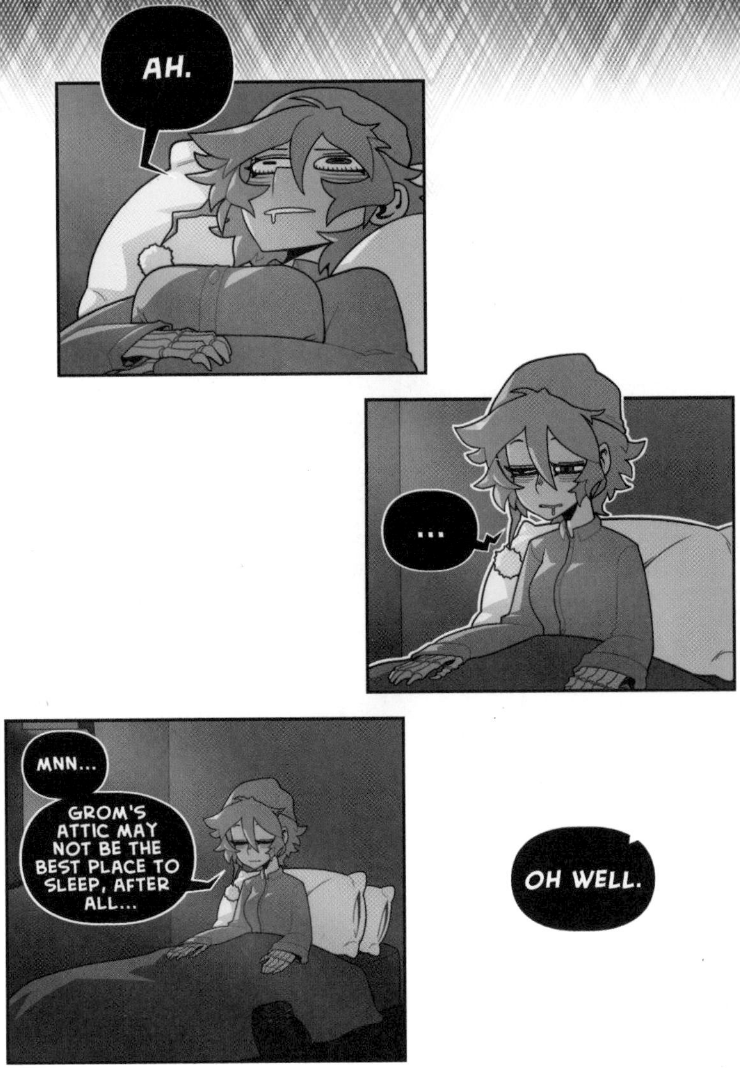
AH.
...
MNN...
GROM'S ATTIC MAY NOT BE THE BEST PLACE TO SLEEP, AFTER ALL...
OH WELL.

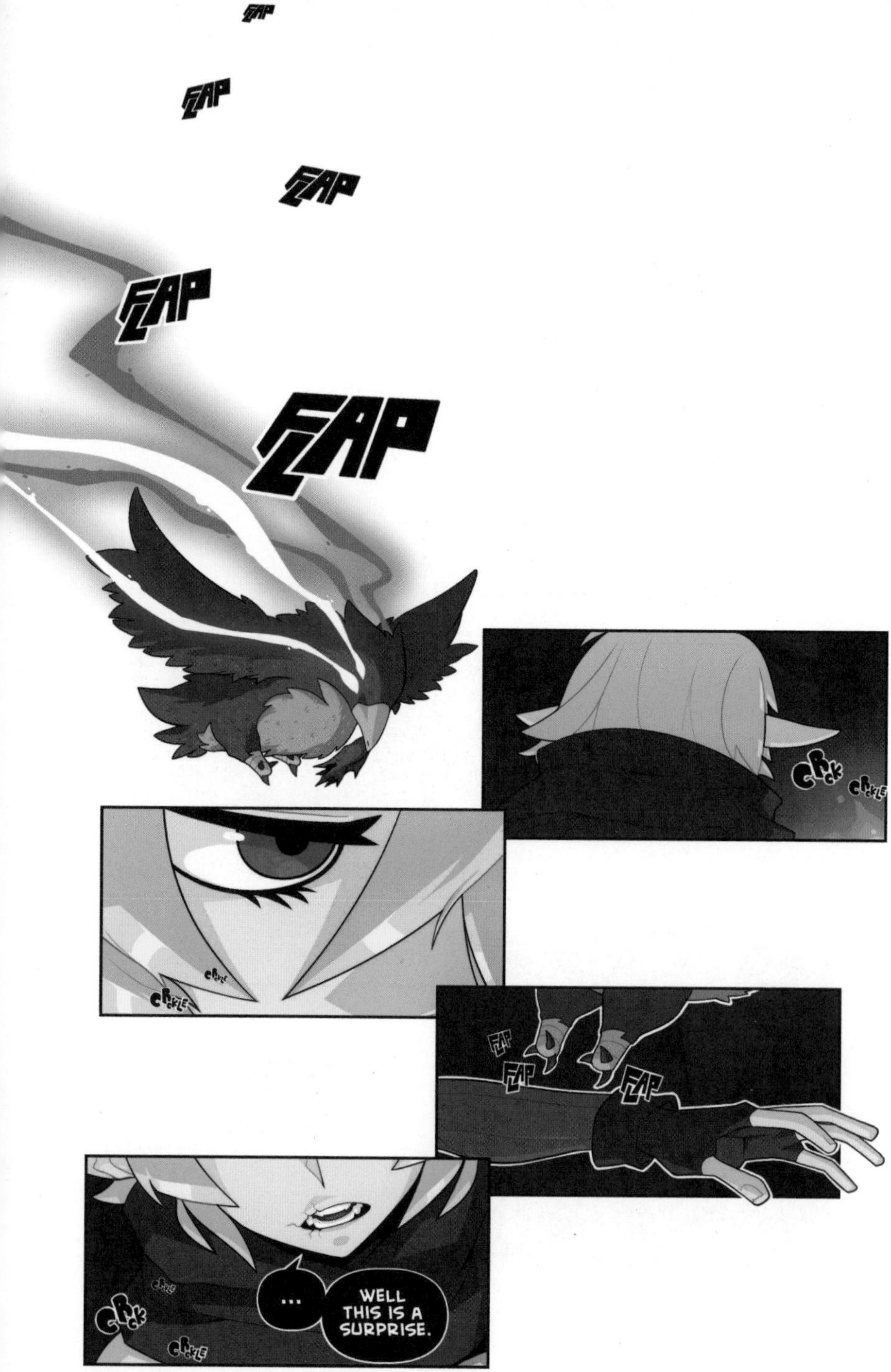
FLAP
FLAP
FLAP
FLAP
FLAP
CRACK
CRACKLE
FLAP
FLAP
FLAP
...
WELL THIS IS A SURPRISE.

A MARK, HUH...
YOUR MASTER MUST WANT THIS PERSON DEAD REAL BAD.
I HOPE HE'S FOUND SOME WORTHY PREY.
CRACKLE
CRACKLE
CRACK

# FLORA
# LEVEL 99

## Chapter 7
# THE HUNTER

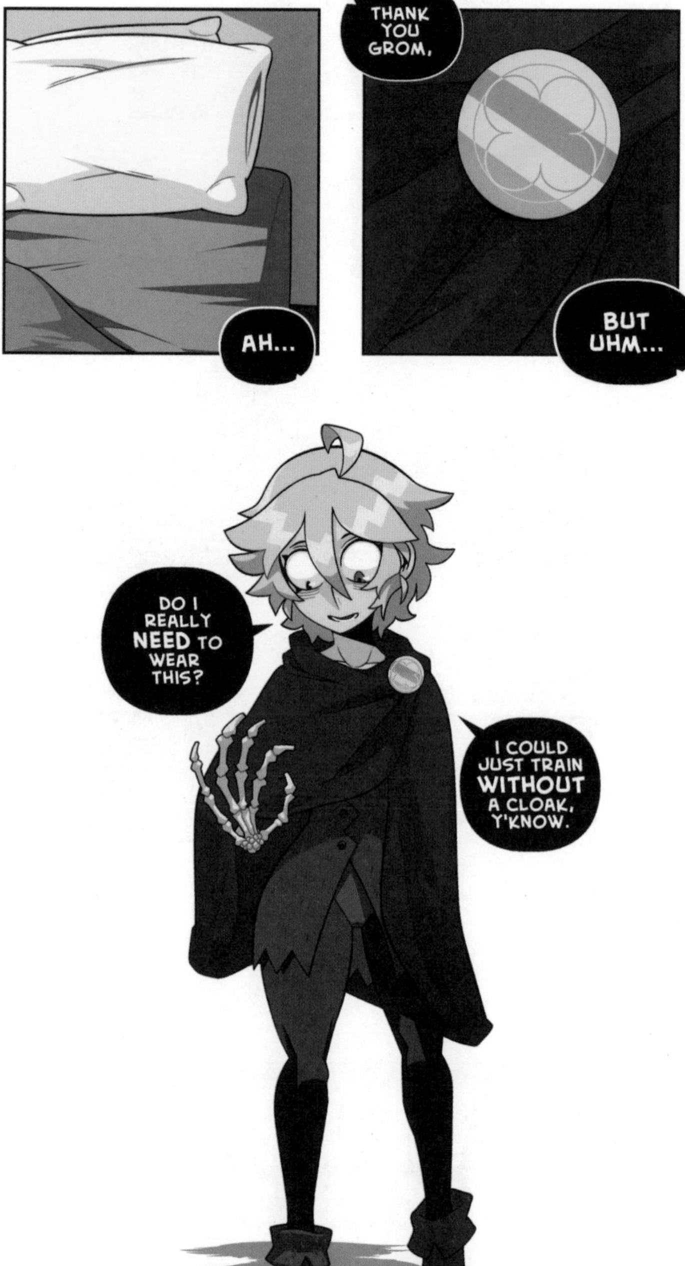

AH...
THANK YOU GROM,
BUT UHM...
DO I REALLY NEED TO WEAR THIS?
I COULD JUST TRAIN WITHOUT A CLOAK, Y'KNOW.

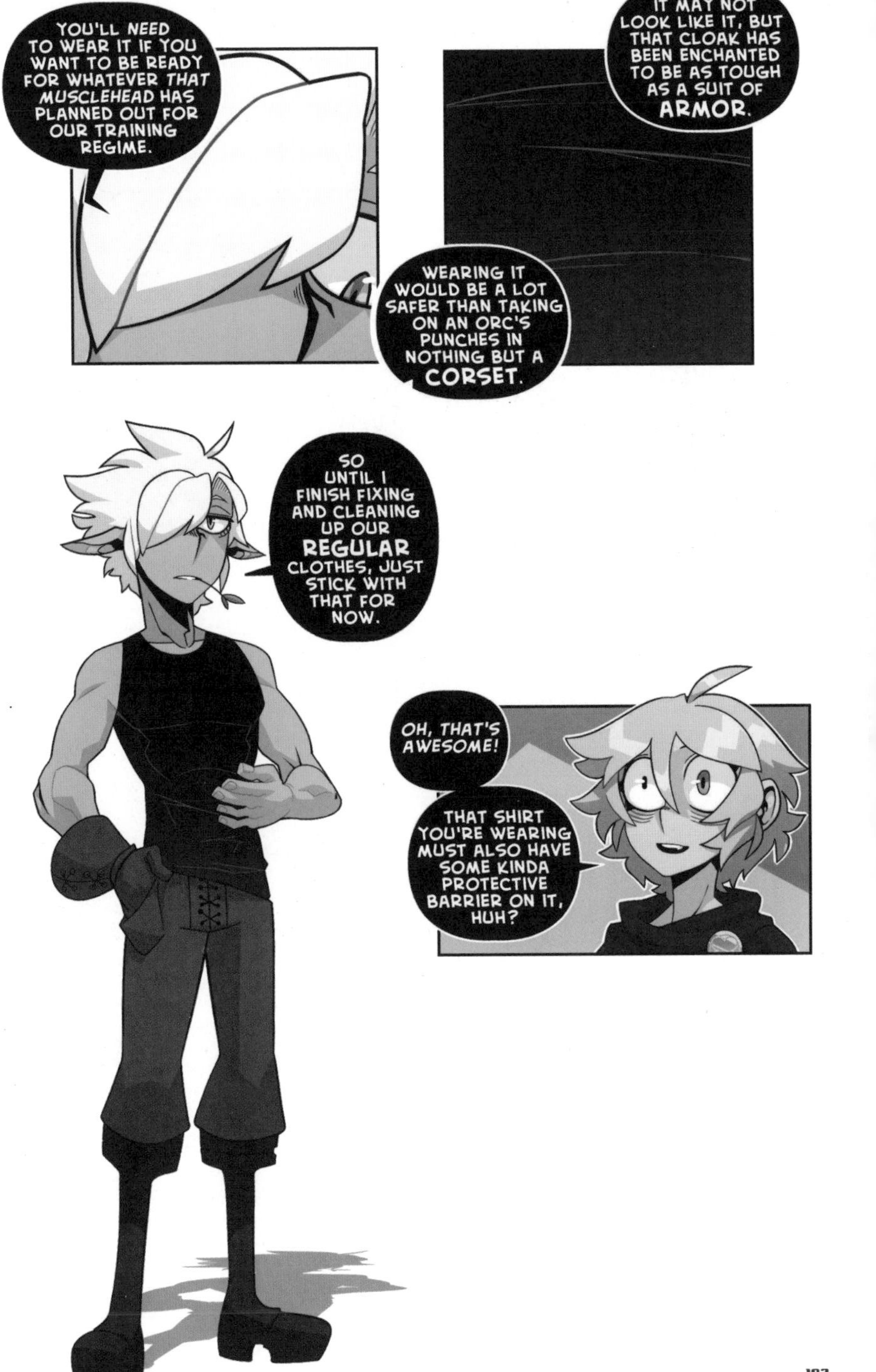
YOU'LL NEED TO WEAR IT IF YOU WANT TO BE READY FOR WHATEVER THAT MUSCLEHEAD HAS PLANNED OUT FOR OUR TRAINING REGIME.
IT MAY NOT LOOK LIKE IT, BUT THAT CLOAK HAS BEEN ENCHANTED TO BE AS TOUGH AS A SUIT OF ARMOR.
WEARING IT WOULD BE A LOT SAFER THAN TAKING ON AN ORC'S PUNCHES IN NOTHING BUT A CORSET.
SO UNTIL I FINISH FIXING AND CLEANING UP OUR REGULAR CLOTHES, JUST STICK WITH THAT FOR NOW.
OH, THAT'S AWESOME!
THAT SHIRT YOU'RE WEARING MUST ALSO HAVE SOME KINDA PROTECTIVE BARRIER ON IT, HUH?

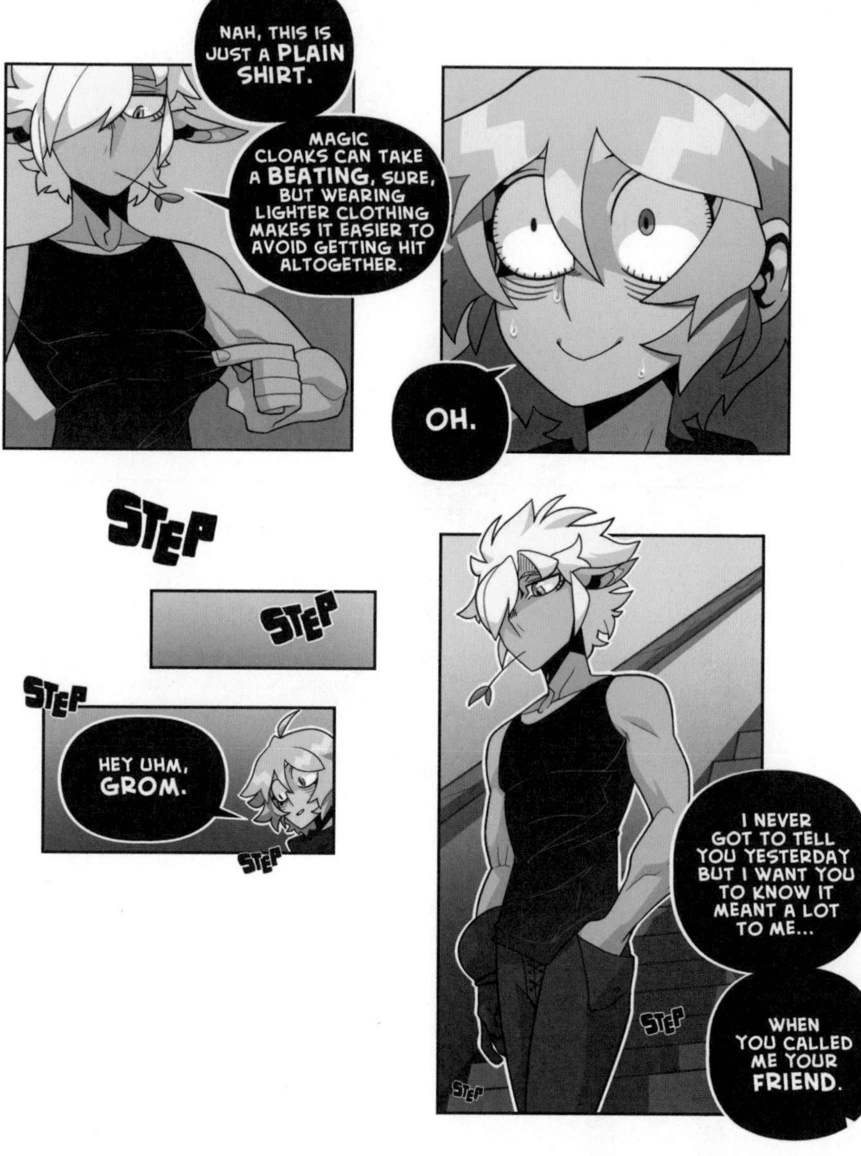
NAH, THIS IS JUST A PLAIN SHIRT.
MAGIC CLOAKS CAN TAKE A BEATING, SURE, BUT WEARING LIGHTER CLOTHING MAKES IT EASIER TO AVOID GETTING HIT ALTOGETHER.
OH.
STEP
STEP
STEP
HEY UHM, GROM.
STEP
I NEVER GOT TO TELL YOU YESTERDAY BUT I WANT YOU TO KNOW IT MEANT A LOT TO ME...
STEP
STEP
WHEN YOU CALLED ME YOUR FRIEND.

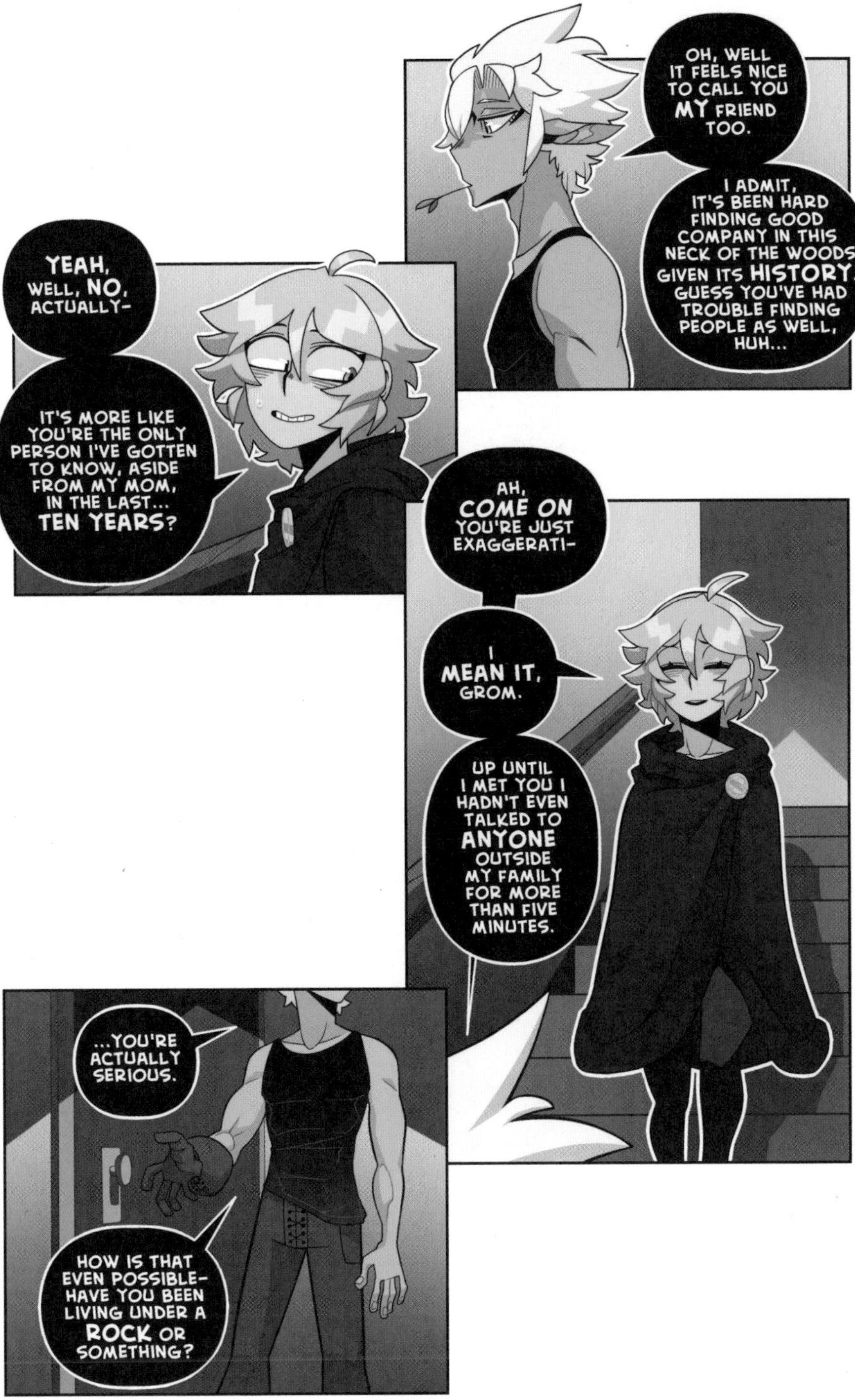
OH, WELL IT FEELS NICE TO CALL YOU MY FRIEND TOO.
I ADMIT, IT'S BEEN HARD FINDING GOOD COMPANY IN THIS NECK OF THE WOODS GIVEN ITS HISTORY. GUESS YOU'VE HAD TROUBLE FINDING PEOPLE AS WELL, HUH...
YEAH, WELL, NO, ACTUALLY-
IT'S MORE LIKE YOU'RE THE ONLY PERSON I'VE GOTTEN TO KNOW, ASIDE FROM MY MOM, IN THE LAST... TEN YEARS?
AH, COME ON YOU'RE JUST EXAGGERATI-
I MEAN IT, GROM.
UP UNTIL I MET YOU I HADN'T EVEN TALKED TO ANYONE OUTSIDE MY FAMILY FOR MORE THAN FIVE MINUTES.
...YOU'RE ACTUALLY SERIOUS.
HOW IS THAT EVEN POSSIBLE- HAVE YOU BEEN LIVING UNDER A ROCK OR SOMETHING?

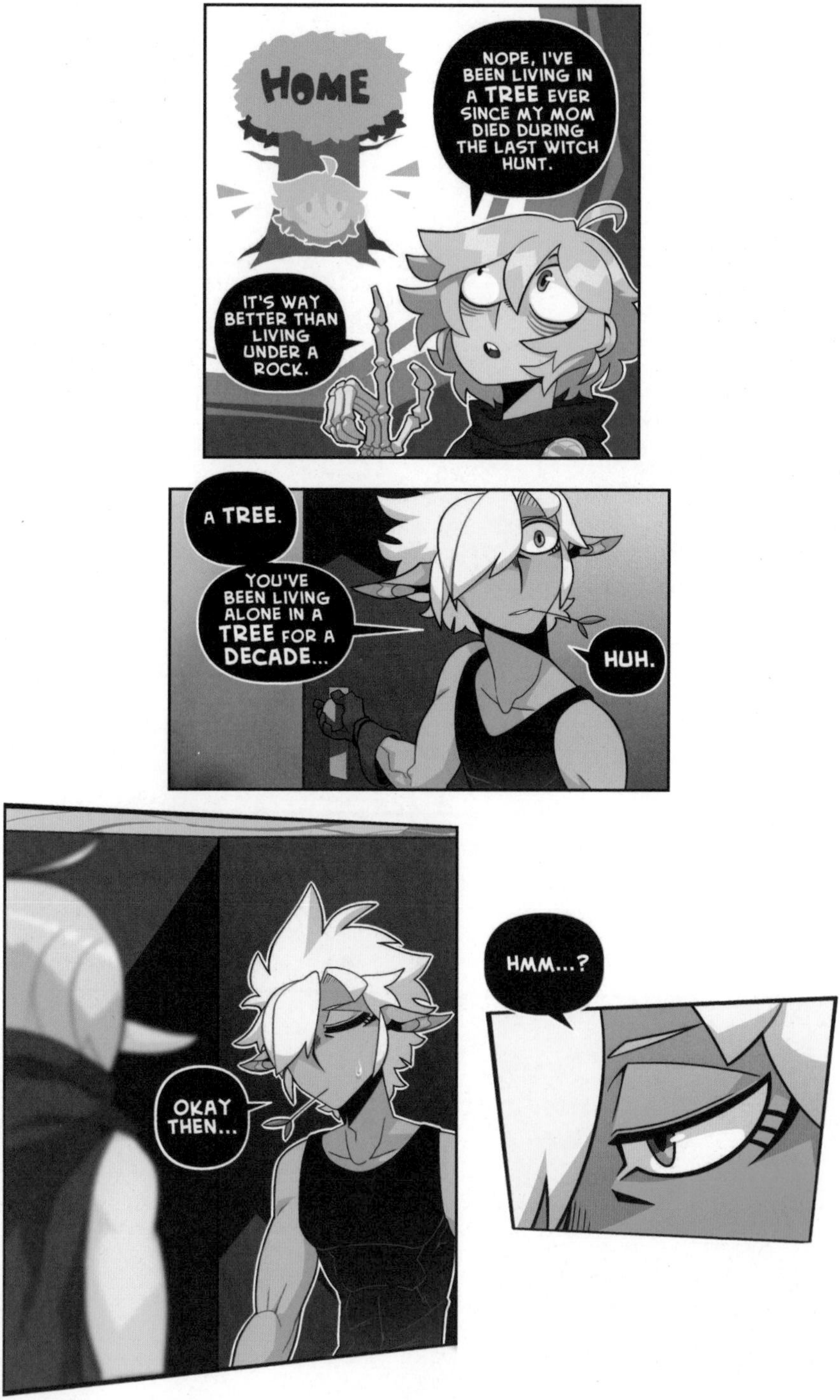
HOME
NOPE, I'VE BEEN LIVING IN A TREE EVER SINCE MY MOM DIED DURING THE LAST WITCH HUNT.
IT'S WAY BETTER THAN LIVING UNDER A ROCK.
A TREE.
YOU'VE BEEN LIVING ALONE IN A TREE FOR A DECADE...
HUH.
OKAY THEN...
HMM...?

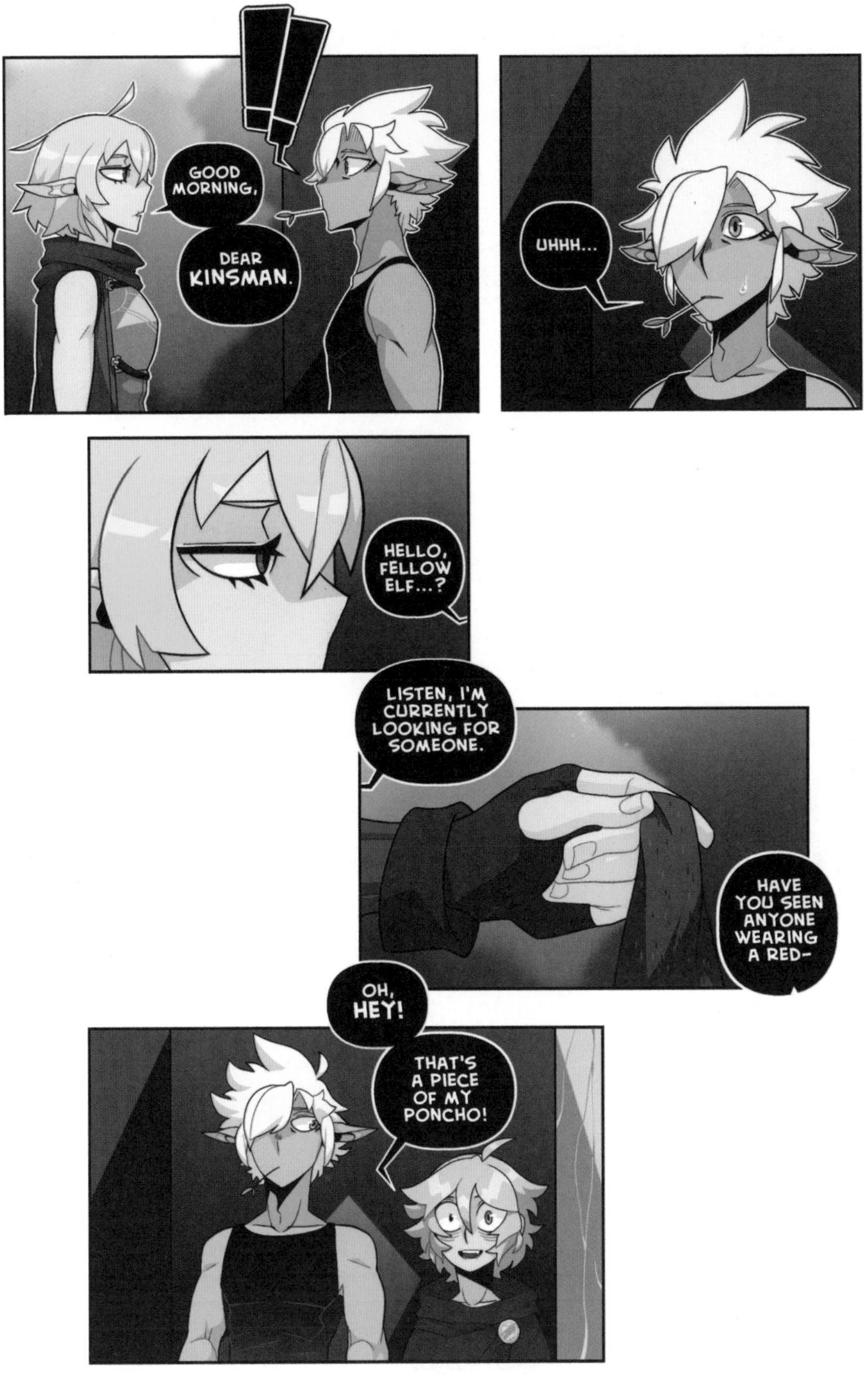
GOOD MORNING,
DEAR KINSMAN.
UHHH...
HELLO, FELLOW ELF...?
LISTEN, I'M CURRENTLY LOOKING FOR SOMEONE.
HAVE YOU SEEN ANYONE WEARING A RED-
OH, HEY!
THAT'S A PIECE OF MY PONCHO!

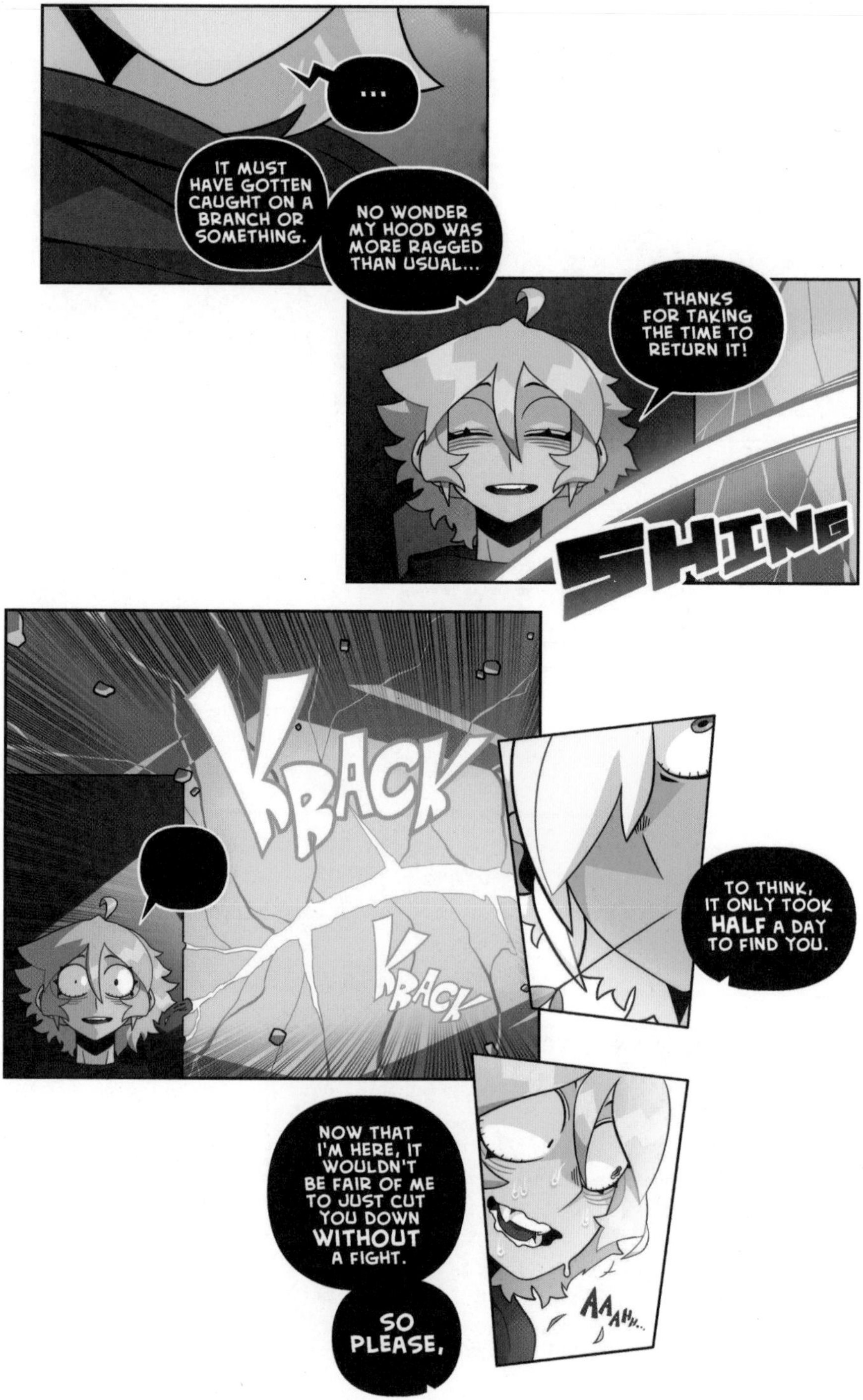

...
IT MUST HAVE GOTTEN CAUGHT ON A BRANCH OR SOMETHING.
NO WONDER MY HOOD WAS MORE RAGGED THAN USUAL...
THANKS FOR TAKING THE TIME TO RETURN IT!
SHING
KRACK
KRACK
TO THINK, IT ONLY TOOK HALF A DAY TO FIND YOU.
NOW THAT I'M HERE, IT WOULDN'T BE FAIR OF ME TO JUST CUT YOU DOWN WITHOUT A FIGHT.
SO PLEASE,
AAAHH...

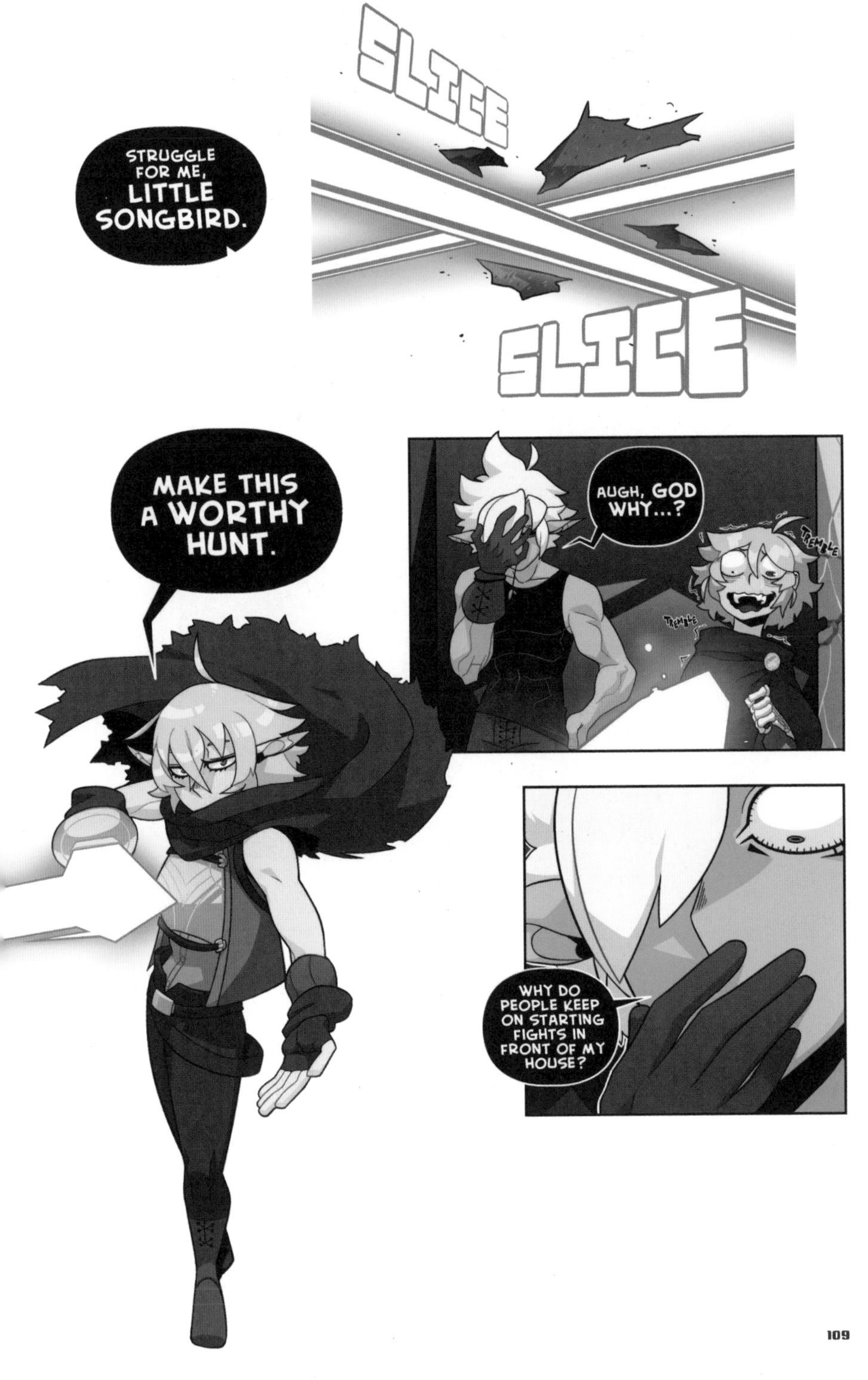
STRUGGLE FOR ME, LITTLE SONGBIRD.
SLICE
SLICE
MAKE THIS A WORTHY HUNT.
AUGH, GOD WHY...?
TREMBLE
TREMBLE
WHY DO PEOPLE KEEP ON STARTING FIGHTS IN FRONT OF MY HOUSE?

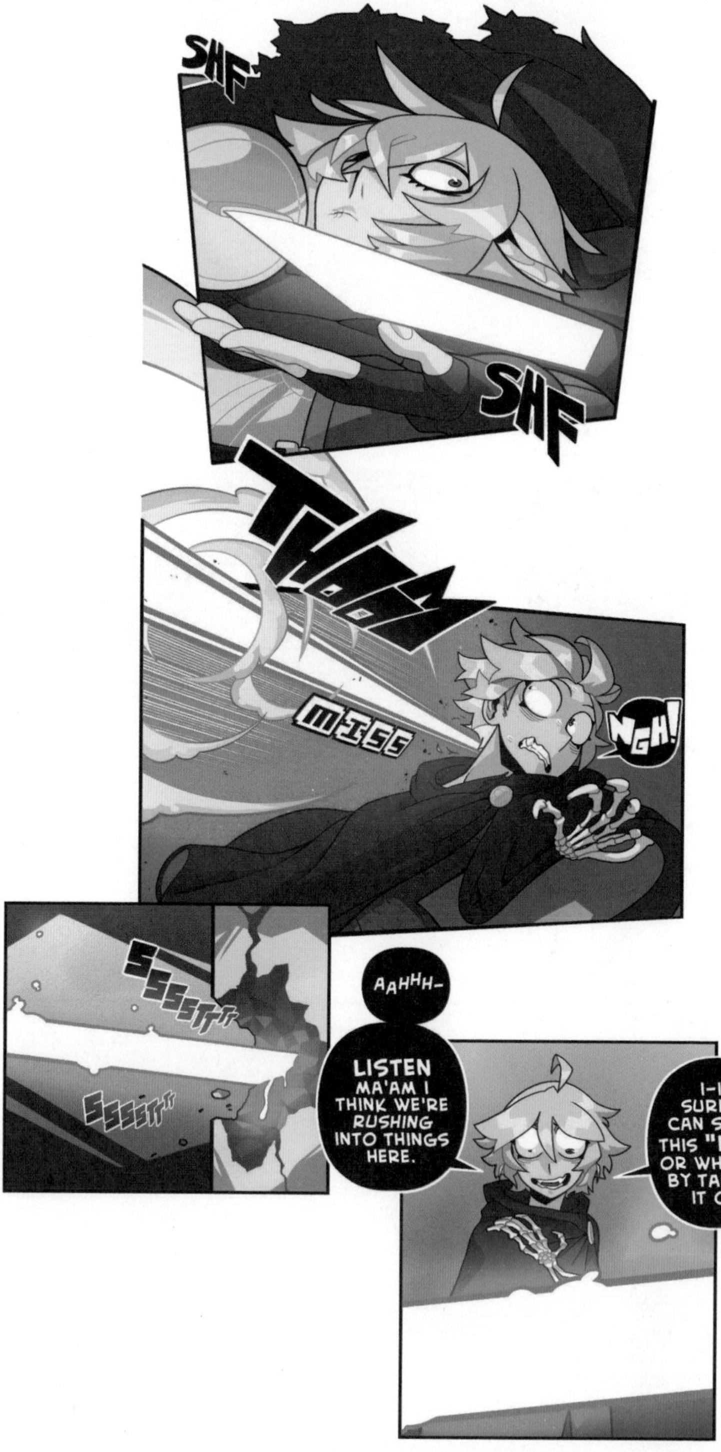
SHF
SHF
THOOM
MISS
NGH!
SSSSTTTT
SSSSTTTT
AAHHH-
LISTEN MA'AM I THINK WE'RE RUSHING INTO THINGS HERE.
I-I'M SURE WE CAN SETTLE THIS "HUNT" OR WHATEVER BY TALKING IT OUT!

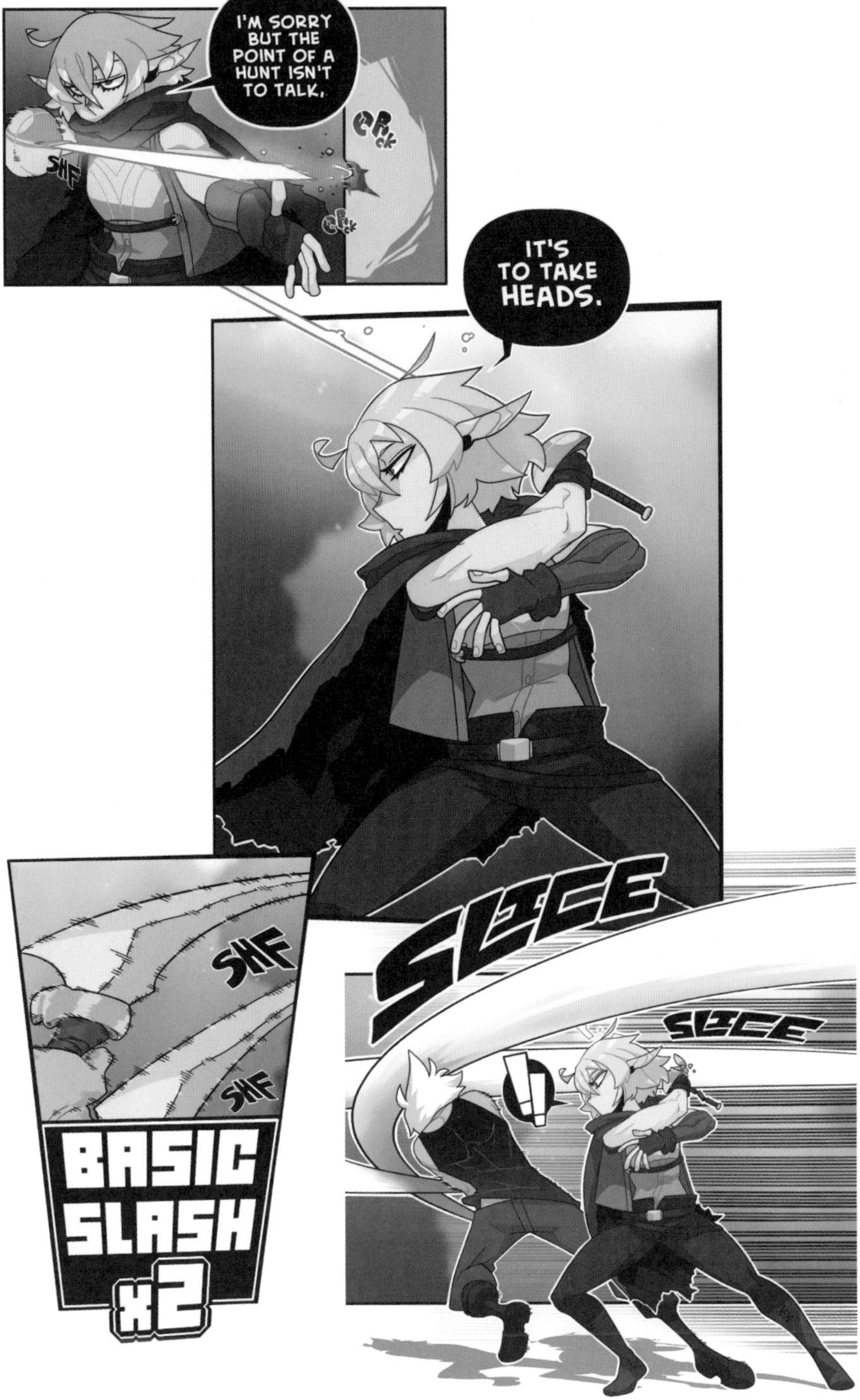
I'M SORRY BUT THE POINT OF A HUNT ISN'T TO TALK,
SHF
CRACK
CRACK
IT'S TO TAKE HEADS.
SHF
SHF
BASIC SLASH x2
SLICE
SLICE
!!

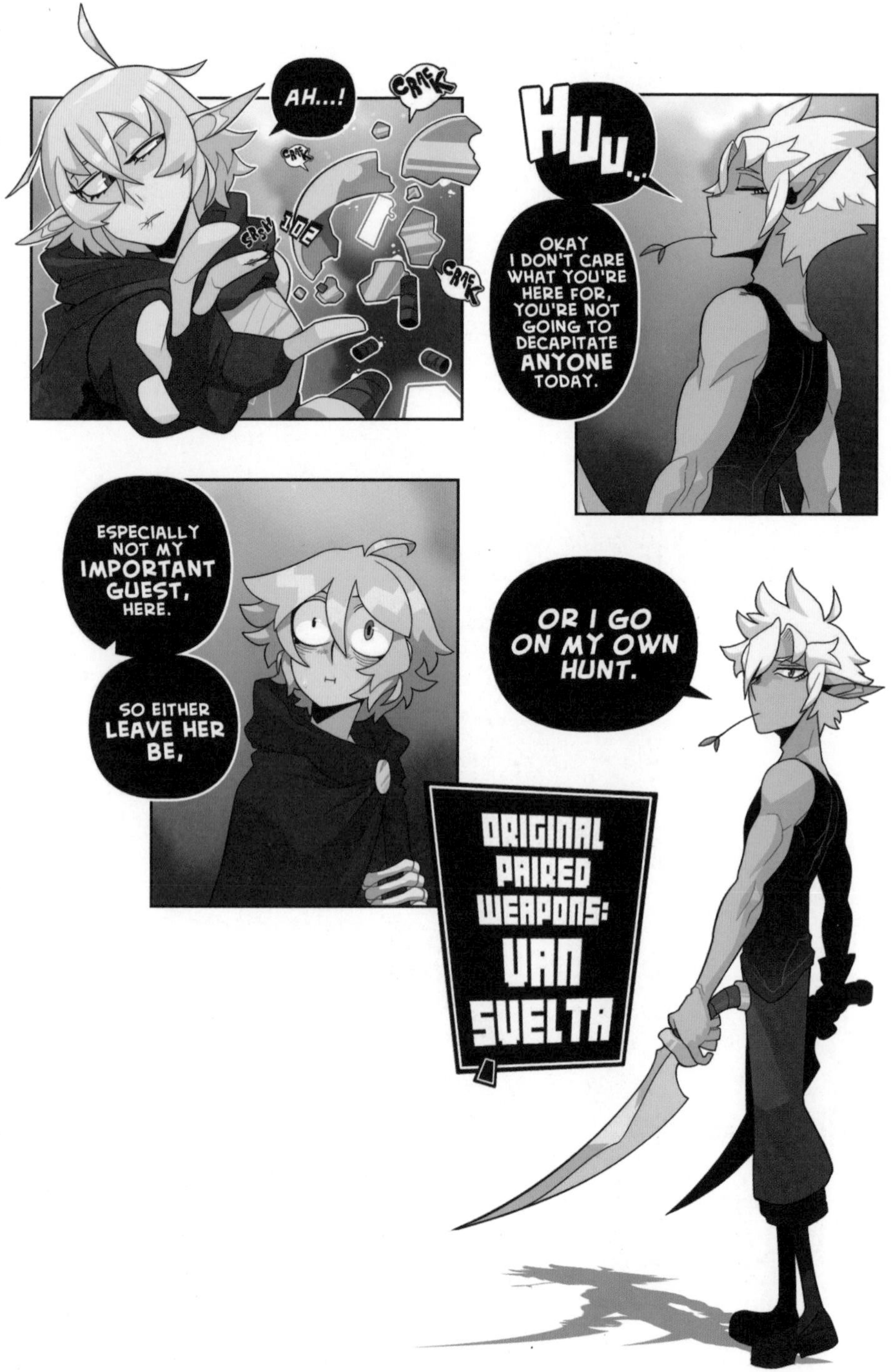
AH...!
HUU...
OKAY I DON'T CARE WHAT YOU'RE HERE FOR, YOU'RE NOT GOING TO DECAPITATE ANYONE TODAY.
ESPECIALLY NOT MY IMPORTANT GUEST, HERE.
SO EITHER LEAVE HER BE,
OR I GO ON MY OWN HUNT.
ORIGINAL PAIRED WEAPONS: VAN SUELTA

OH MY KINSMAN...

YOU DON'T SEEM TO UNDERSTAND ME AT ALL.

THWP

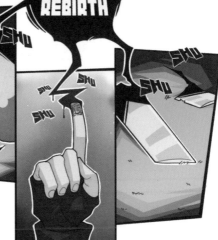

BLOODCRAFT SKILL: REBIRTH

SHU SHU SHU SHU SHU SHU

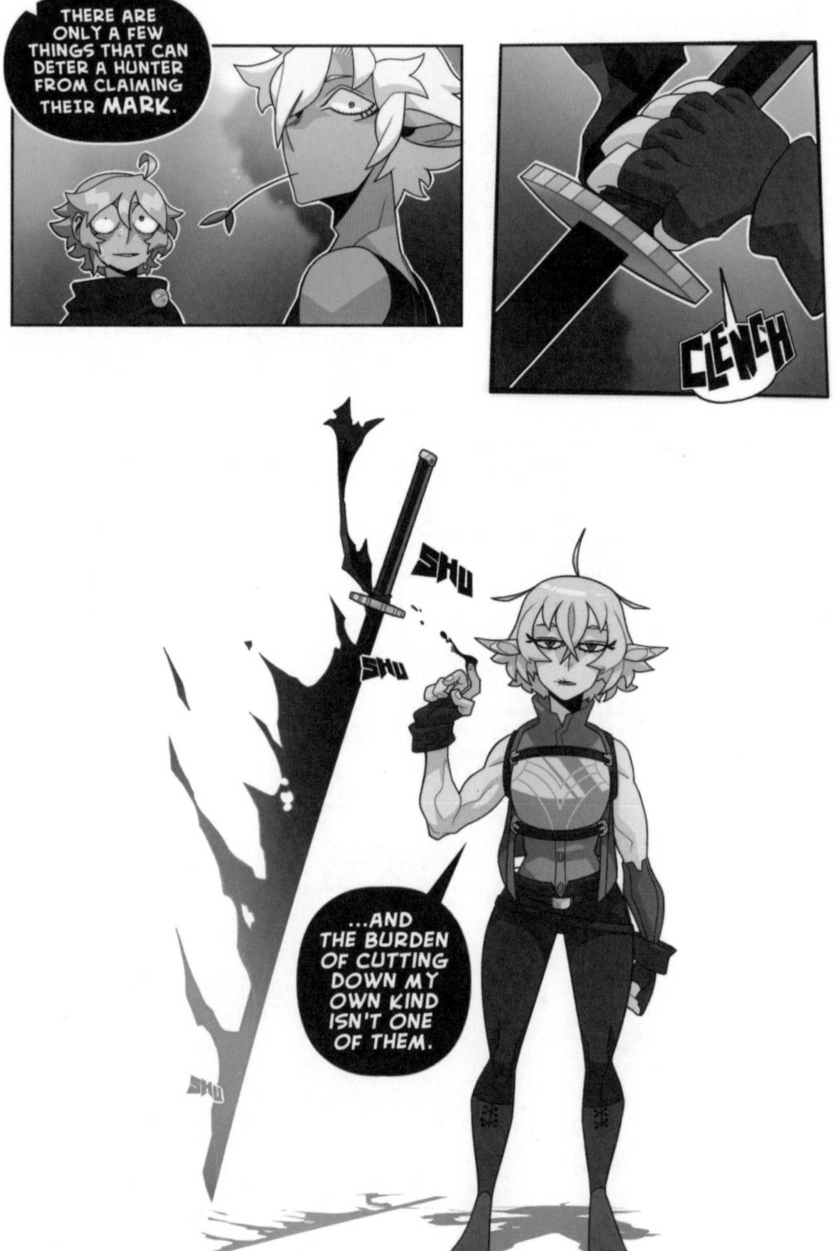
THERE ARE ONLY A FEW THINGS THAT CAN DETER A HUNTER FROM CLAIMING THEIR MARK.
CLENCH
SHU
SHU
SHU
...AND THE BURDEN OF CUTTING DOWN MY OWN KIND ISN'T ONE OF THEM.

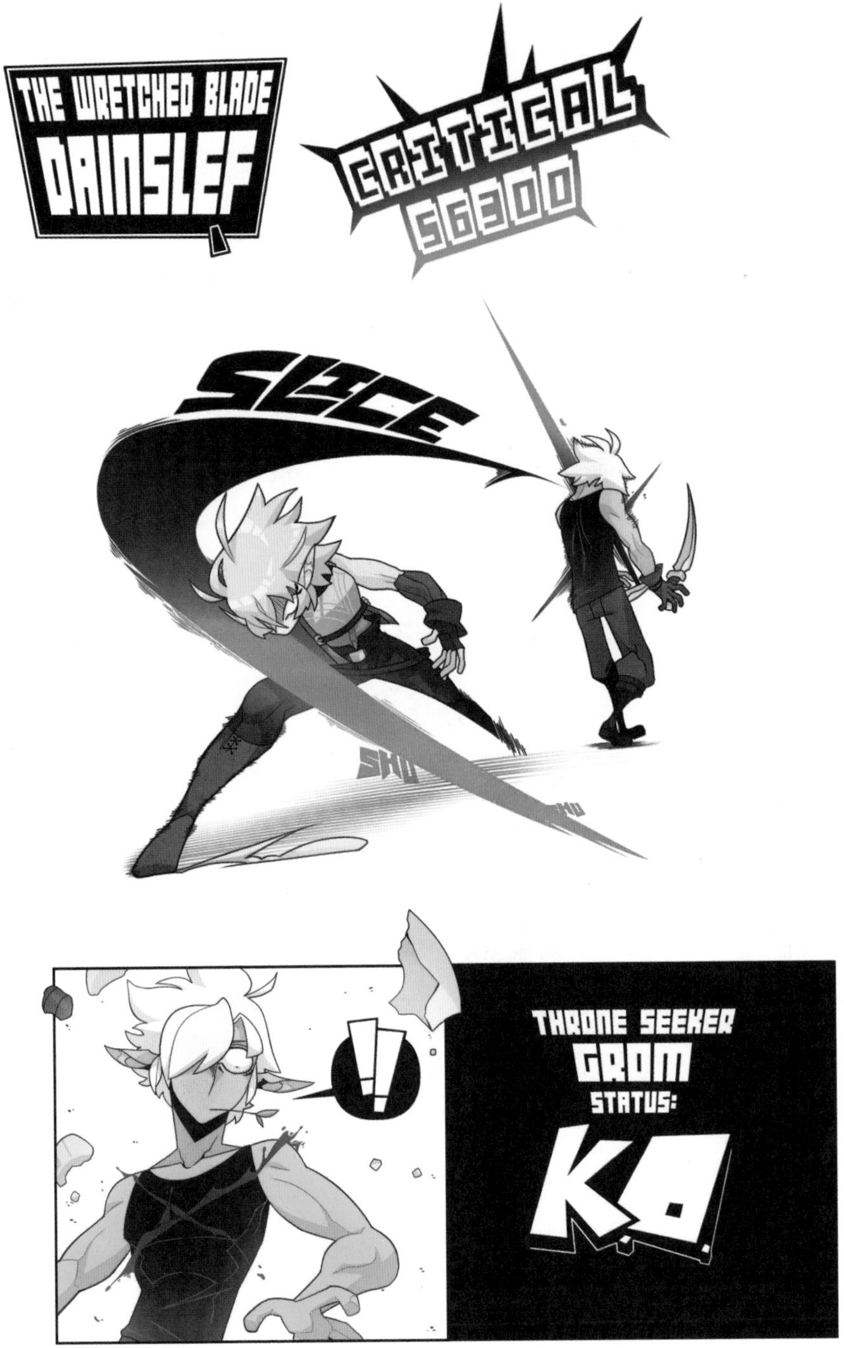
THE WRETCHED BLADE
DAINSLEF
CRITICAL
56300
SLICE
SHU
!!
THRONE SEEKER
GROM
STATUS:
K.O.

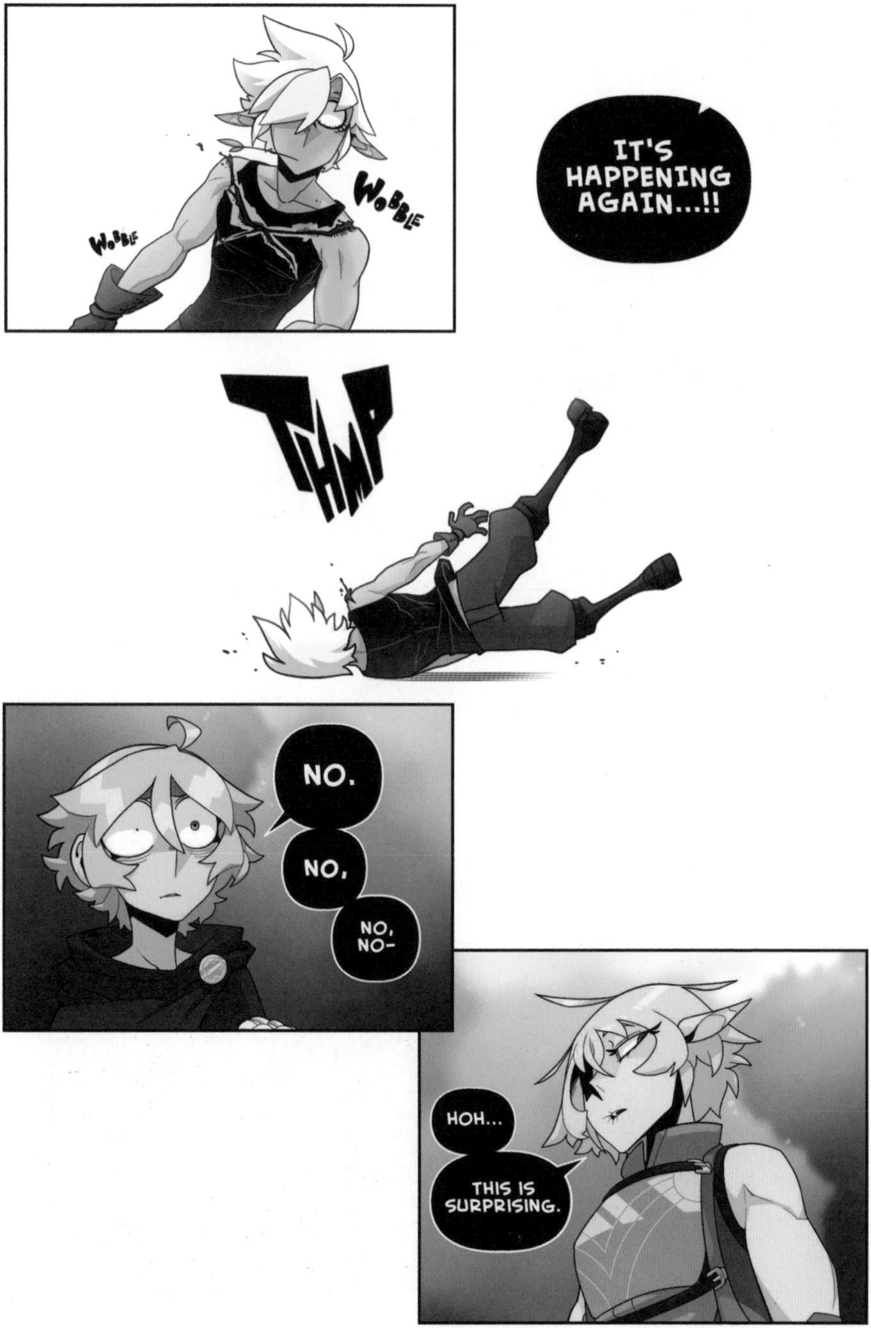
WOBBLE
WOBBLE
IT'S HAPPENING AGAIN...!!
THMP
NO.
NO,
NO, NO-
HOH...
THIS IS SURPRISING.

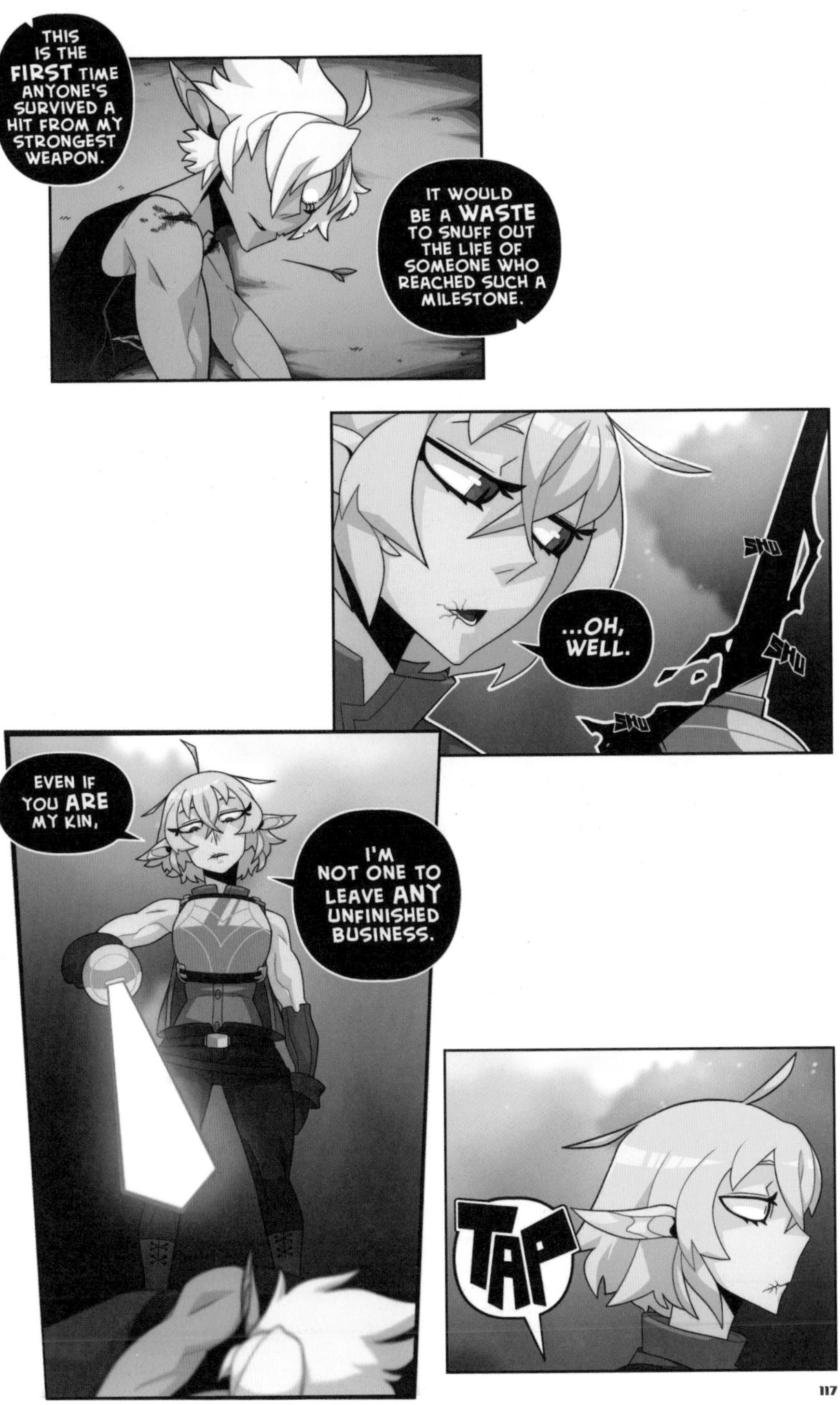
THIS IS THE FIRST TIME ANYONE'S SURVIVED A HIT FROM MY STRONGEST WEAPON.
IT WOULD BE A WASTE TO SNUFF OUT THE LIFE OF SOMEONE WHO REACHED SUCH A MILESTONE.
SHU
...OH, WELL.
SHU
SHU
EVEN IF YOU ARE MY KIN,
I'M NOT ONE TO LEAVE ANY UNFINISHED BUSINESS.
TAP

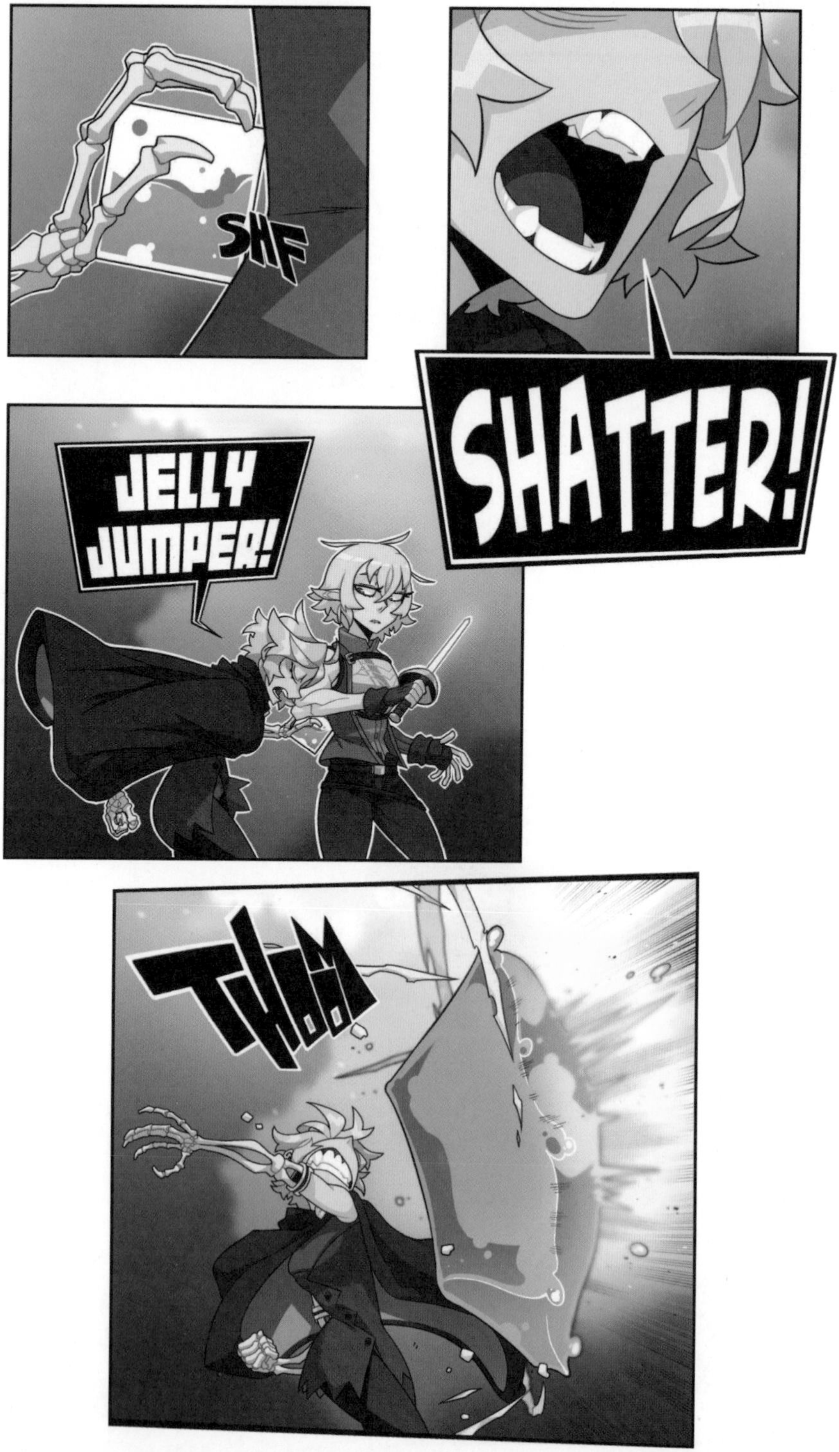
SHF
SHATTER!
JELLY JUMPER!
THOOM

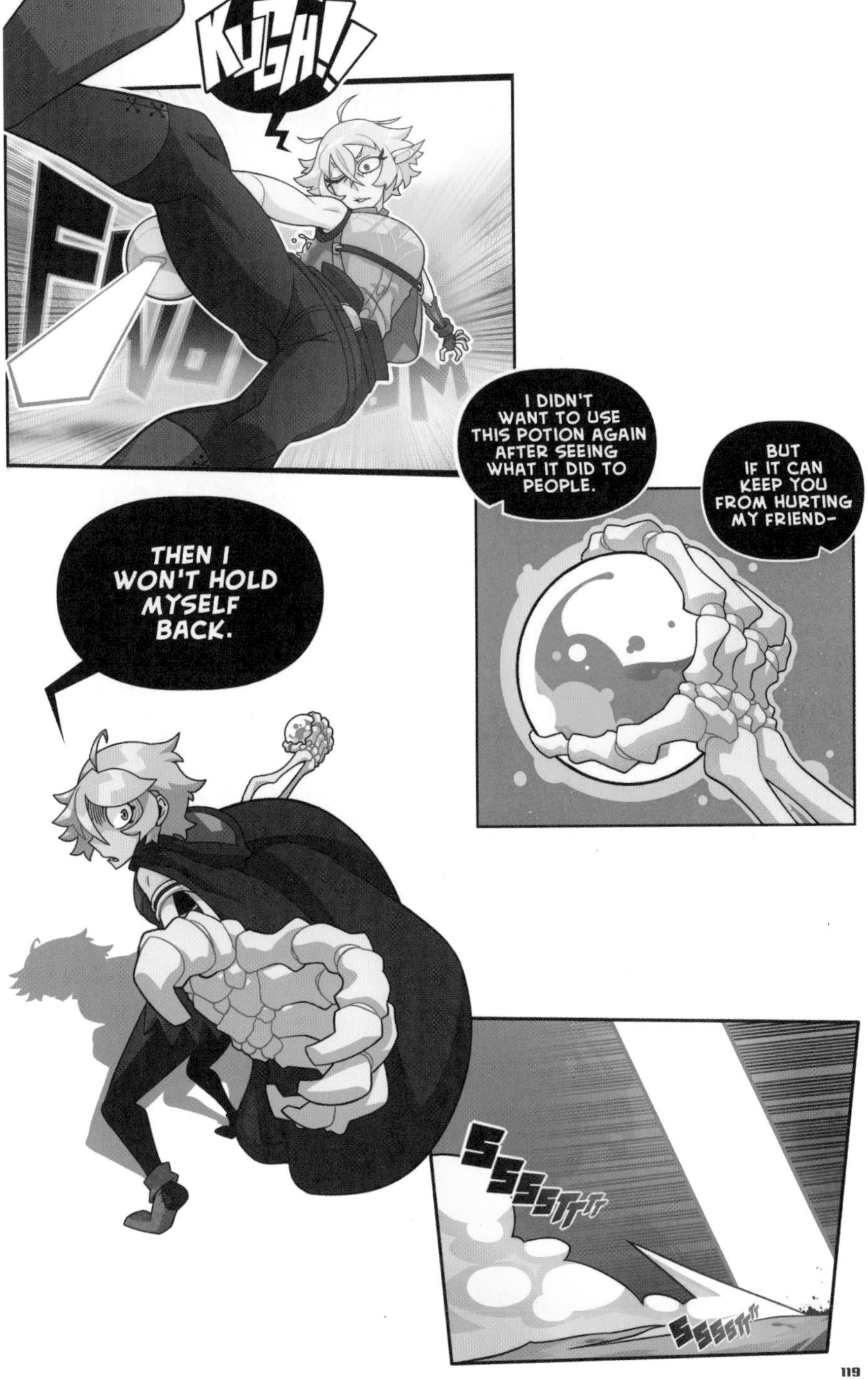
KUGH!!
I DIDN'T WANT TO USE THIS POTION AGAIN AFTER SEEING WHAT IT DID TO PEOPLE.
BUT IF IT CAN KEEP YOU FROM HURTING MY FRIEND-
THEN I WON'T HOLD MYSELF BACK.
SSSSTT
SSSSTT

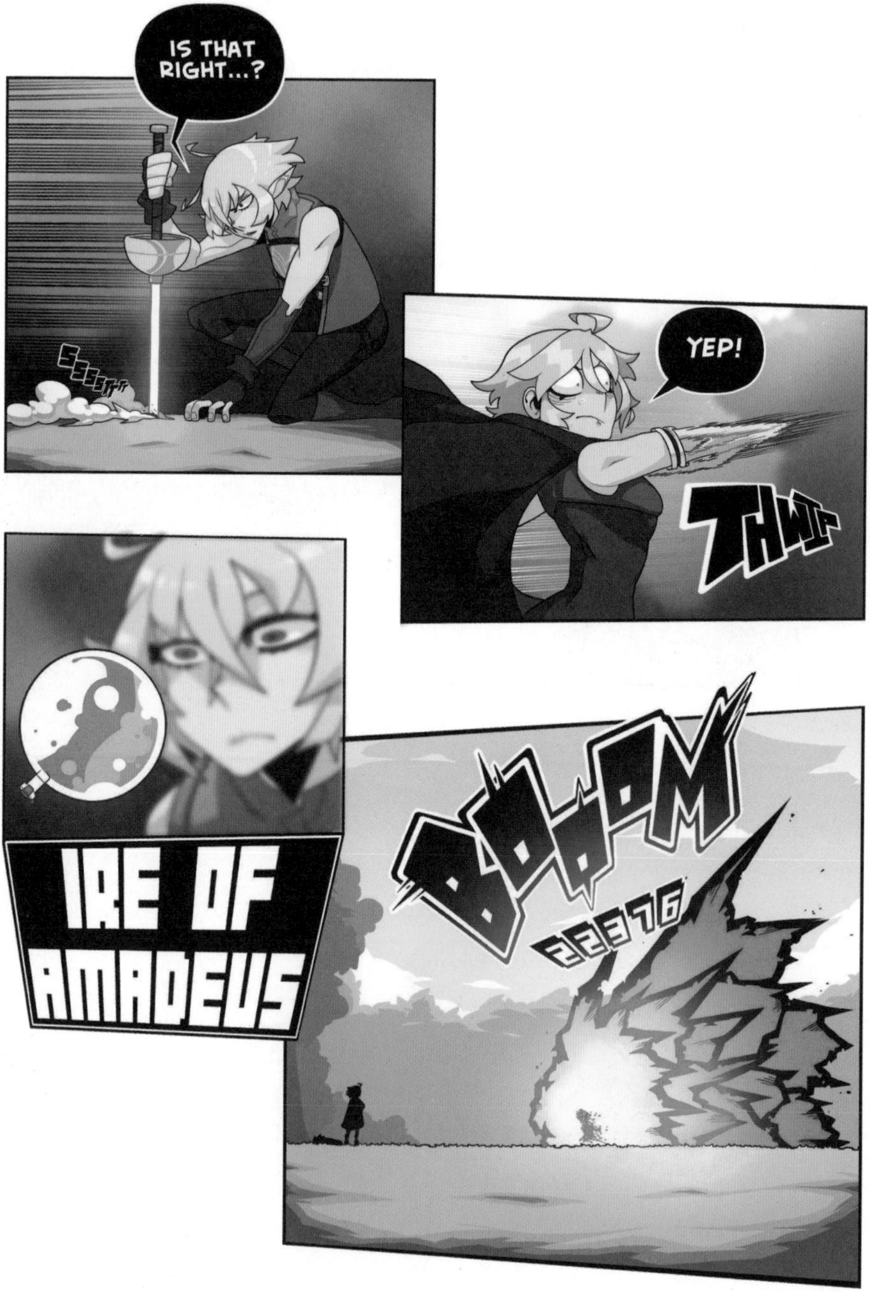
IS THAT RIGHT...?
SSSSTTrr
YEP!
THWIP
IRE OF AMADEUS
BOOOOM
22376

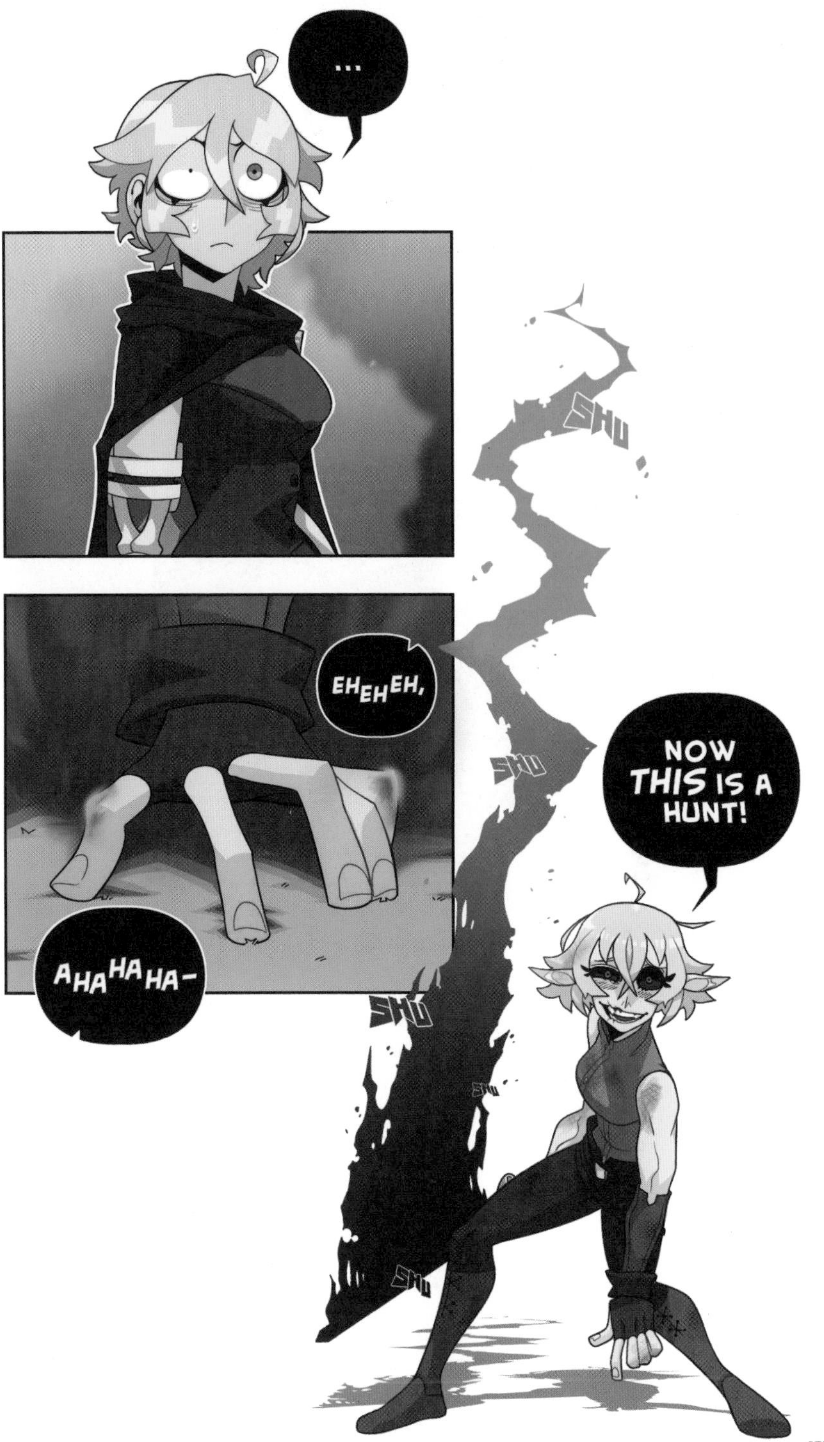
...
SHU
EHEHEH,
AHAHAHAHA-
SHU
NOW THIS IS A HUNT!
SHU
SHU
SHU

# BLOODCRAFT SKILL: MORTAL HIGH

LET ME SEE WHAT YOU CAN DO LITTLE SONGBIRD!

...OH JEEZ.

## Chapter 8
# THE MARK

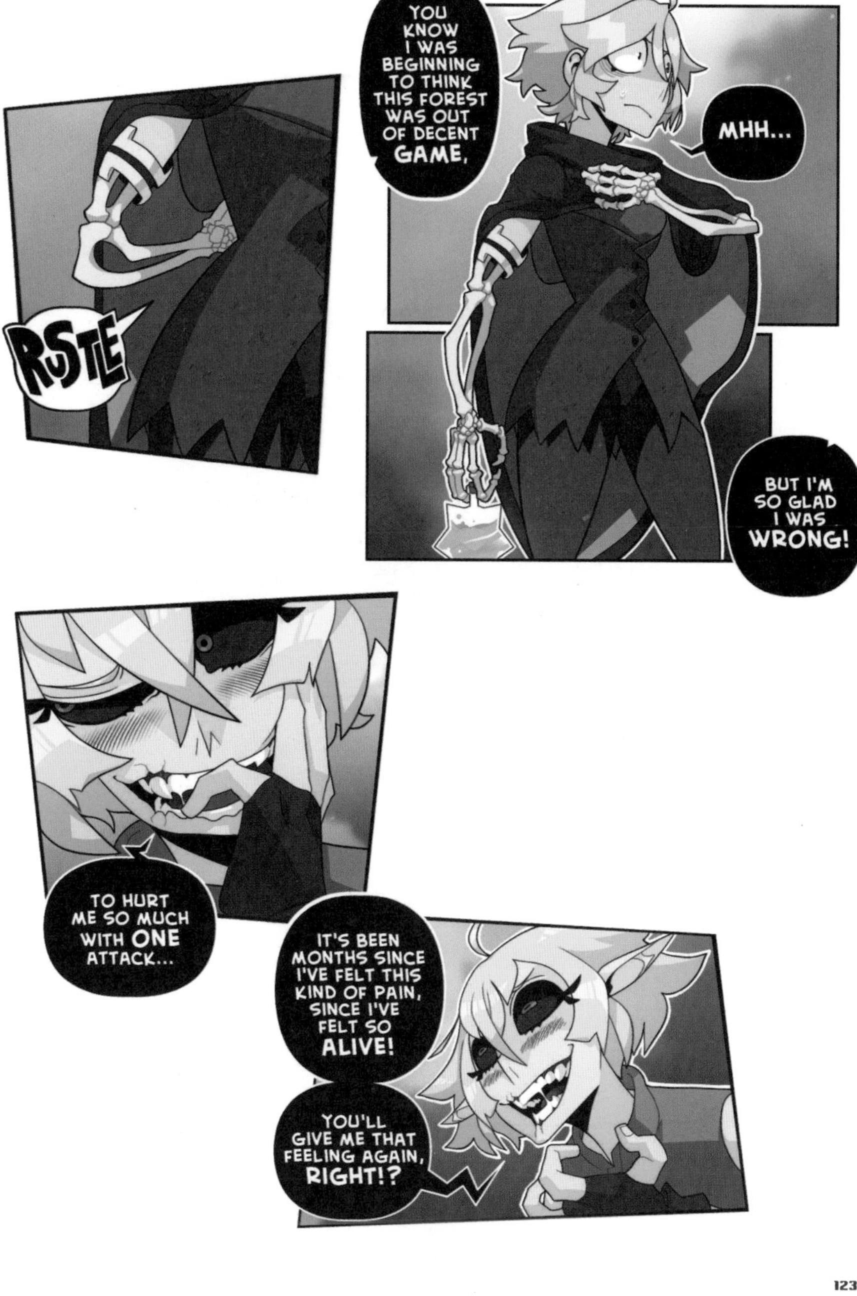
RUSTLE
YOU KNOW I WAS BEGINNING TO THINK THIS FOREST WAS OUT OF DECENT GAME,
MHH...
BUT I'M SO GLAD I WAS WRONG!
TO HURT ME SO MUCH WITH ONE ATTACK...
IT'S BEEN MONTHS SINCE I'VE FELT THIS KIND OF PAIN, SINCE I'VE FELT SO ALIVE!
YOU'LL GIVE ME THAT FEELING AGAIN, RIGHT!?

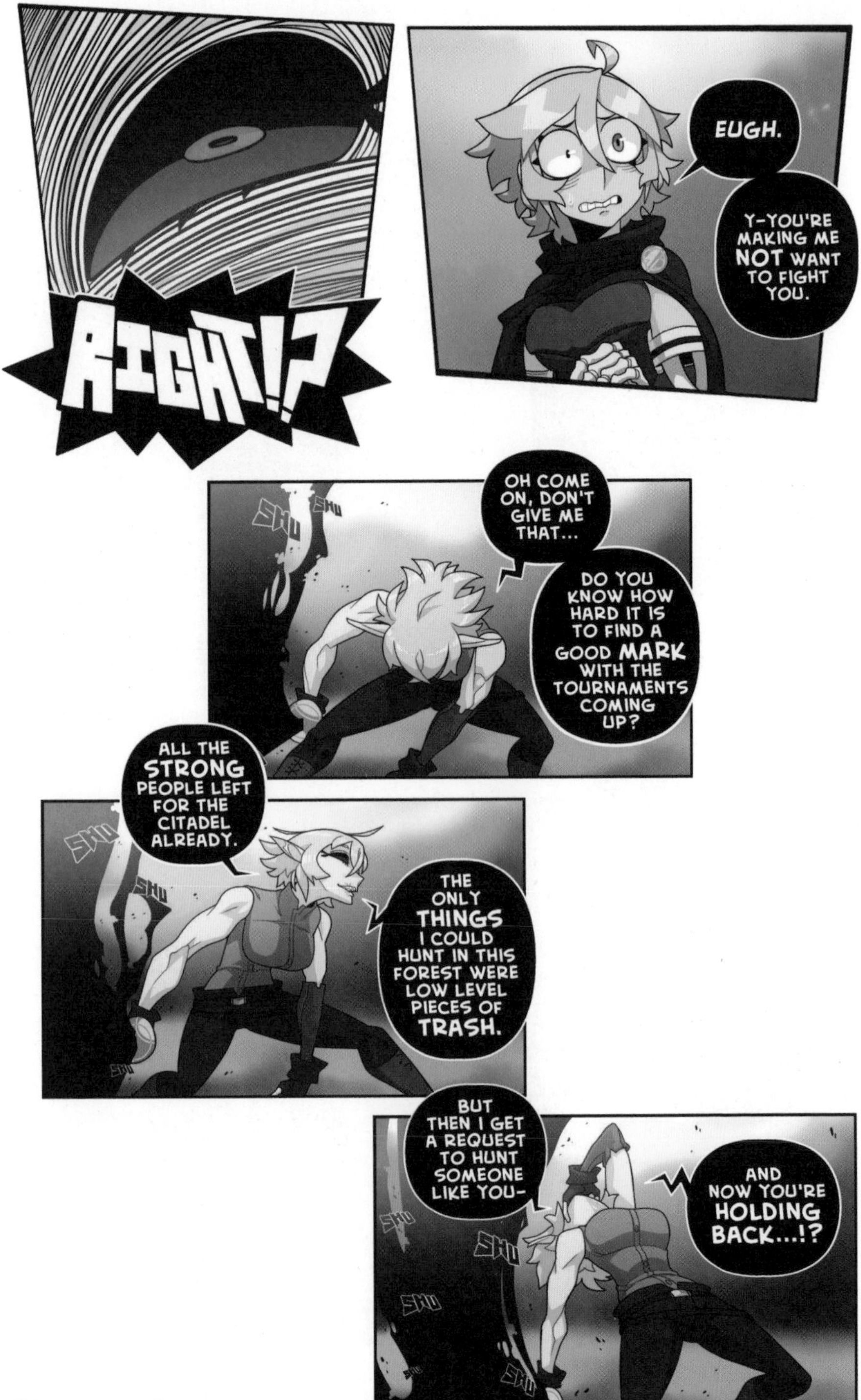
RIGHT!?
EUGH.
Y-YOU'RE MAKING ME NOT WANT TO FIGHT YOU.
SHU SHU
OH COME ON, DON'T GIVE ME THAT...
DO YOU KNOW HOW HARD IT IS TO FIND A GOOD MARK WITH THE TOURNAMENTS COMING UP?
ALL THE STRONG PEOPLE LEFT FOR THE CITADEL ALREADY.
SHU SHU SHU
THE ONLY THINGS I COULD HUNT IN THIS FOREST WERE LOW LEVEL PIECES OF TRASH.
BUT THEN I GET A REQUEST TO HUNT SOMEONE LIKE YOU-
AND NOW YOU'RE HOLDING BACK...!?
SHU SHU SHU SHU SHU

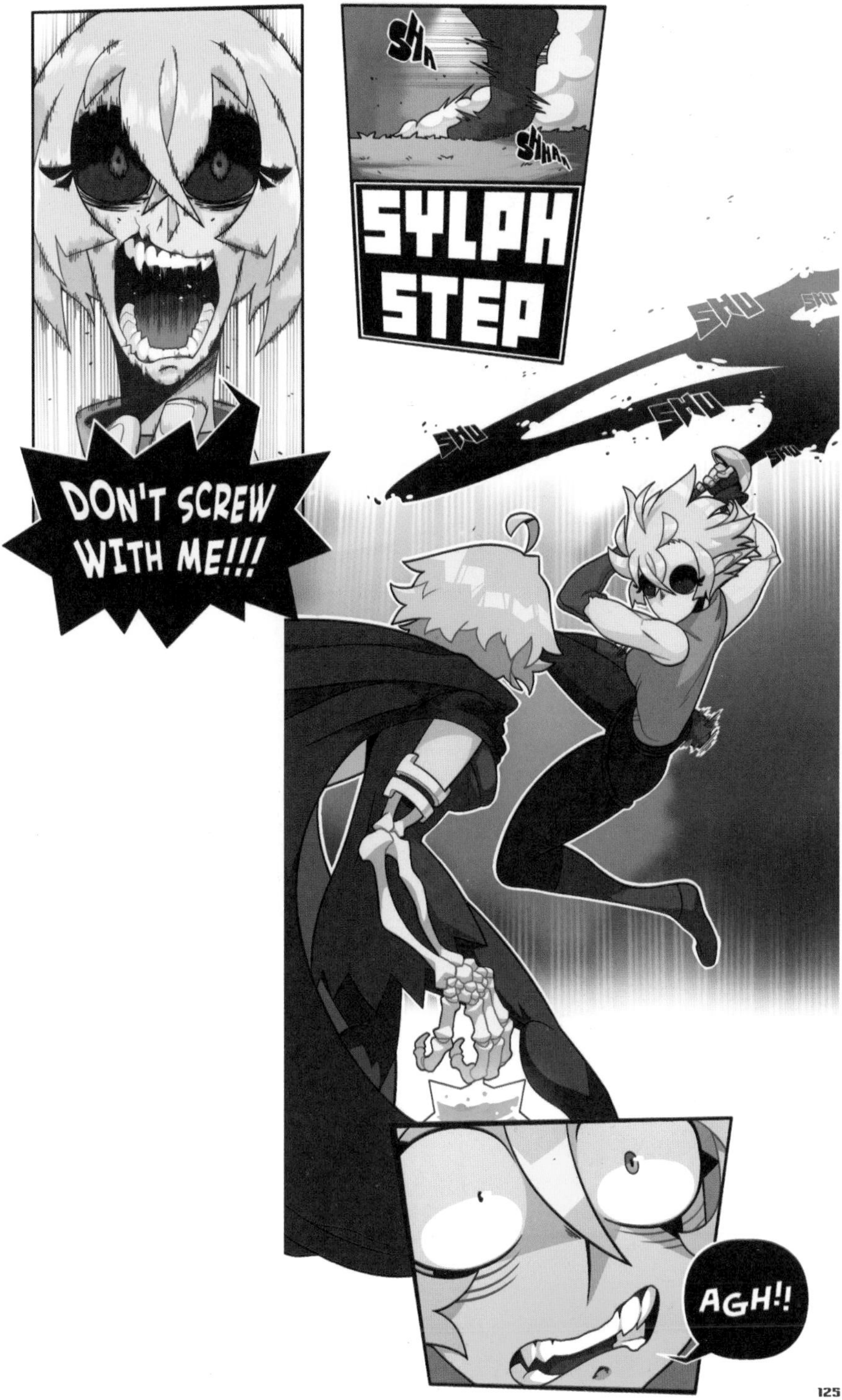
DON'T SCREW WITH ME!!!
SHA
SHHAA
SYLPH STEP
SHU
SHU
SHU
SHU
SHU
AGH!!

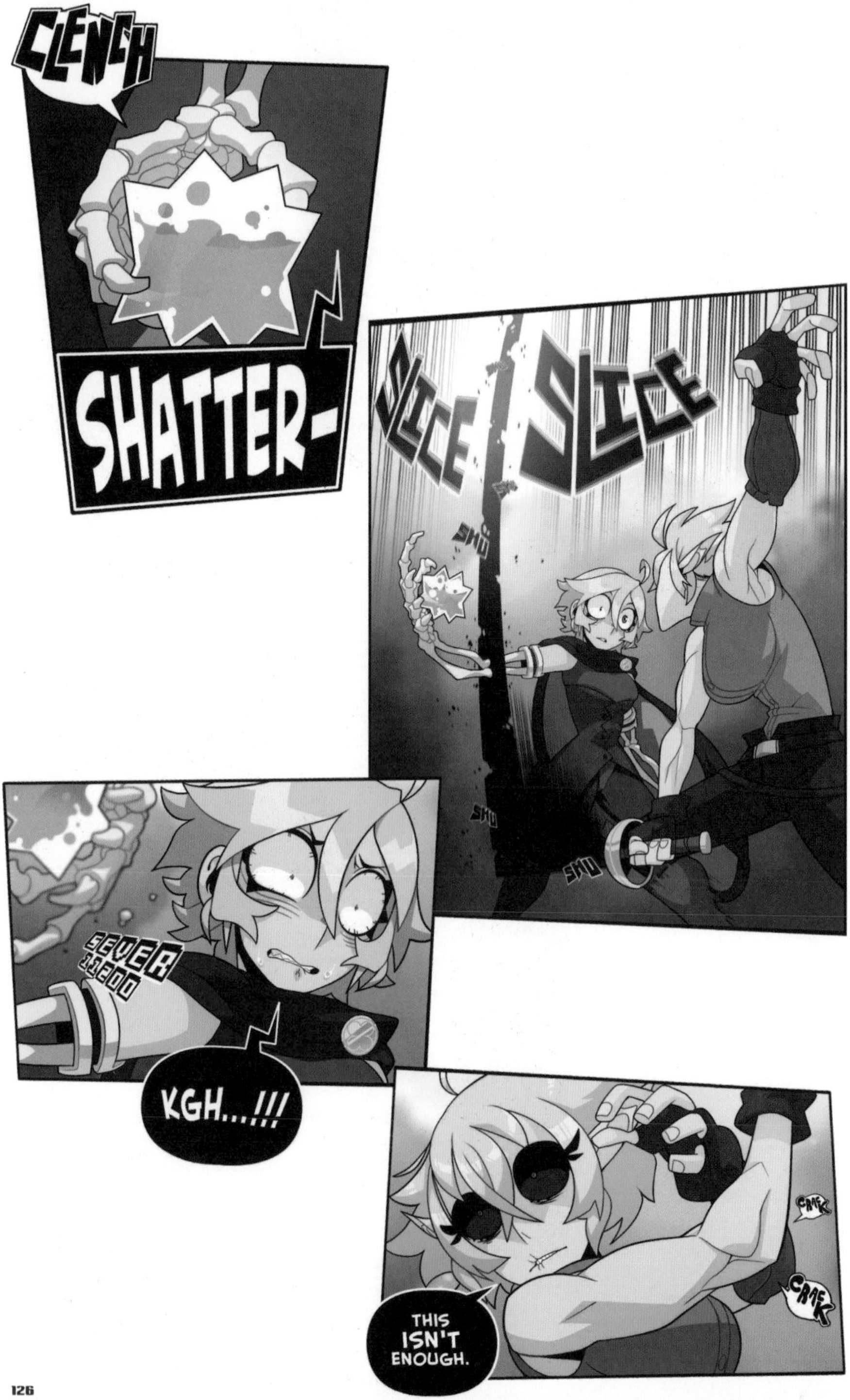
CLENCH
SHATTER-
SLICE
SLICE
SEVER
KGH...!!!
THIS ISN'T ENOUGH.

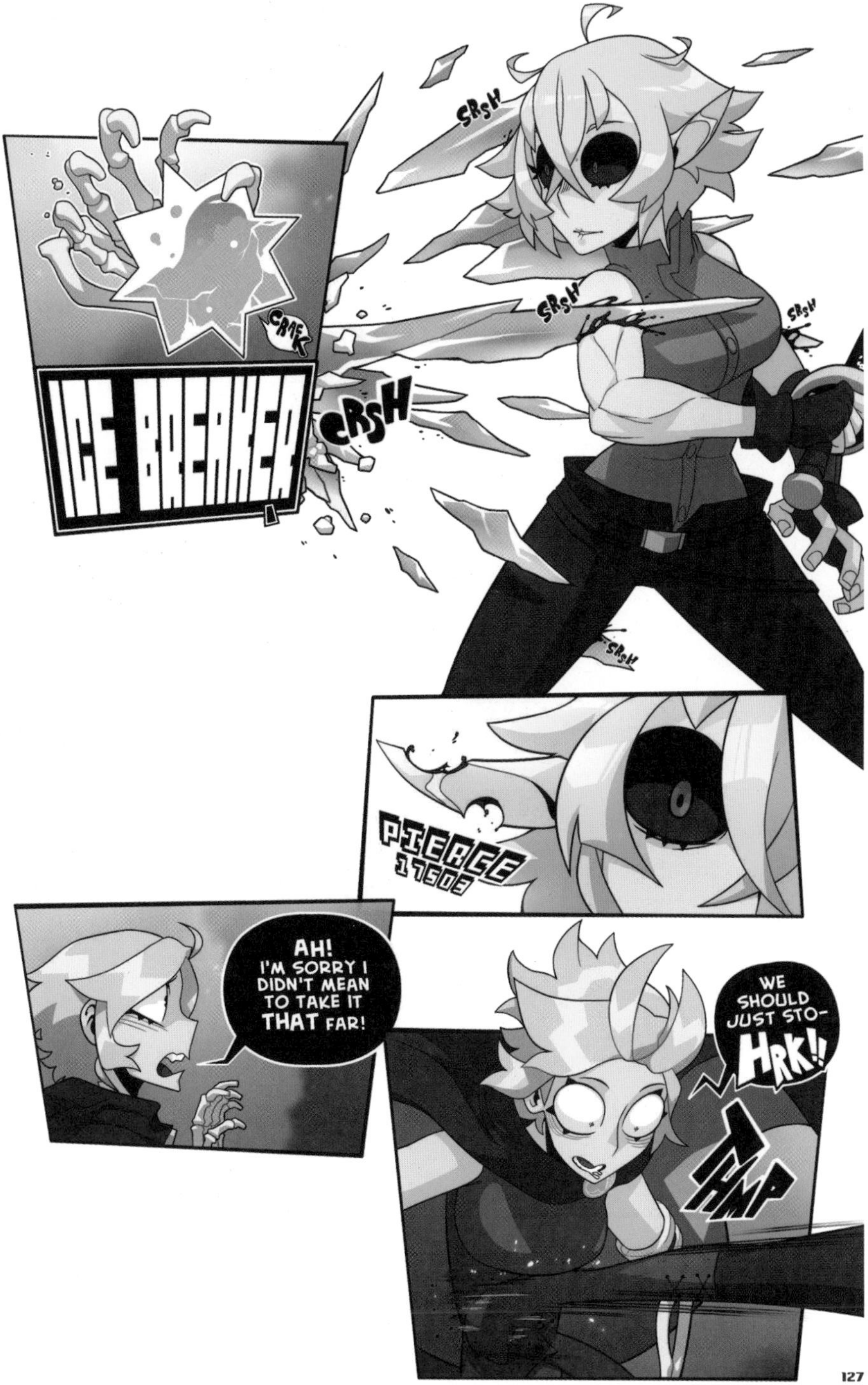
SRSH
CRAEK
ICE BREAKER
CRSH
SRSH
SRSH
SRSH
PIERCE
17503
AH! I'M SORRY I DIDN'T MEAN TO TAKE IT THAT FAR!
WE SHOULD JUST STO-
HRK!!
THMP

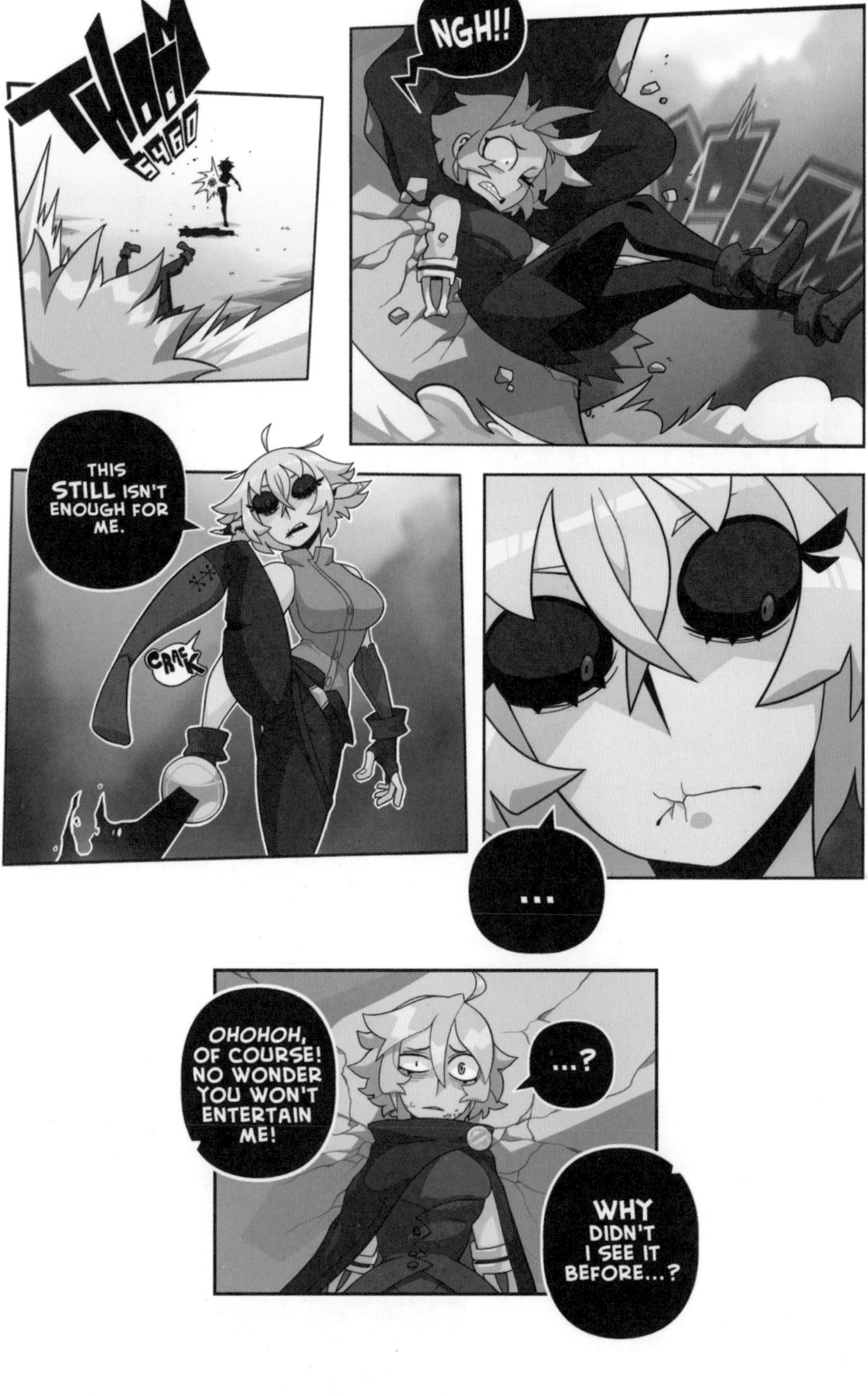
THOOM
NGH!!
THIS STILL ISN'T ENOUGH FOR ME.
CRACK
...
OHOHOH, OF COURSE! NO WONDER YOU WON'T ENTERTAIN ME!
...?
WHY DIDN'T I SEE IT BEFORE...?

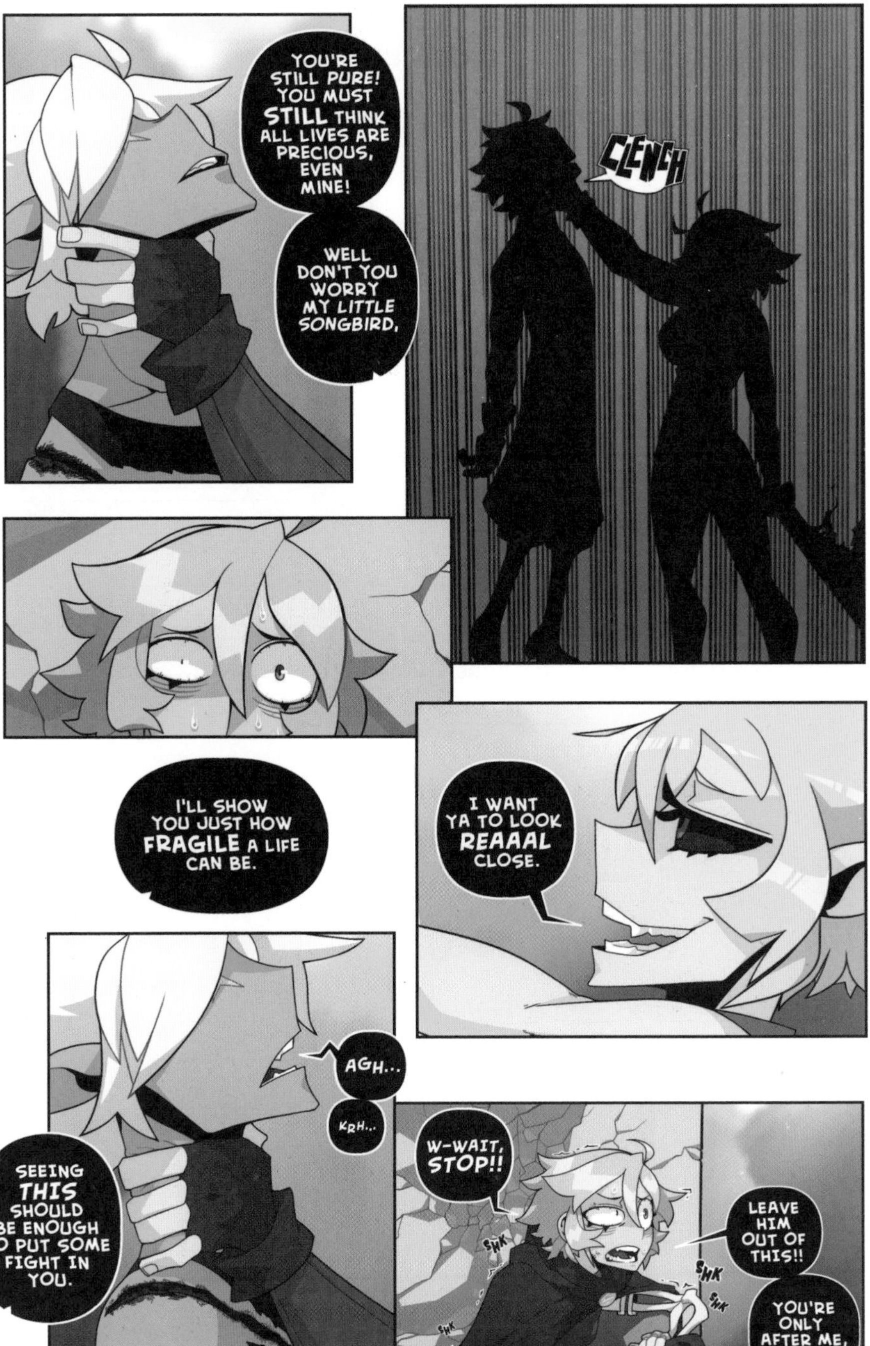
YOU'RE STILL PURE! YOU MUST STILL THINK ALL LIVES ARE PRECIOUS, EVEN MINE!
WELL DON'T YOU WORRY MY LITTLE SONGBIRD,
CLENCH
I'LL SHOW YOU JUST HOW FRAGILE A LIFE CAN BE.
I WANT YA TO LOOK REAAAL CLOSE.
AGH...
KRH...
SEEING THIS SHOULD BE ENOUGH TO PUT SOME FIGHT IN YOU.
W-WAIT, STOP!!
SHK
SHK
SHK
SHK
LEAVE HIM OUT OF THIS!!
YOU'RE ONLY AFTER ME, RIGHT?!

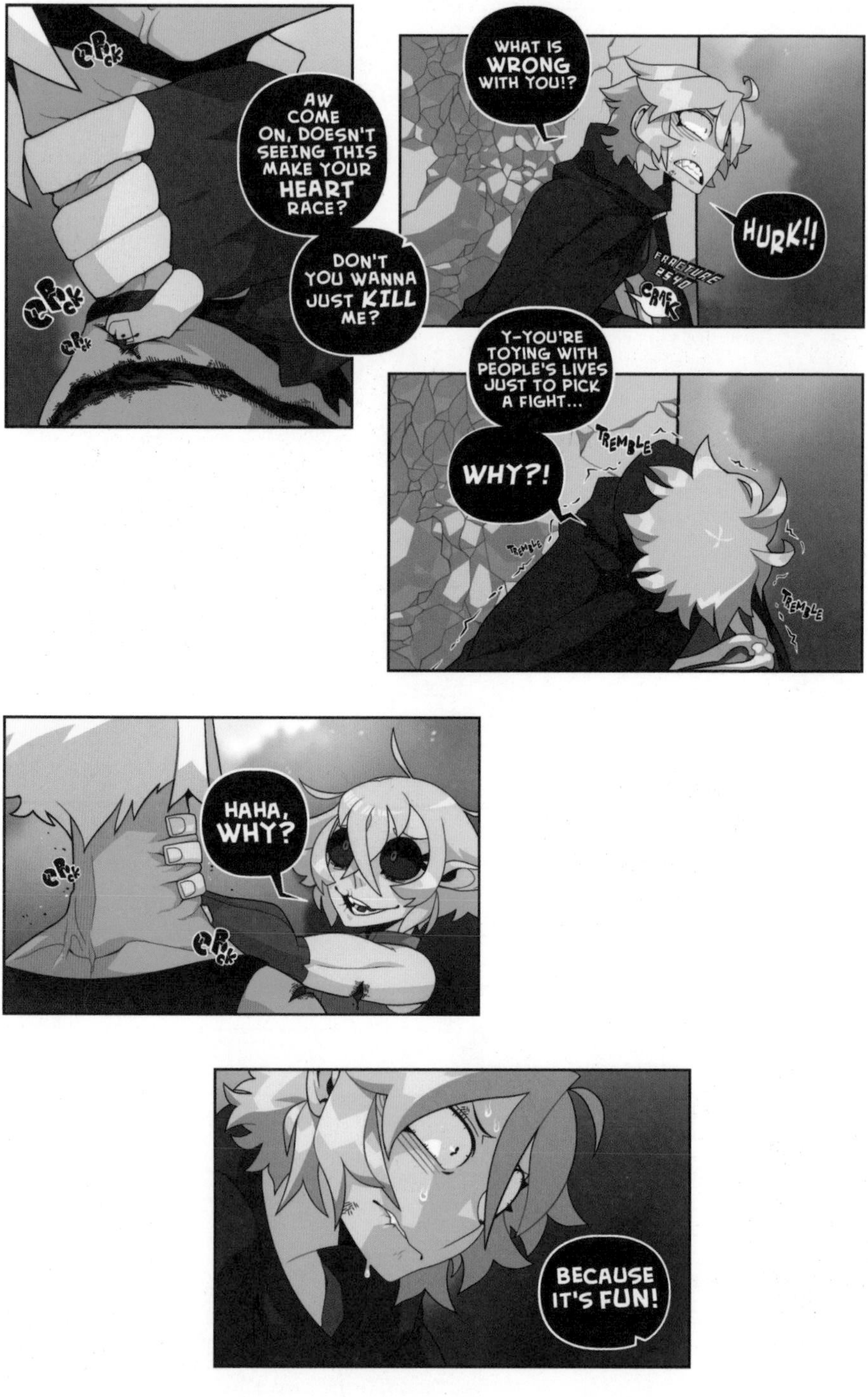
CRACK
AW COME ON, DOESN'T SEEING THIS MAKE YOUR HEART RACE?
DON'T YOU WANNA JUST KILL ME?
CRACK
CRACK
WHAT IS WRONG WITH YOU!?
HURK!!
FRACTURE 2540
CRACK
Y-YOU'RE TOYING WITH PEOPLE'S LIVES JUST TO PICK A FIGHT...
WHY?!
TREMBLE
TREMBLE
TREMBLE
HAHA, WHY?
CRACK
CRACK
BECAUSE IT'S FUN!

LIFE IS A GAME LITTERED WITH OBSTACLES AND HARDSHIP.

IF YOU'RE GOING TO PLAY, YOU MAY AS WELL TRY TO **ENJOY** IT.

AND TO **ME** THERE'S NOTHING MORE ENJOYABLE THAN SEEKING OUT A BEAUTIFUL SOUL,

REACHING OUT TO THEM,

IN THEIR **PRIME**...

AND **CRUSHING** THEM

WITH **ALL** OF MY MIGHT.

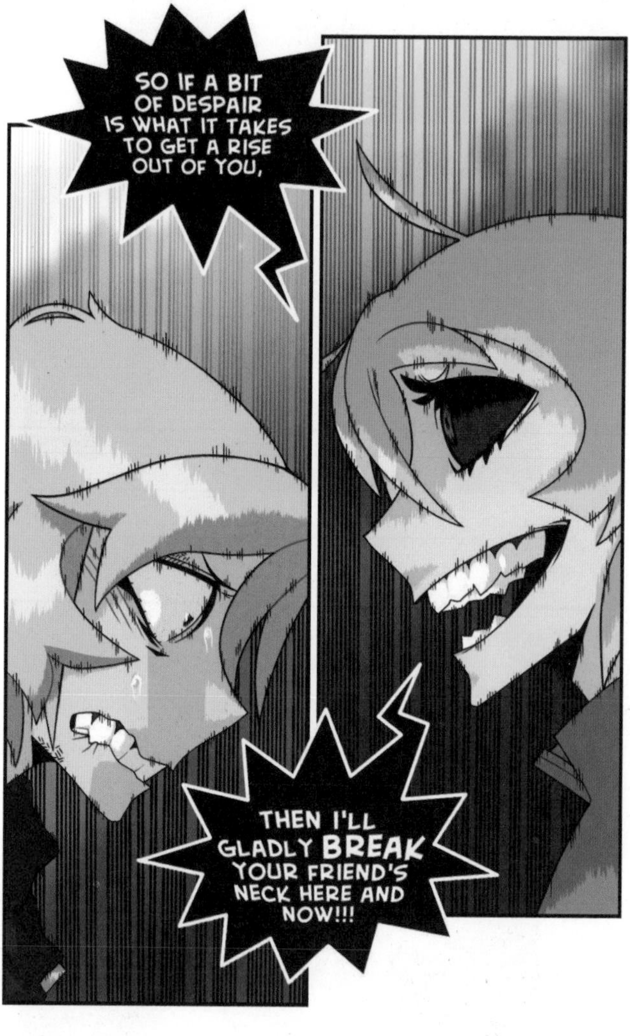
SO IF A BIT OF DESPAIR IS WHAT IT TAKES TO GET A RISE OUT OF YOU,
THEN I'LL GLADLY **BREAK** YOUR FRIEND'S NECK HERE AND NOW!!!

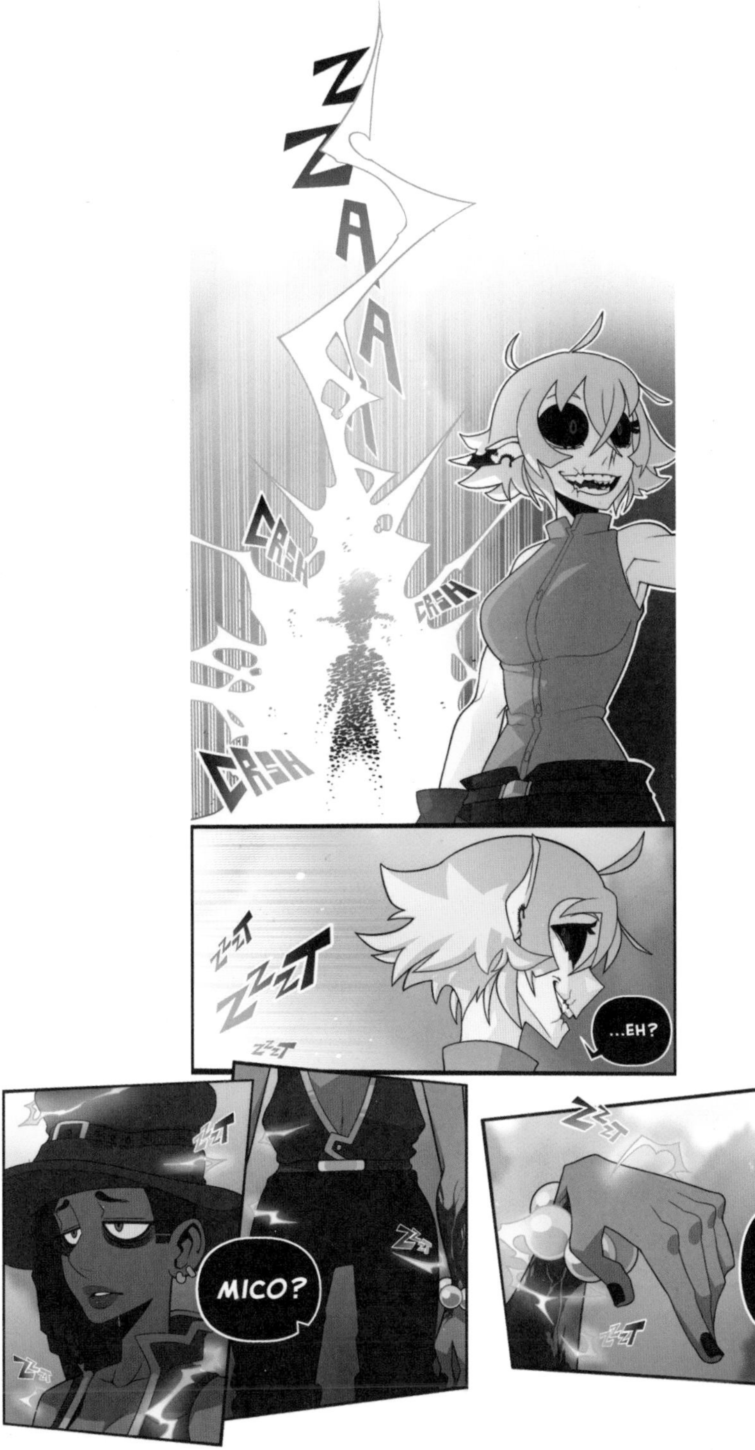
ZZAAA
CRSH
CRSH
CRSH
ZZZT
ZZZT
ZZZT
...EH?
ZZZT
ZZZT
ZZZT
MICO?
ZZZT
ZZZT
WHAT THE **HELL** ARE YOU DOING HERE-

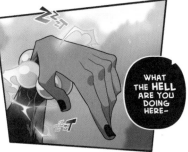

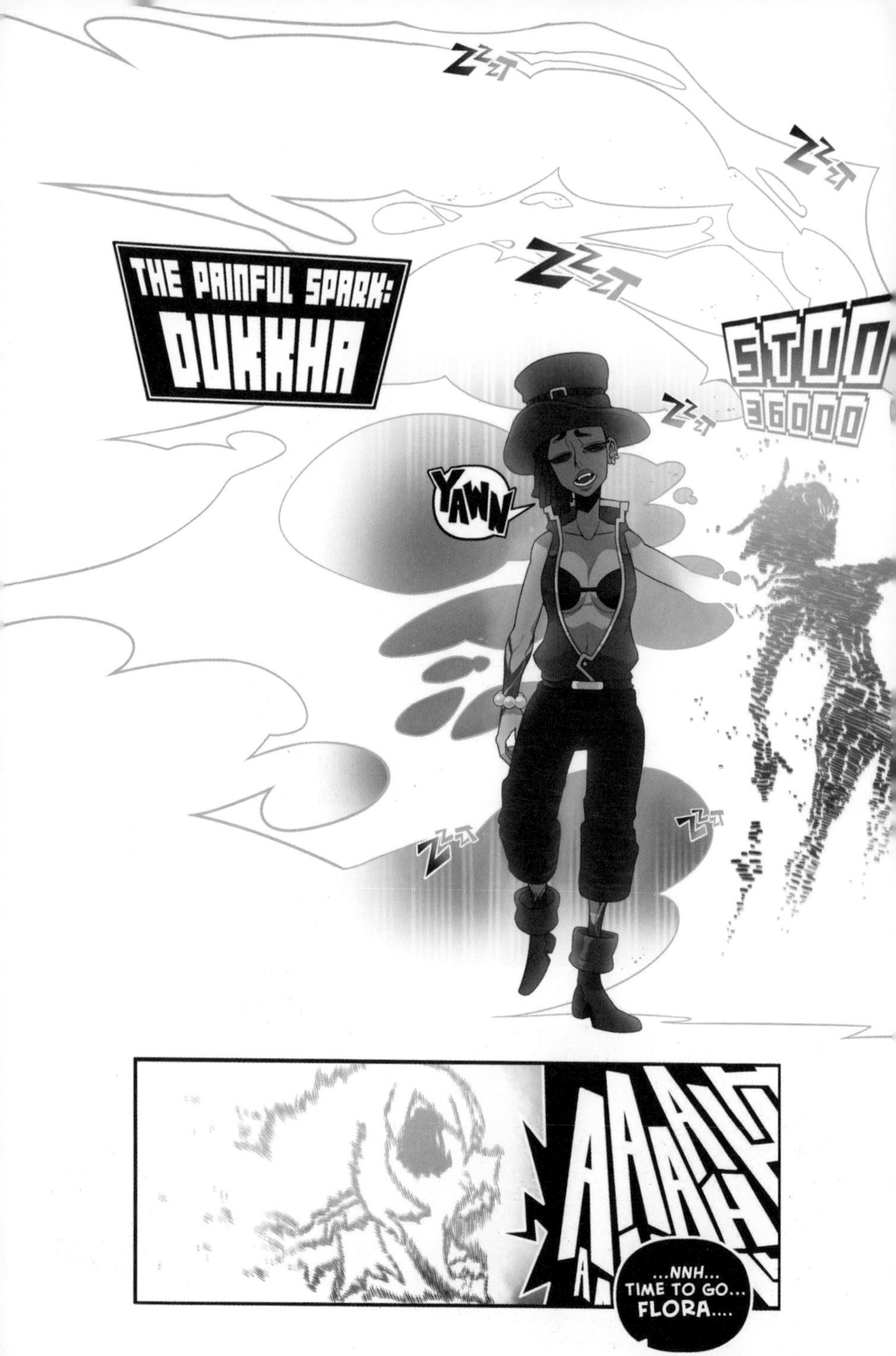
THE PAINFUL SPARK:
DUKKHA
ZZZT
ZZZT
ZZZT
STUN
36000
ZZZT
YAWN
ZZZT
ZZZT
...NNH...
TIME TO GO...
FLORA....

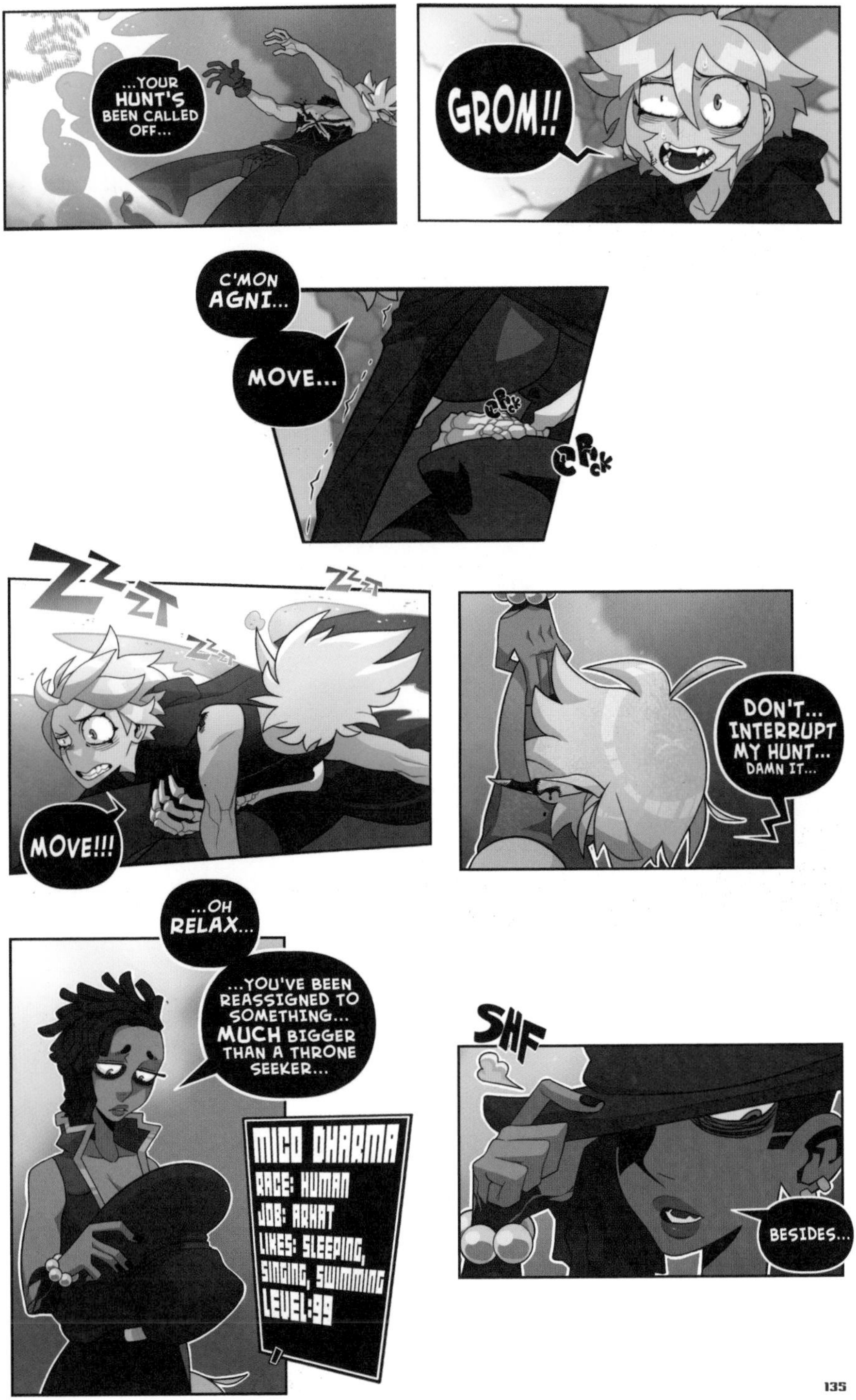

...YOUR HUNT'S BEEN CALLED OFF...
GROM!!
C'MON AGNI...
MOVE...
CRACK
CRACK
ZZZT
ZZZT
ZZZT
MOVE!!!
DON'T... INTERRUPT MY HUNT... DAMN IT...
...OH RELAX...
...YOU'VE BEEN REASSIGNED TO SOMETHING... MUCH BIGGER THAN A THRONE SEEKER...
MICO DHARMA
RACE: HUMAN
JOB: ARHAT
LIKES: SLEEPING, SINGING, SWIMMING
LEVEL:99
SHF
BESIDES...

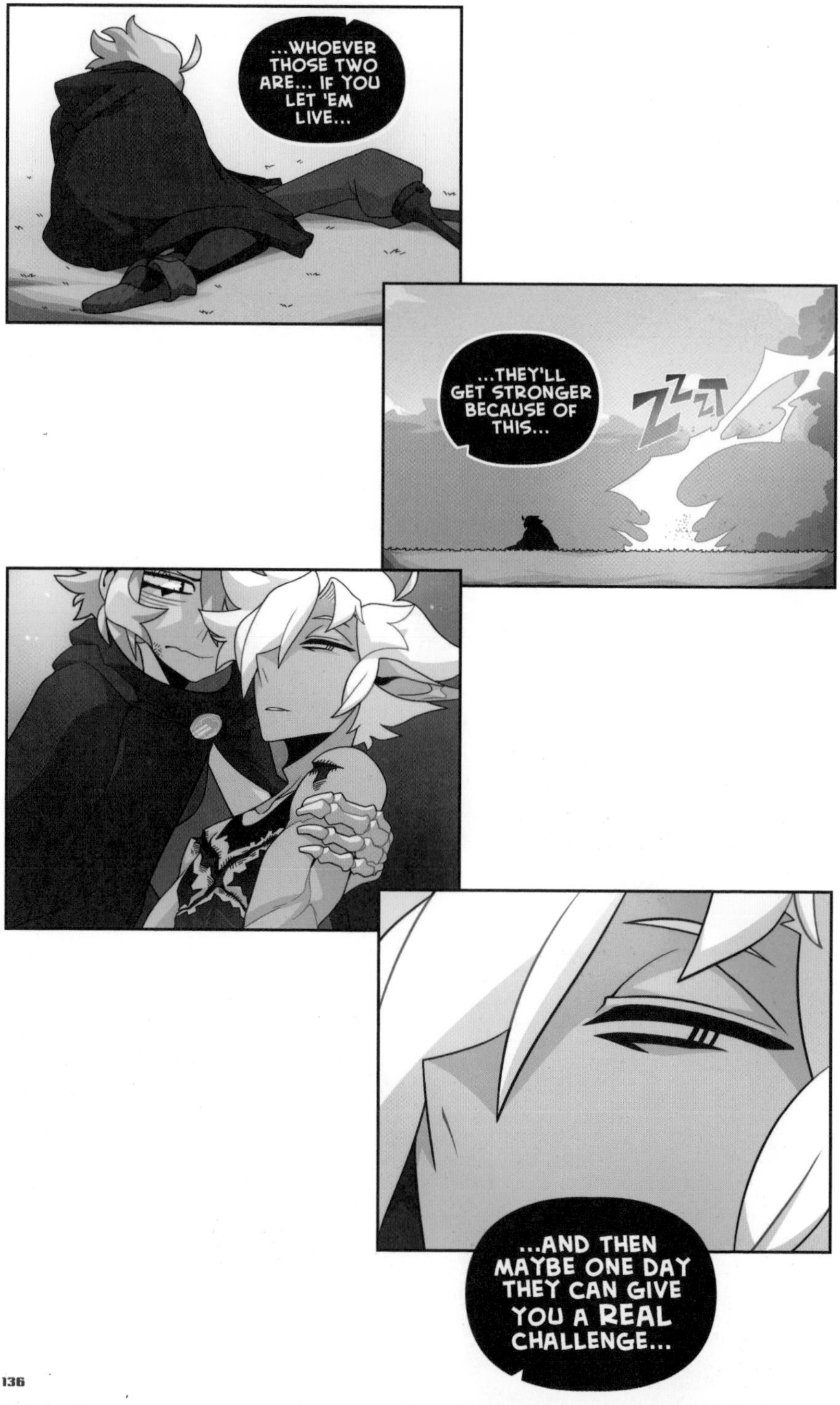
...WHOEVER THOSE TWO ARE... IF YOU LET 'EM LIVE...
...THEY'LL GET STRONGER BECAUSE OF THIS...
ZZZT
...AND THEN MAYBE ONE DAY THEY CAN GIVE YOU A REAL CHALLENGE...

## Chapter 9
# THE RESOLVE

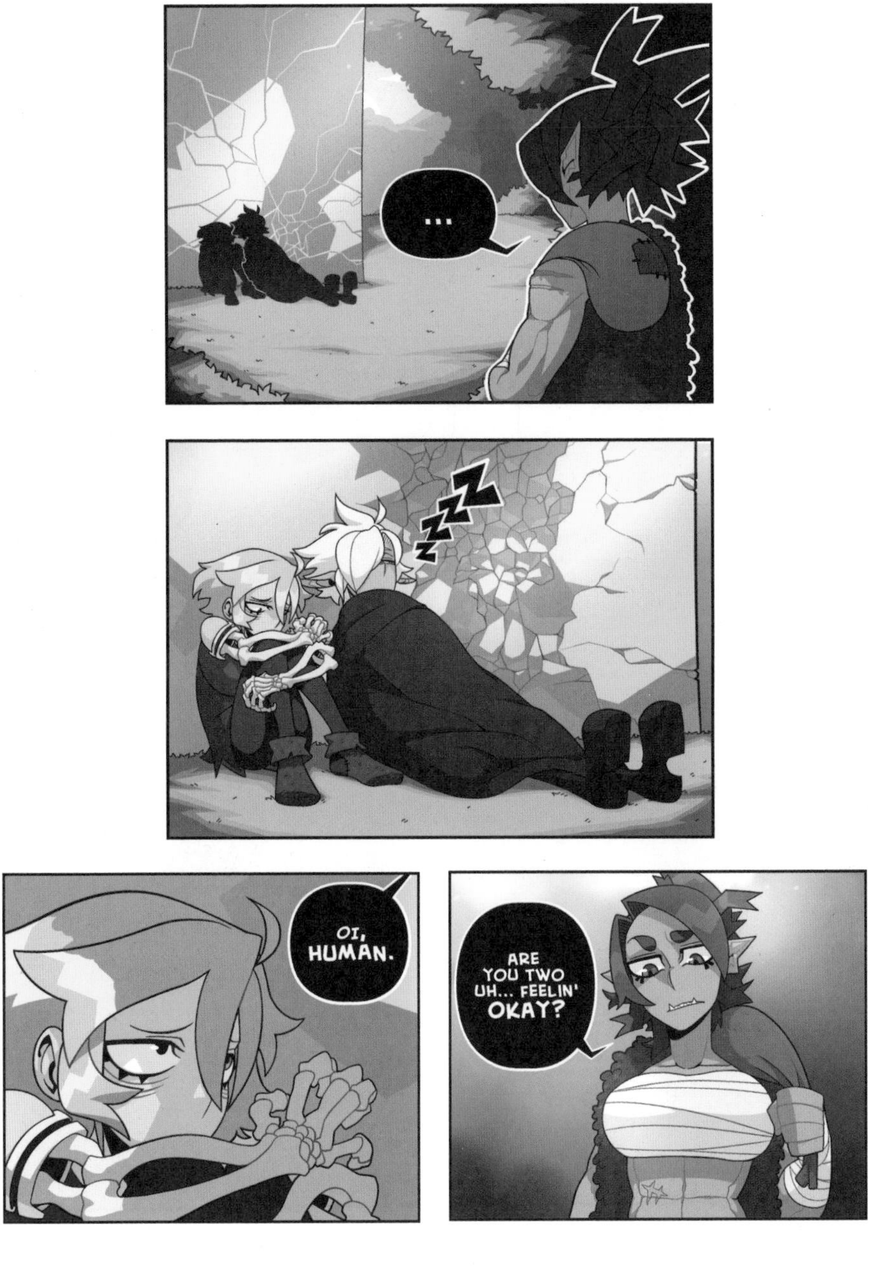
...
OI, HUMAN.
ARE YOU TWO UH... FEELIN' OKAY?

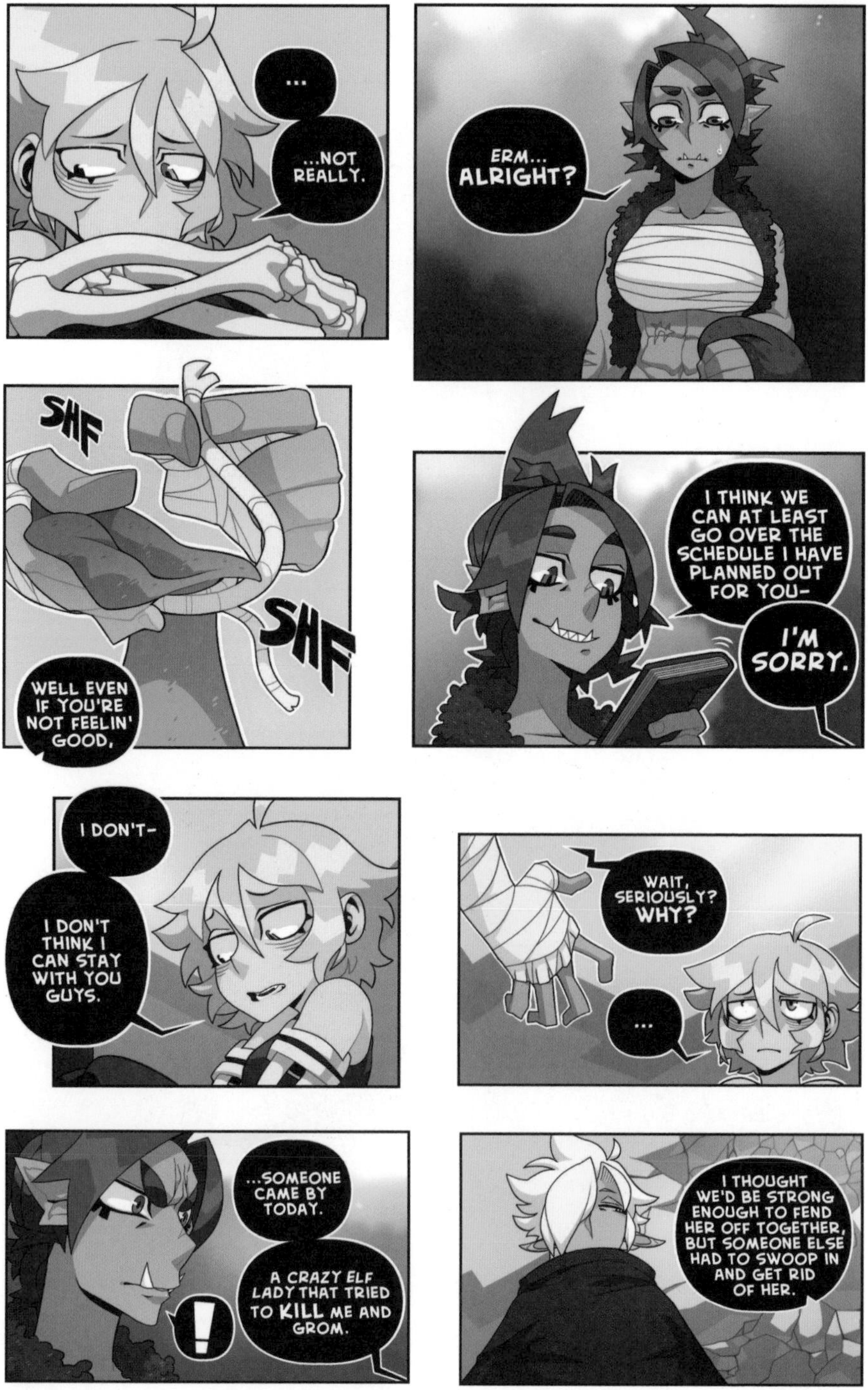
...
...NOT REALLY.
ERM... ALRIGHT?
SHF
SHF
WELL EVEN IF YOU'RE NOT FEELIN' GOOD,
I THINK WE CAN AT LEAST GO OVER THE SCHEDULE I HAVE PLANNED OUT FOR YOU-
I'M SORRY.
I DON'T-
I DON'T THINK I CAN STAY WITH YOU GUYS.
WAIT, SERIOUSLY? WHY?
...
...SOMEONE CAME BY TODAY.
!
A CRAZY ELF LADY THAT TRIED TO KILL ME AND GROM.
I THOUGHT WE'D BE STRONG ENOUGH TO FEND HER OFF TOGETHER, BUT SOMEONE ELSE HAD TO SWOOP IN AND GET RID OF HER.

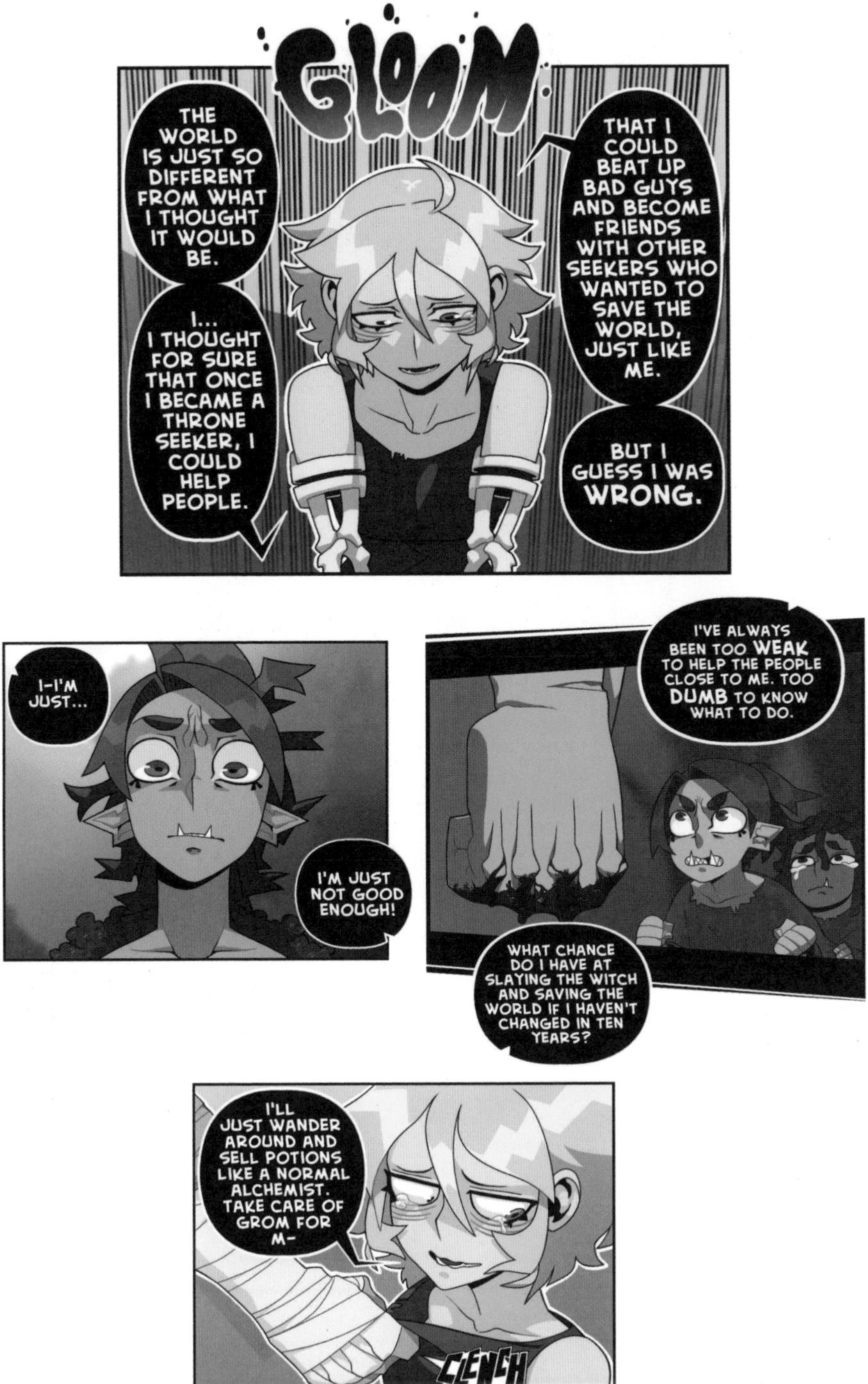
GLOOM
THE WORLD IS JUST SO DIFFERENT FROM WHAT I THOUGHT IT WOULD BE.
I... I THOUGHT FOR SURE THAT ONCE I BECAME A THRONE SEEKER, I COULD HELP PEOPLE.
THAT I COULD BEAT UP BAD GUYS AND BECOME FRIENDS WITH OTHER SEEKERS WHO WANTED TO SAVE THE WORLD, JUST LIKE ME.
BUT I GUESS I WAS WRONG.
I-I'M JUST...
I'M JUST NOT GOOD ENOUGH!
I'VE ALWAYS BEEN TOO WEAK TO HELP THE PEOPLE CLOSE TO ME. TOO DUMB TO KNOW WHAT TO DO.
WHAT CHANCE DO I HAVE AT SLAYING THE WITCH AND SAVING THE WORLD IF I HAVEN'T CHANGED IN TEN YEARS?
I'LL JUST WANDER AROUND AND SELL POTIONS LIKE A NORMAL ALCHEMIST. TAKE CARE OF GROM FOR M-
CLENCH

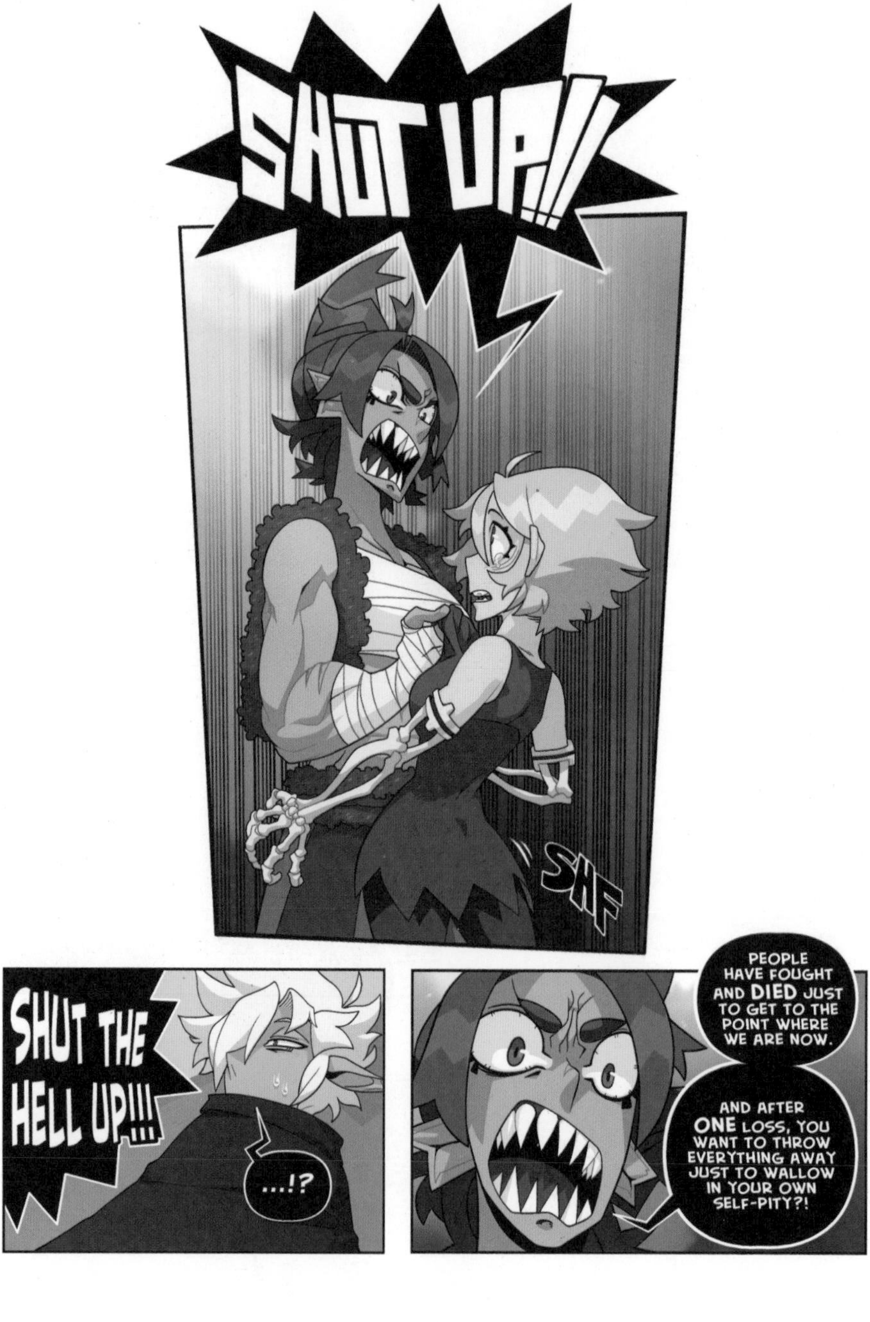
SHUT UP!!!
SHF
SHUT THE HELL UP!!!
...!?
PEOPLE HAVE FOUGHT AND DIED JUST TO GET TO THE POINT WHERE WE ARE NOW.
AND AFTER ONE LOSS, YOU WANT TO THROW EVERYTHING AWAY JUST TO WALLOW IN YOUR OWN SELF-PITY?!

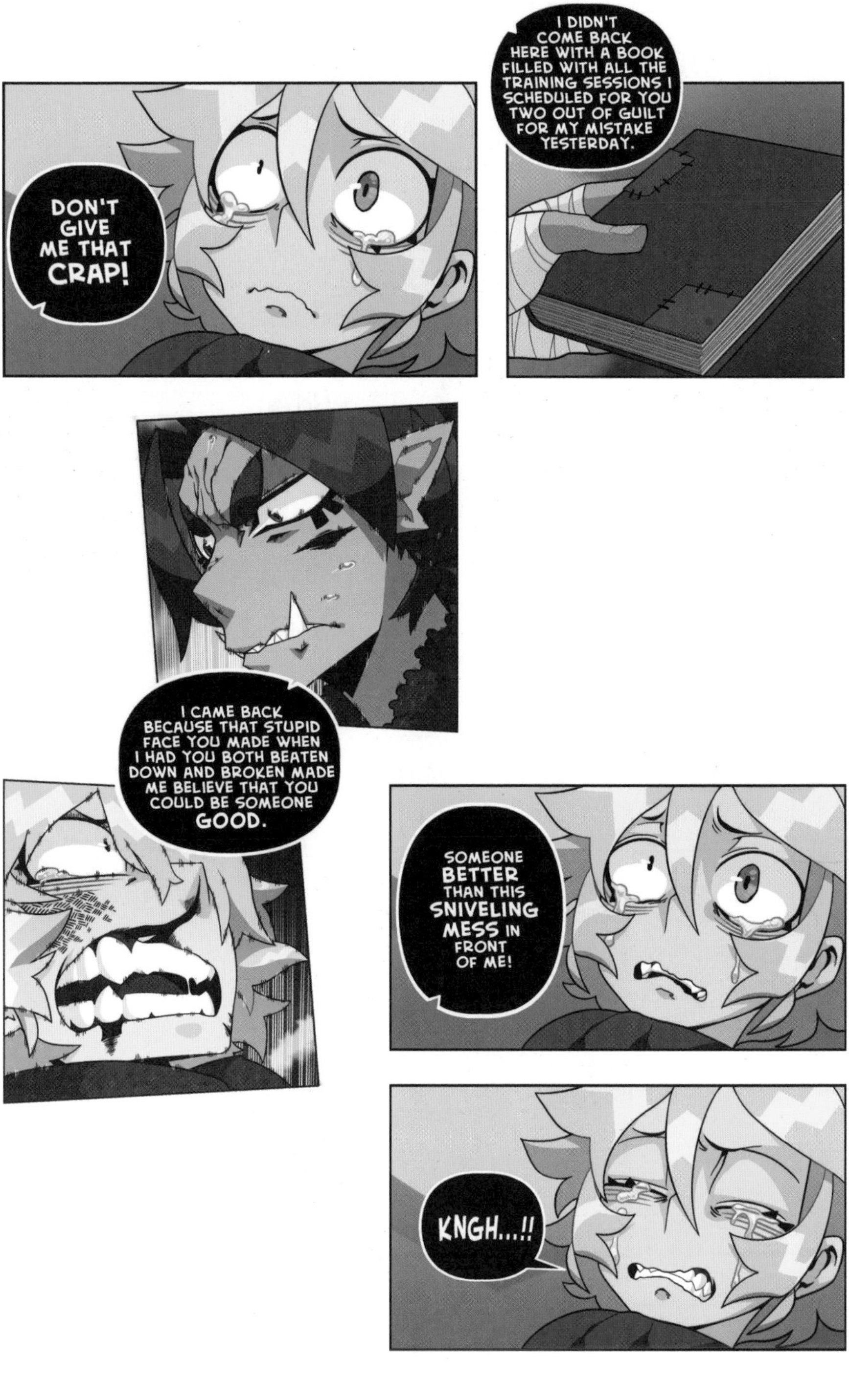
DON'T GIVE ME THAT CRAP!
I DIDN'T COME BACK HERE WITH A BOOK FILLED WITH ALL THE TRAINING SESSIONS I SCHEDULED FOR YOU TWO OUT OF GUILT FOR MY MISTAKE YESTERDAY.
I CAME BACK BECAUSE THAT STUPID FACE YOU MADE WHEN I HAD YOU BOTH BEATEN DOWN AND BROKEN MADE ME BELIEVE THAT YOU COULD BE SOMEONE GOOD.
SOMEONE BETTER THAN THIS SNIVELING MESS IN FRONT OF ME!
KNGH...!!

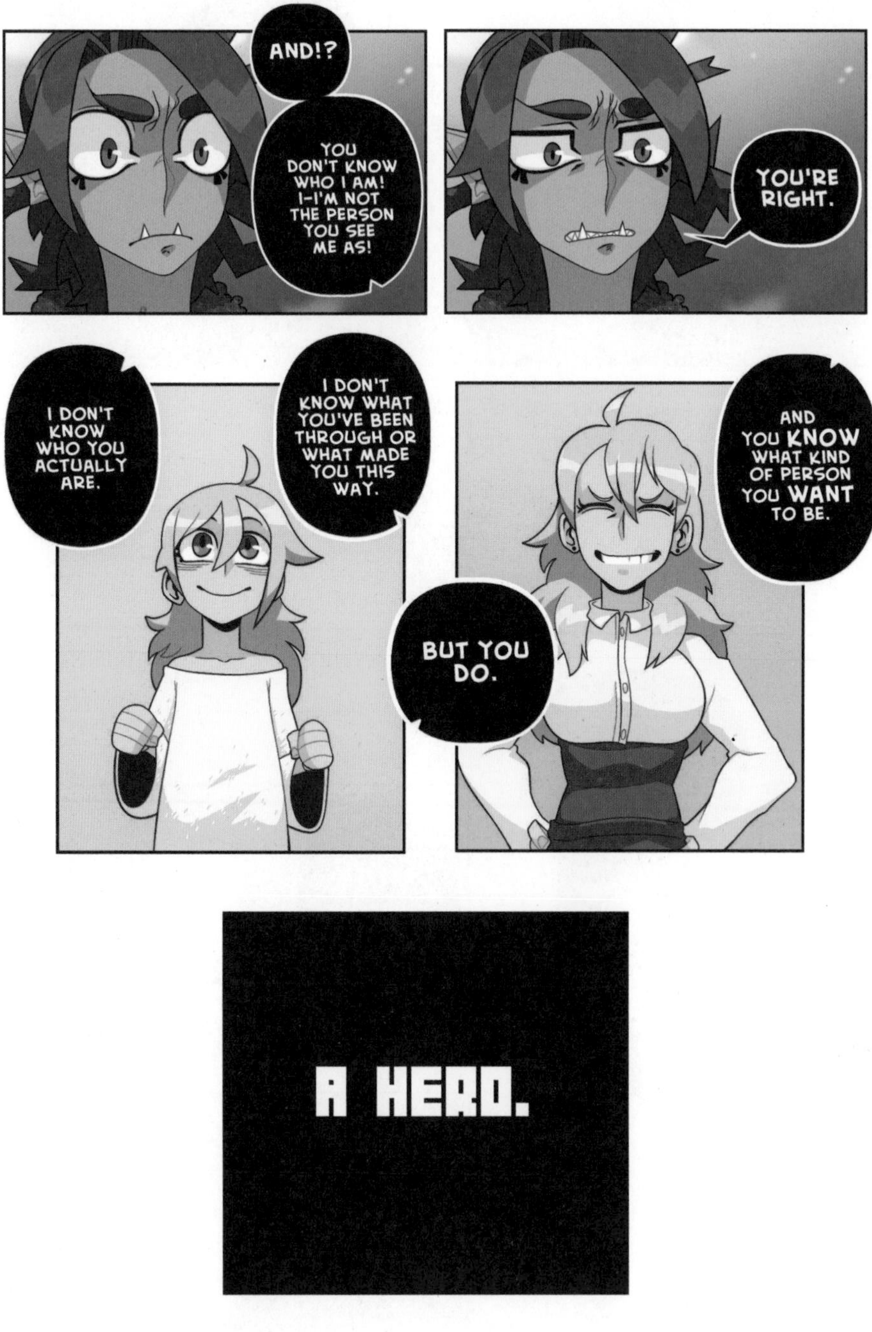
AND!?
YOU DON'T KNOW WHO I AM! I-I'M NOT THE PERSON YOU SEE ME AS!
YOU'RE RIGHT.
I DON'T KNOW WHO YOU ACTUALLY ARE.
I DON'T KNOW WHAT YOU'VE BEEN THROUGH OR WHAT MADE YOU THIS WAY.
BUT YOU DO.
AND YOU KNOW WHAT KIND OF PERSON YOU WANT TO BE.
A HERO.

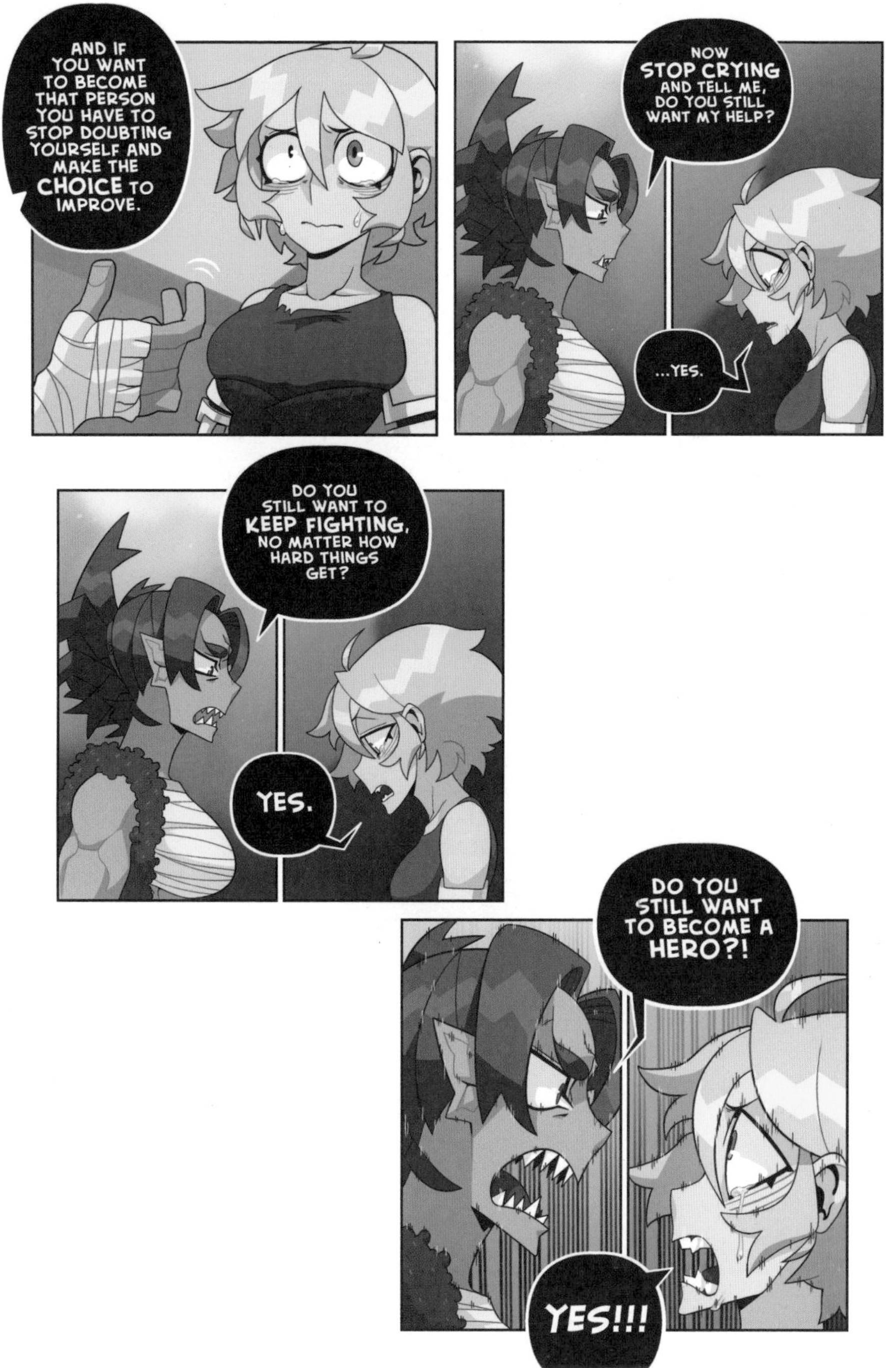
AND IF YOU WANT TO BECOME THAT PERSON YOU HAVE TO STOP DOUBTING YOURSELF AND MAKE THE CHOICE TO IMPROVE.
NOW STOP CRYING AND TELL ME, DO YOU STILL WANT MY HELP?
...YES.
DO YOU STILL WANT TO KEEP FIGHTING, NO MATTER HOW HARD THINGS GET?
YES.
DO YOU STILL WANT TO BECOME A HERO?!
YES!!!

GOOD.

THEN
LET'S START
TRAINING.

...I WANT TO SAY
SOMETHING,
BUT I REALLY
SHOULDN'T RUIN
THE MOMENT.

## Chapter 10
# THE WARM UP

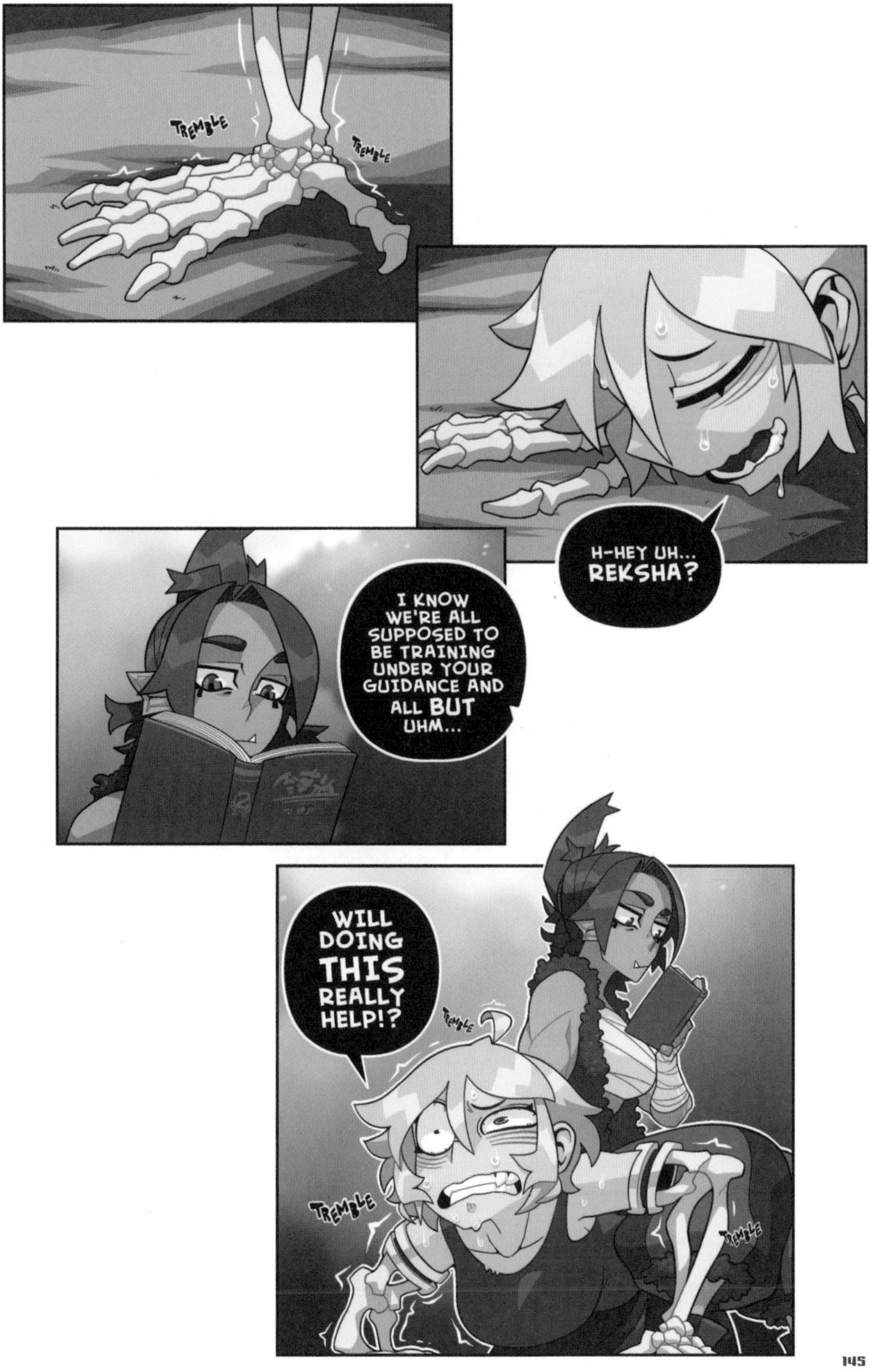
TREMBLE
TREMBLE
H-HEY UH... REKSHA?
I KNOW WE'RE ALL SUPPOSED TO BE TRAINING UNDER YOUR GUIDANCE AND ALL BUT UHM...
WILL DOING THIS REALLY HELP!?
TREMBLE
TREMBLE
TREMBLE

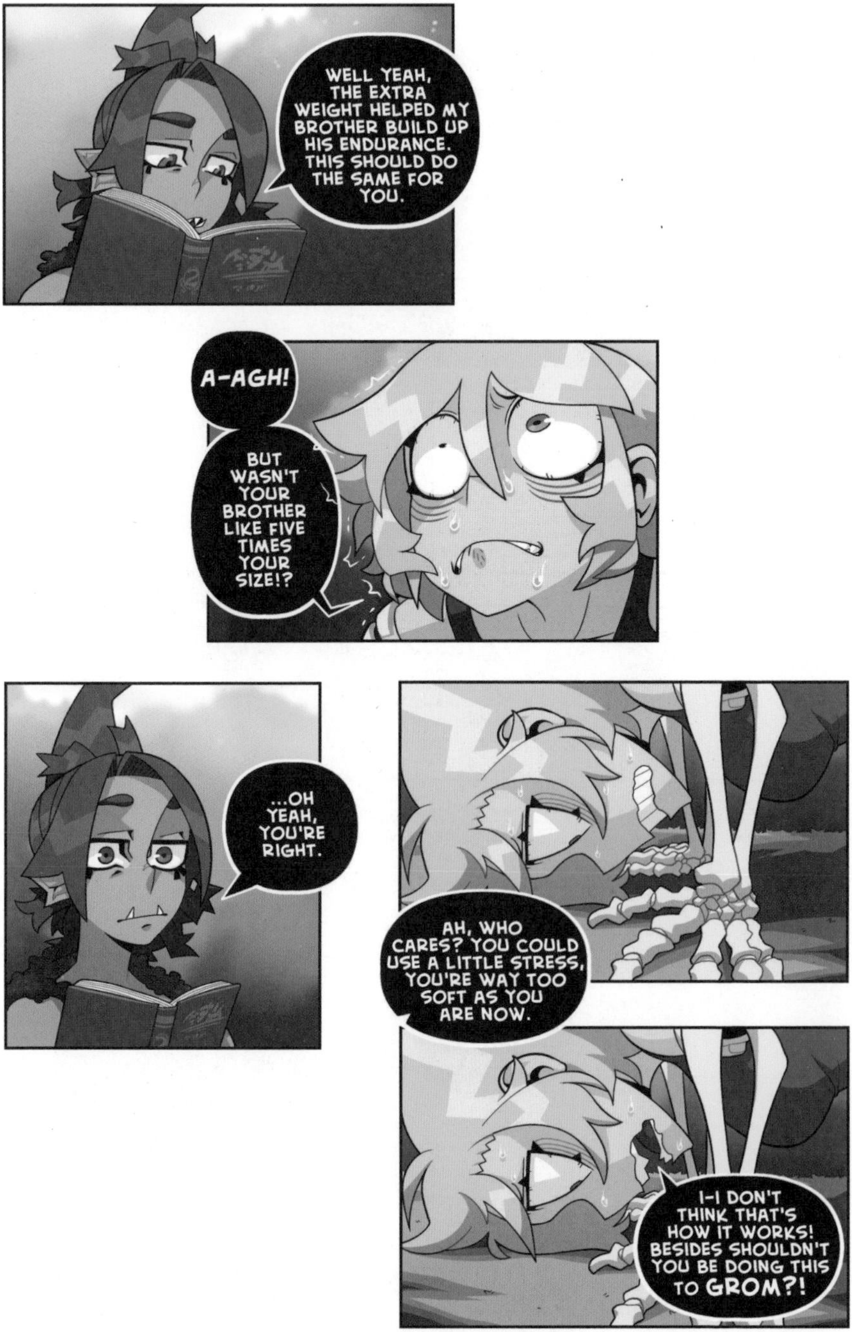
WELL YEAH, THE EXTRA WEIGHT HELPED MY BROTHER BUILD UP HIS ENDURANCE. THIS SHOULD DO THE SAME FOR YOU.
A-AGH!
BUT WASN'T YOUR BROTHER LIKE FIVE TIMES YOUR SIZE!?
...OH YEAH, YOU'RE RIGHT.
AH, WHO CARES? YOU COULD USE A LITTLE STRESS, YOU'RE WAY TOO SOFT AS YOU ARE NOW.
I-I DON'T THINK THAT'S HOW IT WORKS! BESIDES SHOULDN'T YOU BE DOING THIS TO GROM?!

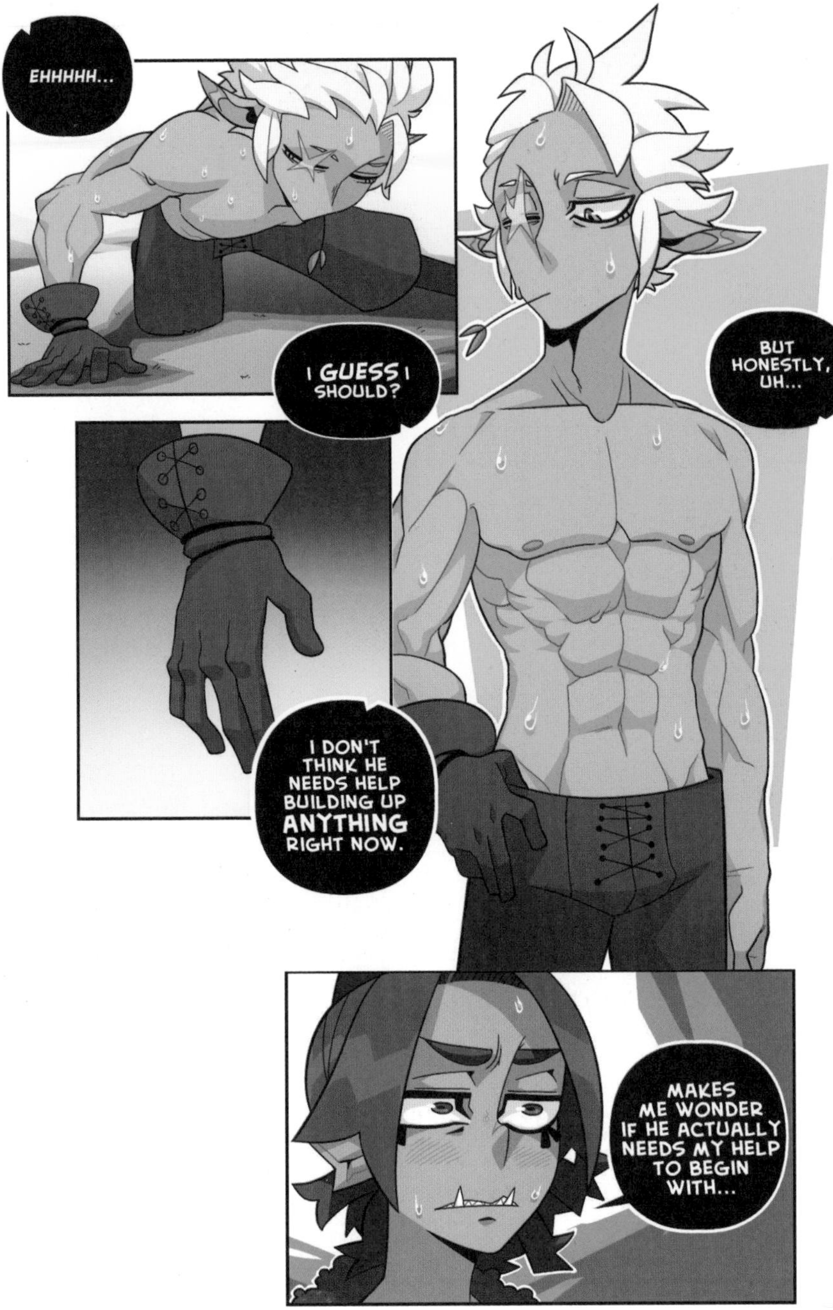
EHHHHH...
I GUESS I SHOULD?
BUT HONESTLY, UH...
I DON'T THINK HE NEEDS HELP BUILDING UP ANYTHING RIGHT NOW.
MAKES ME WONDER IF HE ACTUALLY NEEDS MY HELP TO BEGIN WITH...

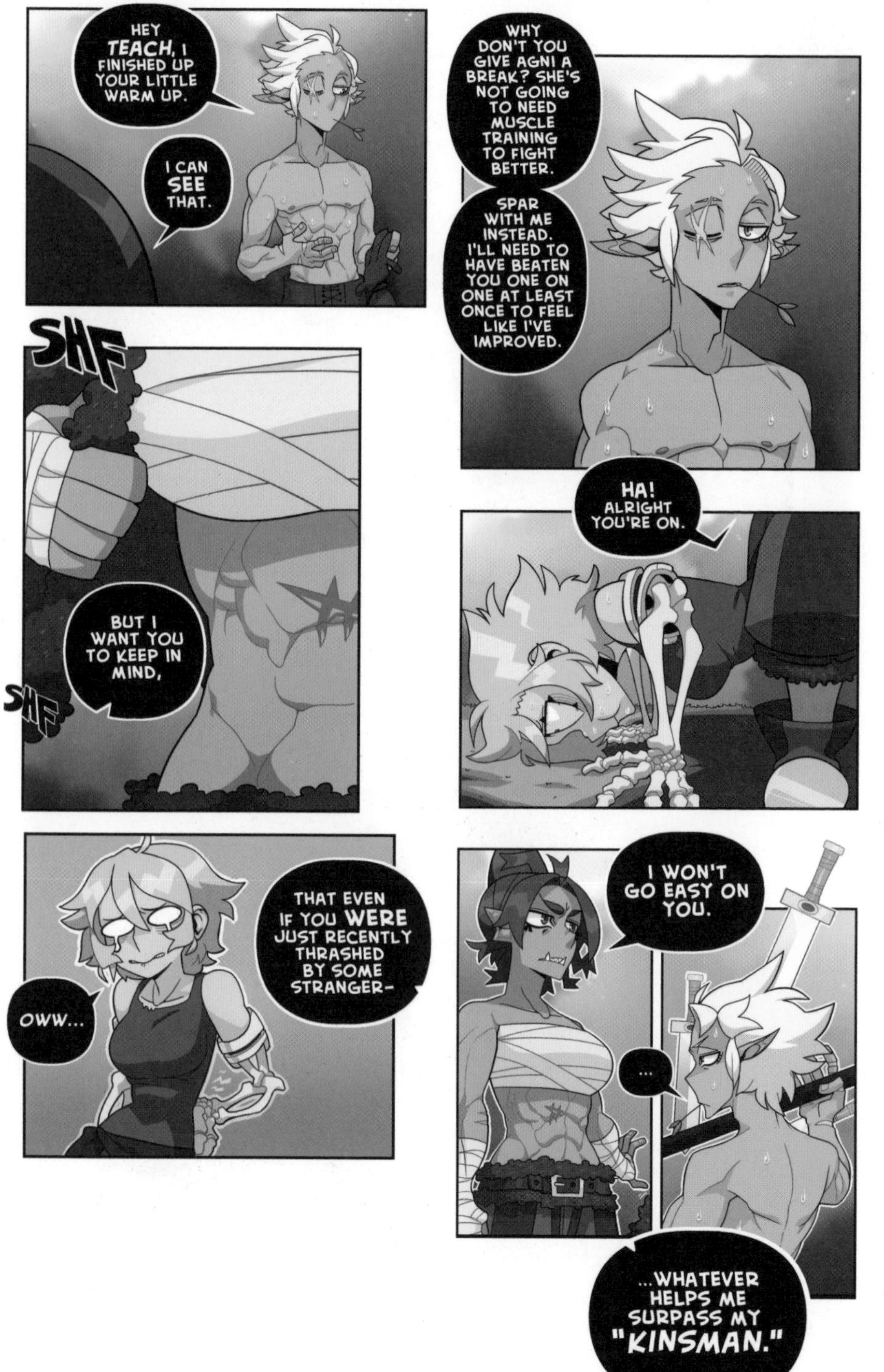
HEY TEACH, I FINISHED UP YOUR LITTLE WARM UP.
I CAN SEE THAT.
WHY DON'T YOU GIVE AGNI A BREAK? SHE'S NOT GOING TO NEED MUSCLE TRAINING TO FIGHT BETTER.
SPAR WITH ME INSTEAD. I'LL NEED TO HAVE BEATEN YOU ONE ON ONE AT LEAST ONCE TO FEEL LIKE I'VE IMPROVED.
SHF
BUT I WANT YOU TO KEEP IN MIND,
SHF
HA! ALRIGHT YOU'RE ON.
OWW...
THAT EVEN IF YOU WERE JUST RECENTLY THRASHED BY SOME STRANGER-
I WON'T GO EASY ON YOU.
...
...WHATEVER HELPS ME SURPASS MY "KINSMAN."

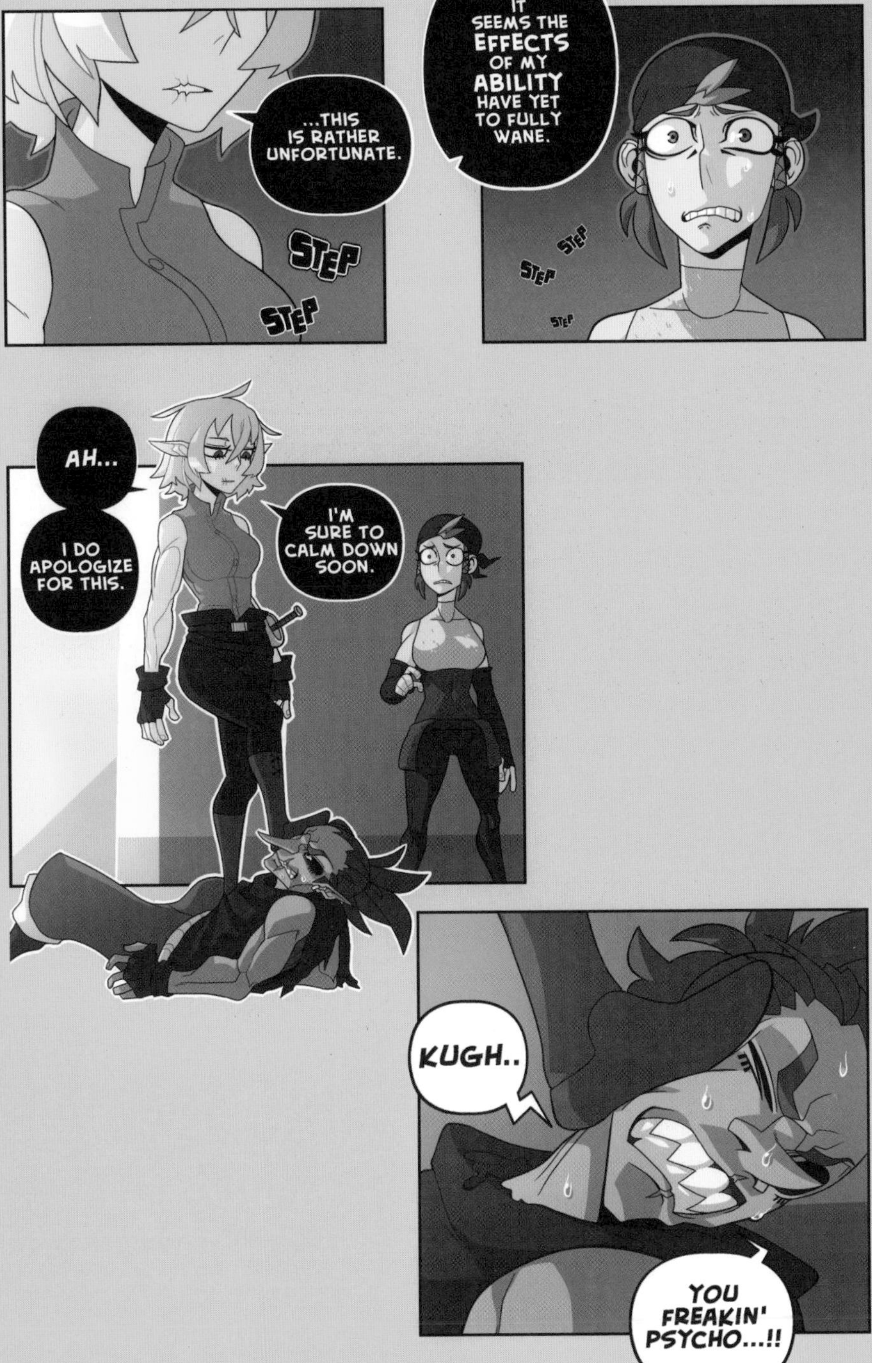

...THIS IS RATHER UNFORTUNATE.
STEP
STEP
IT SEEMS THE EFFECTS OF MY ABILITY HAVE YET TO FULLY WANE.
STEP
STEP
STEP
AH...
I DO APOLOGIZE FOR THIS.
I'M SURE TO CALM DOWN SOON.
KUGH..
YOU FREAKIN' PSYCHO...!!

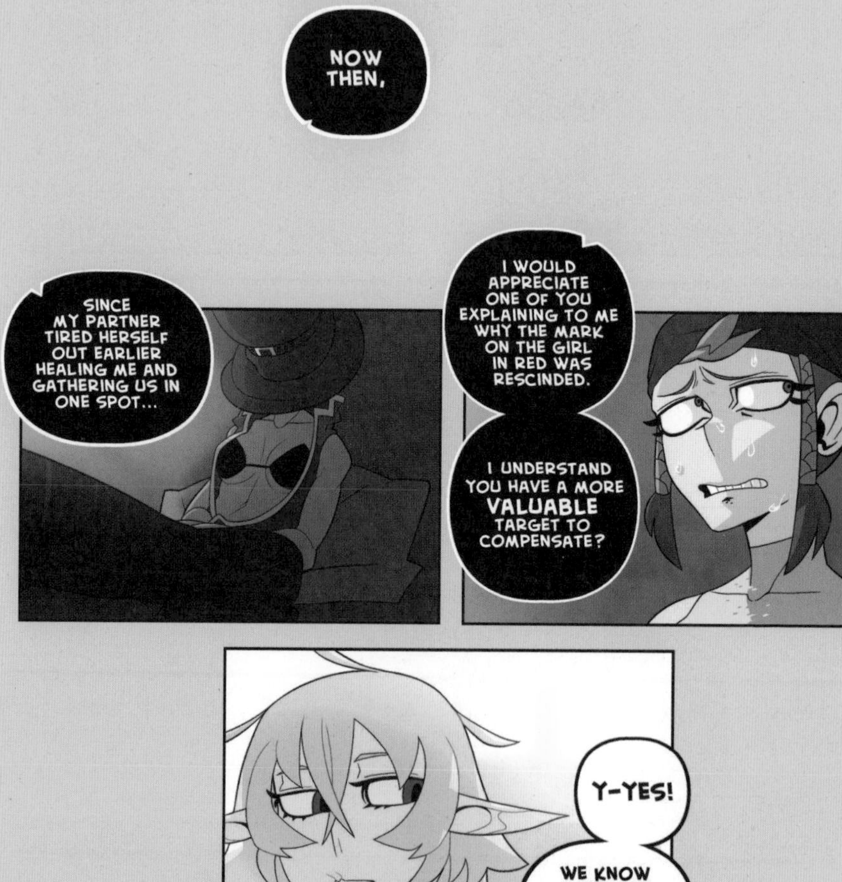
NOW THEN,
SINCE MY PARTNER TIRED HERSELF OUT EARLIER HEALING ME AND GATHERING US IN ONE SPOT...
I WOULD APPRECIATE ONE OF YOU EXPLAINING TO ME WHY THE MARK ON THE GIRL IN RED WAS RESCINDED.
I UNDERSTAND YOU HAVE A MORE VALUABLE TARGET TO COMPENSATE?
Y-YES!
WE KNOW A THRONE SEEKE- A HUNTER'S TIME IS VERY IMPORTANT.

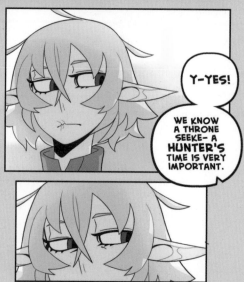

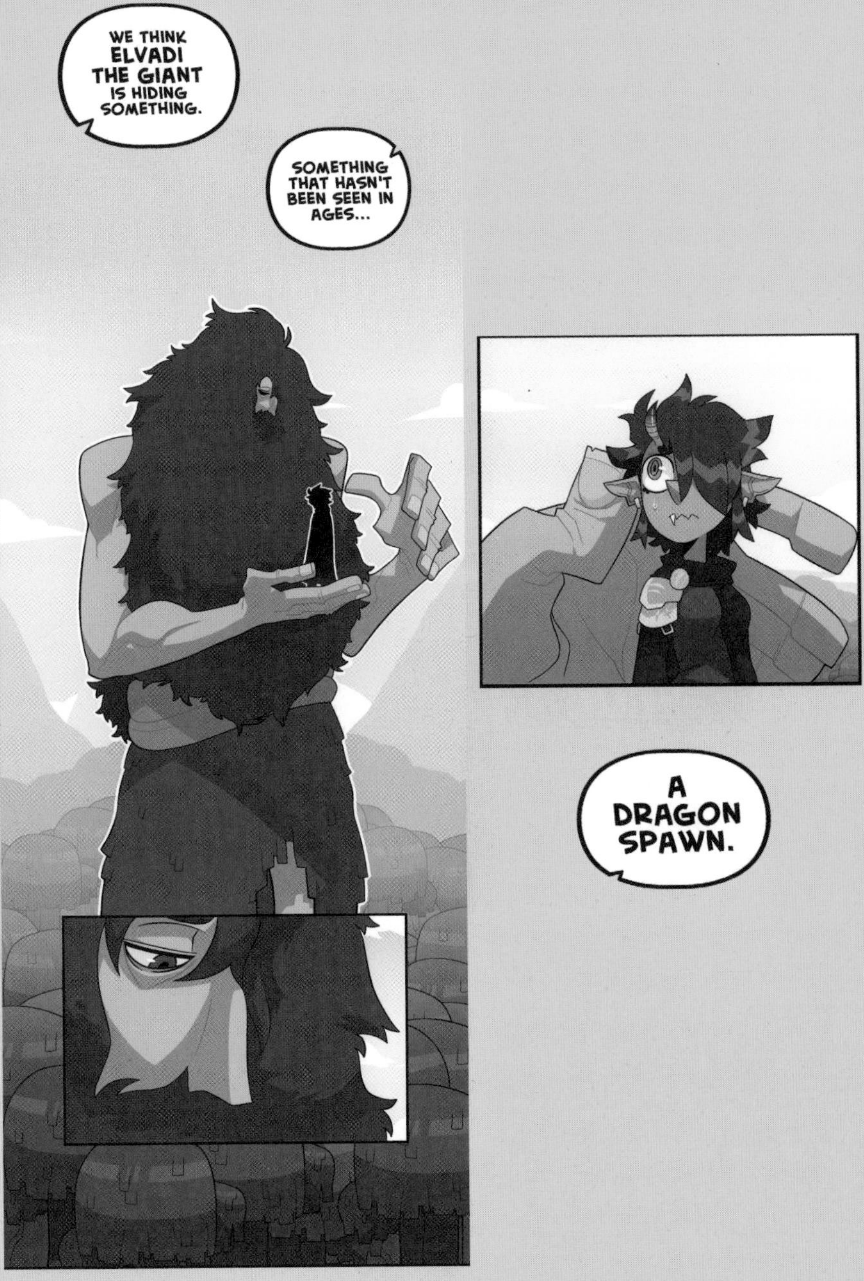
WE THINK ELVADI THE GIANT IS HIDING SOMETHING.
SOMETHING THAT HASN'T BEEN SEEN IN AGES...
A DRAGON SPAWN.

## Chapter 11
# THE HAND

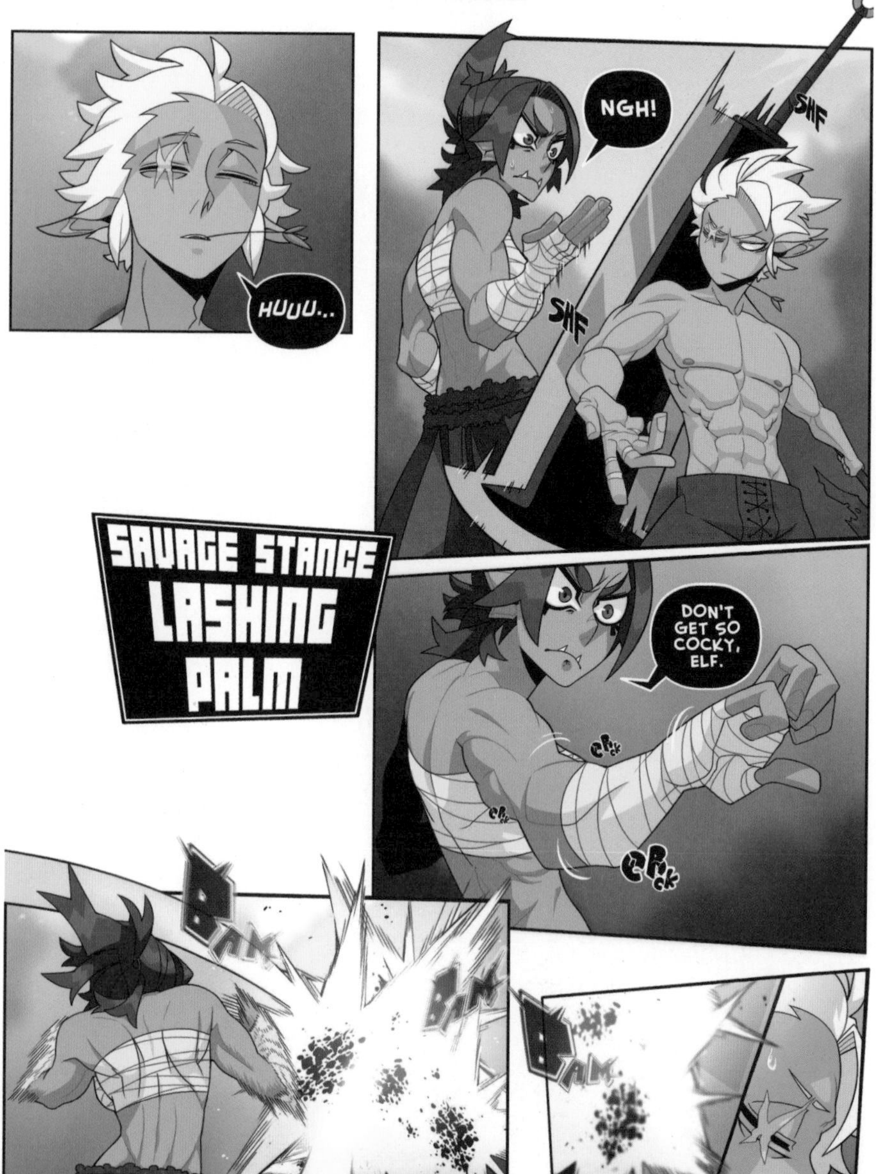
HUUU...
NGH!
SHF
SHF
SAVAGE STANCE
LASHING PALM
DON'T GET SO COCKY, ELF.
BAM
BAM
BAM
BAM

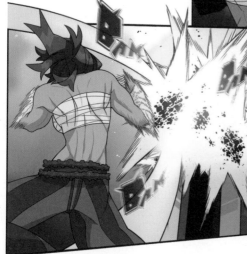

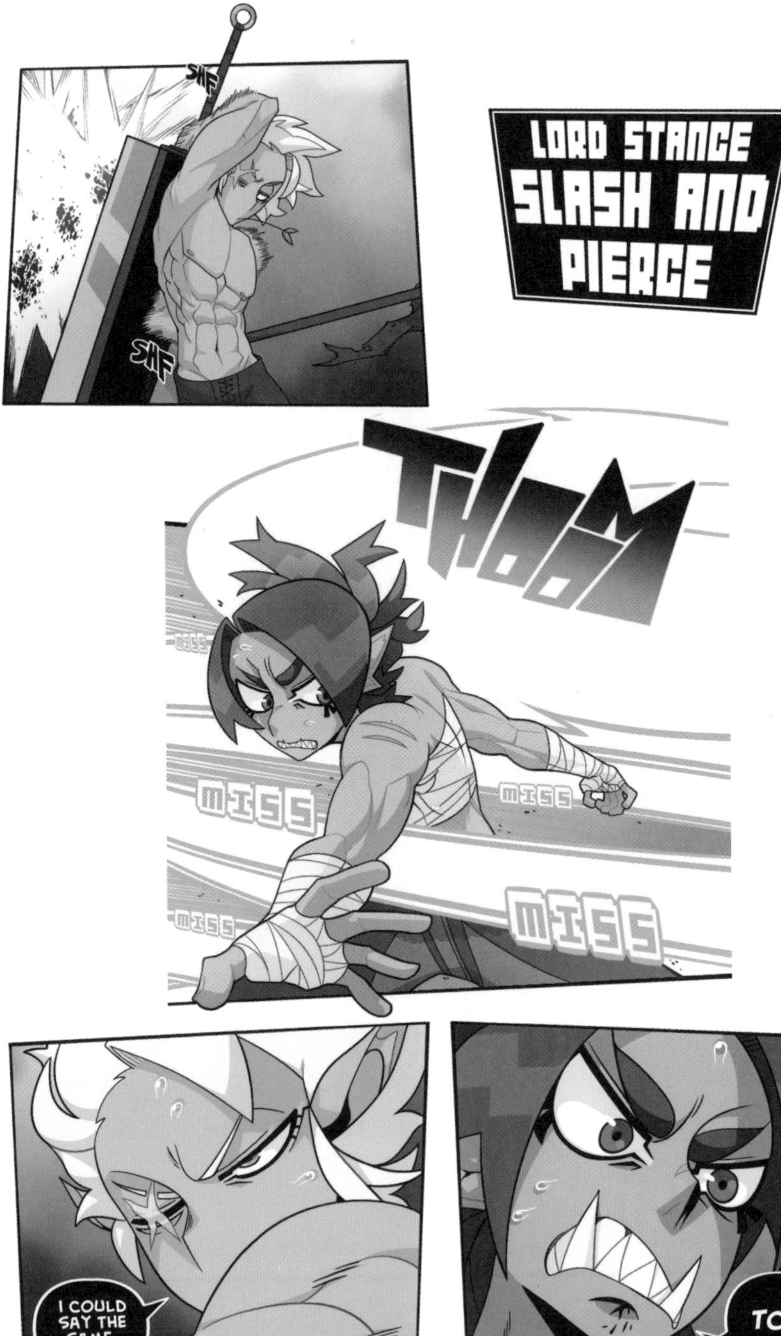
SHF
SHF
LORD STANCE
SLASH AND PIERCE
THOOM
MISS
MISS
MISS
MISS
MISS
I COULD SAY THE SAME, ORC.
TCH!!

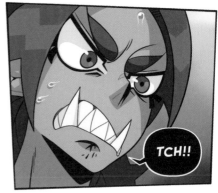

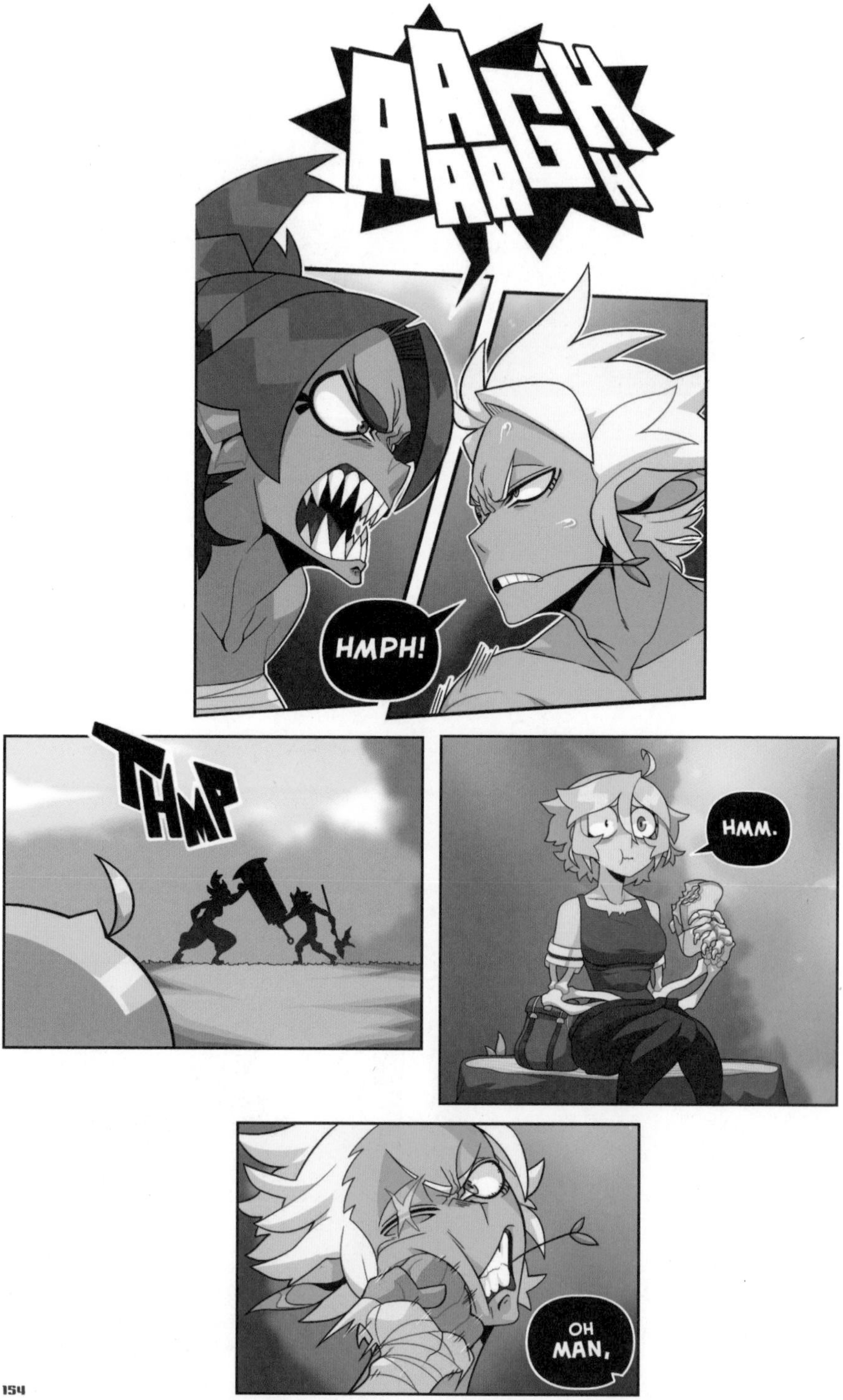
AAAAGHH
HMPH!
THMP
HMM.
OH MAN,

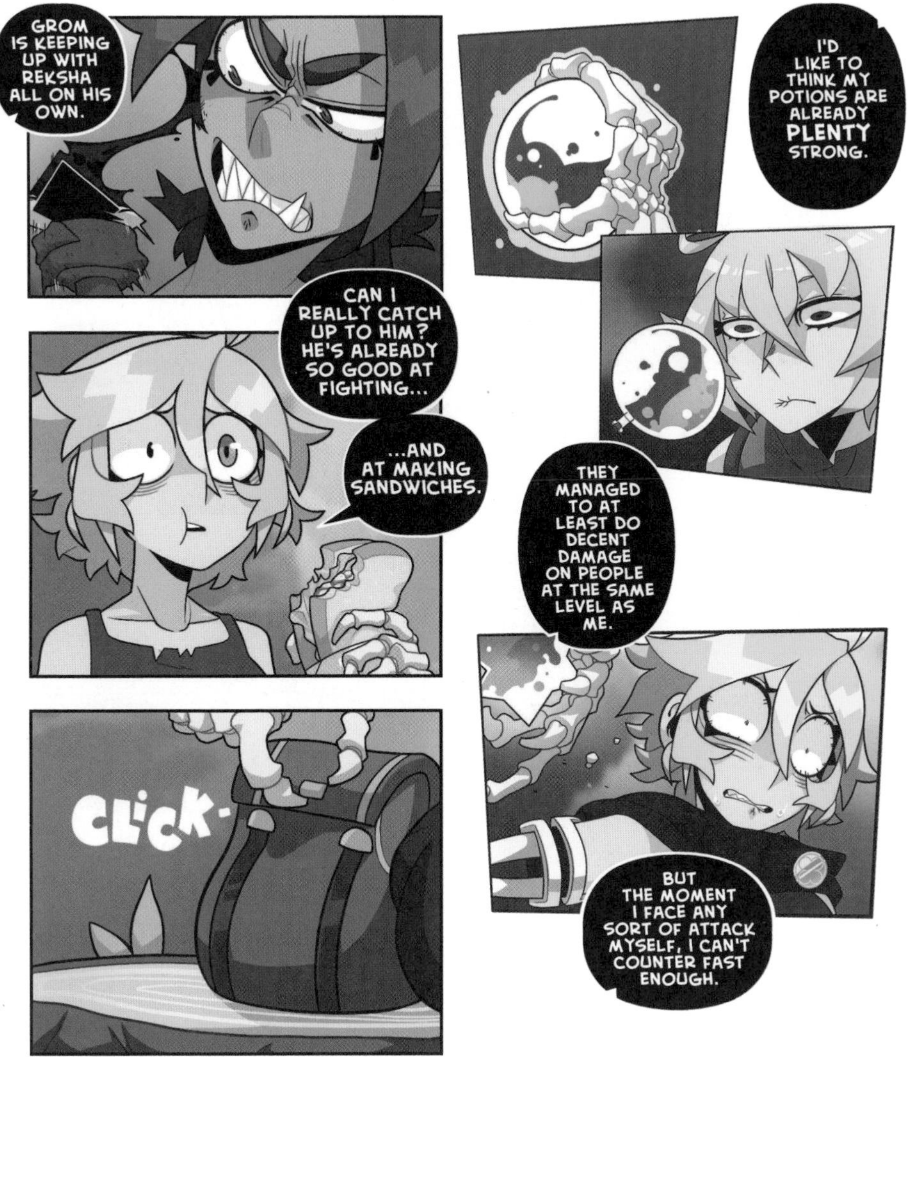
GROM IS KEEPING UP WITH REKSHA ALL ON HIS OWN.
CAN I REALLY CATCH UP TO HIM? HE'S ALREADY SO GOOD AT FIGHTING...
...AND AT MAKING SANDWICHES.
CLICK-
I'D LIKE TO THINK MY POTIONS ARE ALREADY **PLENTY** STRONG.
THEY MANAGED TO AT LEAST DO DECENT DAMAGE ON PEOPLE AT THE SAME LEVEL AS ME.
BUT THE MOMENT I FACE ANY SORT OF ATTACK MYSELF, I CAN'T COUNTER FAST ENOUGH.

...

IF I WANT A SHOT AT WINNING ONE OF THE TOURNAMENTS,

I'LL HAVE TO BE AS STRONG AS THAT LIGHTNING LADY FROM BEFORE.

SHOULD I TRY AND MAKE MORE OFFENSIVE POTIONS? MAYBE SOMETHING THAT WILL TAKE EFFECT QUICKLY...

EITHER WAY, IT WON'T BE ENOUGH TO JUST WAVE A POTION AROUND AND SAY *BREAK—*

!

CRSH

EUGH, WHAT THE HECK?

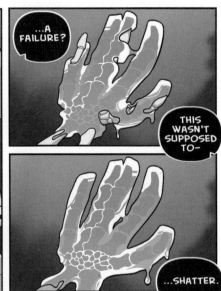

...A FAILURE?

THIS WASN'T SUPPOSED TO—

...SHATTER.

AH.

THAT'S IT!!!

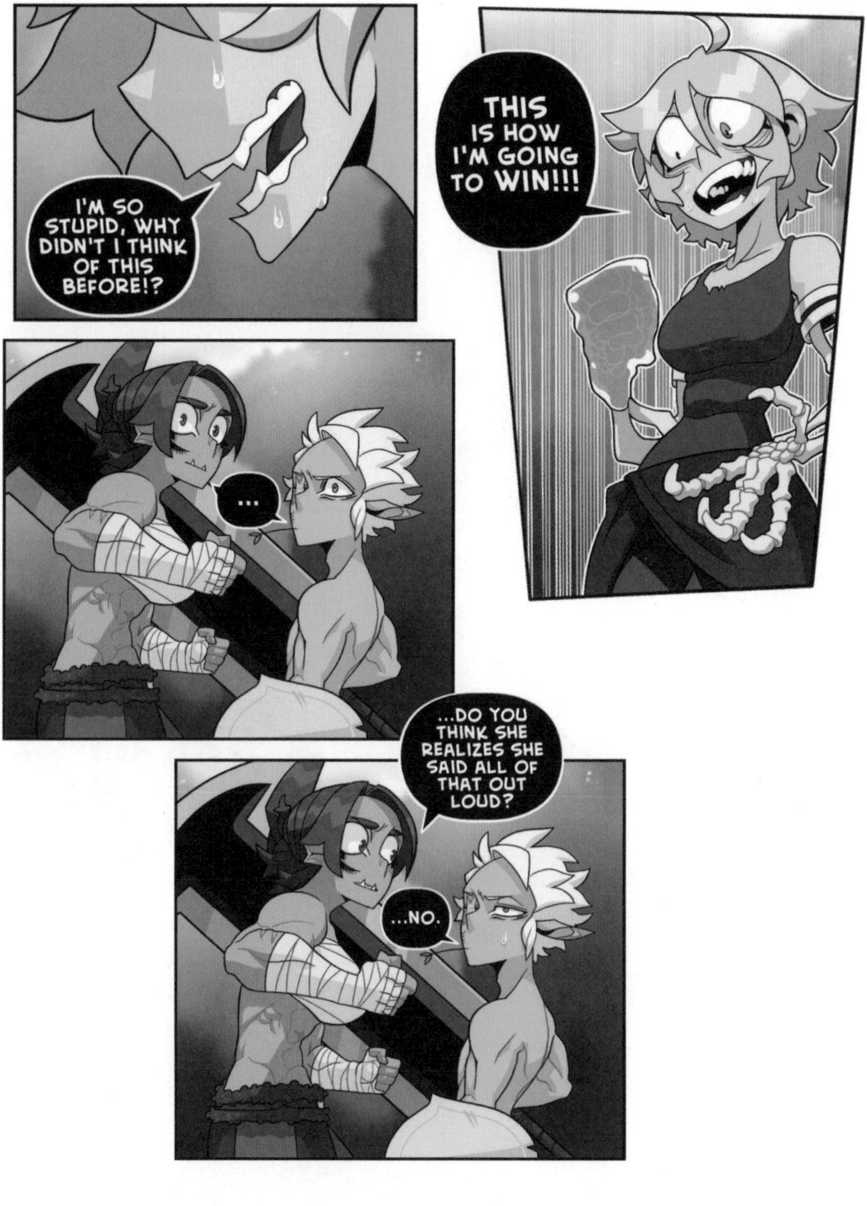
I'M SO STUPID, WHY DIDN'T I THINK OF THIS BEFORE!?
THIS IS HOW I'M GOING TO WIN!!!
...
...DO YOU THINK SHE REALIZES SHE SAID ALL OF THAT OUT LOUD?
...NO.

# Chapter 12
## THE BIG FOUR

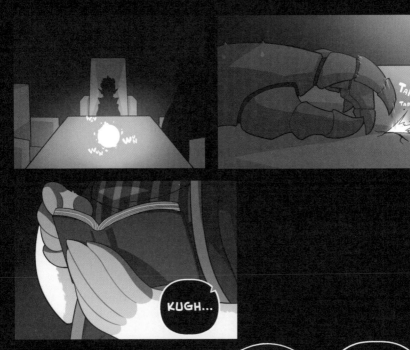

KUGH...

JUST HOW LONG ARE THEY GOING TO KEEP US WAITING...!?

HUNTER'S GUILD LEADER: HINOKA TSUJIN

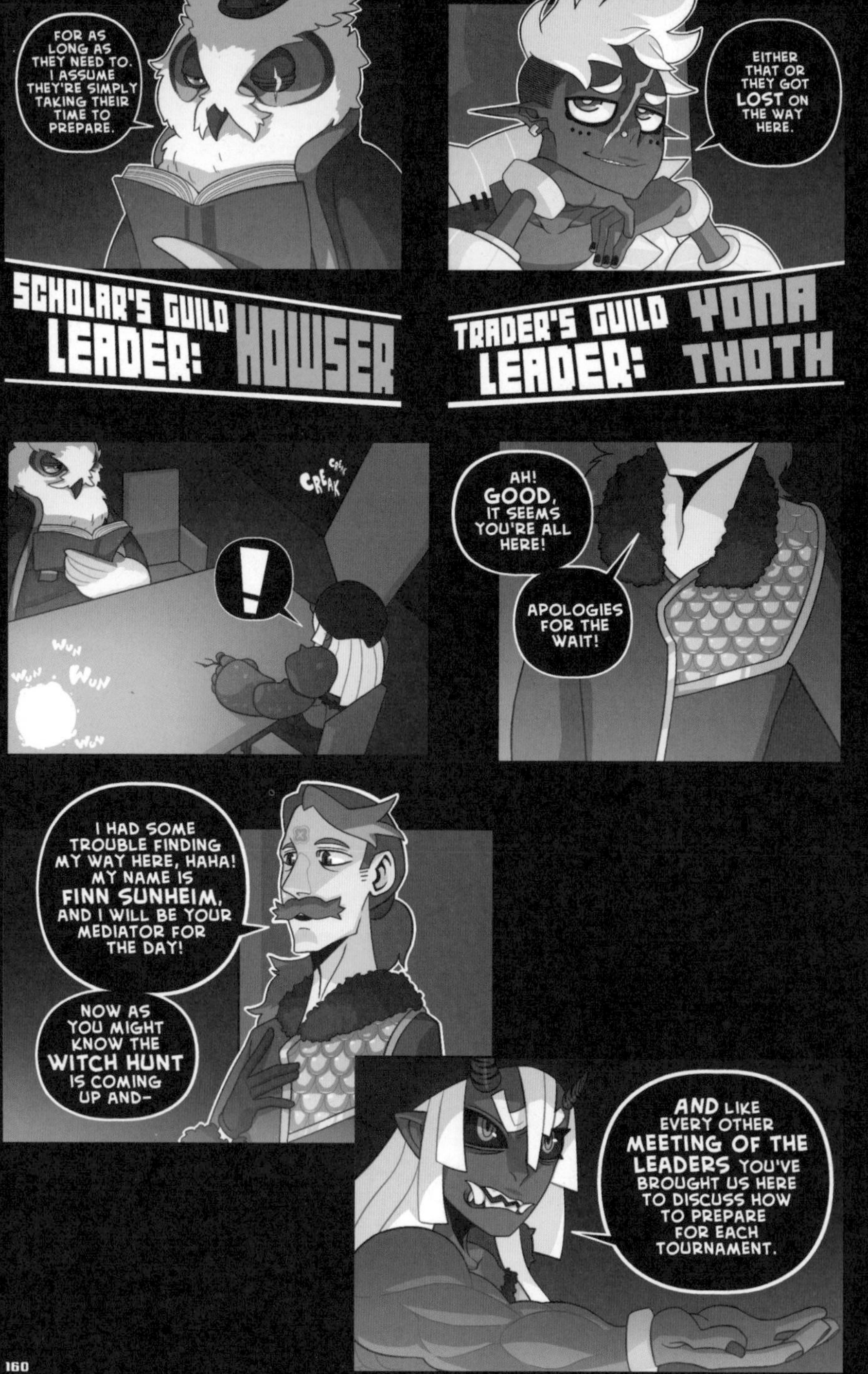
FOR AS LONG AS THEY NEED TO. I ASSUME THEY'RE SIMPLY TAKING THEIR TIME TO PREPARE.
EITHER THAT OR THEY GOT LOST ON THE WAY HERE.
SCHOLAR'S GUILD LEADER: HOWSER
TRADER'S GUILD LEADER: YONA THOTH
CREAK
CREAK
!
WUN
WUN
WUN
WUN
AH! GOOD, IT SEEMS YOU'RE ALL HERE!
APOLOGIES FOR THE WAIT!
I HAD SOME TROUBLE FINDING MY WAY HERE, HAHA! MY NAME IS FINN SUNHEIM, AND I WILL BE YOUR MEDIATOR FOR THE DAY!
NOW AS YOU MIGHT KNOW THE WITCH HUNT IS COMING UP AND-
AND LIKE EVERY OTHER MEETING OF THE LEADERS YOU'VE BROUGHT US HERE TO DISCUSS HOW TO PREPARE FOR EACH TOURNAMENT.

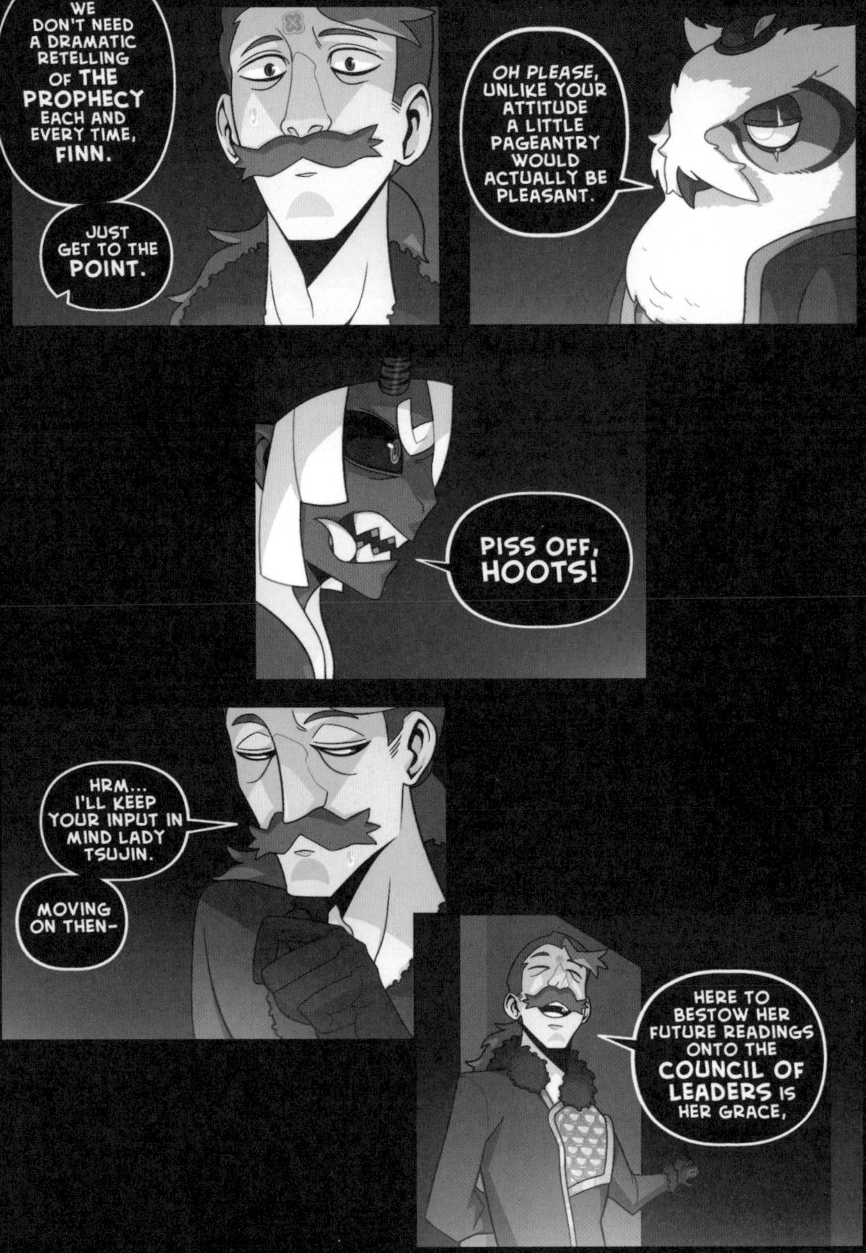
WE DON'T NEED A DRAMATIC RETELLING OF THE PROPHECY EACH AND EVERY TIME, FINN.
JUST GET TO THE POINT.
OH PLEASE, UNLIKE YOUR ATTITUDE A LITTLE PAGEANTRY WOULD ACTUALLY BE PLEASANT.
PISS OFF, HOOTS!
HRM... I'LL KEEP YOUR INPUT IN MIND LADY TSUJIN.
MOVING ON THEN-
HERE TO BESTOW HER FUTURE READINGS ONTO THE COUNCIL OF LEADERS IS HER GRACE,

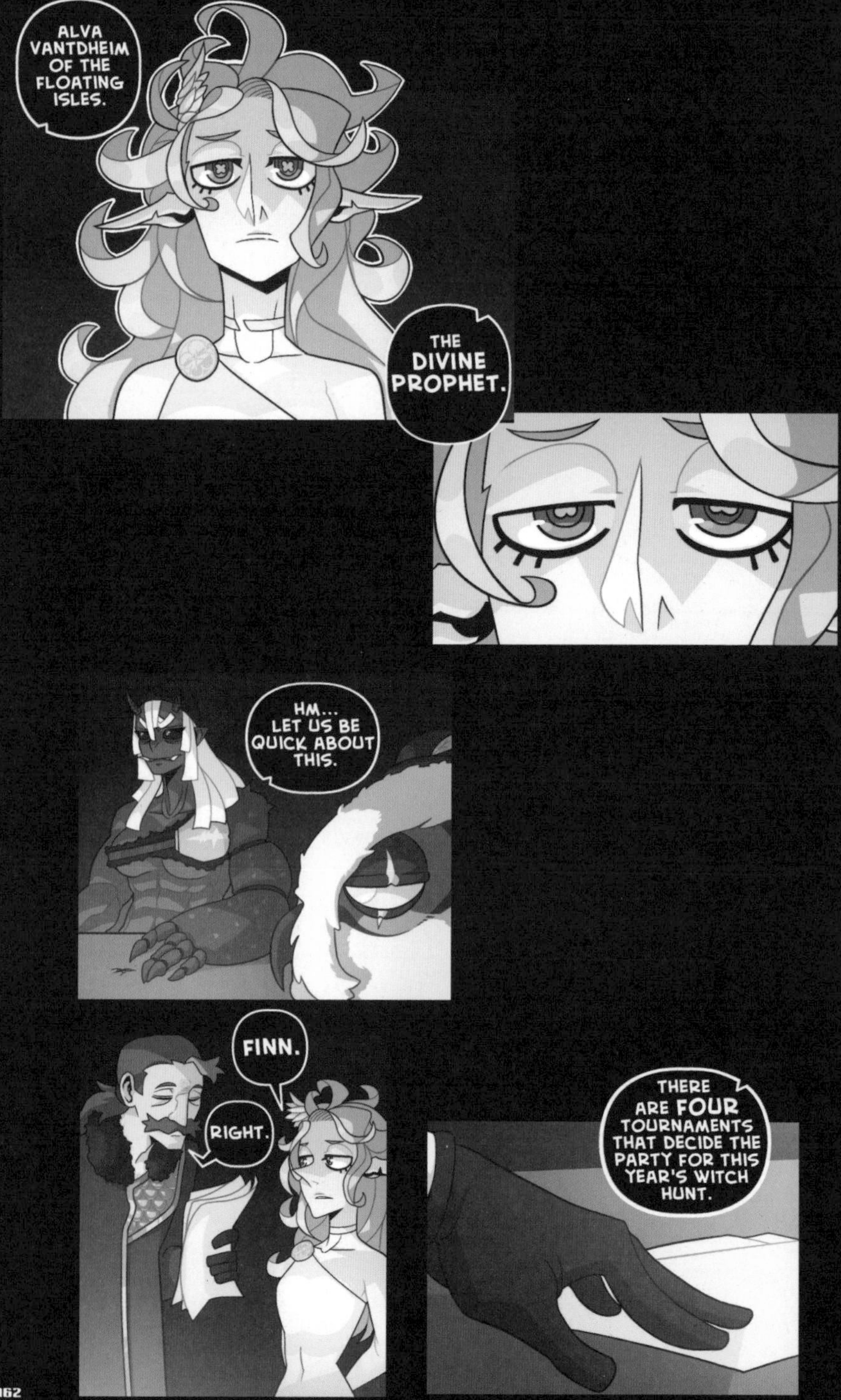
ALVA VANTDHEIM OF THE FLOATING ISLES.
THE DIVINE PROPHET.
HM... LET US BE QUICK ABOUT THIS.
FINN.
RIGHT.
THERE ARE FOUR TOURNAMENTS THAT DECIDE THE PARTY FOR THIS YEAR'S WITCH HUNT.

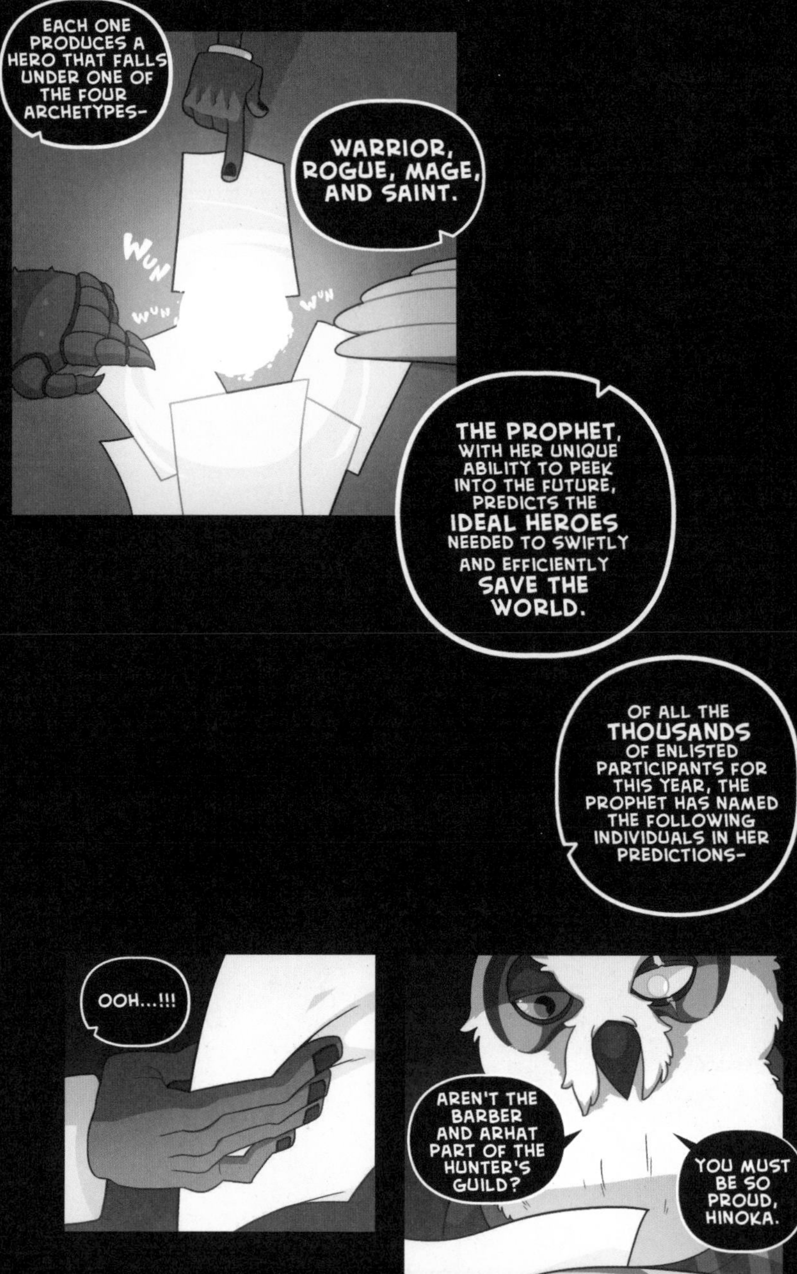
EACH ONE PRODUCES A HERO THAT FALLS UNDER ONE OF THE FOUR ARCHETYPES-
WARRIOR, ROGUE, MAGE, AND SAINT.
WUN
WUN
WUN
THE PROPHET, WITH HER UNIQUE ABILITY TO PEEK INTO THE FUTURE, PREDICTS THE IDEAL HEROES NEEDED TO SWIFTLY AND EFFICIENTLY SAVE THE WORLD.
OF ALL THE THOUSANDS OF ENLISTED PARTICIPANTS FOR THIS YEAR, THE PROPHET HAS NAMED THE FOLLOWING INDIVIDUALS IN HER PREDICTIONS-
OOH...!!!
AREN'T THE BARBER AND ARHAT PART OF THE HUNTER'S GUILD?
YOU MUST BE SO PROUD, HINOKA.

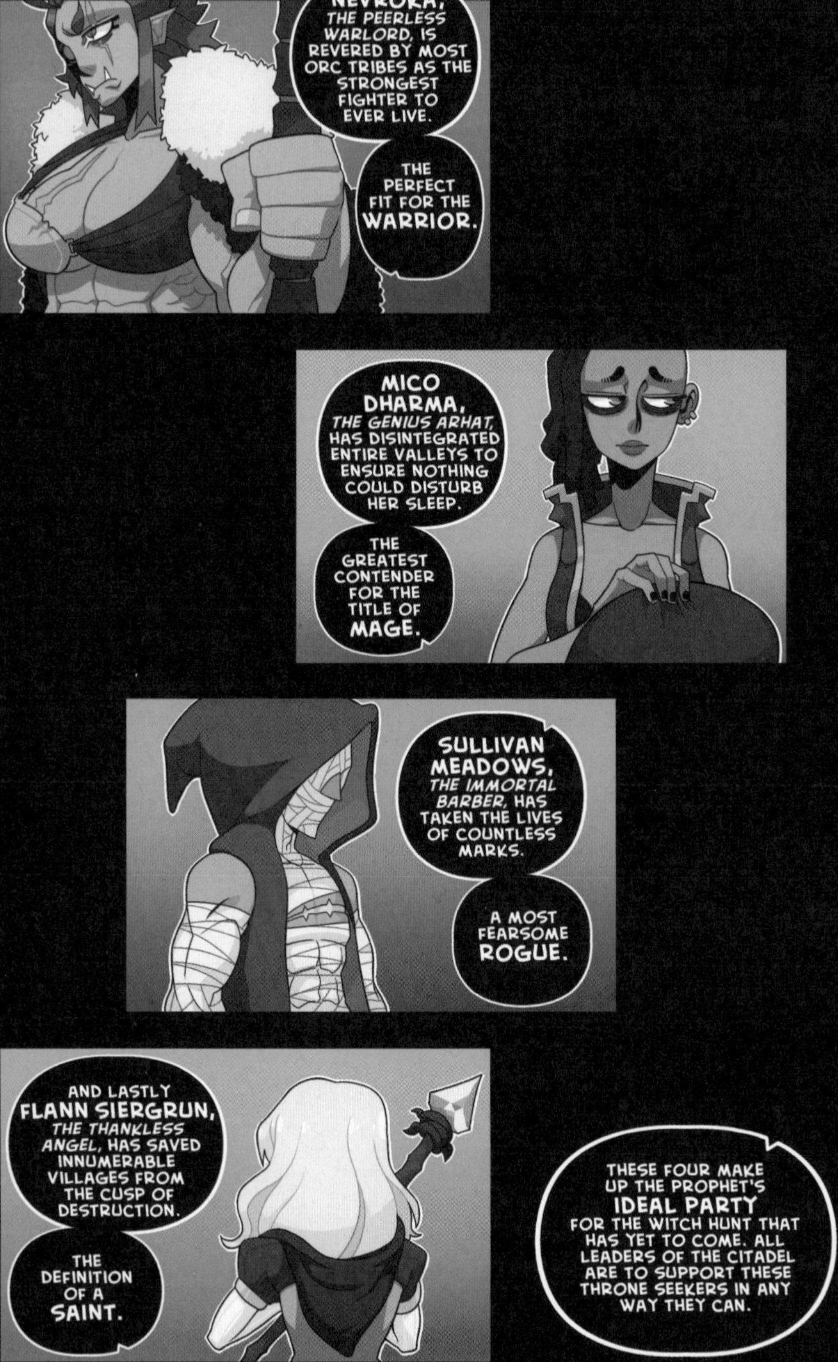
NEVROKA, THE PEERLESS WARLORD, IS REVERED BY MOST ORC TRIBES AS THE STRONGEST FIGHTER TO EVER LIVE.
THE PERFECT FIT FOR THE WARRIOR.
MICO DHARMA, THE GENIUS ARHAT, HAS DISINTEGRATED ENTIRE VALLEYS TO ENSURE NOTHING COULD DISTURB HER SLEEP.
THE GREATEST CONTENDER FOR THE TITLE OF MAGE.
SULLIVAN MEADOWS, THE IMMORTAL BARBER, HAS TAKEN THE LIVES OF COUNTLESS MARKS.
A MOST FEARSOME ROGUE.
AND LASTLY FLANN SIERGRUN, THE THANKLESS ANGEL, HAS SAVED INNUMERABLE VILLAGES FROM THE CUSP OF DESTRUCTION.
THE DEFINITION OF A SAINT.
THESE FOUR MAKE UP THE PROPHET'S IDEAL PARTY FOR THE WITCH HUNT THAT HAS YET TO COME. ALL LEADERS OF THE CITADEL ARE TO SUPPORT THESE THRONE SEEKERS IN ANY WAY THEY CAN.

HMPH.

IT'S ONLY NATURAL.

INTERESTING.

KEEP IN MIND MY PREDICTIONS ARE NOT ABSOLUTE.

NOT ALL THAT I HAVE NAMED ARE CERTAIN TO WIN.

IN THE PAST SOME THRONE SEEKERS HAVE DEFIED MY EXPECTATIONS AND FELL TO THOSE OF EVEN GREATER POTENTIAL.

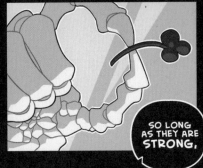

SO LONG AS THEY ARE STRONG,

ANY THRONE SEEKER CAN BECOME A HERO.

## Chapter 13
# THE POWER-UP

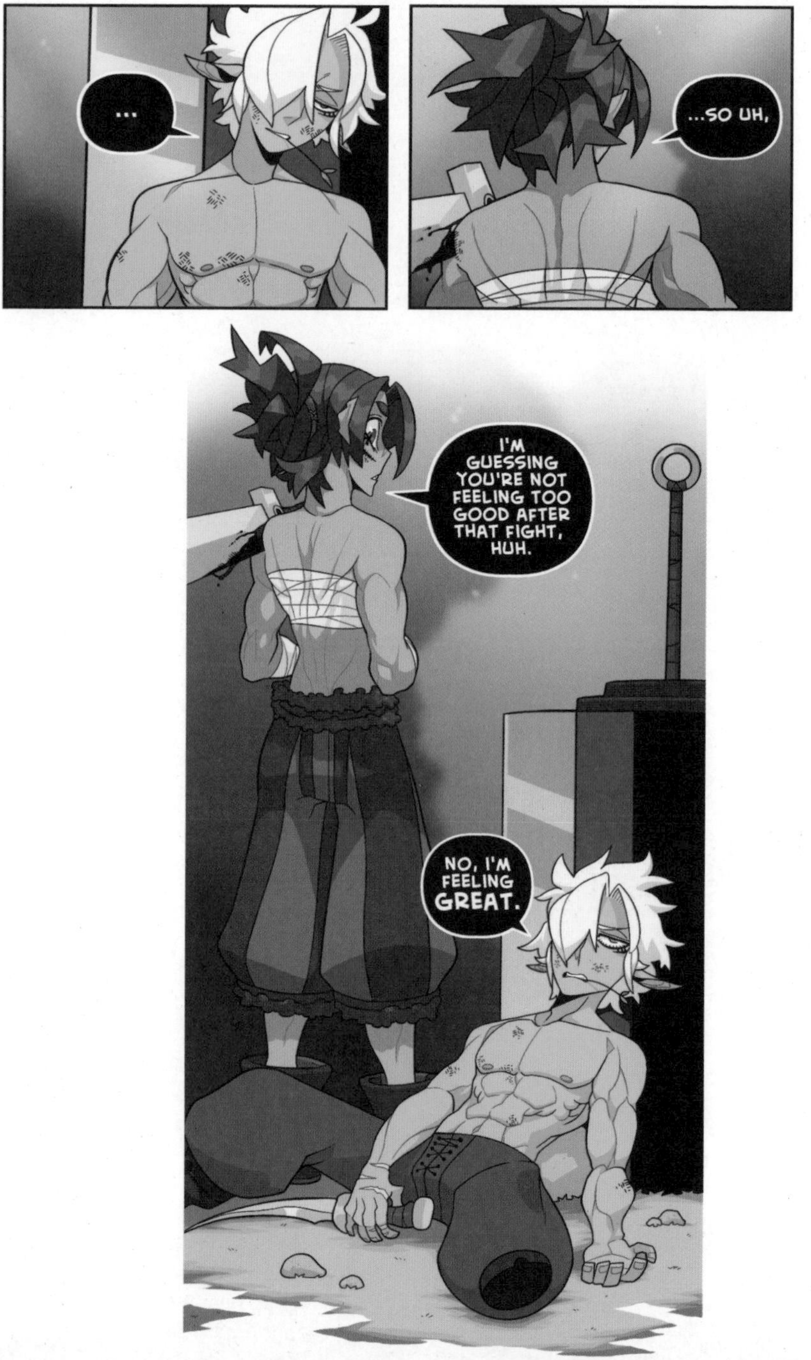
...
...SO UH,
I'M GUESSING YOU'RE NOT FEELING TOO GOOD AFTER THAT FIGHT, HUH.
NO, I'M FEELING GREAT.

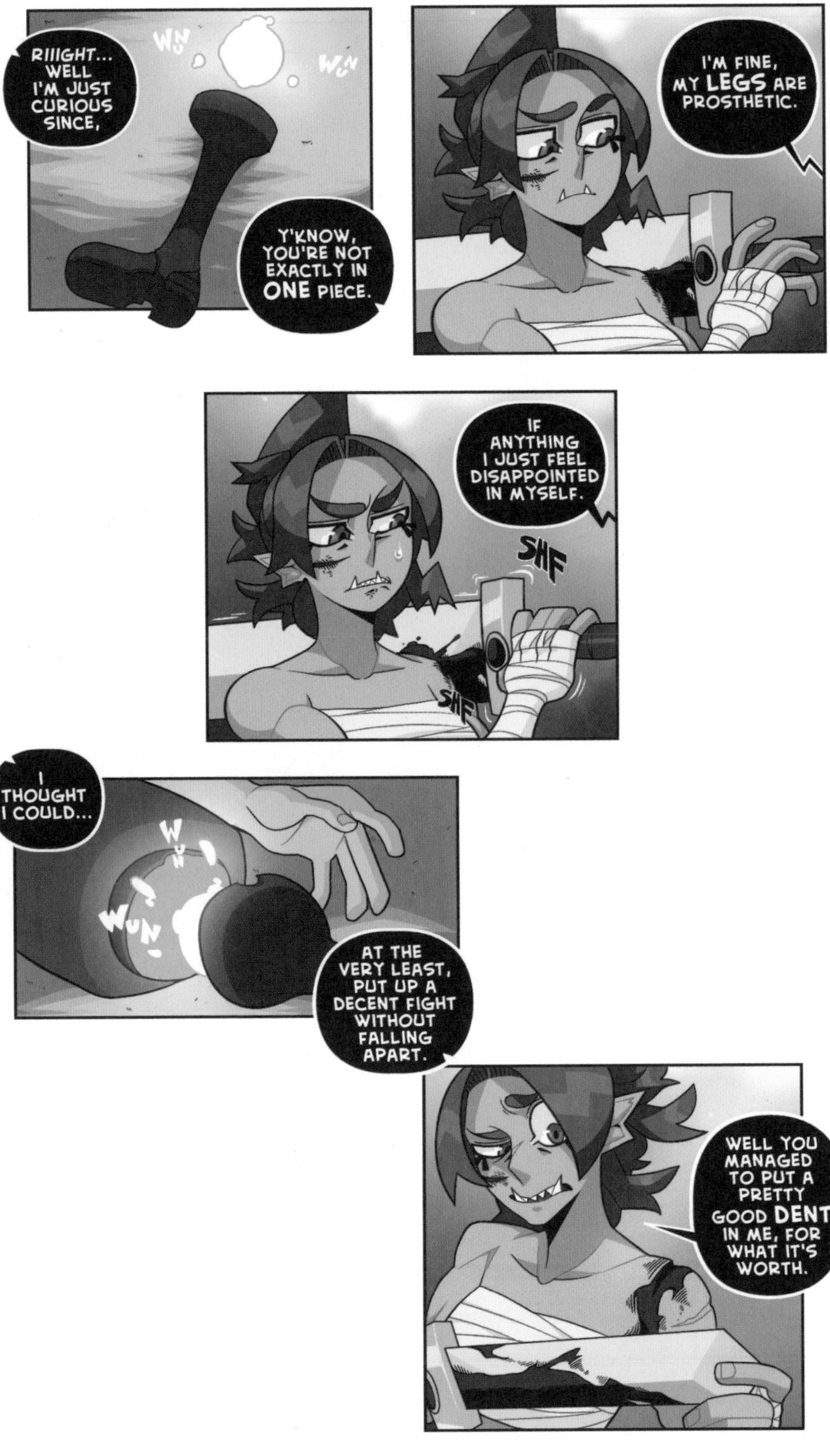
RIIIGHT... WELL I'M JUST CURIOUS SINCE,
WUN
WUN
Y'KNOW, YOU'RE NOT EXACTLY IN ONE PIECE.
I'M FINE, MY LEGS ARE PROSTHETIC.
IF ANYTHING I JUST FEEL DISAPPOINTED IN MYSELF.
SHF
SHF
I THOUGHT I COULD...
WUN
WUN
AT THE VERY LEAST, PUT UP A DECENT FIGHT WITHOUT FALLING APART.
WELL YOU MANAGED TO PUT A PRETTY GOOD DENT IN ME, FOR WHAT IT'S WORTH.

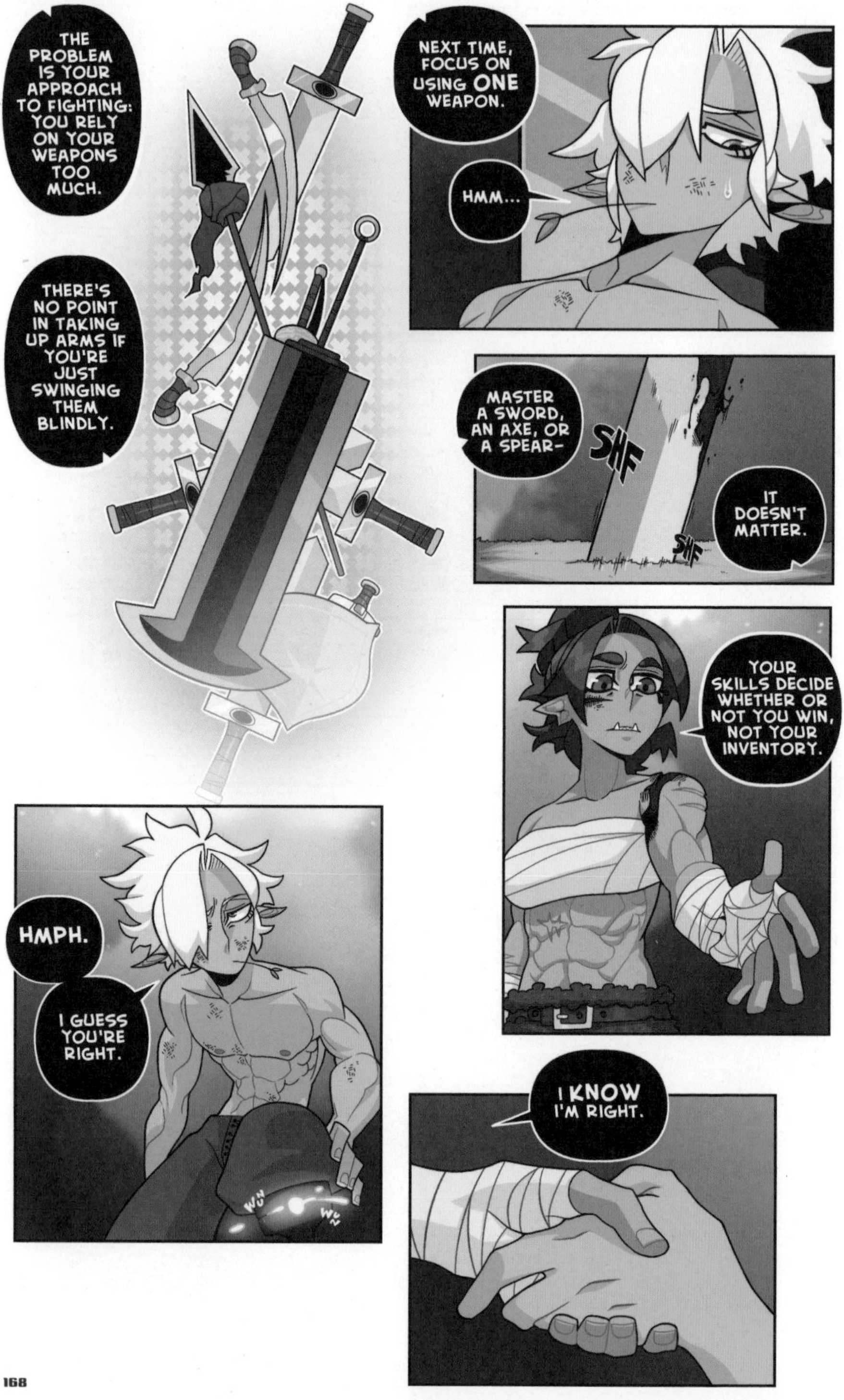
THE PROBLEM IS YOUR APPROACH TO FIGHTING: YOU RELY ON YOUR WEAPONS TOO MUCH.
THERE'S NO POINT IN TAKING UP ARMS IF YOU'RE JUST SWINGING THEM BLINDLY.
NEXT TIME, FOCUS ON USING ONE WEAPON.
HMM...
MASTER A SWORD, AN AXE, OR A SPEAR-
SHF
IT DOESN'T MATTER.
SHF
YOUR SKILLS DECIDE WHETHER OR NOT YOU WIN, NOT YOUR INVENTORY.
HMPH.
I GUESS YOU'RE RIGHT.
WUN
WUN
I KNOW I'M RIGHT.

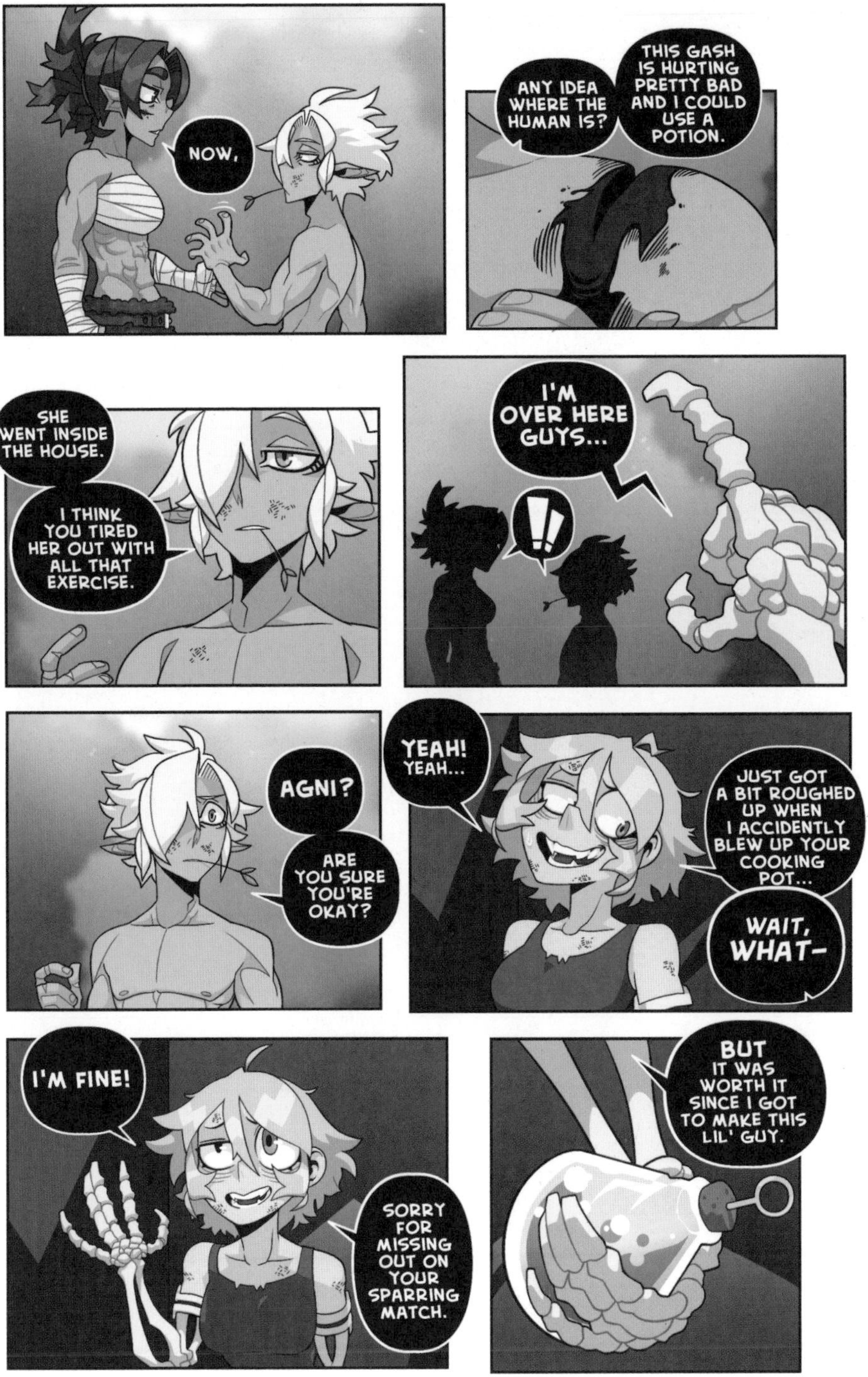

NOW,
ANY IDEA WHERE THE HUMAN IS?
THIS GASH IS HURTING PRETTY BAD AND I COULD USE A POTION.
SHE WENT INSIDE THE HOUSE.
I THINK YOU TIRED HER OUT WITH ALL THAT EXERCISE.
I'M OVER HERE GUYS...
!!
AGNI?
ARE YOU SURE YOU'RE OKAY?
YEAH! YEAH...
JUST GOT A BIT ROUGHED UP WHEN I ACCIDENTLY BLEW UP YOUR COOKING POT...
WAIT, WHAT-
I'M FINE!
SORRY FOR MISSING OUT ON YOUR SPARRING MATCH.
BUT IT WAS WORTH IT SINCE I GOT TO MAKE THIS LIL' GUY.

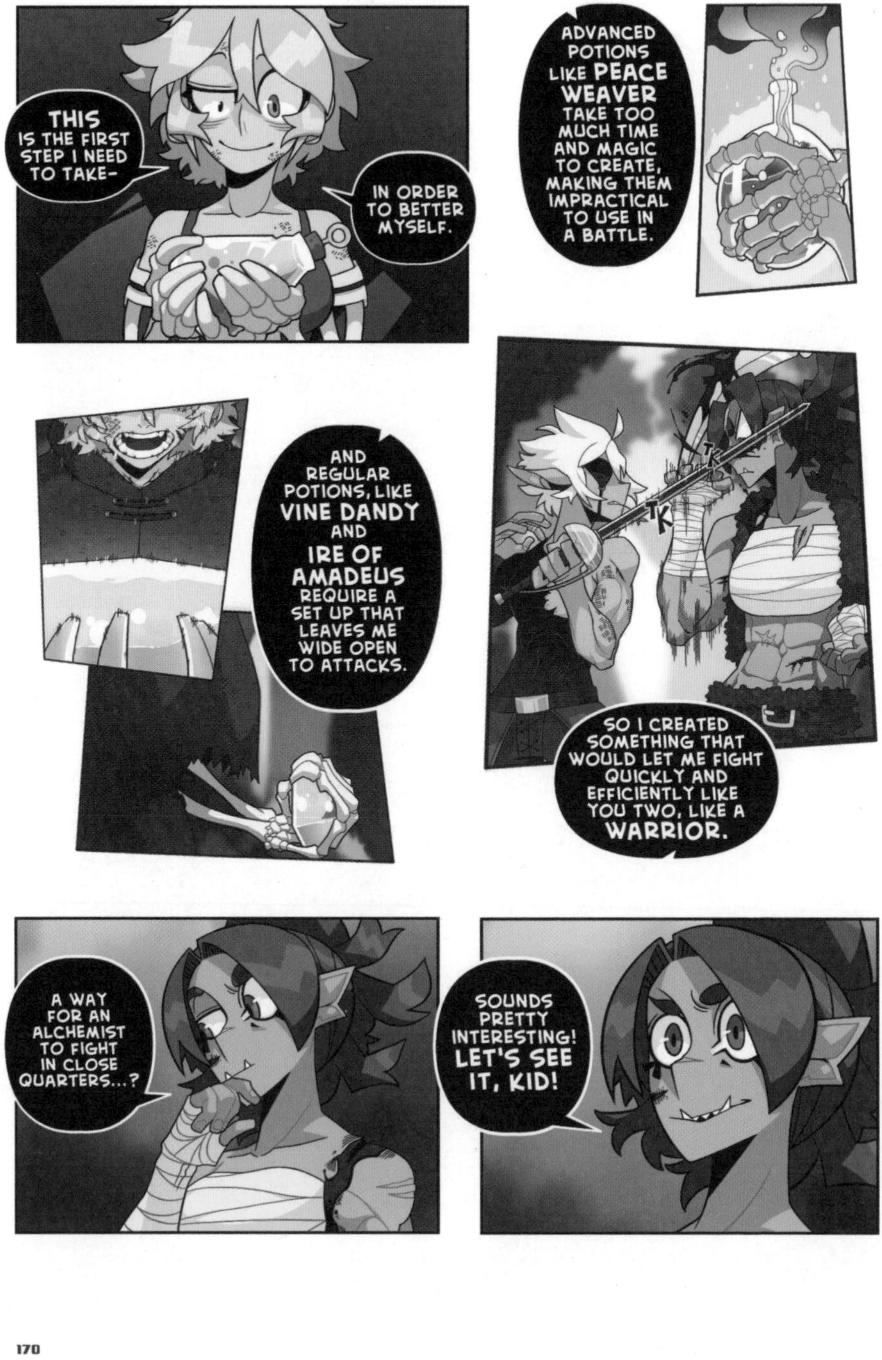
THIS IS THE FIRST STEP I NEED TO TAKE-
IN ORDER TO BETTER MYSELF.
ADVANCED POTIONS LIKE PEACE WEAVER TAKE TOO MUCH TIME AND MAGIC TO CREATE, MAKING THEM IMPRACTICAL TO USE IN A BATTLE.
AND REGULAR POTIONS, LIKE VINE DANDY AND IRE OF AMADEUS REQUIRE A SET UP THAT LEAVES ME WIDE OPEN TO ATTACKS.
SO I CREATED SOMETHING THAT WOULD LET ME FIGHT QUICKLY AND EFFICIENTLY LIKE YOU TWO, LIKE A WARRIOR.
A WAY FOR AN ALCHEMIST TO FIGHT IN CLOSE QUARTERS...?
SOUNDS PRETTY INTERESTING! LET'S SEE IT, KID!

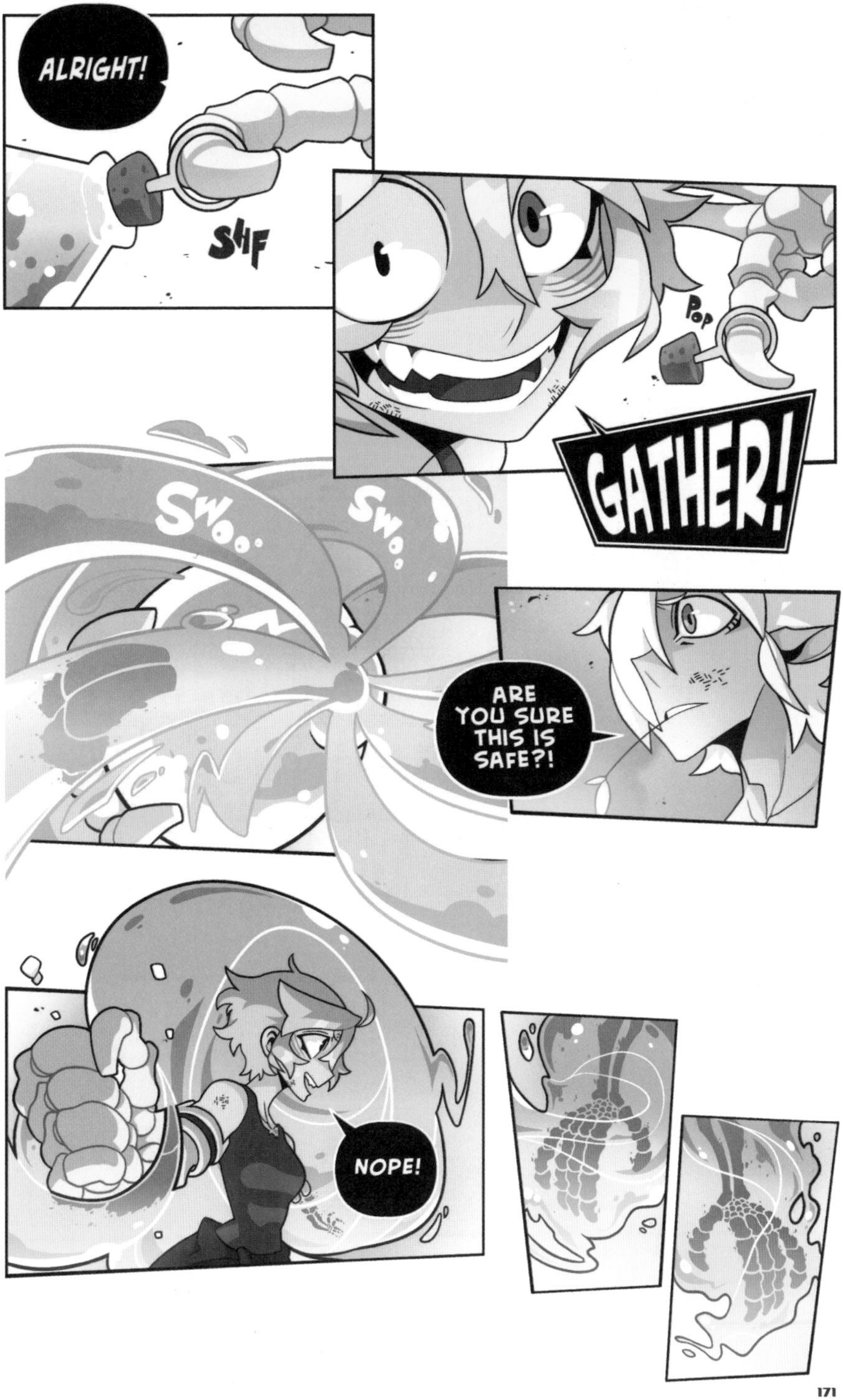
ALRIGHT!
SHF
POP
GATHER!
SWOOO
SWOOO
ARE YOU SURE THIS IS SAFE?!
NOPE!

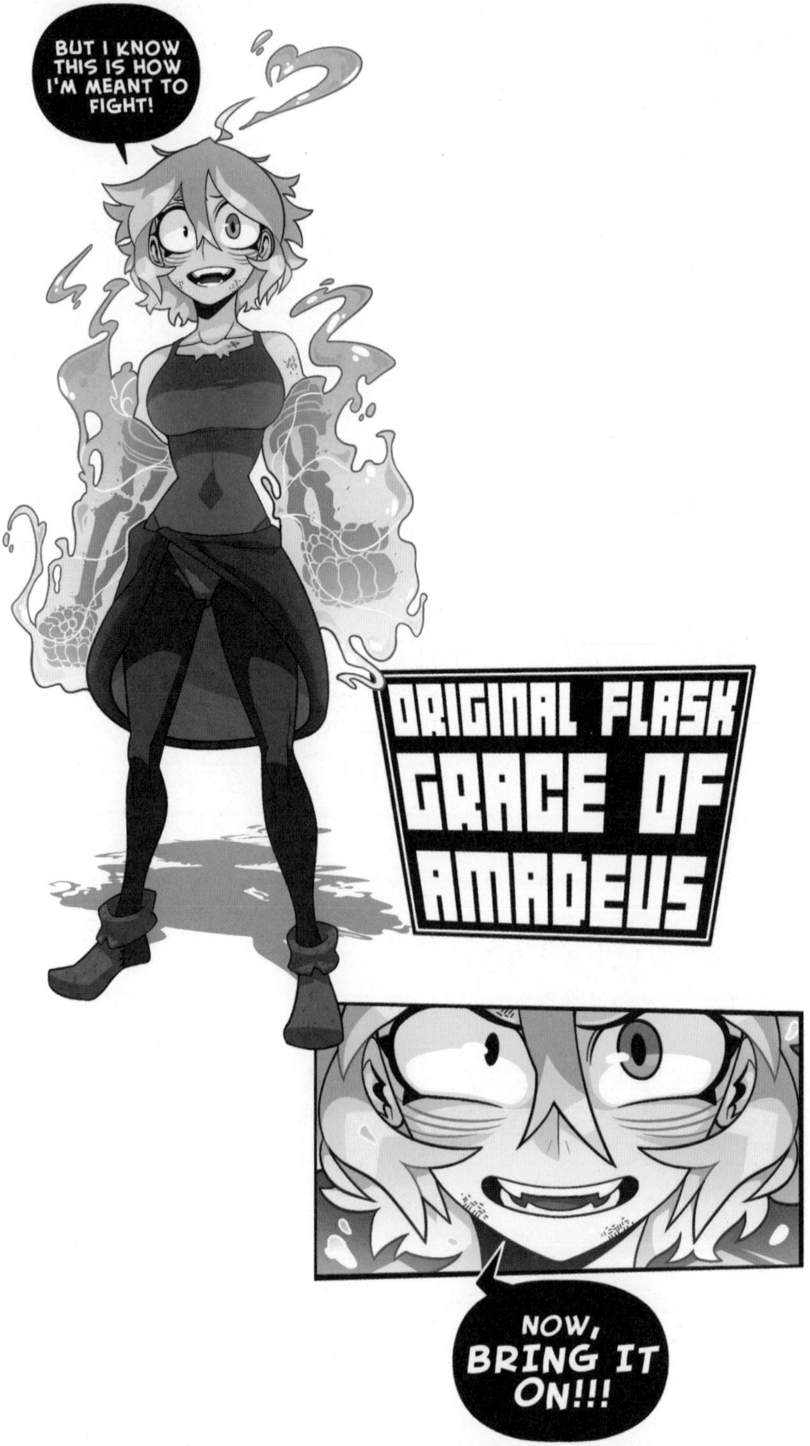
BUT I KNOW THIS IS HOW I'M MEANT TO FIGHT!
ORIGINAL FLASK GRACE OF AMADEUS
NOW, BRING IT ON!!!

## Chapter 14
# THE PUNCH

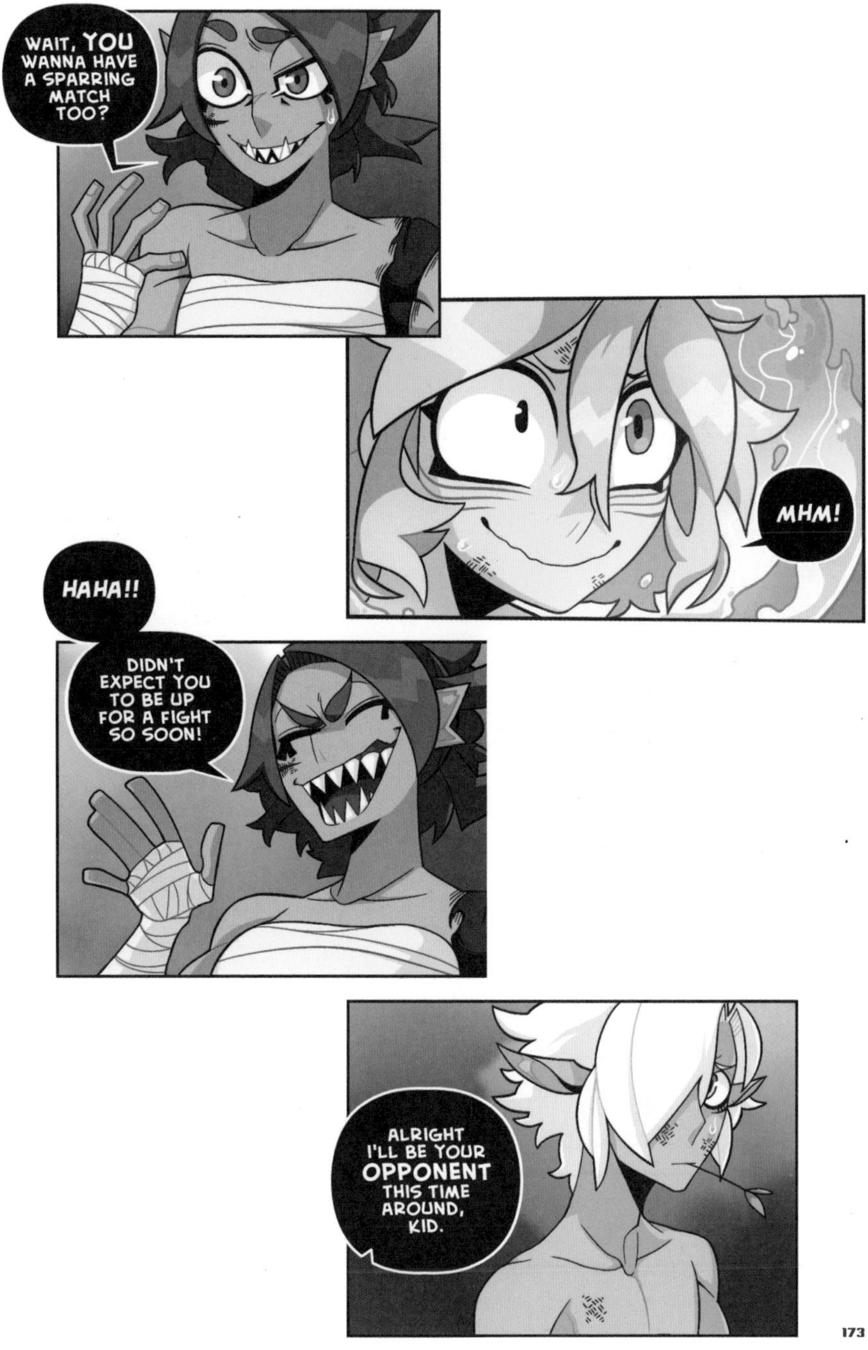
WAIT, YOU WANNA HAVE A SPARRING MATCH TOO?
MHM!
HAHA!!
DIDN'T EXPECT YOU TO BE UP FOR A FIGHT SO SOON!
ALRIGHT I'LL BE YOUR OPPONENT THIS TIME AROUND, KID.

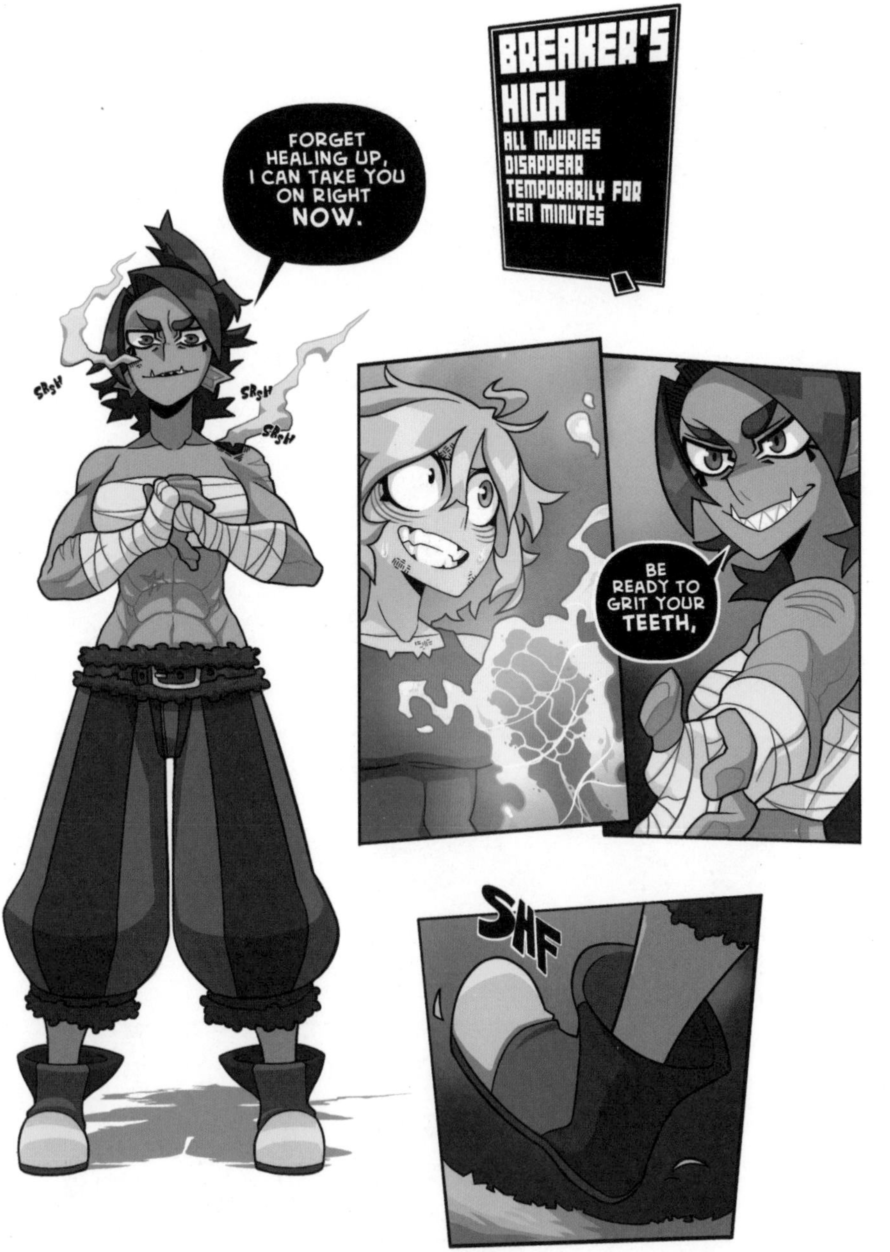
FORGET HEALING UP, I CAN TAKE YOU ON RIGHT NOW.
SRSH
SRSH
SRSH
BREAKER'S HIGH
ALL INJURIES DISAPPEAR TEMPORARILY FOR TEN MINUTES
BE READY TO GRIT YOUR TEETH,
SHF

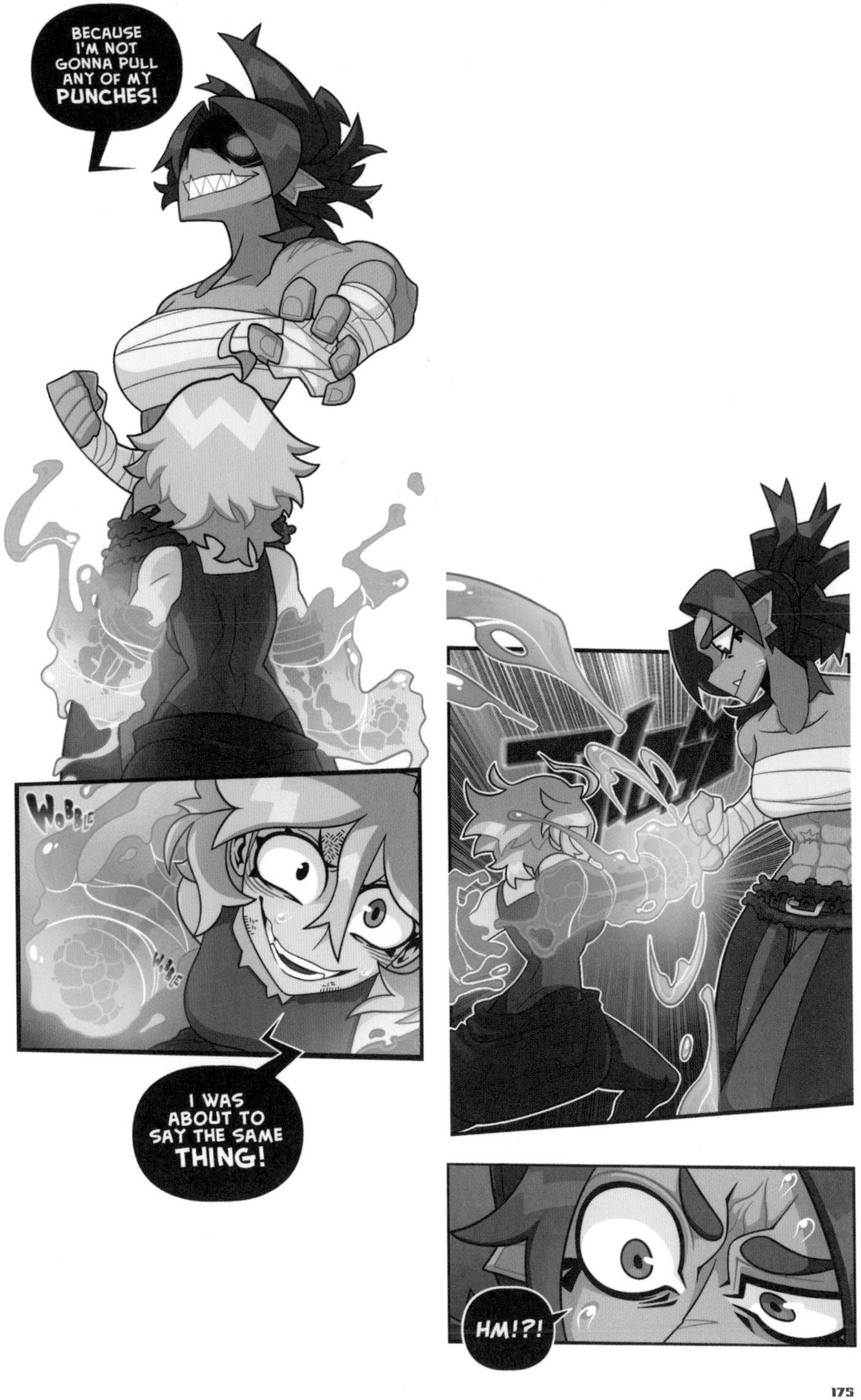
BECAUSE I'M NOT GONNA PULL ANY OF MY PUNCHES!
WOBBLE
I WAS ABOUT TO SAY THE SAME THING!
HM!?!

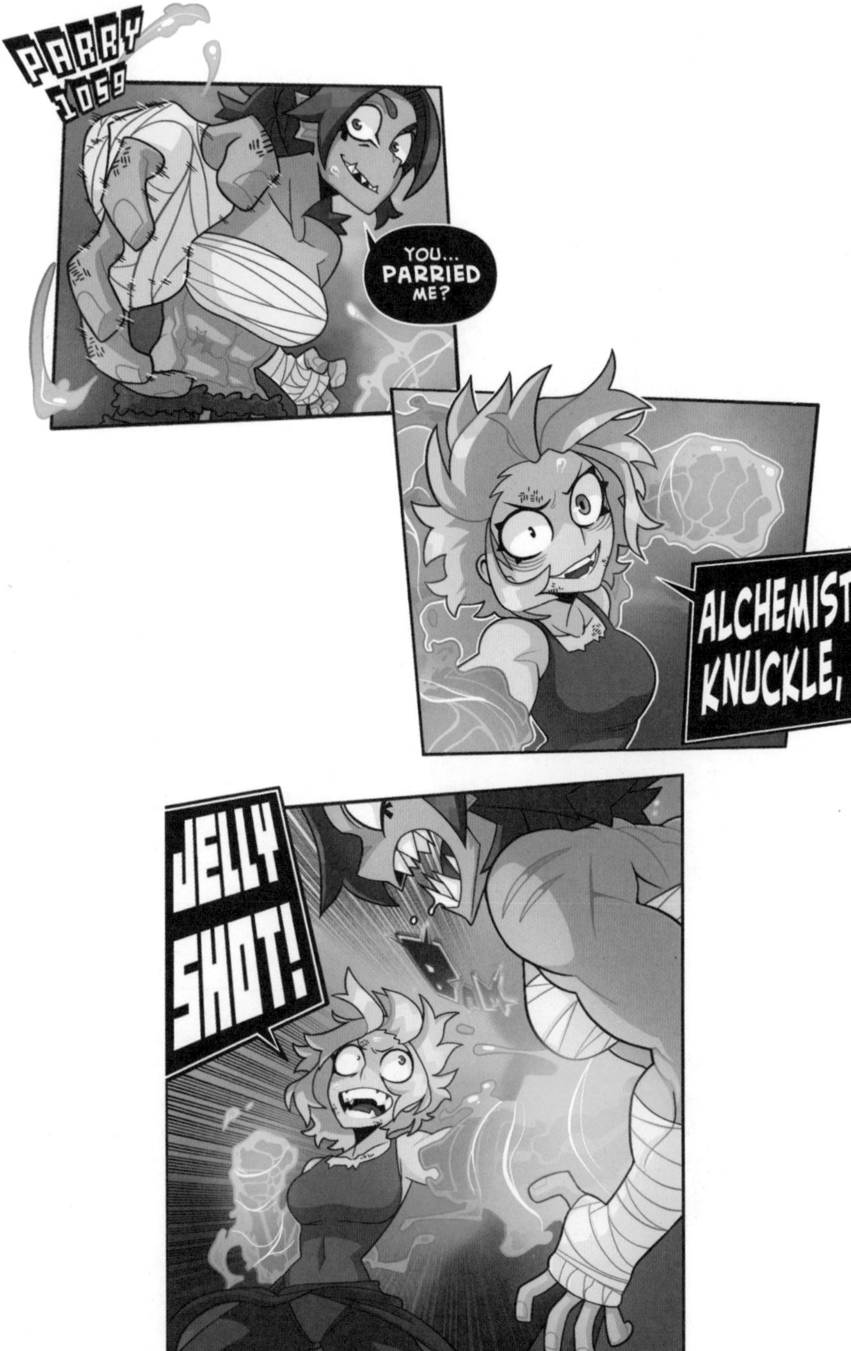
PARRY 1059
YOU... PARRIED ME?
ALCHEMIST KNUCKLE,
JELLY SHOT!

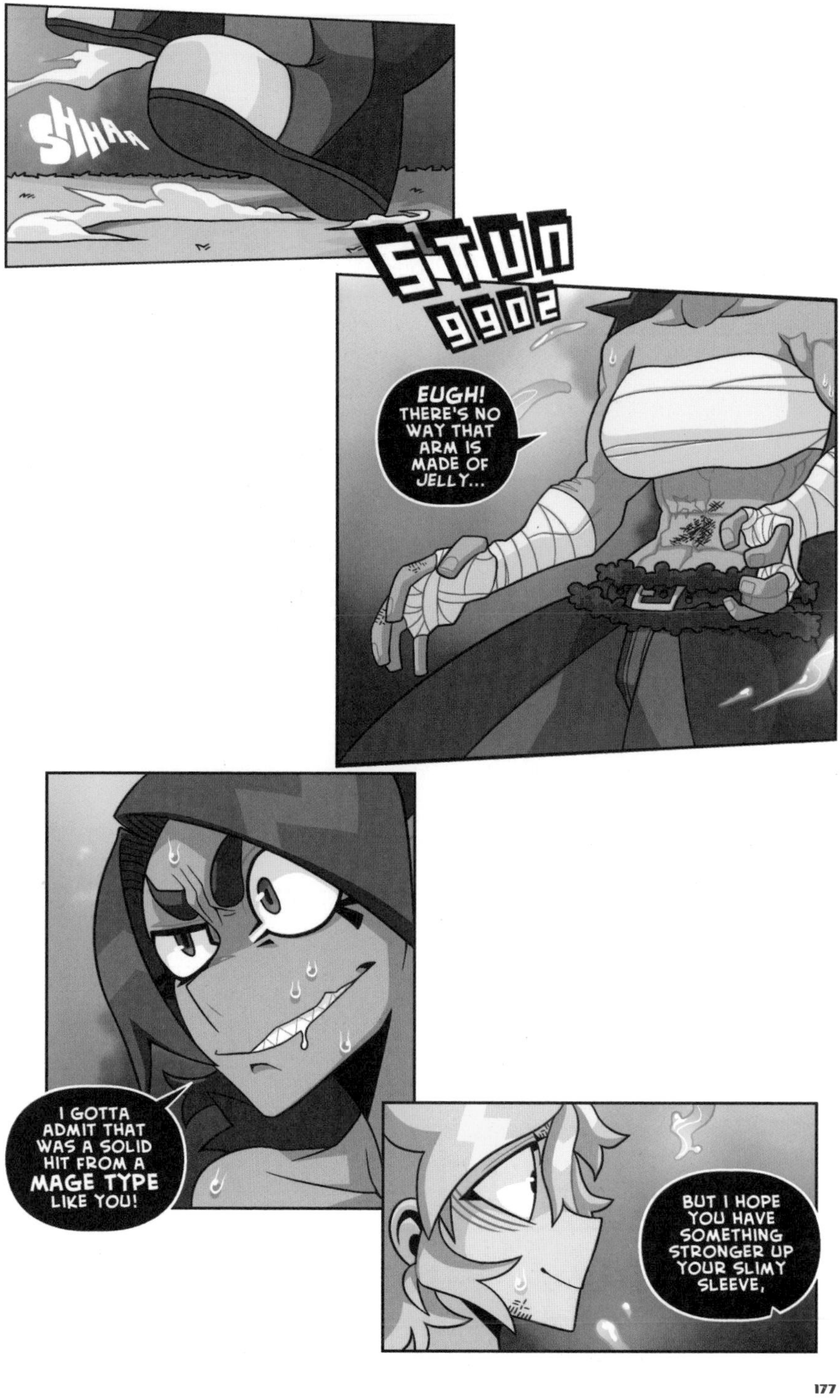
SHHAA
STUN 9902
EUGH! THERE'S NO WAY THAT ARM IS MADE OF JELLY...
I GOTTA ADMIT THAT WAS A SOLID HIT FROM A MAGE TYPE LIKE YOU!
BUT I HOPE YOU HAVE SOMETHING STRONGER UP YOUR SLIMY SLEEVE,

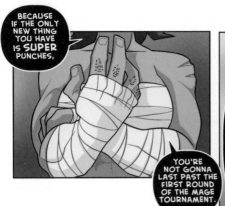

BECAUSE IF THE ONLY NEW THING YOU HAVE IS **SUPER** PUNCHES,

YOU'RE NOT GONNA LAST PAST THE FIRST ROUND OF THE MAGE TOURNAMENT.

THERE ARE PEOPLE OUT THERE BORN WITH MAGE TYPE JOBS THAT COULD WIPE OUT WHOLE **ARMIES** WITH THEIR SPELLS.

IF YOU WANNA KEEP UP YOU HAVE TO GO ABOVE AND BEYOND THE LIMITS OF AN **ALCHEMIST**.

SRsh

SRsh

SRsh

# REKSHA
## STATUS:
## FULL HEALTH

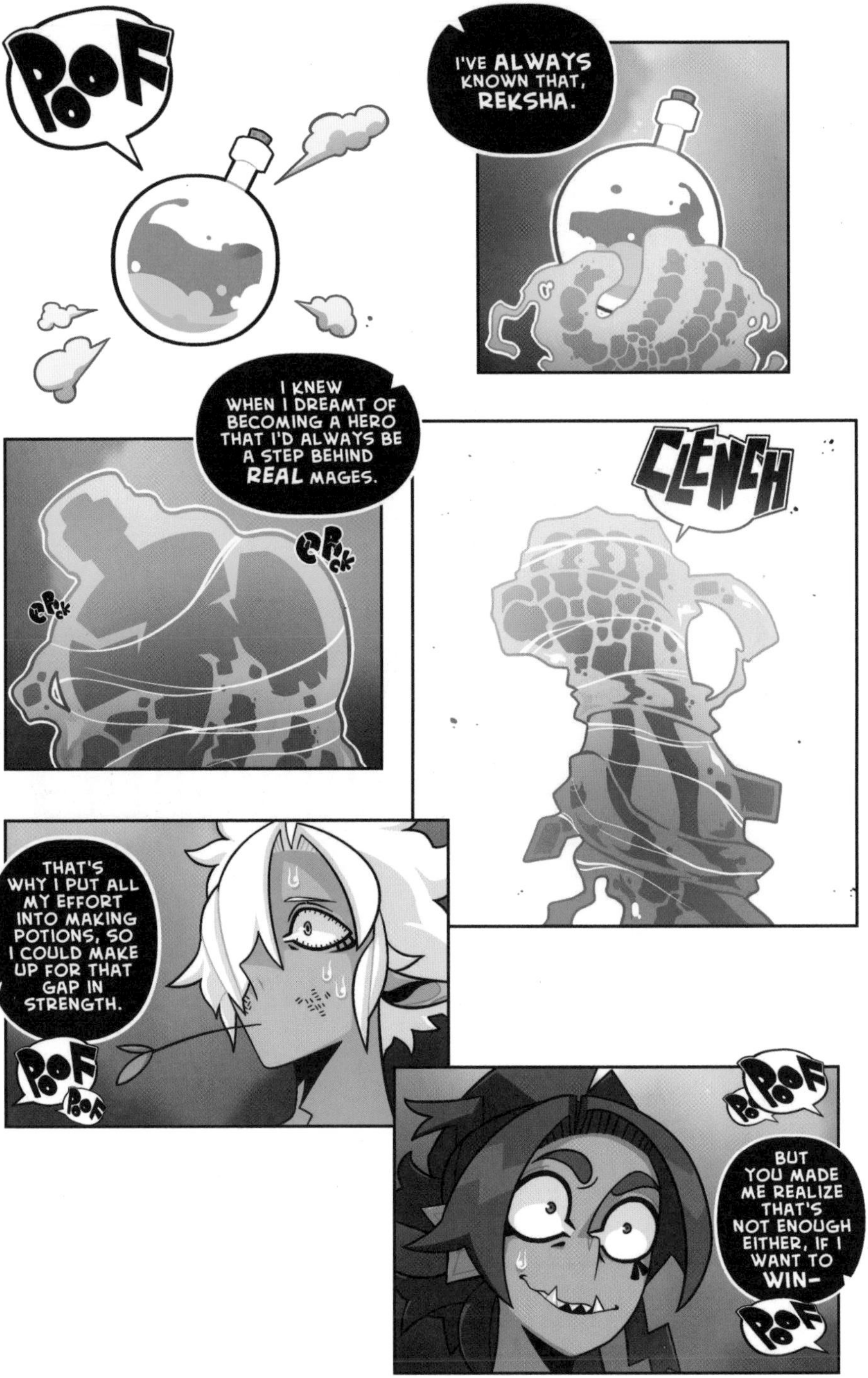
POOF
I'VE ALWAYS KNOWN THAT, REKSHA.
I KNEW WHEN I DREAMT OF BECOMING A HERO THAT I'D ALWAYS BE A STEP BEHIND REAL MAGES.
CRACK
CRACK
CLENCH
THAT'S WHY I PUT ALL MY EFFORT INTO MAKING POTIONS, SO I COULD MAKE UP FOR THAT GAP IN STRENGTH.
POOF
POOF
POOF
POOF
BUT YOU MADE ME REALIZE THAT'S NOT ENOUGH EITHER, IF I WANT TO WIN-
POOF

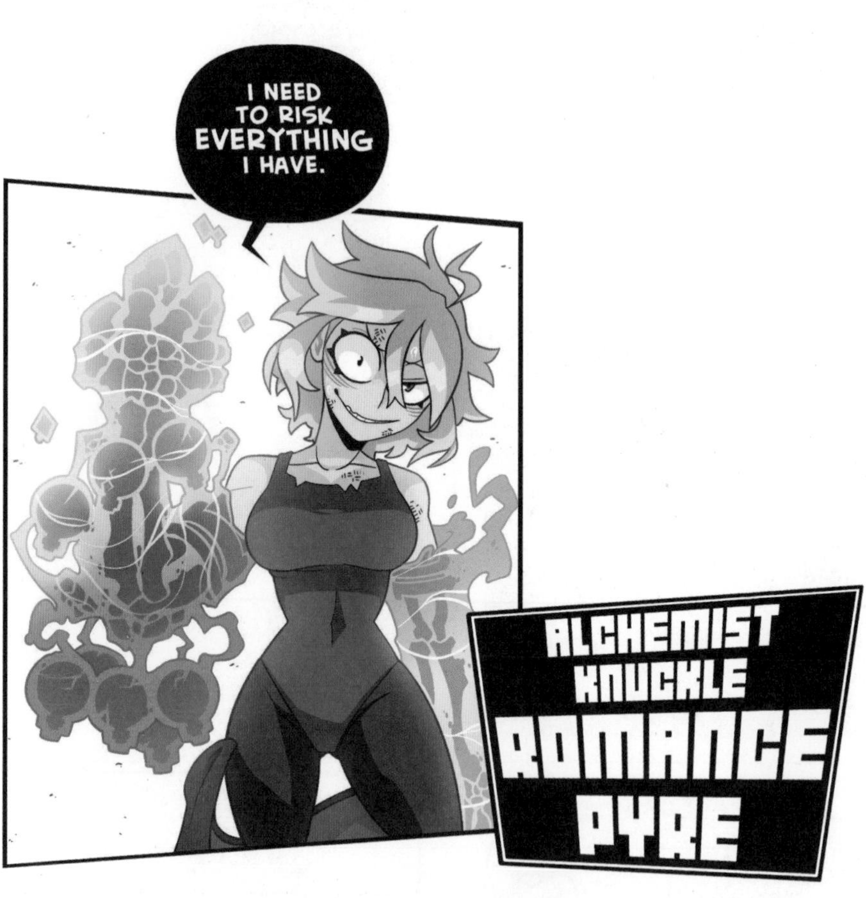
I NEED TO RISK EVERYTHING I HAVE.
ALCHEMIST KNUCKLE ROMANCE PYRE

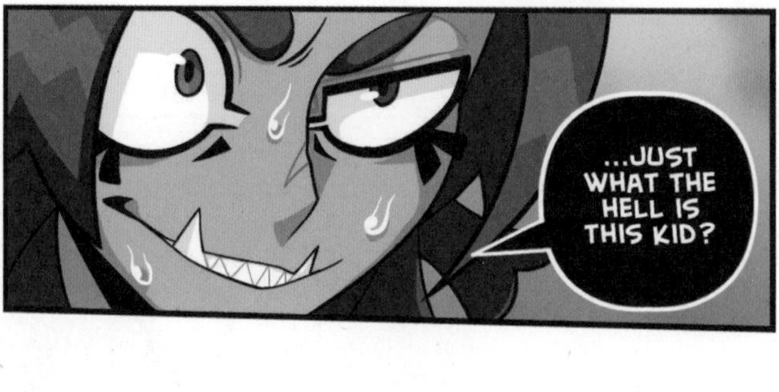
...JUST WHAT THE HELL IS THIS KID?

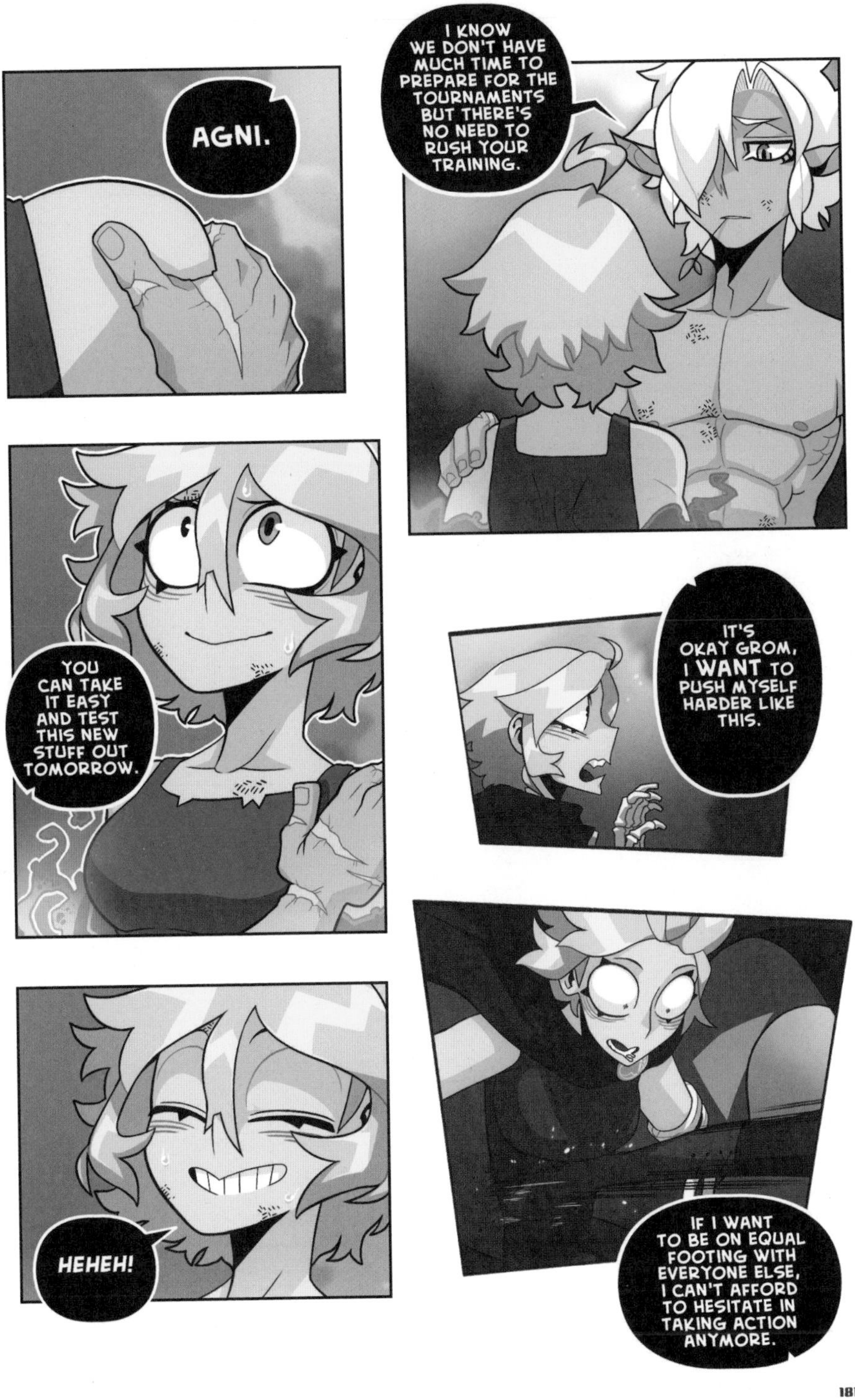

AGNI.
I KNOW WE DON'T HAVE MUCH TIME TO PREPARE FOR THE TOURNAMENTS BUT THERE'S NO NEED TO RUSH YOUR TRAINING.
YOU CAN TAKE IT EASY AND TEST THIS NEW STUFF OUT TOMORROW.
IT'S OKAY GROM, I **WANT** TO PUSH MYSELF HARDER LIKE THIS.
HEHEH!
IF I WANT TO BE ON EQUAL FOOTING WITH EVERYONE ELSE, I CAN'T AFFORD TO HESITATE IN TAKING ACTION ANYMORE.

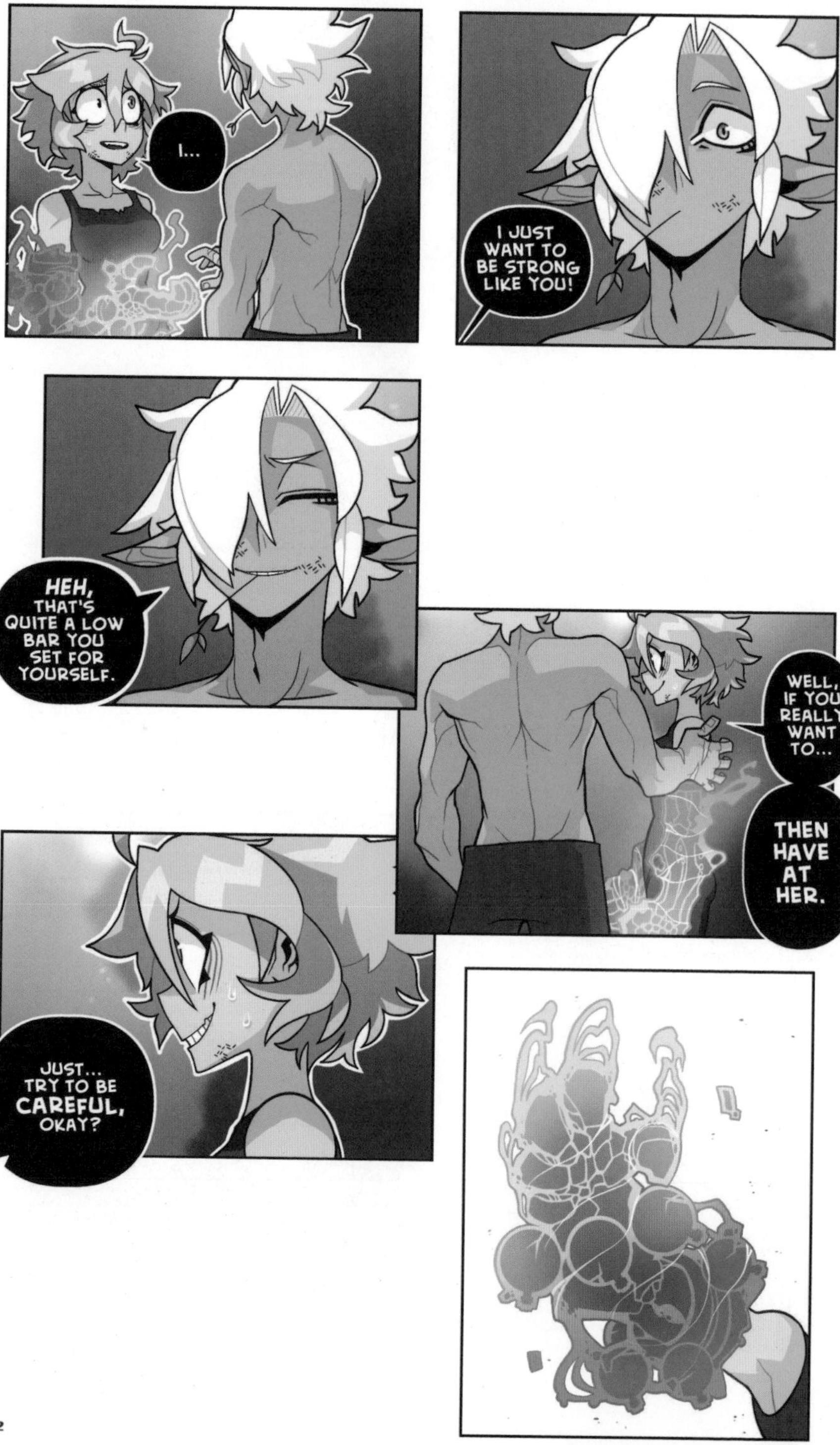
I...
I JUST WANT TO BE STRONG LIKE YOU!
HEH, THAT'S QUITE A LOW BAR YOU SET FOR YOURSELF.
WELL, IF YOU REALLY WANT TO...
THEN HAVE AT HER.
JUST... TRY TO BE CAREFUL, OKAY?

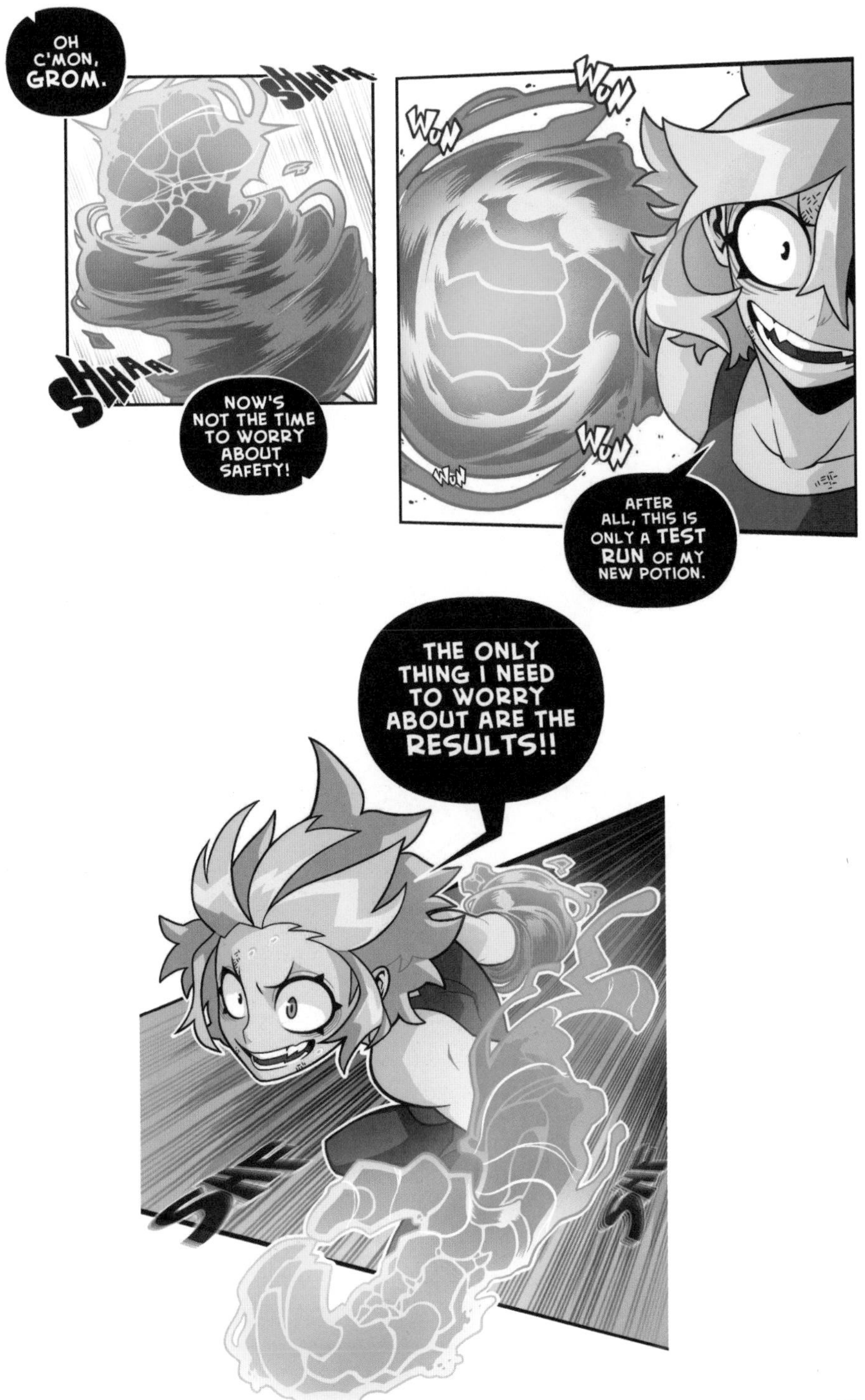
OH C'MON, GROM.
SHHAA
SHHAA
NOW'S NOT THE TIME TO WORRY ABOUT SAFETY!
WUN
WUN
WUN
WUN
AFTER ALL, THIS IS ONLY A TEST RUN OF MY NEW POTION.
THE ONLY THING I NEED TO WORRY ABOUT ARE THE RESULTS!!

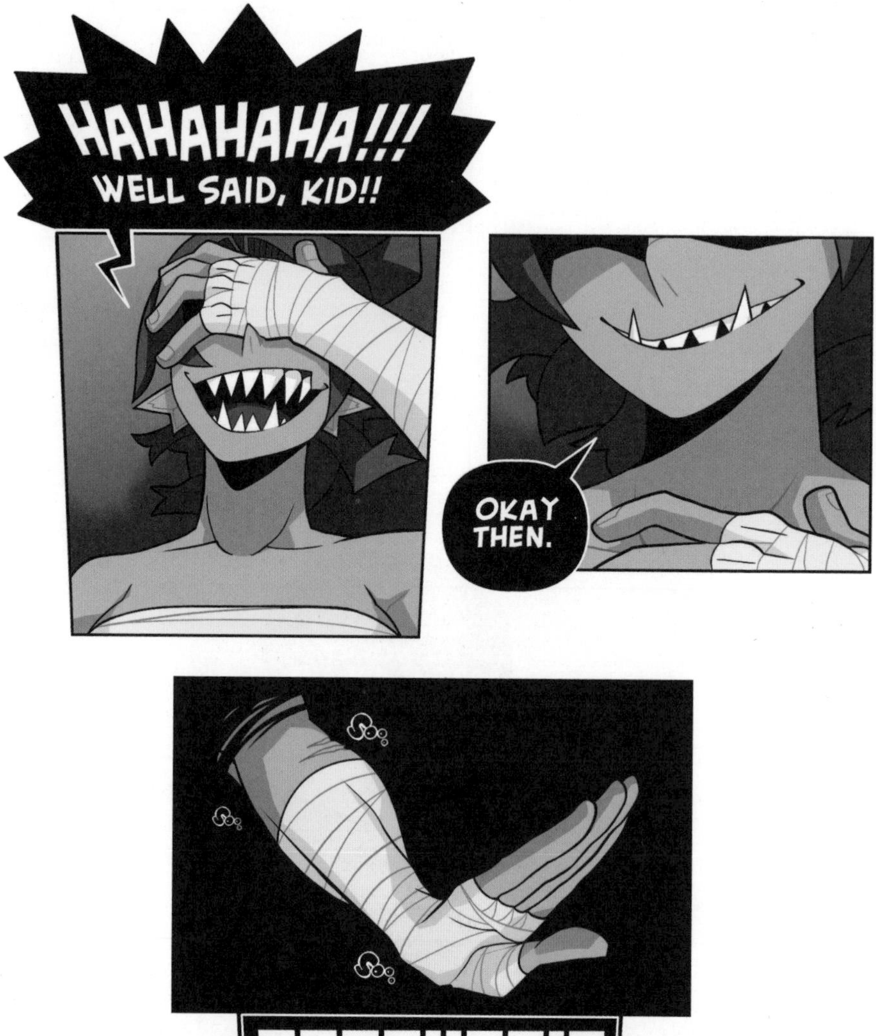
HAHAHAHA!!! WELL SAID, KID!!
OKAY THEN.
BREAKER'S STANCE

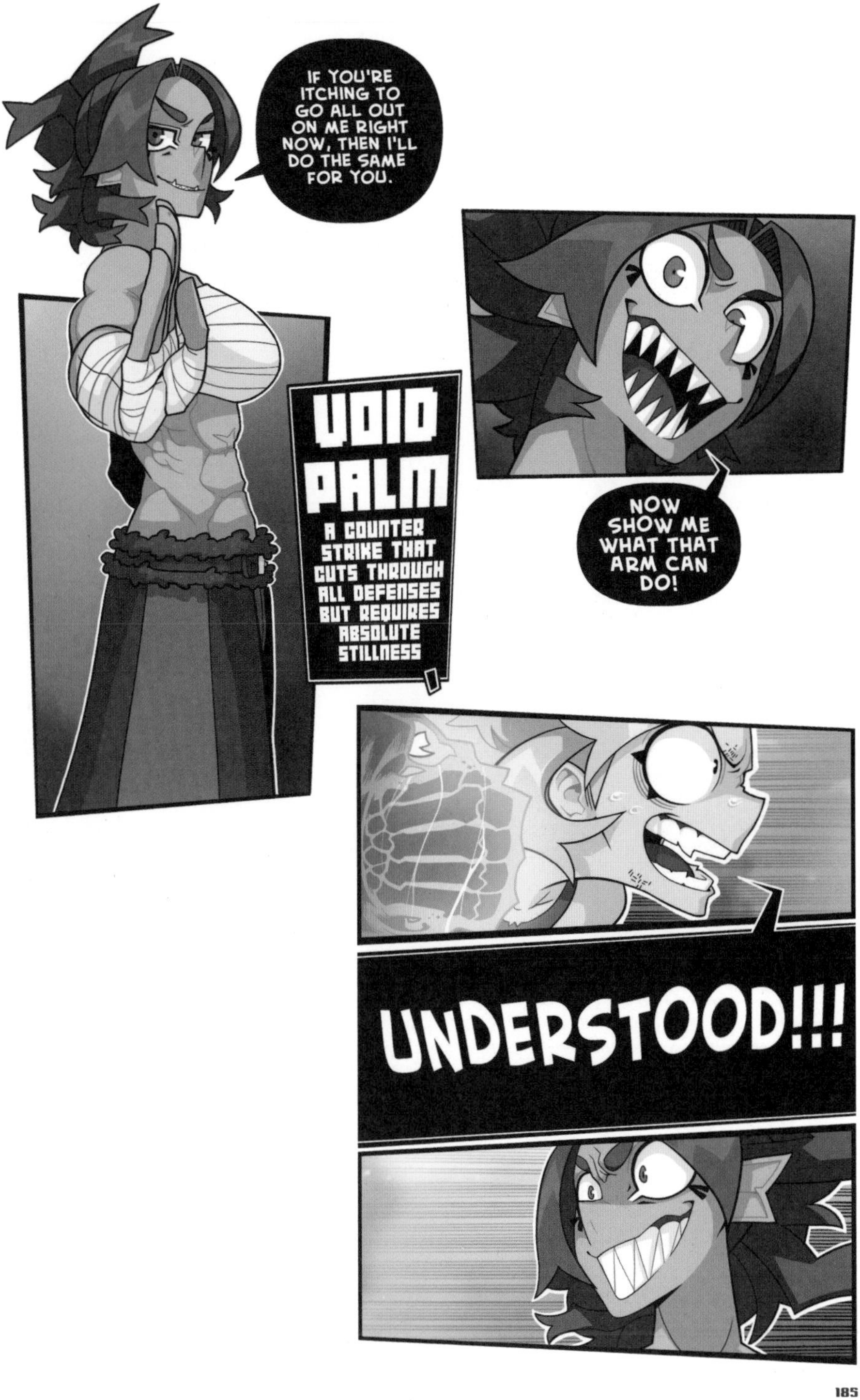
IF YOU'RE ITCHING TO GO ALL OUT ON ME RIGHT NOW, THEN I'LL DO THE SAME FOR YOU.
VOID PALM
A COUNTER STRIKE THAT CUTS THROUGH ALL DEFENSES BUT REQUIRES ABSOLUTE STILLNESS
NOW SHOW ME WHAT THAT ARM CAN DO!
UNDERSTOOD!!!

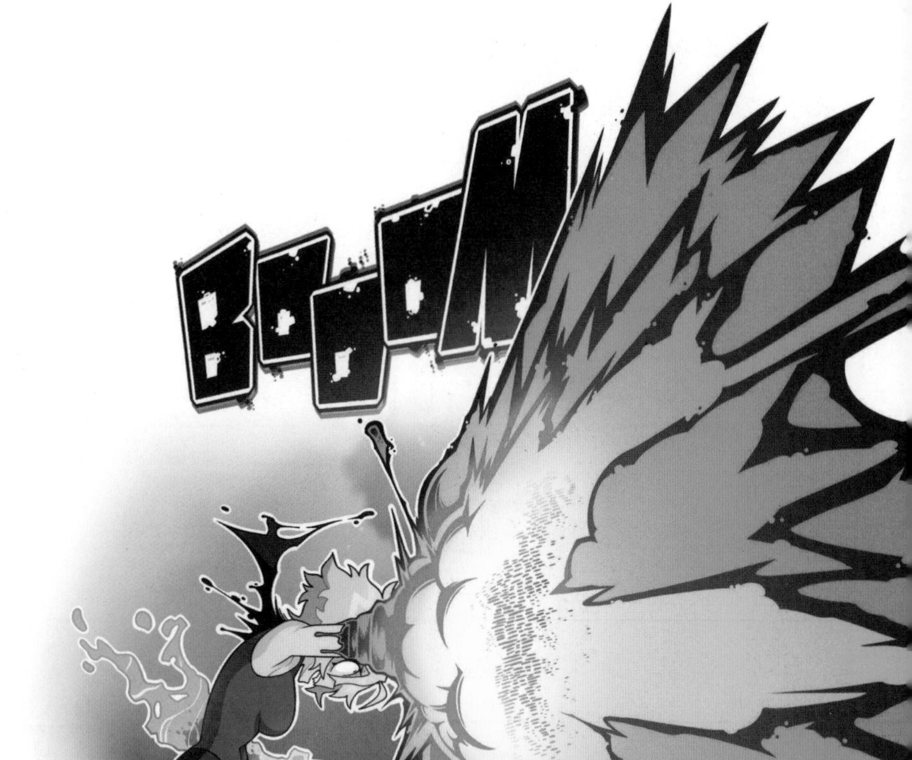
BOOM

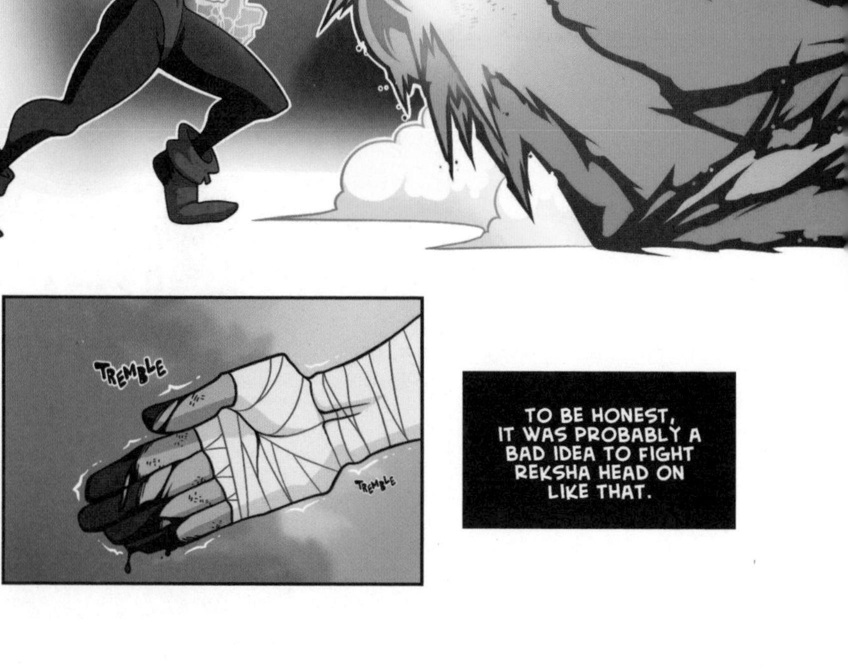
TREMBLE
TREMBLE

TO BE HONEST,
IT WAS PROBABLY A
BAD IDEA TO FIGHT
REKSHA HEAD ON
LIKE THAT.

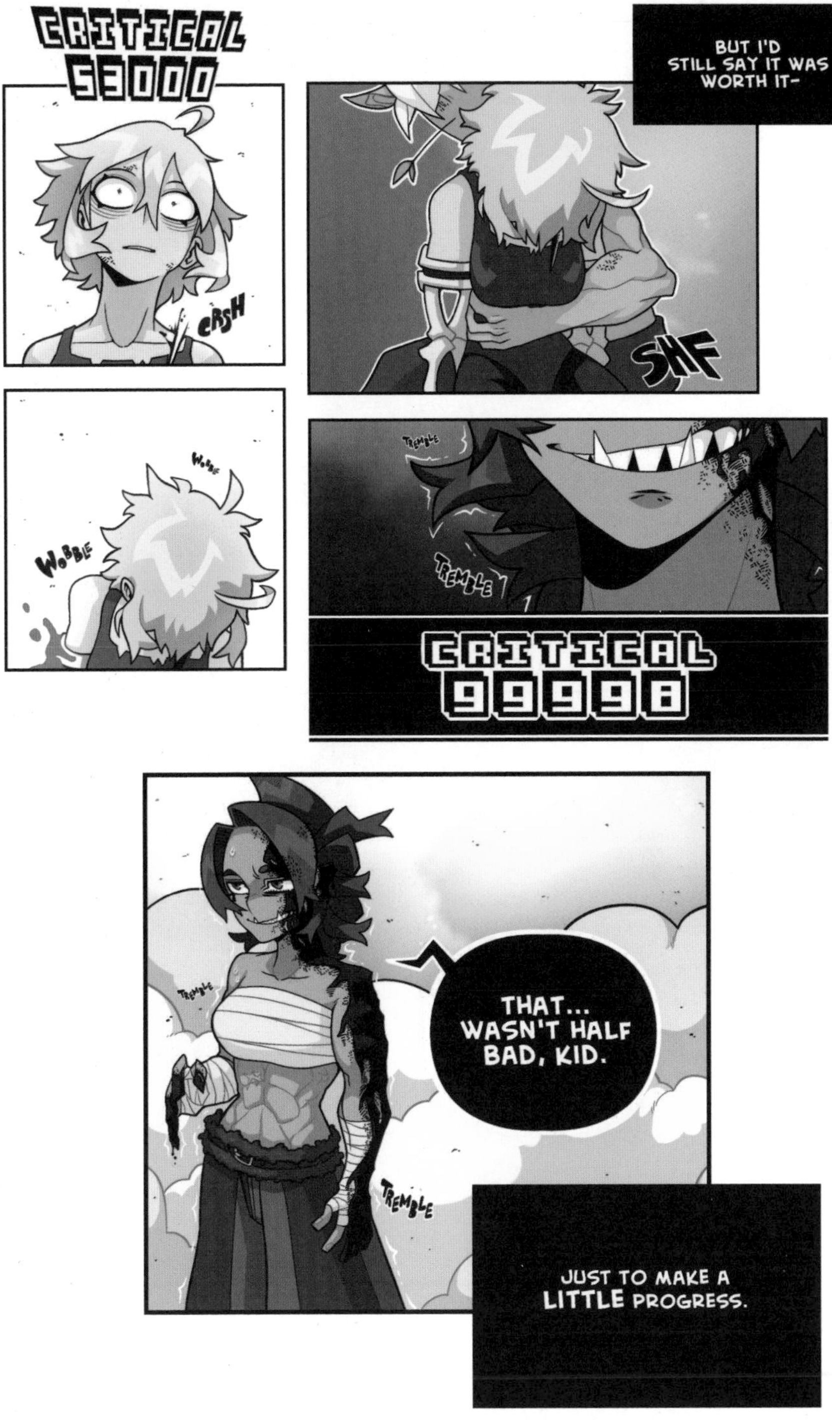
CRITICAL
53000
CRSH
BUT I'D STILL SAY IT WAS WORTH IT-
SHF
WOBBLE
WOBBLE
TREMBLE
TREMBLE
CRITICAL
99998
TREMBLE
THAT... WASN'T HALF BAD, KID.
TREMBLE
JUST TO MAKE A LITTLE PROGRESS.

## Chapter 15
# THE REST

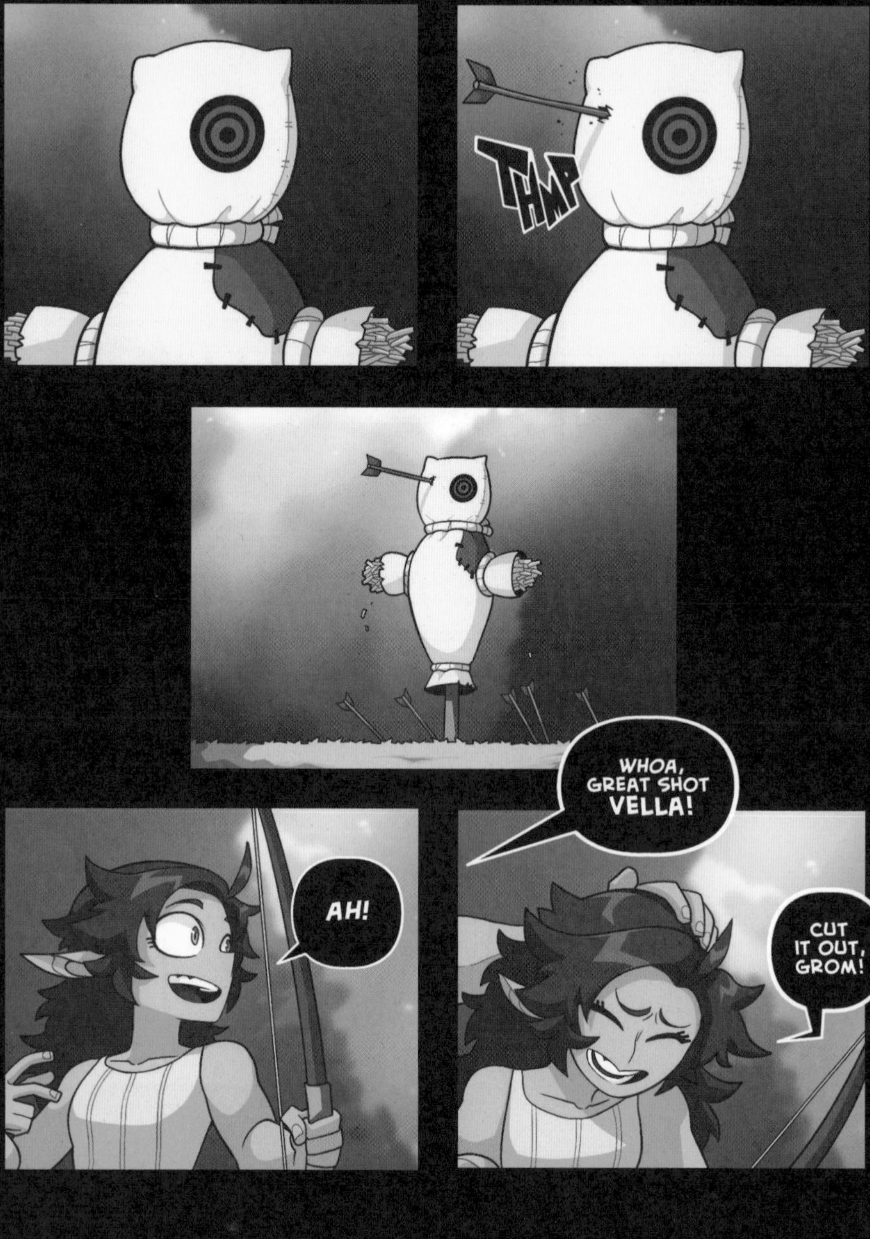

THMP
AH!
WHOA, GREAT SHOT VELLA!
CUT IT OUT, GROM!

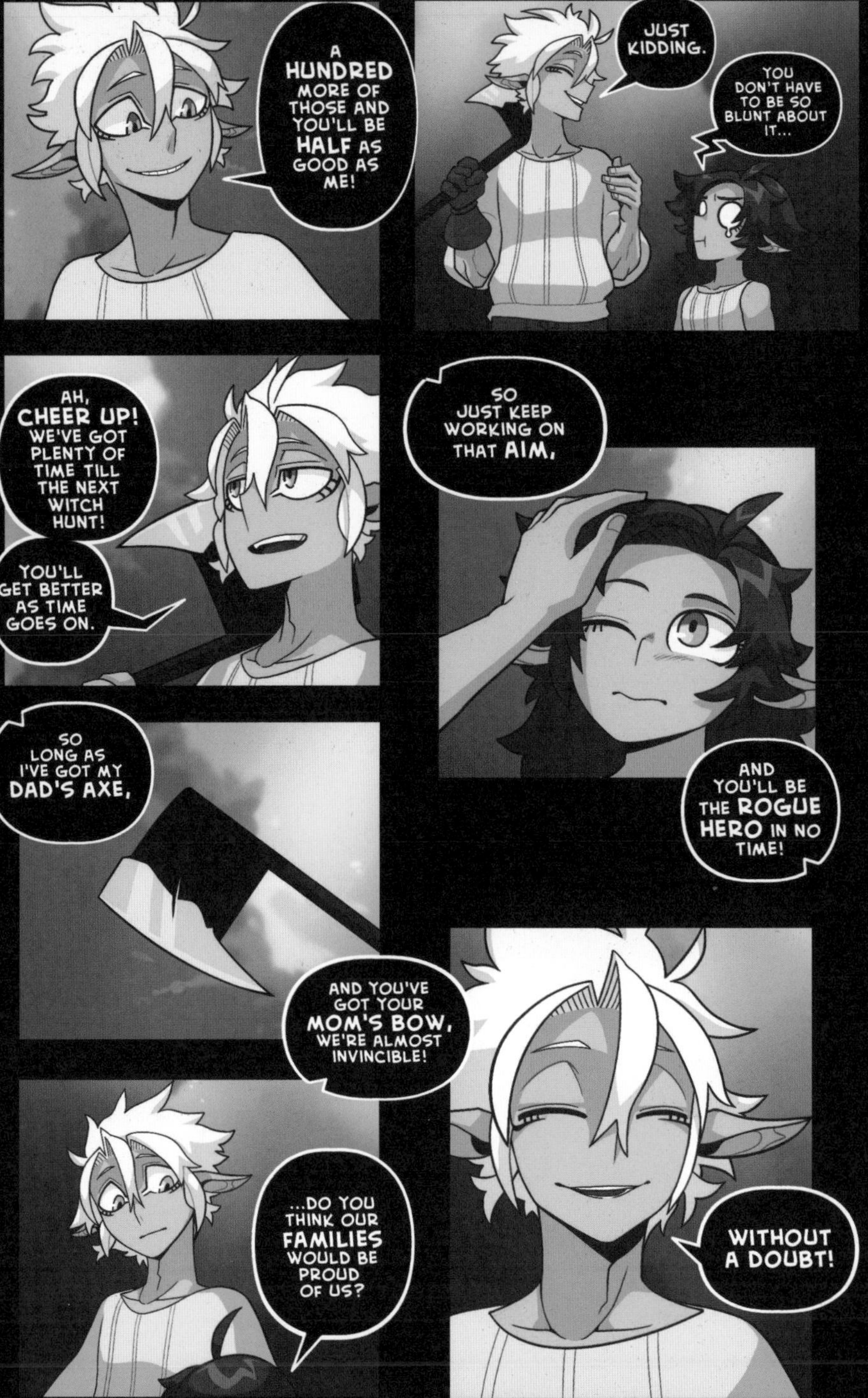
A HUNDRED MORE OF THOSE AND YOU'LL BE HALF AS GOOD AS ME!
JUST KIDDING.
YOU DON'T HAVE TO BE SO BLUNT ABOUT IT...
AH, CHEER UP! WE'VE GOT PLENTY OF TIME TILL THE NEXT WITCH HUNT!
YOU'LL GET BETTER AS TIME GOES ON.
SO JUST KEEP WORKING ON THAT AIM,
AND YOU'LL BE THE ROGUE HERO IN NO TIME!
SO LONG AS I'VE GOT MY DAD'S AXE,
AND YOU'VE GOT YOUR MOM'S BOW, WE'RE ALMOST INVINCIBLE!
...DO YOU THINK OUR FAMILIES WOULD BE PROUD OF US?
WITHOUT A DOUBT!

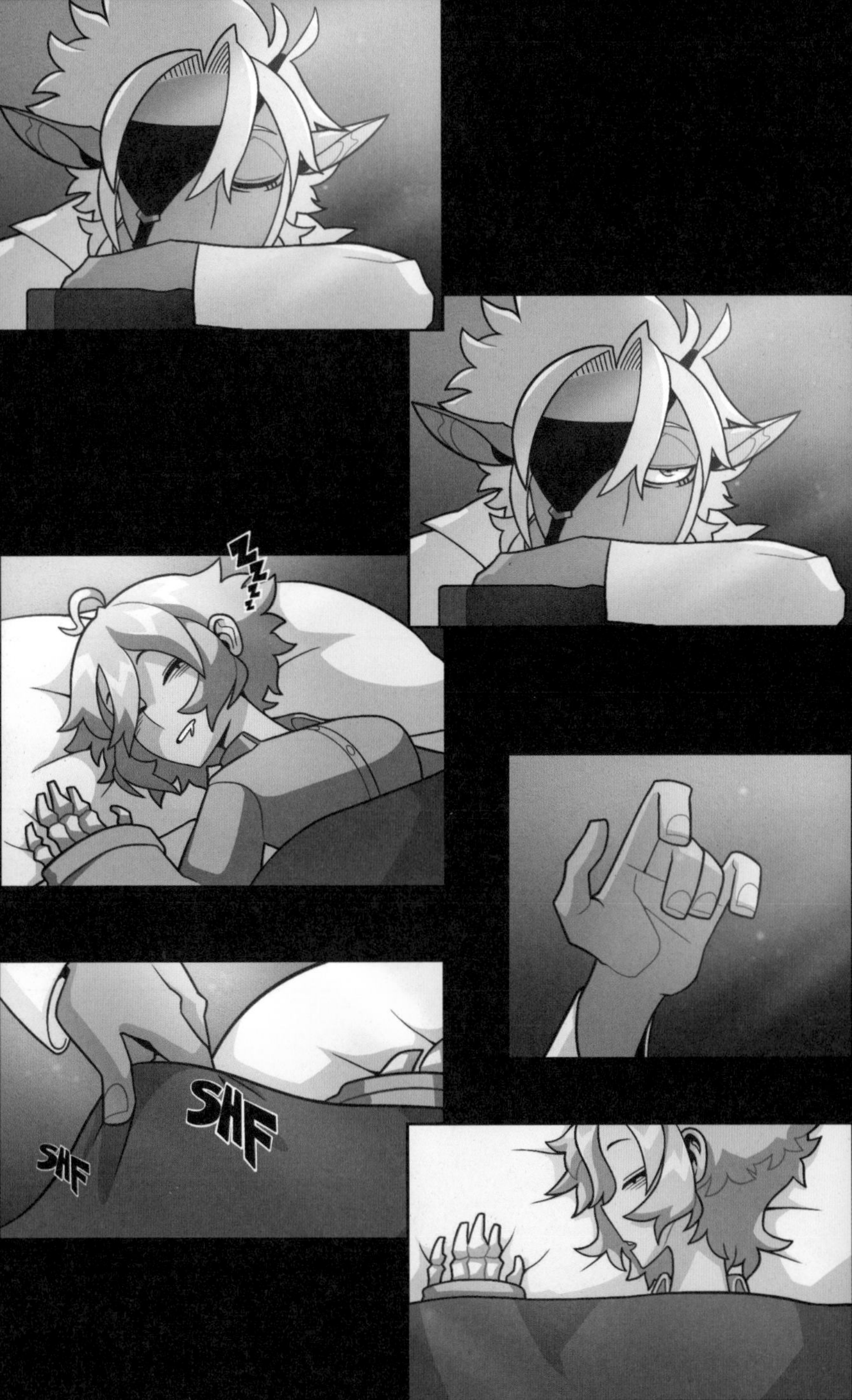
ZZZ
SHF
SHF

KNOCK, KNOCK.

FIGURED I SHOULD CHECK IN ON LIL' RED.

I'M ABOUT TO HEAD OUT, AND I WANNA MAKE SURE SHE'S HEALING UP JUST FINE.

SHE UH, DOING OKAY?

TO BE ABLE TO SLEEP WITH A SMILE AFTER TAKING A HIT LIKE THAT... SHE'S A TOUGH LITTLE NUT.

HAH...

...YEAH, SHE'S SLEEPING WELL.

...DO YOU THINK SHE'S TOUGH ENOUGH TO BECOME THE MAGE HERO?

THAT'S A BIT HARD TO SAY FOR SURE, BUT SHE DOES HAVE POTENTIAL.

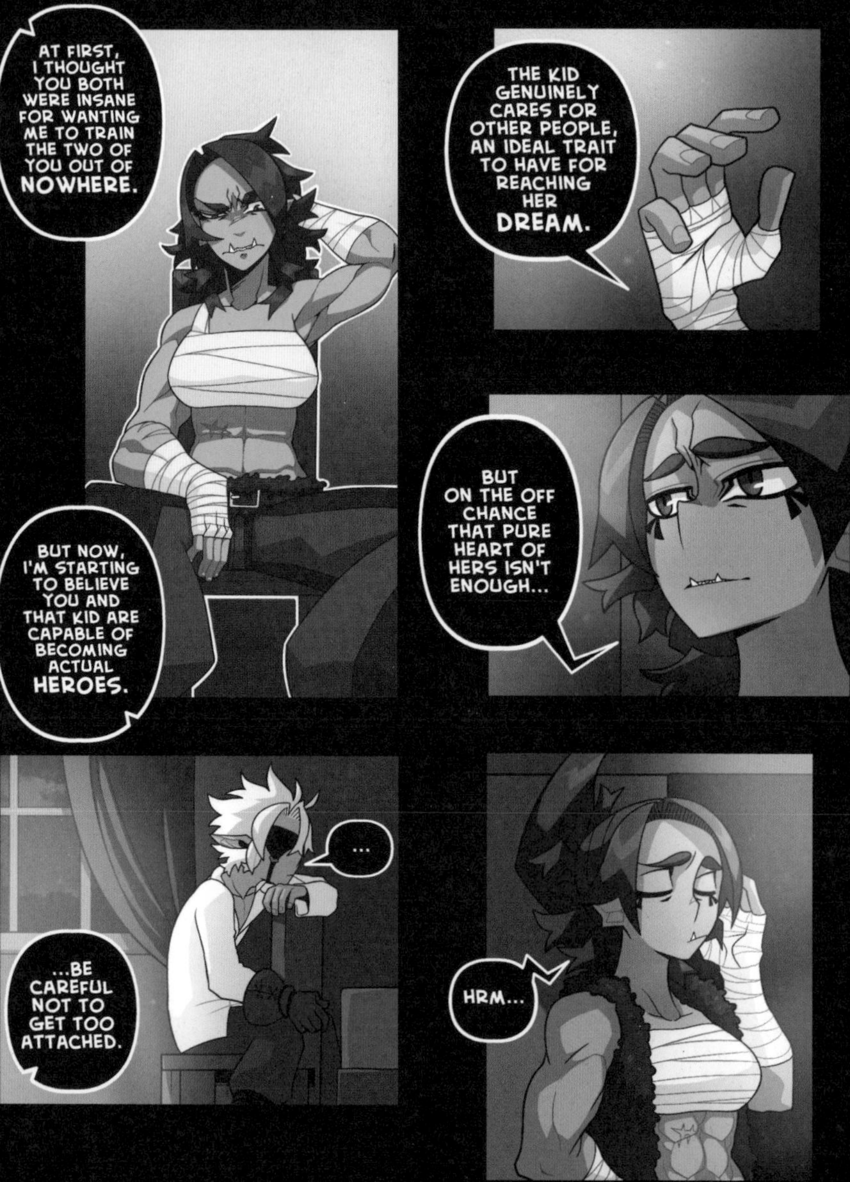
AT FIRST, I THOUGHT YOU BOTH WERE INSANE FOR WANTING ME TO TRAIN THE TWO OF YOU OUT OF NOWHERE.
BUT NOW, I'M STARTING TO BELIEVE YOU AND THAT KID ARE CAPABLE OF BECOMING ACTUAL HEROES.
THE KID GENUINELY CARES FOR OTHER PEOPLE, AN IDEAL TRAIT TO HAVE FOR REACHING HER DREAM.
BUT ON THE OFF CHANCE THAT PURE HEART OF HERS ISN'T ENOUGH...
...
...BE CAREFUL NOT TO GET TOO ATTACHED.
HRM...

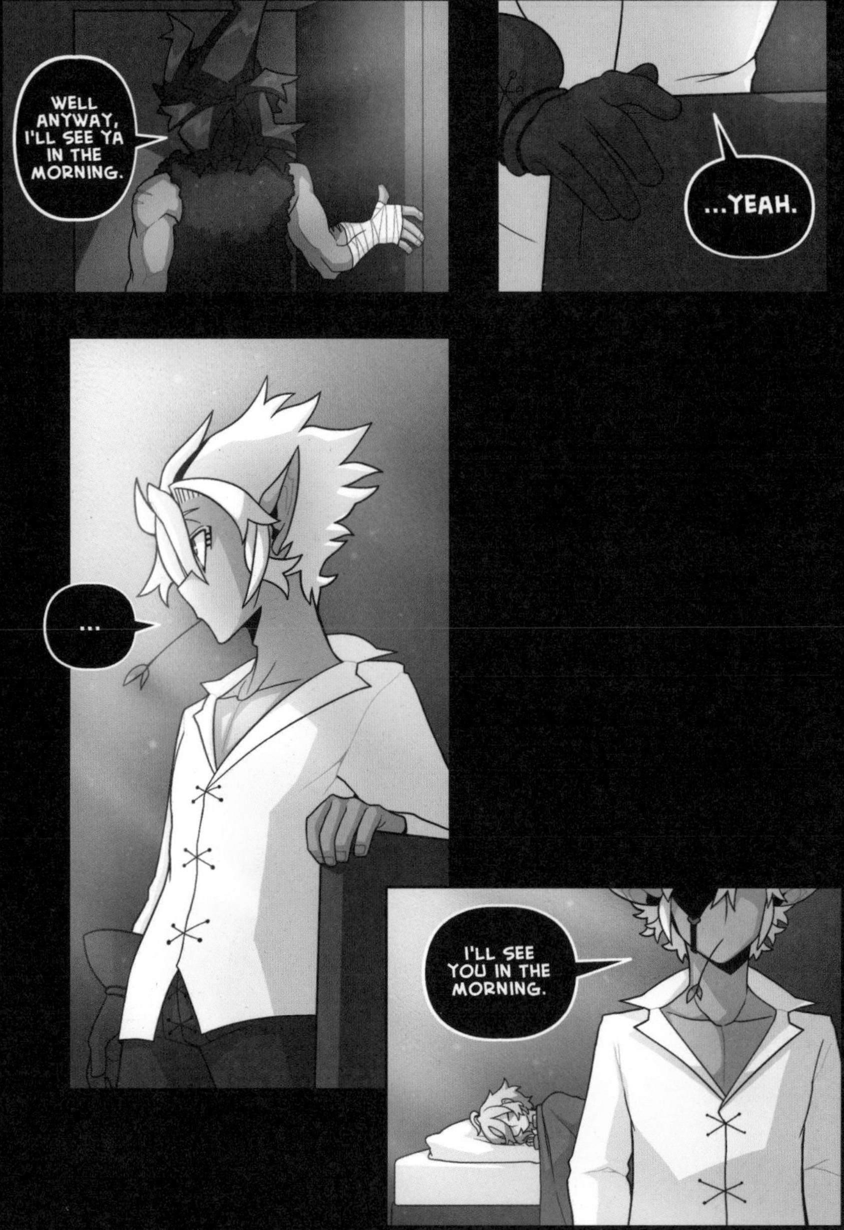
WELL ANYWAY, I'LL SEE YA IN THE MORNING.
...YEAH.
...
I'LL SEE YOU IN THE MORNING.

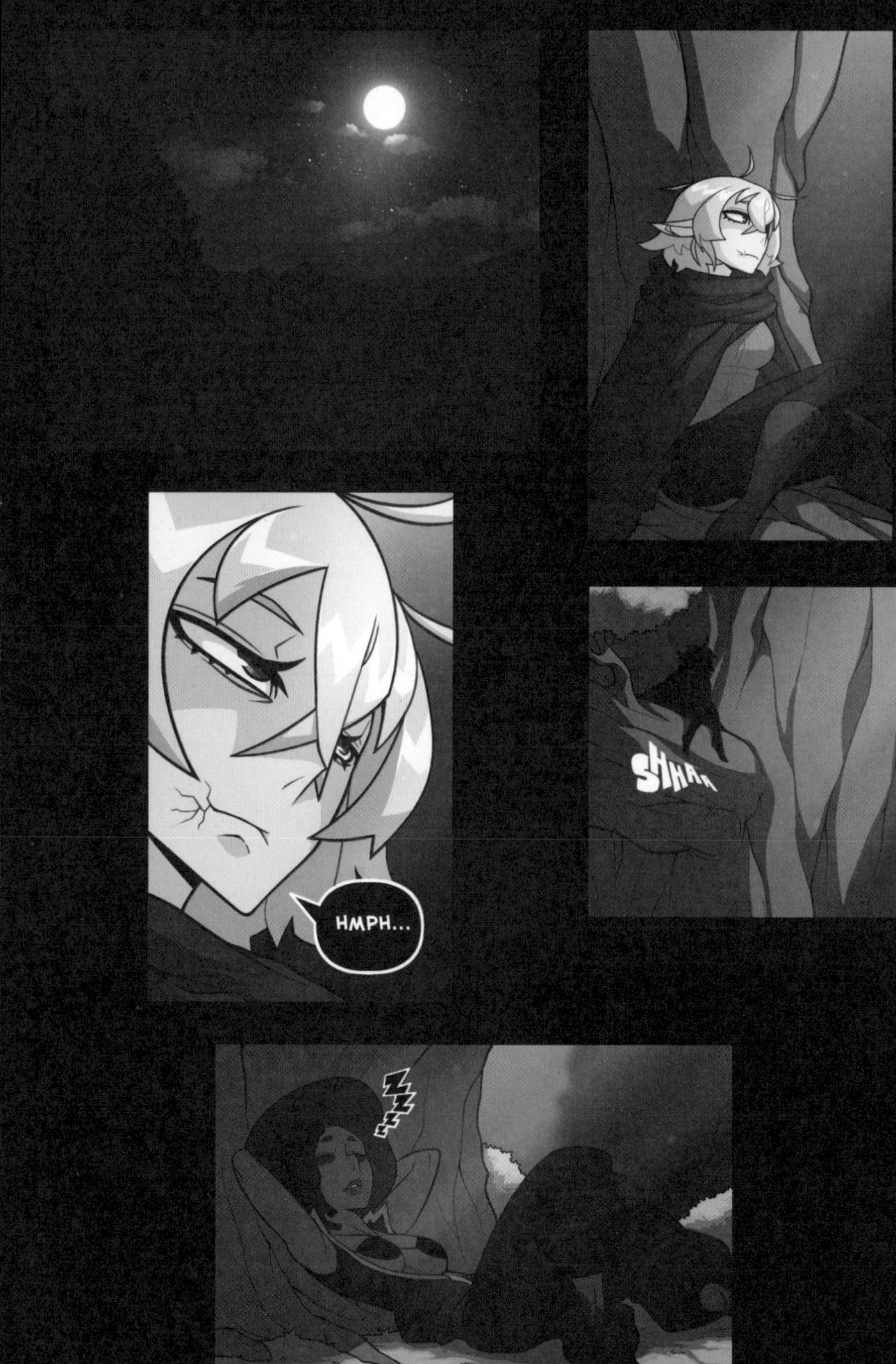
HMPH...
SHHAA
ZZZ

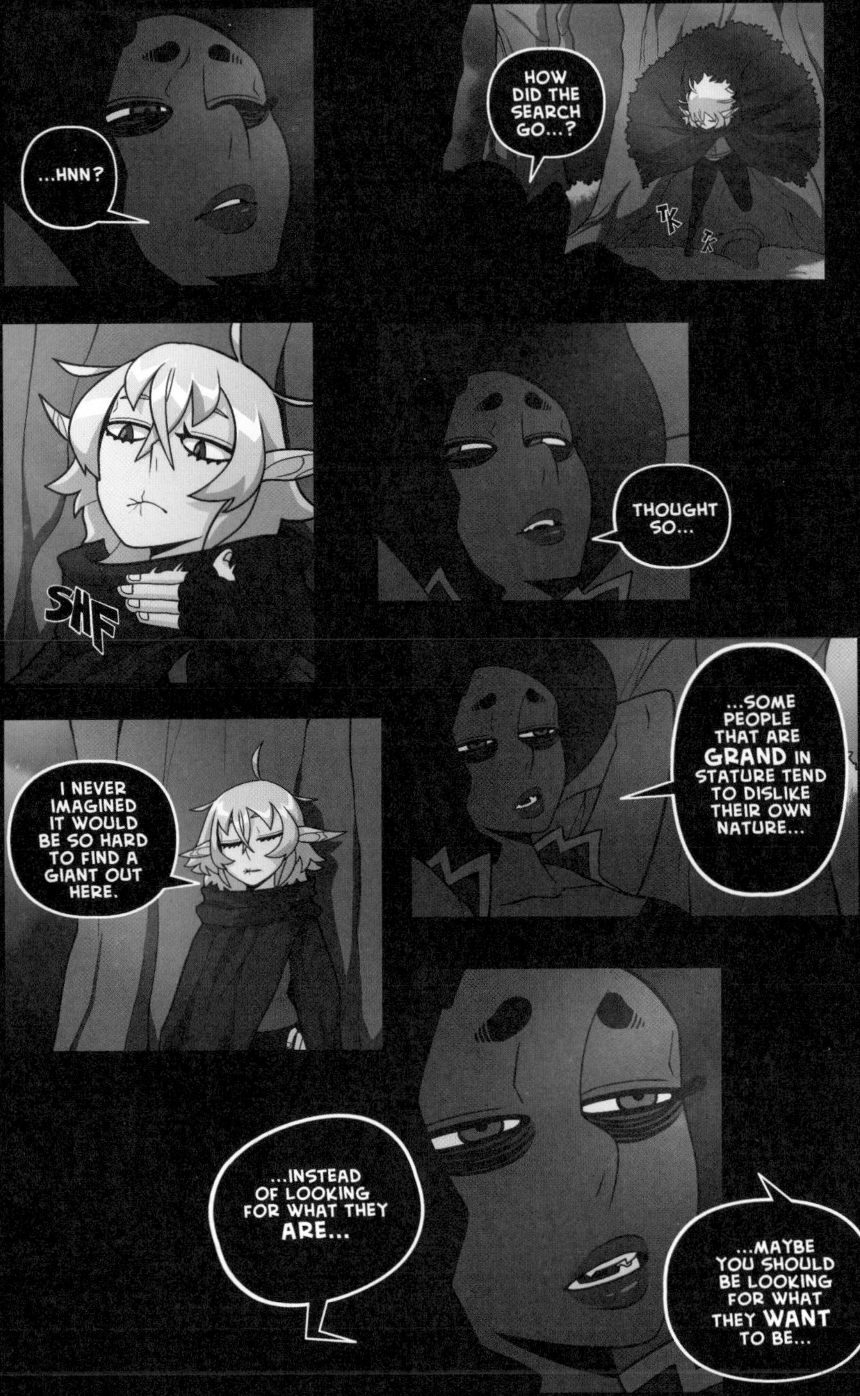

...HNN?
HOW DID THE SEARCH GO...?
TK TK
SHF
THOUGHT SO...
I NEVER IMAGINED IT WOULD BE SO HARD TO FIND A GIANT OUT HERE.
...SOME PEOPLE THAT ARE GRAND IN STATURE TEND TO DISLIKE THEIR OWN NATURE...
...INSTEAD OF LOOKING FOR WHAT THEY ARE...
...MAYBE YOU SHOULD BE LOOKING FOR WHAT THEY WANT TO BE...

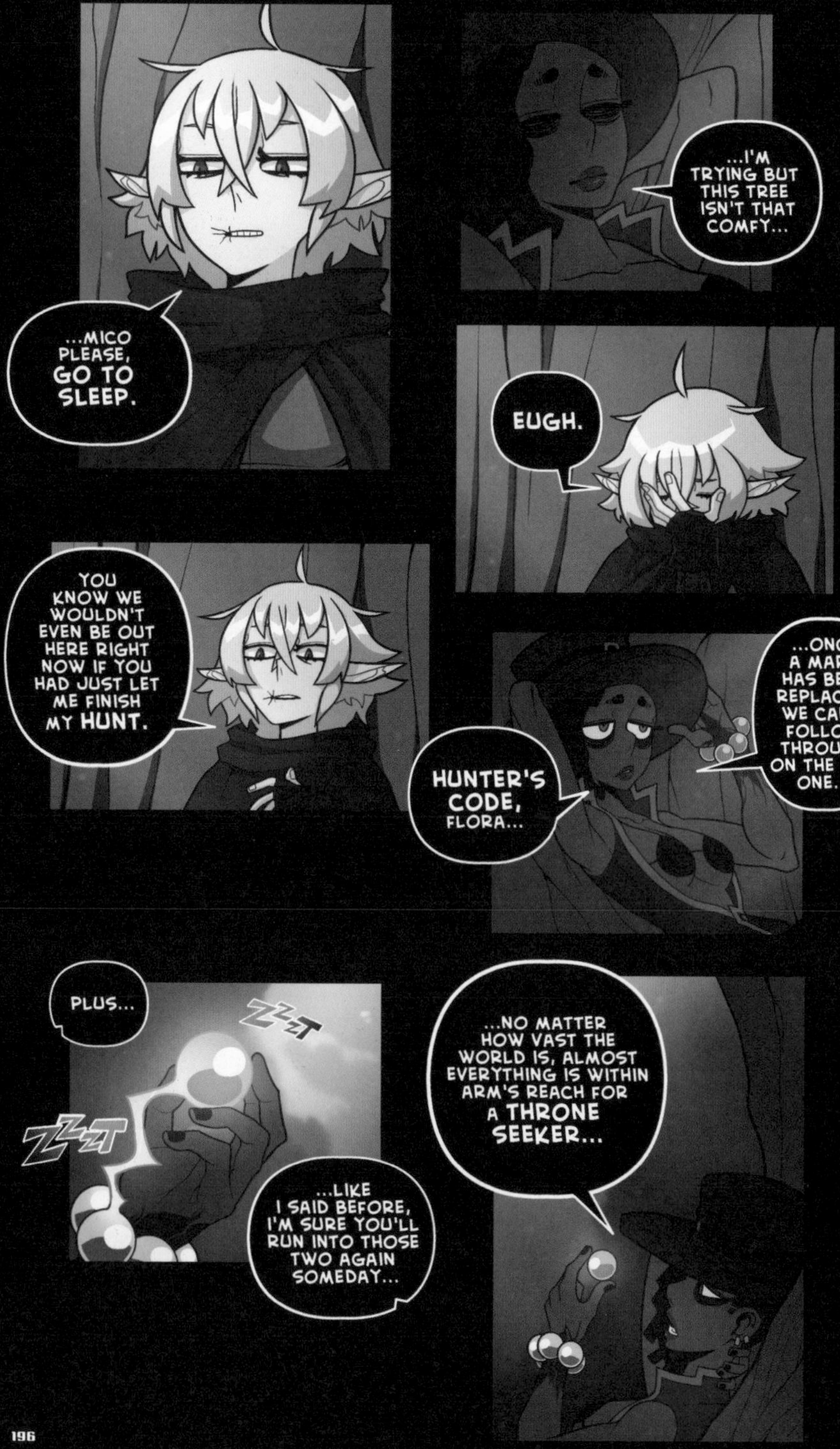
...MICO PLEASE, GO TO SLEEP.
...I'M TRYING BUT THIS TREE ISN'T THAT COMFY...
EUGH.
YOU KNOW WE WOULDN'T EVEN BE OUT HERE RIGHT NOW IF YOU HAD JUST LET ME FINISH MY HUNT.
HUNTER'S CODE, FLORA...
...ONCE A MARK HAS BEEN REPLACED, WE CAN'T FOLLOW THROUGH ON THE OLD ONE...
PLUS...
ZZZT
ZZZT
...LIKE I SAID BEFORE, I'M SURE YOU'LL RUN INTO THOSE TWO AGAIN SOMEDAY...
...NO MATTER HOW VAST THE WORLD IS, ALMOST EVERYTHING IS WITHIN ARM'S REACH FOR A THRONE SEEKER...

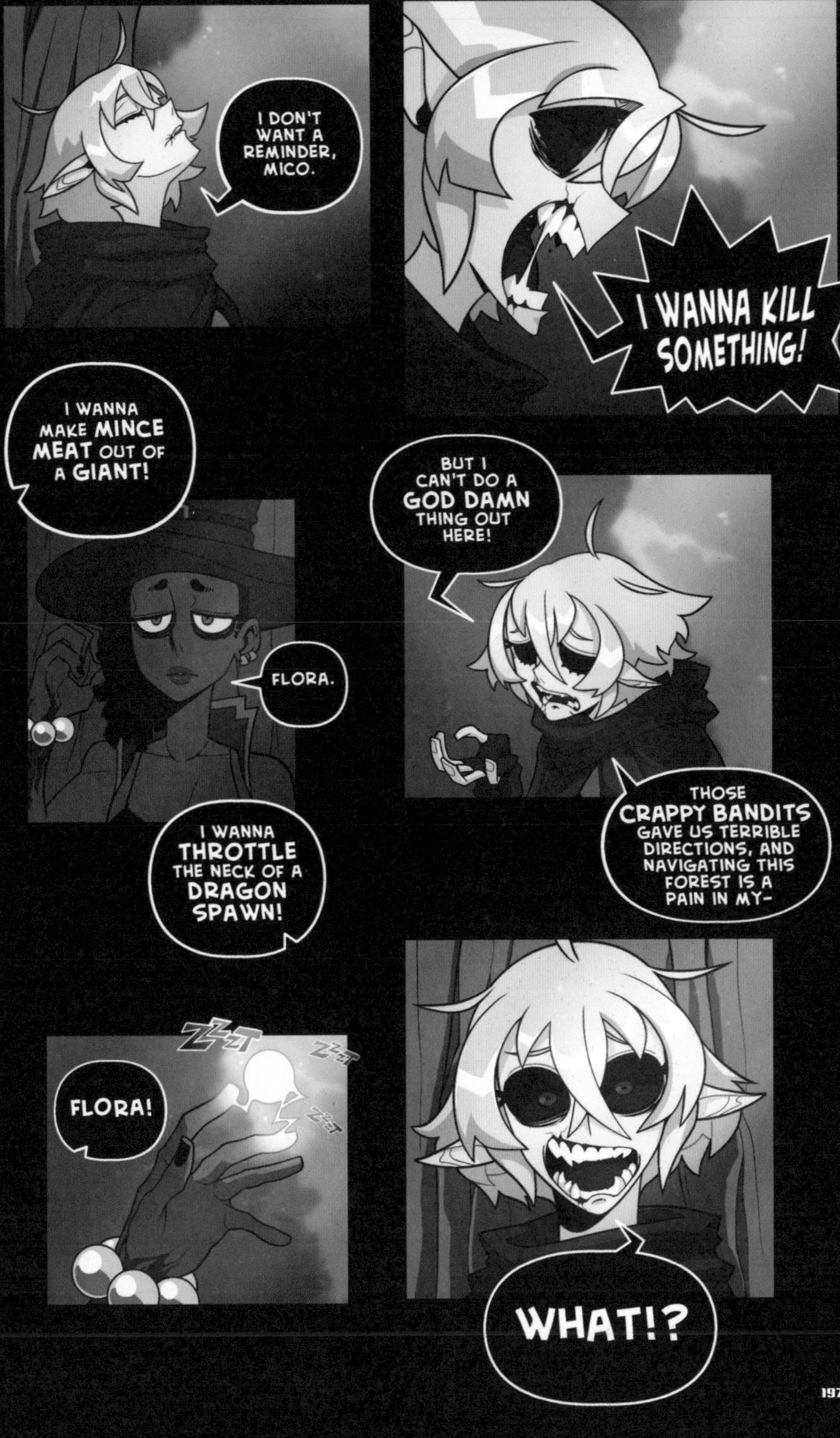
I DON'T WANT A REMINDER, MICO.
I WANNA KILL SOMETHING!
I WANNA MAKE MINCE MEAT OUT OF A GIANT!
FLORA.
I WANNA THROTTLE THE NECK OF A DRAGON SPAWN!
BUT I CAN'T DO A GOD DAMN THING OUT HERE!
THOSE CRAPPY BANDITS GAVE US TERRIBLE DIRECTIONS, AND NAVIGATING THIS FOREST IS A PAIN IN MY-
ZZZT
ZZZT
ZZZT
FLORA!
WHAT!?

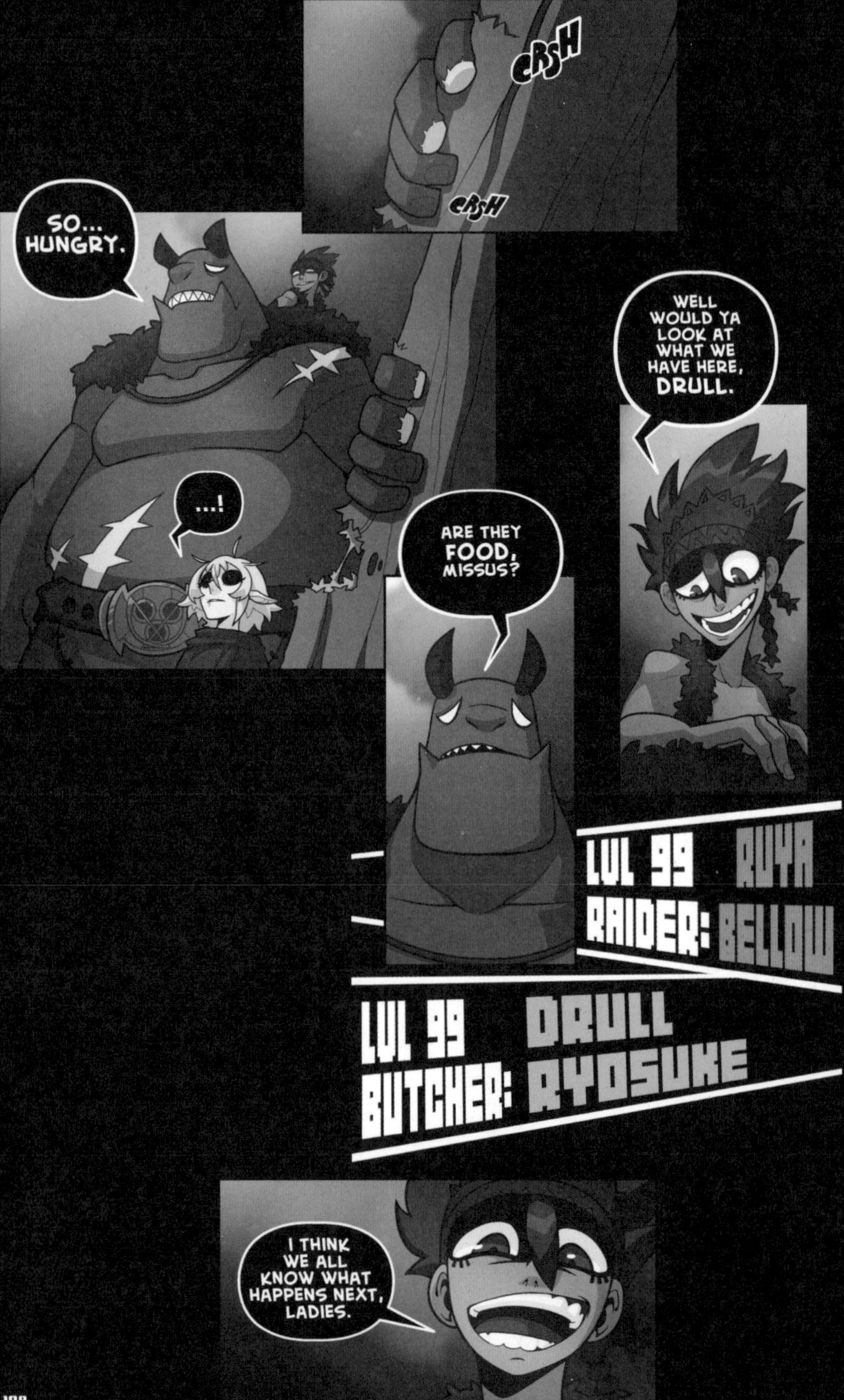
CRSH
CRSH
SO... HUNGRY.
...!
WELL WOULD YA LOOK AT WHAT WE HAVE HERE, DRULL.
ARE THEY FOOD, MISSUS?
LVL 99 RUYA
RAIDER: BELLOW
LVL 99 DRULL
BUTCHER: RYOSUKE
I THINK WE ALL KNOW WHAT HAPPENS NEXT, LADIES.

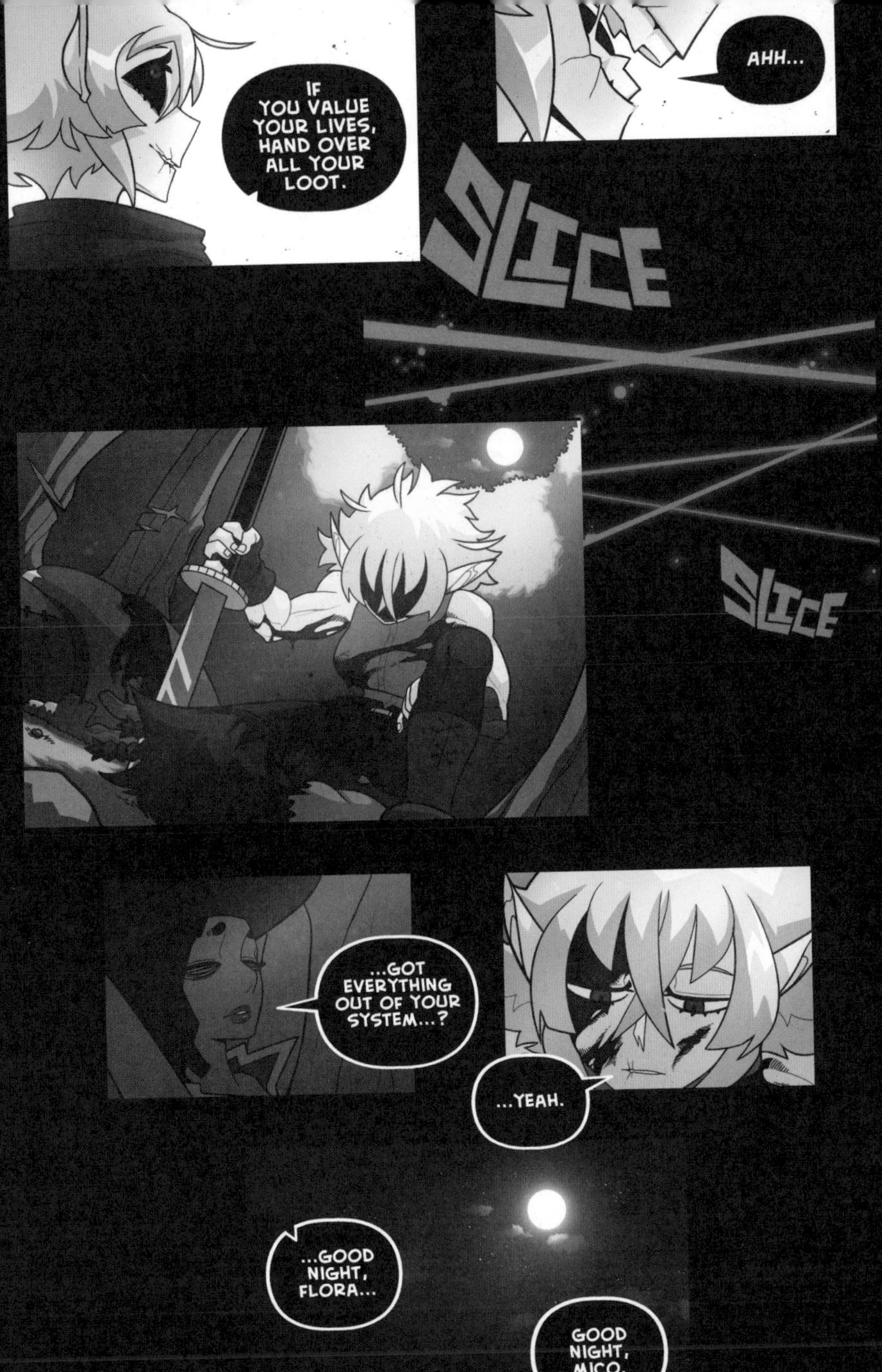
IF YOU VALUE YOUR LIVES, HAND OVER ALL YOUR LOOT.
AHH...
SLICE
SLICE
...GOT EVERYTHING OUT OF YOUR SYSTEM...?
...YEAH.
...GOOD NIGHT, FLORA...
GOOD NIGHT, MICO.

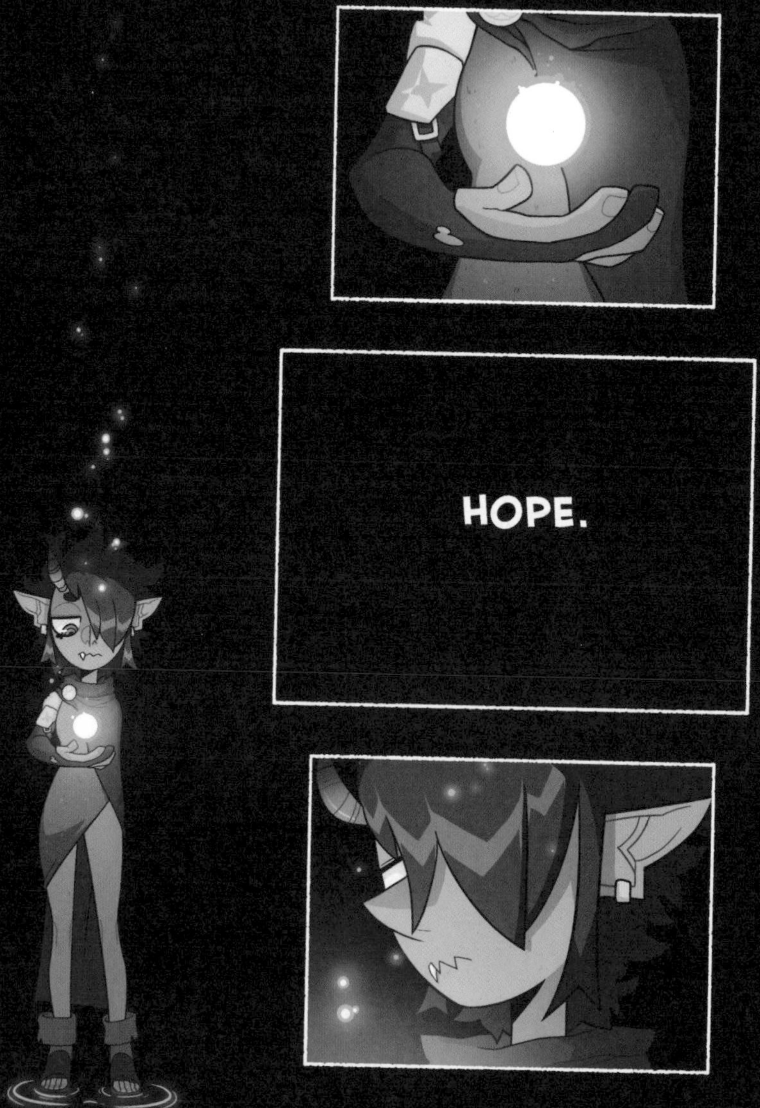
HOPE.

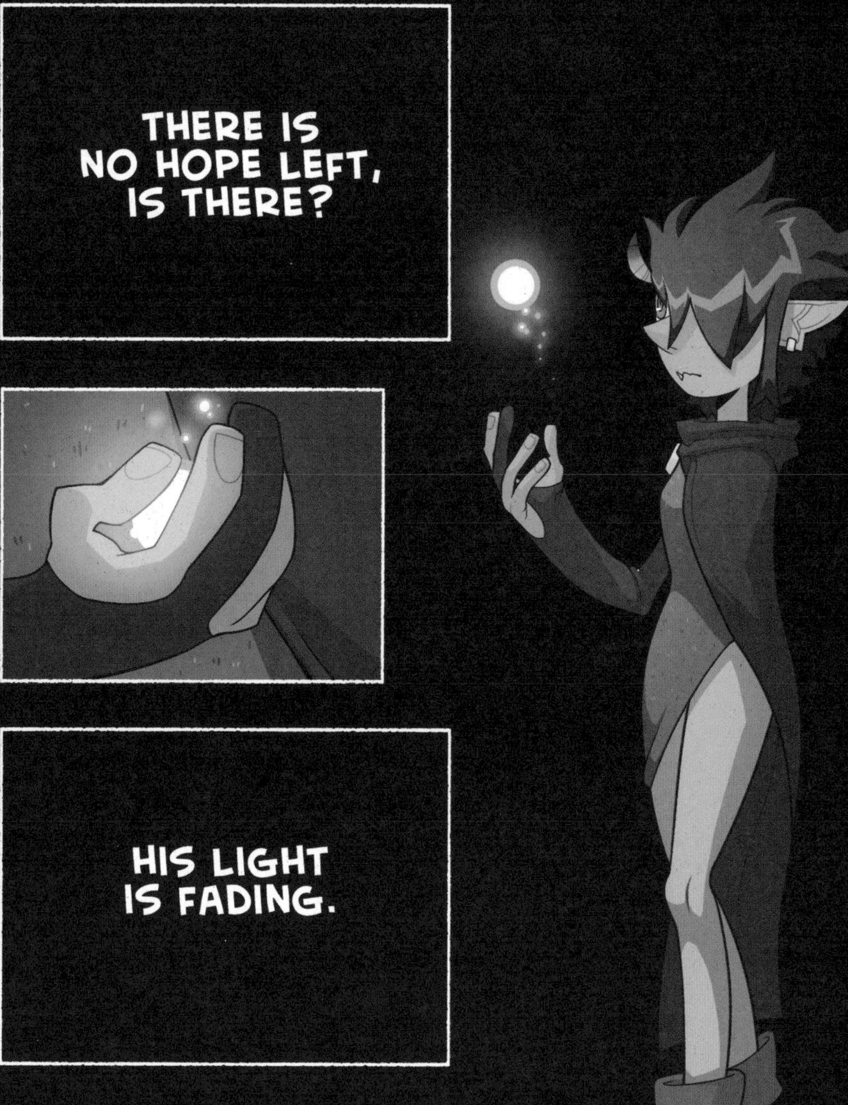
THERE IS
NO HOPE LEFT,
IS THERE?
HIS LIGHT
IS FADING.

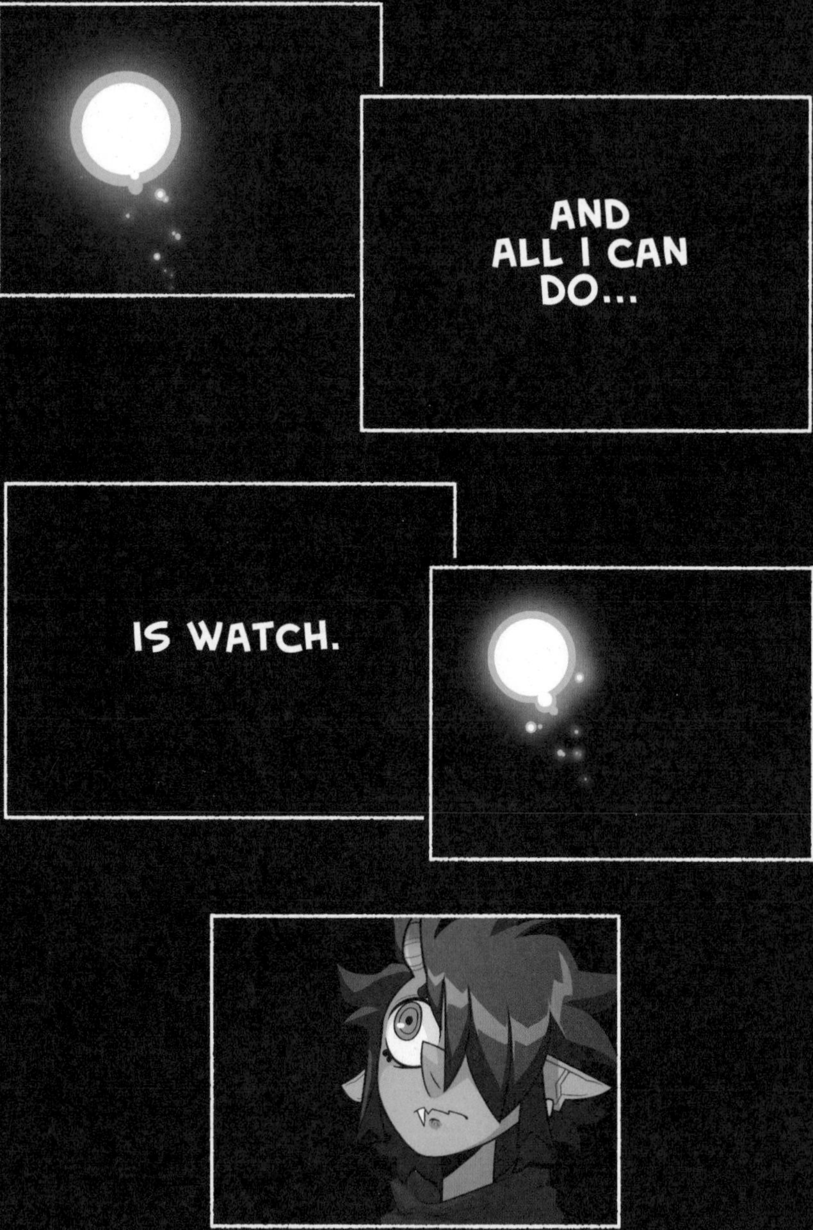
AND ALL I CAN DO...
IS WATCH.

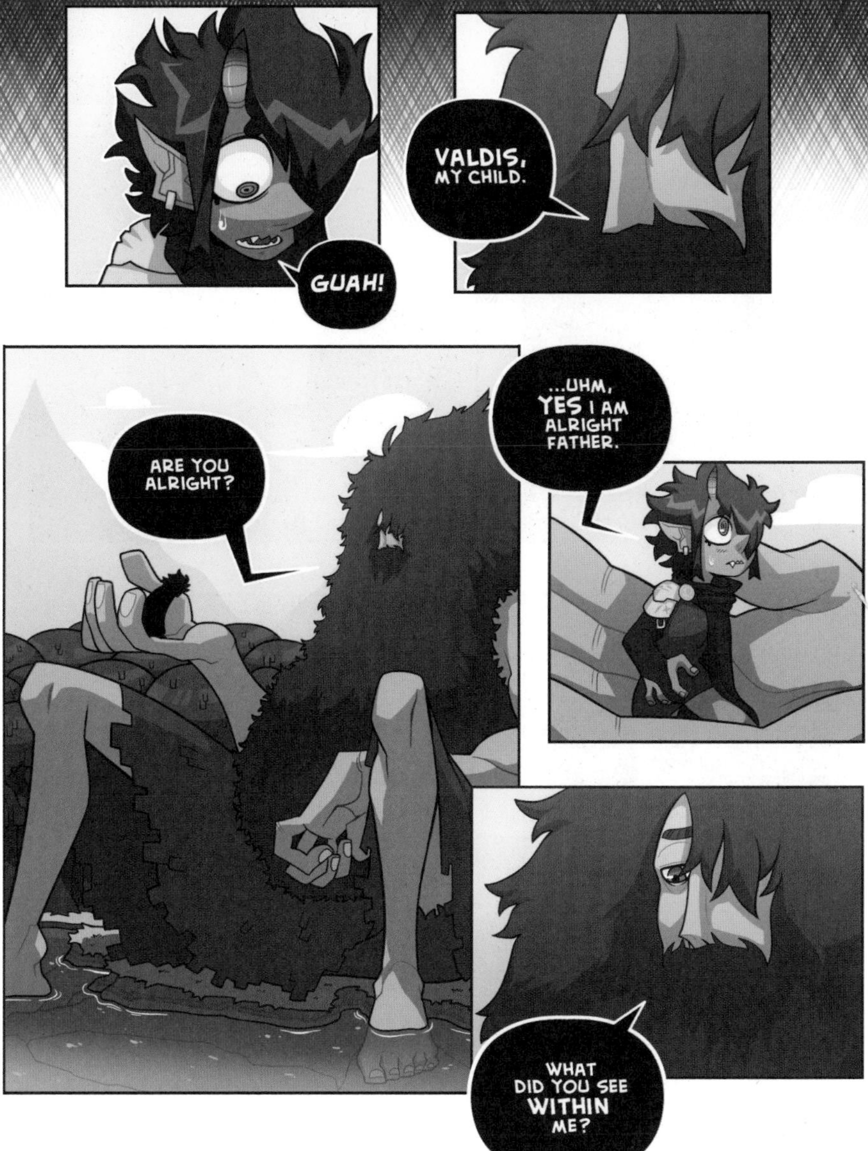
GUAH!
VALDIS, MY CHILD.
ARE YOU ALRIGHT?
...UHM, YES I AM ALRIGHT FATHER.
WHAT DID YOU SEE WITHIN ME?

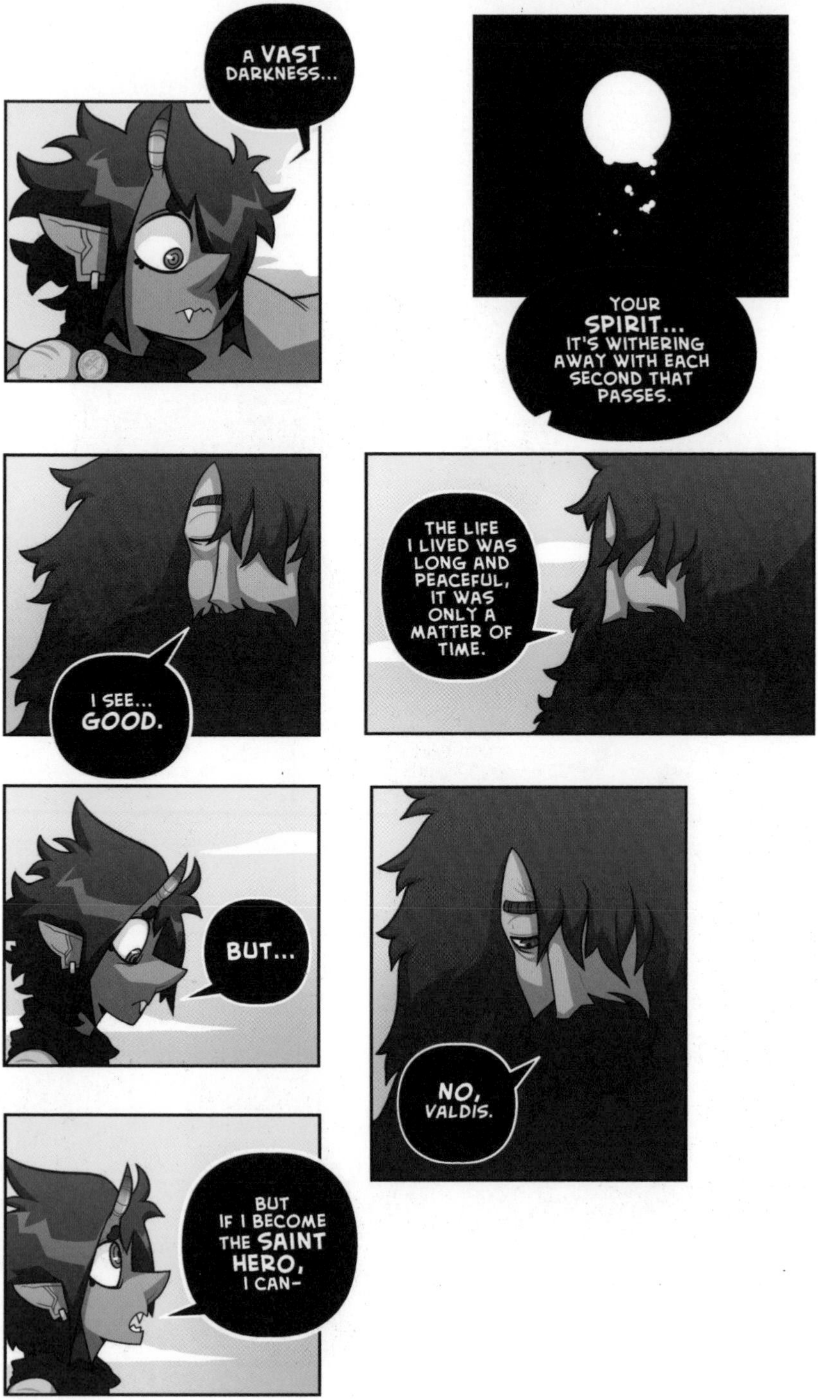
A VAST DARKNESS...
YOUR SPIRIT... IT'S WITHERING AWAY WITH EACH SECOND THAT PASSES.
I SEE... GOOD.
THE LIFE I LIVED WAS LONG AND PEACEFUL, IT WAS ONLY A MATTER OF TIME.
BUT...
NO, VALDIS.
BUT IF I BECOME THE SAINT HERO, I CAN-

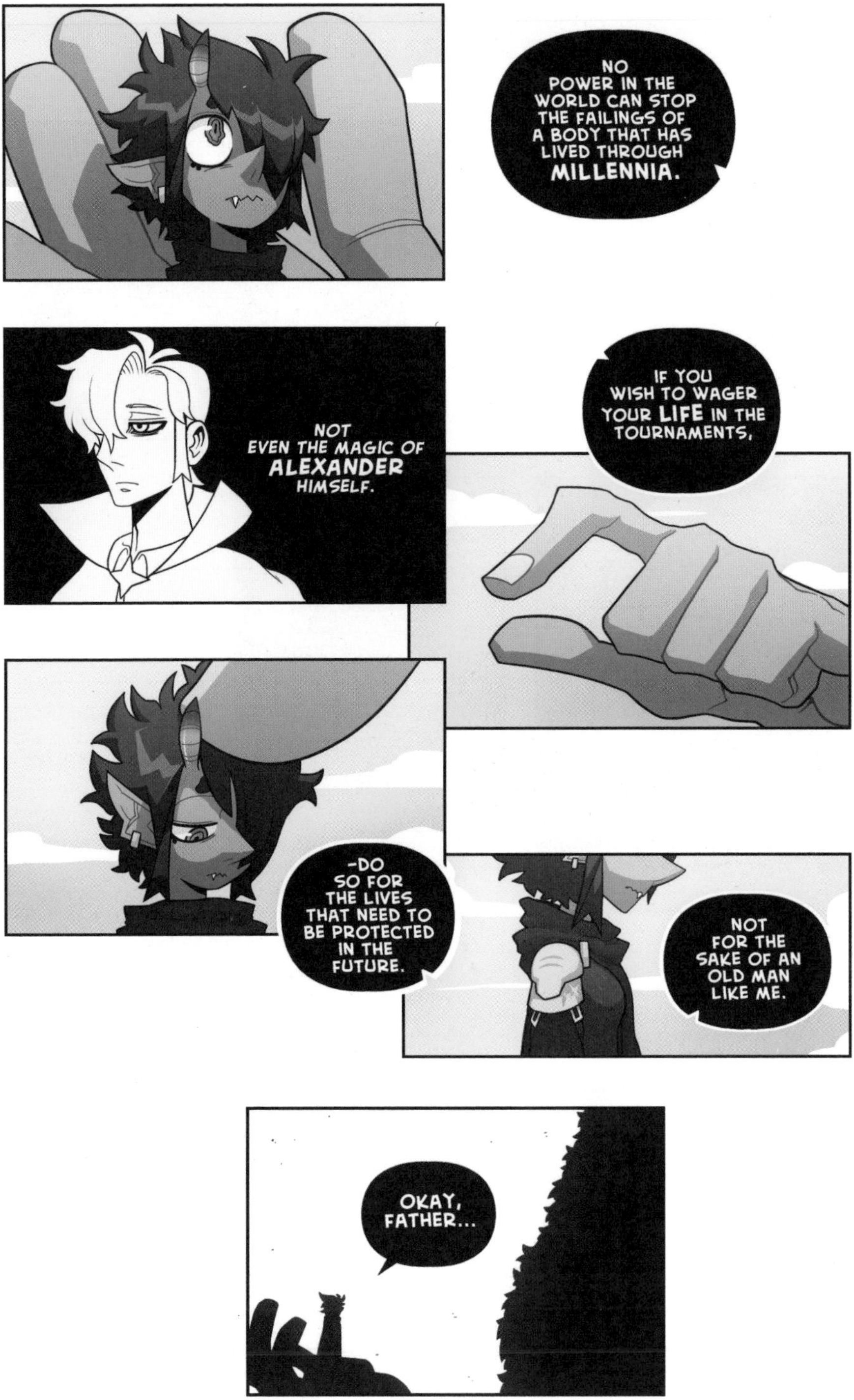
NO POWER IN THE WORLD CAN STOP THE FAILINGS OF A BODY THAT HAS LIVED THROUGH MILLENNIA.
NOT EVEN THE MAGIC OF ALEXANDER HIMSELF.
IF YOU WISH TO WAGER YOUR LIFE IN THE TOURNAMENTS,
-DO SO FOR THE LIVES THAT NEED TO BE PROTECTED IN THE FUTURE.
NOT FOR THE SAKE OF AN OLD MAN LIKE ME.
OKAY, FATHER...

## Chapter 18
# THE STARTING LINE

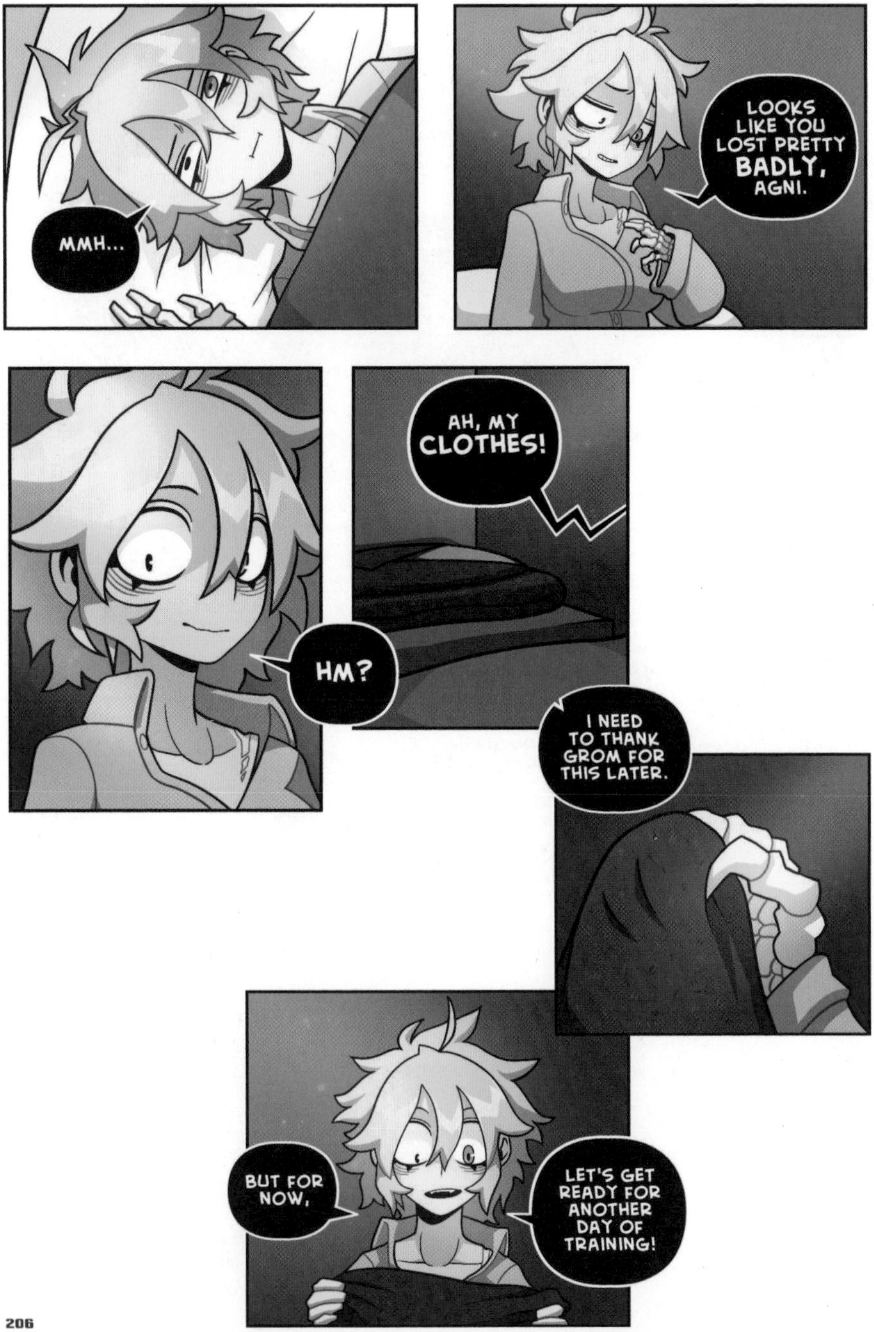
MMH...
LOOKS LIKE YOU LOST PRETTY BADLY, AGNI.
HM?
AH, MY CLOTHES!
I NEED TO THANK GROM FOR THIS LATER.
BUT FOR NOW,
LET'S GET READY FOR ANOTHER DAY OF TRAINING!

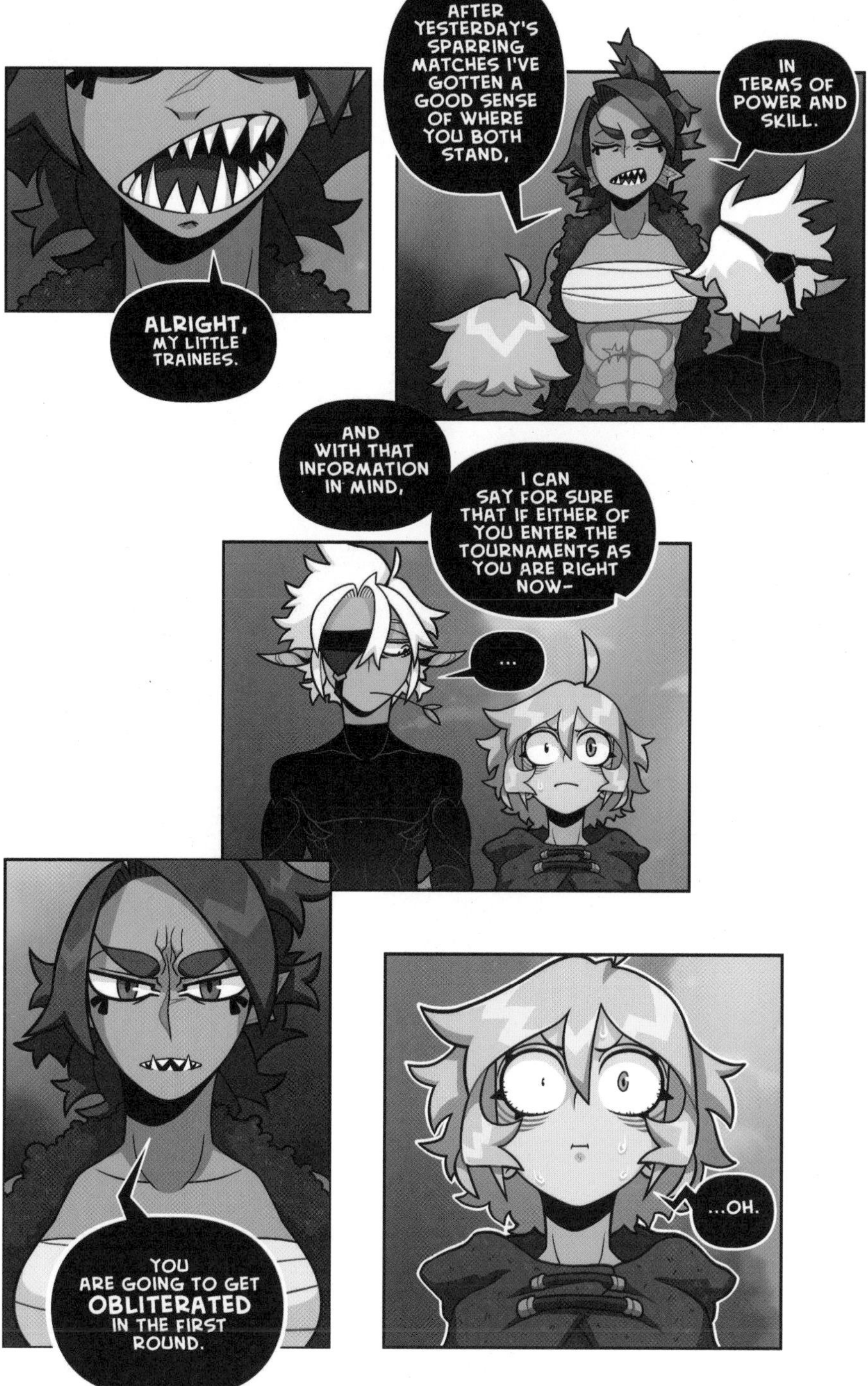
ALRIGHT, MY LITTLE TRAINEES.
AFTER YESTERDAY'S SPARRING MATCHES I'VE GOTTEN A GOOD SENSE OF WHERE YOU BOTH STAND,
IN TERMS OF POWER AND SKILL.
AND WITH THAT INFORMATION IN MIND,
I CAN SAY FOR SURE THAT IF EITHER OF YOU ENTER THE TOURNAMENTS AS YOU ARE RIGHT NOW-
...
YOU ARE GOING TO GET OBLITERATED IN THE FIRST ROUND.
...OH.

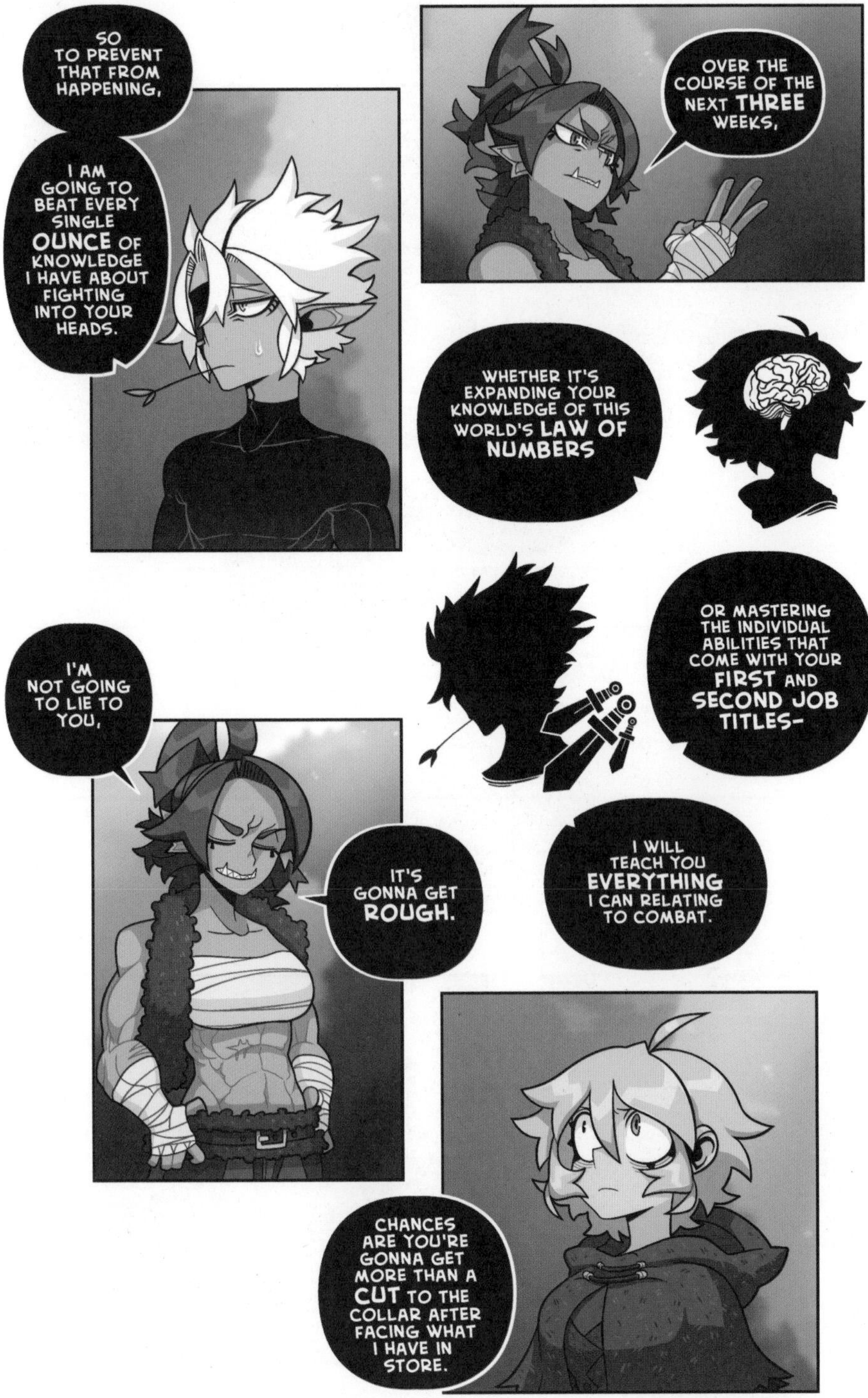
SO TO PREVENT THAT FROM HAPPENING,
I AM GOING TO BEAT EVERY SINGLE OUNCE OF KNOWLEDGE I HAVE ABOUT FIGHTING INTO YOUR HEADS.
OVER THE COURSE OF THE NEXT THREE WEEKS,
WHETHER IT'S EXPANDING YOUR KNOWLEDGE OF THIS WORLD'S LAW OF NUMBERS
OR MASTERING THE INDIVIDUAL ABILITIES THAT COME WITH YOUR FIRST AND SECOND JOB TITLES-
I WILL TEACH YOU EVERYTHING I CAN RELATING TO COMBAT.
I'M NOT GOING TO LIE TO YOU,
IT'S GONNA GET ROUGH.
CHANCES ARE YOU'RE GONNA GET MORE THAN A CUT TO THE COLLAR AFTER FACING WHAT I HAVE IN STORE.

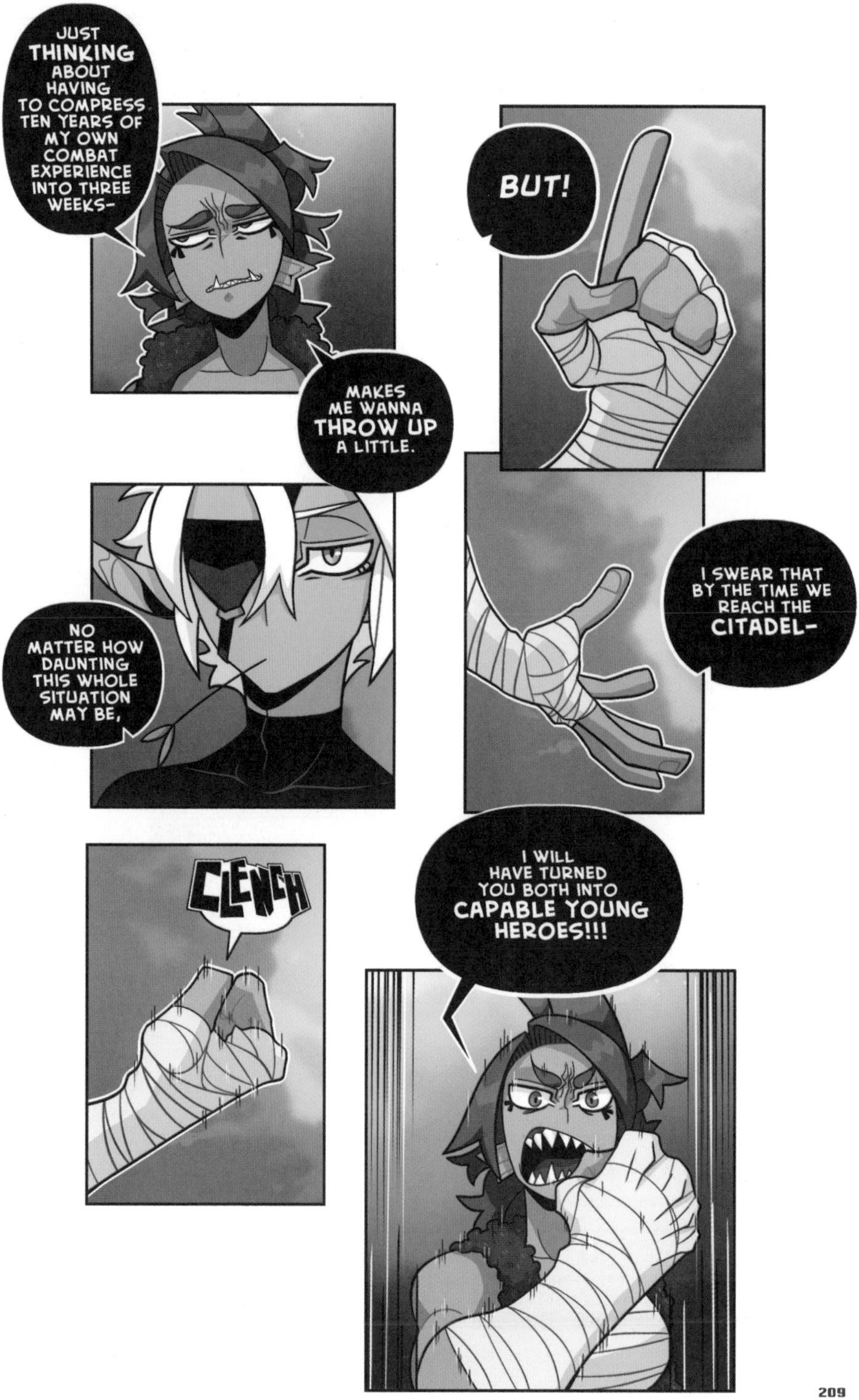
JUST THINKING ABOUT HAVING TO COMPRESS TEN YEARS OF MY OWN COMBAT EXPERIENCE INTO THREE WEEKS-
MAKES ME WANNA THROW UP A LITTLE.
BUT!
NO MATTER HOW DAUNTING THIS WHOLE SITUATION MAY BE,
I SWEAR THAT BY THE TIME WE REACH THE CITADEL-
CLENCH
I WILL HAVE TURNED YOU BOTH INTO CAPABLE YOUNG HEROES!!!

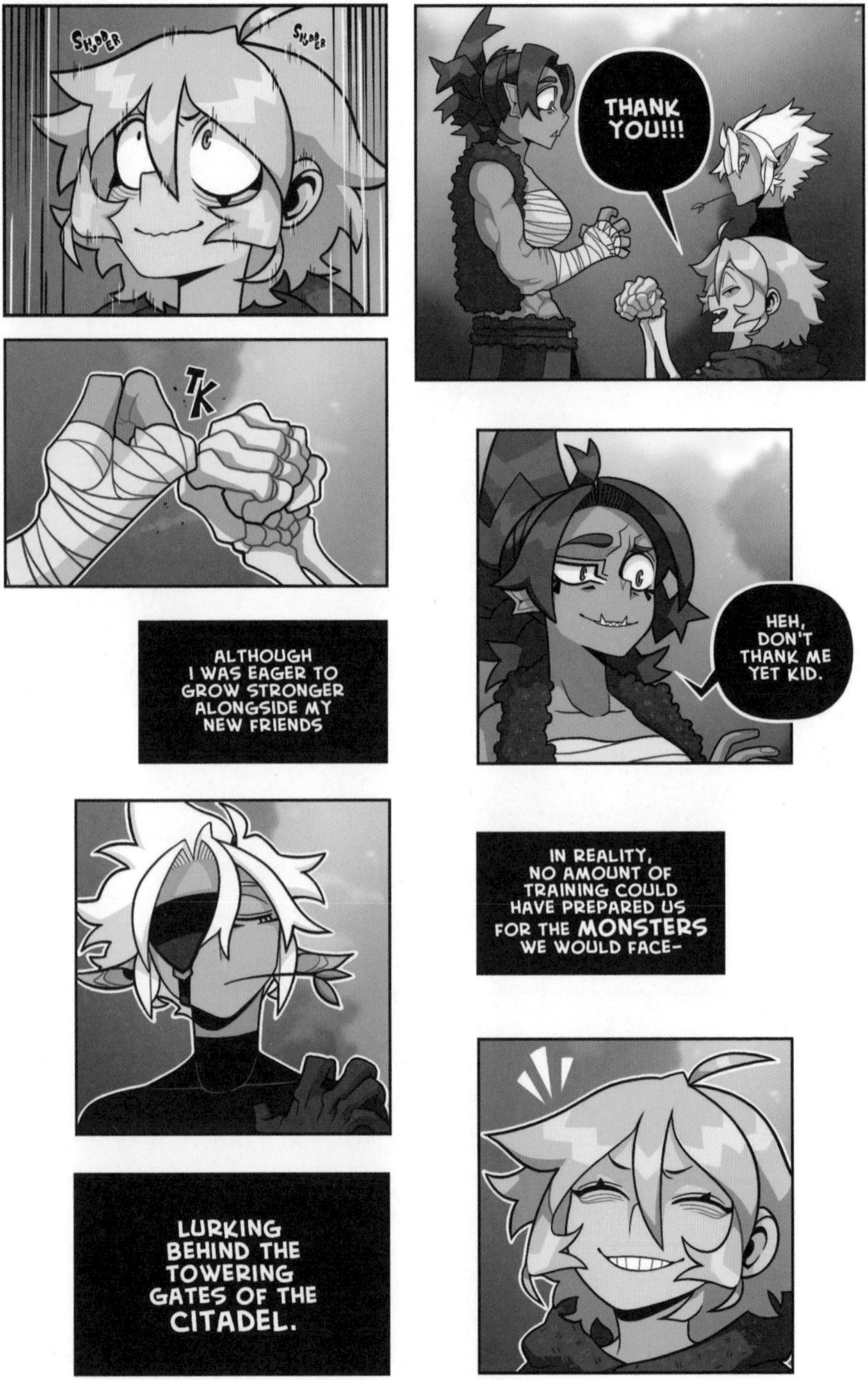
SHUDDER
SHUDDER
THANK YOU!!!
TK
HEH, DON'T THANK ME YET KID.
ALTHOUGH I WAS EAGER TO GROW STRONGER ALONGSIDE MY NEW FRIENDS
IN REALITY, NO AMOUNT OF TRAINING COULD HAVE PREPARED US FOR THE MONSTERS WE WOULD FACE-
LURKING BEHIND THE TOWERING GATES OF THE CITADEL.

# Chapter 19
## THE ROUTINE

THE THREE WEEKS WE SPENT TRAINING UNDER REKSHA WENT BY IN A FLASH.

ALTHOUGH SHE HAD TOLD US IT WOULD BE A GRUELING TEST OF OUR ABILITIES,

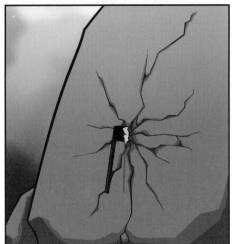

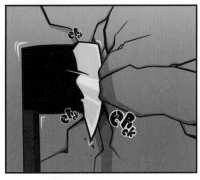

BY THE END OF OUR TRAINING, I COULD ONLY REMEMBER HOW MUCH I CHERISHED OUR TIME TOGETHER.

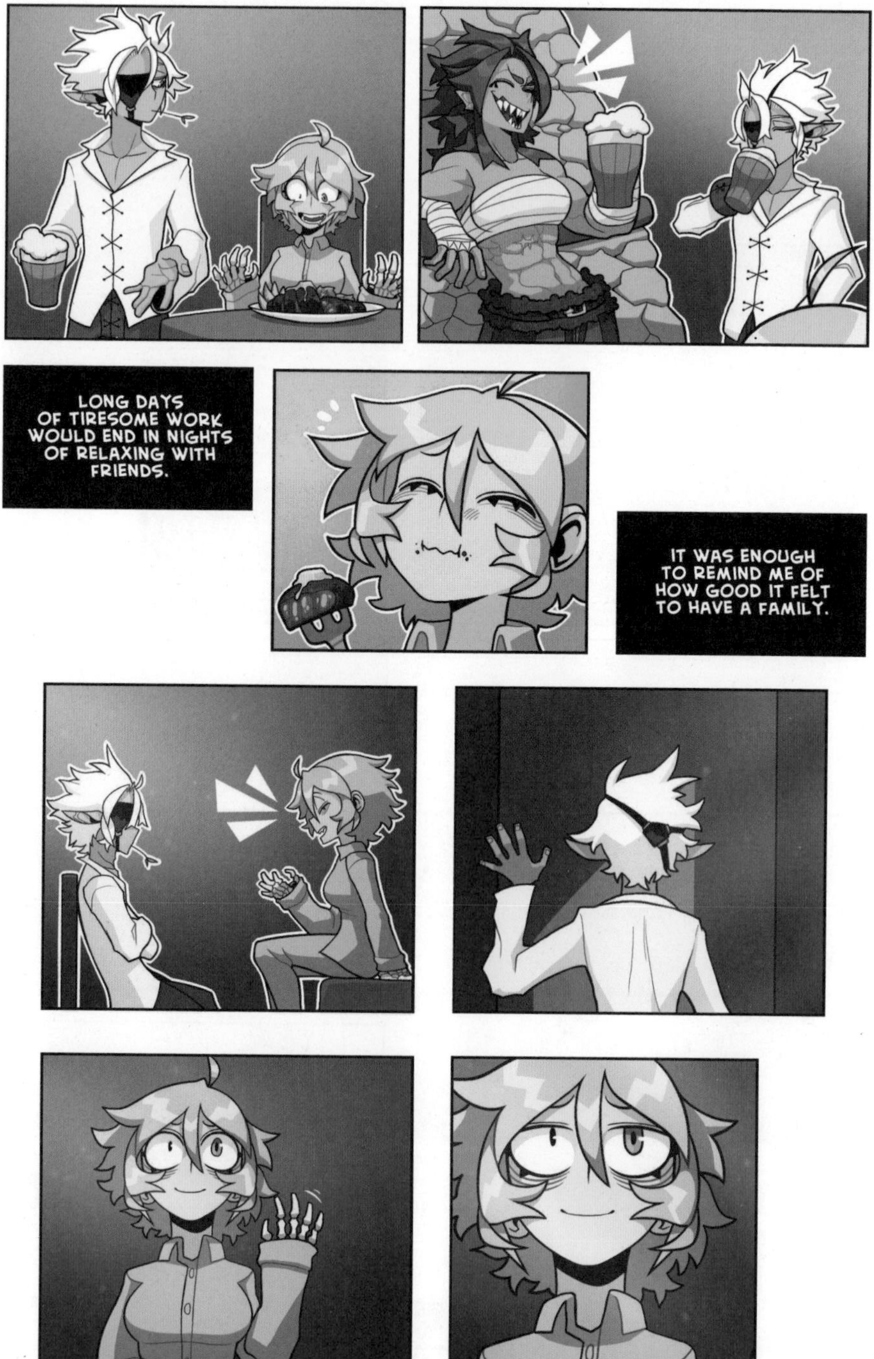
LONG DAYS OF TIRESOME WORK WOULD END IN NIGHTS OF RELAXING WITH FRIENDS.
IT WAS ENOUGH TO REMIND ME OF HOW GOOD IT FELT TO HAVE A FAMILY.

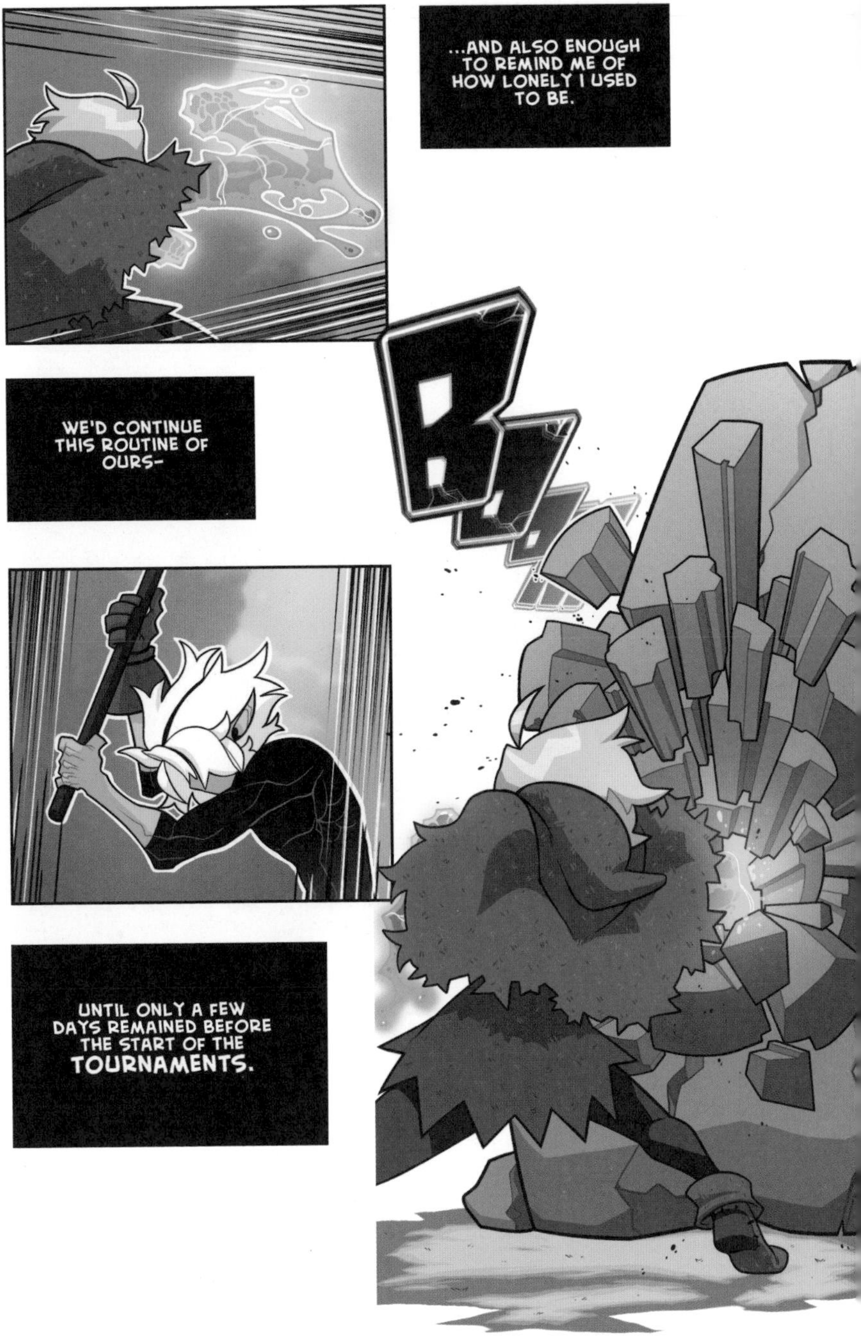
...AND ALSO ENOUGH TO REMIND ME OF HOW LONELY I USED TO BE.
WE'D CONTINUE THIS ROUTINE OF OURS-
UNTIL ONLY A FEW DAYS REMAINED BEFORE THE START OF THE TOURNAMENTS.

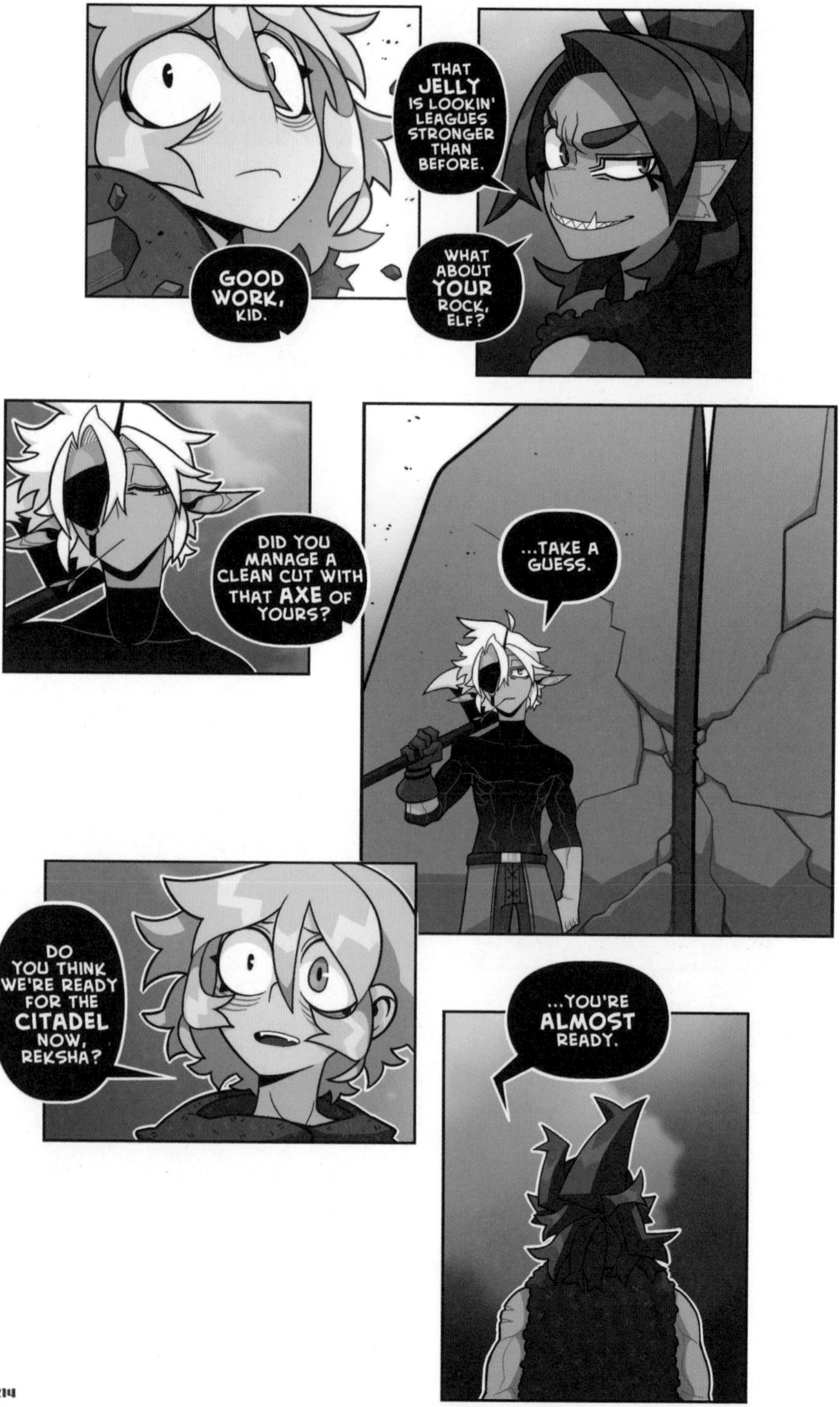
GOOD WORK, KID.
THAT JELLY IS LOOKIN' LEAGUES STRONGER THAN BEFORE.
WHAT ABOUT YOUR ROCK, ELF?
DID YOU MANAGE A CLEAN CUT WITH THAT AXE OF YOURS?
...TAKE A GUESS.
DO YOU THINK WE'RE READY FOR THE CITADEL NOW, REKSHA?
...YOU'RE ALMOST READY.

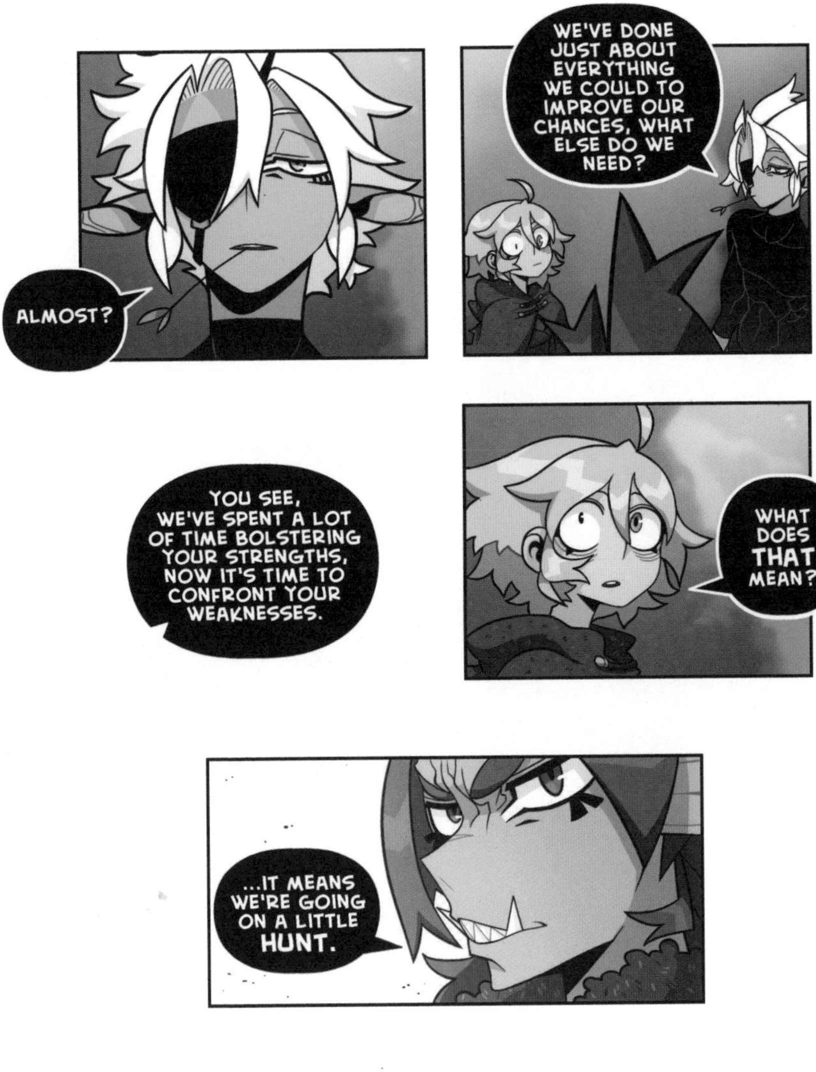
ALMOST?
WE'VE DONE JUST ABOUT EVERYTHING WE COULD TO IMPROVE OUR CHANCES, WHAT ELSE DO WE NEED?
YOU SEE, WE'VE SPENT A LOT OF TIME BOLSTERING YOUR STRENGTHS, NOW IT'S TIME TO CONFRONT YOUR WEAKNESSES.
WHAT DOES THAT MEAN?
...IT MEANS WE'RE GOING ON A LITTLE HUNT.

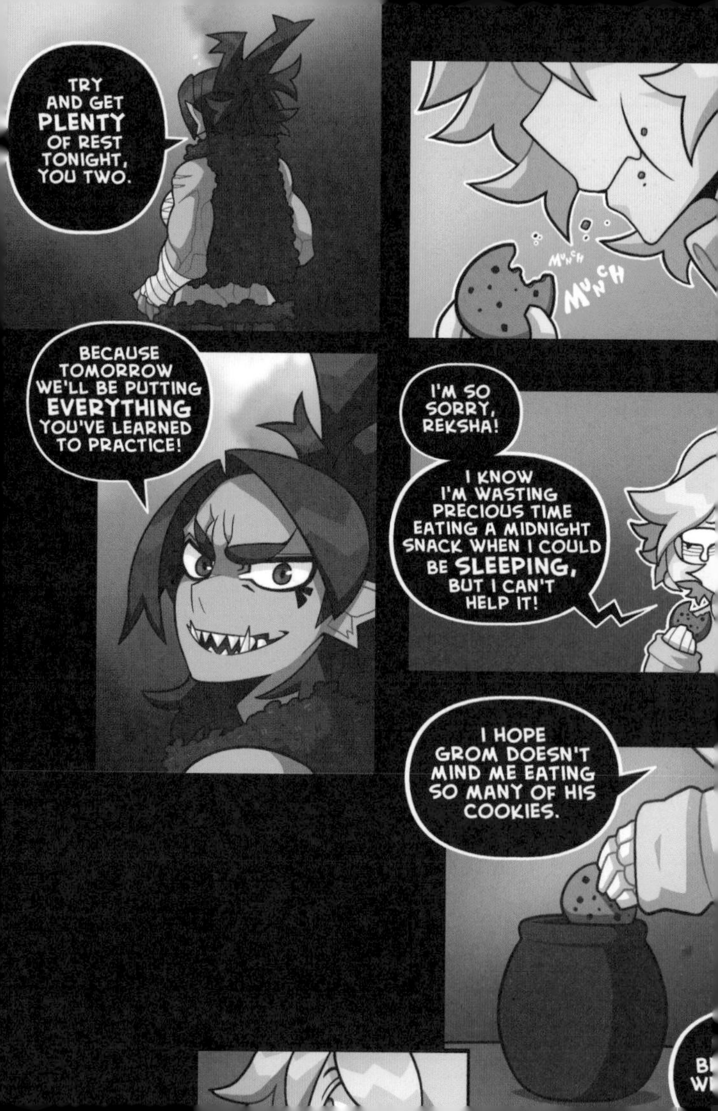
TRY AND GET **PLENTY** OF REST TONIGHT, YOU TWO.
MUNCH MUNCH
BECAUSE TOMORROW WE'LL BE PUTTING **EVERYTHING** YOU'VE LEARNED TO PRACTICE!
I'M SO SORRY, REKSHA!
I KNOW I'M WASTING PRECIOUS TIME EATING A MIDNIGHT SNACK WHEN I COULD BE **SLEEPING,** BUT I CAN'T HELP IT!
I HOPE GROM DOESN'T MIND ME EATING SO MANY OF HIS COOKIES.

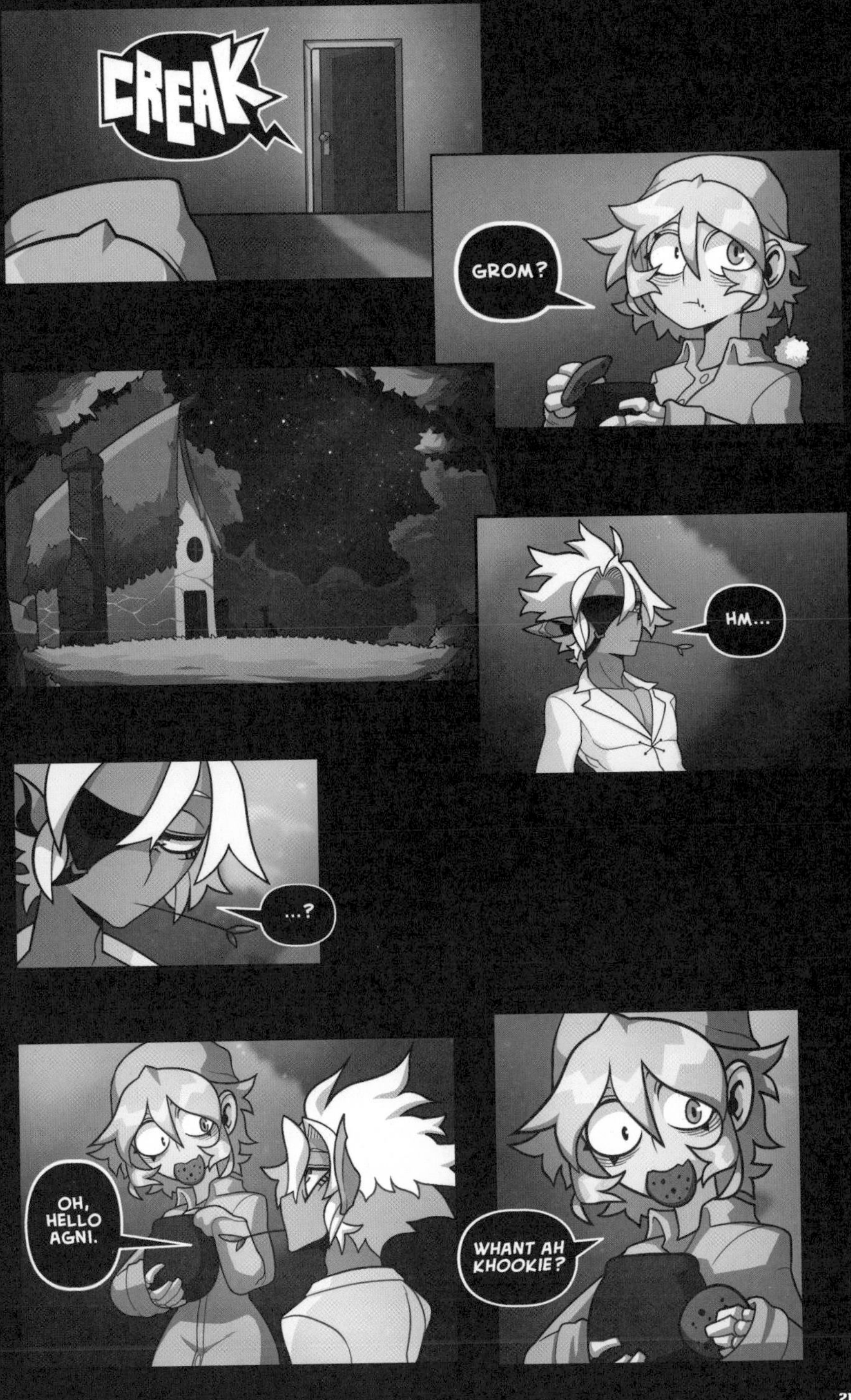
CREAK
GROM?
HM...
...?
OH, HELLO AGNI.
WHANT AH KHOOKIE?

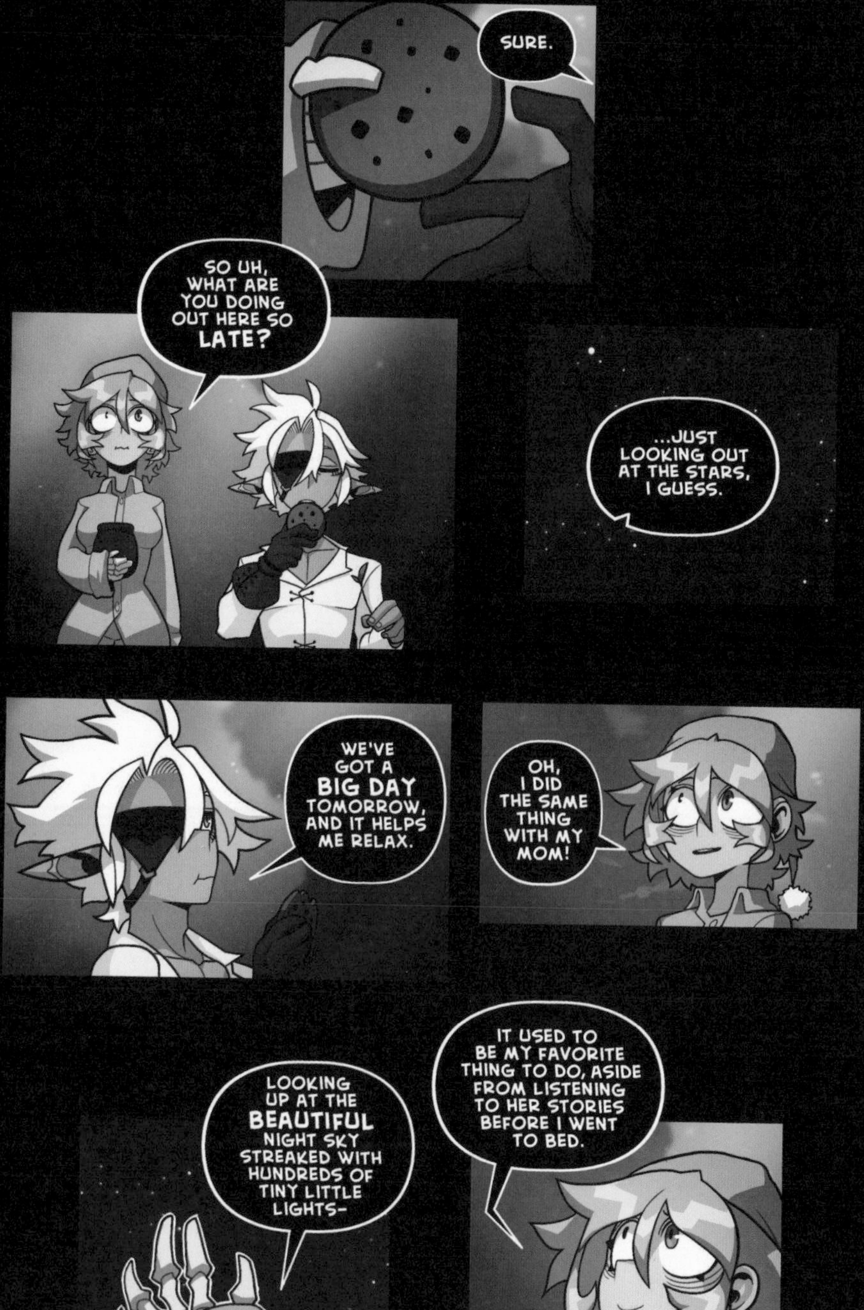
SURE.
SO UH, WHAT ARE YOU DOING OUT HERE SO LATE?
...JUST LOOKING OUT AT THE STARS, I GUESS.
WE'VE GOT A BIG DAY TOMORROW, AND IT HELPS ME RELAX.
OH, I DID THE SAME THING WITH MY MOM!
LOOKING UP AT THE BEAUTIFUL NIGHT SKY STREAKED WITH HUNDREDS OF TINY LITTLE LIGHTS-
IT USED TO BE MY FAVORITE THING TO DO, ASIDE FROM LISTENING TO HER STORIES BEFORE I WENT TO BED.

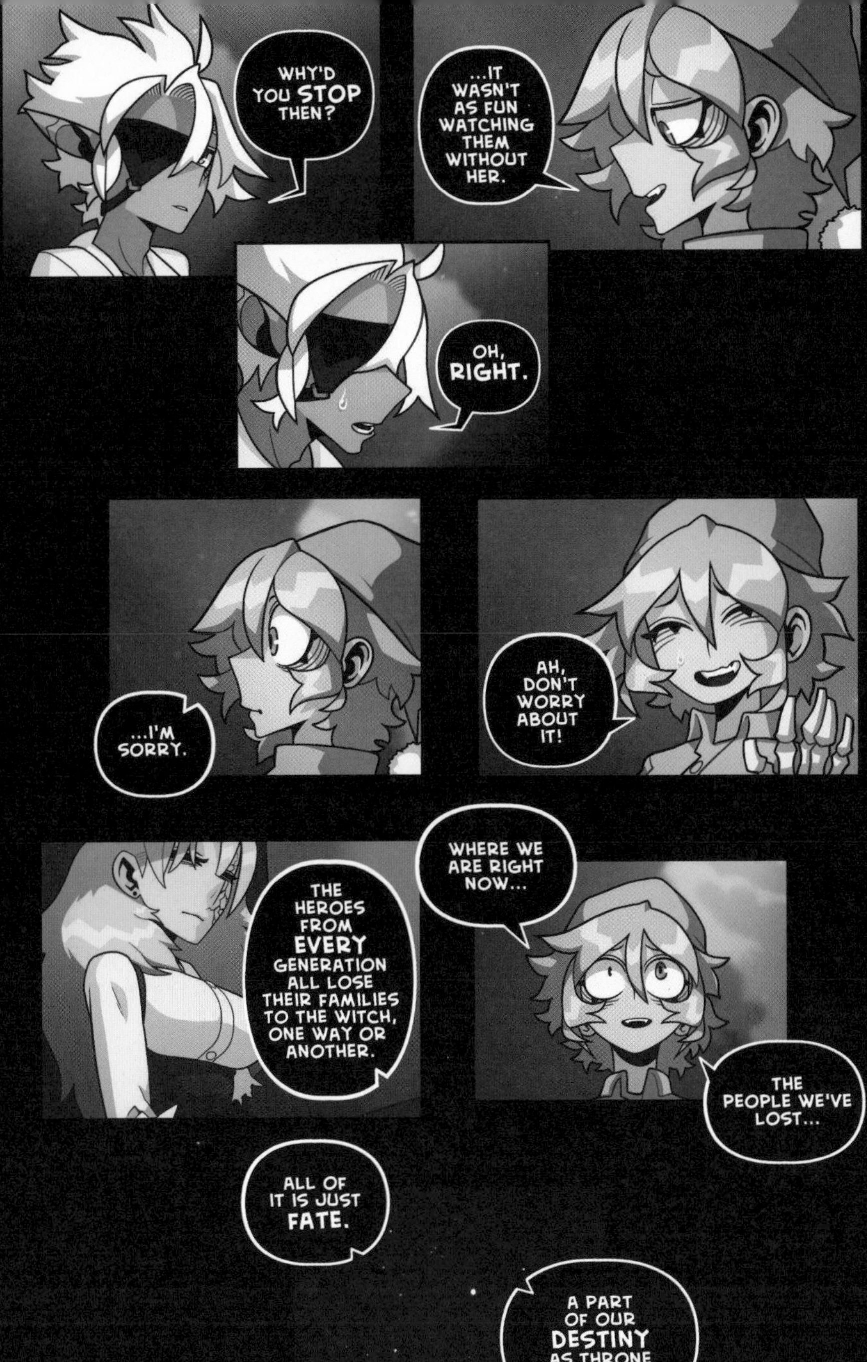
WHY'D YOU STOP THEN?
...IT WASN'T AS FUN WATCHING THEM WITHOUT HER.
OH, RIGHT.
...I'M SORRY.
AH, DON'T WORRY ABOUT IT!
THE HEROES FROM EVERY GENERATION ALL LOSE THEIR FAMILIES TO THE WITCH, ONE WAY OR ANOTHER.
WHERE WE ARE RIGHT NOW...
THE PEOPLE WE'VE LOST...
ALL OF IT IS JUST FATE.
A PART OF OUR DESTINY AS THRONE SEEKERS.

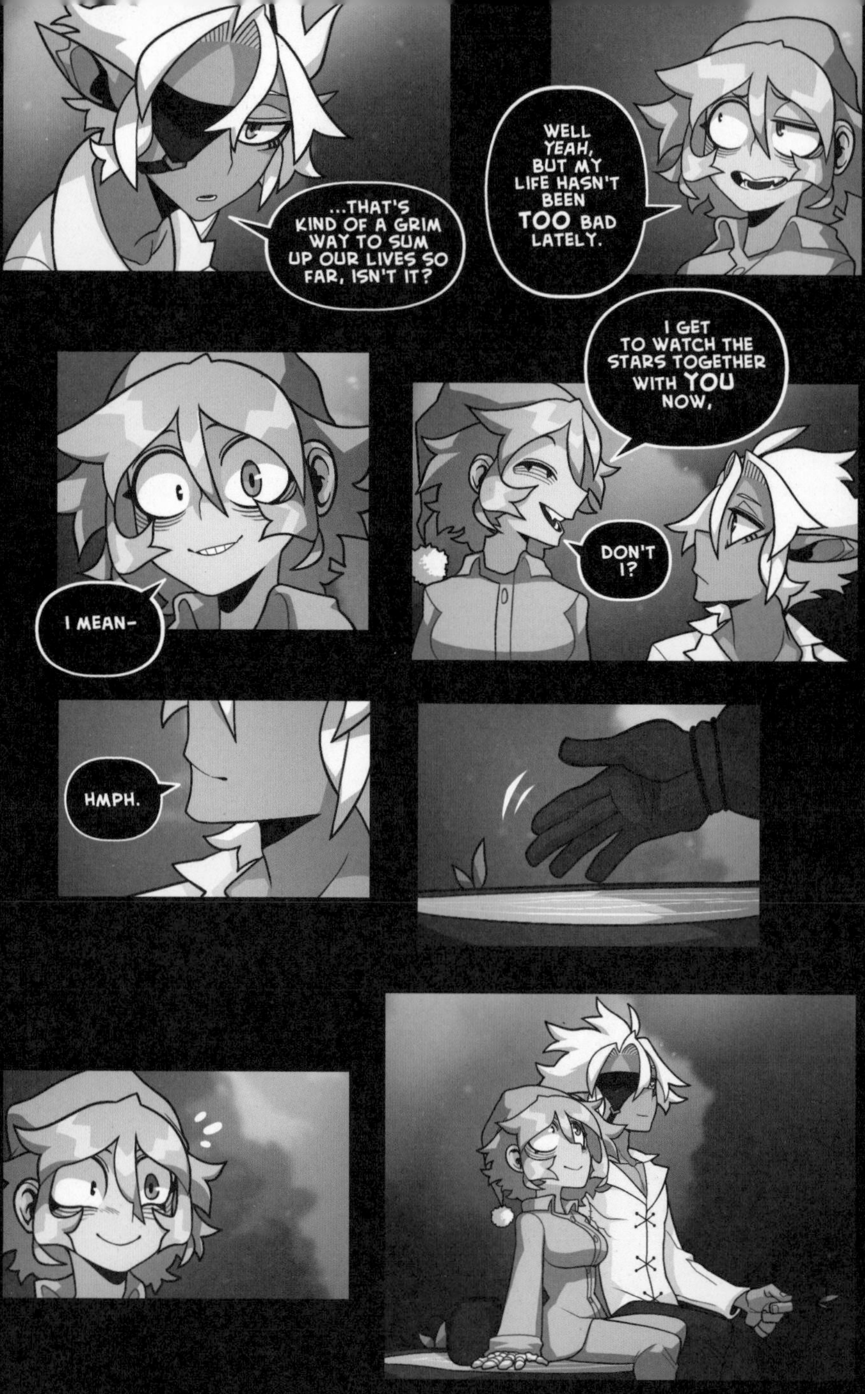

...THAT'S KIND OF A GRIM WAY TO SUM UP OUR LIVES SO FAR, ISN'T IT?
WELL YEAH, BUT MY LIFE HASN'T BEEN TOO BAD LATELY.
I MEAN-
I GET TO WATCH THE STARS TOGETHER WITH YOU NOW,
DON'T I?
HMPH.

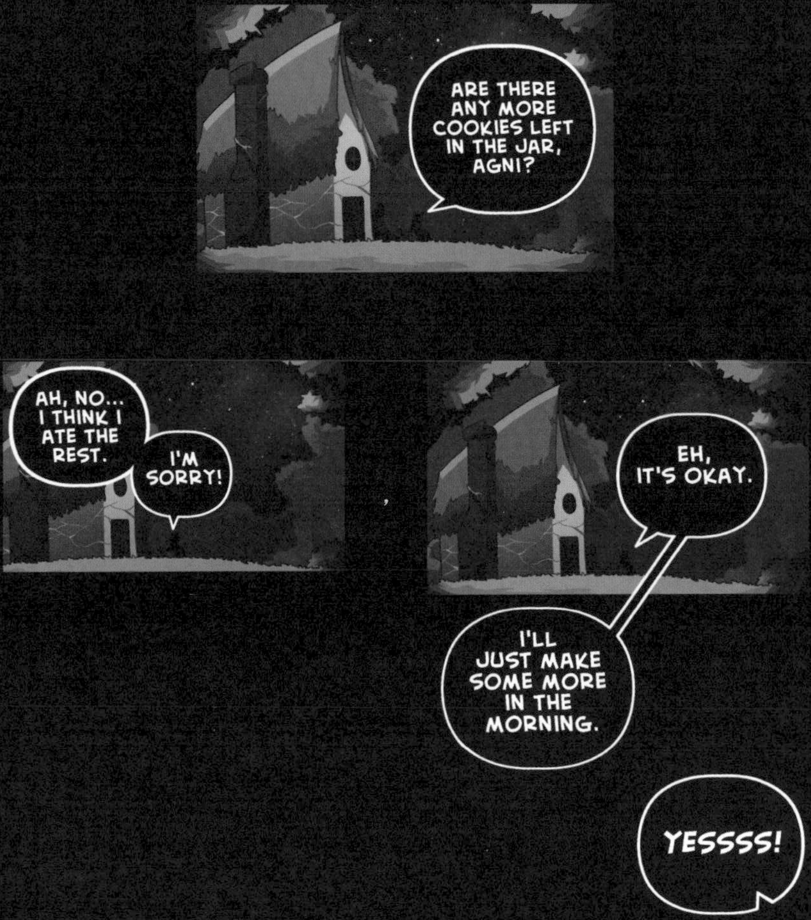

ARE THERE ANY MORE COOKIES LEFT IN THE JAR, AGNI?
AH, NO... I THINK I ATE THE REST.
I'M SORRY!
EH, IT'S OKAY.
I'LL JUST MAKE SOME MORE IN THE MORNING.
YESSSS!

## Chapter 21
# THE BEASTS

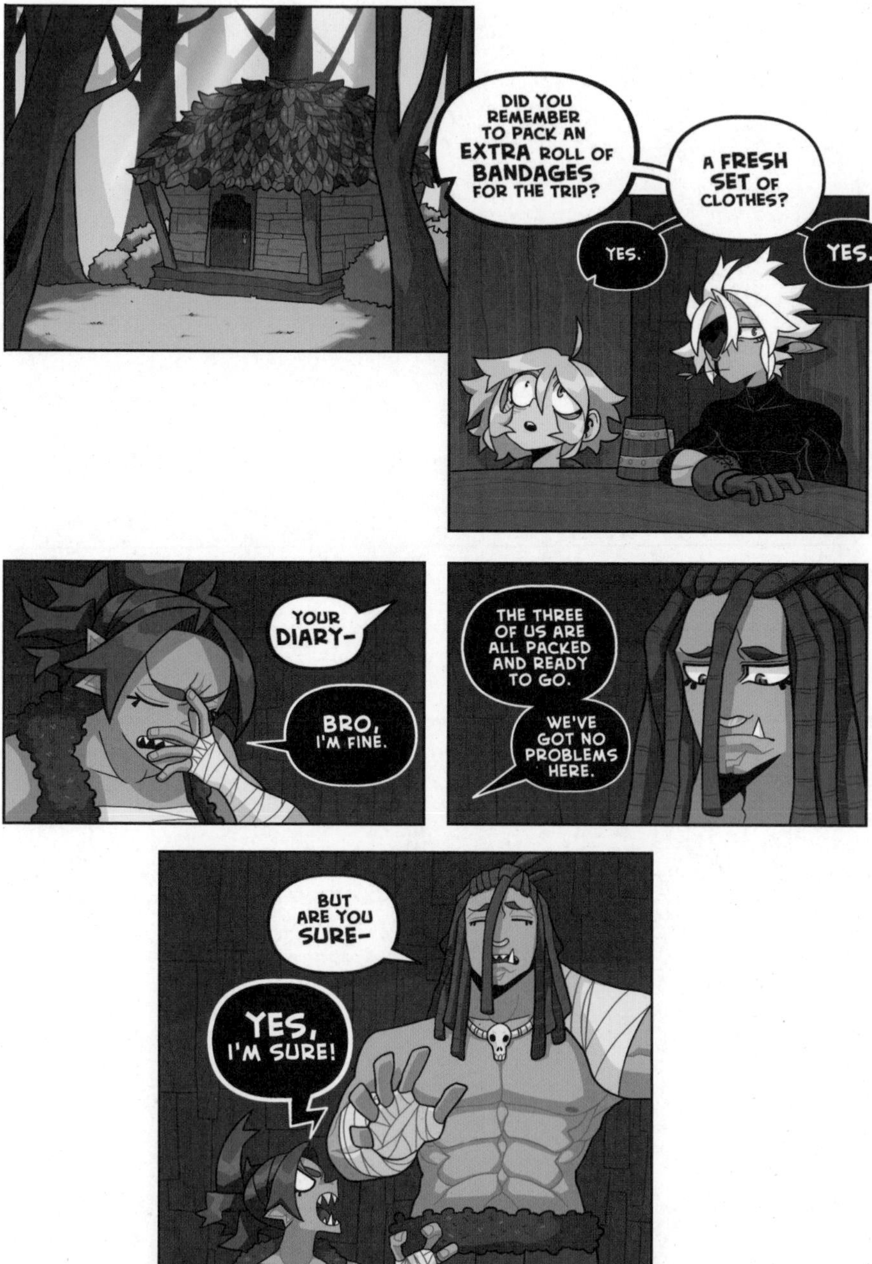
DID YOU REMEMBER TO PACK AN EXTRA ROLL OF BANDAGES FOR THE TRIP?
YES.
A FRESH SET OF CLOTHES?
YES.
YOUR DIARY-
BRO, I'M FINE.
THE THREE OF US ARE ALL PACKED AND READY TO GO.
WE'VE GOT NO PROBLEMS HERE.
BUT ARE YOU SURE-
YES, I'M SURE!

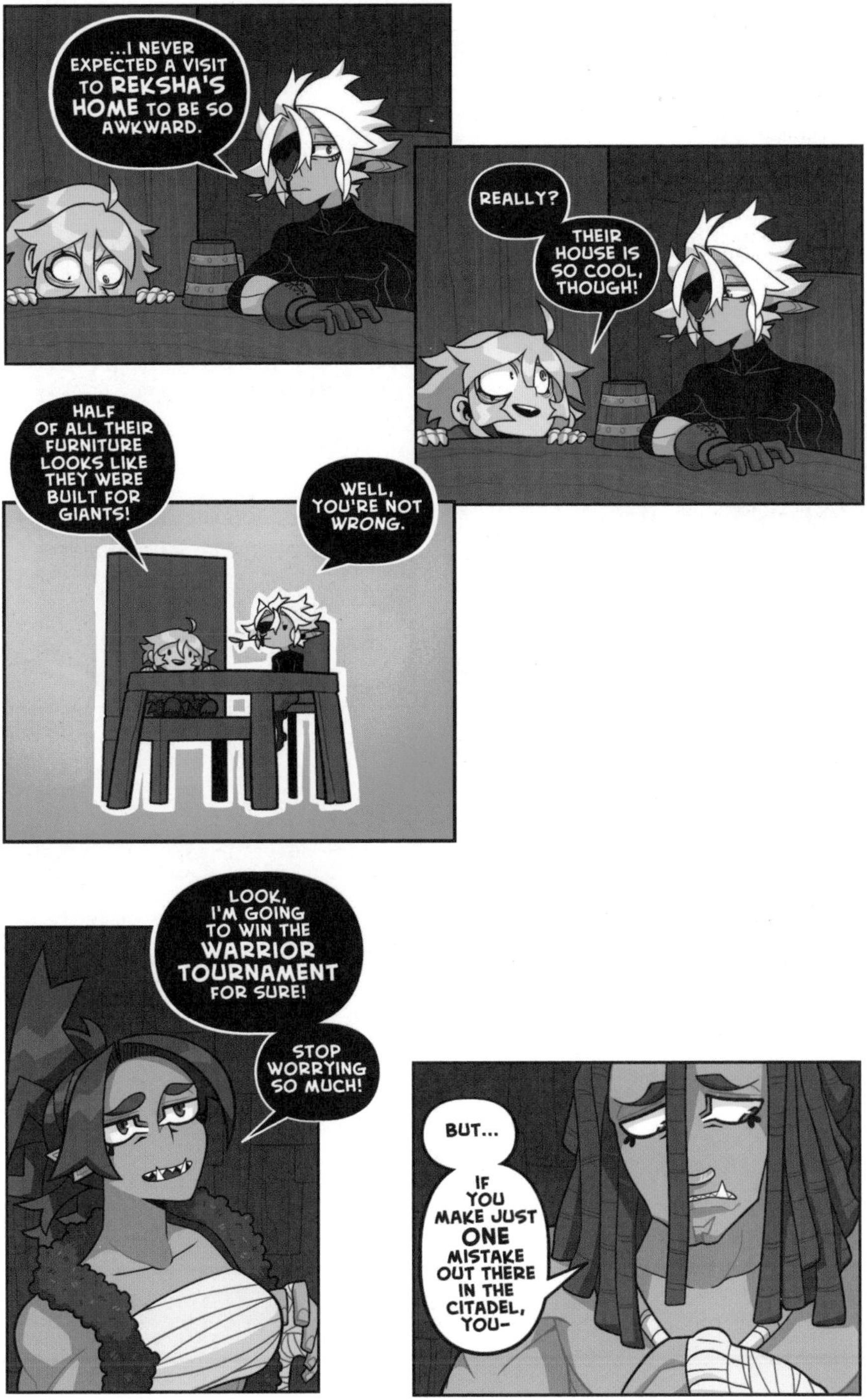
...I NEVER EXPECTED A VISIT TO REKSHA'S HOME TO BE SO AWKWARD.
REALLY?
THEIR HOUSE IS SO COOL, THOUGH!
HALF OF ALL THEIR FURNITURE LOOKS LIKE THEY WERE BUILT FOR GIANTS!
WELL, YOU'RE NOT WRONG.
LOOK, I'M GOING TO WIN THE WARRIOR TOURNAMENT FOR SURE!
STOP WORRYING SO MUCH!
BUT...
IF YOU MAKE JUST ONE MISTAKE OUT THERE IN THE CITADEL, YOU-

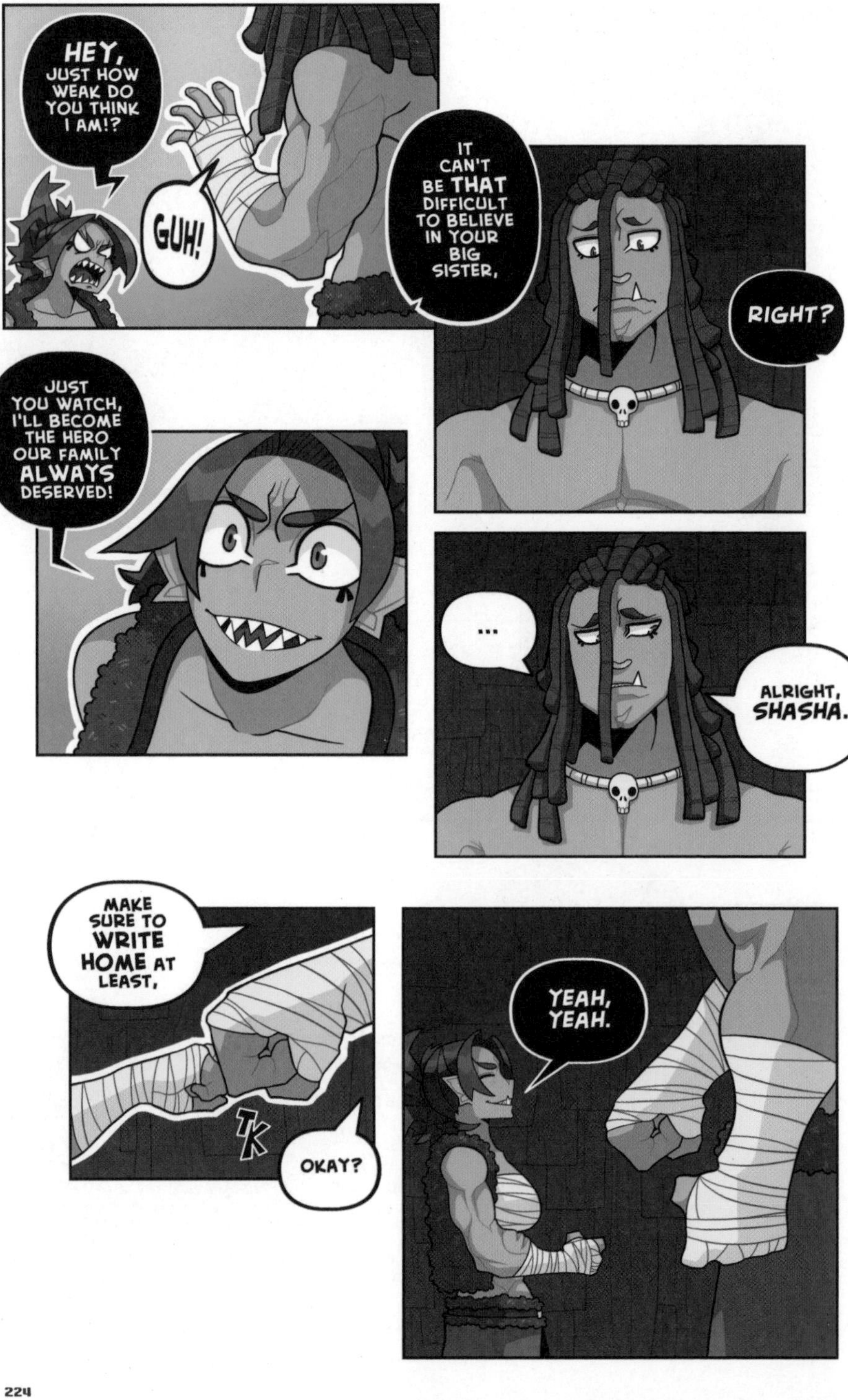
HEY, JUST HOW WEAK DO YOU THINK I AM!?
GUH!
IT CAN'T BE THAT DIFFICULT TO BELIEVE IN YOUR BIG SISTER,
RIGHT?
JUST YOU WATCH, I'LL BECOME THE HERO OUR FAMILY ALWAYS DESERVED!
...
ALRIGHT, SHASHA.
MAKE SURE TO WRITE HOME AT LEAST,
TK
OKAY?
YEAH, YEAH.

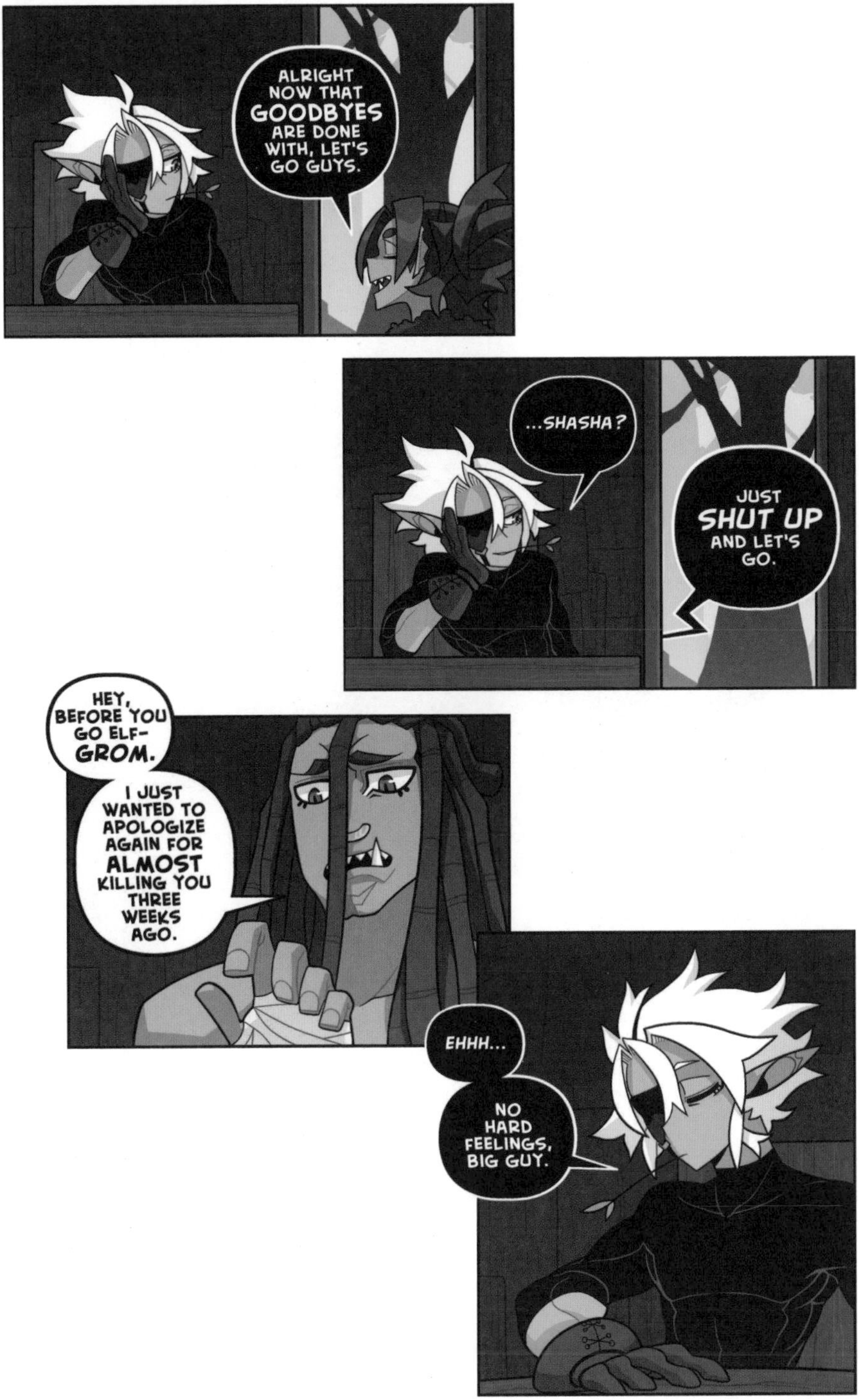
ALRIGHT NOW THAT GOODBYES ARE DONE WITH, LET'S GO GUYS.
...SHASHA?
JUST SHUT UP AND LET'S GO.
HEY, BEFORE YOU GO ELF-GROM.
I JUST WANTED TO APOLOGIZE AGAIN FOR ALMOST KILLING YOU THREE WEEKS AGO.
EHHH...
NO HARD FEELINGS, BIG GUY.

I NEEDED TO GET USED TO THAT SORT OF THING, ANYWAY.

DRIP

GOODBYE REKSHA'S GIANT LITTLE BROTHER!

MY NAME IS FAHREN, BUT OKAY HALF-DEAD HUMAN...

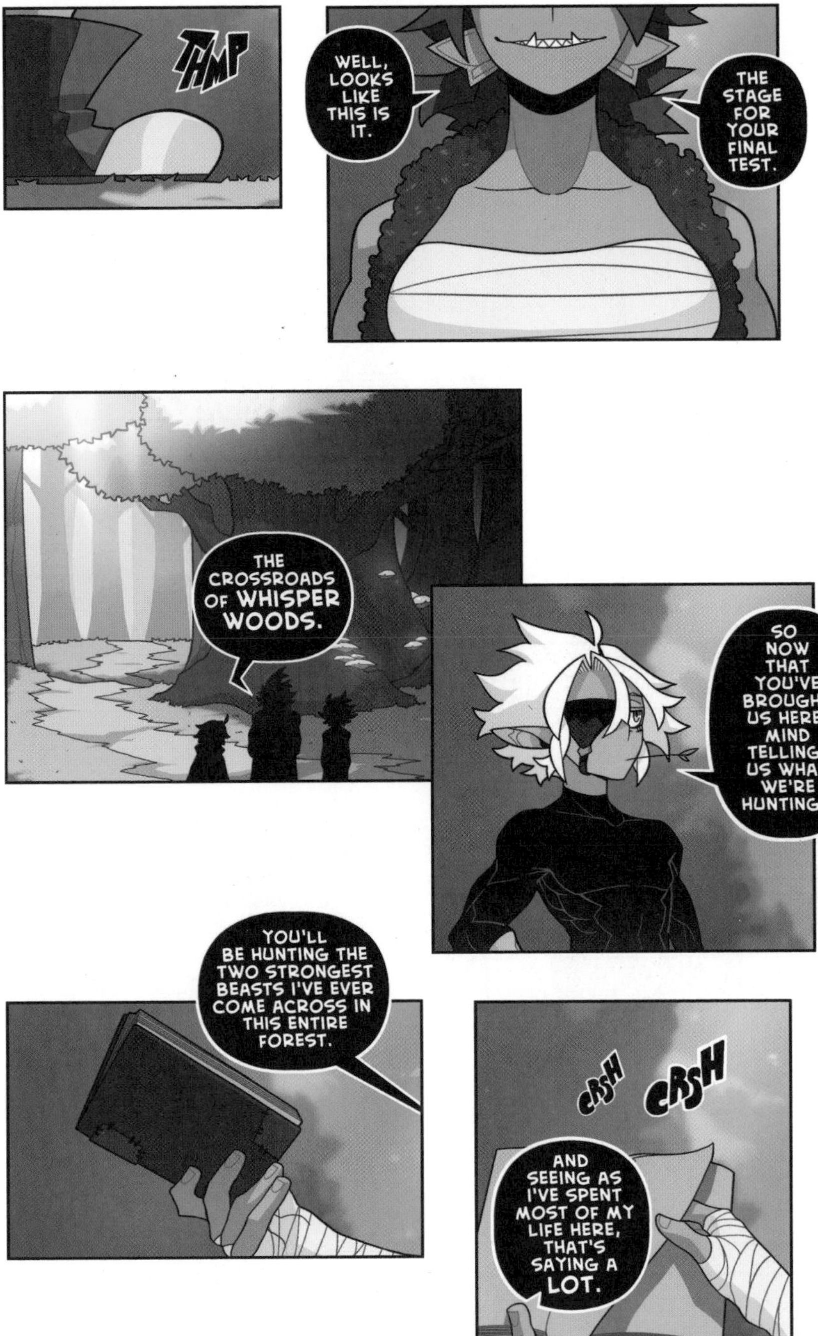
THMP
WELL, LOOKS LIKE THIS IS IT.
THE STAGE FOR YOUR FINAL TEST.
THE CROSSROADS OF WHISPER WOODS.
SO NOW THAT YOU'VE BROUGHT US HERE, MIND TELLING US WHAT WE'RE HUNTING?
YOU'LL BE HUNTING THE TWO STRONGEST BEASTS I'VE EVER COME ACROSS IN THIS ENTIRE FOREST.
CRSH
CRSH
AND SEEING AS I'VE SPENT MOST OF MY LIFE HERE, THAT'S SAYING A LOT.

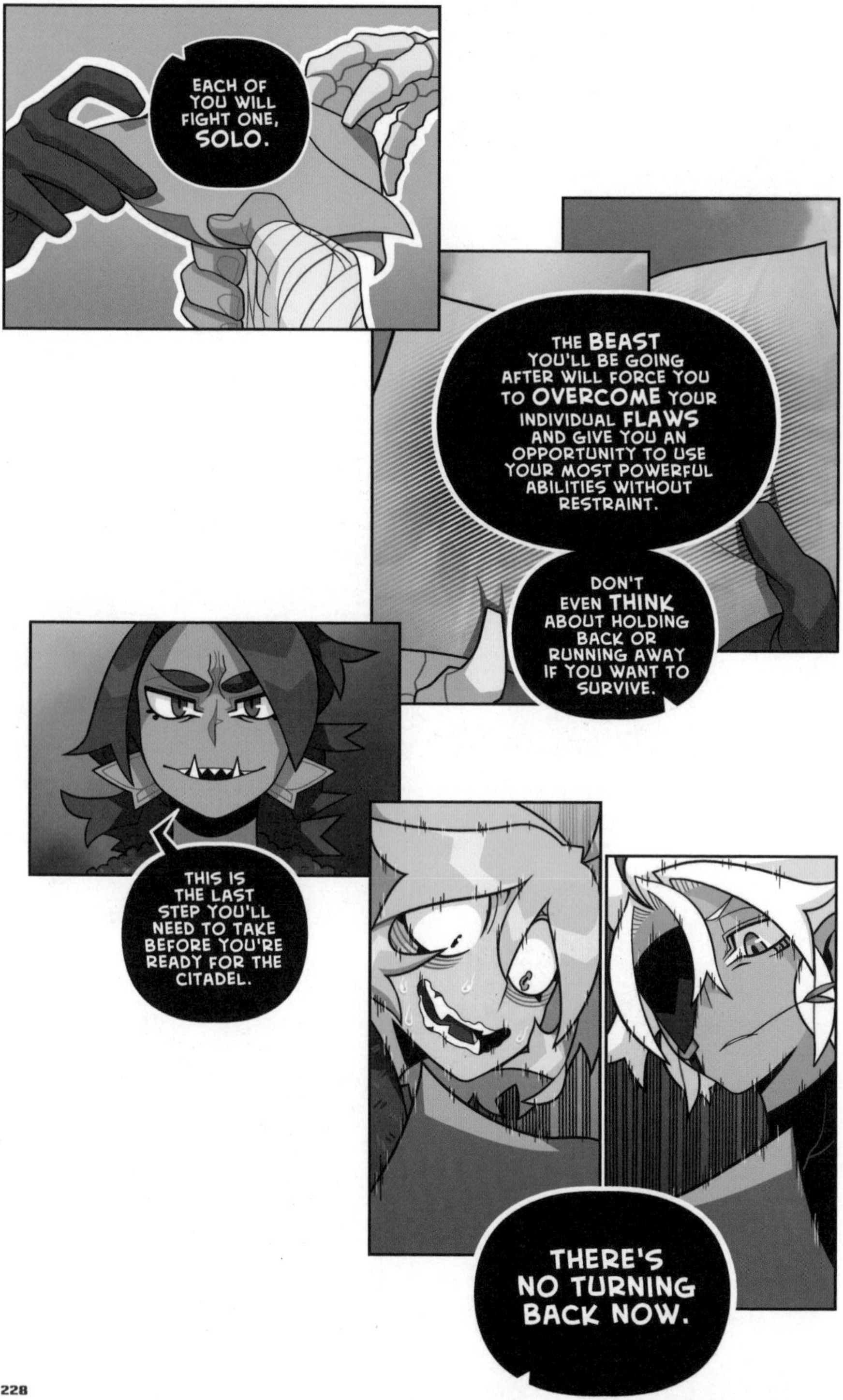
EACH OF YOU WILL FIGHT ONE, SOLO.
THE BEAST YOU'LL BE GOING AFTER WILL FORCE YOU TO OVERCOME YOUR INDIVIDUAL FLAWS AND GIVE YOU AN OPPORTUNITY TO USE YOUR MOST POWERFUL ABILITIES WITHOUT RESTRAINT.
DON'T EVEN THINK ABOUT HOLDING BACK OR RUNNING AWAY IF YOU WANT TO SURVIVE.
THIS IS THE LAST STEP YOU'LL NEED TO TAKE BEFORE YOU'RE READY FOR THE CITADEL.
THERE'S NO TURNING BACK NOW.

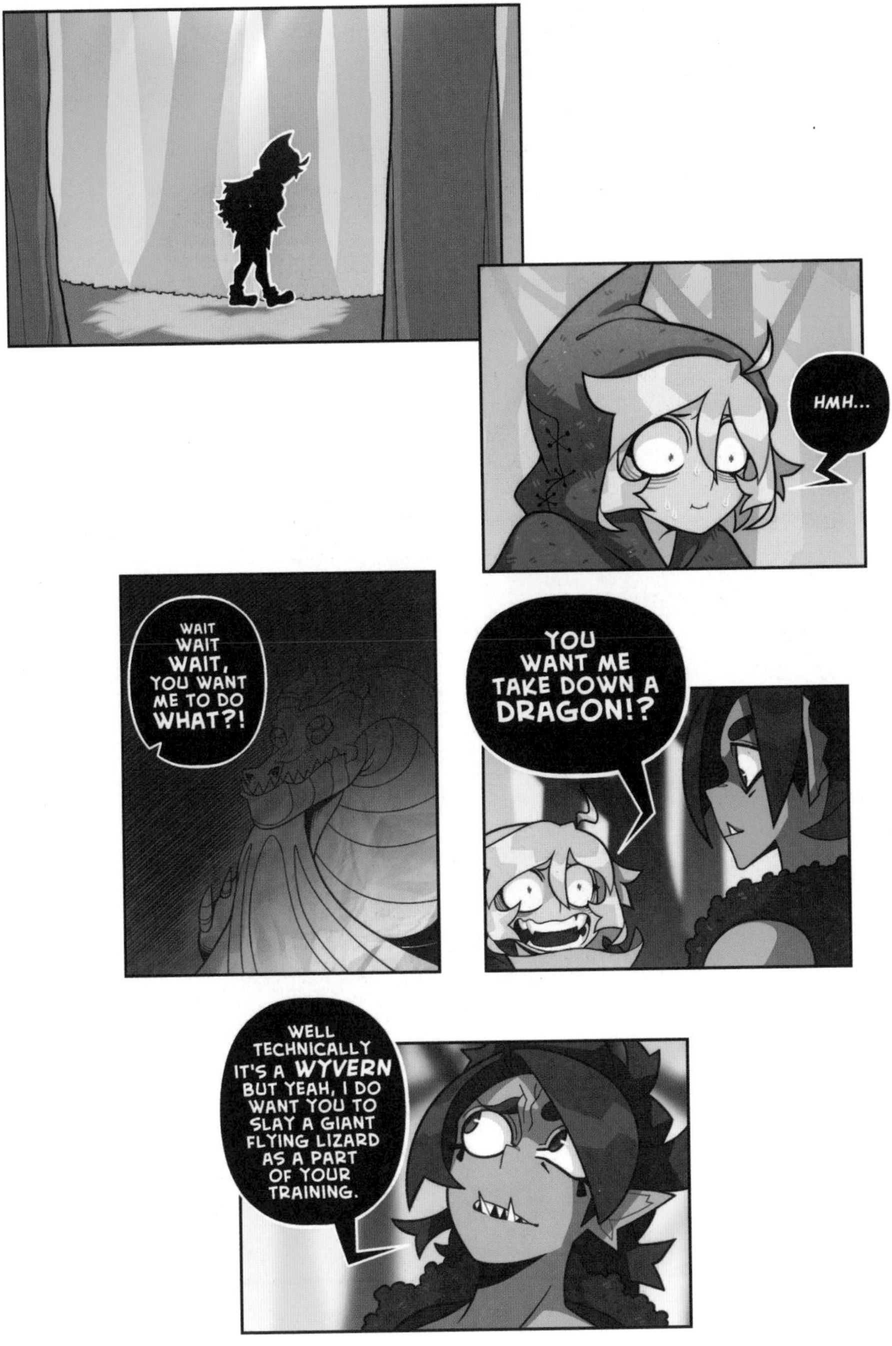
HMH...
WAIT WAIT WAIT, YOU WANT ME TO DO WHAT?!
YOU WANT ME TAKE DOWN A DRAGON!?
WELL TECHNICALLY IT'S A WYVERN BUT YEAH, I DO WANT YOU TO SLAY A GIANT FLYING LIZARD AS A PART OF YOUR TRAINING.

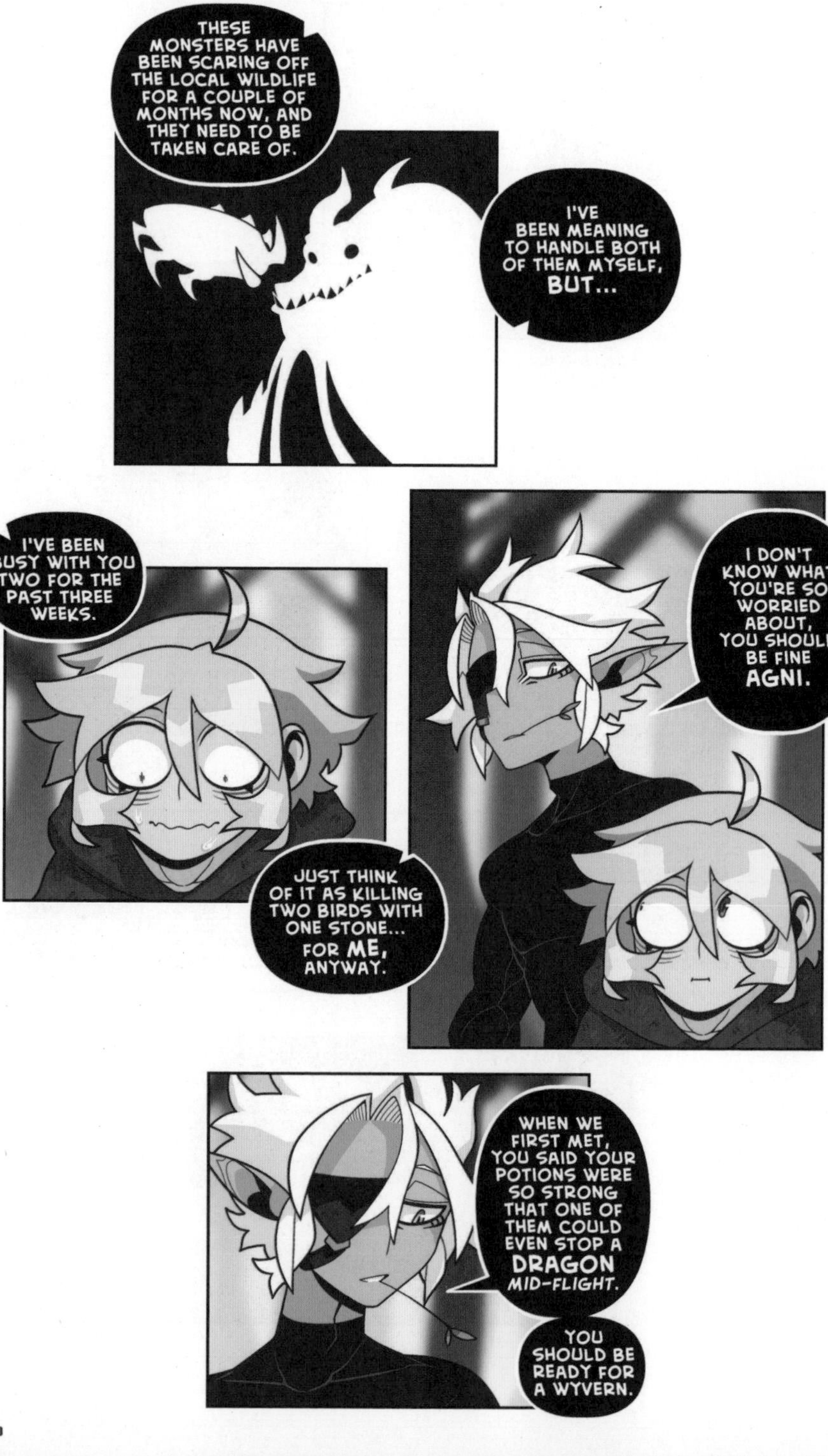
THESE MONSTERS HAVE BEEN SCARING OFF THE LOCAL WILDLIFE FOR A COUPLE OF MONTHS NOW, AND THEY NEED TO BE TAKEN CARE OF.
I'VE BEEN MEANING TO HANDLE BOTH OF THEM MYSELF, BUT...
I'VE BEEN BUSY WITH YOU TWO FOR THE PAST THREE WEEKS.
JUST THINK OF IT AS KILLING TWO BIRDS WITH ONE STONE... FOR ME, ANYWAY.
I DON'T KNOW WHAT YOU'RE SO WORRIED ABOUT, YOU SHOULD BE FINE AGNI.
WHEN WE FIRST MET, YOU SAID YOUR POTIONS WERE SO STRONG THAT ONE OF THEM COULD EVEN STOP A DRAGON MID-FLIGHT.
YOU SHOULD BE READY FOR A WYVERN.

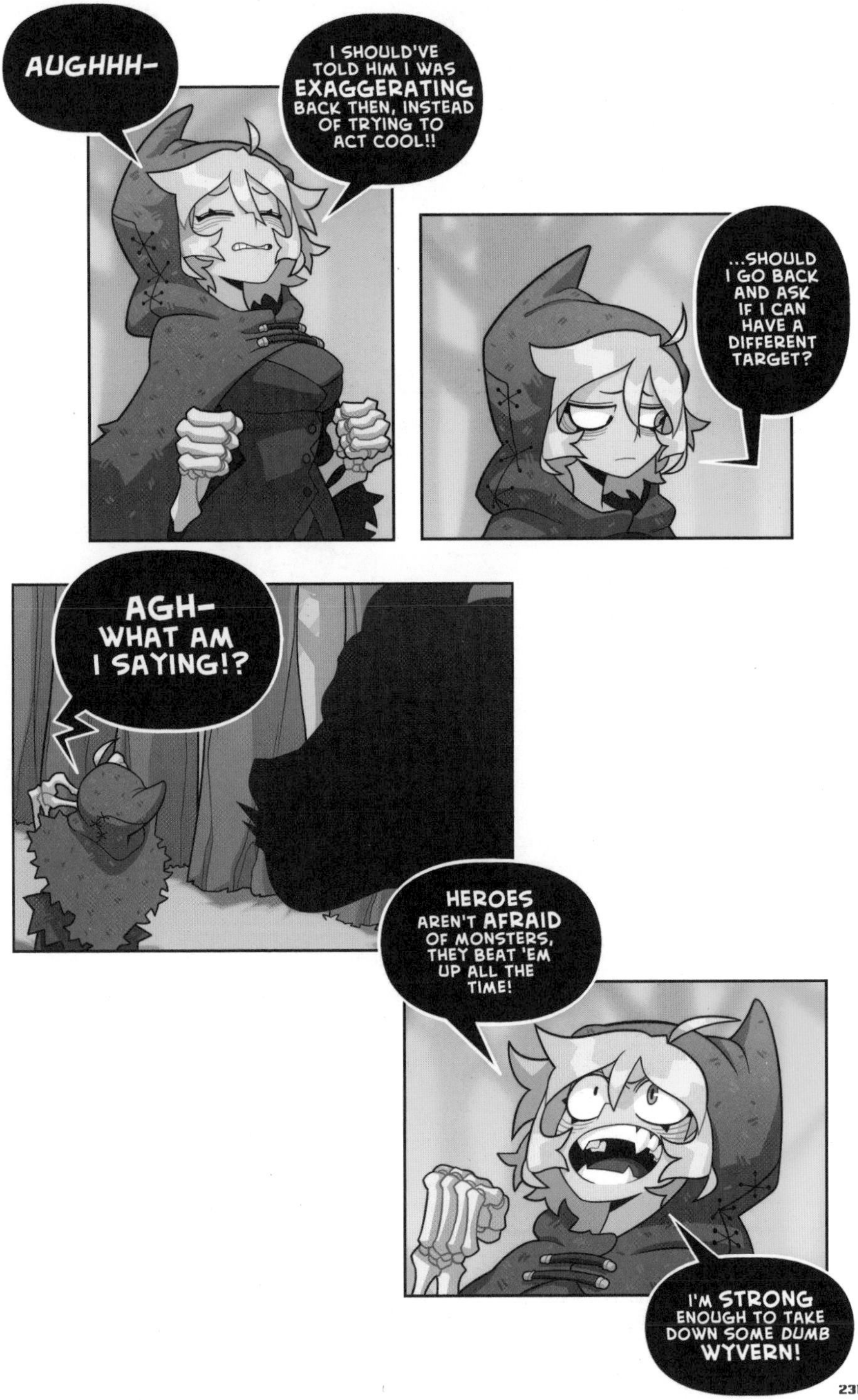
AUGHHH-
I SHOULD'VE TOLD HIM I WAS EXAGGERATING BACK THEN, INSTEAD OF TRYING TO ACT COOL!!
...SHOULD I GO BACK AND ASK IF I CAN HAVE A DIFFERENT TARGET?
AGH- WHAT AM I SAYING!?
HEROES AREN'T AFRAID OF MONSTERS, THEY BEAT 'EM UP ALL THE TIME!
I'M STRONG ENOUGH TO TAKE DOWN SOME DUMB WYVERN!

I MAY NOT BE ABLE TO STOP TALKING TO MYSELF RIGHT NOW,
BUT I CAN **DEFINITELY** DO THIS–
!!
GRRRRR
...EEP.

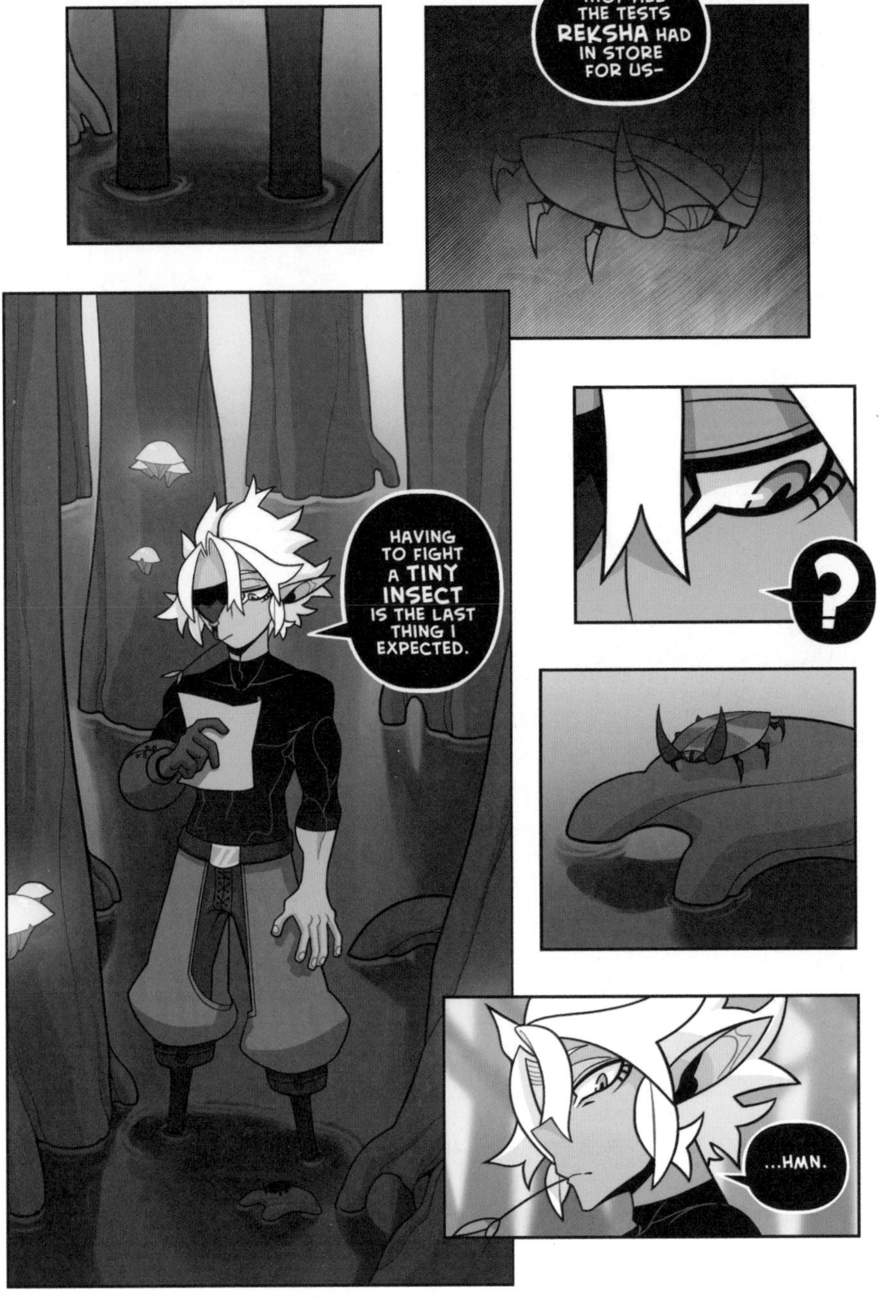
...OF ALL THE TESTS REKSHA HAD IN STORE FOR US-
HAVING TO FIGHT A TINY INSECT IS THE LAST THING I EXPECTED.
?
...HMN.

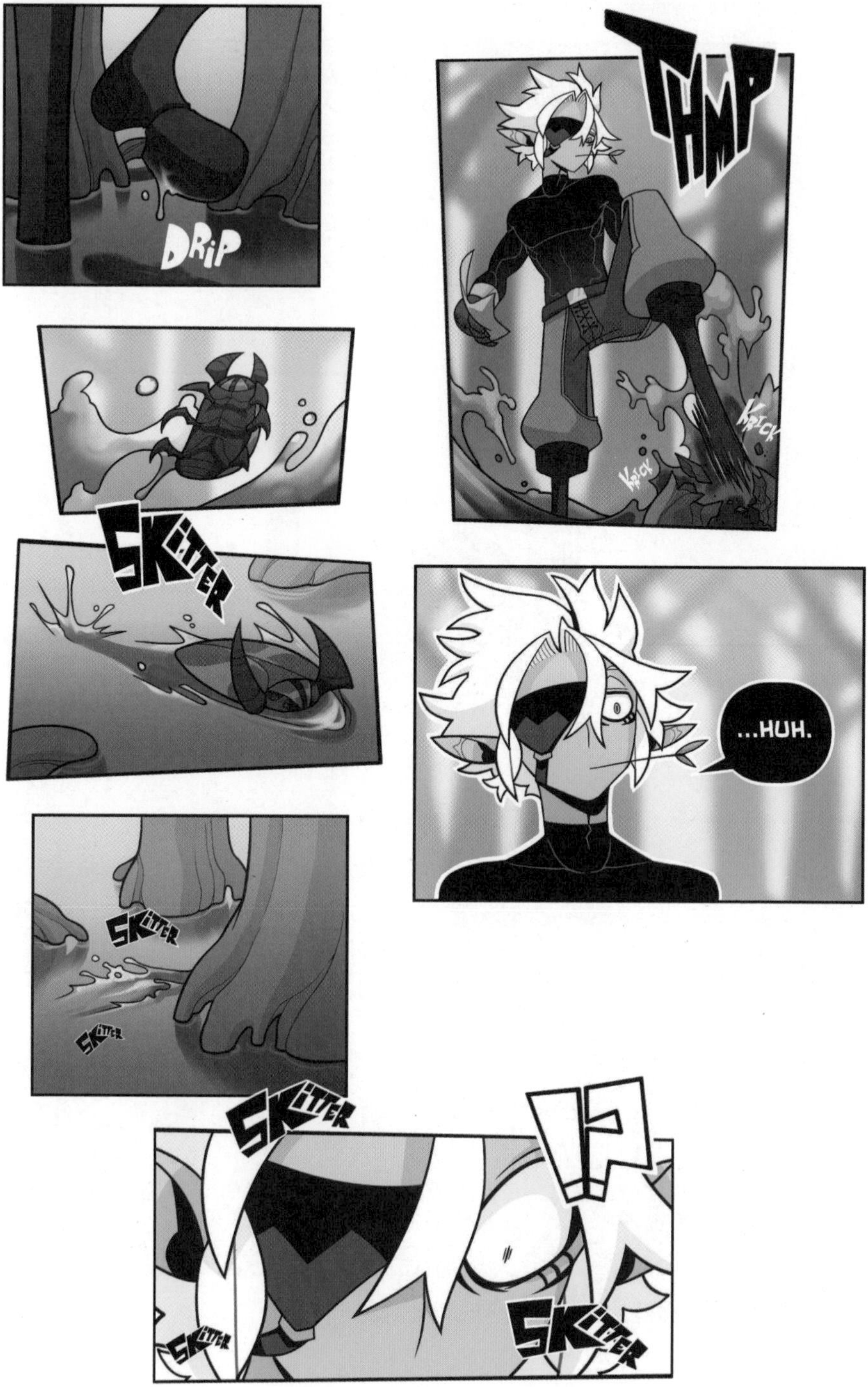
DRIP
SKITTER
SKITTER
SKITTER
THMP
KRICK
KRICK
...HUH.
SKITTER
!?
SKITTER
SKITTER

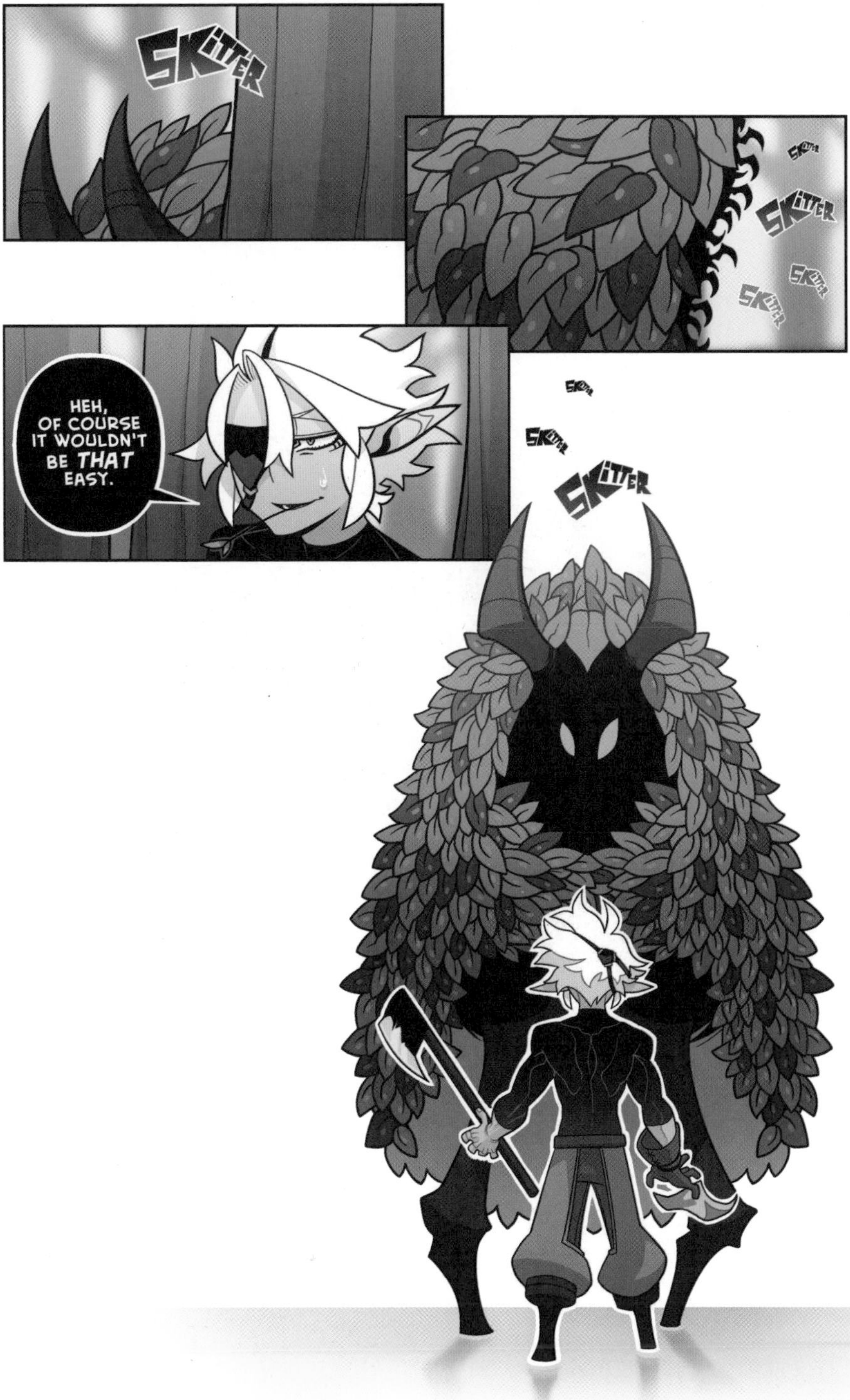
SKITTER
SKITTER
SKITTER
SKITTER
SKITTER
HEH, OF COURSE IT WOULDN'T BE THAT EASY.
SKITTER
SKITTER
SKITTER

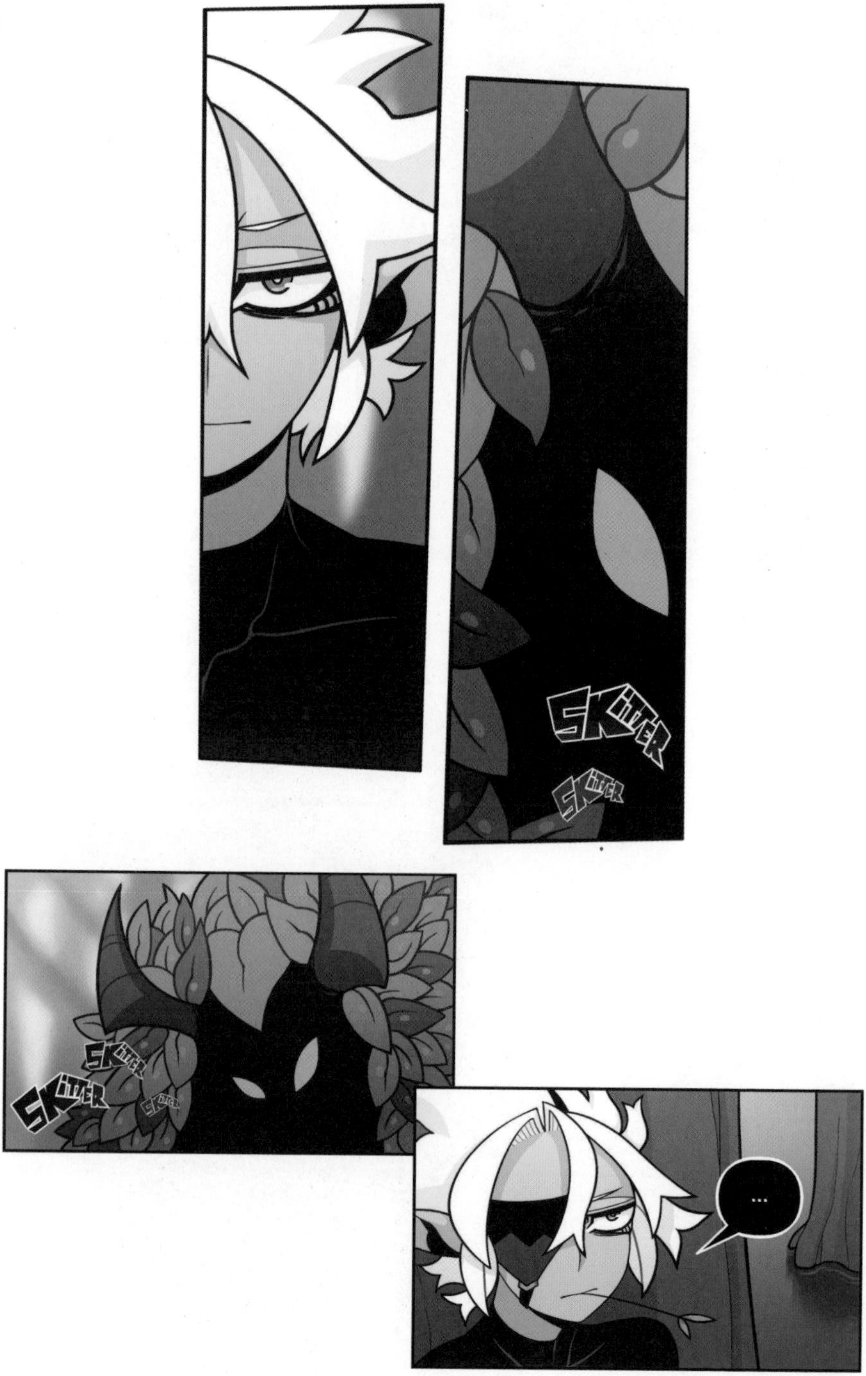
SKITTER
SKITTER
SKITTER
SKITTER
SKITTER
...

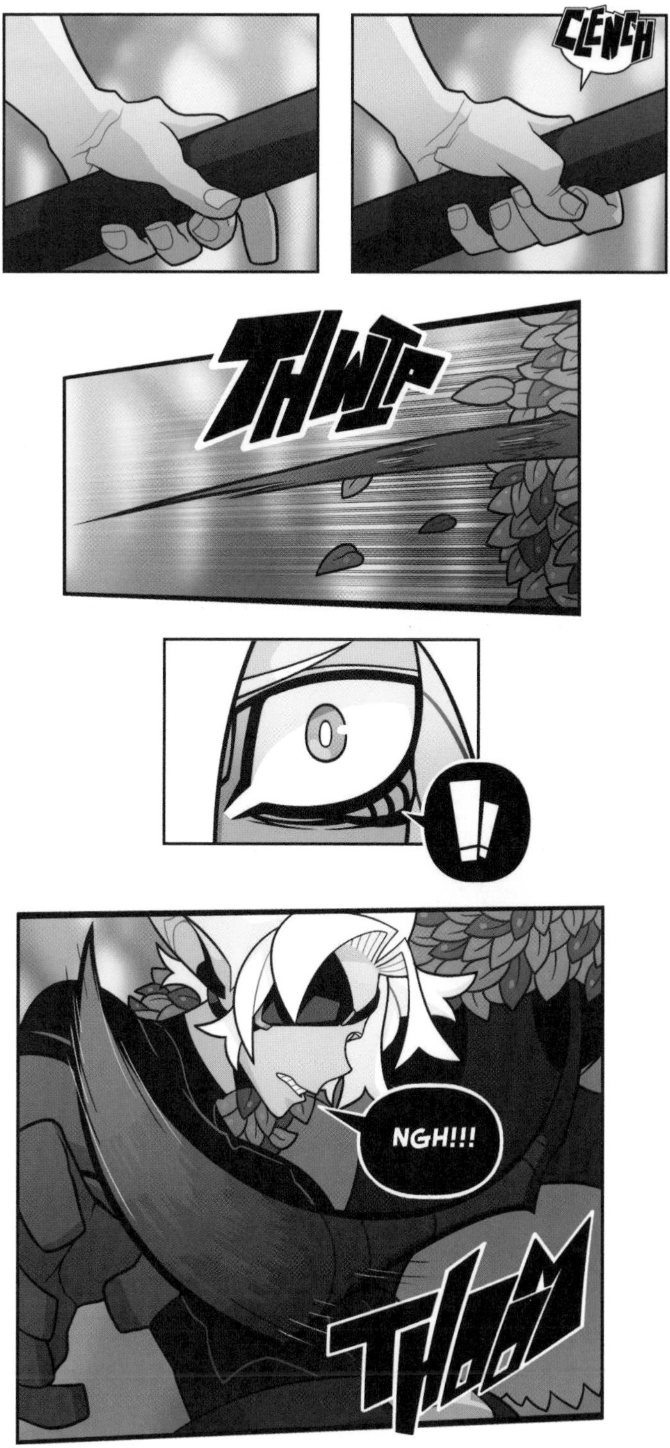
CLENCH
THWIP
!!
NGH!!!
THOOM

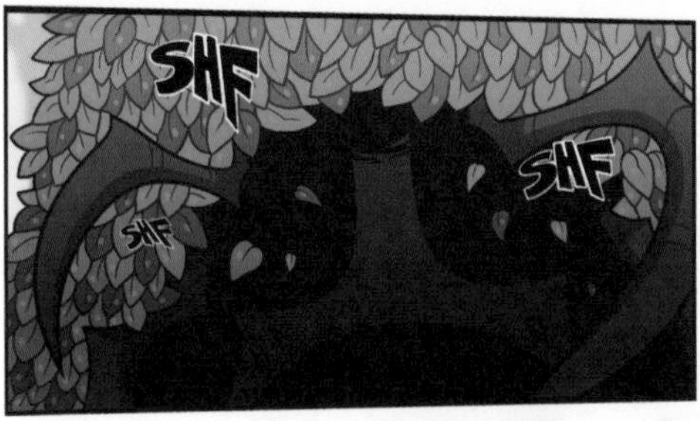
SHF
SHF
SHF
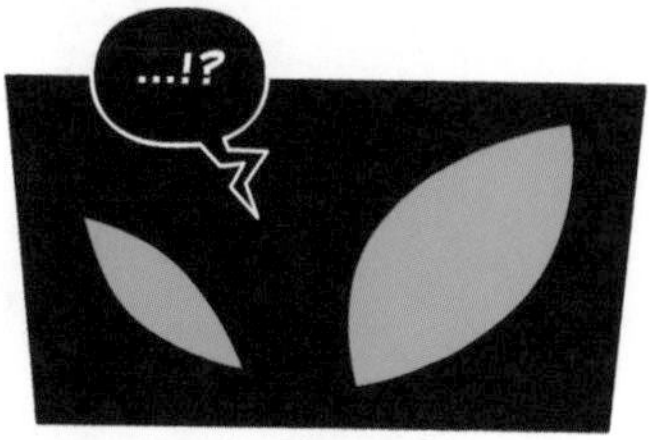
...!?
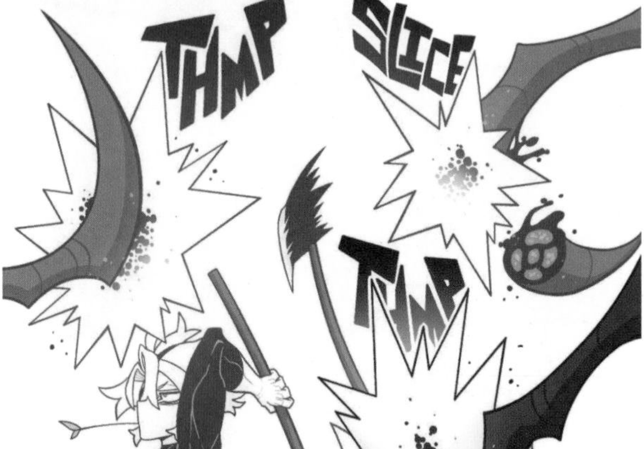
THMP
SLICE
THMP
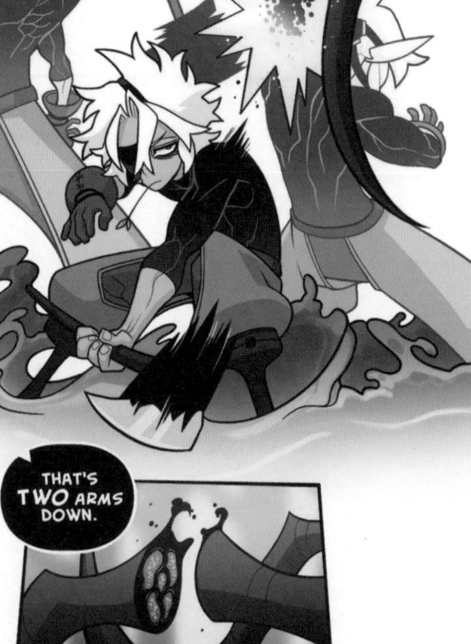
THAT'S TWO ARMS DOWN.

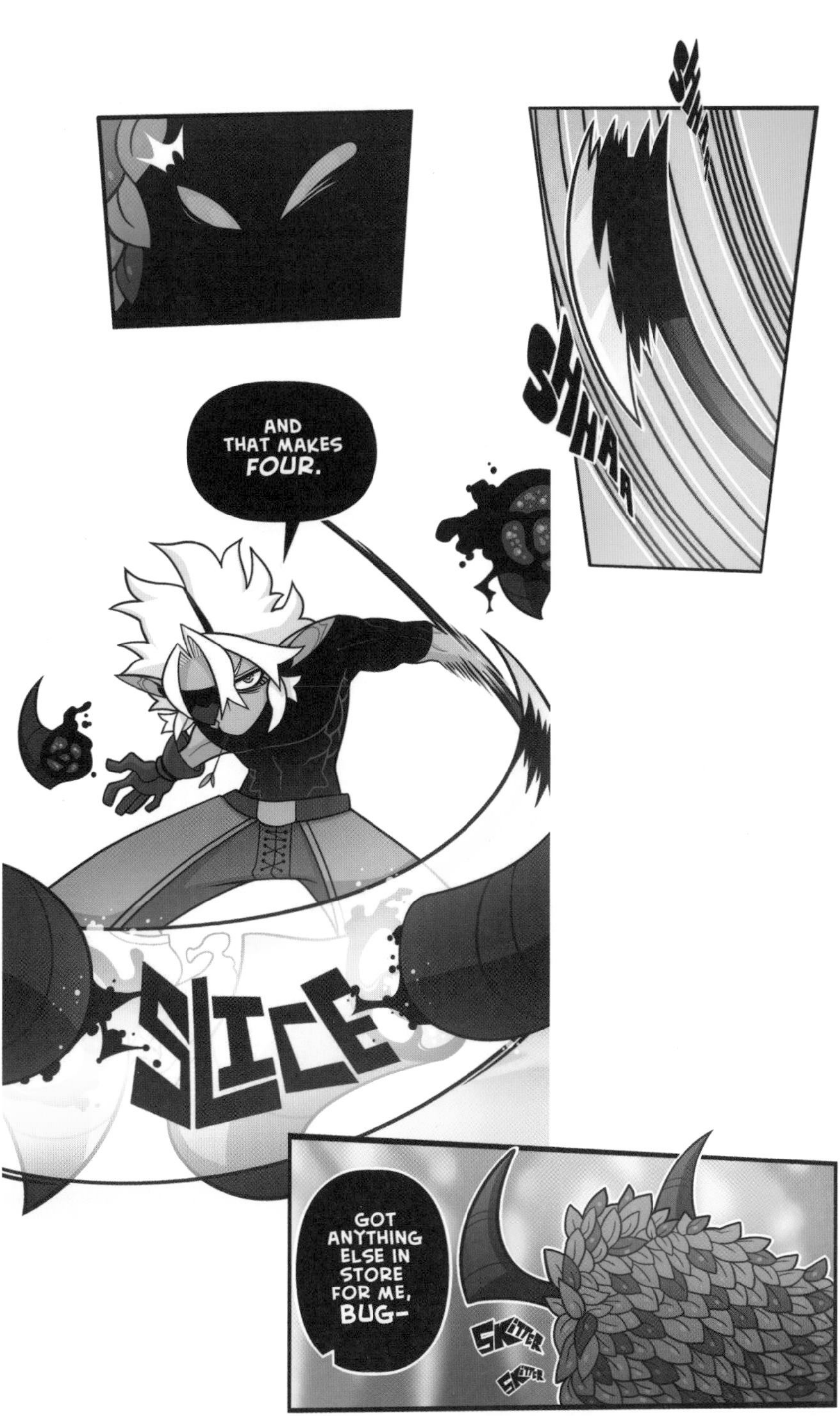
SHHAA
SHHAA
AND THAT MAKES FOUR.
SLICE
GOT ANYTHING ELSE IN STORE FOR ME, BUG-
SKITTER
SKITTER

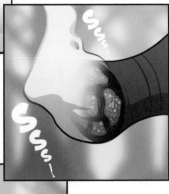

LIMBS THAT REGENERATE AS FAST AS I CAN CUT...

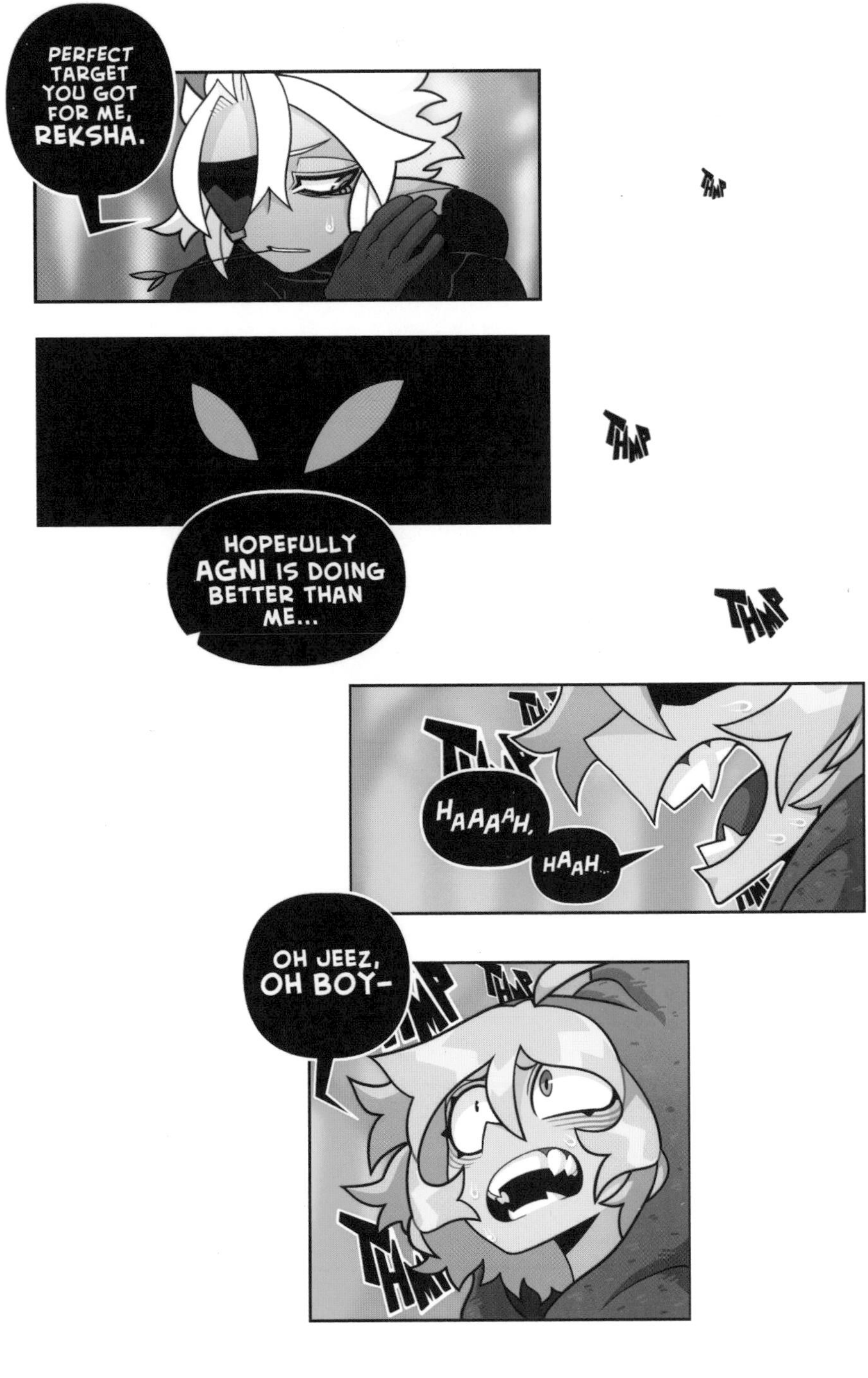
PERFECT TARGET YOU GOT FOR ME, REKSHA.
THMP
THMP
HOPEFULLY AGNI IS DOING BETTER THAN ME...
THMP
HAAAAH,
HAAH...
OH JEEZ, OH BOY-
THMP

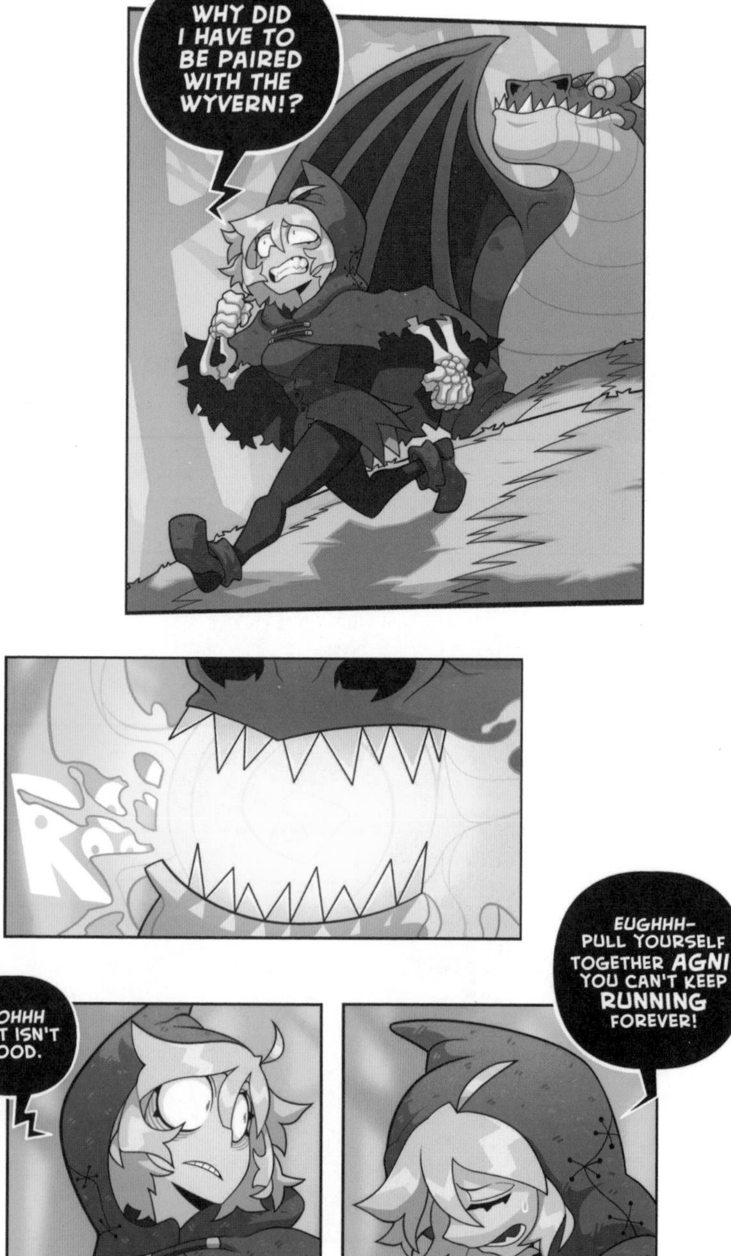
WHY DID I HAVE TO BE PAIRED WITH THE WYVERN!?
OOHHH THAT ISN'T GOOD.
EUGHHH- PULL YOURSELF TOGETHER AGNI, YOU CAN'T KEEP RUNNING FOREVER!

NO MORE HESITATING IN THE FACE OF DANGER—

NO MORE DOUBTING WHETHER OR NOT I CAN DO IT!

SHF

IF I WANT TO BECOME THE HERO I'VE ALWAYS WANTED TO BE—

I CAN'T BACK DOWN FROM THIS!!!

WOBBLE

WOBBLE

WOBBLE

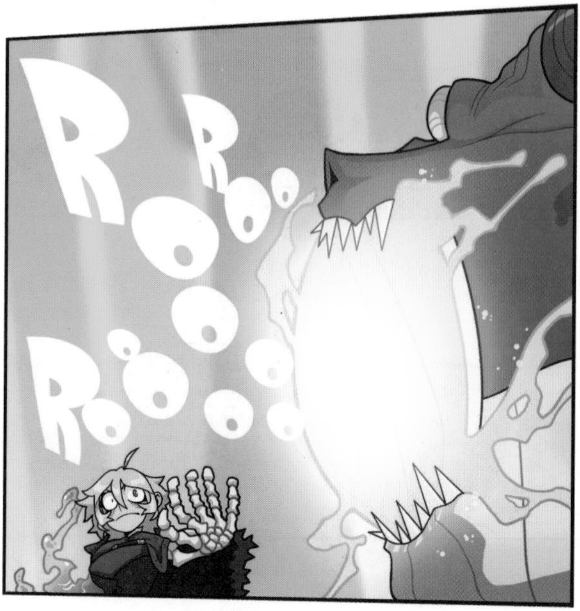
ROOOO
ROOOOO

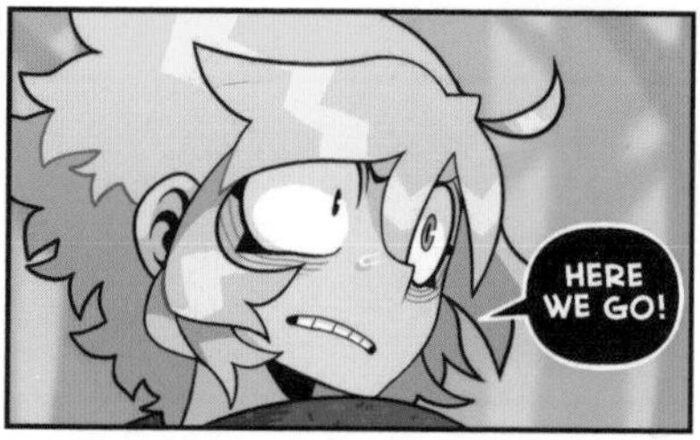
HERE WE GO!

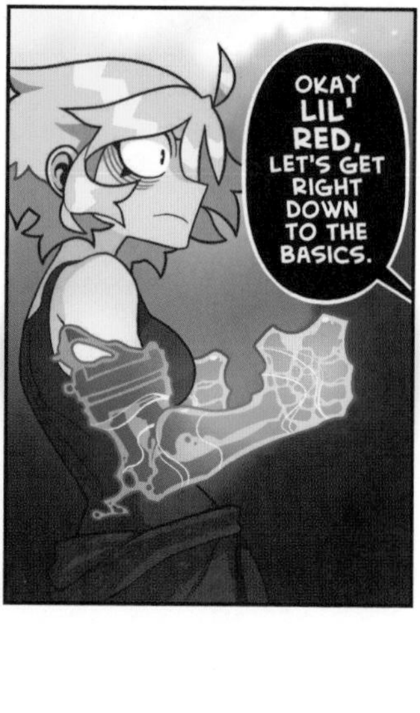
OKAY LIL' RED, LET'S GET RIGHT DOWN TO THE BASICS.

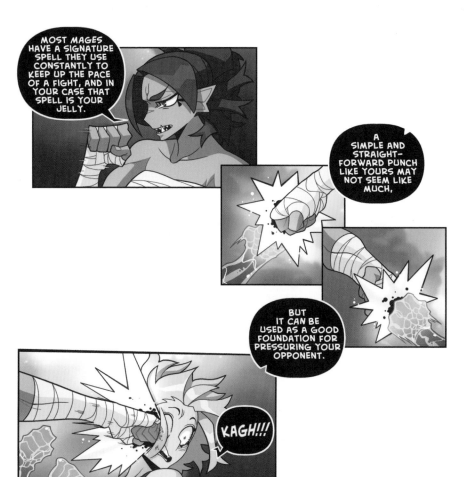

MOST MAGES HAVE A SIGNATURE SPELL THEY USE CONSTANTLY TO KEEP UP THE PACE OF A FIGHT, AND IN YOUR CASE THAT SPELL IS YOUR JELLY.

A SIMPLE AND STRAIGHT-FORWARD PUNCH LIKE YOURS MAY NOT SEEM LIKE MUCH,

BUT IT CAN BE USED AS A GOOD FOUNDATION FOR PRESSURING YOUR OPPONENT.

KAGH!!!

TO IMPROVE ON THIS, WE'LL HAVE YOU MASTER A TECHNIQUE CALLED A PARRY.

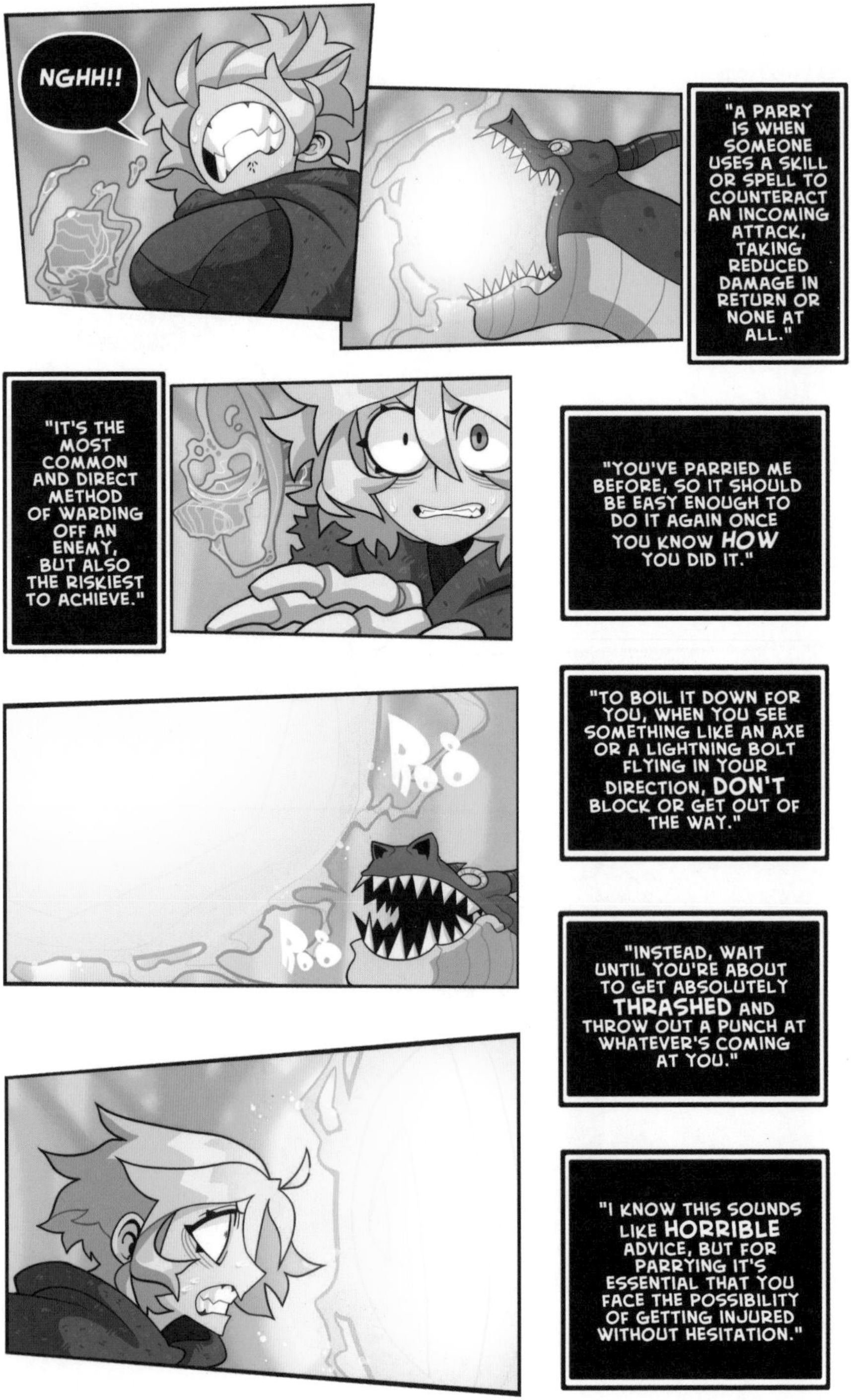
NGHH!!
"A PARRY IS WHEN SOMEONE USES A SKILL OR SPELL TO COUNTERACT AN INCOMING ATTACK, TAKING REDUCED DAMAGE IN RETURN OR NONE AT ALL."
"IT'S THE MOST COMMON AND DIRECT METHOD OF WARDING OFF AN ENEMY, BUT ALSO THE RISKIEST TO ACHIEVE."
"YOU'VE PARRIED ME BEFORE, SO IT SHOULD BE EASY ENOUGH TO DO IT AGAIN ONCE YOU KNOW HOW YOU DID IT."
ROO
ROO
"TO BOIL IT DOWN FOR YOU, WHEN YOU SEE SOMETHING LIKE AN AXE OR A LIGHTNING BOLT FLYING IN YOUR DIRECTION, DON'T BLOCK OR GET OUT OF THE WAY."
"INSTEAD, WAIT UNTIL YOU'RE ABOUT TO GET ABSOLUTELY THRASHED AND THROW OUT A PUNCH AT WHATEVER'S COMING AT YOU."
"I KNOW THIS SOUNDS LIKE HORRIBLE ADVICE, BUT FOR PARRYING IT'S ESSENTIAL THAT YOU FACE THE POSSIBILITY OF GETTING INJURED WITHOUT HESITATION."

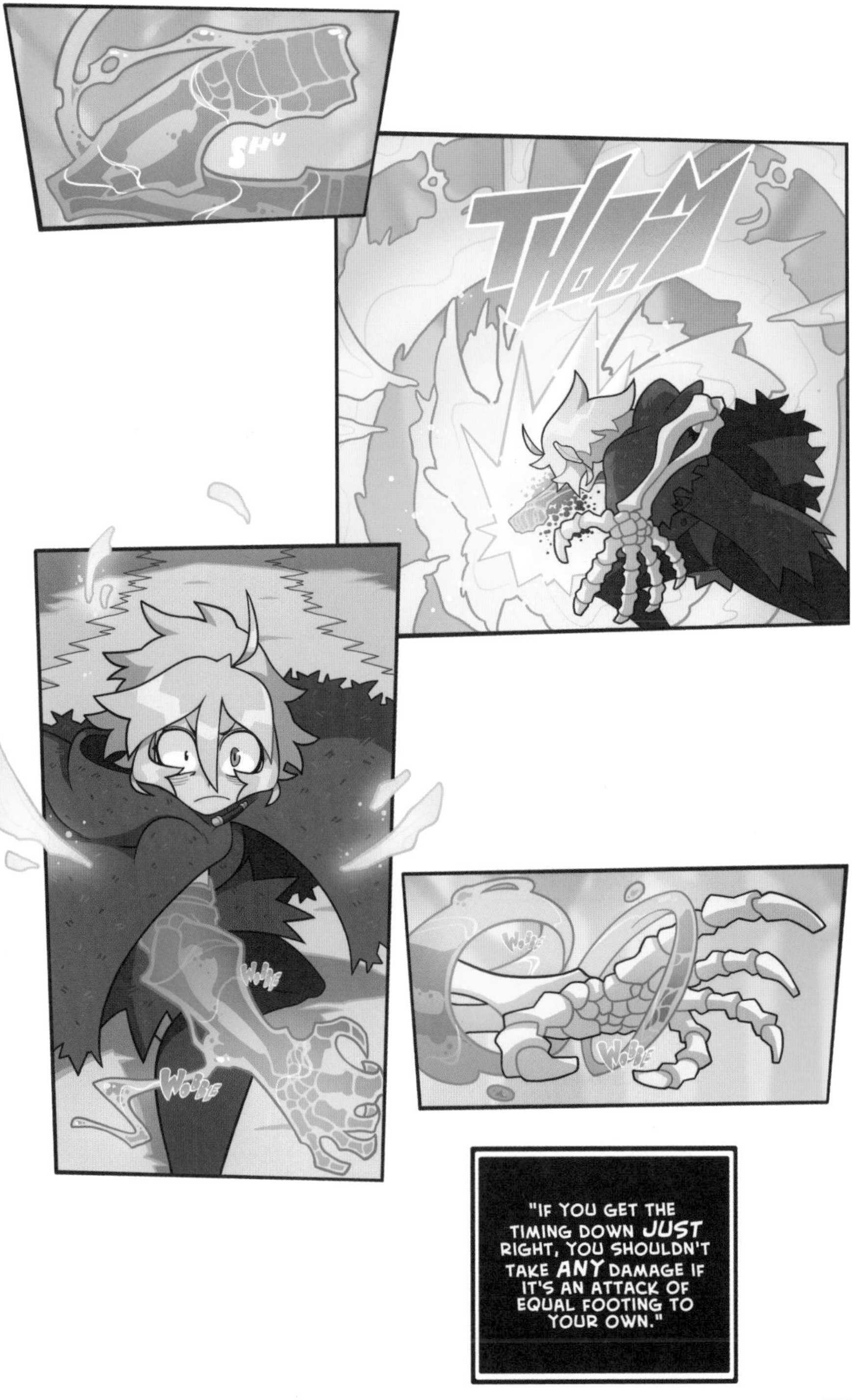
SHU
THOOM
WOBBLE
WOBBLE
WOBBLE
WOBBLE
"IF YOU GET THE TIMING DOWN JUST RIGHT, YOU SHOULDN'T TAKE ANY DAMAGE IF IT'S AN ATTACK OF EQUAL FOOTING TO YOUR OWN."

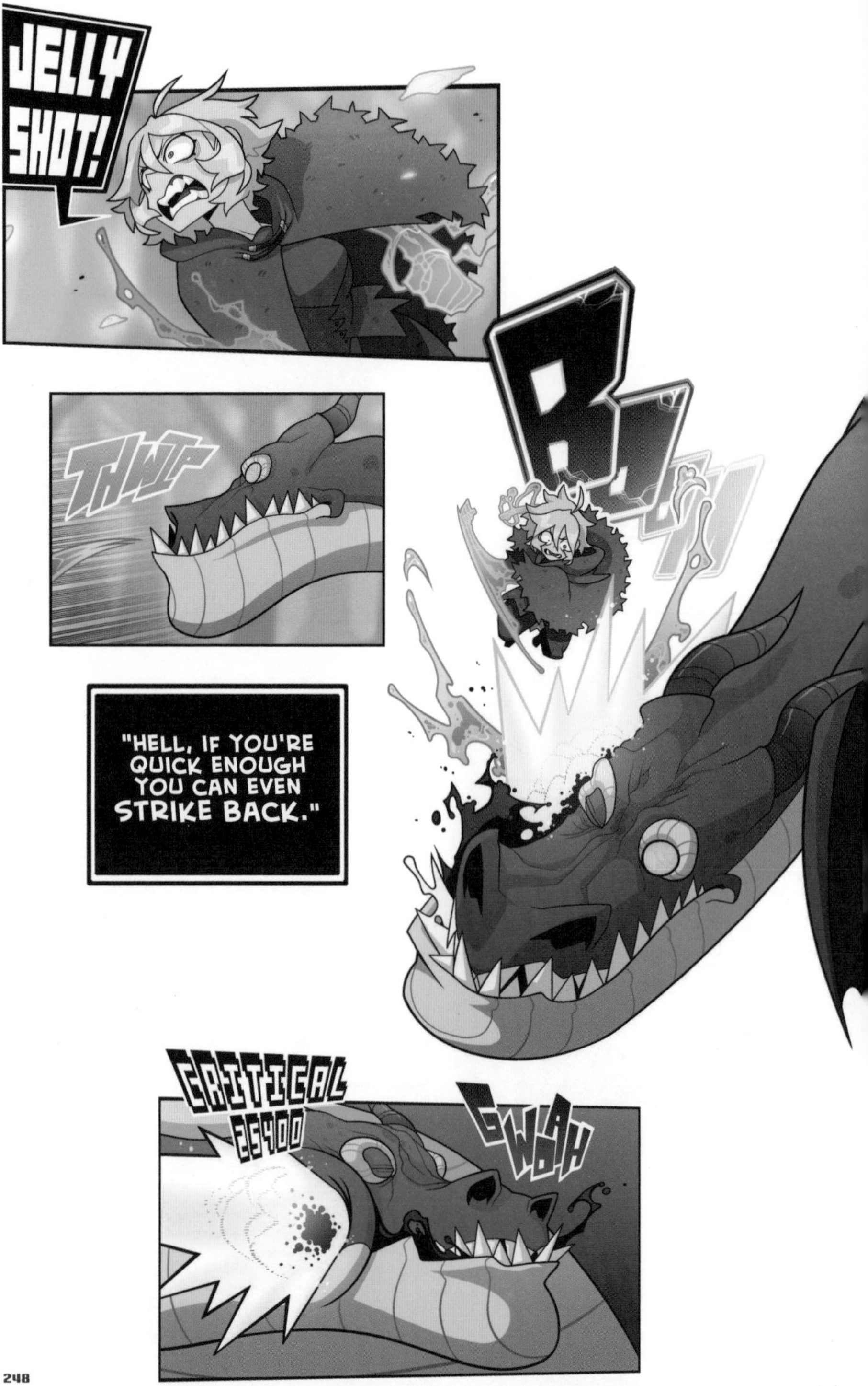
JELLY SHOT!
THWIP
BLAM
"HELL, IF YOU'RE QUICK ENOUGH YOU CAN EVEN STRIKE BACK."
CRITICAL 25400
GWAAH

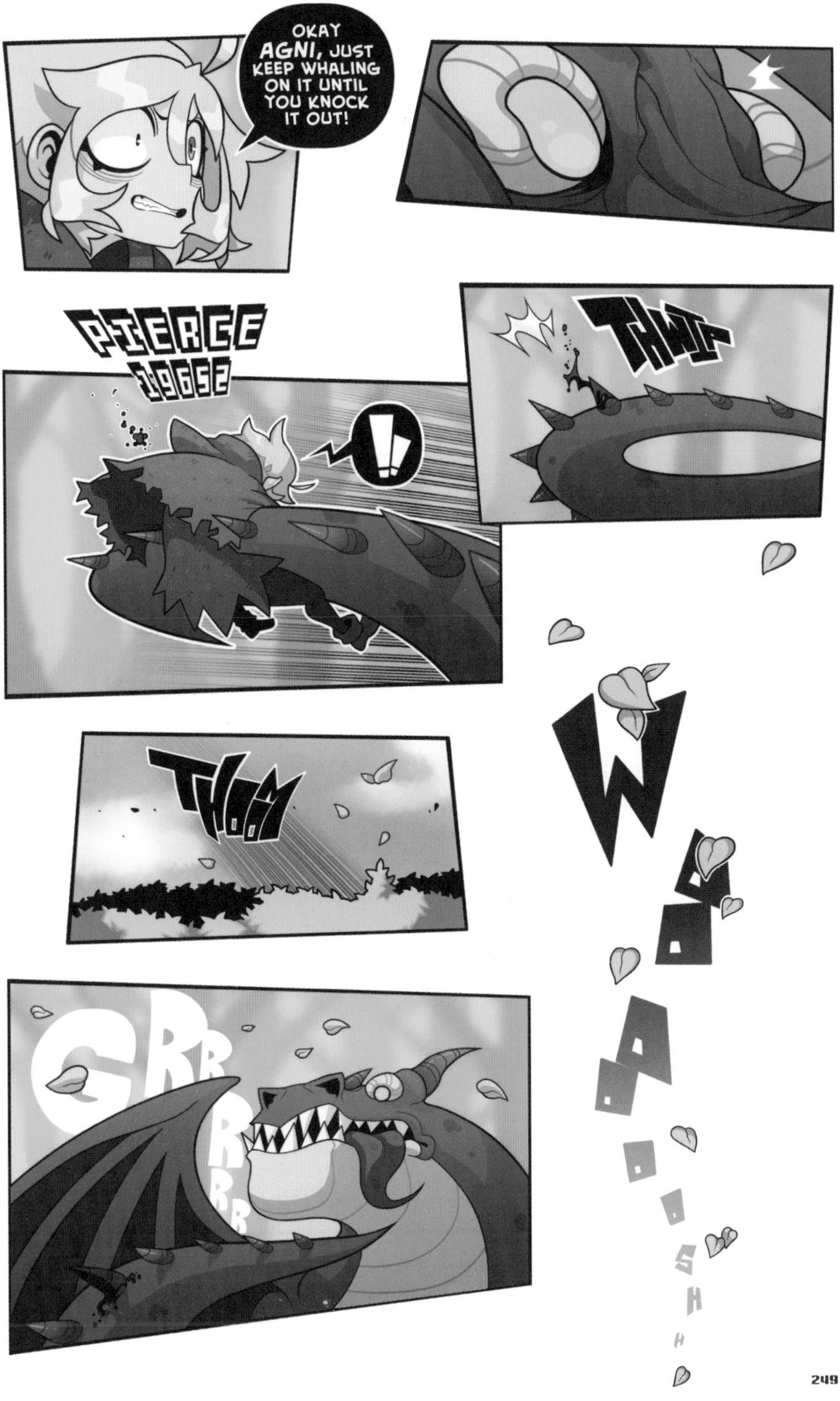
OKAY AGNI, JUST KEEP WHALING ON IT UNTIL YOU KNOCK IT OUT!
PIERCE 19652
!
THWIP
THOOM
WAOAOOOSHH
GRRRRR

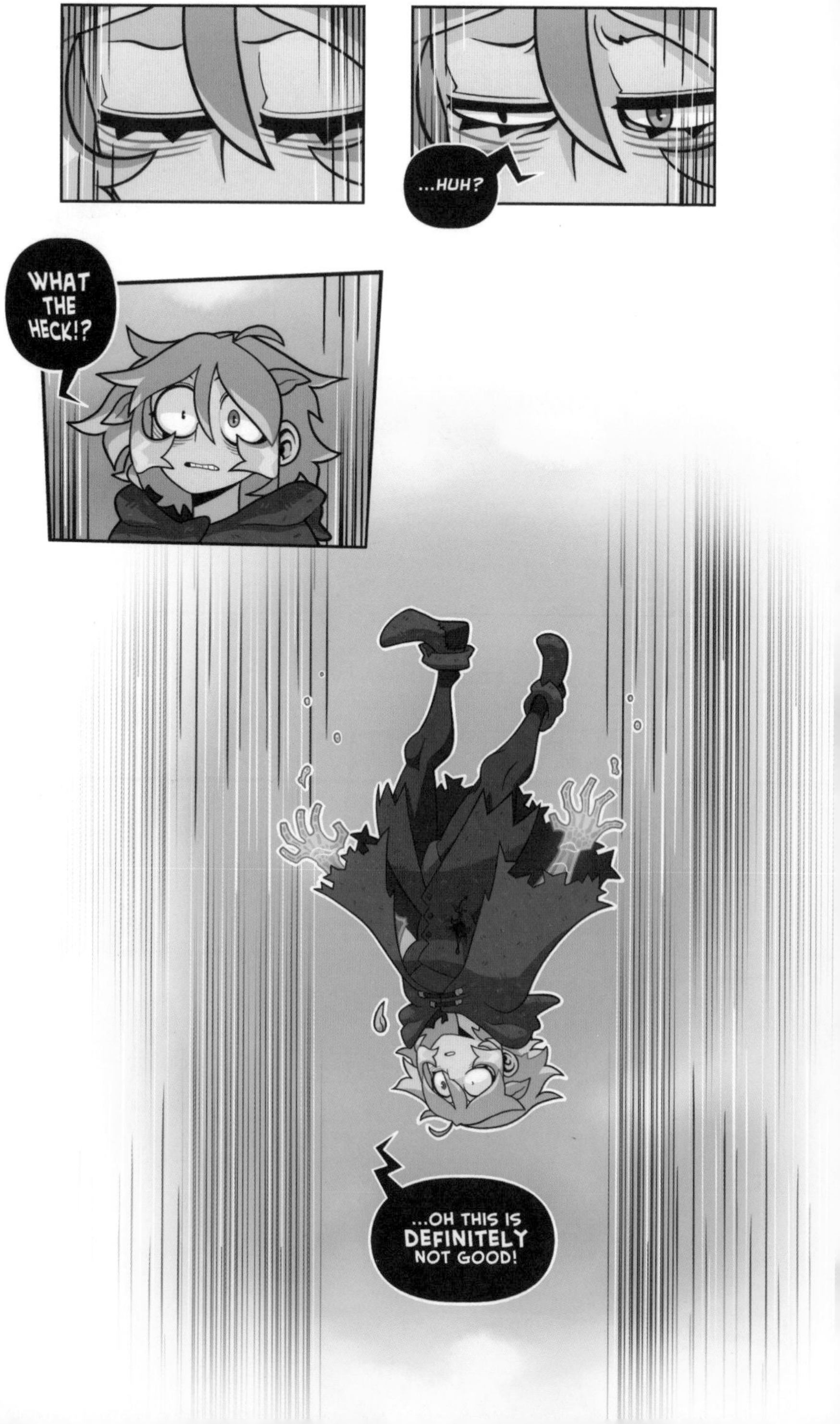
...HUH?
WHAT THE HECK!?
...OH THIS IS DEFINITELY NOT GOOD!

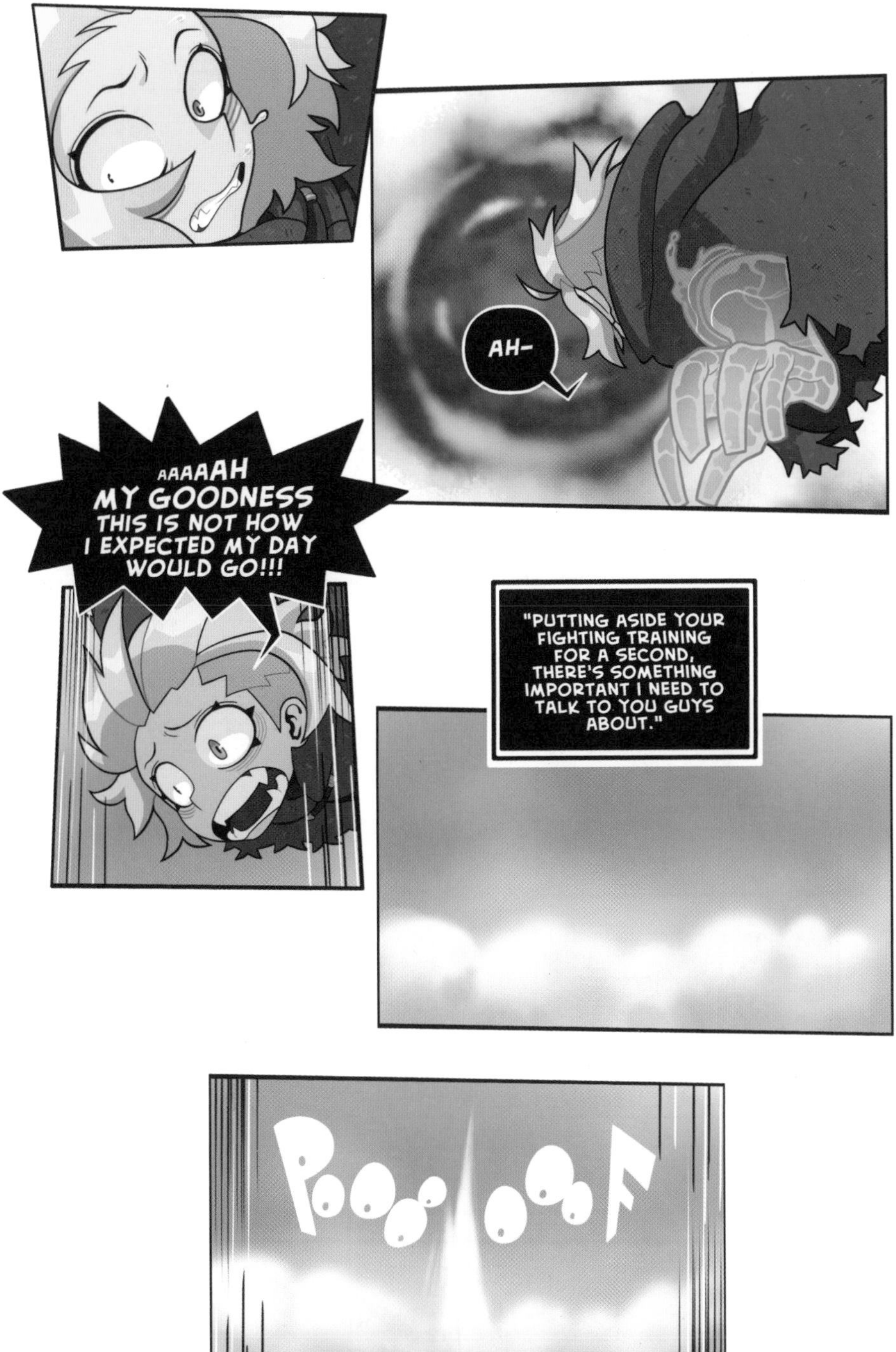
AH-
AAAAAH
MY GOODNESS
THIS IS NOT HOW
I EXPECTED MY DAY
WOULD GO!!!
"PUTTING ASIDE YOUR FIGHTING TRAINING FOR A SECOND, THERE'S SOMETHING IMPORTANT I NEED TO TALK TO YOU GUYS ABOUT."
POOOF

"ALTHOUGH I DID PROMISE I'D HELP YOU BOTH BECOME GREAT FIGHTERS, I'M NOT ABLE TO PROVIDE A SOLUTION FOR EVERY LITTLE HURDLE YOU MIGHT FACE IN THE FUTURE."

WHAT THE-
YOU'RE STILL COMING AFTER ME UP HERE?!

"THERE ARE THINGS YOU TWO HAVE AFFINITIES FOR THAT I CAN NEVER FULLY GRASP."

IT ALREADY HIT ME PRETTY BAD-

"I CAN'T TEACH YOU ABOUT MAGIC AND WEAPONS, I CAN ONLY HELP YOU UNDERSTAND HOW THEY CAN FIT INTO THE FLOW OF BATTLE."

BLEED
1252

"YOUR EXPERIENCES WITH CONFLICT WILL NEVER BE THE SAME AS MINE."

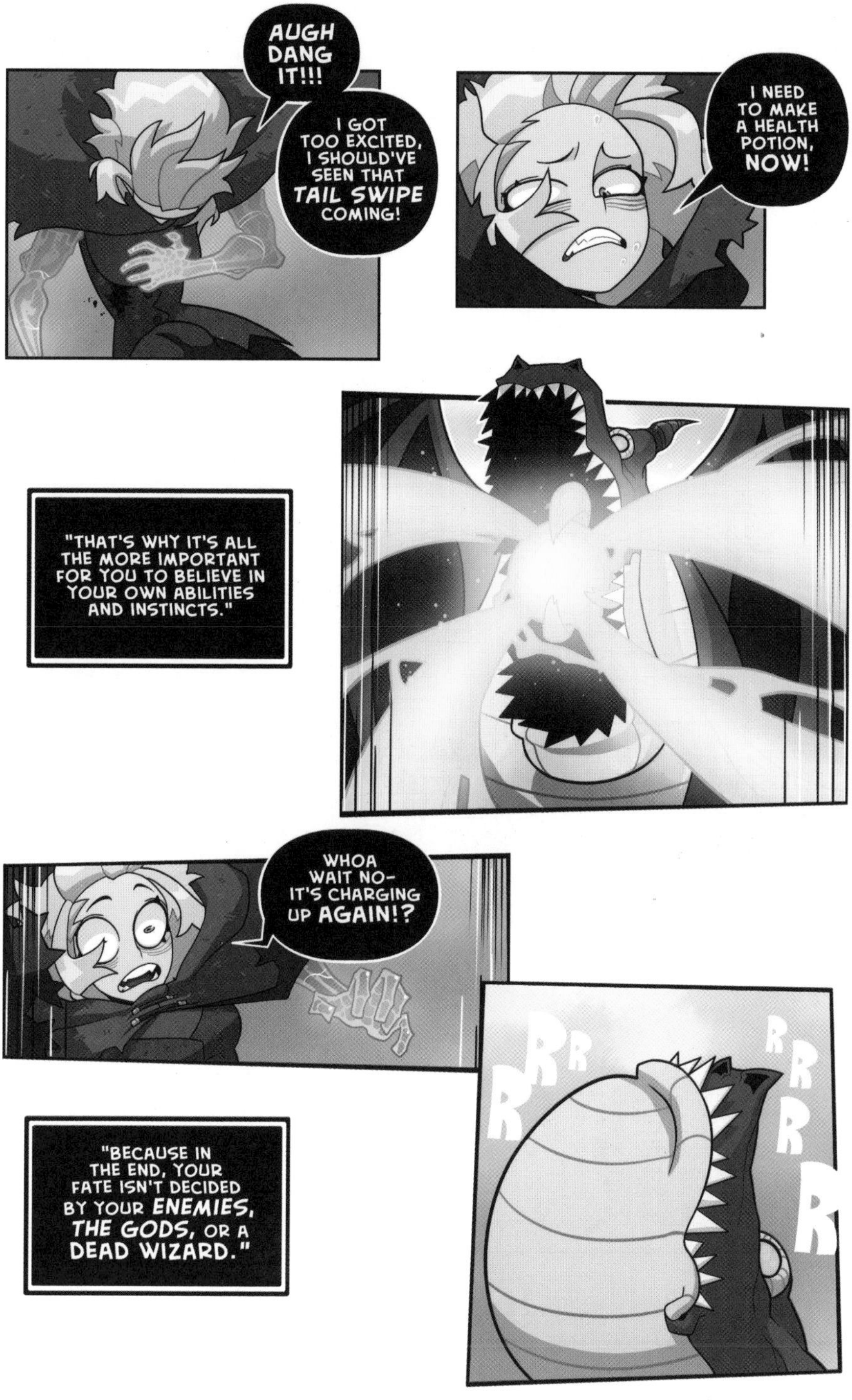
AUGH DANG IT!!!
I GOT TOO EXCITED, I SHOULD'VE SEEN THAT TAIL SWIPE COMING!
I NEED TO MAKE A HEALTH POTION, NOW!
"THAT'S WHY IT'S ALL THE MORE IMPORTANT FOR YOU TO BELIEVE IN YOUR OWN ABILITIES AND INSTINCTS."
WHOA WAIT NO- IT'S CHARGING UP AGAIN!?
"BECAUSE IN THE END, YOUR FATE ISN'T DECIDED BY YOUR ENEMIES, THE GODS, OR A DEAD WIZARD."
RRR
RRRRR

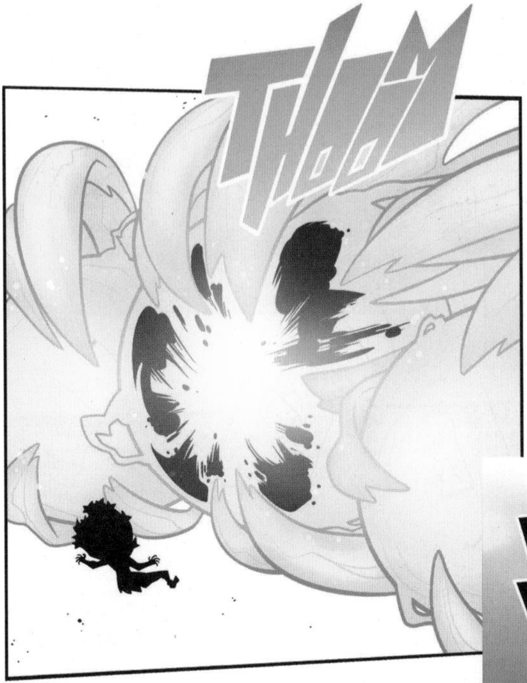
THOOM

"THE ONLY ONE WHO DECIDES YOUR FATE IS YOU."

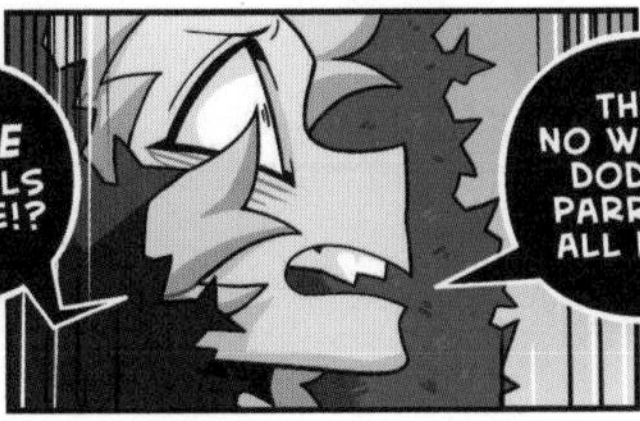
THREE FIREBALLS AT ONCE!?
THERE'S NO WAY I CAN DODGE OR PARRY THEM ALL IN TIME!

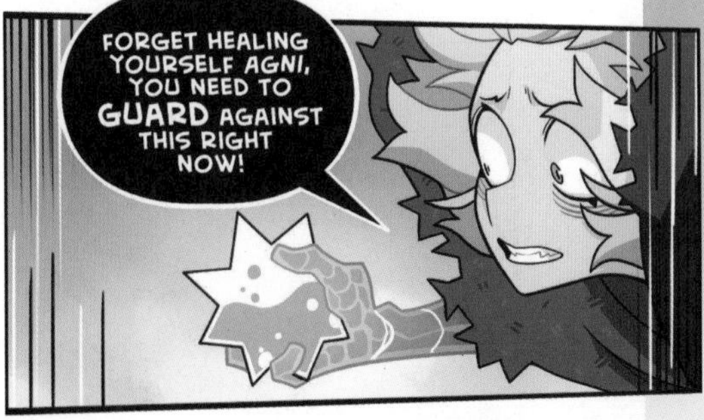
FORGET HEALING YOURSELF AGNI, YOU NEED TO GUARD AGAINST THIS RIGHT NOW!

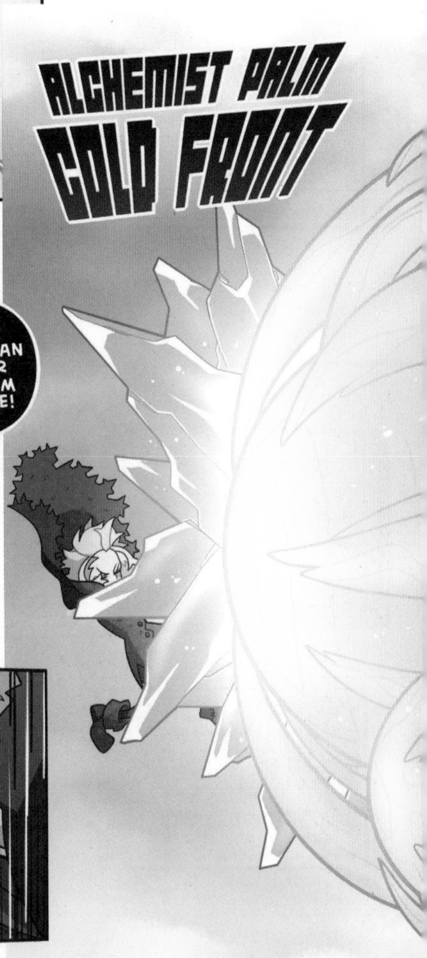
ALCHEMIST PALM
COLD FRONT

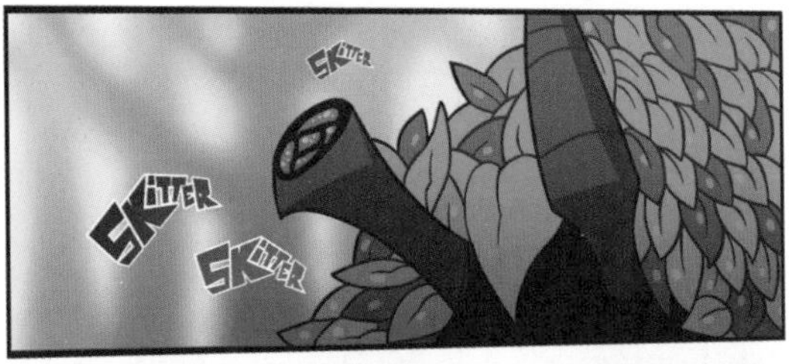
SKITTER
SKITTER
SKITTER

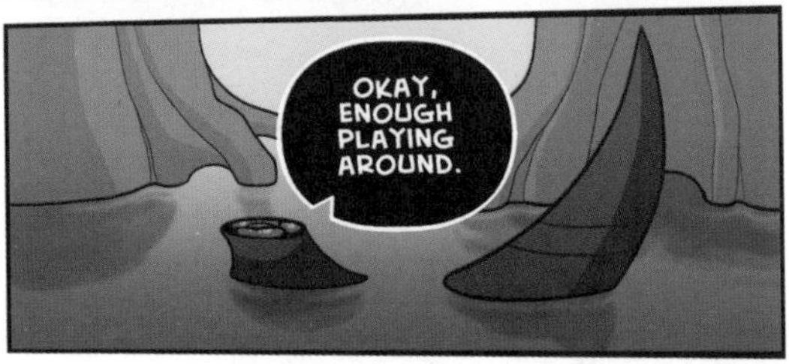
OKAY, ENOUGH PLAYING AROUND.

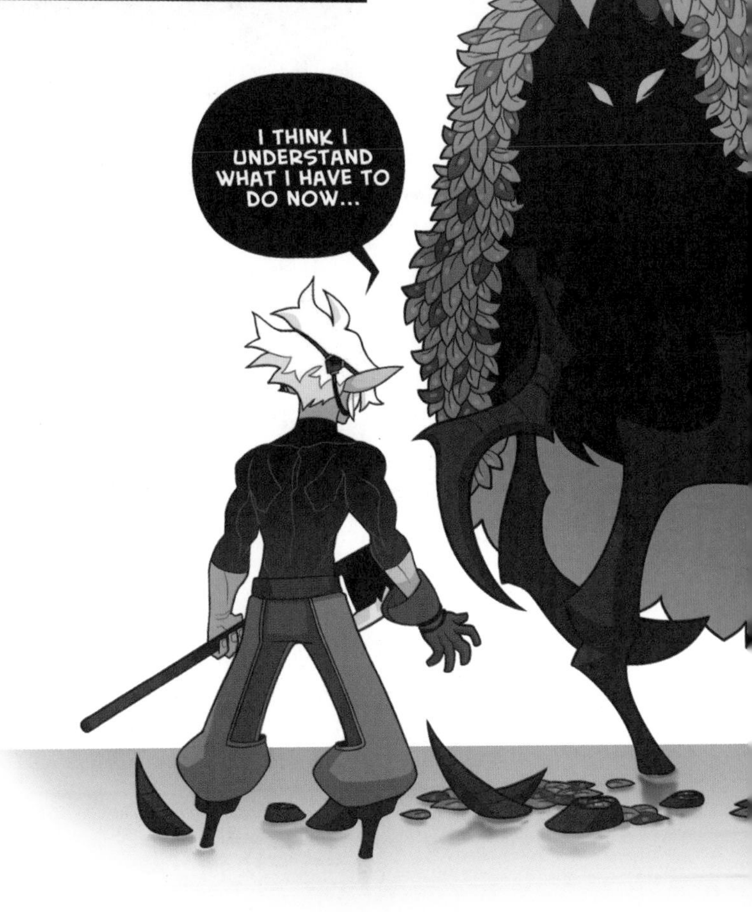
I THINK I UNDERSTAND WHAT I HAVE TO DO NOW...

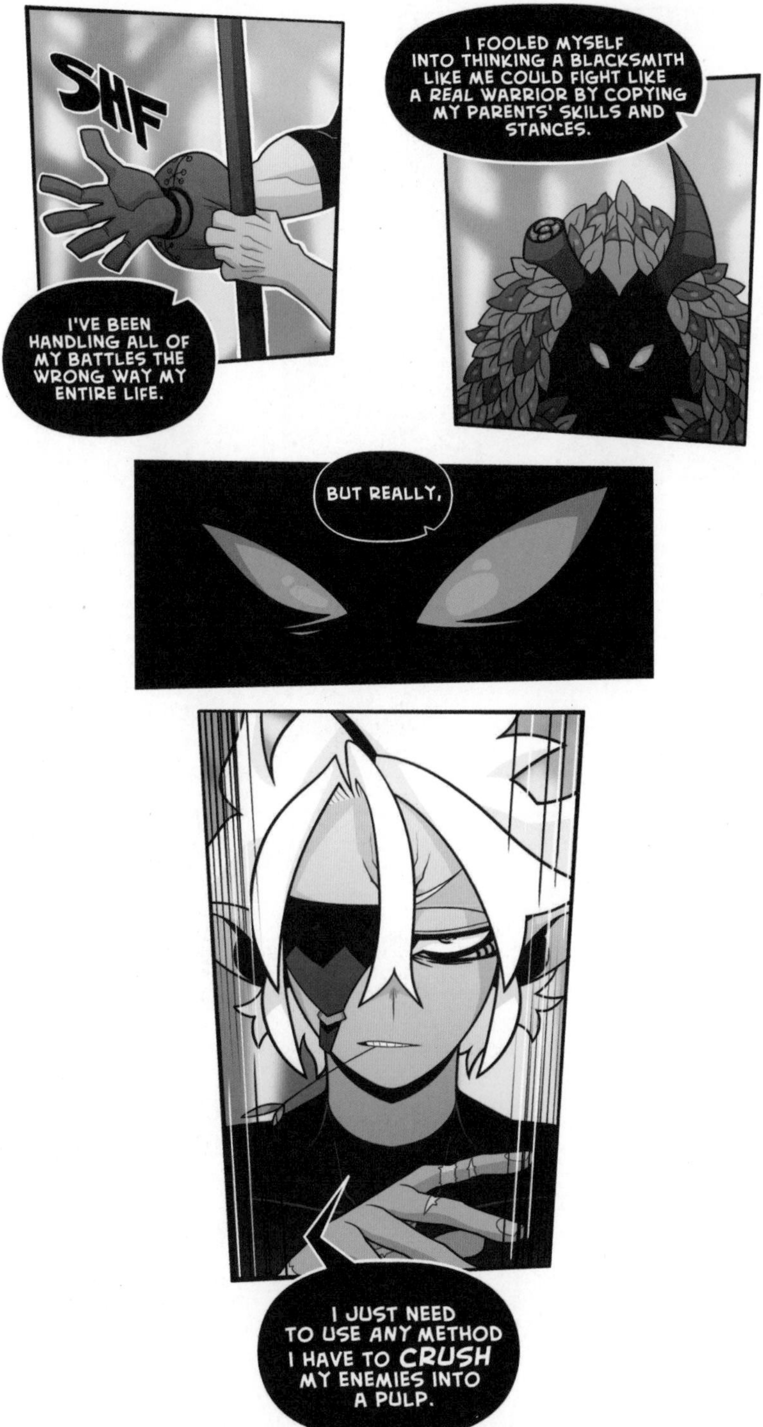
SHF
I'VE BEEN HANDLING ALL OF MY BATTLES THE WRONG WAY MY ENTIRE LIFE.
I FOOLED MYSELF INTO THINKING A BLACKSMITH LIKE ME COULD FIGHT LIKE A REAL WARRIOR BY COPYING MY PARENTS' SKILLS AND STANCES.
BUT REALLY,
I JUST NEED TO USE ANY METHOD I HAVE TO CRUSH MY ENEMIES INTO A PULP.

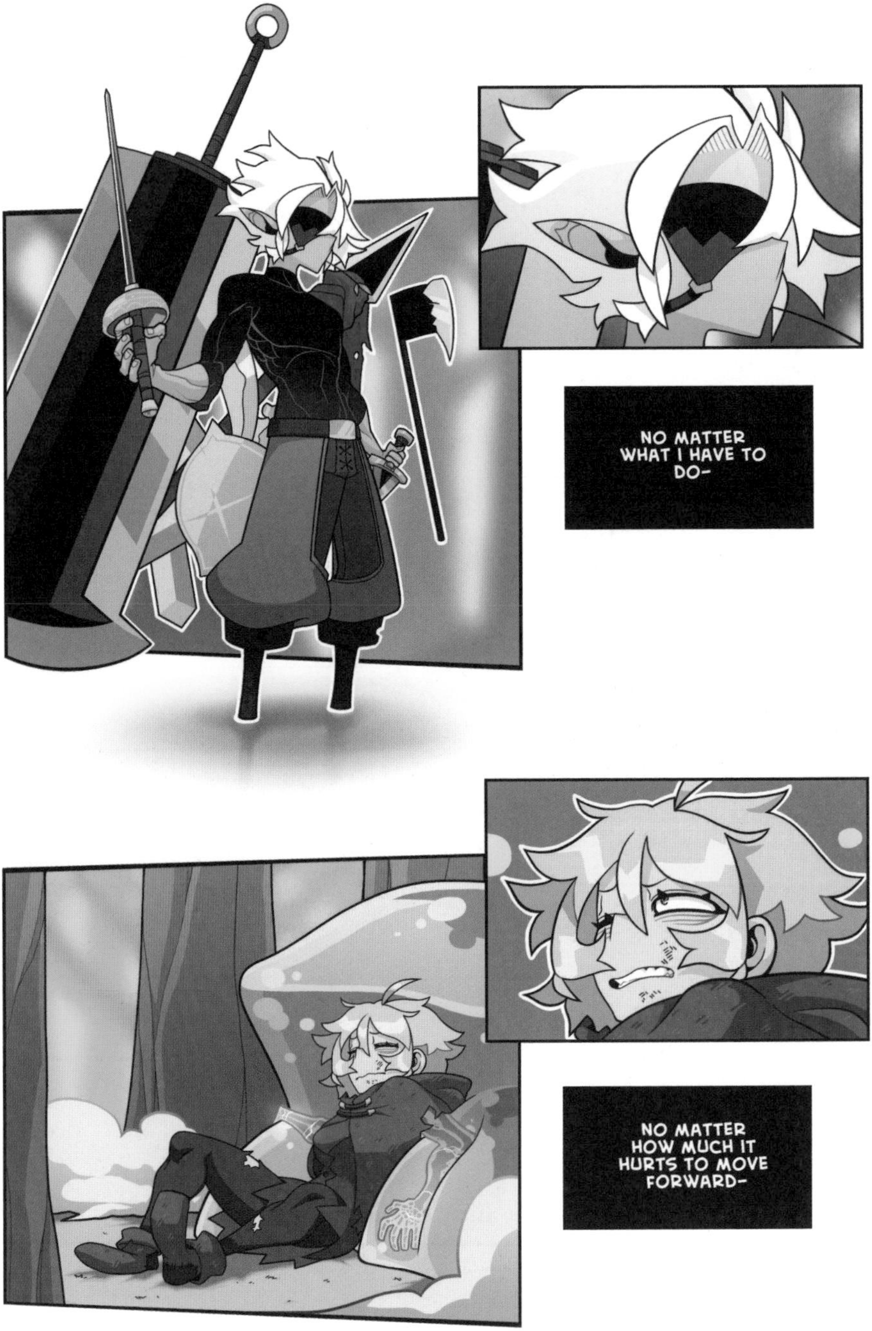
NO MATTER WHAT I HAVE TO DO-
NO MATTER HOW MUCH IT HURTS TO MOVE FORWARD-

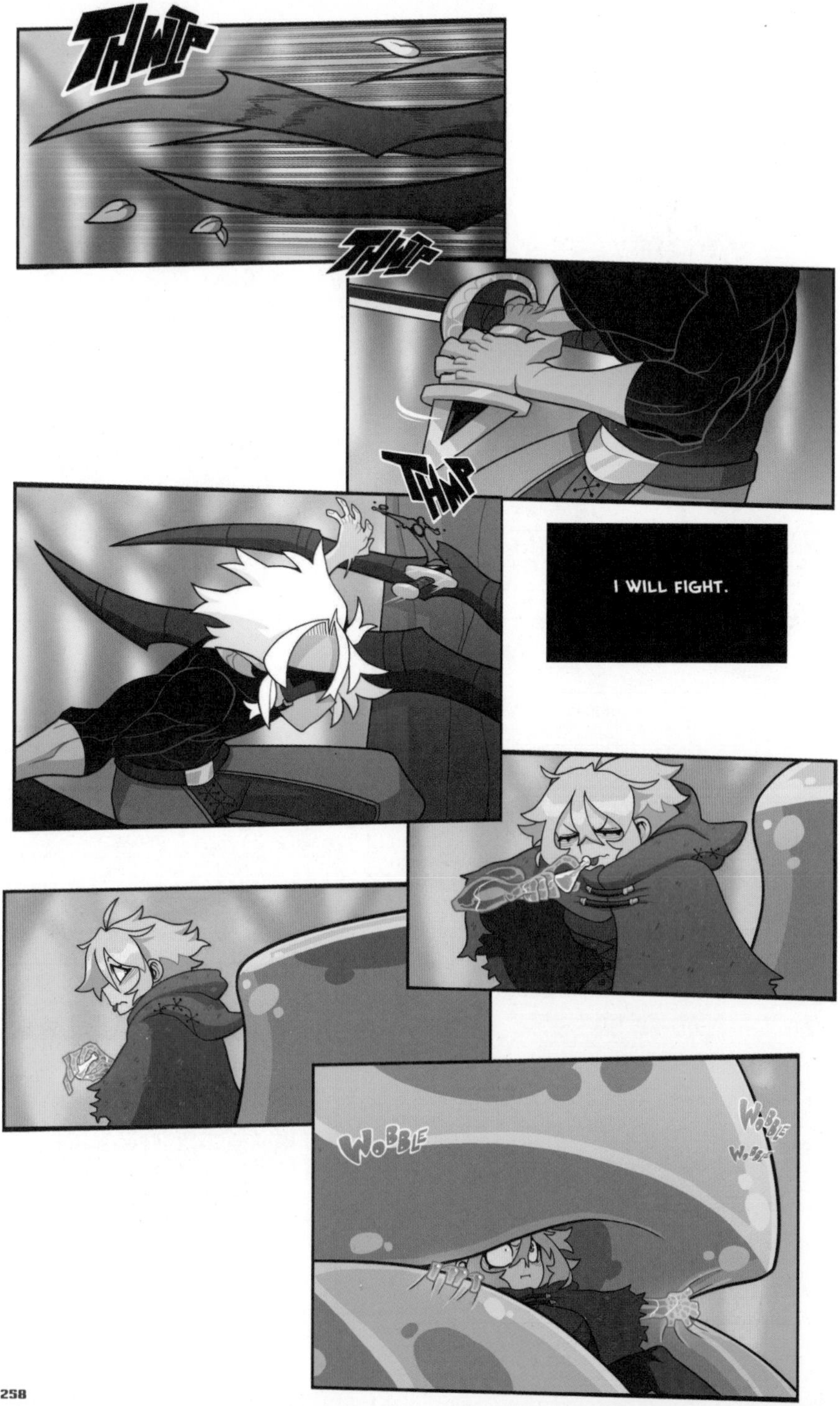
THWIP
THWIP
THMP
I WILL FIGHT.
WOBBLE
WOBBLE
WOBBLE

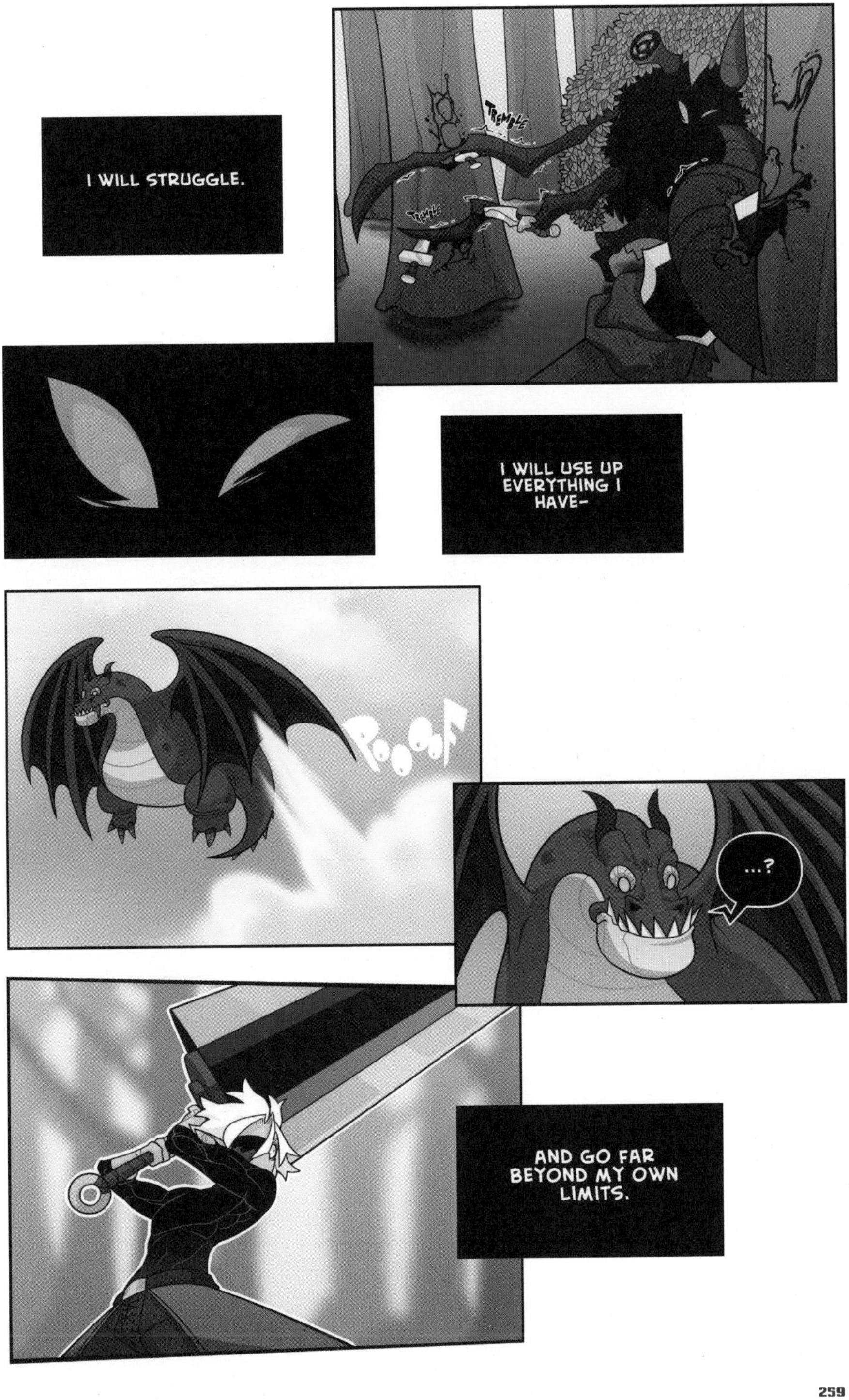
I WILL STRUGGLE.
TREMBLE
TREMBLE
I WILL USE UP EVERYTHING I HAVE-
POOOF
...?
AND GO FAR BEYOND MY OWN LIMITS.

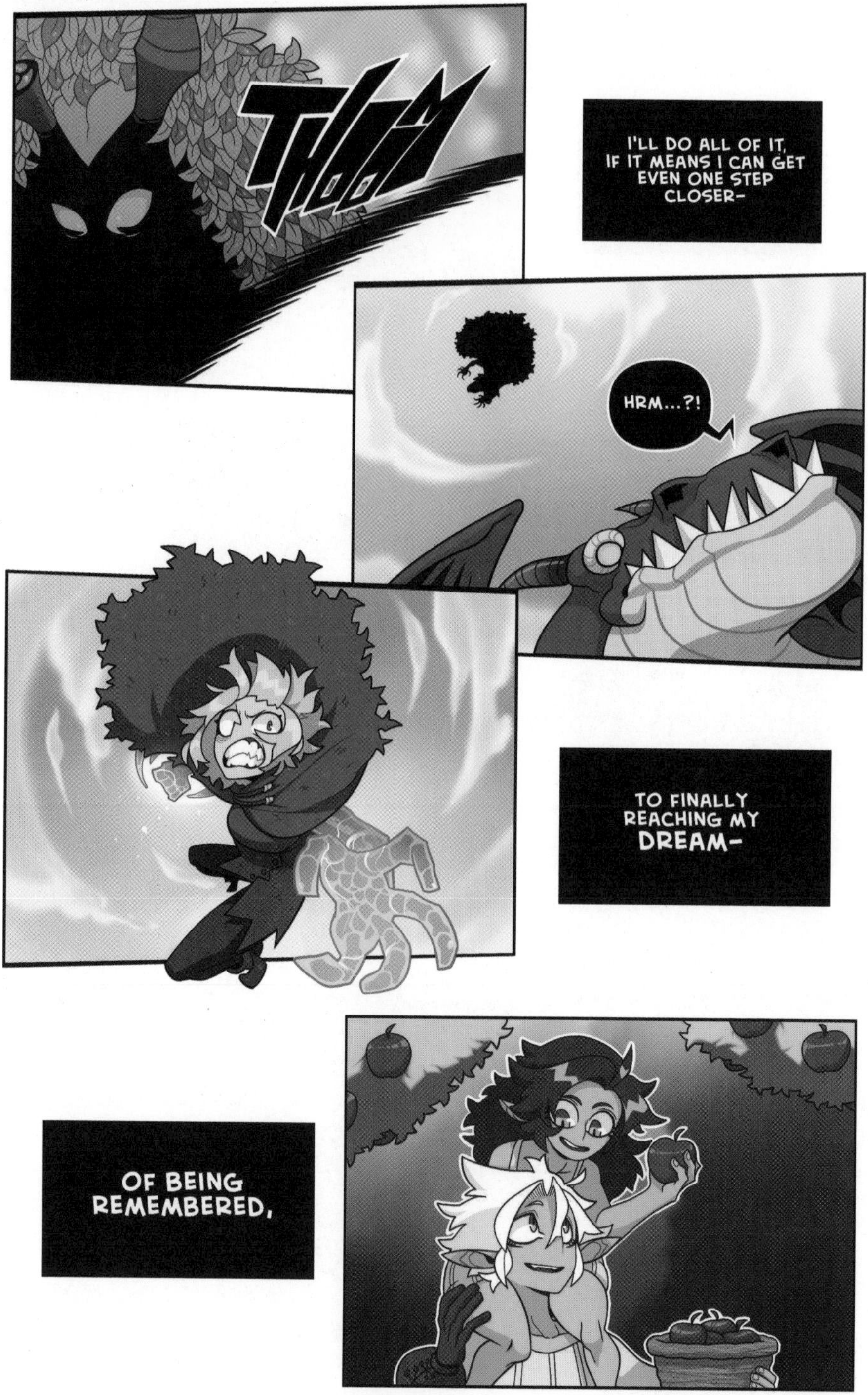
THOOM
I'LL DO ALL OF IT, IF IT MEANS I CAN GET EVEN ONE STEP CLOSER-
HRM...?!
TO FINALLY REACHING MY DREAM-
OF BEING REMEMBERED,

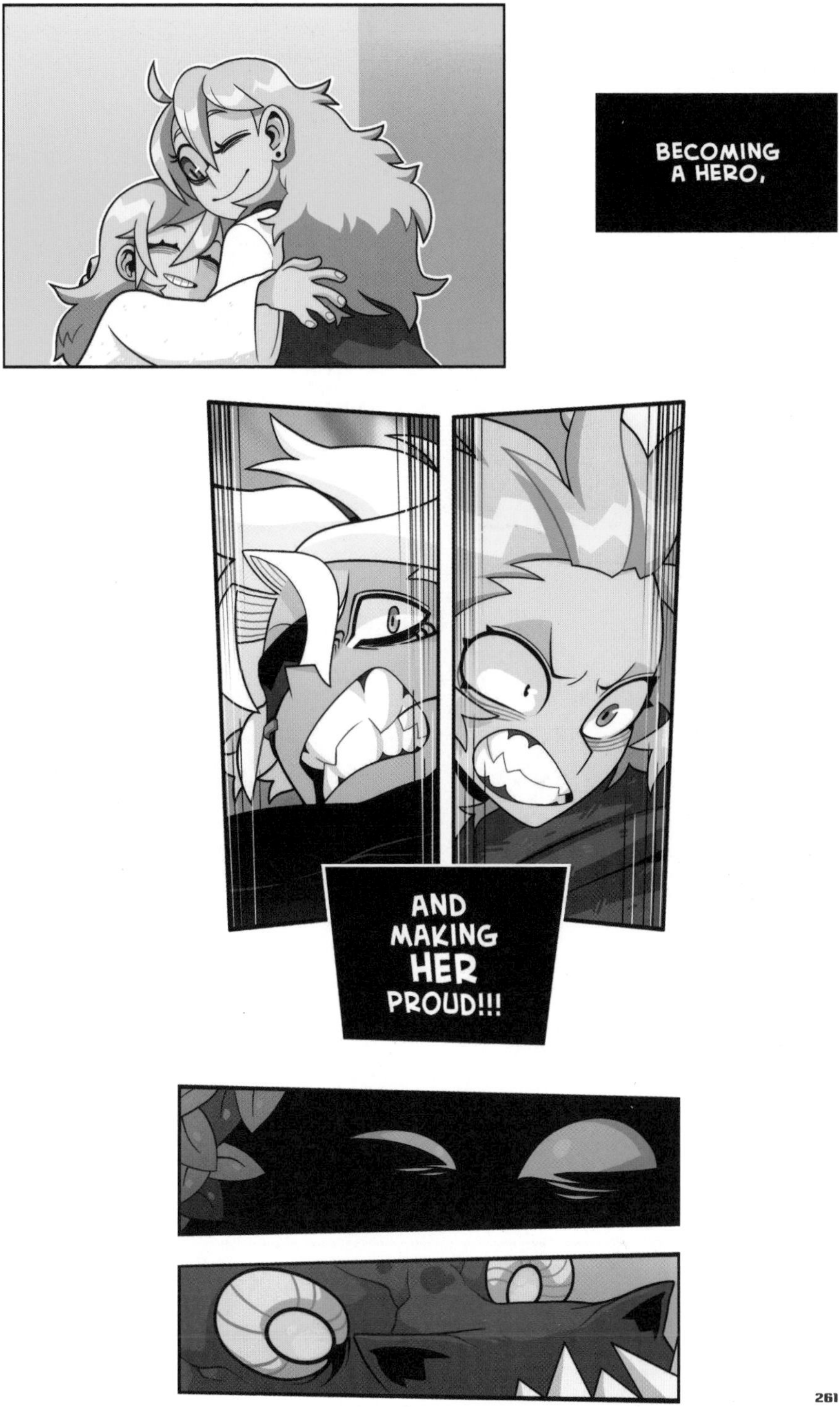
BECOMING A HERO,
AND MAKING HER PROUD!!!

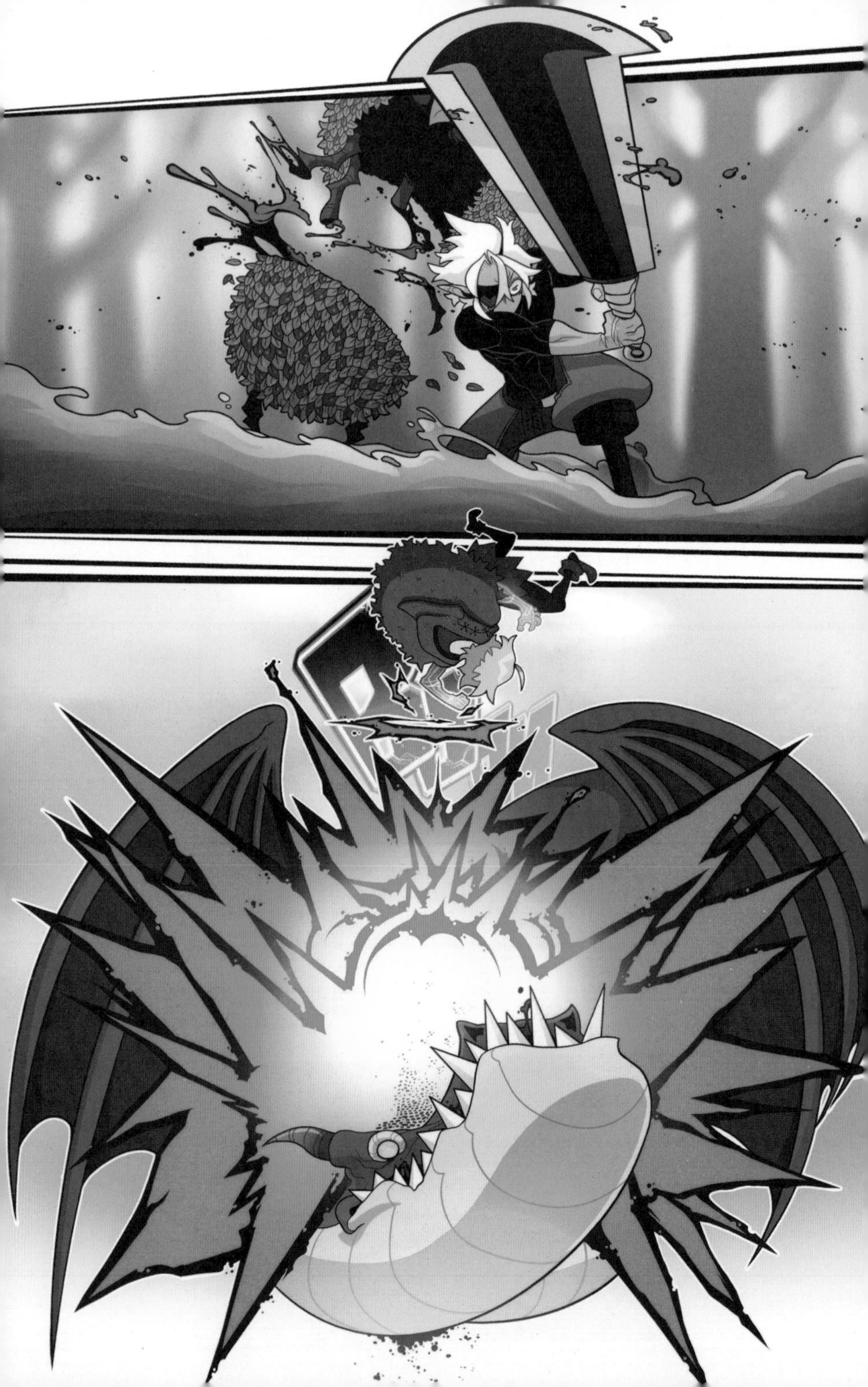

# Chapter 22
# THE HIDDEN

YOU
AREN'T MUCH
OF A LOOKER,
EVEN WITHOUT
ALL THOSE
BUGS NESTING
IN YOUR
FACE.

WOW,
YOU UH...

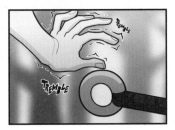

AUGH!

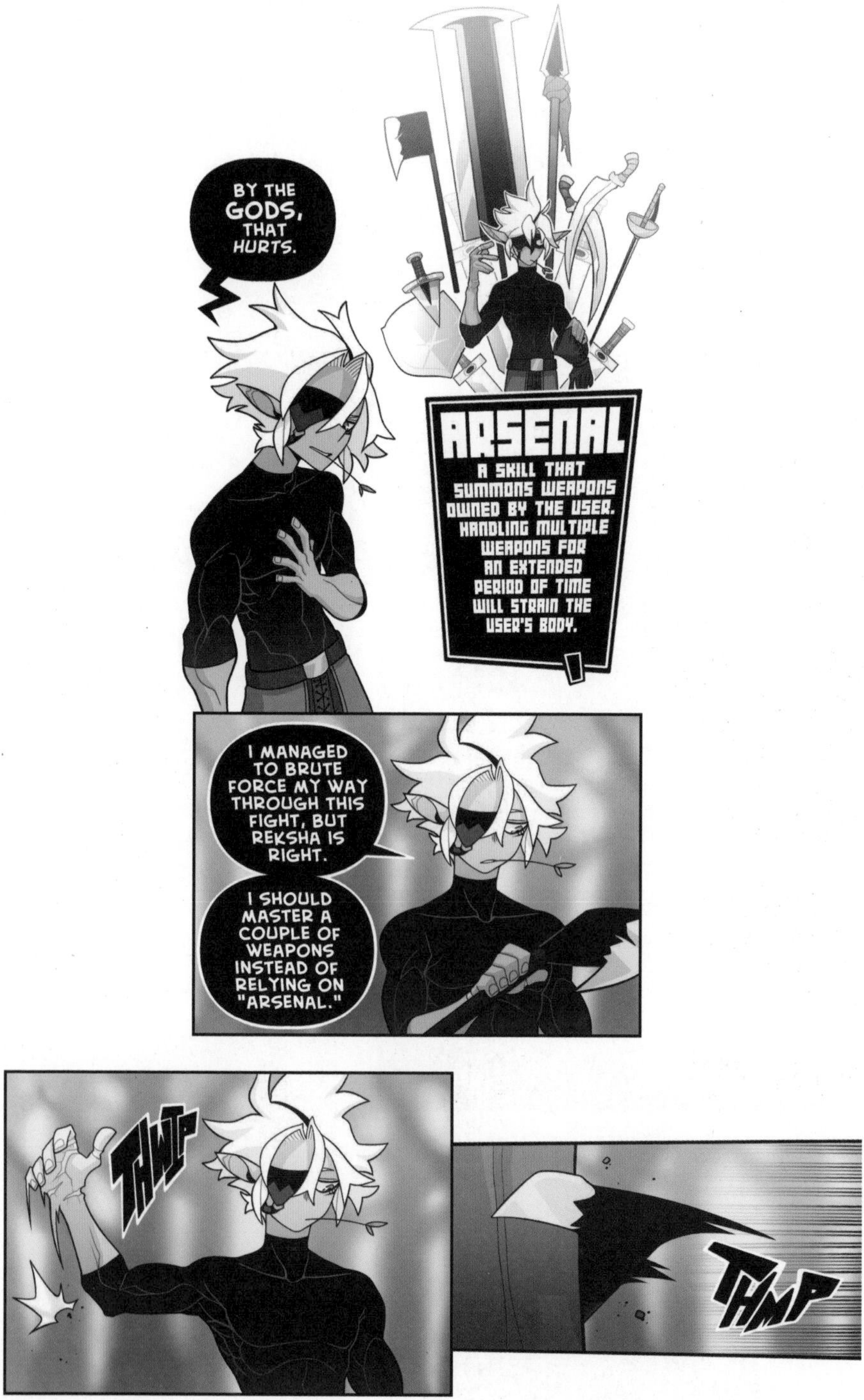
BY THE GODS, THAT HURTS.
ARSENAL
A SKILL THAT SUMMONS WEAPONS OWNED BY THE USER. HANDLING MULTIPLE WEAPONS FOR AN EXTENDED PERIOD OF TIME WILL STRAIN THE USER'S BODY.
I MANAGED TO BRUTE FORCE MY WAY THROUGH THIS FIGHT, BUT REKSHA IS RIGHT.
I SHOULD MASTER A COUPLE OF WEAPONS INSTEAD OF RELYING ON "ARSENAL."
THWIP
THMP

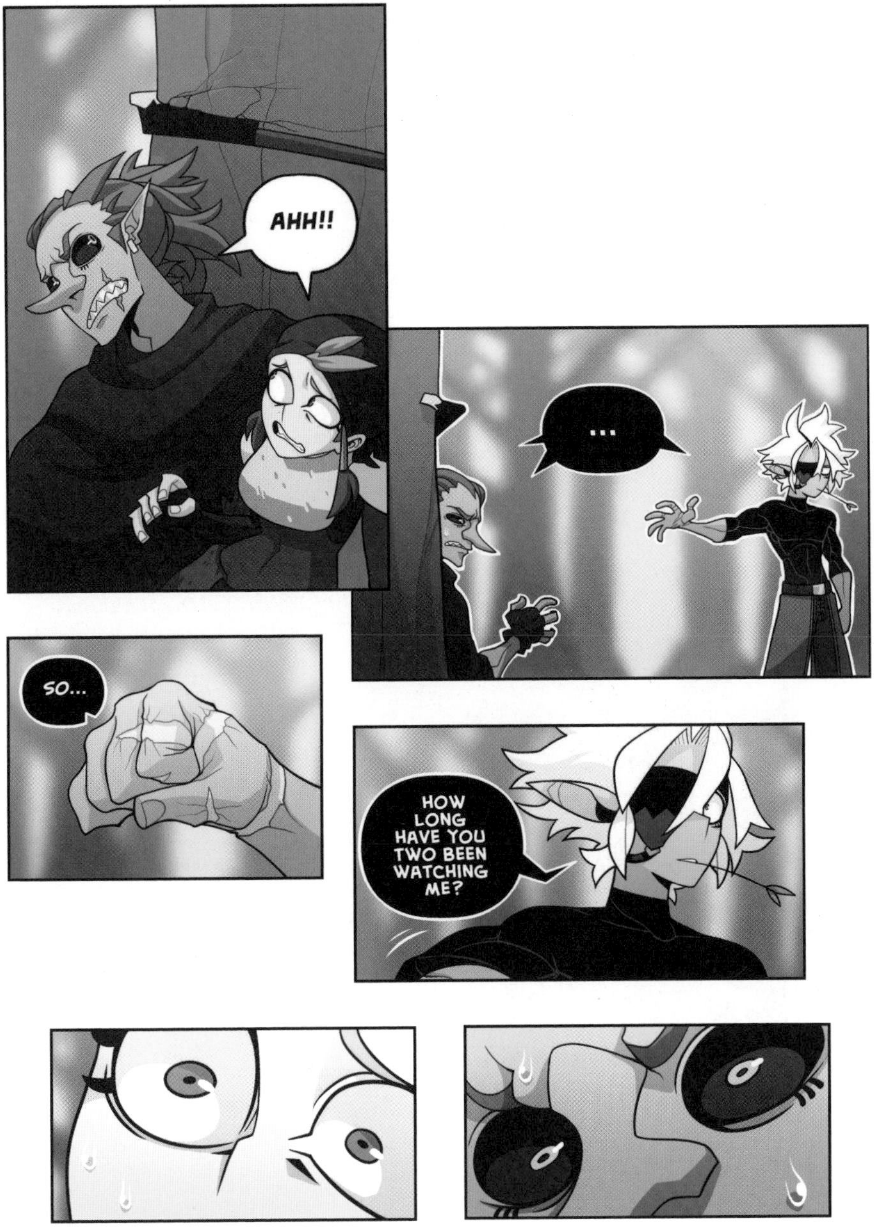
AHH!!
...
SO...
HOW LONG HAVE YOU TWO BEEN WATCHING ME?

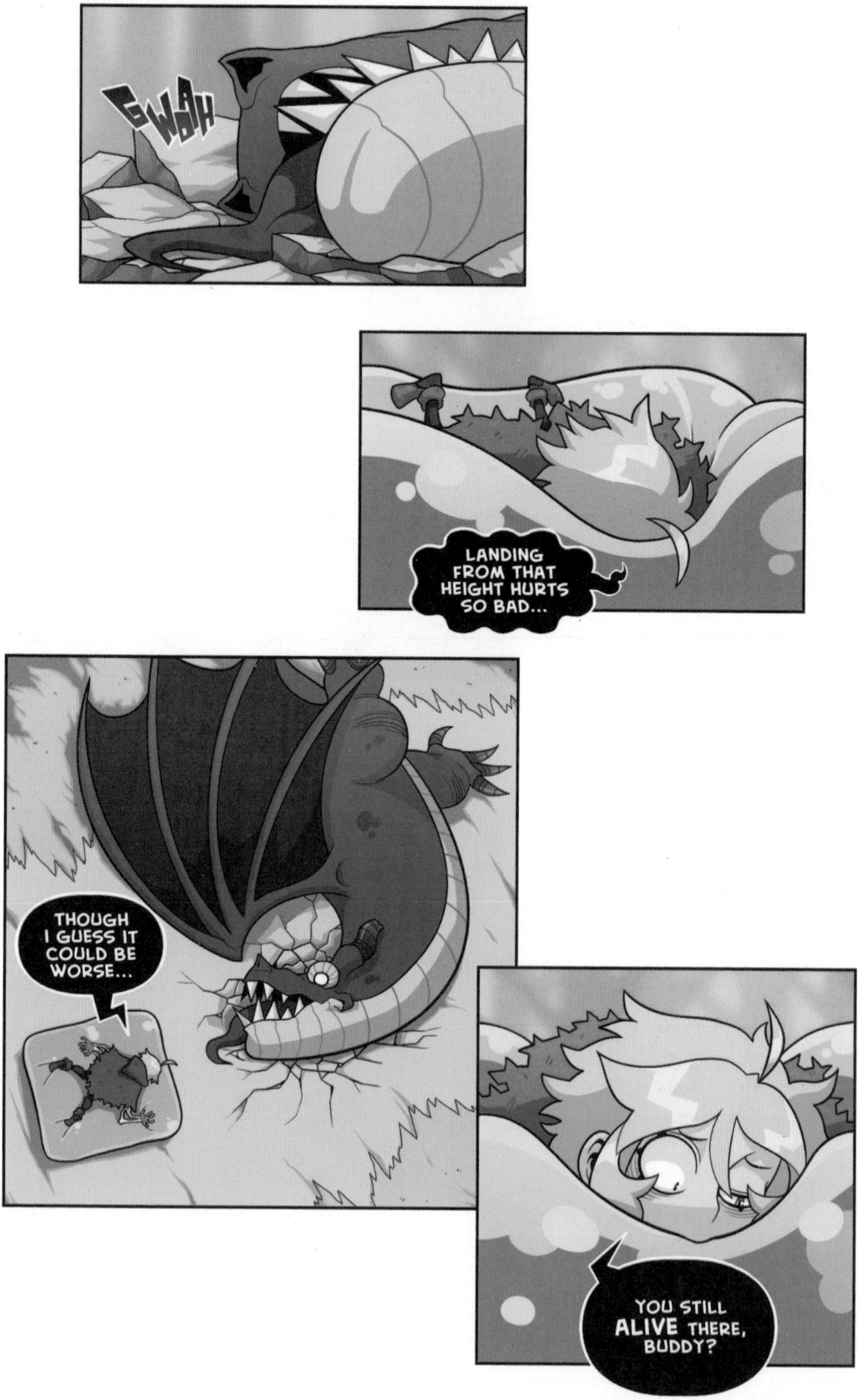
GWAAH
LANDING FROM THAT HEIGHT HURTS SO BAD...
THOUGH I GUESS IT COULD BE WORSE...
YOU STILL ALIVE THERE, BUDDY?

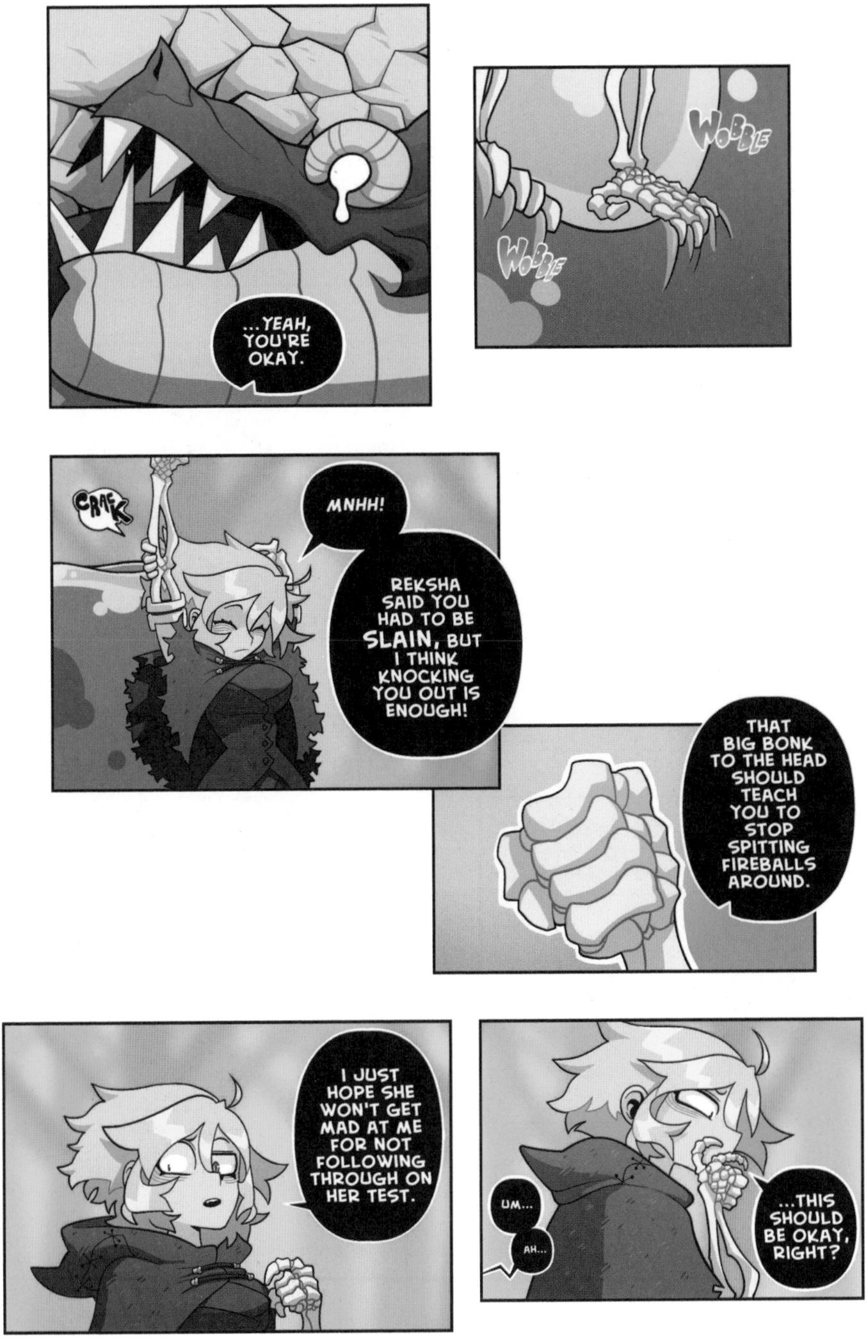
...YEAH, YOU'RE OKAY.
WOBBLE
WOBBLE
CRACK
MNHH!
REKSHA SAID YOU HAD TO BE **SLAIN,** BUT I THINK KNOCKING YOU OUT IS ENOUGH!
THAT BIG BONK TO THE HEAD SHOULD TEACH YOU TO STOP SPITTING FIREBALLS AROUND.
I JUST HOPE SHE WON'T GET MAD AT ME FOR NOT FOLLOWING THROUGH ON HER TEST.
UM...
AH...
...THIS SHOULD BE OKAY, RIGHT?

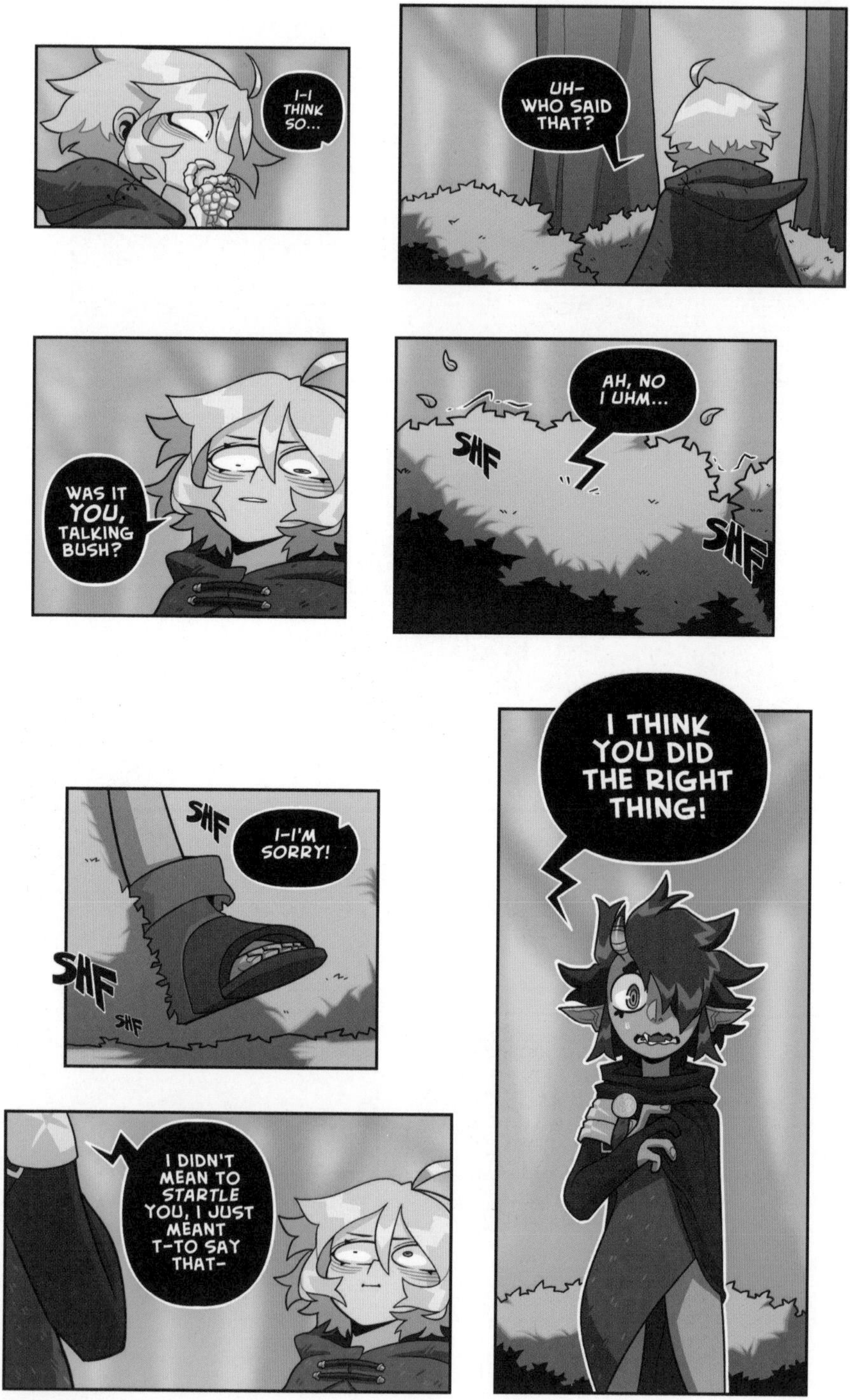
I-I THINK SO...
UH- WHO SAID THAT?
WAS IT YOU, TALKING BUSH?
SHF
AH, NO I UHM...
SHF
SHF
I-I'M SORRY!
SHF
SHF
I DIDN'T MEAN TO STARTLE YOU, I JUST MEANT T-TO SAY THAT-
I THINK YOU DID THE RIGHT THING!

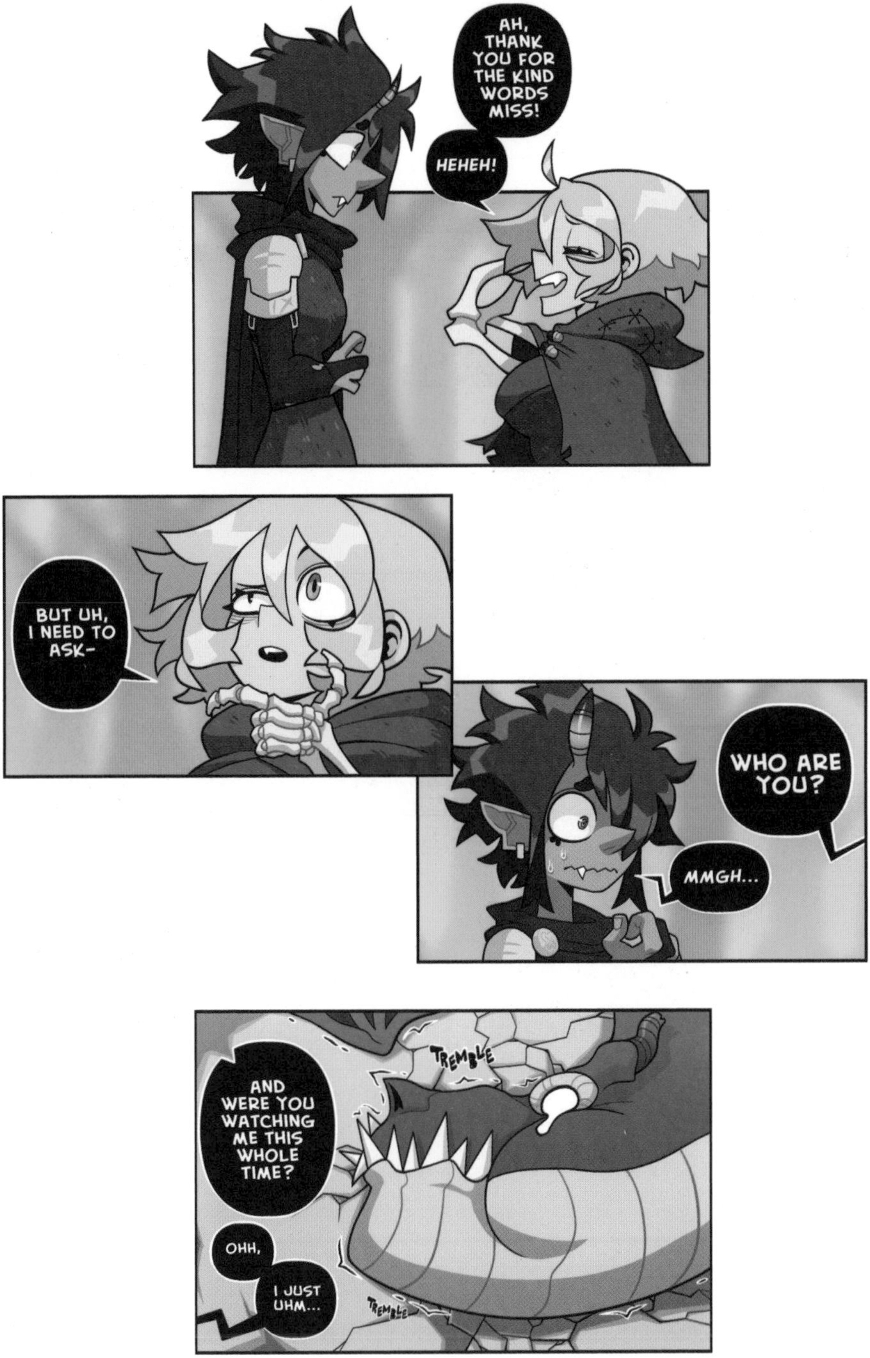
AH, THANK YOU FOR THE KIND WORDS MISS!
HEHEH!
BUT UH, I NEED TO ASK-
WHO ARE YOU?
MMGH...
TREMBLE
AND WERE YOU WATCHING ME THIS WHOLE TIME?
OHH,
I JUST UHM...
TREMBLE

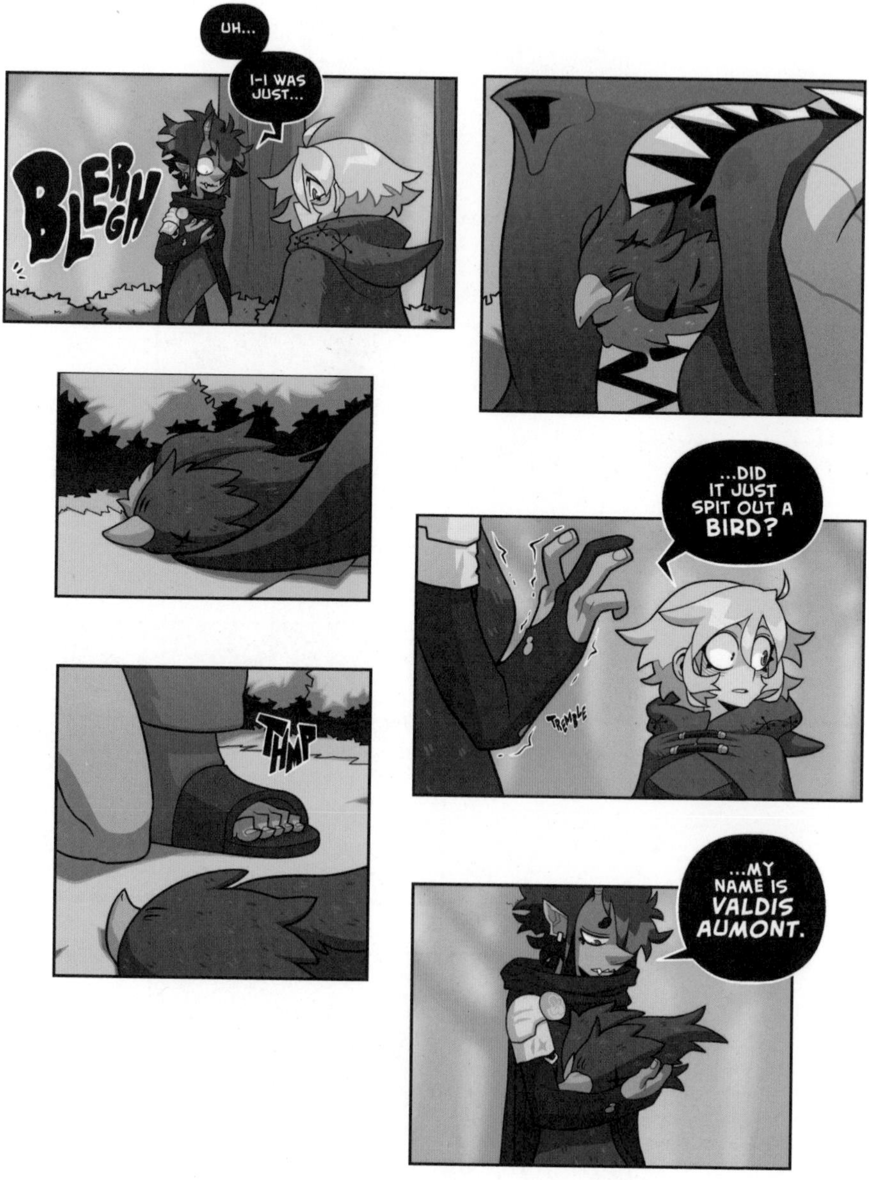
UH...
I-I WAS JUST...
BLERGH
...DID IT JUST SPIT OUT A BIRD?
TREMBLE
THMP
...MY NAME IS VALDIS AUMONT.

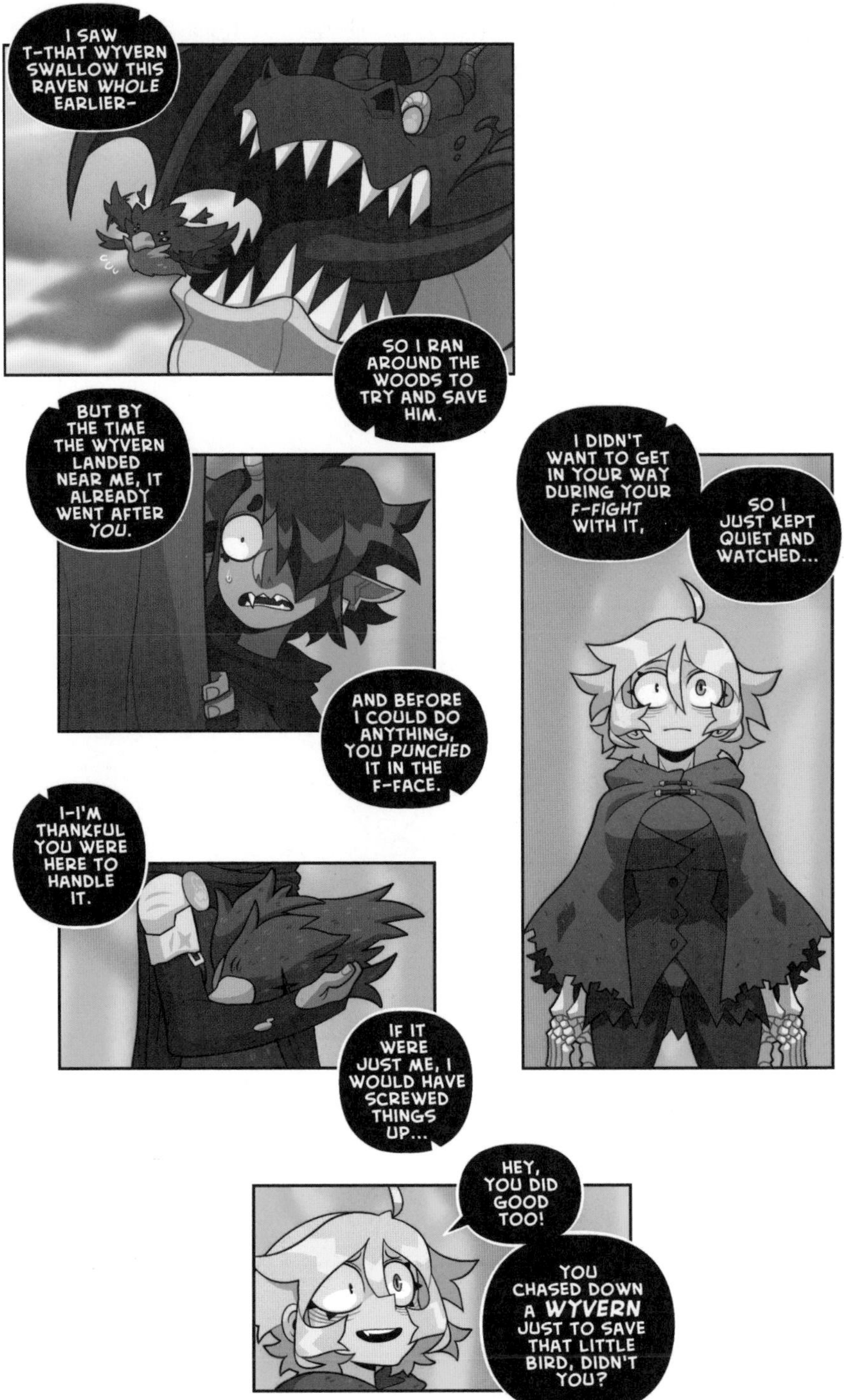
I SAW T-THAT WYVERN SWALLOW THIS RAVEN *WHOLE* EARLIER-
SO I RAN AROUND THE WOODS TO TRY AND SAVE HIM.
BUT BY THE TIME THE WYVERN LANDED NEAR ME, IT ALREADY WENT AFTER *YOU*.
AND BEFORE I COULD DO ANYTHING, YOU *PUNCHED* IT IN THE F-FACE.
I-I'M THANKFUL YOU WERE HERE TO HANDLE IT.
IF IT WERE JUST ME, I WOULD HAVE SCREWED THINGS UP...
I DIDN'T WANT TO GET IN YOUR WAY DURING YOUR *F-FIGHT* WITH IT,
SO I JUST KEPT QUIET AND WATCHED...
HEY, YOU DID GOOD TOO!
YOU CHASED DOWN A **WYVERN** JUST TO SAVE THAT LITTLE BIRD, DIDN'T YOU?

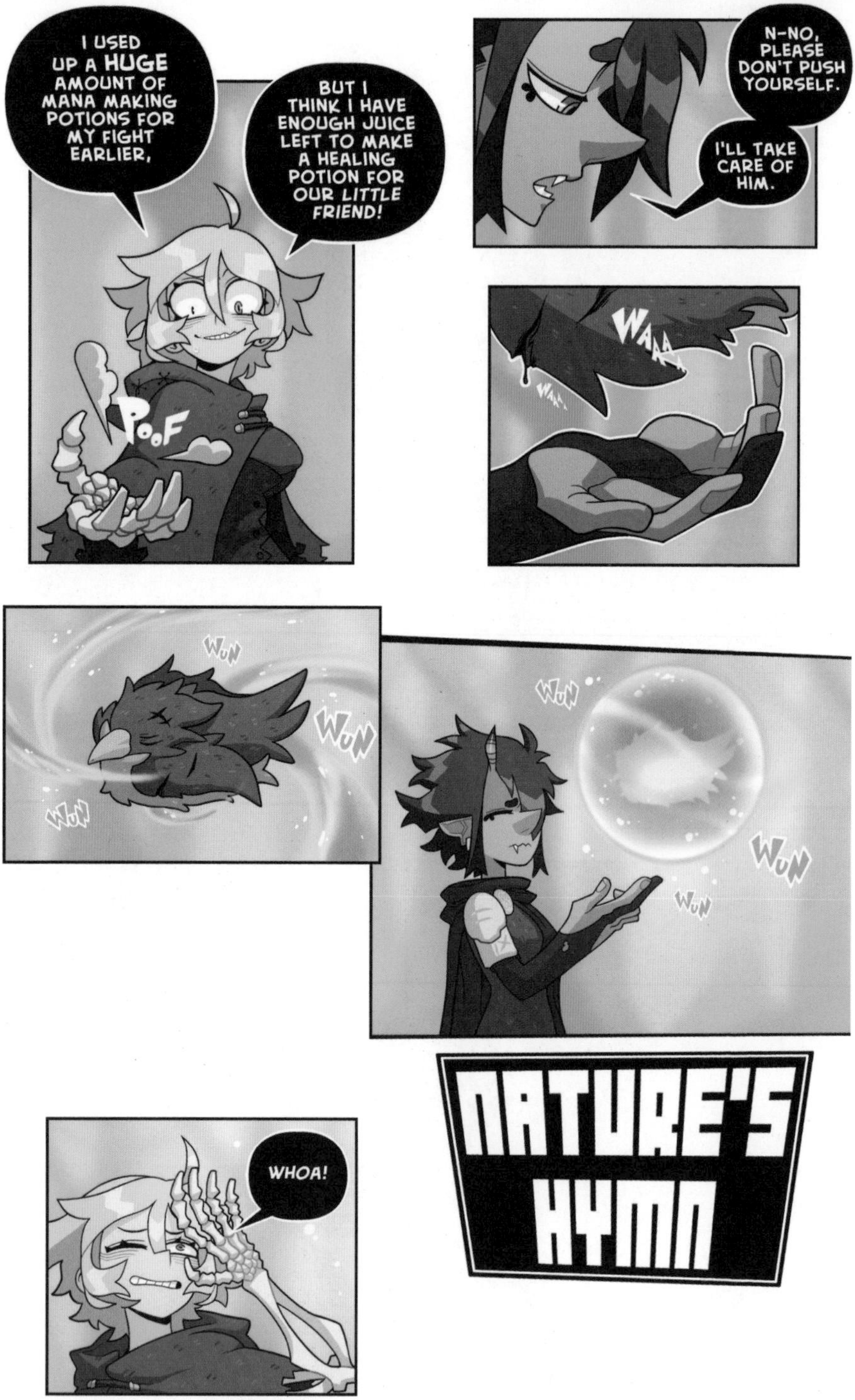
I USED UP A **HUGE** AMOUNT OF MANA MAKING POTIONS FOR MY FIGHT EARLIER,
BUT I THINK I HAVE ENOUGH JUICE LEFT TO MAKE A HEALING POTION FOR OUR *LITTLE* FRIEND!
POOF
N-NO, PLEASE DON'T PUSH YOURSELF.
I'LL TAKE CARE OF HIM.
WAAAA
WUN
WUN
WUN
WUN
WUN
WUN
NATURE'S HYMN
WHOA!

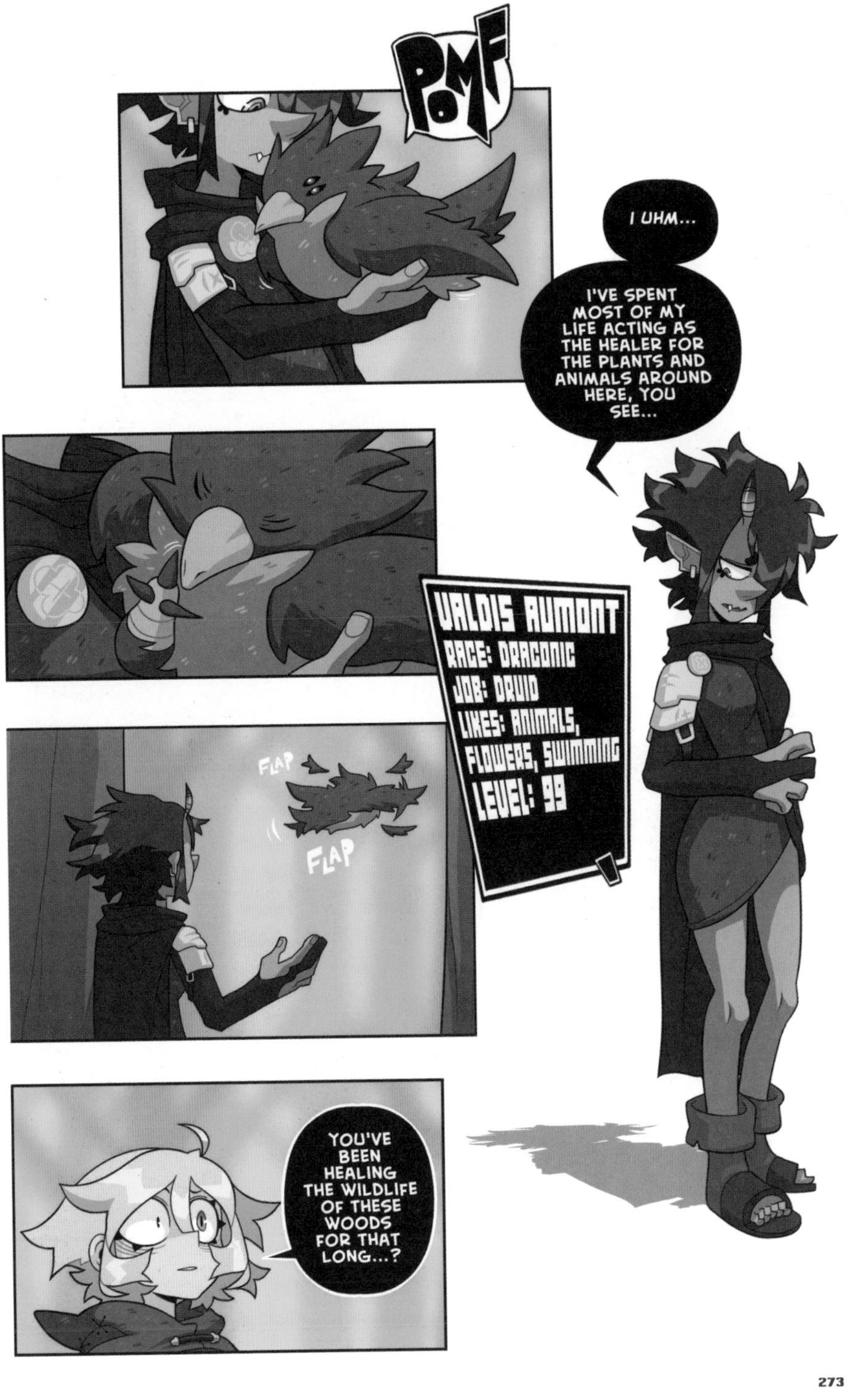
POMF
I UHM...
I'VE SPENT MOST OF MY LIFE ACTING AS THE HEALER FOR THE PLANTS AND ANIMALS AROUND HERE, YOU SEE...
VALOIS AUMONT
RACE: DRACONIC
JOB: DRUID
LIKES: ANIMALS, FLOWERS, SWIMMING
LEVEL: 99
FLAP
FLAP
YOU'VE BEEN HEALING THE WILDLIFE OF THESE WOODS FOR THAT LONG...?

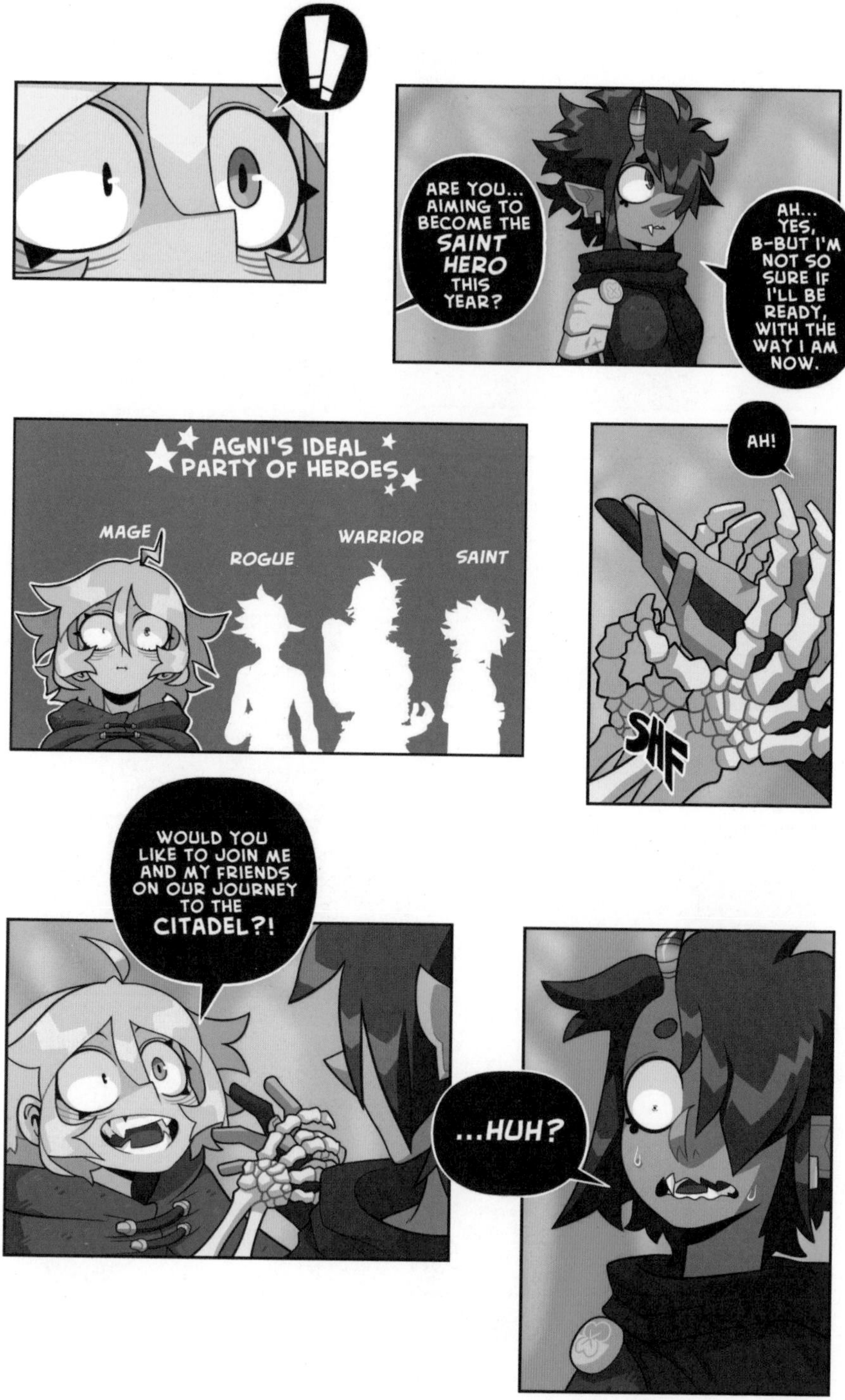

!!
ARE YOU... AIMING TO BECOME THE SAINT HERO THIS YEAR?
AH... YES, B-BUT I'M NOT SO SURE IF I'LL BE READY, WITH THE WAY I AM NOW.
AGNI'S IDEAL PARTY OF HEROES
MAGE
ROGUE
WARRIOR
SAINT
AH!
SHF
WOULD YOU LIKE TO JOIN ME AND MY FRIENDS ON OUR JOURNEY TO THE CITADEL?!
...HUH?

# Chapter 23
# THE PAST

...

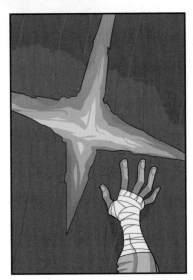

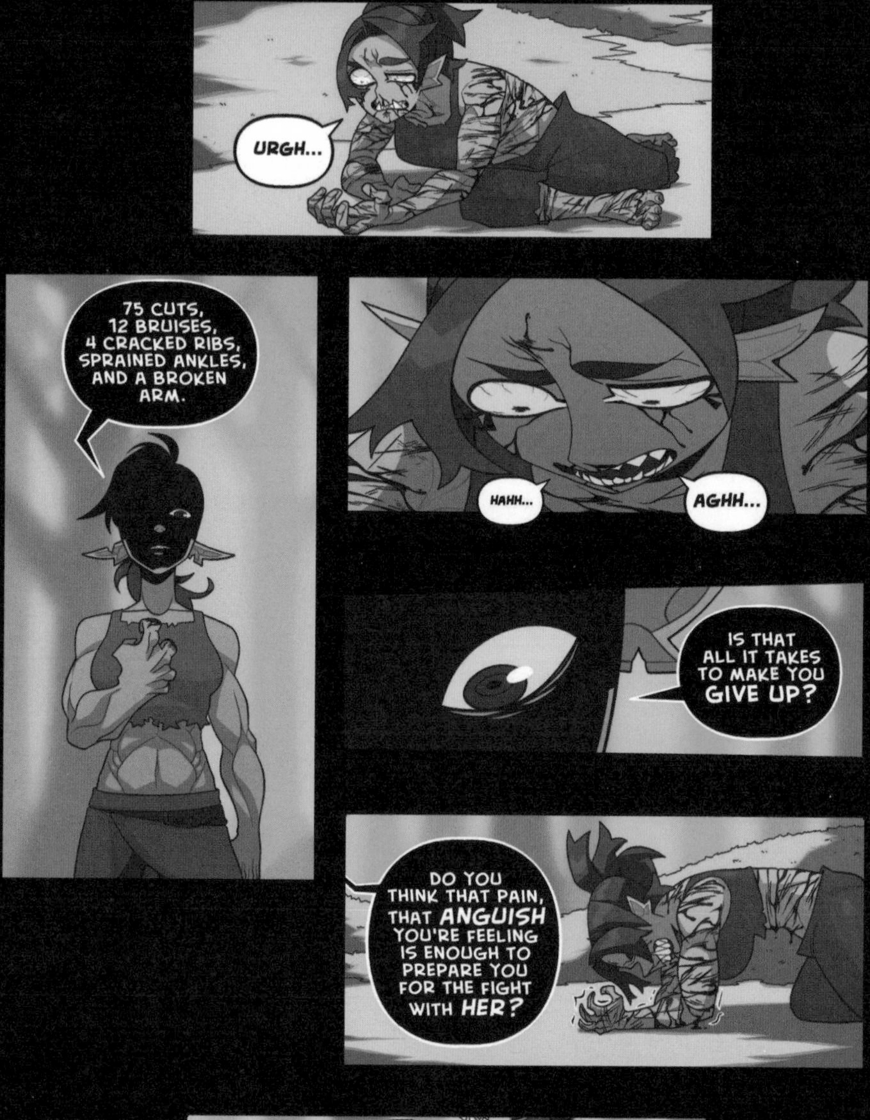
URGH...
75 CUTS, 12 BRUISES, 4 CRACKED RIBS, SPRAINED ANKLES, AND A BROKEN ARM.
HAHH...
AGHH...
IS THAT ALL IT TAKES TO MAKE YOU GIVE UP?
DO YOU THINK THAT PAIN, THAT ANGUISH YOU'RE FEELING IS ENOUGH TO PREPARE YOU FOR THE FIGHT WITH HER?
NGHH..!
YOU HAVE TO BE ABLE TO ENDURE FAR MORE THAN THIS.

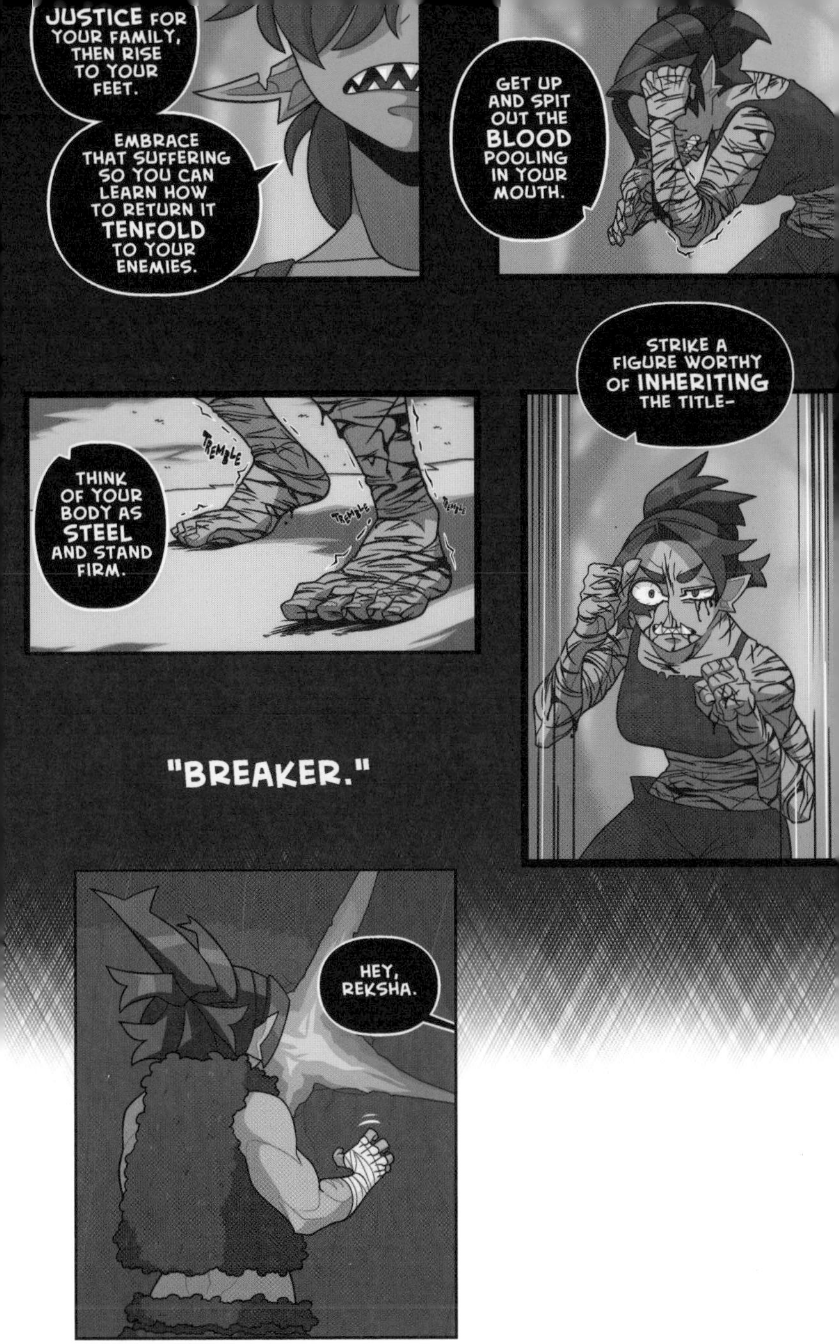
JUSTICE FOR YOUR FAMILY, THEN RISE TO YOUR FEET.
EMBRACE THAT SUFFERING SO YOU CAN LEARN HOW TO RETURN IT TENFOLD TO YOUR ENEMIES.
GET UP AND SPIT OUT THE BLOOD POOLING IN YOUR MOUTH.
TREMBLE
THINK OF YOUR BODY AS STEEL AND STAND FIRM.
TREMBLE
TREMBLE
STRIKE A FIGURE WORTHY OF INHERITING THE TITLE-
"BREAKER."
HEY, REKSHA.

I FINISHED MY LITTLE "TEST."

O-OH, GOOD JOB!

I FIGURED YOU'D BE THE FIRST ONE TO COME BACK.

...NOT EXACTLY THE WARM WELCOME I EXPECTED FOR MAKING IT BACK IN ONE PIECE, BUT ALRIGHT.

BY THE WAY, MIND TELLING ME WHY I FOUND YOU SPACING OUT IN FRONT OF A TREE?

NO REASON REALLY, I'M JUST THINKING BACK ON MY TRAINING DAYS.

MY MASTER TOOK ME OUT HERE TO TEST MY ABILITIES AS WELL.

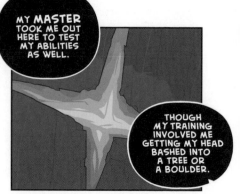

THOUGH MY TRAINING INVOLVED ME GETTING MY HEAD BASHED INTO A TREE OR A BOULDER.

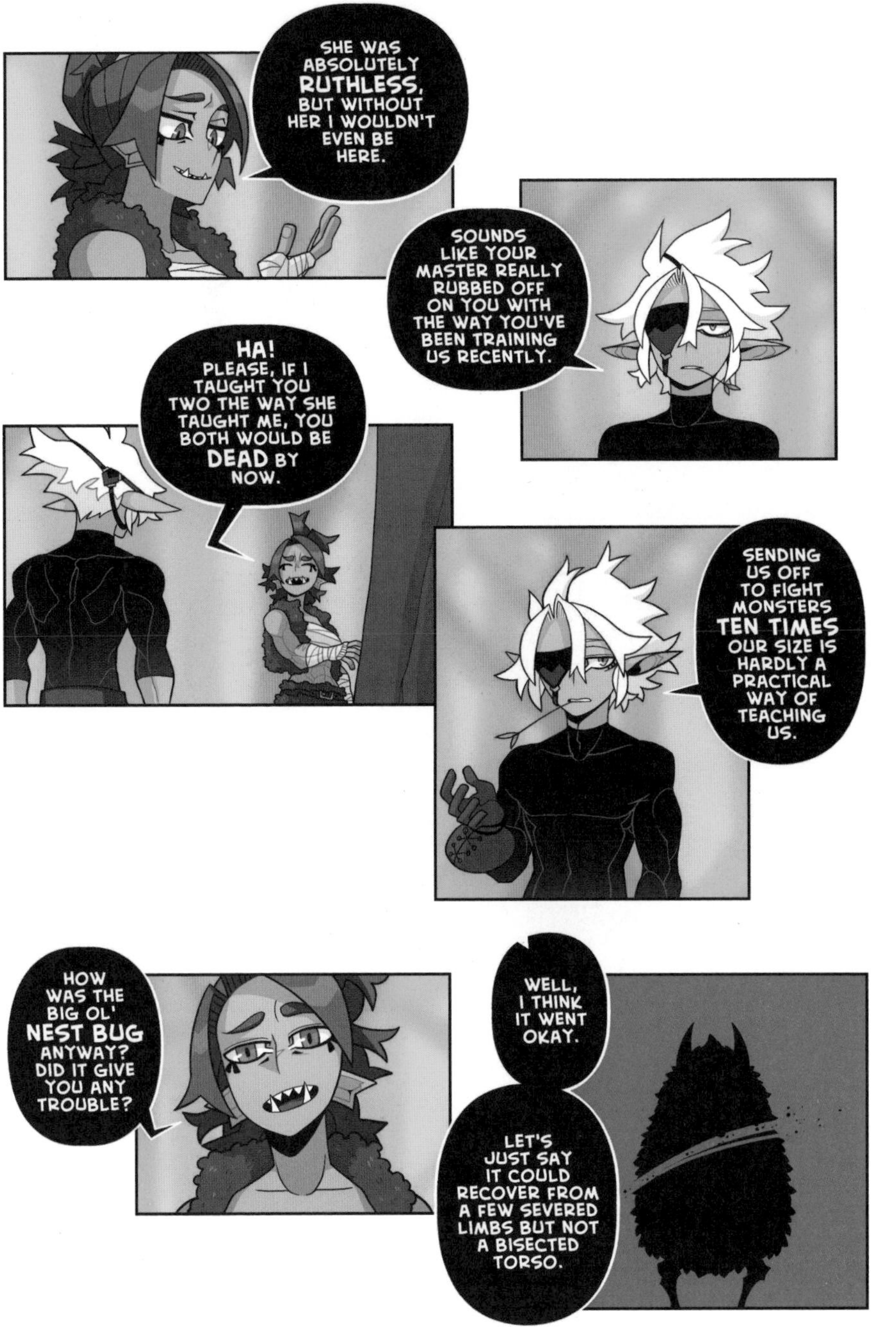
SHE WAS ABSOLUTELY RUTHLESS, BUT WITHOUT HER I WOULDN'T EVEN BE HERE.
SOUNDS LIKE YOUR MASTER REALLY RUBBED OFF ON YOU WITH THE WAY YOU'VE BEEN TRAINING US RECENTLY.
HA! PLEASE, IF I TAUGHT YOU TWO THE WAY SHE TAUGHT ME, YOU BOTH WOULD BE DEAD BY NOW.
SENDING US OFF TO FIGHT MONSTERS TEN TIMES OUR SIZE IS HARDLY A PRACTICAL WAY OF TEACHING US.
HOW WAS THE BIG OL' NEST BUG ANYWAY? DID IT GIVE YOU ANY TROUBLE?
WELL, I THINK IT WENT OKAY.
LET'S JUST SAY IT COULD RECOVER FROM A FEW SEVERED LIMBS BUT NOT A BISECTED TORSO.

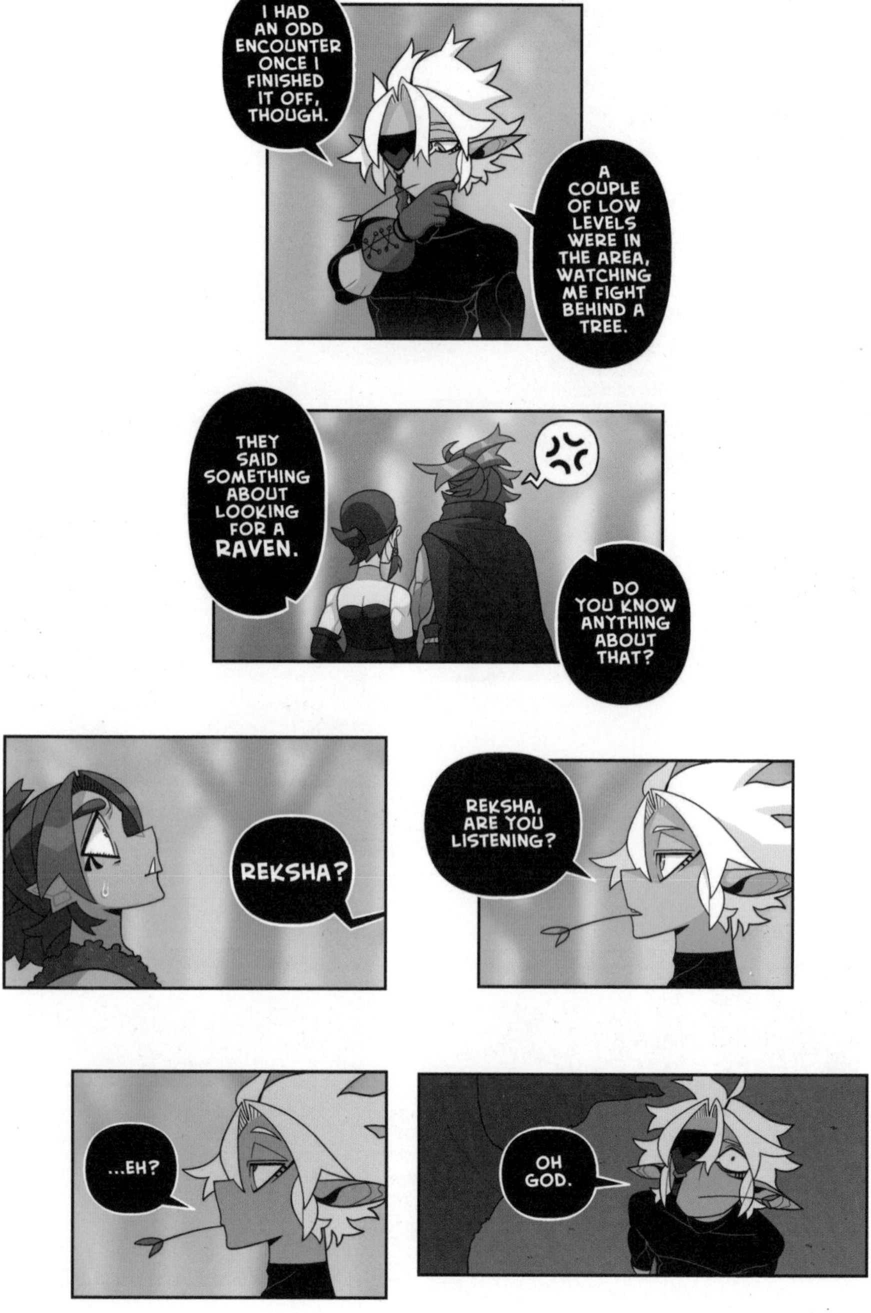
I HAD AN ODD ENCOUNTER ONCE I FINISHED IT OFF, THOUGH.
A COUPLE OF LOW LEVELS WERE IN THE AREA, WATCHING ME FIGHT BEHIND A TREE.
THEY SAID SOMETHING ABOUT LOOKING FOR A RAVEN.
DO YOU KNOW ANYTHING ABOUT THAT?
REKSHA?
REKSHA, ARE YOU LISTENING?
...EH?
OH GOD.

HEY GUYS!

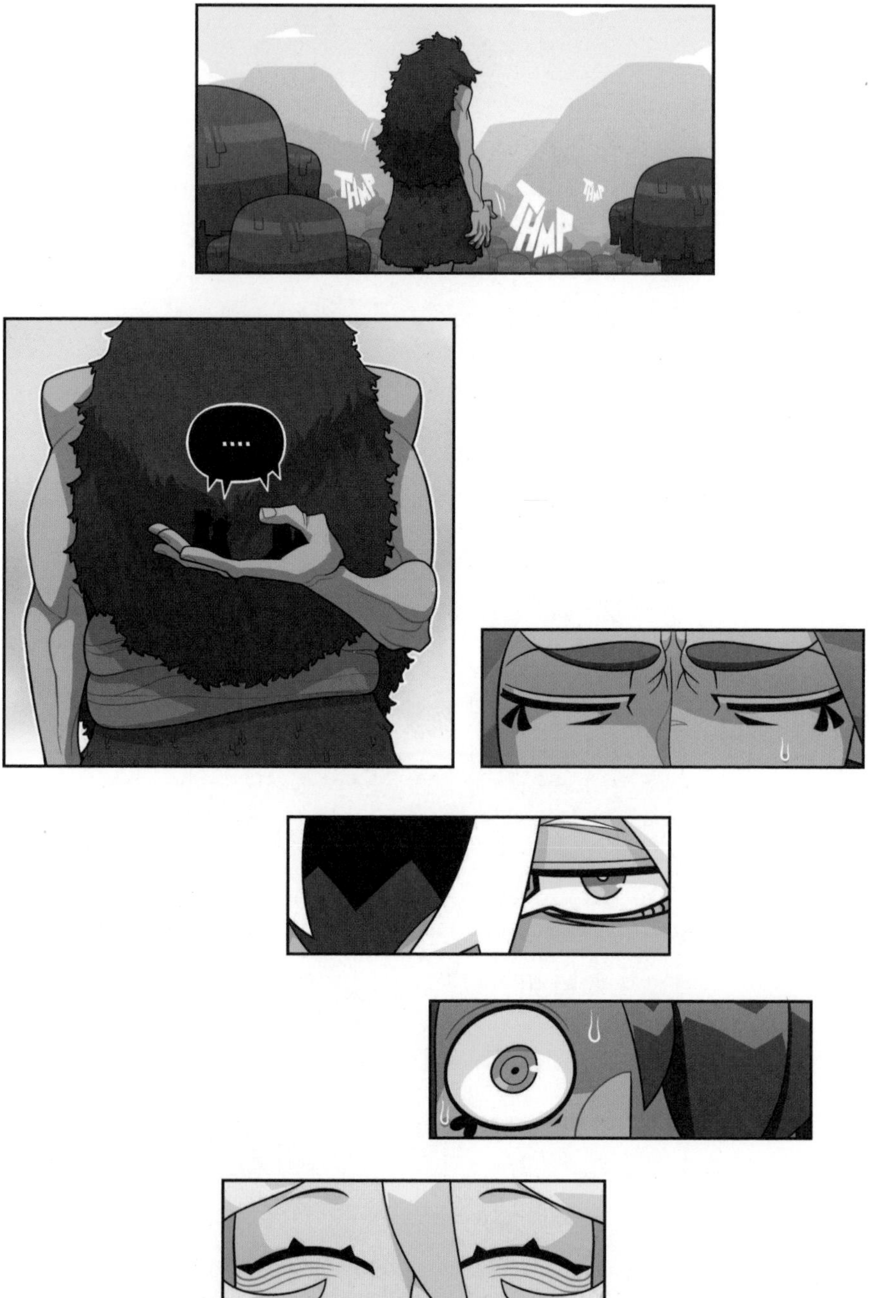
THMP
THMP
THMP
....

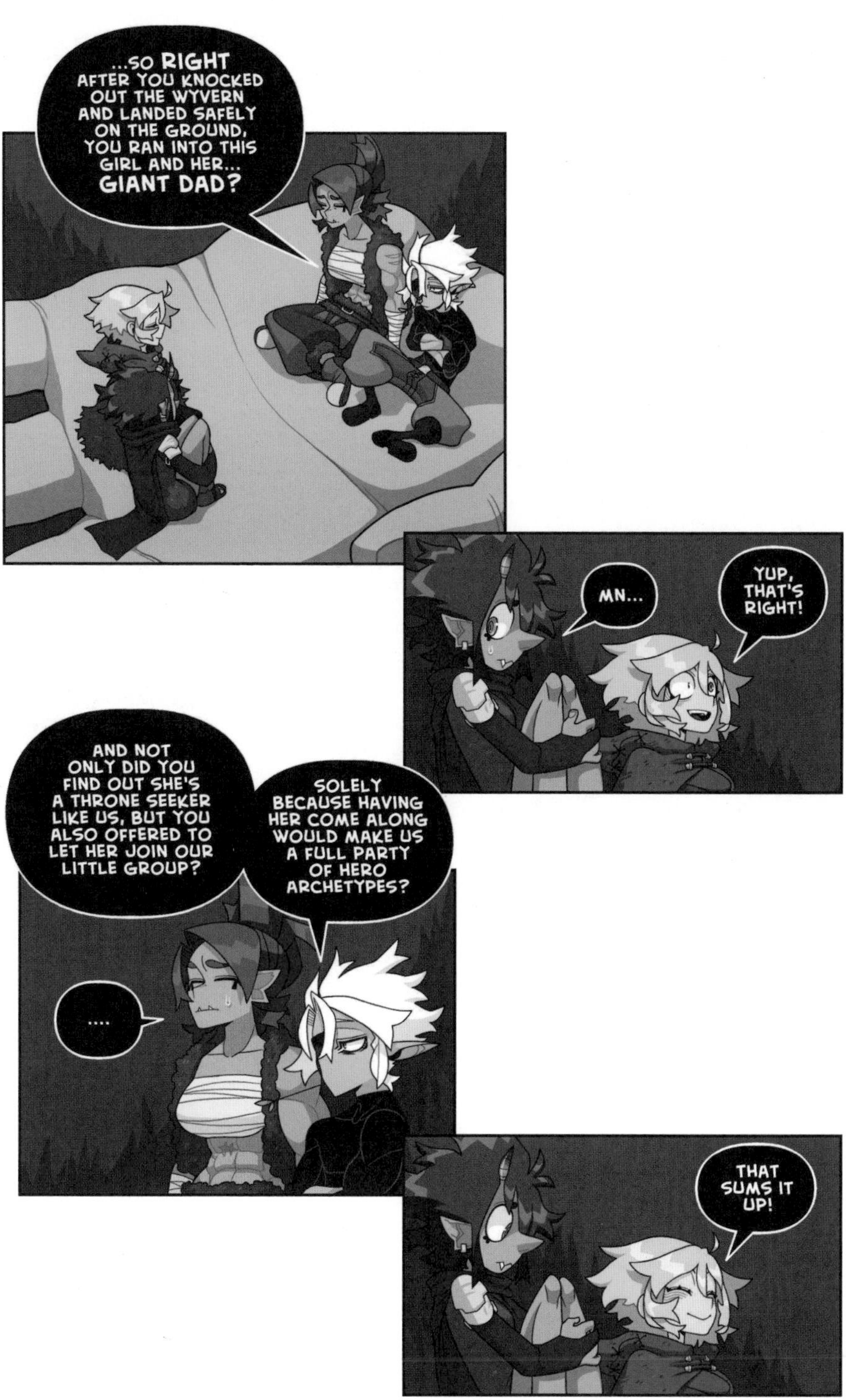
...SO RIGHT AFTER YOU KNOCKED OUT THE WYVERN AND LANDED SAFELY ON THE GROUND, YOU RAN INTO THIS GIRL AND HER... GIANT DAD?
MN...
YUP, THAT'S RIGHT!
AND NOT ONLY DID YOU FIND OUT SHE'S A THRONE SEEKER LIKE US, BUT YOU ALSO OFFERED TO LET HER JOIN OUR LITTLE GROUP?
SOLELY BECAUSE HAVING HER COME ALONG WOULD MAKE US A FULL PARTY OF HERO ARCHETYPES?
....
THAT SUMS IT UP!

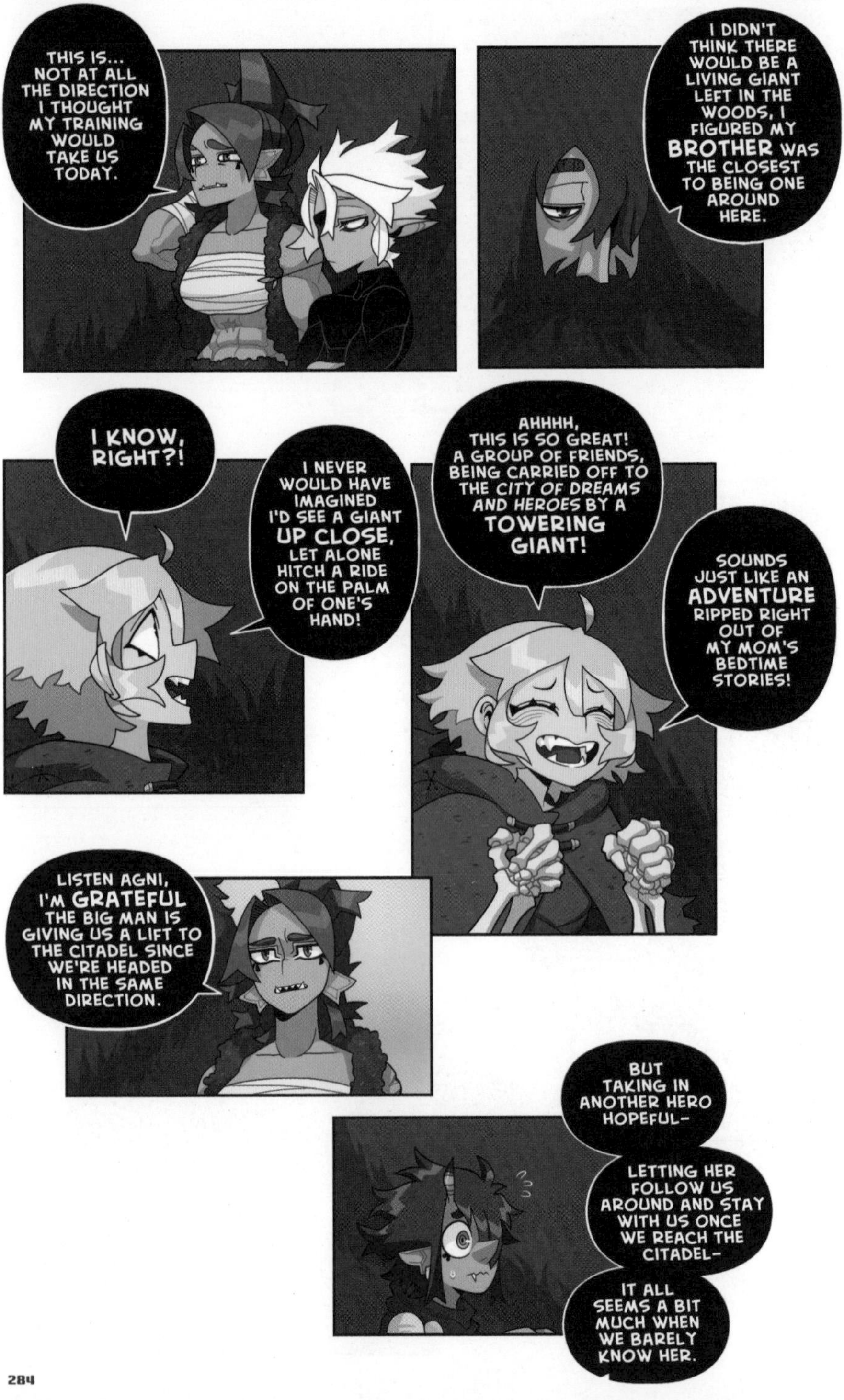
THIS IS... NOT AT ALL THE DIRECTION I THOUGHT MY TRAINING WOULD TAKE US TODAY.
I DIDN'T THINK THERE WOULD BE A LIVING GIANT LEFT IN THE WOODS, I FIGURED MY **BROTHER** WAS THE CLOSEST TO BEING ONE AROUND HERE.
I KNOW, RIGHT?!
I NEVER WOULD HAVE IMAGINED I'D SEE A GIANT **UP CLOSE,** LET ALONE HITCH A RIDE ON THE PALM OF ONE'S HAND!
AHHHH, THIS IS SO GREAT! A GROUP OF FRIENDS, BEING CARRIED OFF TO THE *CITY OF DREAMS AND HEROES* BY A **TOWERING GIANT!**
SOUNDS JUST LIKE AN **ADVENTURE** RIPPED RIGHT OUT OF MY MOM'S BEDTIME STORIES!
LISTEN AGNI, I'M **GRATEFUL** THE BIG MAN IS GIVING US A LIFT TO THE CITADEL SINCE WE'RE HEADED IN THE SAME DIRECTION.
BUT TAKING IN ANOTHER HERO HOPEFUL-
LETTING HER FOLLOW US AROUND AND STAY WITH US ONCE WE REACH THE CITADEL-
IT ALL SEEMS A BIT MUCH WHEN WE BARELY KNOW HER.

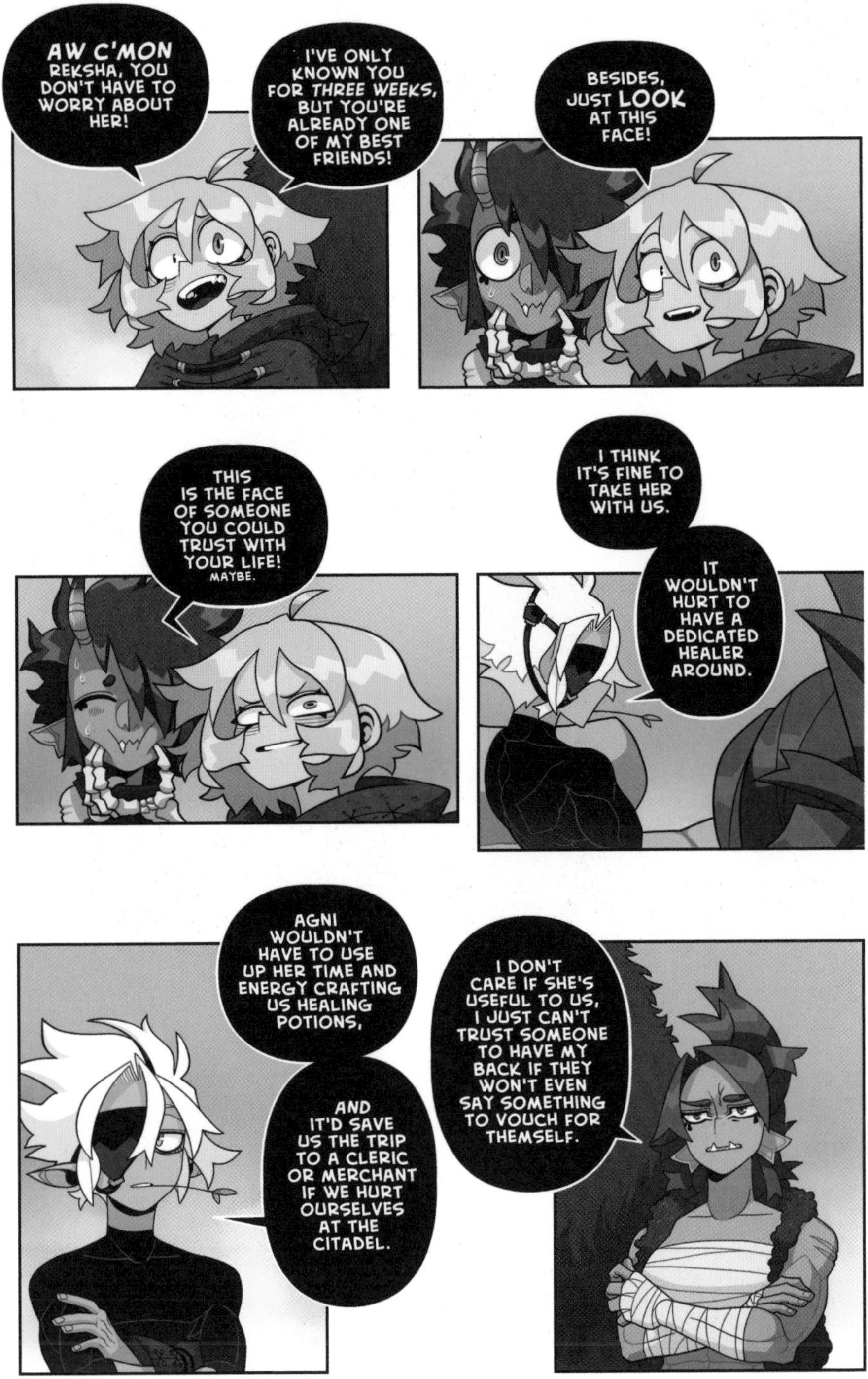
AW C'MON REKSHA, YOU DON'T HAVE TO WORRY ABOUT HER!
I'VE ONLY KNOWN YOU FOR THREE WEEKS, BUT YOU'RE ALREADY ONE OF MY BEST FRIENDS!
BESIDES, JUST LOOK AT THIS FACE!
THIS IS THE FACE OF SOMEONE YOU COULD TRUST WITH YOUR LIFE! MAYBE.
I THINK IT'S FINE TO TAKE HER WITH US.
IT WOULDN'T HURT TO HAVE A DEDICATED HEALER AROUND.
AGNI WOULDN'T HAVE TO USE UP HER TIME AND ENERGY CRAFTING US HEALING POTIONS,
AND IT'D SAVE US THE TRIP TO A CLERIC OR MERCHANT IF WE HURT OURSELVES AT THE CITADEL.
I DON'T CARE IF SHE'S USEFUL TO US, I JUST CAN'T TRUST SOMEONE TO HAVE MY BACK IF THEY WON'T EVEN SAY SOMETHING TO VOUCH FOR THEMSELF.

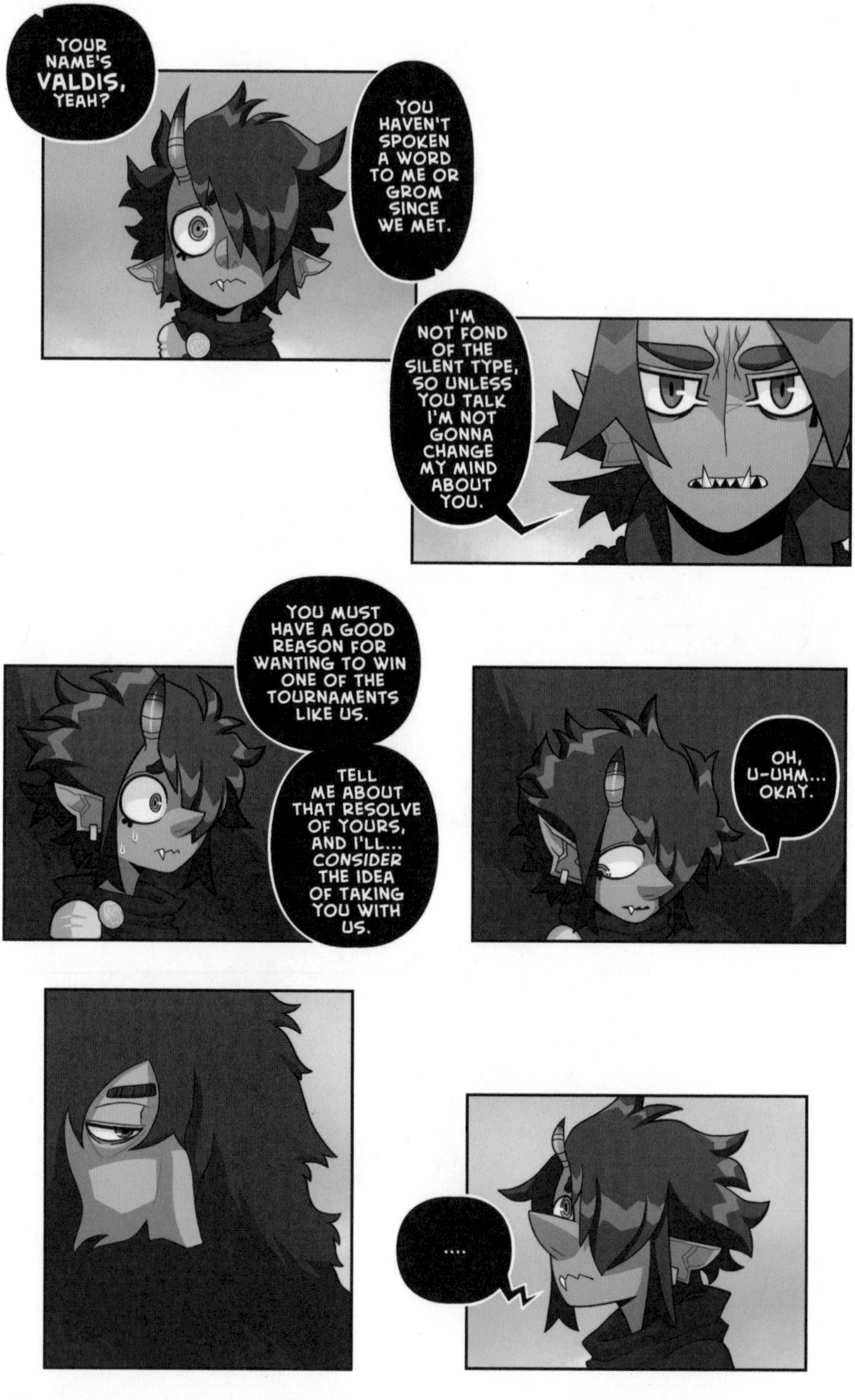
YOUR NAME'S VALDIS, YEAH?
YOU HAVEN'T SPOKEN A WORD TO ME OR GROM SINCE WE MET.
I'M NOT FOND OF THE SILENT TYPE, SO UNLESS YOU TALK I'M NOT GONNA CHANGE MY MIND ABOUT YOU.
YOU MUST HAVE A GOOD REASON FOR WANTING TO WIN ONE OF THE TOURNAMENTS LIKE US.
TELL ME ABOUT THAT RESOLVE OF YOURS, AND I'LL... CONSIDER THE IDEA OF TAKING YOU WITH US.
OH, U-UHM... OKAY.
....

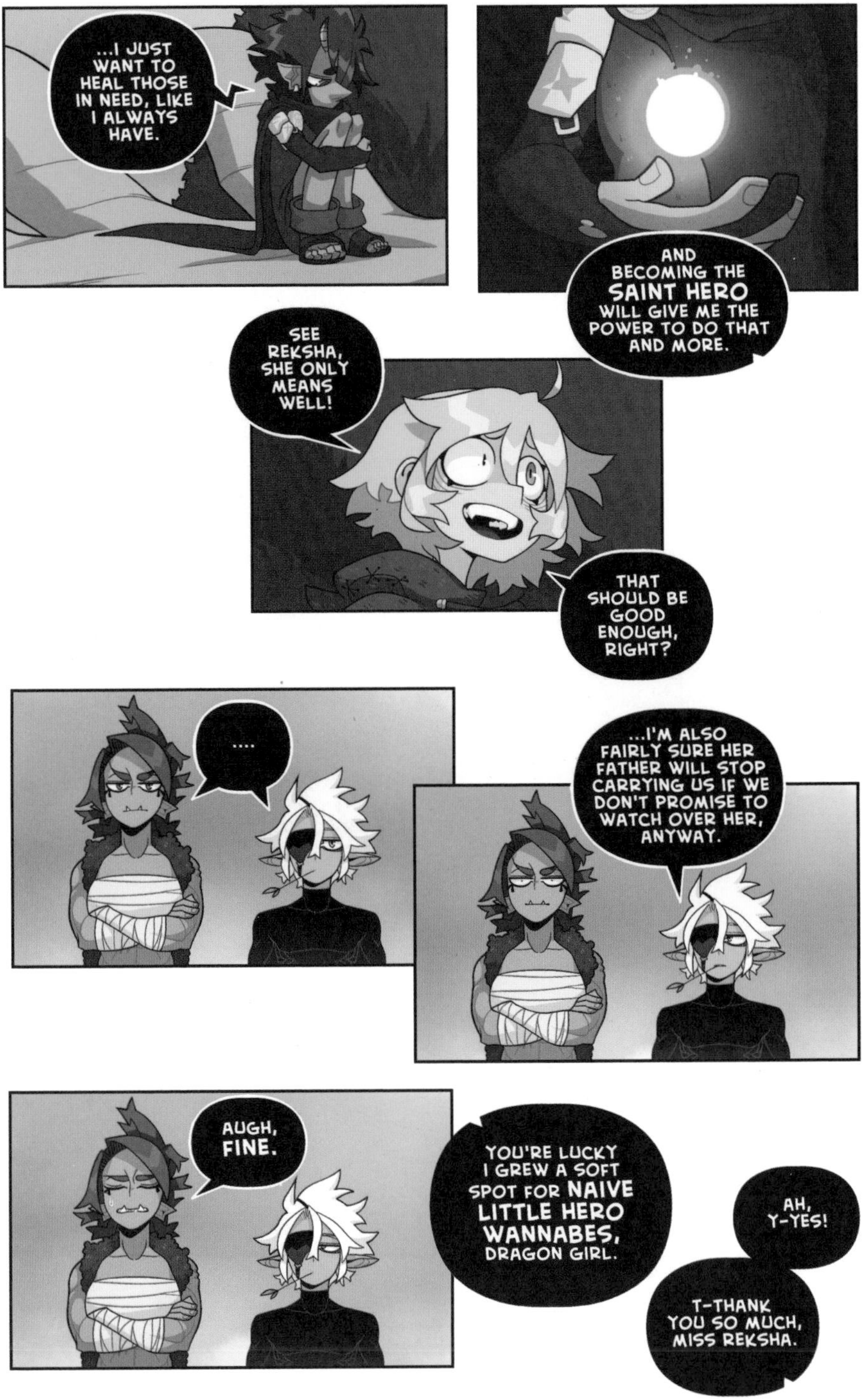
...I JUST WANT TO HEAL THOSE IN NEED, LIKE I ALWAYS HAVE.
AND BECOMING THE SAINT HERO WILL GIVE ME THE POWER TO DO THAT AND MORE.
SEE REKSHA, SHE ONLY MEANS WELL!
THAT SHOULD BE GOOD ENOUGH, RIGHT?
....
...I'M ALSO FAIRLY SURE HER FATHER WILL STOP CARRYING US IF WE DON'T PROMISE TO WATCH OVER HER, ANYWAY.
AUGH, FINE.
YOU'RE LUCKY I GREW A SOFT SPOT FOR NAIVE LITTLE HERO WANNABES, DRAGON GIRL.
AH, Y-YES!
T-THANK YOU SO MUCH, MISS REKSHA.

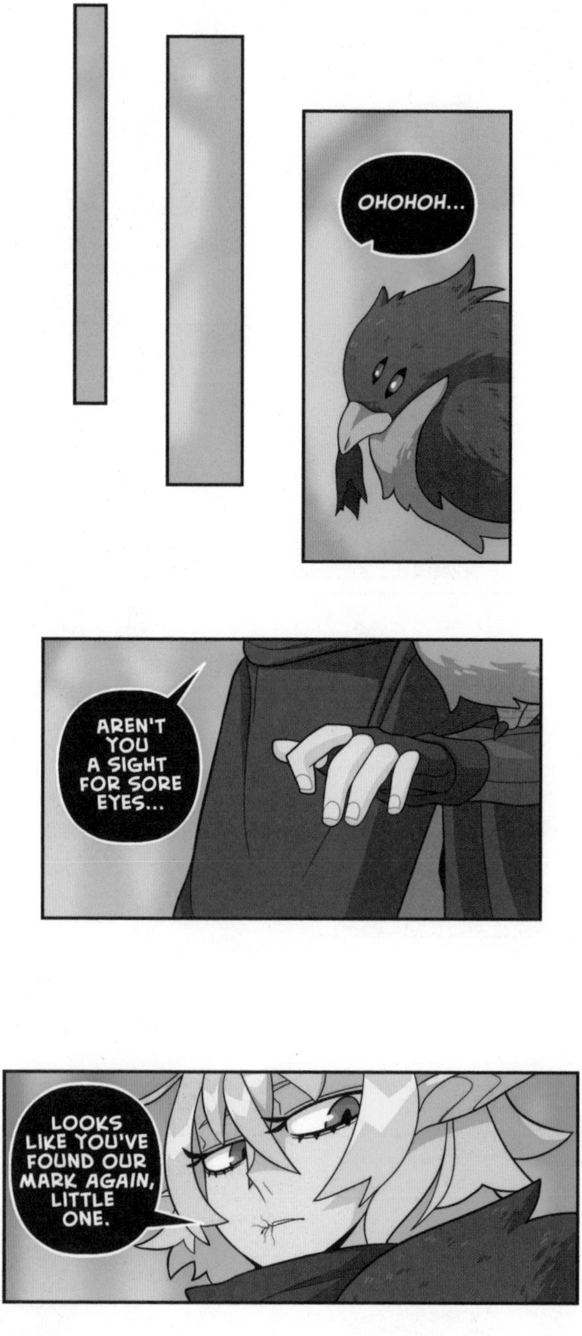
OHOHOH...
AREN'T YOU A SIGHT FOR SORE EYES...
LOOKS LIKE YOU'VE FOUND OUR MARK AGAIN, LITTLE ONE.

ALRIGHT
WE'RE
MAKING
**GREAT**
TIME HERE,
GUYS.

ANOTHER
DAY OF BEING
CARRIED AND
WE'LL MAKE IT
TO THE CITADEL
GATES EARLY!

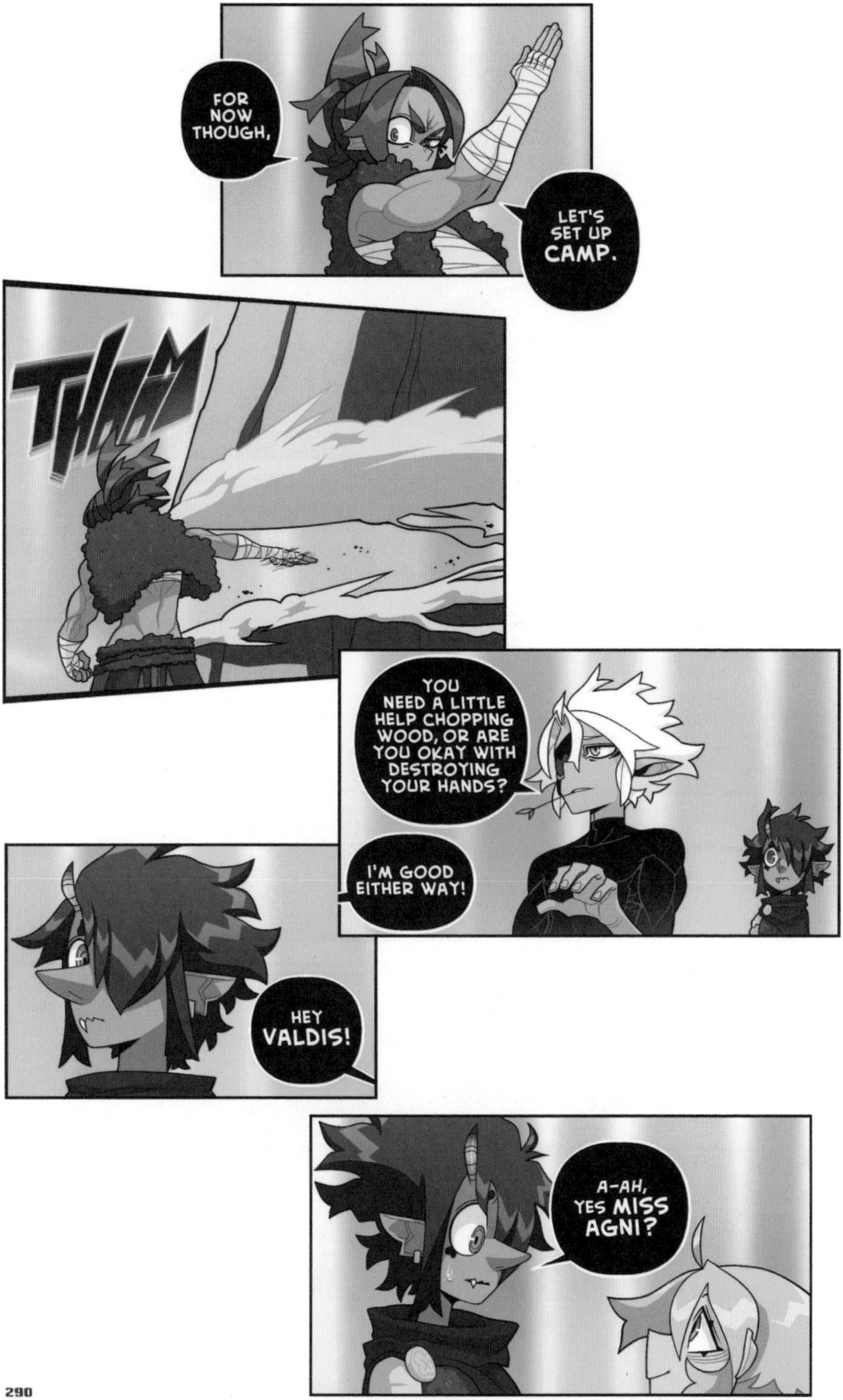
FOR NOW THOUGH,
LET'S SET UP CAMP.
THWOM
YOU NEED A LITTLE HELP CHOPPING WOOD, OR ARE YOU OKAY WITH DESTROYING YOUR HANDS?
I'M GOOD EITHER WAY!
HEY VALDIS!
A-AH, YES MISS AGNI?

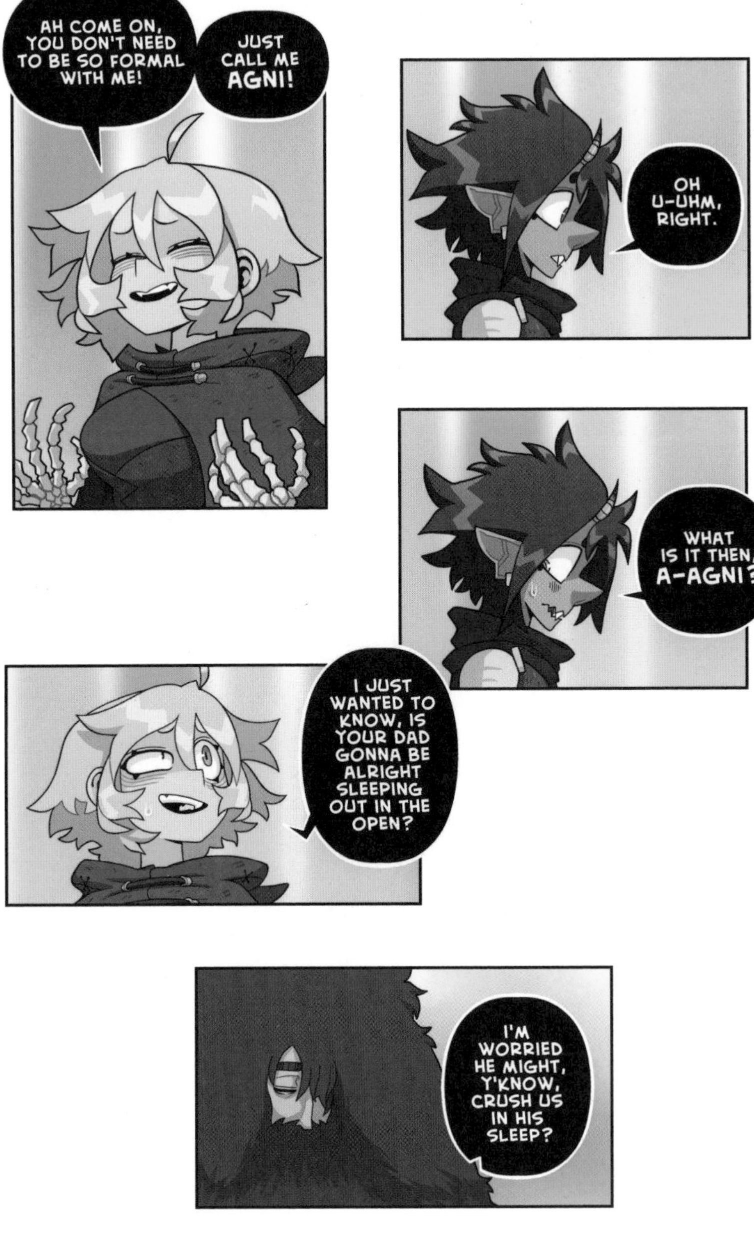
AH COME ON, YOU DON'T NEED TO BE SO FORMAL WITH ME!
JUST CALL ME AGNI!
OH U-UHM, RIGHT.
WHAT IS IT THEN, A-AGNI?
I JUST WANTED TO KNOW, IS YOUR DAD GONNA BE ALRIGHT SLEEPING OUT IN THE OPEN?
I'M WORRIED HE MIGHT, Y'KNOW, CRUSH US IN HIS SLEEP?

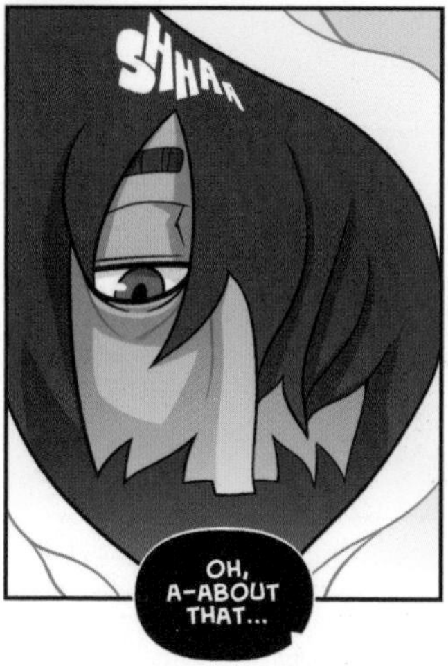
SHHAA
OH, A-ABOUT THAT...

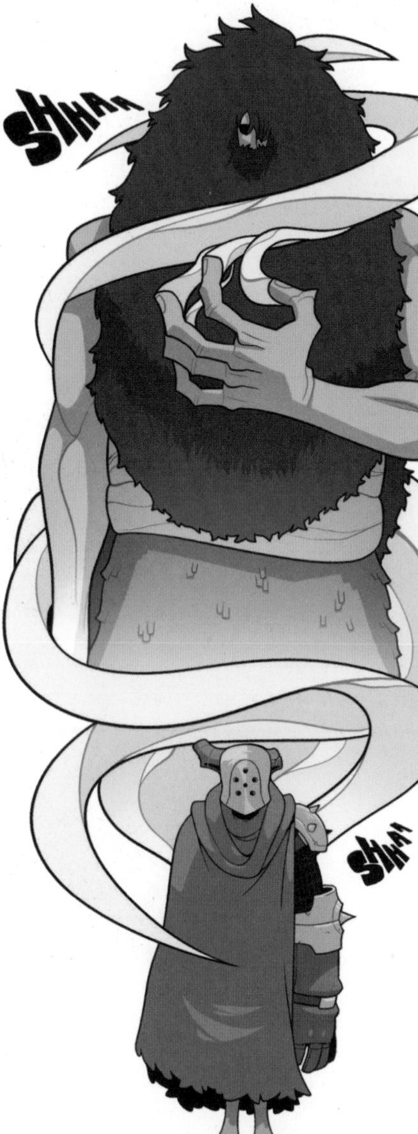
SHHAA
SHHAA

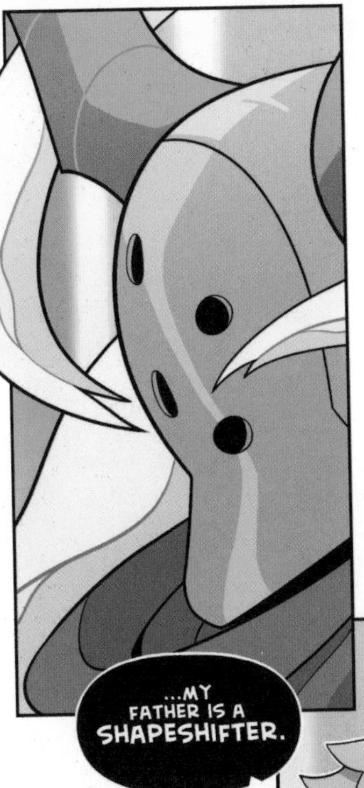
...MY FATHER IS A SHAPESHIFTER.
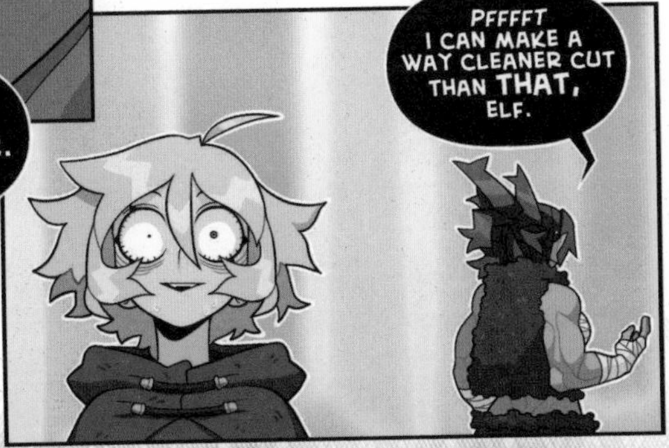
PFFFFT I CAN MAKE A WAY CLEANER CUT THAN THAT, ELF.
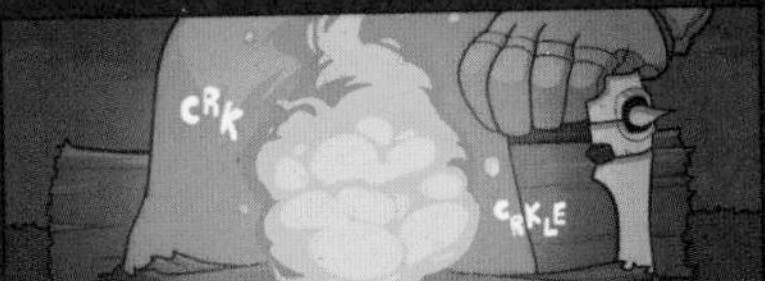
CRK
CRKLE

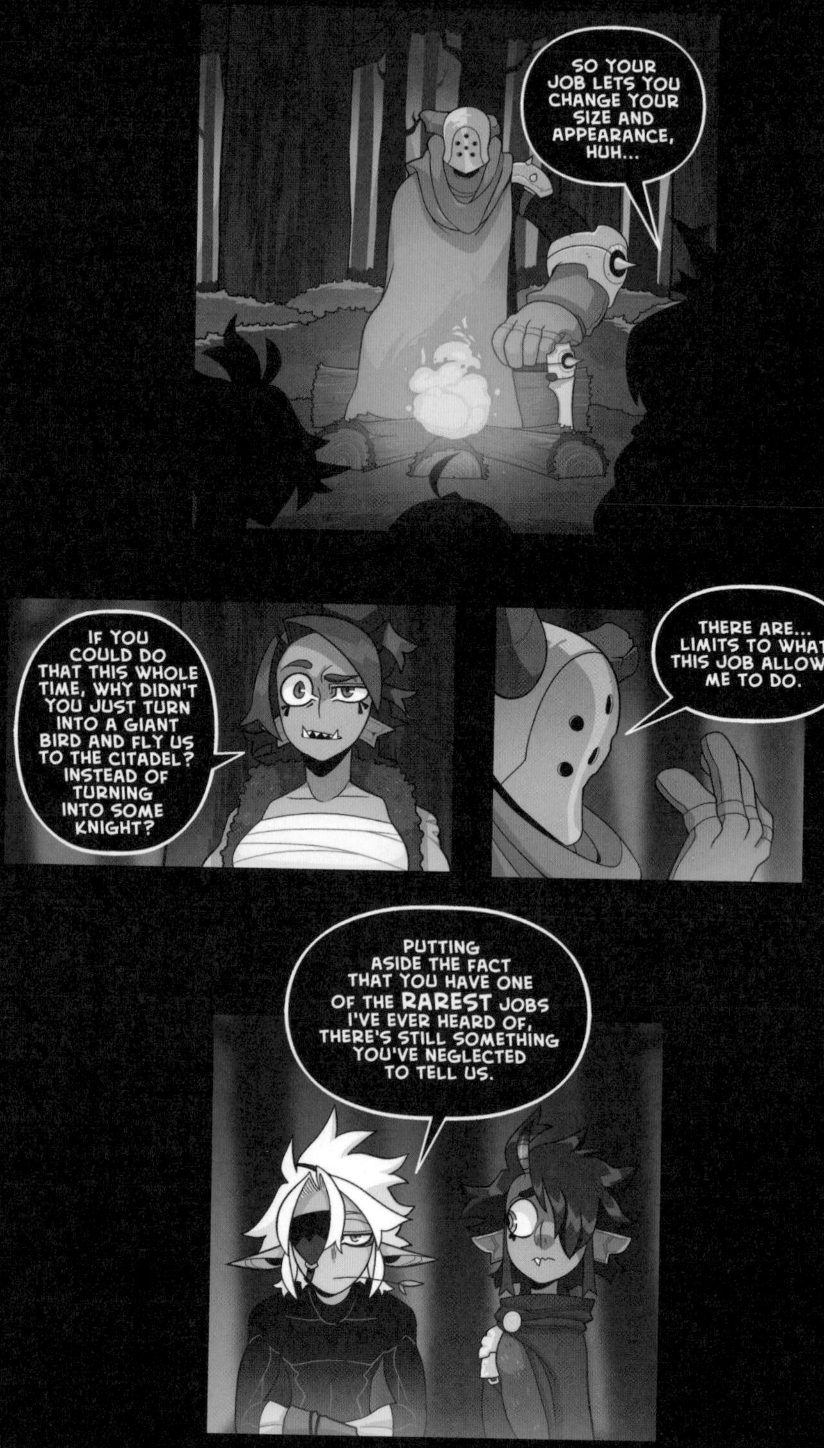
SO YOUR JOB LETS YOU CHANGE YOUR SIZE AND APPEARANCE, HUH...
IF YOU COULD DO THAT THIS WHOLE TIME, WHY DIDN'T YOU JUST TURN INTO A GIANT BIRD AND FLY US TO THE CITADEL? INSTEAD OF TURNING INTO SOME KNIGHT?
THERE ARE... LIMITS TO WHAT THIS JOB ALLOWS ME TO DO.
PUTTING ASIDE THE FACT THAT YOU HAVE ONE OF THE **RAREST** JOBS I'VE EVER HEARD OF, THERE'S STILL SOMETHING YOU'VE NEGLECTED TO TELL US.

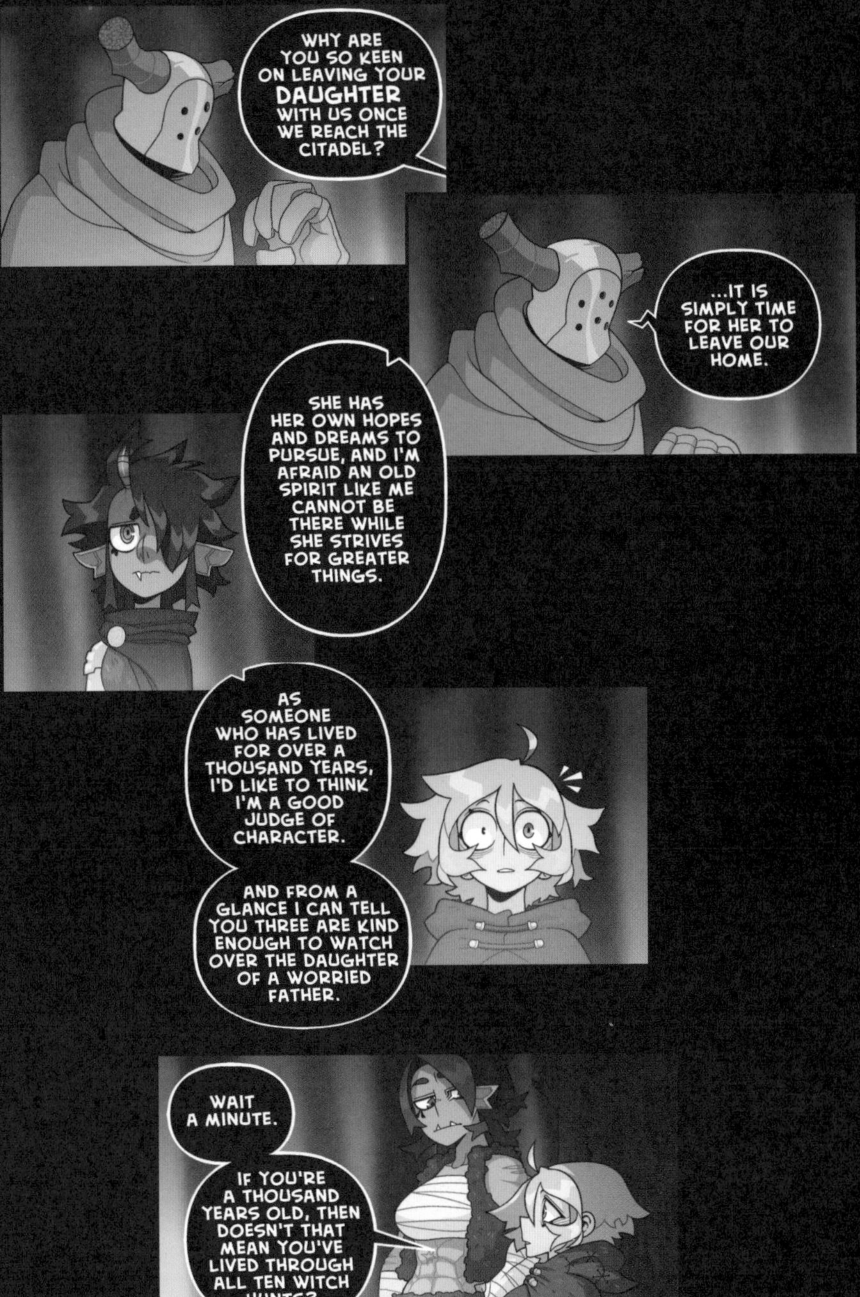
WHY ARE YOU SO KEEN ON LEAVING YOUR DAUGHTER WITH US ONCE WE REACH THE CITADEL?
...IT IS SIMPLY TIME FOR HER TO LEAVE OUR HOME.
SHE HAS HER OWN HOPES AND DREAMS TO PURSUE, AND I'M AFRAID AN OLD SPIRIT LIKE ME CANNOT BE THERE WHILE SHE STRIVES FOR GREATER THINGS.
AS SOMEONE WHO HAS LIVED FOR OVER A THOUSAND YEARS, I'D LIKE TO THINK I'M A GOOD JUDGE OF CHARACTER.
AND FROM A GLANCE I CAN TELL YOU THREE ARE KIND ENOUGH TO WATCH OVER THE DAUGHTER OF A WORRIED FATHER.
WAIT A MINUTE.
IF YOU'RE A THOUSAND YEARS OLD, THEN DOESN'T THAT MEAN YOU'VE LIVED THROUGH ALL TEN WITCH HUNTS?

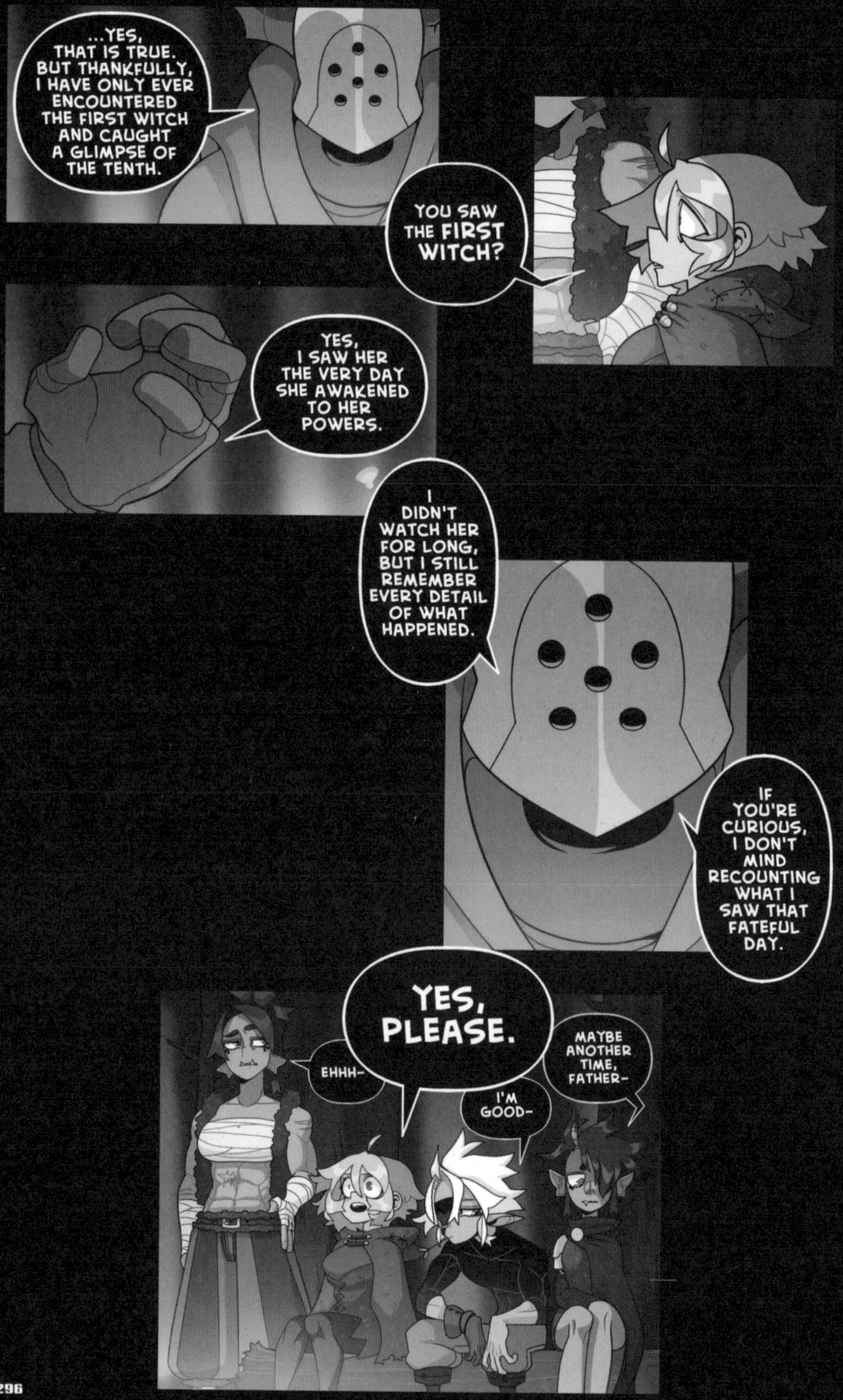
...YES, THAT IS TRUE. BUT THANKFULLY, I HAVE ONLY EVER ENCOUNTERED THE FIRST WITCH AND CAUGHT A GLIMPSE OF THE TENTH.
YOU SAW THE FIRST WITCH?
YES, I SAW HER THE VERY DAY SHE AWAKENED TO HER POWERS.
I DIDN'T WATCH HER FOR LONG, BUT I STILL REMEMBER EVERY DETAIL OF WHAT HAPPENED.
IF YOU'RE CURIOUS, I DON'T MIND RECOUNTING WHAT I SAW THAT FATEFUL DAY.
EHHH-
YES, PLEASE.
I'M GOOD-
MAYBE ANOTHER TIME, FATHER-

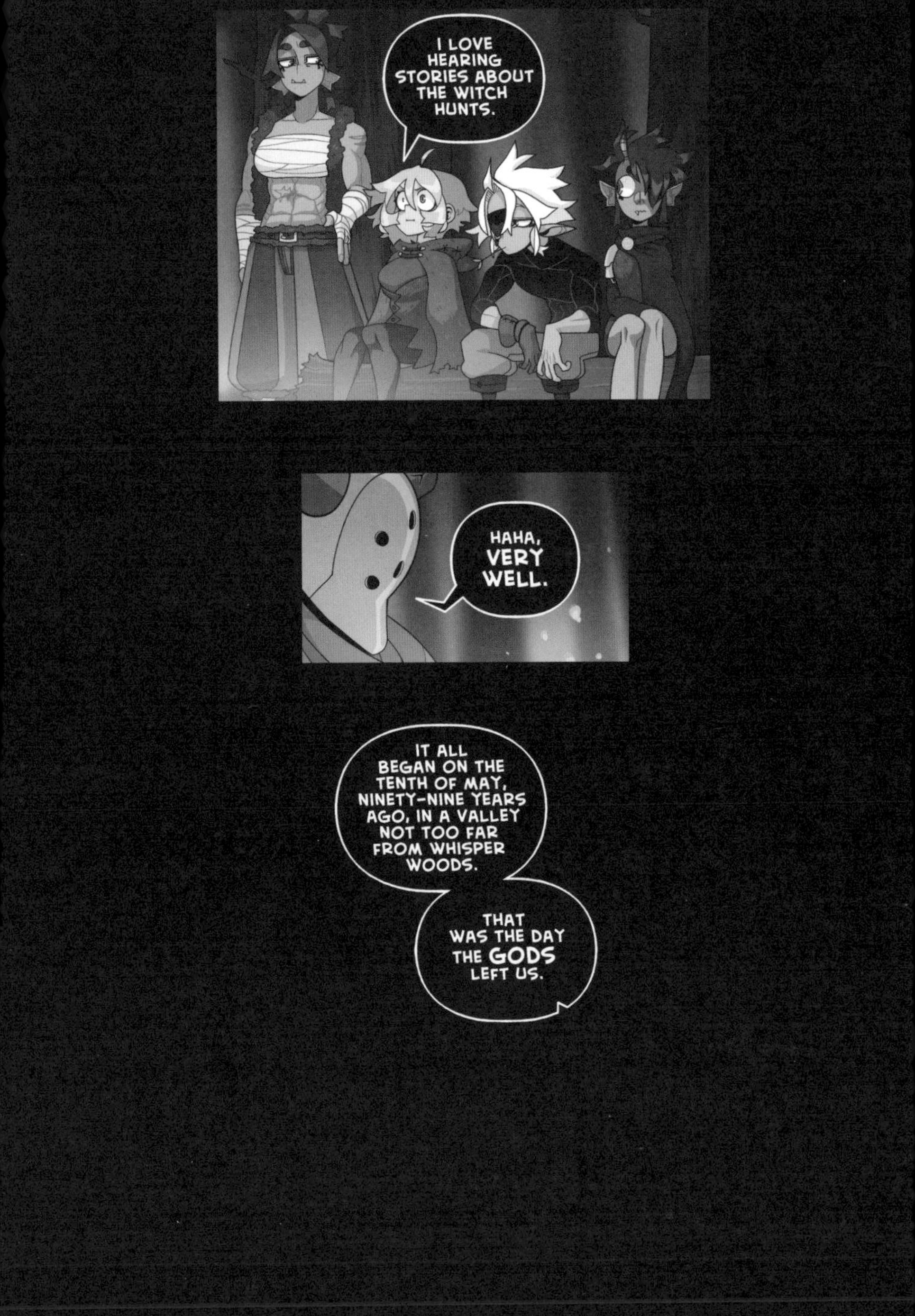
I LOVE HEARING STORIES ABOUT THE WITCH HUNTS.
HAHA, VERY WELL.
IT ALL BEGAN ON THE TENTH OF MAY, NINETY-NINE YEARS AGO, IN A VALLEY NOT TOO FAR FROM WHISPER WOODS.
THAT WAS THE DAY THE GODS LEFT US.

I STILL SEE IT IN MY
WORST NIGHTMARES
SOMETIMES.

THE
SILHOUETTE
OF A SINGLE
THRONE
PROPPED UP
BY A TWISTING
SPIRE,

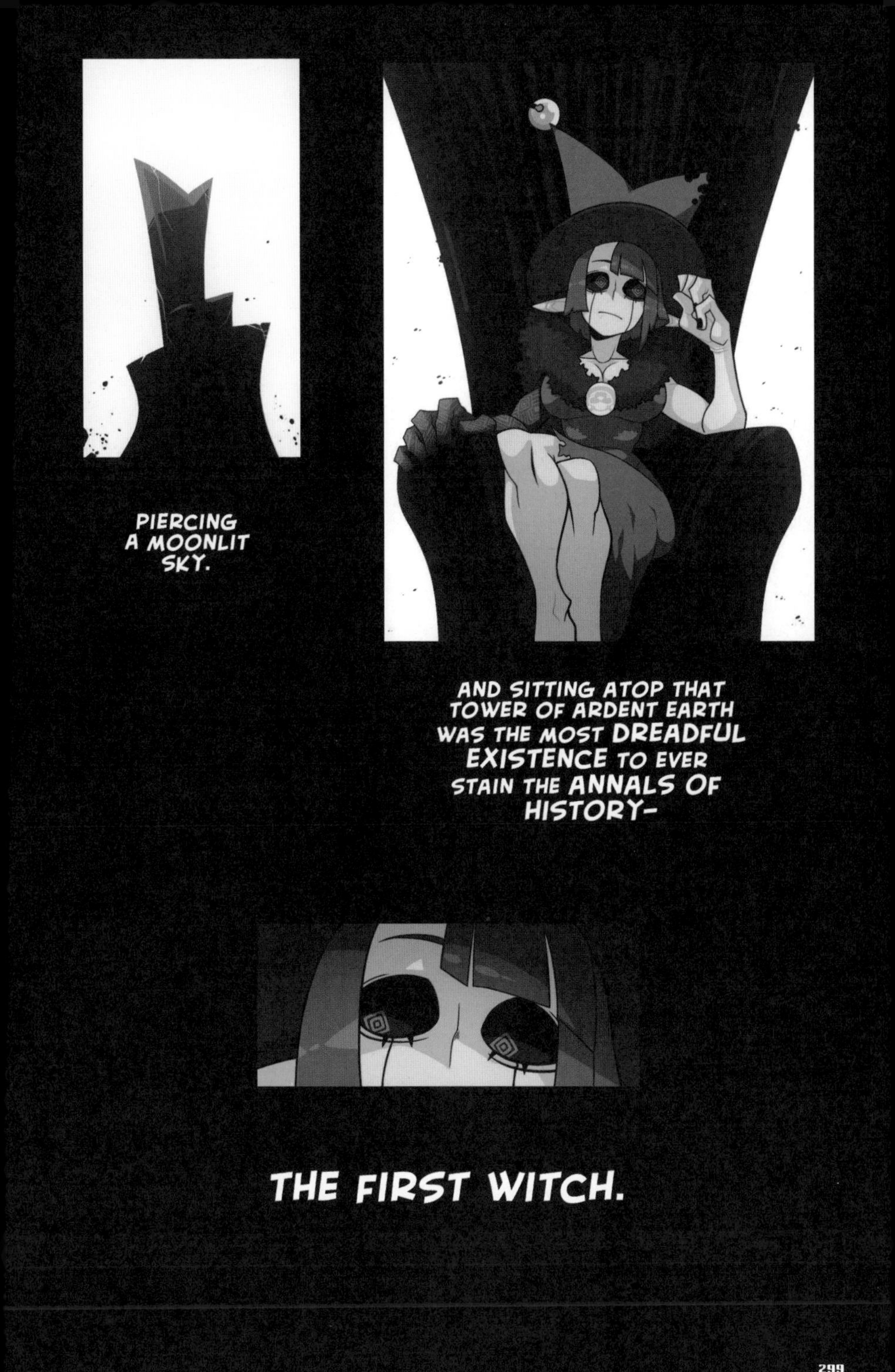
PIERCING A MOONLIT SKY.
AND SITTING ATOP THAT TOWER OF ARDENT EARTH WAS THE MOST DREADFUL EXISTENCE TO EVER STAIN THE ANNALS OF HISTORY-
THE FIRST WITCH.

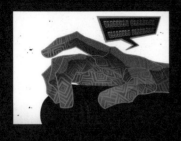

I COULD ONLY
WATCH IN HORROR
AND DISBELIEF AS A
BALL OF FIRE SUDDENLY
APPEARED OUT OF
THIN AIR–

AND RAINED
HELL UPON
THE VILLAGES
BELOW IT.

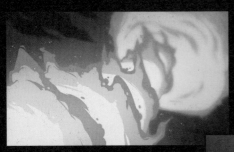

I COULD HEAR
THEM.

DESPITE THE
DISTANCE BETWEEN
ME AND THE HUMANS
WITHIN THE VALLEY, I
COULD STILL HEAR THEIR
SCREAMS.

EVERY FIBER OF MY BEING
SCREAMED AT ME TO RUN.

RUN AWAY FROM WHATEVER
HORRIBLE **THING** IT WAS THAT
HAD CAUGHT MY GAZE.

I SOUGHT
WHATEVER
SHELTER
COULD
POSSIBLY
ACCOMMODATE
MY SIZE AND
HELP ME HIDE
FROM THE EVIL
THAT STOOD
FAR BEHIND
ME.

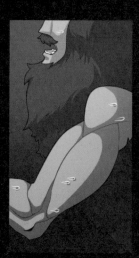

A CAVE IN
THE SIDE OF A
MOUNTAIN
WAS MY ONLY
CHOICE.

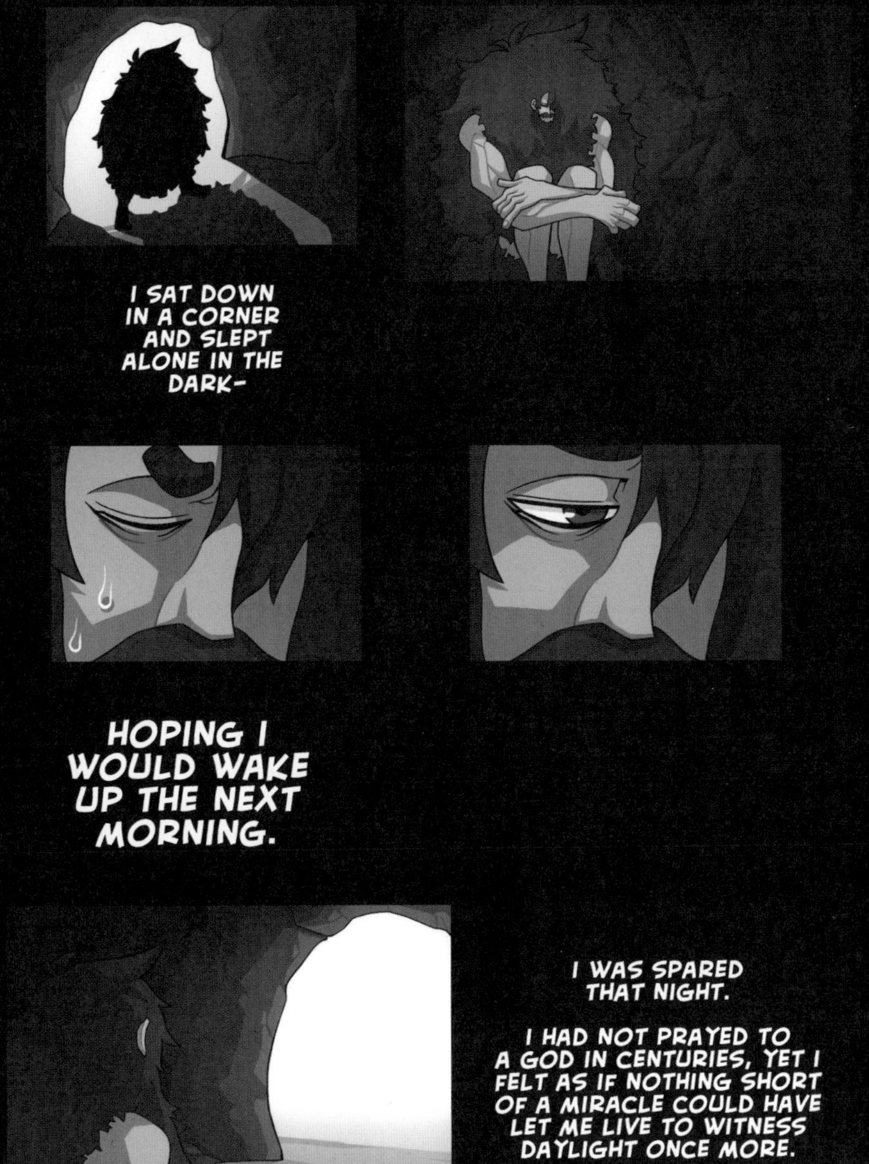
I SAT DOWN IN A CORNER AND SLEPT ALONE IN THE DARK-
HOPING I WOULD WAKE UP THE NEXT MORNING.
I WAS SPARED THAT NIGHT.
I HAD NOT PRAYED TO A GOD IN CENTURIES, YET I FELT AS IF NOTHING SHORT OF A MIRACLE COULD HAVE LET ME LIVE TO WITNESS DAYLIGHT ONCE MORE.

HOWEVER,
THAT FEELING
OF GRATITUDE
WAS FLEETING...

FOR ONCE
I EXITED THAT
CAVE, ALL MY
FAITH IN THE
GODS ABOVE
DISAPPEARED.

 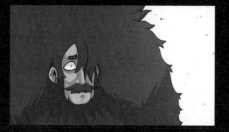

THERE WAS NOTHING.

NOTHING REMAINED
OF THE VALLEY I SAW
THE DAY BEFORE.

ALL THAT WAS
LEFT WAS SMOKE
AND RUIN.

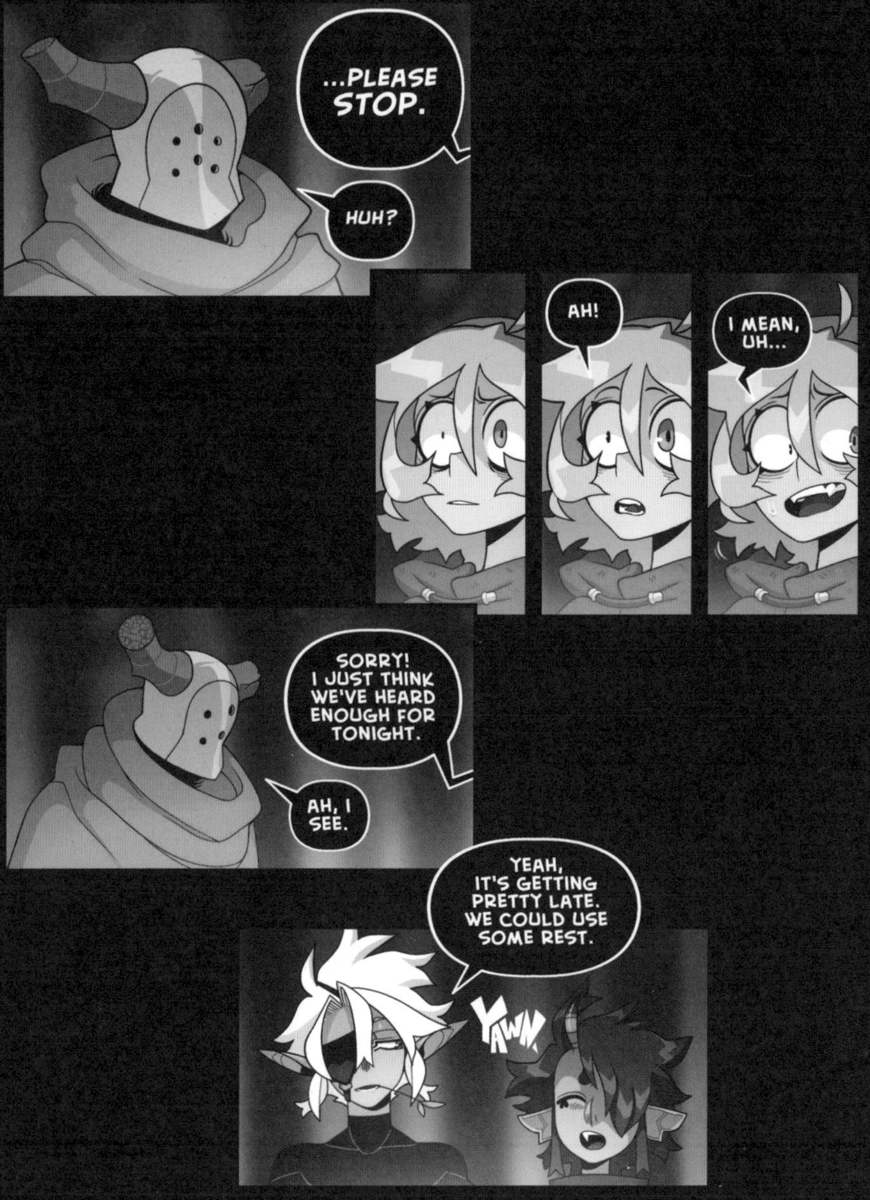
...PLEASE STOP.
HUH?
AH!
I MEAN, UH...
SORRY! I JUST THINK WE'VE HEARD ENOUGH FOR TONIGHT.
AH, I SEE.
YEAH, IT'S GETTING PRETTY LATE. WE COULD USE SOME REST.
YAWN.

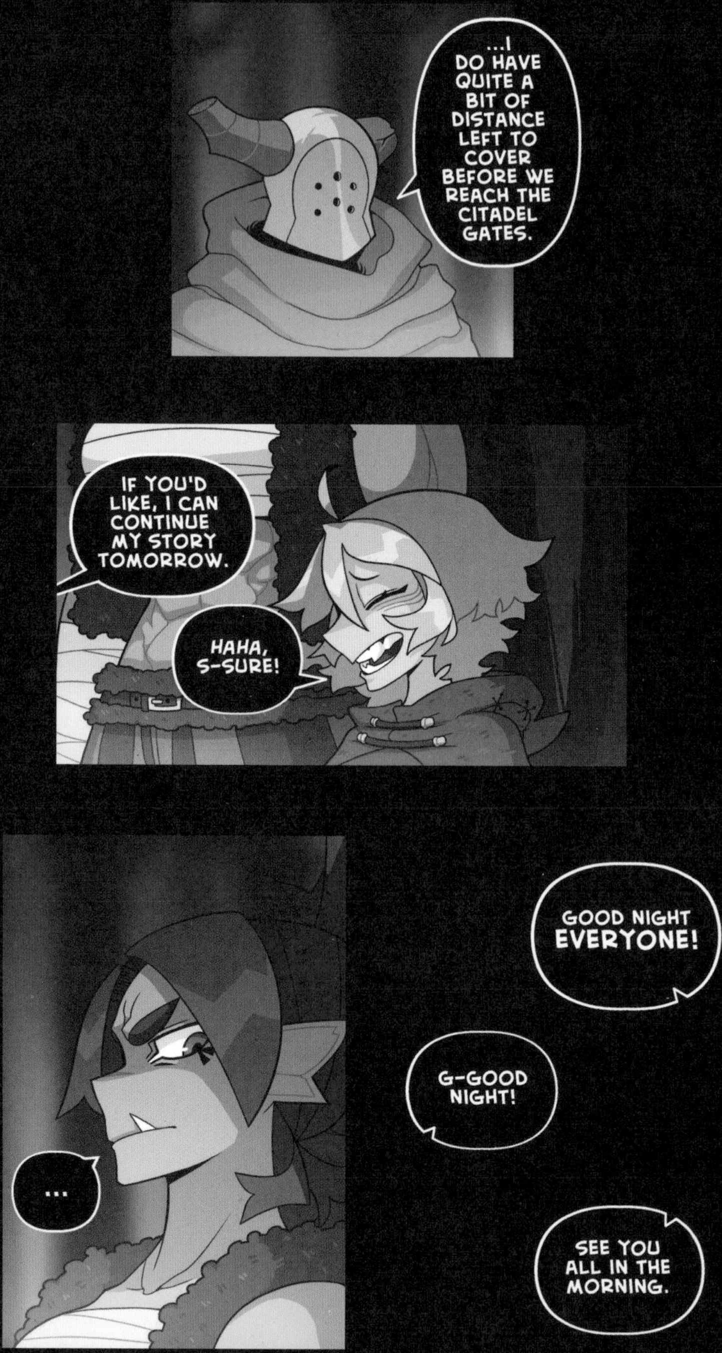
...I DO HAVE QUITE A BIT OF DISTANCE LEFT TO COVER BEFORE WE REACH THE CITADEL GATES.
IF YOU'D LIKE, I CAN CONTINUE MY STORY TOMORROW.
HAHA, S-SURE!
...
GOOD NIGHT EVERYONE!
G-GOOD NIGHT!
SEE YOU ALL IN THE MORNING.

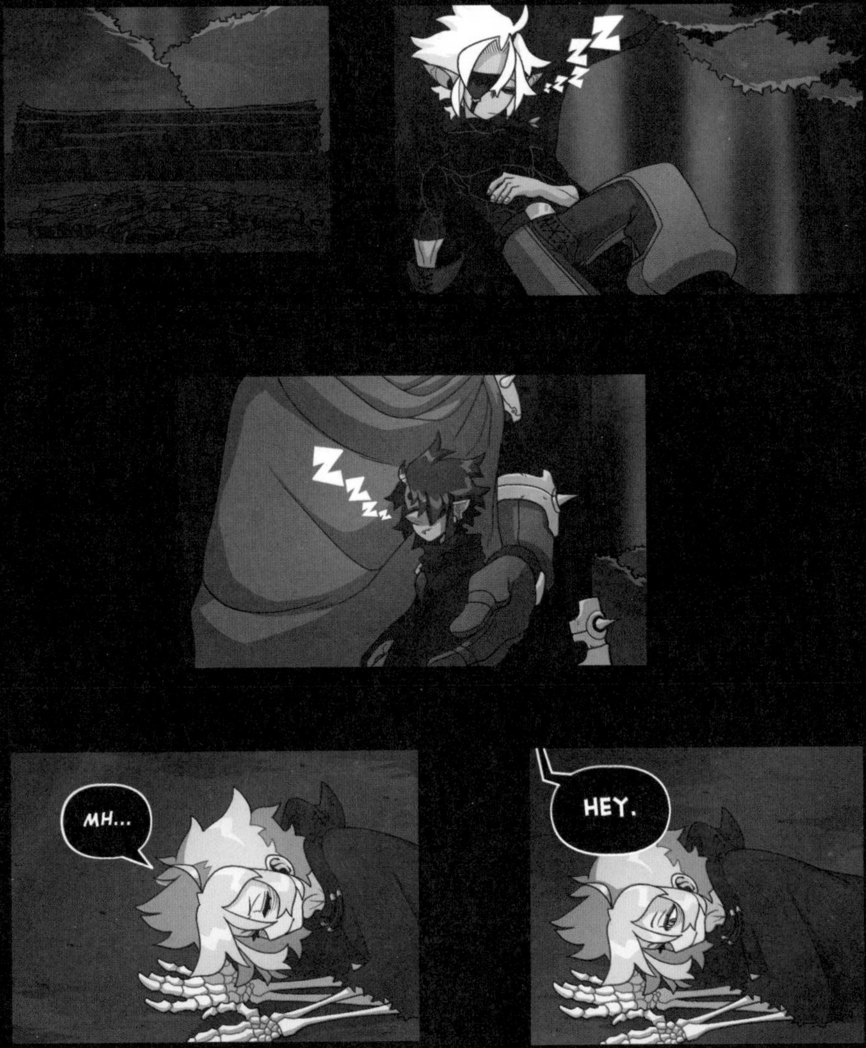
MH...
HEY.

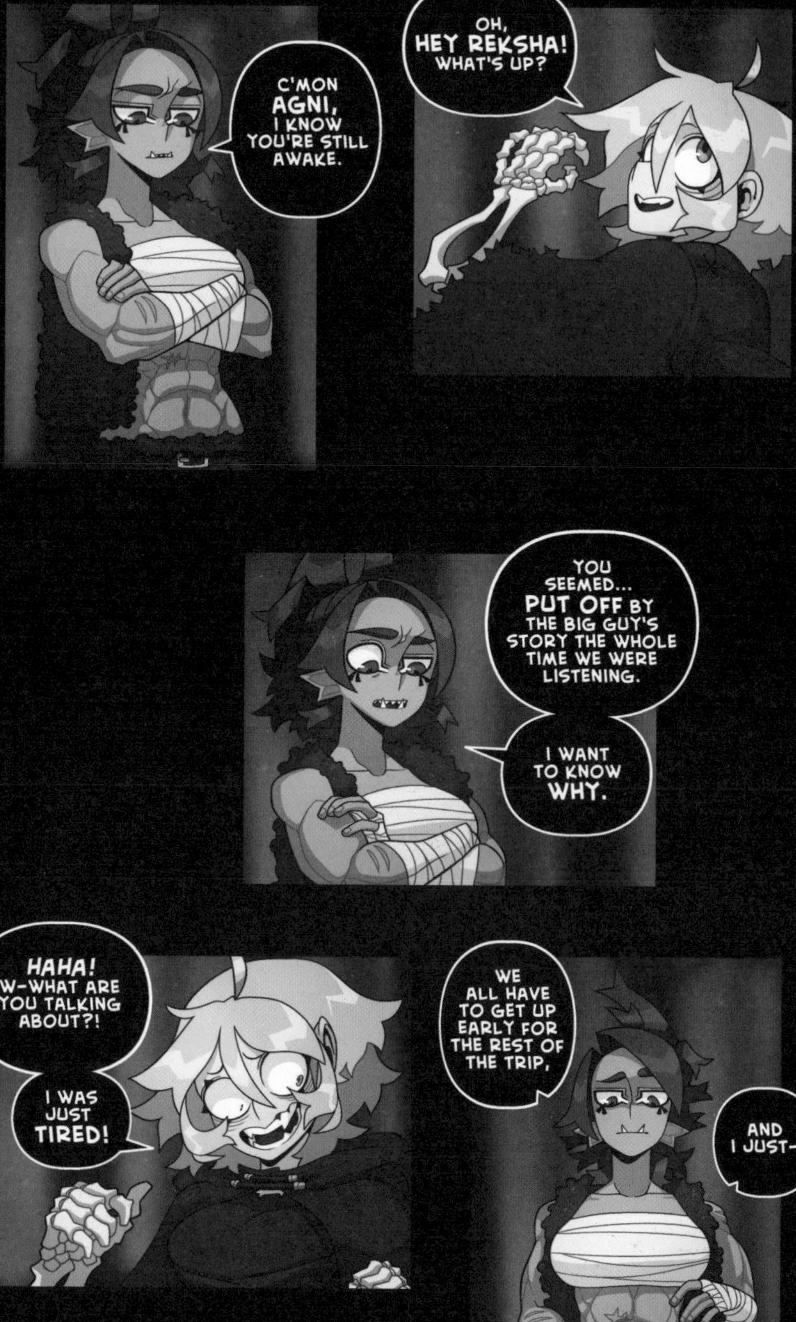
C'MON AGNI, I KNOW YOU'RE STILL AWAKE.
OH, HEY REKSHA! WHAT'S UP?
YOU SEEMED... PUT OFF BY THE BIG GUY'S STORY THE WHOLE TIME WE WERE LISTENING.
I WANT TO KNOW WHY.
HAHA! W-WHAT ARE YOU TALKING ABOUT?!
I WAS JUST TIRED!
WE ALL HAVE TO GET UP EARLY FOR THE REST OF THE TRIP,
AND I JUST-

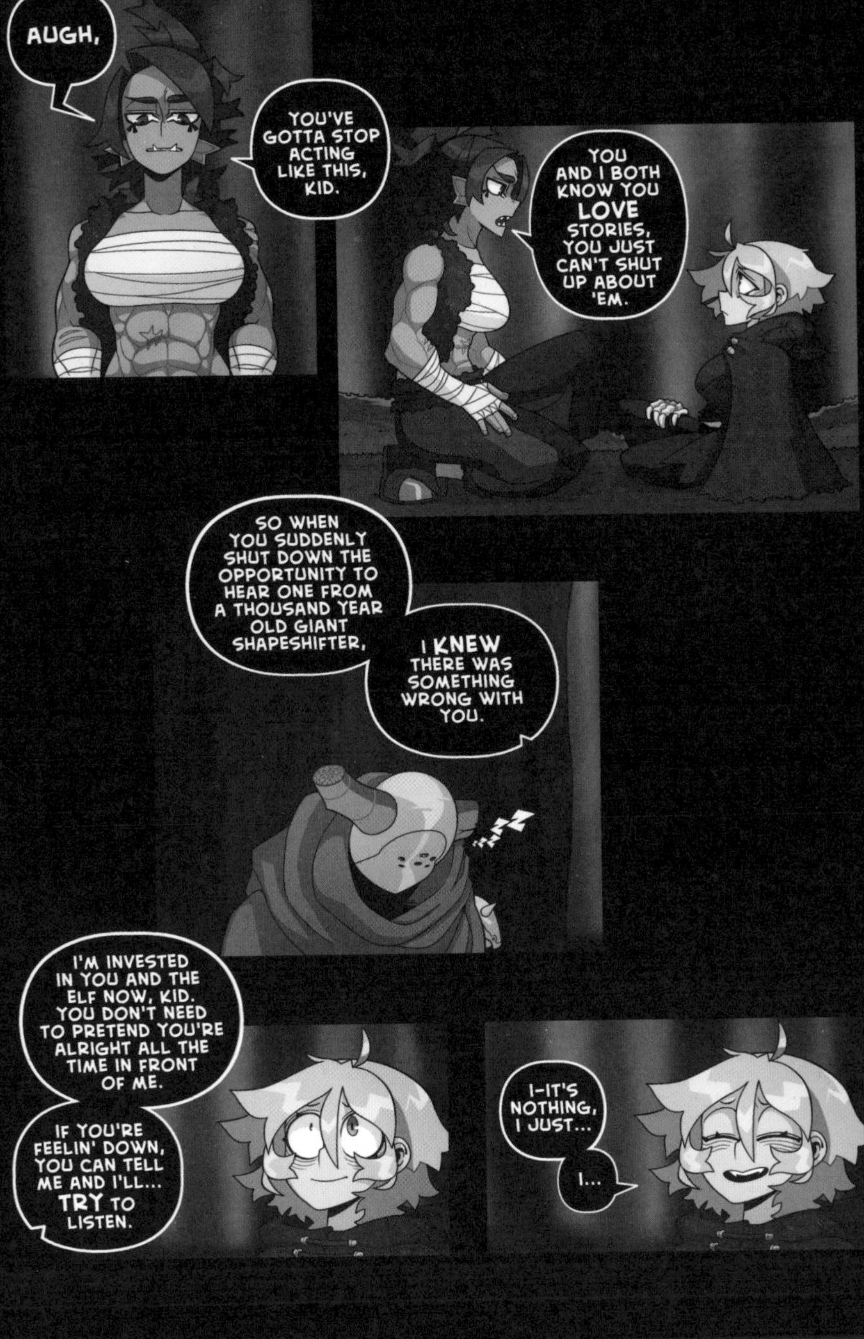
AUGH,
YOU'VE GOTTA STOP ACTING LIKE THIS, KID.
YOU AND I BOTH KNOW YOU **LOVE** STORIES, YOU JUST CAN'T SHUT UP ABOUT 'EM.
SO WHEN YOU SUDDENLY SHUT DOWN THE OPPORTUNITY TO HEAR ONE FROM A THOUSAND YEAR OLD GIANT SHAPESHIFTER,
I **KNEW** THERE WAS SOMETHING WRONG WITH YOU.
I'M INVESTED IN YOU AND THE ELF NOW, KID. YOU DON'T NEED TO PRETEND YOU'RE ALRIGHT ALL THE TIME IN FRONT OF ME.
IF YOU'RE FEELIN' DOWN, YOU CAN TELL ME AND I'LL... **TRY** TO LISTEN.
I-IT'S NOTHING, I JUST...
I...

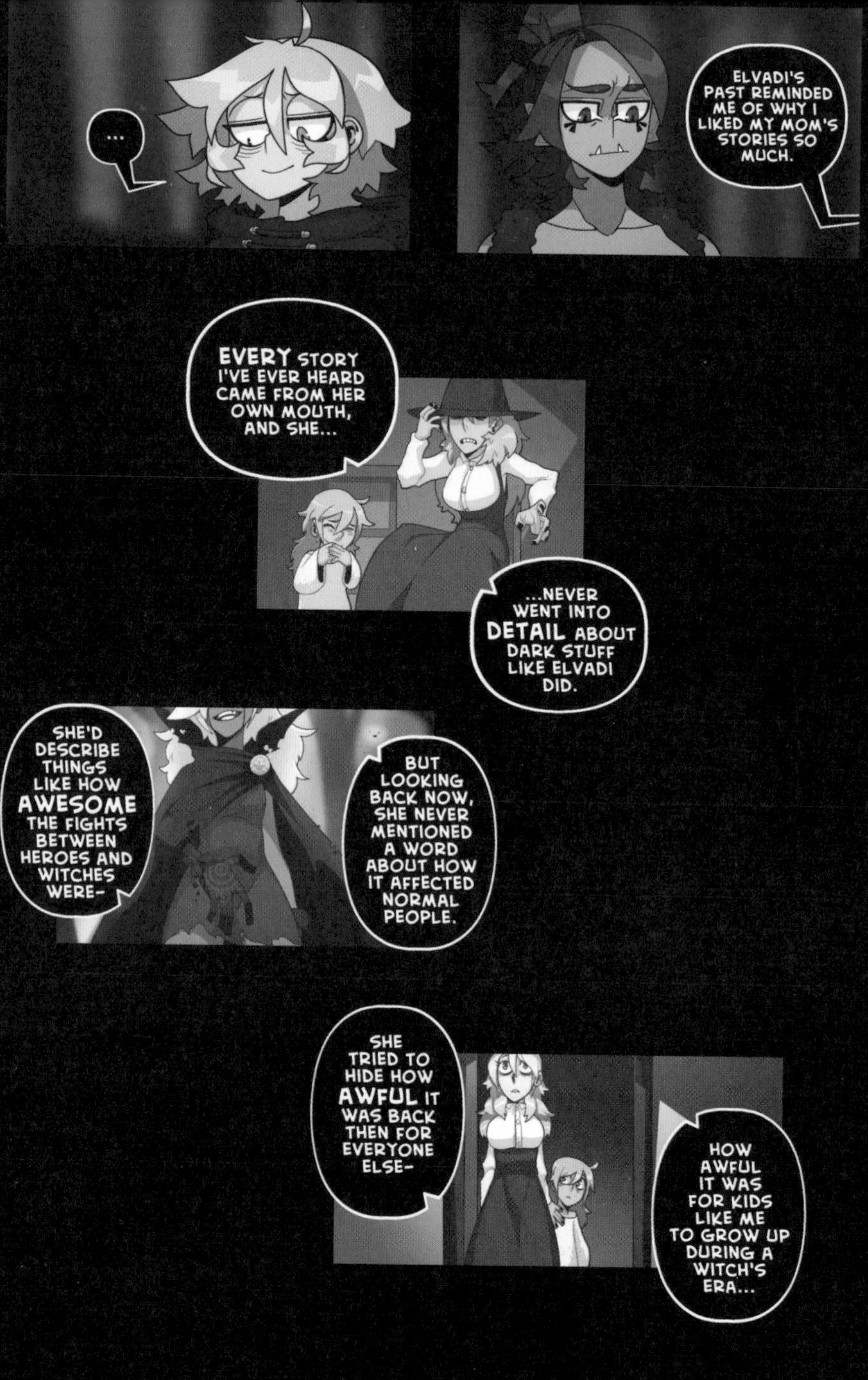
...
ELVADI'S PAST REMINDED ME OF WHY I LIKED MY MOM'S STORIES SO MUCH.
EVERY STORY I'VE EVER HEARD CAME FROM HER OWN MOUTH, AND SHE...
...NEVER WENT INTO DETAIL ABOUT DARK STUFF LIKE ELVADI DID.
SHE'D DESCRIBE THINGS LIKE HOW AWESOME THE FIGHTS BETWEEN HEROES AND WITCHES WERE-
BUT LOOKING BACK NOW, SHE NEVER MENTIONED A WORD ABOUT HOW IT AFFECTED NORMAL PEOPLE.
SHE TRIED TO HIDE HOW AWFUL IT WAS BACK THEN FOR EVERYONE ELSE-
HOW AWFUL IT WAS FOR KIDS LIKE ME TO GROW UP DURING A WITCH'S ERA...

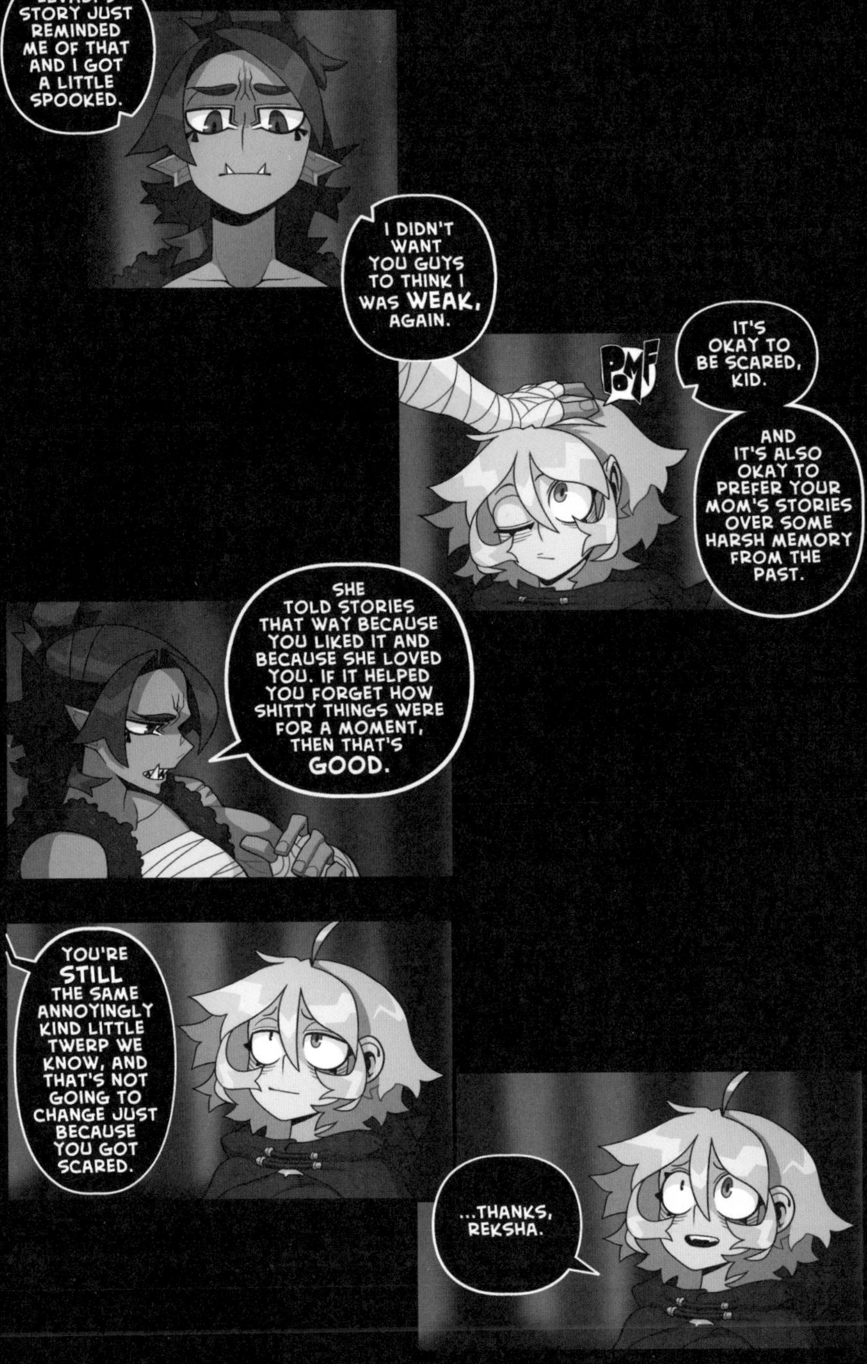
ELVADI'S STORY JUST REMINDED ME OF THAT AND I GOT A LITTLE SPOOKED.
I DIDN'T WANT YOU GUYS TO THINK I WAS WEAK, AGAIN.
POMF
IT'S OKAY TO BE SCARED, KID.
AND IT'S ALSO OKAY TO PREFER YOUR MOM'S STORIES OVER SOME HARSH MEMORY FROM THE PAST.
SHE TOLD STORIES THAT WAY BECAUSE YOU LIKED IT AND BECAUSE SHE LOVED YOU. IF IT HELPED YOU FORGET HOW SHITTY THINGS WERE FOR A MOMENT, THEN THAT'S GOOD.
YOU'RE STILL THE SAME ANNOYINGLY KIND LITTLE TWERP WE KNOW, AND THAT'S NOT GOING TO CHANGE JUST BECAUSE YOU GOT SCARED.
...THANKS, REKSHA.

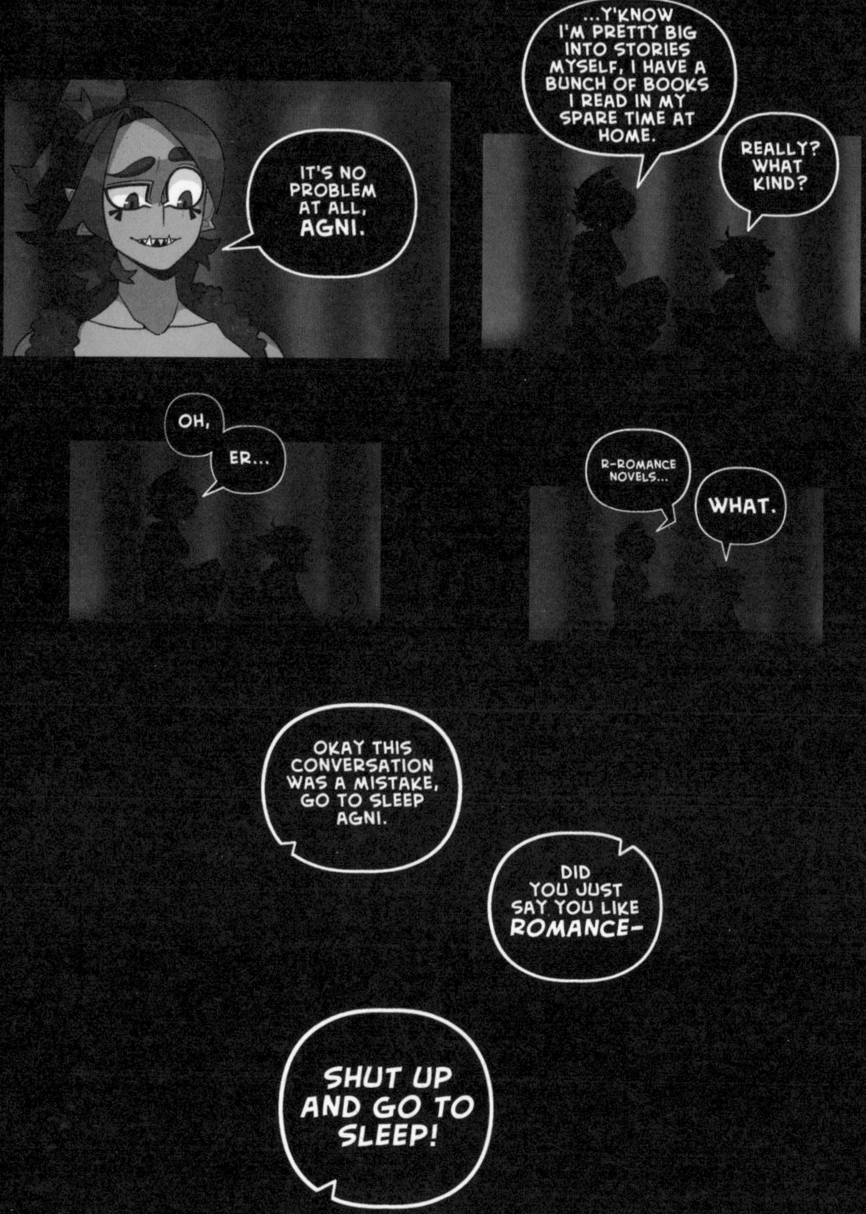
IT'S NO PROBLEM AT ALL, AGNI.
...Y'KNOW I'M PRETTY BIG INTO STORIES MYSELF, I HAVE A BUNCH OF BOOKS I READ IN MY SPARE TIME AT HOME.
REALLY? WHAT KIND?
OH,
ER...
R-ROMANCE NOVELS...
WHAT.
OKAY THIS CONVERSATION WAS A MISTAKE, GO TO SLEEP AGNI.
DID YOU JUST SAY YOU LIKE ROMANCE-
SHUT UP AND GO TO SLEEP!

Don't miss

# THE WITCH'S THRONE

Volume 2!

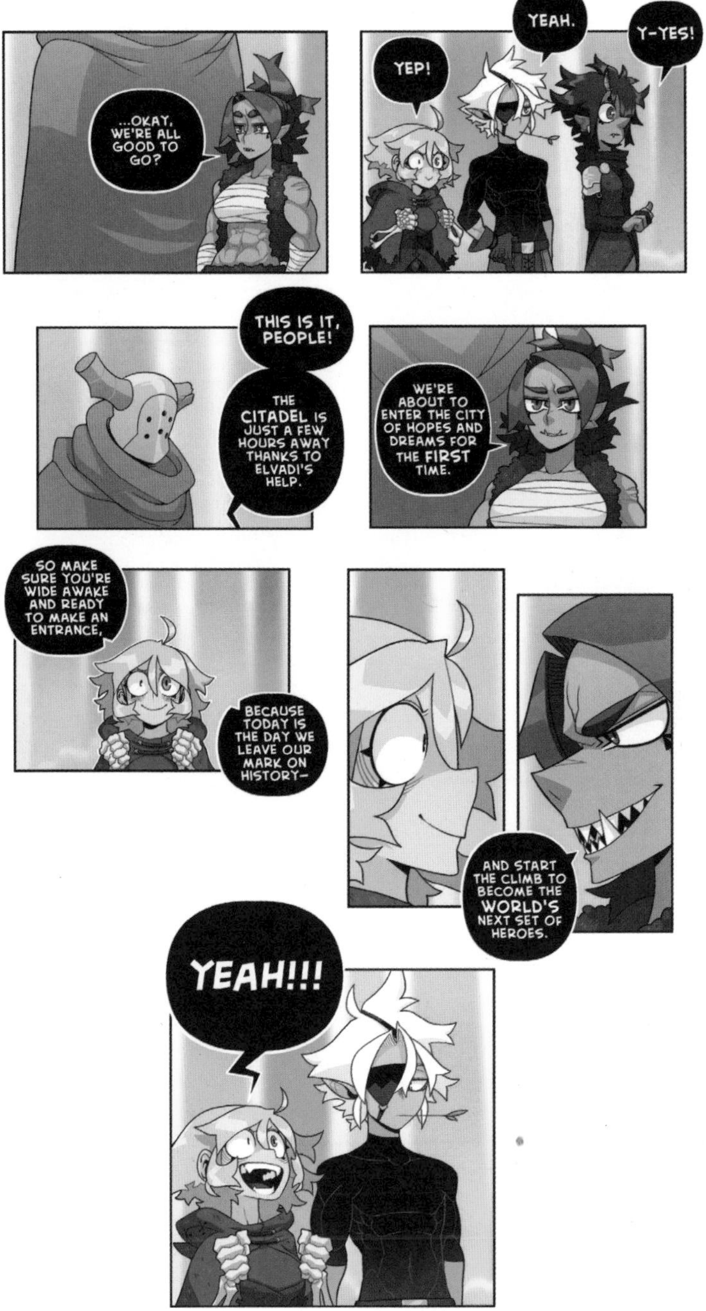

...OKAY, WE'RE ALL GOOD TO GO?
YEP!
YEAH.
Y-YES!
THIS IS IT, PEOPLE!
THE CITADEL IS JUST A FEW HOURS AWAY THANKS TO ELVADI'S HELP.
WE'RE ABOUT TO ENTER THE CITY OF HOPES AND DREAMS FOR THE FIRST TIME.
SO MAKE SURE YOU'RE WIDE AWAKE AND READY TO MAKE AN ENTRANCE,
BECAUSE TODAY IS THE DAY WE LEAVE OUR MARK ON HISTORY-
AND START THE CLIMB TO BECOME THE WORLD'S NEXT SET OF HEROES.
YEAH!!!

# Acknowledgments

First and foremost, I would like to thank my first editor, Brooke Huang, for her continued counsel and supervision over all the years I've worked with the Tapas publishing team. I'm thankful to Dojo Gubser, my dear friend and coloring assistant, who swooped in to help me stay on track with my busy work schedule. For reaching out to publishers and securing the opportunity to create this book, I'm grateful to Alex Carr, Tapas's senior director of publisher development. For showing a great interest in my work and giving me the chance to make a name for myself on the Tapas platform, I'm grateful to Michael Son, Tapas's vice president of content. For taking the time to go through and adapt my work into print, I'm also grateful to all of the hardworking people at Andrews McMeel Publishing.

Over the course of my webcomic-making journey, I made friends with a myriad of amazing people, all of whom I'd like to extend my thanks. For making me laugh and giving me fun memories to look back on, I'm thankful to Jordan Ronis, Joshua Medley, Ben Duckett, Zac Garmon, Jarod Johnson, Mitchell Meritt, Anandé Robinson, Zoray, Hemlock, Maf, and Jesseca. I would also like to extend a special thanks to Selena Ahmed and Kenny Tran, two of my best friends who now work alongside me on my webcomic.

Finally, I would like to express my sincerest gratitude to my close family—my parents, Cristina and Zorro; my sister, Chelsea; my grandmother, Luz; and my cousins, Nicholai, Monica, and Joy, for cheering me on in my artistic endeavors.

This book would not be possible without the love and support of all these wonderful individuals, and I feel nothing short of blessed to have them in my life.

**Cedric Caballes** is a die-hard RPG fan and the creator of the hit Tapas webcomic *The Witch's Throne*. Cedric was born in the Philippines and raised in the United States, growing up with plenty of unsupervised access to video games and the internet. Throughout his childhood, he displayed an affinity for drawing and was "the kid everyone wanted for group art projects" in school. After years of gluing his eyes to a computer screen, Cedric developed a keen interest in fantasy role-playing games and hot-blooded shonen manga. He cites his fascination with both mediums to be what inspired most of his artwork, which range from character designs to multiple webcomic concepts under his pen name WhatAHero. He currently lives in eastern Maryland, daydreaming of magic, dragons, and level-up notifications whenever he's not busy drawing or writing.

You can find Cedric doodling something on Twitter or Instagram at @whatatruehero.

Andrews McMeel Publishing
a division of Andrews McMeel Universal
1130 Walnut Street, Kansas City, Missouri 64106

www.andrewsmcmeel.com

22 23 24 25 26 TEN 10 9 8 7 6 5 4 3 2 1

ISBN: 978-1-5248-7650-0

Library of Congress Control Number: 2022937860

Book Editor: Betty Wong
Art Director: Holly Swayne
Designer: Lisa Martin
Production Editor: Dave Shaw
Production Manager: Tamara Haus

Studio Tapas
Editor: Brooke Huang
Editor-in-Chief: Jamie S. Rich
Coloring Assistance: Dojo Gubser

ATTENTION: SCHOOLS AND BUSINESSES
Andrews McMeel books are available at quantity discounts with bulk
purchase for educational, business, or sales promotional use. For information,
please e-mail the Andrews McMeel Publishing Special Sales Department:
specialsales@amuniversal.com.